Strangers in a Stranger Land

Strangers in a Stranger Land

*How One Country's Jews Fought an Unwinnable War
alongside Nazi Troops . . . and Survived*

John B. Simon

HAMILTON BOOKS
Lanham • Boulder • New York • London

Published by Hamilton Books
An imprint of The Rowman & Littlefield Publishing Group, Inc.
4501 Forbes Boulevard, Suite 200, Lanham, Maryland 20706
www.rowman.com

6 Tinworth Street, London SE11 5AL, United Kingdom

British Library Cataloguing in Publication Information Available

Library of Congress Cataloging-in-Publication Data

ISBN 978-0-7618-7149-1 (pbk. : alk. paper)
ISBN 978-0-7618-7150-7 (electronic)

∞™ The paper used in this publication meets the minimum requirements of American
National Standard for Information Sciences—Permanence of Paper for Printed Library
Materials, ANSI/NISO Z39.48-1992.

For Maggie

Contents

~

Preface

This narrative begins with the story of a Finnish Jew being awarded the Iron Cross by the German military during World War II, an event that made so little sense to me when I first heard about it that I felt compelled to seek an explanation. At a time when Nazi leaders were planning the extermination of Europe's entire Jewish population, openly Jewish soldiers in the Finnish army were being awarded medals by the German military. Furthermore, despite the presence of hundreds of thousands of German soldiers on Finnish soil between 1941 and 1944, not a single Finnish Jew was imprisoned or harmed by the German forces. How was this possible?

To answer these questions, I first had to understand what it was about Finland that differentiated it from all the other countries that fought alongside Germany in the war. Did the Finns somehow protect their Jews, and if so, how and why? I also needed to understand something about Finland's tiny Jewish minority. Where did they come from, how well were they integrated into the exceptionally homogeneous Finnish society by the time war broke out, and was there something special about them that contributed to their unprecedented escape from Nazi violence?

Outside their own congregations, little is known about Finland's Jews. I would argue that without understanding their community's origins in the Russian Imperial Army's Cantonist[1] system and the tensions existing in the Finnish society that became their home, it is impossible to understand how Finnish Jews came to be fighting alongside German troops. Therefore, this book has many historical sections that retrace these developments.

My real interest, however, is in the human contours of this story. By the time I began my research, survivors of WWII were in their seventies, eighties or nineties. There weren't many Jewish Finnish war veterans still alive. While those I was able to speak with generously shared their stories, I did not think it right to choose one or more of them to represent all Finnish Jews who fought in the war. Instead, I used the information I gathered from interviews with them as well as from extensive reading to create three generations of a fictional family, not exactly typical, perhaps, but facing many of the same situations and challenges as the real parents, grandparents and great-grandparents of today's Finnish Jews. I situated them, to the extent I was able, in actual historical locations and events with real people. Thus, for example, while Benjamin, his relatives and friends are fictional and so could not actually have worked in the shops or served in the military units or hospitals where you will encounter them, most of their experiences are rigorously faithful to the circumstances and experiences of real people who would have been their contemporaries.

Fictional characters are introduced early in the book. In monologues, 95-year-old Benjamin recalls not only the war in which he fought but his experiences growing up in the cosmopolitan Finnish city of Viipuri in the 1920s and 1930s. We meet his grandfather, Peisach, who is abducted from a *shtetl*[2] near Vitebsk in what is today Belarus and ends up in the Finnish city of Viipuri. We subsequently follow Benjamin's father, Mendel, as he tries, despite numerous setbacks, to climb into the middle class and make a better life for his wife and children. Benjamin reappears as a young man growing up in the period between Finland's independence and WWII, experiencing the tensions that arise within Finland's Jewish community and society as a whole at a time when Europe is sliding down the slippery slope to war.

The story of these three generations plays out against the background of a Finland that sees its status as eight outer provinces of Sweden transformed into that of an autonomous grand duchy of Russia, then struggles to break away and survive as an independent country. For centuries, little more than pawns between two world powers, the Finnish people manage to find ways to assert themselves despite wars, deprivation and oppression. In the process of achieving nationhood, the Finns define themselves first through linguistic, cultural and historical differences with their neighbors. By investing in education, economic development and the rule of law, they transform their young country into a modern nation. The Jews of Finland, for their part, are content at first to plead for basic human rights, realizing that equality and citizenship are out of reach. Shortly after Finland gains independence in 1917, however, and less than twenty years before WWII, the first Jews are finally allowed to apply for full citizenship. Along with their Romanian co-religionists, they are the last Jews of Europe to achieve full emancipation.

A contrapuntal score emerges from these four stories—the veteran's reminiscence, the emergence of independent Finland, the travails of three generations of Finland's Jews, and the experiences of Benjamin, David and Rachel in the years leading up to and into the war. While the introduction of numerous characters and shifts back and forth in time may present some challenges to the reader at first, the way they interconnect becomes clearer as the book proceeds and the context assumes its historical shape.

How a small group of Jews came to fight alongside German troops in WWII, and how they and their families survived the experience without falling victim to Nazi terror, is one of the strangest stories to come out of the war. I do not claim to be adding much original research to what has already been written about it, but I hope to tell this counterintuitive tale in a way that will reach a far wider audience than has previously been exposed to it as well as to correct some of the misconceptions that exist about Finland and its role in WWII. Located in the remotest northeast corner of Europe, it has always been sandwiched along the political and cultural divide between East and West. For most of their history, Finns, like Jews, were forced to eat the unleavened bread of poverty and powerlessness.

The story of the tiny Jewish community of Finland, which still proudly affirms its place in a society where it accounts for barely .02 percent of the population, is fascinating but not more so than the story of how the Finnish people not only achieved nationhood and independence but defended their right to exist against almost insurmountable odds. Like the braid of a loaf of Sabbath *challah*[3], these narratives are intricately intertwined.

John Simon
Vantaa, Finland, 2019

Notes

1. Regional organization for military conscription and training of young boys
2. Small town in Eastern Europe with a considerable Jewish population (Yiddish)
3. In this text, the gutteral "h" sound is represented by "ch" in words such as challah, cheder and chapper.

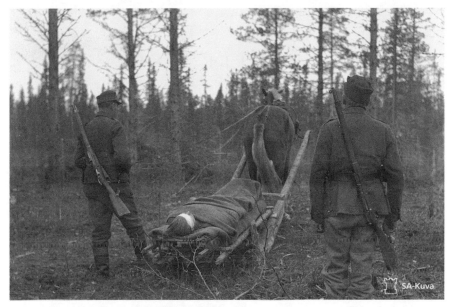

Figure 1.1. A severely wounded Finnish soldier being evacuated from the Kiestingin motti along the Kapustnaya River's Via Dolorosa. (Finland's Military Museum)

Those of us at the Foreign Section of the General Staff Headquarters knew well enough what was going on. You saw the reports, and you could read between the lines. I was trained as an intelligence officer so I soon learned what different expressions really meant. There were Finnish liaison officers in the German headquarters on the Eastern Front, and we got hints from them about what was going on there. Some of the documents were passed on. If they came to us, they'd be sent to the General Staff, and they would come back with four or five signatures. . . . After they'd been returned to my desk, I'd put them in the safe for secret documents, for which I had a key. There were two keys, and I had one of them.

From what I was able to see, it became absolutely clear that the Germans would not spare one single Jew. At some point, I started to think, "What if I were to bring all this out into the open?" In a way, I was guilty of an offense against my co-religionists and my family for not saying anything.

Having analyzed the situation, I came to the conclusion that by talking, I'd break my military oath. And if I broke my oath as an officer, I'd give those Finns who were Nazi sympathizers an excuse to destroy Judaism in Finland. They'd say, "You can't trust them, they can't keep a secret."

By bringing it out in the open, I'd be signing a death sentence for Judaism in Finland.

Leo Jakobson*

**Daavid: Stories of Honor and Shame,* documentary film by Taru Makela, ForRealProductions in cooperation with the Finnish Broadcasting Company's Channel 2, 1997.

CHAPTER ONE

~

Iron Cross for a Jew?

Kananainen, Finland, 1941—"Tell them, My Good General, that I wipe my ass with their medal!"

What Finnish Medical Captain (later Major) Leo Skurnik—son of Ben-Zion Skurnik and grandson of Schmuel Skurnik—was really saying with that outburst was: "Tell *the Nazis* who want to give me one, General Siilasvuo, that *I wipe my Jewish ass with their Iron Cross!*"

Against all logic and in stark contrast to the Third Reich's murderous antisemitic policies, the *Wehrmacht* (the German Army) had awarded this particular Iron Cross to a Jew—not a clandestine Jew but an openly Jewish soldier—serving in a unit of the Finnish Army subordinated to the German *Armeeoberkommando Norwegen* (Army Norway). Finnish Major General Hjalmar Siilasvuo, commander of Finland's Third Army Corps, knew that Skurnik was Jewish, temperamental, and extremely uncomfortable serving alongside German troops under a German-led chain of command and could hardly have been surprised by his reaction. The recommendation to award Skurnik the medal, after all, must have crossed Siilasvuo's desk on its way to General Waldemar Erfurth, the *Wehrmacht's* liaison officer in the headquarters of the Finnish Army, who, in turn, had to forward it to Berlin for final approval.

Dr. Skurnik had distinguished himself for bravery on at least two occasions during his tour of duty with Finland's 53rd Infantry Regiment in 1941. In the first, under heavy Soviet fire, he rescued wounded soldiers—at least one of whom was German—from the field of battle while the rest of their comrades cowered in their foxholes. Skurnik would later confide to his son that this was less an act of bravery than of foolhardiness.

During the Kiestinki *motti*,[1] one of the bloodiest encounters of the Continuation War, Skurnik successfully planned and carried out the evacuation of some 800 people, including an entire field hospital of more than 600 sick and wounded soldiers. At least 70 of those survivors were German. The rescue, which took place under concentrated artillery fire, began August 23, 1941 and lasted nearly two weeks. An accomplished musician, Skurnik timed the intervals between enemy artillery barrages and orchestrated the departure of small clusters of evacuees, limping along or dragged on crude horse-drawn litters across rocky terrain and through treacherous swamps during brief lulls in the shelling. The evacuees—the last of whom were personally escorted to safety by Skurnik on September 4 along the 10-kilometer path that became known as the *Kapustnaya River's Via Dolorosa*—were all that remained of the 2,800 Finnish and German soldiers who had advanced confidently towards the river less than a month earlier.

Samuli Skurnik[2] insists his father never considered himself a hero. Leo Skurnik had a deep-seated fear and resentment of his German co-belligerents and never had any intention of accepting their medal. He wanted to see, however, how long it would take for the Germans to realize their mistake: that they were awarding their medal to a Jew. When it became clear that the medal was really going to be awarded as planned, he told General Siilasvuo to put a stop to the proceedings.

Siilasvuo passed on Skurnik's message to the German high command (although it is not known the extent to which he first toned down the language). Furious at the snub, the Germans demanded that Skurnik be arrested and delivered to them. "Hand over one of my best soldiers?" the Finnish general replied. "Certainly not!"

Two other Finnish Jews were nominated for the Iron Cross during the war. Neither of them accepted it. Lieutenant (later Captain) Salomon Klass was designated for the award in 1942 after distinguishing himself in battle on the Uhtua front as a company commander in General Siilasvuo's III Army Corps. Upon hearing that he was being recommended for the medal, Klass immediately asked that his name be withdrawn from the list of recipients. *Lotta Svärd* (Women's Auxiliary) member Dina Poljakoff, on the other hand, waited until the day of the awards ceremony, checked the table where the medals were displayed to make sure that there really was one intended for her, and then left without accepting it. Lieutenant Leo Jakobson, who handled communications from German military and diplomatic sources for the Finnish army headquarters foreign office, quietly removed his own name from a list of potential recipients before it could even be considered.

Not One War but Three

For most of Europe, there was just one World War II. For Finland, however, there were three: first the Winter War (November 30, 1939–March 13, 1940) against the Soviet Union; then the Continuation War (June 25, 1941–September 5, 1944), also against the Soviet Union; and finally the Lapland War (September 15, 1944–April 27, 1945) against Germany.

The Winter War was an unambiguous defensive struggle. On August 23, 1939, as Germany and the Soviet Union prepared for war in Europe, their leaders agreed to a mutual non-aggression treaty that became known after its main architects, Soviet foreign minister Vyacheslav Molotov and German foreign minister Joachim von Ribbentrop, as the Molotov-Ribbentrop Pact. One week later, Germany invaded Poland, and WWII began.

A secret protocol attached to the Molotov-Ribbentrop Pact consigned Finland to the Soviets' sphere of influence, stating that "in the event of a territorial and political rearrangement in the areas belonging to the Baltic States, the northern boundary of Lithuania shall represent the boundary of the spheres of influence of Germany and the U.S.S.R." In plain language, Germany would not interfere in any Soviet attempt to take over Estonia, Latvia, and Finland, and the Soviets would concede control over Lithuania to the Germans. The two countries would divide Poland, with the Germans taking the larger, western slice.

The Soviet Union, in an effort to shore up its defense of Leningrad, had been demanding territorial concessions that the Finns proved unwilling to grant. On November 30, 1939, on the pretext that the Soviet border town of Mainila had been shelled four days earlier by Finnish artillery, supposedly resulting in the death of four Soviet soldiers, Stalin ordered the bombing of Helsinki and the invasion of Finland. The League of Nations condemned the Soviet attack as unwarranted—the Mainila shelling was a Soviet ruse (i.e., fake news)—and expelled the U.S.S.R. on appeal from the Finnish government.

The Soviets fully expected to be able to march straight across Finland, taking Viipuri[3] in four days and Helsinki in less than two weeks, overcoming with little difficulty whatever resistance they might meet along the way. They even printed a handbook for their troops, with maps and timetables and the reminder that, "Upon arrival at the Swedish and Norwegian borders, in no way should they be violated."[4]

The Finns were only able to muster some nine poorly prepared field army divisions of fewer than the prescribed 15,400 men each, 56 small tanks,[5] 114 combat planes, and a three-week supply of artillery shells to face considerably more than three times as many Soviet troops (26–29 divisions of 18,700 men each), nearly 40 times as many tanks (2,000) and 20 times as many aircraft (2,500). Yet despite their overwhelming superiority in troops and firepower, Soviet forces suffered far greater casualties than the Finns and were only able to advance across approximately 10 percent of Finland's territory before Stalin began to think twice about further alienating the Western powers, whose leaders and citizens admired the plucky Finns. After 105 days of brutal and exhausting combat in the dead of winter, an uneasy truce was reached.

Finland suffered heavy losses in the Winter War: 24,000 dead or missing and 43,500 injured (together almost 2 percent of its total population of 3.7 million). In addition, the Soviet Union annexed 11 percent of Finland's land, including its second largest city, Viipuri, causing some 430,000 Karelians, or 12 percent of Finland's population, to evacuate their homes and seek refuge in the remaining 89 percent of the country.

Unfinished Business

For the displaced Karelians as well as most Finns, the peace agreement ending the Winter War left many scores unsettled. That is why the second war became known in Finland as the Continuation War, emphasizing that it was a continuation of Finland's response to the unprovoked Soviet aggression that had ended only fifteen months earlier.

The Continuation War officially began June 25, 1941 with Finland's Prime Minister Jukka Rangell acknowledging in a radio address that a state of war existed once again between Finland and the Soviet Union. Although Soviet planes had begun bombing Finnish airfields and cities that morning, and President Risto Ryti in a speech the next day blamed the war on Soviet aggression, this was not the same kind of one-sided encroachment that had set off the Winter War. The hostilities had actually been initiated on June 22nd by Germany's massive assault, code-named *Barbarossa*, along the Soviet Union's European border from the Barents Sea to the Carpathian Mountains. *Luftwaffe* squadrons from eastern Prussia bombed Soviet targets before refueling at Finnish airfields on the return flight, and Finland's navy coordinated the laying down of mines in the Baltic Sea with its German counterparts.

In an attempt to create the impression that Germany was acting alone while Finland remained a bystander, the Finnish government kept its troops in defensive positions and did not participate directly in the first days of Operation Barbarossa. Nevertheless, Finland had clearly been complicit in the planning and staging of the part of the invasion that was launched from its territory.

After German forces from Norway crossed into Finland and took up positions along the Soviet border, there were 80,000 (the number would later grow to exceed 250,000) German troops on Finnish soil. On June 22, a 27,500-man assault force of Germany's Mountain Corps Norway marched along the coast of the Barents Sea into the nickel-rich Kola Peninsula. Three days later and more than 500 kilometers to the south, Finland's Third Army Corps, which was subordinated to Germany's XXXVI Corps, also launched an attack to cut the Soviets' vital Murmansk rail line. The Continuation War was underway, and Finland was an active combatant. The war would last more than three years, cost Finland more than 63,000 lives, and leave 142,000 citizens seriously injured (taken together, 5.5 percent of the population).

The third and final war Finland had to fight in this northernmost sideshow to the great powers' conflict was the Lapland War. This was an absurd struggle in which the Finns, having agreed for a second time to an armistice with the Soviets but still technically at war, were forced to pursue their former German comrades in arms and expel them violently from Finland. The Germans, already retreating towards Norway, laid waste to Lapland, and the Finns, who had no enthusiasm whatsoever for this operation, had to attack convincingly enough to keep the Soviets from surging into Lapland to finish the job for them. Giving the Russians an excuse for further military intervention on their soil was not an option for the Finns, who feared the prospect of Russian occupation far more than any damage the retreating Germans might inflict on them. The Lapland War lasted seven months and resulted in the death of approximately 1,000 Finnish soldiers and serious injury to 3,000 more.

Between a Rock and a Hard Place

Why was Finland ready in 1941 to enter into war against the Soviet Union as Germany's co-belligerent? In the fall of 1939, before the start of the Winter War, Finland had nervously watched as the Soviets compelled the Estonian, Latvian and Lithuanian governments to sign mutual assistance pacts that called for Russian troops to be stationed on their soil. Then, in June 1940, just three months after the end of the Winter War, the Soviet army occupied all three Baltic republics and installed pro-Soviet regimes. Within a few days, these previously independent countries "requested" to join the Soviet Union.

Following the annexation of the Baltic states, the Soviets demanded (and received) the right to transport troops by rail across Finland to the Hanko Peninsula, the southernmost point on Finland's coast, where a Soviet garrison had been established as a condition for ending the Winter War hostilities. The Finnish government was facing increasing demands for concessions from the Soviets, and to many Finns it seemed only a matter of time before the Soviets would once again move to occupy their country.

Germany's alliance with the Soviet Union (the Molotov-Ribbentrop pact), had ruled out the Third Reich as a potential ally for Finland in 1939, when the latter desperately needed to arm itself against the threat of Soviet attack. The Finnish government sought help at that point from Sweden and then from the Americans, British, and French, but the moral encouragement it received from the Allied Powers was not backed by timely military support. France and Great Britain eventually promised military aid, including the dispatch of troops to Finland, but Norway and Sweden, warned by both Germany and the Soviet Union that Scandinavia would be transformed into a major theater of war if Allied troops were allowed to set foot on their territory, refused to allow the Allies safe passage. As the Soviet threat turned into overt aggression, and help from the West was not forthcoming, the Finns were left to face the Soviet onslaught on their own.[6]

By the spring of 1940, Finland's options were reduced even further. As it struggled to get back on its feet after the Winter War, the country was faced with a rapidly changing geopolitical environment. Germany invaded and occupied Denmark and Norway in April; France, Belgium and the Netherlands buckled in May. Sweden and Finland, desperately clinging to aspirations of neutrality, were surrounded on all sides by belligerent totalitarian regimes or helpless countries occupied by them. When the two Nordic countries proposed a neutrality alliance, the Soviets reacted vigorously, saying it would constitute a violation by Finland of the conditions agreed to at the end of the Winter War. Germany also opposed the alliance, fearing it would interfere with German access to Sweden's iron and Finland's nickel reserves.

Finland's meager supply of arms and ammunition had been depleted by the Winter War, and to the threat of invasion from the East was now added Germany's willingness to overrun Nordic countries by force. The Finns clearly understood that doing nothing would lead to occupation by one side or the other with the additional possibility of becoming a battleground between the two sides. They needed weapons to defend themselves and a strategy that would prevent occupation of their country and the loss of sovereignty that would surely follow.

Another pressing issue was hunger. When the ceasefire ending the Winter War was reached, Finland lost the rich farmland of Karelia to the Soviet Union and had to feed the displaced Karelians. During peacetime, resettling and feeding these refugees would have been difficult enough for a poor country with reduced agricultural capacity, but the war between the Axis

Figure 1.2. Northern Europe in 1940 (Marja Leskelä)

and Allied powers made it nearly impossible. Finland—which relied on the export of lumber, pulp and paper, dairy products and copper for currency with which to import essential grain, fertilizer, fuel and raw materials for its textile industry—found its shipping lanes through the Baltic Sea cut off, leaving it unable to supply its trading partners in the West. Food supplies began shrinking at an alarming rate.

Help from the Only Available Source

In August 1940, as pressure from the Soviet Union mounted once again, Finland's Commander in Chief, Field Marshal C.G.E. Mannerheim,[7] was approached by the Germans with an offer he would find hard to refuse: the opportunity to buy badly needed military hardware and ammunition as well as grain and other foodstuffs in exchange for Germany's right to transport troops stationed in northern Norway across Finnish territory on the way to and from Germany. Mannerheim well understood that the presence of German troops on Finnish soil would cause Stalin to think twice about invading again. The agreement was finalized in September, and before long Germany accounted for the lion's share of Finland's foreign trade.

By the early months of 1941, the Molotov-Ribbentrop Pact, a union of convenience that allowed the Germans to carry out their assault on the West without having to worry about their eastern flank while the Soviets gained valuable time to build up their arsenal, was unraveling under the twin pres sures of territorial ambition and ideological passion. Hitler envisioned diverting the agricultural capacity of Russia and the Ukraine to feed the German people and its army. His deep-seated hatred of what he called "Jewish world Bolshevization" was also fueling his plans for the destruction of the Soviet Union. He called the Soviet leaders "common blood-stained criminals" and "the scum of humanity. . . . The fight against Jewish world Bolshevization," he said, "requires a clear attitude toward Soviet Russia."

As Germany prepared to invade the Soviet Union, Finland grew in strategic importance for the Third Reich, thanks primarily to having both the West's longest border with Russia and large deposits of weapons-grade nickel ore. Field Marshal Mannerheim sent his trusted emissary, Major General Paavo Talvela, to Berlin several times in 1940 for secret discussions. Testimony given at the Nuremberg Trials, which may not have been entirely reliable, claimed that during these discussions, "an agreement was reached between the German and Finnish General Staffs for joint preparation for a war of aggression against the Soviet Union," Although such discussions were more likely of an exploratory nature than "joint preparation for a war of aggression," Finland's military leadership certainly knew by the end of January 1941, when Chief of Staff Lieutenant General Erik Heinrichs returned from a visit with his German counterpart, General Franz Halder, that Germany intended to attack the Soviet Union via Finland. German plans called for launching attacks from Norway to ensure control of nickel mines on the Kola Peninsula and from Salla in northeast Finland toward Kantalahti (Kandalaksha)[8] to sever the crucial Soviet rail link between Murmansk and Leningrad.

Driven to collaboration with Germany largely by geopolitical circumstance, Finland was not a passive "drifting log" as the post-war exculpatory narrative adopted by many in Finland would have it. By early 1941, the Finns were sandwiched between Soviet troops massed along their eastern border and German troops stationed on the Norwegian stretch of their northwestern border. The Soviets, on the one hand, had deceitfully annexed three Baltic countries and carved off 11 percent of Finland's territory as spoils of an unjust war. The Germans, on the other hand, were offering desperately needed arms and food. Western democracies had failed to provide Finland with timely material assistance in the Winter War and were now effectively cut off from doing so by German control of the western rim of Continental Europe. For most Finns, including many in the government and military command, the choice was simple: the prospect of another war against the Soviets without adequate air power, artillery or ammunition for the troops was enough to tip the scales in favor of cooperation with Germany.

The Devil and the Angel Gabriel

Today, many in the West still refer to WWII in American journalist Studs Terkel's memorable phrase as "The Good War" and Nazi Germany as the epitome of evil. In 1940, however, much of what we know today about the horrors of the Nazi program was still unfolding, largely out of public view. As Timothy Snyder notes in *Bloodlands*, his chilling account of the murderous reigns of both Hitler and Stalin, "In the 1930s, the Soviet Union was the only state in Europe carrying out policies of mass killing. Before the Second World War, in the first six and a half years after Hitler came to power, the Nazi regime killed no more than about ten thousand people. The Stalinist regime had already starved millions and shot the better part of a million." In 1941, when Winston Churchill defended his decision to provide aid to the Soviet Union by telling the Members of Parliament that "If Hitler invaded Hell, I would make at least a favorable reference to the Devil in the House of Commons," he knew exactly what he was saying.

The Soviet Union was a hermetic society from which little accurate information made its way to the West, and it is difficult today to determine how much was known in Finland during the years approaching WWII about Stalin's Great Terror of the 1930s. In 1918, at the end of Finland's Civil War, some 30,000 Finnish communists and sympathizers had fled to the Soviet Union, where they were joined by Finnish-American and Finnish-Canadian idealists who arrived in the 1920s and early 1930s to help build a utopian socialist society. When the Karelian Autonomous Socialist Republic's political and economic decision-making powers were revoked by Stalin in 1935 and its leadership removed (and eventually liquidated), a few refugees were able to escape to the West, bearing tales of horror. As many as 20,000 of the comrades they left behind were executed or died in prison camps.

Finland's Civil War of 1918, which pitted Reds and Whites against one another in bloodletting that involved atrocities on both sides, had left Finnish society deeply divided. As the sons of both the victims and victors of that bloody fratricidal combat would be called upon to fight side-by-side in the Winter, Continuation and Lapland Wars, the transformation of bitter division into national unity became an urgent priority for the nation and its politicians in the years leading up to the Winter War.

By the time the Winter War started, the radical elements on both the left and right in Finnish politics had been effectively marginalized, and the population was ready to unite in a desperate struggle for survival. Although the Continuation War was a very different kind of conflict, most of the Finns who were called up for military service once again dutifully reported. Some, however—mainly communists and communist sympathizers—saw it as an unjustified adventure. A small number went underground, spreading anti-war propaganda and carrying out occasional terrorist acts such as blowing up railway track.

Although the vast majority of Finnish citizens supported the government's decision to take up arms once again, they did not all agree on the ultimate goal of the undertaking. Some felt that Finland should do no more than defend its post-Winter War borders against renewed Soviet aggression. Most, including the 450,000 displaced Karelians whose homes were now on the "wrong" side of the border, wanted to take back the land that had been unfairly wrested from Finland in 1940. And then there were those adventurists who wanted to take advantage of the alliance with mighty Germany to push the Soviets beyond the pre-war border and create a Greater Finland that would encompass Eastern Karelia and Ingria.

Comrades in Arms but Not Allies?

Despite their complicity in Operation Barbarossa, the Finns steadfastly refused to call themselves "allies" of the Germans. They held that they were fighting a separate war and the Germans just happened to be fighting against the same enemy at the same time. This argument was primarily aimed at enabling Finland to maintain normal relations with Great Britain and the United States, important trading partners and democracies with republican values closely aligned with those held by most Finns.

Critics since then have increasingly argued that Finland's claim of non-alliance was self-serving and basically dishonest. While the choice between Russian and German dictatorships may have been for the Finns a distasteful one made under duress, choose they did; and although their decision enabled them to avoid the awful fate of their Baltic brethren, their carefully crafted co-belligerence became a moral stigma that cast a long and compromising shadow over Finland's status as a liberal democracy. When the Finnish Army crossed the pre-Winter War frontier and drove deep into Soviet territory that had never been part of Finland, even many in the West who originally sympathized with the Finns as victims of Soviet aggression began to see them as willing participants in the Nazi juggernaut.

Contemporary reports suggest that Finnish public opinion was largely supportive of the arrival of German troops on Finnish soil and remained so at least as long as the Germans seemed likely to win the war. Historian Arvi Korhonen wrote years later about the protective aura cast by the German presence as follows: "If the Angel Gabriel steps down from Heaven offering gifts, one doesn't organize meetings to consider what to do, one accepts the offer."

Because Finnish soldiers fought side-by-side with the Germans, there remains even today a misconception that Finland's leadership and its people were Nazi sympathizers. There is plenty of evidence that this was not the case. Although a relatively small group of Nazi sympathizers certainly did exist in the country, they never held significant power nor exerted much influence over public opinion. The *Wehrmacht's* own chief liaison officer in Finland's military headquarters, General Waldemar Erfurth, wrote in his post-war memoirs of the period:

> Finland's political rapprochement with Germany, which began prior to the Winter War and grew stronger during the brief period of peace between the Winter War and the [Continuation] War, resulted from a clear-sighted and realistic assessment of the world situation and not at all from sympathy for national socialism. The Nazi world view did not—with the exception of a few exceptional cases—prior to the war or during it, achieve any degree of support in Finland.[9]

The Role of Finland's Jews

The participation in the war by one small group, Finland's approximately 1,800 Jewish citizens, strongly suggests that Finland was fighting for its own survival and not in support of Nazi ideology. The 267 Finnish Jews who served in the military during the Continuation War plus several dozen Jewish women in the women's auxiliary knew full well that they might find themselves in close contact with their country's German co-belligerents.

Their attitude, then and since, is encapsulated in this comment by Jewish veteran Aron Livson. "When I am asked," he said, "I reply that Finns didn't fight at all on the German side. They fought for Finland's independence, and that's a fact."[10]

The Jewish community had provided vital support for hundreds of Central European Jewish refugees from Nazi terror, some of whom passed through Finland on their way to Sweden or the United States while others remained in Finland throughout the war. The full horror of *Die Endlösung*, the Nazis' "Final Solution," would only be revealed to Finland's Jewish soldiers after the conclusion of the war, but they knew enough about Nazi ideology at the outset to find their situation absurd and frightening. Many of them had lost relatives in Russian pogroms and would lose more in the gas chambers of the German death camps or in the killing fields and forests of Eastern Europe. Yet they answered the call to arms and did so without any effort to disguise their Jewish identity.

Captain Leo Skurnik was one of those who suffered terribly from the existential contradiction of being a Jewish soldier under German command. His son, Samuli, says that Skurnik's experiences as a regimental doctor in charge of a field hospital in the midst of some of the most intense fighting of the war exposed him as a doctor and as a person to such horrors that he apparently never fully recovered.

> According to his own account, as told to me by a very close wartime friend of his, Father was very afraid because of the Germans. As a physician, he felt it was his duty to treat all patients brought before him regardless of their national origin, but he was fully aware of the Germans' attitudes and behavior towards Jews and was therefore unable to feel completely safe.[11]

Nevertheless, Skurnik and 266 other Finnish Jews dutifully served in the Finnish armed forces during the Continuation War. Their family members on the home front contributed to the war effort in whatever ways they could. Their country was being threatened, and they were being offered an opportunity to prove their patriotism to the rest of their countrymen once and for all. The story of why and how Jewish soldiers fought and in some cases died on the same side of the battle lines as German soldiers is one of the most curious and intriguing stories to come out of "The Good War,"

From 1945 through 1989, Finland's need to reach an accommodation with its overbearing Soviet neighbor made frank and open public discussion of the Continuation War impolitic if not impossible. The official Soviet position still held that Finland's fictitious shelling of Mainila was the cause of the Winter War and the Continuation War was an act of Nazi adventurism on the part of the Finns. At the personal level, the brutal and traumatizing war often caused Finnish veterans to bury their war stories in stoical silence. Almost without exception, their children will say, "Father never spoke of the war." In their old age, however, a few were finally willing to unspool for the rest of us their tightly wrapped memories.

Notes

1. A *motti* (Finnish) is one cubic meter of cut and split firewood. In Finnish military jargon, it came to mean an entrapment in which the enemy was pinned down, surrounded and unable to escape.

2. Interviewed by the author, 24 January, 2012.

3. Although the city is called Vyborg in English, it seems more appropriate to use the Finnish name, Viipuri, for a city in which the Finnish language was dominant, than the Russian name (Выборг or Vyborg), which found its way into English usage.

4. *Puna-armeijan marssiopas Suomeen 1939*, ed. Antero Kautto, Karisto, Hämeenlinna, 1989, p. 50.

5. Of these, some were outdated Renault FT-19s left over from WWI and 32 were Vickers Mark E models without artillery. According to Seppo Jyrkinen, it would be better to acknowledge that at the start of the war, Finland really had no useful tanks at all.

6. Some 8,000 volunteers from Sweden and 700 from Norway did fight valiantly alongside the Finns in the Winter War but not as official representatives of their countries.

7. Although his full name was Carl Gustaf Emil Mannerheim, he detested the name Emil and signed his name "Gustaf Mannerheim" or simply "Mannerheim,"

8. Russian place names, many of them given to Karelian municipalities as part of Stalin's Russification of the area, are provided so the reader can locate them on contemporary maps.

9. Erfurth, Waldemar, *Suomi sodan myrskyssä 1941–1944*, Werner Söderström, Porvoo, 1951, pp. 174–175.

10. Interviewed by the author, April 3, 2012.

11. Interviewed by the author, 24 January, 2012.

Figure 2.1. Viipuri's castle viewed from the Salakkalahti Harbor in the 1930s (Eino Partanen)

Many labels have been hung on the old city of Viipuri: Finland's most joyful city, most cosmopolitan city, German Hansa city, city of the sea, city of trade, guard on the border between East and West, "old Russian city" and capital city of Karelia. As none of these labels can be completely removed, as none of them invalidates any other and as each one contains its own truth, if only for the duration of a century, we are certainly talking about a city which is like no other in Finland.

Katri Veltheim*

**Kävelyllä Viipurissa,* Kustannusosakeyhtiö Tammi, Helsinki, 1985, p. 6.

CHAPTER TWO

~

Benjamin Reminisces
about his Childhood

When I was growing up in Viipuri in the 1920s and 1930s, children died from diseases you almost never hear about any more, horrible diseases like diphtheria and the Spanish flu. There was no television, there were more horses than cars on the streets, and Old Man Lassila ladled creamy unpasteurized milk into the galvanized pails we brought to his shop on Sammonkatu early each morning. Radio was the new thing then, radio and moving pictures with our own movie stars like Tauno Palo and Hanna Taini.

Sometimes, when I'm especially tired, I imagine that I am still a teenager, Viipuri is still a part of Finland, the smell of boiling cabbage fills the air, and the Harmony Sisters are singing "Tähtikirkas on sää" on the radio. But Viipuri isn't part of Finland any more, it's part of Russia, and the milk from the supermarket doesn't taste anything like the milk we used to drink. I still listen to the radio, though. I used to watch television, but my eyesight got so bad that I had to sit with my nose practically touching the screen. Now I don't even bother turning it on.

My wife and children are gone, olehem hashalom,[1] and only the grandchildren and great-grandchildren are left. I rarely leave these two rooms any more, and hardly anyone comes to see me except the woman who comes in the morning to clean and prepare my meals. All that is left to connect me to the world are 95 years of memories. I guess that's what happens when you live this long.

Some things are better not to remember. I don't like thinking about the war. It was a shreklekhe tsayt, a terrible time! I was 19 when the Winter War began and 20 when I was called up to serve. At that age, you don't know much about life. Some of my friends were eager to fight. Viipuri had been handed over to the Russkies after the Winter War. Of course, we all wanted to get it back. But I wasn't excited about fighting. It was my duty, that was all.

We did get Viipuri back at the beginning of the war, but the Russkies took it away again at the end. I went there once with my youngest daughter, Sara, about thirty years ago, before she got so sick and when I could still walk pretty good. I think it was 1986 or 1987. I wish I hadn't gone. It was pitiful! Viipuri was such a great city when I was growing up. What we saw was nothing like that. Everything was a mess. Imagine! Some of the buildings that had been destroyed in the fighting in 1944 were still in ruins more than forty years later! The ones that were left standing needed paint and repairs. The people looked depressed, the shops were empty, and there were only a few stalls in the market square selling berries, mushrooms and tins of sardines. I wanted to show the wonderful places of my childhood to Sara, but they were all lost, and in their place was only some kind of shell, a hollow, bloodless city. It broke my heart.

I took her to see the building on Ainonkatu where my family lived before the war. The stairwell was filthy, and the only light was from a single bulb on the second-floor landing. When I knocked, an old woman opened the door to what had been our apartment. In my broken Russian I explained that I once lived there. I think at first she was afraid we wanted to take back the apartment, but when she understood I only wanted to show it to my daughter, she let us in and served us tea. The apartment was cold and damp. The old woman apologized for not having any cake to offer us, but we thanked her and took our leave as quickly as we could.

Our family lived in Viipuri for over 90 years. Zayde[2] Peisach was brought there by the Russian Army sometime around 1850. We don't know exactly where he was born, but it was somewhere around Vitebsk in what we used to call White Russia. He was a Cantonist, one of the children forced into the Russian Army when he was only a boy. He ended up stationed in the Viipuri garrison. When he got out of the army, he didn't know if anyone in his family was still alive or how to find them. He had nowhere to go so he stayed in Viipuri. My grandmother's family was from St. Petersburg. Bubbe[3] Feige came to Viipuri with her sister and another woman, all looking for husbands. Her sister married the father of Dov Weinstein. When I was growing up, the Weinsteins still had a clothing shop on Karjalankatu, No. 27. It was right around the corner from the Maxim Cinema.

Our home was like the Tower of Babel. Bubbe Feige lived with us after Zayde Peisach died. She spoke Russian, and my parents spoke Yiddish. We children went to a Finnish school and spoke Finnish to each other, but we spoke Yiddish with our parents and Russian with our grandmother. Sometimes we were speaking all three languages at the same time. When we all spoke together, though, it was in Yiddish. Religious services were in Hebrew, of course, and we boys had Hebrew lessons twice a week with Bortnovsky. He was a nice man and a good teacher, but we would rather have been playing football than sitting in his class. At least I would have.

Almost all the Jewish families kept kosher then. Two sets of dishes we had, even when we didn't have much to put on them. I still keep a kosher home, but my grandchildren and great-grandchildren don't. Not many live the old way anymore.

Back then we ate fish soup, chicken, potatoes, rye bread, all the same foods everyone else in Viipuri did except, of course, for the pork. And we had Russian food, too, like borscht, pelmeni, pirozhki, *and all kinds of pickles. For shabbos[4] we usually had* cholent *because Mameh could cook it the day before and keep the pot warm until the evening meal. And then there were the holidays with* challah, kreplakh, gefilte fish, herring *and onions in sour cream. . . . Ah, the Jewish food was the best!*

Tate[5] started as an apprentice in Meyer Steinbock's hat factory on Pohjolankatu and then moved to Eckert's to work as a cutter, but he was not the kind of person to work for someone else. He wanted to do everything his own way. When he and Mameh[6] got married, her father gave them enough money for Tate to leave Eckert, rent a small store front on Maununkatu, and start making hats on his own. The business was slow getting off the ground. During World War I, it was impossible to get the cloth and fur he needed from abroad for his hats, but that meant that no one else could import material or hats, either. He would be able to sell whatever he could make with the cloth he could find. His business was just picking up in 1917 when along came the Russian Revolution. Finland became independent, the border with Russia was closed, and suddenly our country was caught up in civil war. By the time the fighting ended more than three months later, Tate had lost everything. The next year when the first Simca Lifson—that's how he spelled his name then, the great-grandfather of the Simon Livson who is now our rabbi—opened his Eastern Finland Hat Factory on Karjalankatu, Tate went to work for him as a cutter. He started all over from nothing.

When I was 14, not long after Tate died, Mameh got Lifson to take me on as an apprentice at his hat factory. We worked with both cloth and fur, but working with fur was the most demanding. Lifson made hats for the army and the Civil Guard. He even made hats for Mannerheim. It was a good business, but eventually it got pretty boring, cutting the same patterns day after day.

Fortunately, there was more to do than just work. Viipuri was a great place to grow up, safe and friendly. We played sports, all kinds of sports, but I loved football the most. In the winter we all skated at the Salakkalahti Rink, and in the summer we swam at the Tervaniemi Beach. Sometimes it was so crowded in the water that all you could do was stand. You couldn't move without bumping into other people.

And then there was music and the theater. Viipuri had grand theaters! There was the Workers' Theater and the Viipuri Stage, which merged to form the Viipuri City Theater. We also had our own Jewish theater group, a Yiddish theater. All the Jews in Viipuri went. Of course, there were only about 250 of us in the whole city so whenever there was a performance at Ahdus,[7] everybody attended. And many of us acted, too. Salomon Eckert and I were in almost every performance from the time we were old enough to play children's roles. Salomon was older and a much better actor than I was. He even got to go to Riga and Vilnius with our theater group's production of Di Nekome fun a Froi. *He fell in the Winter War.*

Ahdus was a real community center, the focus of Jewish community life. The name means something like "solidarity," The entire community took up a collection and bought the property in 1919. That was only the second year that Jews had civil rights in this country. Before that, any Jew could be deported for any reason.

The location of Ahdus was perfect, right in the middle of town on Linnankatu, next to the Parade Ground. There were five buildings, most of them two or three stories tall, with a yard in the middle. People said there had been a bakery there in the old days. There were club rooms, meeting rooms, and a big library full of books in Yiddish. The biggest room was where we held our theater productions and concerts.

I sang in the choir and sometimes played the piano a little. Mameh said that when she was pregnant with me, she attended the first concerts at Ahdus. She always claimed I got my musical talent from being exposed to the wonderful music there. Who knows, maybe she was right. I certainly didn't get it from her or Tate. Neither of them could carry a tune. I sang in the Jewish choir in Helsinki until a few years ago and played the piano every day until Rachel died, ole hashalom![8] It's been years now since I opened the piano, but I still like to go to choir rehearsals when I can find someone to take me. I don't sing any more, but they always let me sit with them anyway.

There really wasn't any antisemitism to speak of in Viipuri. We Jews were just like any other kids. Maybe every once in a while some boys would yell "Jutku"[9] or wave a pig's ear at us and grunt a few times, though, and then we would have to fight. Wuli Gurevitsch's little brother was a year older than me, and Wuli had taught him how to box. I knew how to box a little, too. Gurevitsch and I would teach those boys a lesson! We were all pretty good athletes—Gurevitsch, Lifson, Eckert, Altschuler, Klimscheffskij, Steinbock, the Kagan brothers, and me—so after a while even the tough boys learned not to bother us. The funny thing was that the working-class kids got along with us just fine. It was the rich boys we had problems with. They thought they were better than us.

We had our own Jewish sports club, Kadur.[10] We played football in the eastern area league against all the other clubs. As teenagers, Tevi Kagan, Aron Lifson and I got to play on the men's team sometimes because there weren't enough grown men to fill the roster. Salomon Altschuler was already a regular in the lineup by that time. Wuli, though, was the only Jew from Viipuri to make a real name for himself in sports. He was the heavyweight boxing champion of Finland and a hero to all of us.

In the evening, when we didn't have practice or a game, we would join all the other young people who were walking back and forth along Torkkelinkatu between the Market Square and Punaisenlähteentori. From Vappu[11] to the end of September, we walked on the park side of the street, and the rest of the year on the other side, where the buildings are. Why did we change sides like that? I don't know, but that is how we did it, year after year. The younger ones would be there first in the late afternoon, and then, as it began to get dark, they would have to go home and leave the sidewalk to the older ones. After a while, if you got lucky, you might get one of the girls to go to Café Espilä or Pursiainen's for hot chocolate or walk with you towards the harbor.

A few of the Finnish girls wouldn't have anything to do with the Jewish boys, but most of them weren't like that. It was a good thing, too, because we would have had no social life at all if the only girls we could socialize with were the Jewish girls! There were so few of them, not even a handful our own age. We all had lots of non-Jewish friends and non-Jewish girlfriends, too. I always knew, though, I would marry a Jewish girl someday, but I never thought she would have to be from Viipuri.

Some of the older boys used to brag about the good time they had with women. Times were hard during the Depression, and it was understood that if you had a little money, you could always find a companion. I was still too young to know, but that's what the older boys said. Most of the easy women in Viipuri were poor Russians from the countryside, but there was one Jewish girl a few years older than us who scandalized the whole community. Her name was Rosalia Gurovitz. She was from Viipuri, but she became known as the Rose of Kotka.[12] She ran around a lot, married a goy,[13] a policeman he was, got divorced, moved to Kotka, drank a lot, and sold bootleg liquor from the back room of her beauty parlor in the Kotka harbor. Oy vey, how the Viipuri women talked about her!

I didn't know anything about women in those days. I was small for my age and shy. I didn't have a girlfriend the whole time we lived in Viipuri, but that didn't really matter. We always did things and went places in groups, boys and girls together. It was easy to fit in, doing what everyone else did. I didn't really get interested in girls until I attended the Scandinavian Jewish Youth Association summer camp the year I turned sixteen, but that's another story.

Notes

1. May they rest in peace (Hebrew)
2. Grandfather (Yiddish)
3. Grandmother (Yiddish)
4. Sabbath (Yiddish)
5. Dad (Yiddish)

6. Mom (Yiddish)
7. Solidarity (Yiddish), the name of Viipuri's Jewish Community Center
8. May she rest in peace (Yiddish)
9. Kike (Finnish, vulgar)
10. Ball (Hebrew), the name of Viipuri's Jewish sports club
11. May Day (Finnish), the 1st of May
12. She was immortalized in a popular 1940s song, *Kotkan ruusu*
13. A gentile

Figure 3.1. Arrival at the SJUF 1936 Summer Camp at Vidablick (Finland's Jewish Archives)

"Judaism in Finland will disappear only if we let it disappear."

"Although it is possible to love us to death . . ."

"Was that a reference to efforts to convert us or to mixed marriage?"

"If you go to sauna and eat sauna sausage, you can think of yourself as a real Finn, but just ask your neighbor!"

The conversation turned increasingly often to this sad reality. Many had long painted a picture for us of how Jews were disappearing from Finland. It was difficult, even impossible, for a small minority community to survive.

*Mindele London**

*London, Mindele, *Kolmastoista tuoli*, Atena Kustannus, Jyväskylä, 2002, p. 28.

CHAPTER THREE

~

Vidablick

Siuntio, August 1936—The *allée* lined by stately spruces was designed to convey a sense of rustic grandeur as one sweeps up the long approach to *Vidablick*. In Benjamin's case, it only reinforces the sense of foreboding that has been building since he first got on the bus. The branches, still dripping from the afternoon shower, shut out the sunlight and envelop the bus in a shroud of misery. *I will never make any friends here, and the girls will ignore me, or worse.*

The animated chatter of those at the back of the 20-seater bus, renewing old acquaintances or making new ones, confirms his worst suspicions. They are speaking Swedish, of course, and from their sing-song inflections he can tell that some of them are actually from Sweden, not just Helsinki or Turku. Benjamin will be the only camper from Viipuri, and that means he will probably be the only one whose mother tongue is Finnish. At 16, he is sure to be one of the youngest in the whole camp as well.

He sits behind the driver, leaning against the window. He hasn't said a word to anyone—nor anyone to him—since he left Viipuri. Not having anyone to talk to was a relief to him at first, but by the time he changed trains in Helsinki for the short ride to Siuntio, he had begun to feel lonely and perhaps a little homesick. He had followed the low-skimming clouds along the shore from the train window, and before he knew it, he was sitting on the camp bus, which now turns away from the golden fields of ripening rye and heads into the pine-dark forest. His stomach is churning, and his sense of foreboding is only slightly eased by knowing he will soon be able to find an outhouse and some relief.

Attending the week-long 1936 Scandinavian Jewish Youth Association Camp was not Benjamin's idea, not at all. Until his departure, everything that summer had been just fine. He had been working at Lifson's Eastern Finland Hat Factory, learning the cutter's trade. On his days off, he played football, went with friends to the beach, or took bike trips into the countryside. Soon, he thinks, the other campers will be returning to school or work, and I will be at Lifson's cutting table and preparing in my spare time for the autumn play at Ahdus. First, though, I have to get through this week.

It was his mother, of course. She is the one who worries that he is spending too much time with gentiles, by which she means with shiksas.[1] The boys don't matter. Good contacts in the wider community can be useful, no? But what if, God forbid, he falls in love with the wrong kind of girl?

The Scandinavian Jewish Youth Association Camp has been held each of the past six years in exotic cities such as Copenhagen, Malmö, Oslo and Gothenburg. This year it is Finland's turn, and Hatchijo, the Helsinki Zionist Youth Organization, has decided to hold the camp at a country school so there will be as few outside distractions as possible. There are participants from Sweden, Norway and Denmark as well as Finland, nearly 90 in all. The flyer sent to his home had emphasized the trips, discussions and sports, but everyone knows that the real purpose of the camp is matchmaking. In many of the Scandinavian Jewish communities, there simply aren't enough eligible partners to go around. Summer camp creates opportunities for young people to meet and, perhaps, fall in love. The old system of arranged marriages, which brought many of their grandparents, and even some of their parents, together, is no longer going to work for this generation.

Curious as he is, Benjamin refuses to turn around and look at the girls behind him. He will meet them later, and he doesn't want them to think he is too interested. Besides, it is taking all his powers of concentration to control his rumbling gut.

* * *

David remembers Rachel from the previous year's camp in Copenhagen. She is slim with dark, shoulder-length hair and large brown eyes. She had seemed very young to him at the time, but the intervening months have worked wonders. He recalls that she had a boyish figure, but that is certainly no longer the case.

Trying not to seem too obvious, he casually slips into the seat next to her on the bus. After a minute or two, he takes a bag of Kiss-Kiss candies from his pocket, unwraps one and pops it into his mouth, and, almost as an afterthought, offers one to Rachel. Later, to overcome her shyness, David brings up some of the funny incidents from the previous year's camp: the skit in which the older campers made fun of the counselors, the time when the boy from Norrköping bragged to everyone how well he could swim but had to be pulled out of the water by a staff member. Before long, they are laughing at each other's Swedish, hers modulated and lilting, his nearly atonal by comparison and full of slang words she finds strange.

David has been looking forward all year to returning to camp. Tall and physically imposing, he is a favorite with the girls. Over the winter he corresponded with a few of the campers from the previous year—two sisters from Gothenburg and a real looker from Oslo—but none of them could come to camp this summer. No matter, he will have no trouble making new conquests.

*   *   *

When the campers get off the bus in front of the large, wooden schoolhouse, "Dafa" Jankeloff is waiting for them. At 25, Dafa is not much older than the oldest campers although his receding hairline and serious demeanor give him the requisite air of authority for a camp director. He assembles the campers, including those who arrived earlier, in front of the flagpole and briefly explains the most important rules. The girls will be housed in the school building and use the outhouse at the far end of the woodshed. The boys will sleep in the army tents at the edge of the field and use the outhouse at the far end of the yard, behind the storage barn. Under no circumstances are boys to be found in the girls' quarters or vice-versa. There is to be absolutely no smoking during the entire week and, of course, no drinking. To ensure that the camp is strictly kosher, no food is to be kept in the tents, either. If anyone has brought food along, it is to be handed over to the staff before the evening meal. Attendance at all meals and activities will be carefully monitored, and only the director can excuse anyone from participating.

Upon arrival, Benjamin had hurriedly explained his stomach problem to Dafa and rushed off behind the storage barn while the others listened to the brief instructions. By the time he returns, the others are already unloading their bags from the bus, and Benjamin is sure his embarrassing absence from the very first meeting has been noted by all. With head down, avoiding eye contact, he searches until he finds his suitcase.

David offers to help Rachel with her bag, but she demurely refuses, pointing out that he isn't allowed up the stairs anyway. She tries hard to pretend that she isn't flattered by the attention, but she knows that the color in her cheeks gives her away. Oh well, there are worse things than being singled out for attention on the first day by one of the handsomest boys in the camp.

When tent assignments are handed out, Benjamin discovers that he shares Tent 7 with David as well as a friendly Norwegian boy named Herman, and a chubby Danish boy called Max. The others have already laid out their bedding so Benjamin takes the remaining cot. Although he has studied Swedish in school and can speak it passably, the fluency of the others only adds to his isolation. He can understand well enough when someone speaks directly to him, but when he retreats into his own thoughts, his tent-mates' chatter wafts over him like a breeze on a hot and humid night that blows by without providing any relief.

Benjamin assumes that David will have no time for him and is surprised to find that, on the contrary, the older boy is quite friendly. David opens a box of *mandelbreyt*[2] his mother has packed in his suitcase and passes it around. "Better to eat it now than give it up to the staff," he says. "They'll just feast on it themselves." Benjamin notices that Max takes several pieces, eating one and hiding the others in his back-pack. David obviously sees it, too, but says nothing. Benjamin has to admit that the *mandelbreyt* is delicious, almost as good as his own mother's, which is saying a lot.

Benjamin keeps waiting for David to ask how old he is or find something to tease him about, but he only asks, "What's your name?"

"Benjamin."

"Where you from, Beni?"

"Viipuri."

"Oh yeah? My mother's cousins are from there. The Maslovats. You probably know some of them."

"Everyone knows them. They're very active in the congregation. When I was younger, our rabbi was a Maslovat."

"I haven't been there since I was little, but I hear it is a great place. Have some more *mandelbreyt*. We have to finish it up before we go to dinner."

*   *   *

Benjamin walks with David to the dining room and sits at the same table, but if he expects to be included in the older boy's conversation or that of the table in general, he is mistaken. David's attention is focused entirely on Rachel, just as it had been on the bus. Benjamin picks distractedly at his chicken pilaf. Probably hasn't been a good idea to eat that *mandelbreyt* before dinner, especially with his stomach the way it is.

He wants to leave the table and go outside, but Dafa says it is time for the evening program, and they begin with the evening quiz. After every evening meal, a sheet of quadrille paper and a pencil are distributed to each table.

The tables compete with each other to answer ten tricky questions covering a wide range of topics, from Biblical history to current events and from classical music to sports. Working together to answer the questions, the campers get to know one another better.

To its members' surprise, Benjamin's table wins the first evening's contest with nine correct answers. Benjamin supplied four of them and Rachel three. Although Benjamin's father was a worker in a hat factory, Mendel was a voracious reader and autodidact. Every evening before dinner, he introduced new words to his children or told them interesting facts he had gleaned that day from a book, newspaper or the *Bible*. The other children sometimes found it boring, but Benjamin shared his father's passion for knowledge and made a point of trying to absorb all the information his father offered them. And then he and his friends are also crazy about sports and music so he knows a lot about those, too. He answers the biblical and sports questions correctly as well as one about the rivers of Africa and the one about the Thirty Years' War but needs Rachel's help for the questions about Goethe's *Die Leiden des jungen Werther*, the names of the starring actors in *It Happened One Night*, and the birthplace of Ze'ev Jabotinsky. Neither of them knows what the chemical symbol Sb stands for.

"I guess I'd better sit with the two of you every meal," says David, who knew the one about antimony but was unable to answer most of the others. Benjamin thinks there is little doubt that his tent-mate will sit with Rachel, anyway, but he is flattered to be publicly included in this way in their inner circle.

*   *   *

Benjamin is wrong about David and Rachel as he finds out that evening at the campfire. A Swedish girl named Naomi has already caught David's eye, and he is now pursuing her as assiduously as he had courted Rachel earlier in the day. Naomi is big-boned and well built. She laughs loudly and tosses her long hair in an alluring way whenever something is said that strikes her as funny. She commands attention and attracts admirers, especially among the older boys. Benjamin can see that the other girls quickly divide into cliques: those who seek Naomi's approval and those who resent her queen bee act.

The next morning's program begins with a discussion led by Rabbi Ehrenpreis from Stockholm on the current situation in Palestine. He has been invited to give a speech at the Nordic Jewish Youth League Congress to be held in Helsinki immediately after the end of camp and has been prevailed upon by the organizers to come to Finland a week early so he can speak to the campers. Rabbi Ehrenpreis explains how the boycott and general strike sparked by the violent death of Sheikh Izaddin al-Qassam have deteriorated into a full-blown Arab revolt against both the British and the Jews. He describes how *kibbutzim* are springing up to establish the presence of Jewish settlers throughout *Eretz Yisrael*.[3] It is the responsibility of the campers and their generation, he says, to support the Zionist cause, and he predicts that it will probably not be long before some of them will be called on to fight.

The lively and sometimes contentious discussion that follows sets the tone for the rest of the camp. The Revisionist Zionists in the group, most of whom are from Finland, feel that it is the duty of every able-bodied Jew to take up arms in support of the establishment of a Jewish homeland in Palestine. Some of them, including David, insist that they are prepared to leave as soon as their congregations can prepare the necessary papers and provide them with tickets.

Others argue that the position of Jews in Europe is growing more precarious all the time, not just as a result of growing Nazi power and the spread of antisemitism but because of Jewish overreaction. Their main obligation, they argue, is to demonstrate that Jews are loyal citizens of the countries in which they live and are neither communist agitators nor untrustworthy outsiders. Modern Jews need to participate in the modern world, not withdraw to utopian settlements or antagonize their friends with unrealistic demands. Benjamin is surprised at how militant some of the girls are about these issues. Back in Viipuri, it is mostly the young men who argue about politics and religion, trying to convince their fathers to let them make *aliyah*[4] to Palestine.

How strongly does Benjamin himself feel about all this? He isn't sure. At home, several of his friends and their older brothers are ardent Zionists, but Benjamin has never been all that interested in politics. He feels uncomfortable speaking out one way or the other and so listens to the debate without taking part.

In the afternoon, the campers are allowed to choose among several activities. Benjamin chooses swimming, in part because he sees Rachel and David signing up for it. A group of them, led by two counselors, mount bicycles and begin the ride down the hill towards *Tjusträsk*, which Benjamin hopes will turn out to be a real lake and not a mud hole.

The swimming area is on the opposite shore of *Tjusträsk* near where the Siuntio River flows out of it towards the sea. In August the water level in the river is low enough for them to leave their bikes on the near river bank and wade across at the end of the path. Trees on the far bank of the lake have been cleared away to create a sunny area where bathers can sit or lie on the grass, and a strong rope has been looped over an overhanging alder branch to enable the more adventurous to swing out over the water in a graceful arc and drop down into the cool water.

When they reach the swimming area, the boys strip to their bathing costumes and rush into the water. David is a strong swimmer but so is Benjamin, and the two soon find themselves treading water about 70 meters offshore. "Isn't this keen?" David says, throwing back his head and then diving under, only to resurface about five yards away. "Race you back to shore!"

Benjamin knows he will lose, but the older boy takes off before he can say anything so there is nothing to do but head after him. By the time Benjamin can stand, David is striding confidently towards the girls, and that puts an end to their conversation for the afternoon. Benjamin starts walking towards their group, but when he sees that David has planted himself next to Rachel in a way that clearly indicates others are not welcome, he proceeds along the clearing and slouches to the ground near a boy who appears to be as lonely as he is. Since neither of them shows any interest in starting up a conversation, they sit there silently staring out over the water until it is time to return to *Vidablick*.

*   *   *

At dinner that evening, Benjamin returns to the same table. David, however, has switched and is sitting across the room, next to Naomi. Benjamin now finds himself next to Rachel. He wants to talk to her but can't figure out how to begin so he is a little startled when she speaks first.

"Wasn't the water cold?"

"Not for me, I'm used to swimming in the sea. Why didn't you go in?"

"Oh, I'm not a very good swimmer. I prefer just to sit on the shore and enjoy the sun."

"Where are you from?" Benjamin asks. "I'm from Viipuri."

"Yes, I know. I'm from Turku. I visited Viipuri once. It is a really beautiful city. I loved the castle and park."

"I've heard Turku is nice, too, but I've never been there."

Benjamin is afraid Rachel will ask his age or what he is studying. If she attended camp the previous year, she has to be at least a year older than he is. And although he isn't exactly ashamed of working in a hat factory, Rachel is probably studying to be something grand, like a teacher or a musician. Benjamin would have wanted to study, too, but after his father died, he had to go to work to help support the family.

"Do you know a lot of people from last year?" he asks.

"A few," she answers. "There are four others from Turku. Of course, I know all of them. There are so few Jews in Turku that we all know each other. In fact," she laughs, "most of us are related to each other."

Benjamin thinks about why his mother has sent him to camp and can't help blushing. That is probably why Rachel is here, too.

When it is time for the evening quiz, Rachel and Benjamin lead their team to a perfect score, but this time another table shares the victory with them. A third team had nine correct but was unable to identify Rahab, the woman who housed the spies who helped Joshua conquer the walled city of Jericho. After the program is over and the flag-lowering ceremony has concluded, Benjamin and Rachel find themselves wandering together down the *allée* leading back to the main road. It is after 9:00 p.m., but the northern sun is still well above the horizon, and the orange light filters warmly through the towering branches.

"I really love this time of year," says Rachel. "Except for the mosquitoes, that is."

"Me, too," replies Benjamin. It isn't something he has thought a lot about, but the way Rachel says it makes him feel as if the idea has been his own as well. The part about the mosquitoes, anyway, is certainly true. Here in the woods, some of them are as big as dragonflies.

The walk, which lasts only about 10 minutes before they return to the schoolhouse, leaves Benjamin feeling curiously lightheaded and somewhat confused. He has seen the way Rachel looks at David and is enough of a realist to recognize she does not feel the same way about him. The curious mixture of elation and depression follows him to his tent and settles next to him on his cot, where it will keep him company through the uneasy night.

Before they go to sleep, David tells his tent-mates how he slipped away with Naomi and she let him kiss her. Not only that, he had slid his hand under her blouse onto her breast, and she had let him keep it there while they kissed. Max and Herman try to get him to say more, but David just rolls over, mumbling something about being tired.

That night, the dreams of the young men in Tent No. 7 are every bit as conflicted as their arguments about their responsibilities as Jews in a world infected with virulent antisemitism had been during the morning's discussion.

* * *

David doesn't carve notches in his belt, but he certainly keeps a detailed mental catalogue of the girls he has bedded. Or maybe "bedded" is the wrong word because there haven't been that many actual beds involved. His first sexual encounter had come when he was only twelve and a teen-aged neighbor had gotten down on all fours and ordered him to mount her "like a dog does," He had no idea what he was supposed to do and didn't get an erection. His next experience a few years later, also with an older girl, helped demystify what older boys and girls do together and made it easier for him to perform adequately when he began "falling in love" in earnest. Why he falls in love so easily he can't say, but it doesn't trouble him all that much, except when he finds himself with strong feelings for more than one girl at a time or has to extract himself from a relationship with a girl who is getting too serious, which has happened more than once.

During his first year as a student at the Polytechnic, David had plenty of opportunity to visit the dance halls and restaurants of Helsinki. His father is so proud to have a son studying to be an engineer that he gives David a generous allowance and encourages him to enjoy life, saying that he, himself, never had the opportunity to do anything but work and wants his son to make friends and have "as good a time as the Finnish boys,"

So David quickly learns to appreciate good food, strong drink and beautiful girls. Even before reaching the legal drinking age, he has no difficulty getting served in Helsinki's restaurants because he looks older. And if you are good-looking and have a little money, it is not difficult to find women or make friends. Tall with regular features, David does not resemble the Jewish stereotype. Although he never tries to disguise his ethnicity, many people do not realize at first that he is Jewish. The girls, especially, don't seem to mind. Often, it is only when a girl expresses curiosity about his circumcised penis that the subject comes up at all.

By the fourth day of camp, David has begun to show a brotherly, protective affection for Benjamin. In football games he makes sure the younger boy gets his share of touches. If Benjamin's imperfect Swedish causes someone to snicker, a sharp look from David puts an end to the laughter. Benjamin's appreciation for David's sponsorship is heavily tinged with admiration, but one thing prevents it from blossoming into full-fledged idolatry: David's treatment of Rachel. David continues to flirt with her. Although he no longer tries to monopolize her attention, he is clearly playing with her feelings.

Each night in the tent, David's update on his romance with Naomi includes bolder revelations. Max and Herman listen with a mixture of awe and envy, but Benjamin's loyalty to Rachel makes David's bragging about his exploits unseemly. Benjamin suspects that David might be exaggerating about how far Naomi lets him go, but the details are pretty convincing. Swedish girls have a reputation for being easy, anyway, although Benjamin always thought that didn't apply to Jewish girls. Now he knows better.

For his own part, Benjamin is just as confused as ever about how to approach Rachel. Although he is spending more and more time with her, he hasn't dared to reveal his feelings in any way and face the likelihood of rejection. David's behavior, which under different circumstances might have encouraged him to be bolder, actually has the opposite effect. Rachel might think he, too, just wants to boast to his tent-mates, one of whom is David. Benjamin is sure she is not the kind of girl to allow a boy to take liberties with her, and any kind of physical contact, however innocent, might be taken the wrong way.

This, of course, is exactly what caused David to change course so abruptly. He thinks Rachel is pretty and clever, but he also knows that a week is too short a time to get anywhere with a girl like that. Since she doesn't live in Helsinki, either, it isn't really worth investing the time and energy to try and break down her defenses. Still, he can't resist flirting with Rachel from time to time, even if only to make Naomi jealous.

* * *

The morning discussion groups grow more heated by the day. Some of the campers apparently have no idea what is going on in Germany or even in their own countries, and this infuriates some of the others. Four Danish campers show up for breakfast one morning wearing yellow stars with the word *Jude* in Hebraic-like letters pinned to their shirts. Dafa is livid and makes them remove the badges immediately, but the discussion that follows is by far the liveliest and most intense of the camp. Examples of antisemitism that campers or their families have personally experienced transform the official discussion topic—"What does Judaism mean to me?"—into a heated debate over whether Jews are safe in Scandinavian countries. Most feel they are—for now, at least—but a few argue that security for Jews is an illusion and will continue to be until a militarily defensible Jewish homeland can be established in Palestine.

Benjamin thinks most of the campers are just repeating what they hear at home. What do they really know about the world? He has experienced antisemitism in the form of some name-calling and a few fights, but does that mean Viipuri is an unsafe place to live? He certainly doesn't feel that way. Big kids have always found ways to bully smaller kids. If he were cross-eyed or spoke with a lisp, they would beat him for that. His mother said that life in Finland had been bad before the Jews won their rights, but now they are citizens like everyone else.

David insists that Jews might be tolerated in Scandinavia for now but would never be fully accepted. The population is so nearly homogeneous that Jews and the handful of other minorities living there—Tatars, Gypsies and Lapps—stand out like sore thumbs. Whenever a scapegoat is needed for social or economic ills, the minorities are always going to be the first to be blamed, he says. If the economy doesn't improve, it will only be a matter of time before the first pogrom is organized. Only where Jews are in the majority can they ever be really secure.

Benjamin watches to see Rachel's reaction. She hasn't said much so far, but now she speaks out strongly in support of David's position. She points out that Finnish Jews, as the last ones in Europe to receive citizenship rights, seem to be in a particularly vulnerable position. She says her family can't seem to figure out which is the greater threat, communism or antisemitism. Both of them make her wonder what the future will be like. "Maybe in Palestine we Jews can create a better society, not just for ourselves but for everyone."

David claps vigorously when she finishes speaking, and Benjamin wonders at first whether she said what she did to win his approval, but on second thought he feels ashamed of himself.

The session gives Benjamin a headache. At lunch, he toys with his fish soup, leaving most of it in his bowl. Rachel, too, seems preoccupied. It is hard to make normal small talk after the morning's heavy discussion. Having finished their meal, Benjamin and Rachel find themselves once again walking side-by-side down the *allée*, saying little.

There are many things Benjamin would like to say to Rachel, but he knows he can never bring himself to say them. Once again, Rachel is the one to break the silence.

"You didn't say anything during the discussion."

"I don't know. I just don't think I know enough to have a strong opinion like you. I've never thought much about these things before."

"If you don't think about them," Rachel scolds, "someone else will do the thinking for you. You can't go through life like a leaf in a stream, floating whichever way the current takes you."

"But how can you be so sure of yourself?" Benjamin replies. "I can have strong opinions when I feel I am right, but I can't see into the future and predict which way the world will go. Sometimes these discussions make me feel like everything is just going to hell and it doesn't matter what I think, anyway."

"That's the way I felt last year, but then I got interested in reading the newspapers and listening to the news. Now I attend WIZO[5] meetings with my mother and my aunt. I think we have a responsibility to try to understand what is going on in the world and be ready to act when the time comes."

"Act how?"

"I don't know, exactly, but there is a lot of scary talk about another world war. If there is one, I don't know what will happen to us. I only know it will be too late to start thinking about what to do when the fighting begins."

Benjamin can see that she is right. He wonders why he always needs someone else to open his eyes like that. Isn't he smart enough to figure things out for himself? Or is he just so self-absorbed that he isn't paying attention to the right things?

Suddenly, Rachel takes the conversation in a totally different direction.

"Why does your friend act that way?"

Benjamin knows exactly whom she means but answers, "Who?"

"You know who I mean. David."

"Acts what way?"

"Don't play dumb. You see that he flirts with me and then runs off with that stupid Naomi. I don't care if he likes her, but why can't he leave me alone? I don't really like him anyway. He's too stuck up."

Benjamin doesn't know how to answer.

"I don't think he's conceited," he says. "I think he likes you, and maybe he respects you too much. I don't know, I guess that's just his way."

"Respects me too much? That's a good one. I don't think he respects anyone, really. Certainly not that Naomi!"

*　　*　　*

Naomi gets her period the next day. As with almost everything Naomi does, it quickly becomes public information, and that puts an abrupt end to David's aspirations. He suspects Naomi wouldn't have let him go all the way until possibly the last night of camp, anyway, and now that is out of the question.

Naomi's altered circumstances leave David without a project for the last days of camp. He thinks about Rachel again, but he knows that one is going nowhere. He has noticed, though, how Benjamin has been mooning after her lately—there really was no other way to describe it. Benjamin clearly needs help, and who better to provide it? If he isn't going to make a serious play for Rachel himself, he can at least give some advice to his forlorn little buddy.

Before dinner, David finds Benjamin down by the well, throwing pebbles distractedly into an empty pail. The older boy throws his arm across the younger boy's shoulder and leads him over to the nearby slant-pole fence.

"How are you and Rachel doing?"

"What do you mean?" Benjamin is taken completely off guard.

"You know, how's that little romance going?"

"We're just friends."

"Come on, don't try to tell me you don't fancy her. Everyone can see it."

Benjamin is horrified. Can it be that everyone is watching him make a fool of himself?

"Hey, there's nothing wrong with that," says David. "She's pretty and smart. But you're never gonna get anywhere unless you make a move. Camp is almost over, and she'll be gone before you work up enough nerve to kiss her. She's not gonna make the first move, you know."

"I don't want to talk about it."

"OK, it's your business, but I'm just trying to help. You see, what you need to do . . ."

*   *   *

Camp ends two days later. Benjamin hasn't kissed Rachel or anyone else, Naomi has stopped talking to David, who has begun thinking about Helsinki night life and treating camp as if it were already in the past. Rachel's friendship with Benjamin remains constant, but their last walk on the *allée* is taken in awkward silence. Before they get on their separate busses, they exchange addresses and Rachel promises to write. David tells both of them to look him up when they come to Helsinki. It has started to rain by the time the campers have to leave. They hug, promise to stay in touch, and climb into the busses. From behind the tiny windows they wave tearfully at the waterlogged staff members, standing on the steps with hands held high, waving.

There will be three more pre-war Scandinavian Jewish Youth Association Camps, the last held in an atmosphere of self-delusion less than a month before Germany invades Poland and plunges Europe into World War II. It is hosted by Norway, which will itself be invaded by the Germans eight months later. Eleven former campers will be among the 762 Norwegian Jews sent to Auschwitz and their death by the German occupiers and their Norwegian collaborators.

Rachel keeps her word and writes to Benjamin a few weeks after camp. He doesn't dare open the envelope at first, but when he does, he finds a pleasant, friendly message lacking even a hint of the affection he hoped against hope to find. She asks whether he has heard from David, which, of course, he hasn't. She writes about her studies and her fear that Europe is headed for another war. The letter is signed, "Your friend, Rachel,"

Benjamin is becoming quite a skilled cutter and is at his happiest while working. He is troubled, however, by thoughts of Viipuri's proximity to the Russian border. If the Soviets decide to cause trouble, they will be in his back yard before anyone knows it. At least he is clear about what he will have to do in that case: he will fight. But what to do about Rachel, he is clueless.

David tries to keep up with his schoolwork, but he finds it hard to concentrate on those subjects he finds boring. Physics and engineering, though, continue to fascinate him, and he begins to see how they might be of use if Finland ends up at war. He devours books about field artillery operations and hopes to be selected for special training in artillery theory and practice one day. He still finds time for socializing, of course, and discovers that the general atmosphere of growing insecurity is a powerful aphrodisiac for certain young women who no longer seem quite so concerned about saving themselves for marriage.

Living in three different cities and leading very different lives, Benjamin, Rachel and David have no idea how tightly their lives will become intertwined. As they return home in the autumn of 1936, they are mostly thinking about the same things as other teenagers throughout Scandinavia: school, work, romance and their future. But the future, as WWII approaches, has its own plans for them, plans that are beginning to take shape far away in Moscow and Berlin.

Like Medical Captain Leo Skurnik, they will find themselves in close proximity to the German military at the same time as the Nazi killing machine is doing everything in its power to exterminate Judaism from Europe. To understand how they came to be in such a precarious situation, we must travel back almost 100 years to a *shtetl* in the Pale of Settlement where Benjamin's paternal grandfather is preparing for his *bar mitzvah*.

Notes

1. Female gentiles (Yiddish, derogatory)
2. Almond bread (Yiddish)
3. Land of Israel (Hebrew)
4. Act of emigrating to Israel (Hebrew)
5. Women's International Zionist Organization.

Figure 4.1. A shtetl not unlike Peisach's home in Byelorussia in the early 19th Century (Alamy Stock Photo)

"You see, they have collected a crowd of cursed little Jew boys of eight or nine years old . . . we are driving them to Kazan. It took them over a hundred *versts** out of their way back there. The officer who handed them over said, 'It's dreadful, and that's all there is to it; a third were left on the way," and he pointed to the earth. "Not half will reach their destination,' he said."

"Have there been epidemics?" I asked, deeply moved.

"No, they just die off like flies . . . I ask you, what use is it to the army? What can they do with little boys?"

Alexander Herzen**

<hr />

*About 60 miles or 96 kilometers

**Quoted in Domnitch, Larry, *The Cantonists: The Jewish Children's Army of the Tsar,* Devorah Publishing, Jerusalem–New York, 2003, p 33.

CHAPTER FOUR

~

Peisach Loses Everything

Vitebsk, Byelorussia, 1842—Suppose, just for example, that you are a twelve-year-old boy living somewhere in a *shtetl* near Vitebsk in what was then called White Russia. The year is 1842. Let's say your name is Peisach, and you have dark, curly hair with long *peyes*,[1] or sidelocks, and slightly bowed legs from a vitamin-deficient diet. Your father, wrapped in a long black coat in your cold, dark and smoke-filled home, seems to spend all his time hunched over religious texts, commentaries on those religious texts, and commentaries on the commentaries. You know this because whenever he is not mumbling over them himself, he is teaching them to you in much the way a French farmer crams food down the throat of a goose whose swollen liver he will later turn into *pâté de foie gras*. The only school you attend is a *cheder*, three afternoons a week, where the rabbi has you and five other twelve-year-olds memorize prayers and portions of the Torah in anticipation of the *bar mitzvah* each of you expects to celebrate during the coming year.

Your family's sole source of income is the sewing your mother does on contract for Moses Sirovitsch. Your older sister, Dvera, helps with the hemming and buttons after she has done the housework, prepared the meals, and looked after the younger children. Fortunately for her, there isn't that much housework to do because your home consists of just two small and sparsely furnished rooms.

You are looking forward to your *bar mitzvah* and the prospect of becoming a full-fledged member of the congregation . . .

. . . and then the *chappers*[2] arrive!

There are two of them, rough men in dirty clothes and muddy boots, reeking of damp soil and dung. At first, they don't seem so bad. They allow you time to say goodbye to your family and wrap your few belongings in a rectangle of cloth. You've heard that some *chappers* just hit boys over the head and carry them off.

Your father, wailing prayers all the while, hands you the *tallit* and *tefillin*[3] you would have received at your *bar mitzvah*, communicating in this silent way his wish for you to remain true to your faith. Your mother sobs loudly

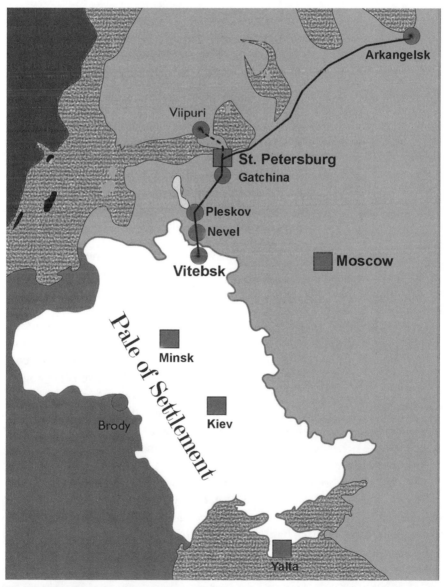

Figure 4.2. The Pale of Settlement, showing Peisach's journey to Arkangelsk and Viipuri (Marja Leskelä)

by the door and hugs the younger ones clinging to her skirt. Dvera must be hiding inside. And then you are off.

No one bothers to tell you where you are going. It wouldn't matter anyway as you have never been outside the *shtetl* you were born in and wouldn't understand if they told you. Before evening there are two other boys with you in the back of the damp cart, and your captors give you half a loaf of dry black bread and a can of water to divide among the three of you. You have to pee, but the *chappers* won't stop so you pee over the side of the cart. Later that night, the larger of the other two boys tries to jump out and run away, but one of the *chappers* catches him, bloodies him with a knobby stick, and tosses him back in the cart like a sack of meal.

It is early spring, and the frozen winter road has turned into a muddy track that sucks at the horses' hooves and the wooden wheels of the cart. Before long there are seven of you as additional boys are grabbed in settlements along the way, and the slathered horses have to struggle to maintain a pace that stills the driver's whip. From time to time, you are all made to descend and push the recalcitrant cart out of the mud or tramp alongside it through the slush.

Long March Begins

On the evening of the fifth day, you arrive in Nevel. There the *chappers* hand you over to the army, receiving six rubles for each of you. In the garrison, you are stripped naked and given a cursory medical examination by an army doctor. Then your head is shaved (How can you stand before the Lord without the *peyes* He has commanded you never to cut off?), and are given a uniform made for a grown man many times your size. You wonder if this is your final destination, but after only one night in musty barracks that smell of cold and damp, you are back on the road. This time, though, there is no wagon, and you are trudging along through the mud with about 50 other boys. You are accompanied by six armed soldiers. One is an officer with a limp, who doesn't seem to be too happy with his assignment. You are not allowed to talk with the other boys while you are walking, and the soldiers only speak to grunt out orders.

The boots you were given fit poorly, and yesterday's blisters are already open sores. The army coat tugs you earthward as its hem drags soddenly through the mud. You repeat over and over again the prayers you had memorized for your *bar mitzvah*, but they do little to lighten your spirits.

The soldier with the limp calls you Yankel Itzkovitsch. When you protest that Yankel Itzkovitsch is not your name, he calls you a liar and hits you with his riding crop. This happens two more times before you realize that the *va'ad* of the *kehile*, the local Jewish council of your *shtetl*, must have given you up to the *chappers* in place of the son of the wealthy merchant Chaim Itzkovitsch. You will not hear your real name again for many years. In the meantime, you will be Itzkovitsch. The loss of your name is another heavy stone to carry in your sack of miseries.

Your march progresses through the spring, which in that part of the world is not a time of flowers and birds but of melting, filthy snow and life-sucking mud. Boys who take sick, forced to keep marching until they drop, are left where they fall without even a few shovelsful of dirt to cover their pathetic little bodies. As the soles of your feet begin to grow hard, so does your heart. If you happen to get your hands on an extra crust of bread, you hide it from the other boys or gobble it down. If you notice another boy exhibiting the white lips and blue rings around the eyes that are the telltale signs of fever, you try to sleep near him so you can get his socks if he dies during the night. You devote all your energy to survival, and your childhood becomes such a distant memory that you will later wonder if it mightn't, after all, have happened to someone else. The soldiers take away your shawl and phylacteries on the absurd grounds that they are slowing you down, leaving nothing of your Jewishness but the prayers you repeat endlessly as you slog along.

As April turns to May, your progress is interrupted by work in the villages you pass through. The soldiers hire you out to help hoe the fields or clear away debris where forest has been slashed and burned to create new farm land. You have never done physical labor of any kind, and your hands easily bleed, blister and swell. You wrap them in strips of cloth you tear from the bundle holding your possessions, but these soon become so soaked with blood and pus that they are of little use.

After weeks on the road (so many you have lost count), having alternated between stretches of field work and day-long marches, you arrive in Pleskov, caked in mud and numb from fatigue. You see arching Cathedrals with glistening golden domes and the sturdy administrative buildings of Imperial Russia for the first time. But you aren't on a sightseeing excursion. The soldiers hurry through the town, stopping only long enough to stock up on vodka for the next leg of the journey and take turns visiting a brothel on the outskirts of the city.

A Sign from Above

It is sometime in July when you approach Gatchina and its 6,000-room palace. You will only see the palace from afar, however, as you are immediately put to work harvesting early cabbage. The work is hard, and the bags of cabbage are heavy, but you are glad to have a respite from walking all day. The midsummer days are long, and your captors keep you in the fields from just after daybreak until evening. The fields are dusty, and the sun beats down relentlessly at midday. One day, a boy picking cabbage in the row next to you collapses from the heat. Two soldiers drag him by his feet to the side of the field, where he lies until feral dogs carry off his twitching body.

One week after you arrive in Gatchina, you are still working in the cabbage field when it suddenly begins to grow cold and dark in the middle of the day. You look up to see if it is going to rain and are startled to see that there is not a cloud in the sky. Instead, a black sun has begun moving in front of the yellow sun. It hurts your eyes to look at it, and you continue to see bright spots as you turn your head away. The others notice it, too, and begin to scream in terror, tearing their clothes and thrashing around on the ground. One of the boys is screaming, "The world is coming to an end!"

You fear that maybe he is right. Maybe *Adonai*[4] is putting out the sun like your mother used to put out the candle in your home before everyone went to sleep. Maybe He who commanded "Let there be light!" has decided to extinguish it as punishment for the darkness in the hearts of men. Or maybe He is sending a sign like the plague of locusts He sent to punish the pharaohs, a sign that the Russians, too, should let His people go.

At this point, your Russian captors are as afraid as you are. They are on their knees, their prayer beads clacking pathetically in their trembling hands, their voices barely audible as they stumble through their prayers. You, too, are reciting prayers, but yours are a different invocation in a different language: "*Sh'ma Yisrael, Adonai Eloheinu, Adonai ehad!*"

After what seems like hours but is in reality only minutes, the black sun begins to move away, and light once again drives out the cold and darkness. The soldiers rise to their feet and begin kicking the boys, telling you to get back to work. For once, you are glad to be alive and suffering no more than the familiar blows from the hard boots of your overseers. Maybe, you think, there will be a Moses to lead you, too, out of bondage one day if only you are patient enough and do your best to remain true to the commandments of your faith.

Ten days later, the splendors of St. Petersburg rise before you like a mirage at the end of the road. The soldiers keep a sharp eye on you at all times now and have tethered you together with coarse rope to keep anyone from running away as you approach the city. You might be able to loosen the ropes when they are not looking, but where would you run? You know no one and have no money, food nor possessions to speak of. Several times daily you repeat your prayers, hoping to convince yourself that the Lord will watch over you, but increasingly you find yourself resigned to whatever fate awaits you, with or without the Lord's protection.

One night, after you have marched through St. Petersburg and onto the open road again, one of the older boys, Scholem by name, explains that you are all being taken somewhere far away to a Cantonist school. If Scholem is right—and he is—your life as you have known it is definitely over. Forget your *bar mitzvah*, Peisach. Forget your family and friends, your home. Forget even your name. Like Joseph almost 4,000 years before you, sold into bondage for 20 shekels by his brothers, you are being taken by these modern-day Ishmaelites on a journey that will eventually lead to a land far stranger than Egypt. You are going to Finland.

Cantonist School

First, though, you will spend five grueling years in a Cantonist school in Arkhangelsk on the shore of the White Sea. Czar Peter the Great (1672–1725) founded the Cantonist school system in 1721, requiring every canton (military district) to provide a school for fifty children. Starting in 1758, the children of all military personnel were required to attend Cantonist schools until the age of 18, after which the "graduates" were required to serve 25 years in the Imperial Army. Other children sent to Cantonist schools included orphans, abandoned children, and young people convicted of criminal activity. From 1827, these requirements were expanded to include quotas of Jewish children.

By the time Peisach arrived at the Arkhangelsk Cantonist school near the end of 1842, most of the "schooling" consisted of military drills and rudimentary training in skills such as carpentry or tailoring that were useful to the Imperial Army. Because they attended Cantonist schools before being transferred to Imperial Army garrisons, Peisach and the other early Jewish settlers in Finland who first arrive as military conscripts will be known as Cantonists.

Peter the Great wanted access to the Baltic Sea and trade with the West. During the Great Northern War of 1700–1721, Russian troops pushed their Swedish rivals westward, acquiring as they advanced the territories of Ingria, Estonia and Livonia at the eastern end of the Baltic. The czar decided to build a new city in the Neva River Delta at the eastern tip of the Baltic. He named it St. Petersburg after his patron saint and made it Russia's capital in 1703. This decision, intended to spur modernization and economic growth, placed the new capital in a most precarious position, vulnerable to German aggression from the south and Swedish invasion from the north as well as to

French or British attack by sea. Remarking on the situation he, himself, had created by moving the capital of his empire to within spitting distance of the frontier with Sweden, Peter the Great said "the ladies of St. Petersburg cannot sleep peacefully" so long as Finland remains in enemy hands.

Forty years later (1743), at the conclusion of one of the many Russo-Swedish Wars, Sweden ceded the southeastern corners of its territory to Russia, creating a deeper buffer zone between Sweden's Eastern Provinces and Russia's fledgling capital city. Later known as Old Finland (*Vanha Suomi*) to distinguish it from the territory Russia would wrest from Sweden in 1809, this land was reattached to the Autonomous Grand Duchy of Finland by mutual agreement in 1812.

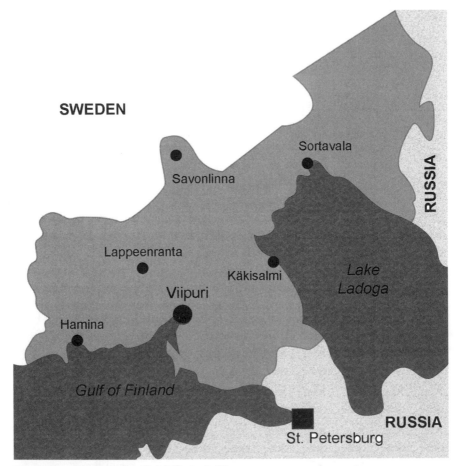

Figure 4.3. "Old Finland" (Marja Leskelä)

Beyond the Pale

The *shtetl* in the village near Vitebsk that Peisach had called home was located in the Pale of Settlement, a broad swath of land between the Baltic and Black Sea that included much of present-day Lithuania, Belarus, Poland, Moldova, Ukraine and parts of Western Russia. Catherine the Great created the Pale in 1791 in order to confine Russia's growing number of Jews to the western fringe of her expanding empire. It became a kind of permanent quarantine zone to keep the Jews from contaminating the rest of her subjects with their Old Testament religion and non-Slavic customs. One hundred years later, between four and five million Jews would be living in the Pale.

Jews from the Pale were not allowed to travel freely and could only settle elsewhere in Russia with special permission. An exception was made for Jews who were in the military or providing services to the Imperial Army.

In 1825, Czar Nicholas I became emperor of Russia and immediately undertook a substantial expansion of the military. One consequence was that from 1827, Jewish communities in the Pale were ordered to fill conscription quotas. Jewish boys could be taken from their families at the age of twelve—in reality, some as young as eight or nine were kidnapped—and sent far away from home. Their term of military service was set at twenty-five years from the time they turned eighteen. Jewish boys, however, were never considered particularly promising conscripts. In Czar Nicholas' own words, "The chief benefit from drafting Jews is the certainty that it will move them to change their religion."

During Nicholas' reign (1825–1855), some 50,000 Jewish children from the Pale were forcibly enrolled in Cantonist schools. In some ways, these "schools" were now more like survival camps than educational institutions. Children were often intentionally underfed and encouraged to steal or scrounge for food to survive. Jewish children were routinely coerced to convert to Christianity by means that often included physical brutality. Some children held out, but many either converted or pretended to do so in order to escape the torture.

Your long march, Peisach, which takes you from St. Petersburg to Arkhangelsk, lasts more than seven months. Of the 50 boys who set out from Pleskov, only 19 arrive in the dead of lightless winter. And while most of the survivors eventually accept baptism, you never do. You stay doggedly focused on survival, one day at a time, and banish all feeling and sentiment to the outskirts of your existence. Whenever they begin to creep back towards your consciousness, you repel them with a fusillade of bitterness and memorized prayer.

The five years of Cantonist school extirpate whatever was still soft and sensitive in you, leaving a personality as gnarled and hardened as a walnut. You make no friends, unburden your heart to no one. You judge people by their usefulness to you and cultivate relationships accordingly.

The year you turn 18 (1848), you are marched with a handful of other 18-year-old Cantonists back along the arduous route from Arkhangelsk to St. Petersburg, where you receive your first military postings. Because the unit to which you are assigned is garrisoned in Viipuri, a city of 8,618 on the Baltic coast some 125 kilometers to the west of St. Petersburg, that is where you will settle and your grandson Benjamin will be born 78 years later.

Three years after you arrive in Viipuri, Czar Nicholas finds himself involved in a disastrous war with the Ottoman Empire. Before long, the Turkish enemy is joined by the British and French in an alliance that is far too strong for the Russian Imperial Army. Resounding defeat in the Crimean War (1856) signals an end to Russia's role as the "Gendarme of Europe" and its reign as a major nineteenth century power.

Alexander II Reforms the Military

A year before the war ends, Nicholas dies and is replaced by his son, Alexander II. Alexander implements a program of radical reform that begins with an overhaul of the military and culminates in the liberation of the serfs in 1861. One of Alexander's first edicts reduces obligatory military service to 12 years, and on March 29, 1858 he signs a decree granting discharged Russian soldiers as well as their children and wives or widows the right to settle in the locations where they have served. In Finland, garrison towns are located in Hamina, Helsinki, Hämeenlinna, Impilahti, Kuopio, Sortavala, Suistamo, Tampere, Turku, Vaasa and Viipuri. Whether intentionally or through oversight, the decree makes no mention of religious affiliation. Finnish law will not recognize that this right also applies to Jewish soldiers until 1867, but the Cantonists who choose to stay in the country are protected in the interim by the czar's decree.

You have already served twelve years in the army when, in the autumn of 1861, you suddenly find yourself discharged onto the streets of Viipuri. While you were in the army, life was governed by the arcane rules and regulations of military service. Now you are out and on your own in an unfamiliar environment.

Santeri Jacobsson, in his authoritative 1951 treatise on the struggle by Finland's Jews to obtain their human rights, notes the unusual circumstances in which these Cantonist settlers found themselves upon their discharge:

When the Russian Army was modernized during the second half of the nineteenth century, long-serving soldiers were discharged. Their ties to their native land and families had loosened to such an extent during their long stint in the military that they had little choice but to begin to try to make a new life for themselves in the foreign land where fate had flung them. They had only dismal memories of their former homeland, which did nothing to encourage them to return.[5]

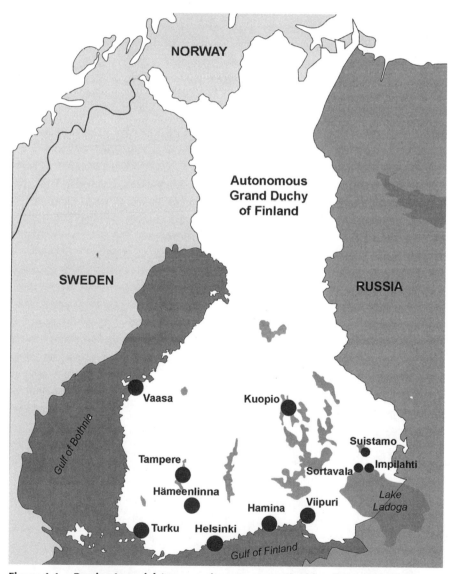

Figure 4.4. Russian Imperial Army garrison towns on Finnish soil (Marja Leskelä)

You are a free man, Peisach, but free to do what? The army has spit you out like a bone that has been picked clean, leaving you with nothing but a passport, a small cash severance payment, and the clothes on your back. You will never see your home or family again. The army has taught you no useful trade and you speak almost no Finnish, but you have something you never previously enjoyed, namely the freedom to find a place to live and seek a livelihood. Now 31 years old and having lived most of your life in military institutions, you find yourself in need of a wife, a means of earning a living, and a roof over your head—although not necessarily in that order.

Notes

1. Sidelocks (Yiddish)
2. Kidnappers (Yiddish)
3. Prayer shawl and small black leather box containing parchment scrolls with verses from the Torah, worn by adult males while praying (Hebrew)
4. The Lord (Hebrew)
5. Jacobsson, Santeri, *Taistelu ihmisoikeuksista*, Gummerus, Jyväskylä, 1951, pp. 85–86, translation by the author.

Figure 5.1. Finland's first Jews were easily distinguished by language, dress and customs from the Finnish population at large. (Finland's Jewish Archives)

Why I must travel to a distant land
Far from the home I love?*

---

*"Far from the Home I Love," song from *Fiddler on the Roof*, lyrics by Sheldon Harnick, 1964, based on *Tevye and His Daughters* by Sholem Aleichem.

CHAPTER FIVE

Benjamin Remembers His Grandfather

You would think my mother would have had more important things to worry about in 1936 than finding me a wife. Jews were being persecuted in Germany, and our family was having a hard time paying the bills on what little my sister and I were earning. But no, Mameh felt she had to beg the congregation for money so I could be bundled off to a Jewish summer camp to fall in love. What meshugas!¹

For me, finding a wife was the last thing on my mind. I was trying to make Kadur's soccer team and become a skilled enough cutter and blocker so I wouldn't have to clean the shop, make deliveries and do all the other things no one else at Lifson's wanted to do. I wasn't really ambitious like my father had been. I didn't dream of owning my own business or anything like that, just having a steady job. What I really would have wanted was to be able to stay in school, but after Tate died, that was out of the question.

Tate had been a hatmaker, and that was going to be good enough for me. Zayde Peisach had been a hatmaker, too, but he had to take a job in a dry goods store after he lost his business. I never knew him. He died before I was born. From what I heard, I think he might have wanted to be a rabbi or a scholar or something like that, but in Viipuri at the time, that was impossible. Anyway, he had no schooling except for what he got in the army and at cheder,² and that wasn't much.

The army, Oy vey! What that must have been like for Zayde Peisach! Bubbe Feige said he was the opposite of a soldier, a man of ideas, not of action. But what could he do?

Finland must be the only country where Jews were brought by force. Most places, Jews either arrive because they had been driven out of somewhere else because they are Jews or are trying to get in so they can make a better life for themselves and their family, but the first Jews came to Finland as soldiers who were marched here without even knowing where they were going. One of the problems they had when they finally got out of the army—and believe me, there were plenty—was that there weren't any Jewish women for them to marry. All the women had to be brought from somewhere else. Some of them came by wagon, some by boat. My grandmother, Bubbe Feige, she came by sleigh from St. Petersburg. My grandparents eventually had seven children, but three of them died very young. Tate was the youngest of the survivors.

At the time Zayde Peisach got out of the army, Jews just did whatever they could to make a living. Like most of them, he started selling second-hand clothes. It wasn't as if he had much choice. That was pretty much all the law allowed Jews to do.

Zayde and Bubbe sold second-hand clothes at the Punaisenlähteenturi narinkka[3] *until they were deported by the governor. That was in 1888. The only place they could think of to go when they were forced to leave was St. Petersburg so they went to live with Bubbe Feige's sister, Tante Golde, and her family. Zayde Peisach found work with the husband of one of Bubbe Feige's cousins. He had a factory where they made hats, men's hats, all kinds of hats. That's where he learned how to cut felt and leather and fur so almost none of it was wasted. He learned how to use wooden blocks, hot blocks, brim blocks and know which materials to use for different models. He learned how to stitch and glue the parts together and how to stiffen a finished hat. Years later Tate learned to do all these things, too, and so did I, but Zayde Peisach had already passed away by that time.*

When my grandparents moved back to Viipuri a year later, they needed a place to live. It had to be near enough to the synagogue so they could walk there on shabbos, of course, even in terrible weather. The new synagogue was on Kalevankatu, and my grandparents found rooms in the back of a courtyard on Juteininkatu. I think it had once been some kind of workshop.

Tante Chana never got to attend school. She had to help at home. Tante Mirjam and Tante Ida went to school for four years and Tate for six. They learned to read, do some math, and write Finnish. Later, even Bubbe Feige learned a little Finnish, too; enough, at least, to deal with customers in the market.

By the time Tate was 14, all his sisters had married, even sickly Tante Ida. Zayde Peisach had been a permitted Cantonist, but his daughters had to marry soldiers with residence permits if they wanted to stay in Finland. Of course, my aunts were quite good-looking so that didn't hurt their chances. By marrying a permitted soldier, a Jewish girl who was born in Finland got the right to settle down here. Otherwise she had to go "back where she came from," It makes no sense, but that was the law. Tante Chana married a history teacher from St. Petersburg and moved there so it didn't matter, and Tante Mirjam married a soldier but they moved to New York, I think it was in 1905. And Tante Ida married a doctor who was working for the army so of course they got to stay.

Tate started working as a delivery boy in Meyer Steinbock's hat factory. Bubbe Feige was good friends with Steinbock's mother, and together they talked Steinbock into giving Tate a chance right after he left school. Because his business was growing, Bubbe told me, Steinbock was willing to take on an apprentice. That would have been about 1903. Tate must have been a quick learner because he got a job at Eckert's as a cutter after only eighteen months at Steinbock's.

Life was hard for my father but nothing like it had been for my grandfather. Every time I think about what Zayde Peisach had to go through, it makes me angry. I think Zayde Peisach's biggest problem was disappointment. He was not an ambitious man, but he wanted security and respect. As a Jew in Finland at that time, he got neither.

He was tough, though, a survivor. He made a life for himself in spite of everything that happened, and because of that I am here today, an old man with poor eyesight but a heart that is still beating after 95 years. If Zayde Peisach hadn't been taken away from his home in Vitebsk and sent to Finland, our family history would have been much shorter. It would have ended 70 years ago in the gas chambers of Majdanek and Treblinka or in mass graves we would have been forced to dig for ourselves in the forests of Byelorussia or Memel before being put out of our misery like crippled horses or diseased cattle. Baruch hashem[4] he came to Finland!

Notes

1. Madness (Yiddish)
2. School where the fundamentals of Judaism are taught to young children (Yiddish)
3. A word derived from the Russian "*na rynke,*" meaning "on the square" and referring to the market square where the first Jewish settlers in Finland peddled second-hand clothing and other goods of little value.
4. Thank God (Hebrew)

Figure 6.1. Emanuel Thelning's portrayal of Russia's Czar Alexander I opening the Diet of Porvoo in 1809 (Public domain)

The early experiences of Jews who settled in Finland were not comforting. Later, they experienced even harder times in which their very existence often hung by a thread. Their legal status caused many tragedies and shocking personal fates. Mothers' tears flowed copiously when they thought about their families' fate and their children's future, and many prayers resembling cries of distress rose toward heaven from the hearts of religious Jews.

*Santeri Jacobsson**

---

*Taistelu ihmisoikeuksista, K.J. Gummerus, Jyväskylä, 1951, p.107.

CHAPTER SIX

~

Finland Becomes Part
of the Russian Empire

Viipuri, 1861—What was the Finland into which Peisach was disgorged in the mid-nineteenth century and which his grandson would be called on to defend almost a century later? To answer that question, we must understand what it had been for most of the second millennium AD: part of the Kingdom of Sweden and a buffer between two of Europe's great powers, Sweden and Russia.

Through the early Middle Ages, *Finlandia* (land of fens) had been a place-filler on Latinate maps for the stretch of land between Sweden and Russia, a geographic concept with no political identity of its own. Then, in the twelfth century, Novgorod (Russia) aggressively expanded its influence westward into Karelia (eastern *Finlandia*). In response, the English-born Bishop Henry (later Saint Henry) led a crusade from Stockholm to repel this incursion, convert non-believers, and strengthen the hold of the Roman Catholic bishopric of Uppsala. Somewhere towards the end of the twelfth century, in the midst of the Swedish-Novgorodian Wars (1142–1322), Sweden annexed *Finlandia* and would rule it for the next six centuries. Fighting continued, however, with Swedes and Russians shedding their blood and that of the Finnish-speaking people—the latter dying in the service of one side or the other or simply caught between them—until the 1323 Treaty of Pähkinäsaari (Schlüsselburg) formalized for the first time the border between Sweden to the West and Novgorod to the East.

The new border did little to stop the bloodshed. Fighting continued with the two sides pushing each other first in one direction and then the other in the Russo-Swedish War of 1495–97, the Russo-Swedish War of 1554–57, the Livonian War (1558–1583), the Russo-Swedish War of 1590–1595, the

Ingrian War (1610–1617), the Russo-Swedish War of 1656–58, the Great Northern War (1700–1721), The Russo-Swedish War of 1741–1743, and Gustavus III's Russian War (1788–1790) before the matter was finally settled for good in the Finnish War of 1808–09, when Russia under Czar Alexander I drove Sweden all the way back to its current eastern border.

During most of the time these wars were going on, what we now call Finland consisted of eight provinces of the Swedish realm, collectively called Österland (Eastern Land). The Finnish people—those who thought of themselves as Finns and spoke the Finnish language—had little influence over their lives in Österland. Swedish kings granted titles and provincial land to Swedish officers and bureaucrats who distinguished themselves in service to the monarchy and were willing to collect taxes from the local peasantry on its behalf. During the reign of Gustavus I Vasa (1523–1560), systematic taxation and administrative rule were imposed on the provinces and would remain in force, with the exception of two brief periods of Russian military occupation (1714–1721 and 1741–1743), until 1809.

Although the Reformation replaced Catholicism with Lutheranism as the dominant form of Christianity in Northern Europe, and the Enlightenment introduced subversive notions of liberty and human rights, the Finnish people remained firmly in vassalage to the Swedish crown. There were no Finnish laws (Österland was ruled by Swedish law), the language of the courts and schools was Swedish (or German or Latin, but never Finnish), and matters such as taxation and representation were decided in far-away Stockholm.

Sweden's status as a Great Power ended abruptly with the crushing defeat it suffered at the hands of Russia in the Finnish War of 1808–1809, followed by the forced abdication of King Gustavus IV Adolphus and the imposition of a constitutional monarchy. The fall of Sweden, and the defeat of Napoleon four years later, left victorious Russia as the guarantor of order and stability in Europe.

As the balance of power was shifting in Russia's favor, one of Czar Alexander I's most pressing tasks was to deal with his newly acquired Swedish provinces. Even before hostilities with Sweden had ended and the Treaty of Hamina (1809) signed, he began weaning the Finns from their long and close association with Sweden in an effort to secure their loyalty. In front of a hastily convened Diet of Finland's Four Estates in Porvoo, halfway between St. Petersburg and the western coastal city of Turku, he proclaimed the provinces to be the Autonomous Grand Duchy of Finland and announced that its inhabitants would be allowed to retain their Lutheran religion, their Swedish legal system, and the privileges that their estates had enjoyed under Swedish rule. These promises addressed important Finnish concerns as Russia's Eastern

Orthodox form of Christianity was anathema to the Protestant Finns, the Swedish legal and administrative systems were far more modern and liberal than their feudalistic Russian counterparts, and Finland's Swedish-speaking elite would surely have rebelled at the loss of its property and privileges.

Alexander was known to be interested in the philosophy of the Enlightenment, but he reportedly feared the chaos it would unleash if introduced into feudalistic Russia. Finland was linguistically and culturally isolated from Mother Russia, making it an ideal place to experiment. Could modernism be introduced into an autocratic empire in a way that would stimulate economic development in one part without contaminating the rest with the French and American Revolutions' egalitarian ideals and ambitions for self-determination?

Winning the allegiance of the Finnish people turned out to be easier than Alexander might have expected. Sweden was a defeated nation in disarray; Russia was a powerful nation on the rise. Furthermore, Sweden had allowed the Finns little say in their own governance, whereas Alexander, instead of imposing harsh restrictions on them, was promising protection, privilege and a considerable degree of autonomy in return for little more than loyalty. If the Finns could be bound by loyalty to the czar, they could potentially be counted on to protect Russia's access to the Baltic Sea and its northwestern flank from attack.

The czar took for himself the honorific of Grand Duke of Finland, a Swedish title that had been vacant for some time. At the close of the Diet, Alexander told the assembled representatives in French, the official language of his court, that Finland had henceforth taken its place among the rank of nations (*"placé désormais au rang des nations"*). Historians still debate what he meant by this locution for Finland was surely not a sovereign nation by the criteria we would apply today. It was ruled by an autocrat from a conquering country who could take away in a heartbeat the privileges he had just promised. Perhaps he meant "nation" in the sense of "people," a political entity loosely defined by a common language, ancestry and location. In any case, his intention was clear: to make them appreciate that they had much to gain from their new status as an autonomous entity, part of the Russian Empire but not part of the Russian "nation,"

Let Us Therefore Be Finns!

In an oft-cited call to nationhood attributed to Finnish patriot Adolf Ivar Arwidsson, the Finns were summoned early in their new "nationhood" to define their status against a double negative: "Swedes we are no longer,

Russians we do not wish to become, let us therefore be Finns!" To the East, the divide with Russia was linguistic, religious, cultural, and embodied in a legal and administrative system inherited from Sweden. To the West, Finland was separated physically from Sweden by the Gulf of Bothnia and in ways political and administrative by the absolute power of the czar and his Imperial Army.

It is worth noting at this point that the Finnish language bears no relation whatsoever to either Swedish or Russian. With its Finno-Ugric vocabulary and complex grammatical structure, it serves, like Basque or Hungarian, as one of the most daunting language barriers between neighbors in all of Europe. There has been for centuries, however, a significant Swedish-speaking population in Finland, especially along the coast and in coastal cities. In 1809, before the addition of Old Finland, approximately 14.5 percent of Finland's total population of 863,000 was Swedish-speaking and 85 percent Finnish-speaking with the remaining 0.5 percent divided among Russian, German, and Sami (the group of languages spoken by the indigenous people of Lapland).

Alexander decided in 1812, the year in which he integrated Old Finland into the Autonomous Grand Duchy, to make Helsinki the capital of Finland. Located halfway from Sweden towards St. Petersburg along the shore of the Baltic, Helsinki had been almost entirely destroyed by fire four years earlier. In the wake of the fire, Helsinki's population had been reduced from 8,000 to about half that figure.

One reason for choosing Helsinki was that it was protected by the harbor fortress of Sveaborg, known today as Suomenlinna, which was home to a large garrison of Russian troops. Under different circumstances, the natural site for the capital would have been Turku, Finland's most populous city at the time and home to both its only university and the bishopric of the Evangelical Lutheran Church of Finland. Turku, however, is located at the point on Finland's southwest shore nearest to Stockholm and for centuries had been the hub of political, commercial and cultural interaction between Sweden and its eastern provinces. By moving Finland's Senate and university to Helsinki, the czar intended to sever the umbilical cord that tied the Finns to Sweden and replace Stockholm with St. Petersburg as the nexus of Finland's commercial and political activity.

One major problem Alexander faced in his attempt to replace Swedish influence in Finland with Russian ways of doing things was the difficulty in finding competent civil servants to run the country. Russia suffered from a chronic lack of skilled civil servants and certainly had no corps of Finnish- and Swedish-speaking bureaucrats available to work in Finland. Finland's

Swedish-speaking civil servants, for their part, knew no Russian. The czar was left with no choice but to allow Finland's existing Swedish-speaking civil service corps to carry on, ensuring a conservative approach to administration and a focus on the rule of (inherited Swedish) law. The same problem surfaced in attempts to reform the university. Insistence that university lectures be delivered in Russian was meaningless as there were very few teachers capable of delivering lectures in Russian and even fewer students who would have been able to understand them. Long before Helsinki University became a hotbed of resistance to Russification, practical obstacles prevented Russian influence from gaining a stronghold in this important institution.

Finnish society in 1809 was overwhelmingly rural (95 percent), agricultural and poor. Significantly, there were few large estates employing large numbers of peasants. Most of the arable land was owned by independent farmers with relatively small holdings, who might use at most a handful of laborers or tenant farmers to till their fields. Even seventy years later (1880), 75 percent of the population would still derive its living from agriculture and just 6.6 percent from crafts and industry. Finland did not get its first mechanized cotton or paper mill until the 1840s, nearly a century after the Industrial Revolution began transforming Europe and North America. Most Finns in 1809 still eked out a living by farming in the short summer growing season and logging in the long, cold winter. Along the coast and lake shores, fishing was the primary source of livelihood.

Finland's largest cities in 1815 were Turku (12,550), Helsinki (4,801) and Oulu (3,543). No other municipality had as many as 3,000 inhabitants, reflecting the lack of work in urban areas. Viipuri, for example, had just 2,740 inhabitants. Turku and Helsinki were predominantly Swedish-speaking, but Viipuri's tiny population represented four different groups of native-language-speakers: Finnish (44 percent), Russian (39 percent), Swedish (14 percent) and German (13 percent). When ranked by economic and social status, that order would have been reversed with German- and Swedish-speakers at the top and Finnish-speakers at the bottom. It is estimated that in 1800, thanks to religious education delivered by itinerant teachers, between 50 percent and 75 percent of Finns could read a little, but only 4 percent could write at all.

So what did "Let us therefore be Finns" mean in this context? There was no Finnish literature or art to inform the discussion, no *History of Finland* to provide a starting point. The educated elite of the country was Swedish-speaking; Finnish was the lingua franca of the poor and poorly educated. Certainly Arwidsson (or whoever actually said it) had not meant, "Let us therefore be poor, uneducated and powerless!" So now there was a third negative to ponder, the socio-politico-economic status of the Finnish people, and there was no one to set about improving it, paradoxically, but the country's Swedish-speaking elite.

Golden Age

Finland may be the only country in the world where a powerful and privileged minority fought for and eventually won the right for the down-trodden majority to participate fully in political, economic and cultural life. The giants of Finland's Golden Age—Lönnrot, Edelfelt, Snellman, Topelius, Cygnaeus, Gallén-Kallela, Kivi (Stenvall), Sibelius, Runeberg, Järnefelt, von Wright, to name just a few—typically had Swedish names and were Swedish-speaking. The dearth of Finnish-speaking intellectuals was hardly surprising as the first government-supported Finnish-language schools weren't opened until the 1850s.

Swedish-speakers were largely responsible for shaping the Finnish people's sense of national awareness, patiently collecting material from which to cobble together a cohesive national narrative. During long trips to Karelia in the second half of the eighteen century, Turku University's Professor Henrik Gabriel Porthan had begun recording oral poetry, and Zachris Topelius the Elder (whose great-great-grandfather, Isak Zebulon, was a Jew who converted to Christianity and moved to Oulu in the seventeenth century) gathered runes from traveling salesmen from Karelia and published them between 1822 and 1831. Matthias Alexander Castrén and Elias Lönnrot traveled to Lapland and Karelia to study first-hand the language and culture of indigenous peoples. Castrén explicitly wanted to "demonstrate to the Finns that we were not some lonely swamp people torn apart from the world but are rather related to at least a sixth of mankind,"

In 1835, Lönnrot published the *Kalevala*, which would become Finland's national epic. The poem, expanded by Lönnrot in 1849, consisted of material gathered primarily from folksingers and poets working exclusively in an oral tradition in which material was handed down from generation to generation. The *Kalevala's* pagan symbolism is woven into a mythology that portrays the ancient roots of the Finnish people as separate and distinct from those of either the Russians or the Swedes, implying that Finnish identity is also worthy of cultural respect and historical standing.

The *Kalevala* became the inspiration for some of Finland's greatest art, literature and music. Composer Jean Sibelius, artist Akseli Gallén-Kallela, and poet Eino Leino were among the cultural giants whose works contributed to the popularity of the *Kalevala* among Finns, many of whom who knew little or nothing of Karelia or its traditions at the time.

Even before publication of the *Kalevala*, nationalist fervor began to percolate to the surface in academic circles. Starting in 1830, a group of Helsinki University students and teachers who called themselves the *Lauantaiseura* (Saturday Society) met regularly to discuss culture and politics, and the *Suomalaisen kirjallisuuden seura* (Finnish Literature Society) was founded in 1831. Although the members of both groups were Swedish speakers, they became strong proponents of the Finnish language, with many going so far as to adopt Finnish names. The two groups included future scientists, literary figures, academics, newspapermen, clergymen and politicians.

Johan Ludvig Runeberg's epic poem, *Fänrik Ståls sägner* (*The Tales of Ensign Stål*) played a leading role in the creation of a positive Finnish self-image. Written in Swedish, published in two installments (1848 and 1860), and translated into Finnish in 1867, it recounts the exploits, some historical and some fictional, of Finnish soldiers in the Finnish War of 1808–1809. The tales praised heroic Finns who held their ground against Russians in battle. The second part, especially, appearing shortly after Russia suffered humiliating defeat in the Crimean War, was an important stimulus to the spread of Finnish nationalistic fervor.

These scholarly activities gave substance to what was called the Fennoman movement. At first, the movement focused on striving for the recognition of Finnish language and culture in a society where the elite still spoke Swedish and literature in Finnish hardly existed. This turning away from Swedish-centered culture was precisely what Czar Alexander I had called for half a century earlier, and many of the Fennomen were, in fact, staunchly loyal to the czar. According to Professor Matti Klinge:

> The Finnish nationalist ideal rested on two pillars. One was the tradition inherited from the period of enlightenment, in which it was thought that improvement in the position of the Finnish language would be a tool for spreading enlightenment and tolerance and developing good and efficient governance and the disposition of justice. On the other hand, it was a matter of romantic nationalism built on ancient history and mythology as well as aesthetic values and was politically more conservative than radical.[1]

The conservative, loyalist faction held the upper hand at the time of the Crimean War. In order to protect St. Petersburg from attacks by the British and French navies in the Baltic Sea, Russia badly needed—and received—Finland's loyalty and support. But Russia's defeat in the war and subsequent decline as a European power dampened Finland's enthusiasm for its dependent status and created space in which more radical nationalism and nascent separatism would begin to grow.

Finland's First Jews

Fifty years before the first Cantonist veterans were allowed to settle in Finland, at the time when the Autonomous Grand Duchy of Finland was created out of former Swedish provinces, there were no Jews—zero—living there. Swedish church law of 1686 specified: "In our kingdom and the lands belonging to it, everyone shall recognize only the teachings and beliefs of Christianity, which is based on the holy word of God." All non-believers were forced to convert to Christianity before being allowed to settle in the kingdom.

The law was modified by Sweden's 1781 Declaration of Religious Freedom, a liberalizing step motivated, at least in part, by the crown's need to raise money. It stipulated that a Jew who wished to settle in Sweden would have to provide evidence of being of good reputation and be in possession of at least 2,000 *rigsdalers* in silver. Upon arrival, he would have to report to the King's Governor, who, having certified his passport, would direct him to a particular neighborhood in a specific city—Stockholm, Gothenburg or Norrköping. None could settle in the eastern provinces. By restricting the right of Jewish immigrants to live in just three cities, the Swedish authorities believed it would be easier for the police to keep close watch over them. This approach would later be reflected in copycat efforts in the second half of the nineteenth century to restrict Jews in Finland to residence in its own three largest cities. If Cantonists released into other garrison towns wanted to move—and most of them would have to relocate in search of work or to join a community with the 10 adult males needed to form a *minyan*[2]—the only places where they could obtain residence permits would have been Helsinki, Turku or Viipuri.

Although there were no Jews living in "New Finland" when Russia took control of it from Sweden, there was one Jewish family living across the border in the area soon to be known as "Old Finland," Tinsmith Jacob Weikaim had arrived in 1799 from either Sloka or Daugavpils in Latvia to work on the installation of street lights during the rebuilding of Russian fortifications. Hamina had been part of Russia for more than half a century, but in 1812 it was integrated into the Autonomous Grand Duchy, along with the rest of Old Finland, by imperial decree. As a consequence, Jacob Weikaim and his family, without moving from their modest home in Hamina, became the first Jewish settlers in Finland and fell under the strictures on Jewish settlement "inherited" from Sweden, placing Weikaim and his family in a potentially precarious position. They quietly lit the Sabbath candles in the privacy of their home and, with no rabbi to lead them or co-religionists to share their celebrations, they observed Jewish holy days and customs as best they could. By practicing Judaism unobtrusively, they managed to avoid running afoul of the authorities.

Were it not for the Imperial Army, the Weikaims might have remained the only Jews in Finland for half a century or more. Although Jews were neither allowed to work nor settle in the Autonomous Grand Duchy, that ruling did not apply to those serving in or employed by the Imperial Army. As the army was busy securing its hold over the acquired territory and fortifying the coast against potential foreign incursion, it became Finland's largest employer of skilled civilians. Tailors, cobblers, smiths, tanners, carpenters and hatters were needed as the huge army was constantly forced to replenish its stock of uniforms, equipment and supplies. A few Jews from the St. Petersburg area and Baltic States were eventually able to secure employment in these trades although they would not have been allowed to practice them without the army's protection. Later even a Jewish doctor or two found their way into the Grand Duchy in this way.

Jacob Weikaim left Hamina and moved to Viipuri in 1815. According to court testimony from the 1830s, there was no poorer family in Viipuri than the Weikaims, who by this time had changed their name to Veikkanen. Between 1814 and 1842 Jacob Weikaim had 11 children, two with his first wife and nine with his second. They lived in a rundown shack at the southernmost corner of *Punaisenlähteentori* (Red Spring Square), which took its name from a small red well-house near the Weikaims' home. Nevertheless, every Saturday, when, in observance of the commandment forbidding Jews to work on the Sabbath, a neighbor was called in to light a fire in the modest oven that was the only source of heat in their home, the Weikaims and their children appeared dressed in their best, freshly washed clothes. In the fall of 1831, Governor General Zakrevski ordered the handful of Jews who had not converted to Christianity banished from Finland. Somehow, the Weikaims obtained permission from the czar to remain. Jacob Weikaim died in 1842, at which time, surprisingly, all eleven of his children were still alive.

The first Jewish soldiers, known as Cantonists, began arriving in Finland about the time of Weikaim's death, but no one knows for certain who were the very first Cantonists to settle in Finland. The 1858 decree allowing them to do so covered a number of Jewish soldiers who had served more than twelve years in the Imperial Army. What we do know is that the circumstances of their release could only have been bewildering to them.

Daniel Weintraub, a teacher at Helsinki's Jewish School and a historian by training, summarizes their situation as follows:

> In these circumstances, they began to learn a new way of living. On the one hand, the Jewish world they had known as children before being forced into Cantonist schools and the army was the only one that was familiar and safe.

On the other hand, their new circumstances, all things considered, offered them considerable freedom and opportunities.[3]

Freedom and opportunities. Although they had not brought Peisach to Finland, they were awaiting him on his discharge from the military. Was there antisemitism in Finland? Yes, of course, but it was not the deadly violent kind that would erupt before long in many cities in Russia, Poland and Ukraine. Although Peisach and his fellow Cantonists would be subject to annoying and often harsh restrictions on travel, employment and where they could live, they were entering a society that was governed by the rule of law. If they obeyed the law, however onerous, they would not have to fear a knock on their door in the dead of night, nor would their grandchildren three quarters of a century later.

Notes

1. Klinge, Matti, *Keisarin Suomi*, Schildts, Helsinki, 1997, p. 154.
2. The quorum required by Jewish law for public worship (Hebrew).
3. Daniel Weintraub, interview with the author, June 5, 2013.

Figure 7.1. Helsinki's narinkka (Finland's Jewish Archives)

Judaism exists in the congregation and in the home, and only after that Judaism exists in the synagogue. Judaism was especially strong in the home because Jews didn't marry outside the faith. I've been told that the wife of one of my relatives committed suicide when her daughter married a Finn.

The Sabbath was extremely important to those religious Jews, but it changed rapidly because their life was determined by their income. First, they had to sell used clothing at a market called *Onnettomuudenmäki* [Accident Hill], but later they were allowed to go to the Central Market, which had been off limits to Jews. Gradually, toward the end of the nineteenth century, they were permitted to open shops of their own, but a Finn had to be legally in charge in case some kind of problem arose. Only when Finland became independent could they officially become owners of their own businesses!

*Jacob Seela**

---

*Interviewed by the author, Turku, August 31, 2012.

CHAPTER SEVEN

~

Annus Mirabilis

Viipuri, 1861—Historian Osmo Jussila identifies 1861, the year when Pei-sach and two friends buy their first sewing machine and open a second-hand clothing stall on *Punaisenlähti* Square, as Finland's *annus mirabilis*, a turning point in the country's history. Finland spent its first half century as an au-tonomous grand duchy adjusting to life under Russian rule and trying to curry favor with Czars Alexander I (1809–1825) and Nicholas I (1825–1855). The czars, in turn, focused on turning Finland away from its historic attachment to Sweden and winning the loyalty of its people. They made numerous de-cisions that encouraged Finns to think of their homeland as separate from Sweden, but this process inevitably led many Finns to see it by the middle of the century as separate from Russia as well. After 1861, Russia's rulers found themselves increasingly at odds with a people who considered Finland to be a nation in its own right. Their allegiance was not to Mother Russia but to *koti* (home), *uskonto* (religion = Lutheranism) and *isänmaa* (fatherland = Fin-land), setting them on a collision course with Russian authorities struggling to hold an increasingly fractious empire together.

Meanwhile Peisach and his co-religionists were left to settle into a soci-ety in which *koti, uskonto* and *isänmaa* (incidentally, the future rallying cry of Finland's anti-communist and antisemitic IKL Party in the 1930s) were either forbidden or just plain alien to them. Finland offered them only tem-porary residence, not a fatherland; they had no desire to become Lutheran and would have said, if asked, that their "home" was somewhere far away in the dimly remembered Pale of Settlement. As the society around them began to form a core identity linked to the Finnish language and a growing sense of the Finnish people as defined by shared values and a common history, these Jews were relegated to the periphery. There were so few of them in Finland in 1861, though, that they were hardly noticed. As the Jews lived in a limited number of cities and were forbidden to travel on business to the countryside where 93 percent of all Finns lived, a typical Finn in the second half of the nineteenth century would never have come face to face with a single Jew during his or her entire lifetime.

Obstacles To Integration
(of Finland into Imperial Russia)

Russia experienced enormous difficulties in trying to integrate the Autonomous Grand Duchy into its empire. Finland maintained its inherited legal system and customs border with Russia. It even set up its own postal system and began issuing its own postage stamps in 1856.

Russia tried to make the ruble the official currency of Finland, but the crisis caused by the disastrous Crimean War forced Russia to detach the ruble from the silver standard. Because Russia could not prevent the resultant decline and instability in the ruble's value, it agreed to allow Finland to create its own currency, the *markka*, which became legal tender in the Grand Duchy alongside the ruble in 1860. Two years later, the country's first commercial bank, the Union Bank of Finland, opened its doors for business.

Two important milestones in the development of infrastructure were reached in the middle of the century. In 1856, the Saimaa Canal was opened to traffic. This 43-kilometer channel made commercial navigation possible, via a chain of lakes, locks and inland waterways, from Kuopio in Central Finland to Viipuri on the coast, a distance of over 300 kilometers. The canal brought lumber and agricultural produce from the countryside to Viipuri for sale or export while simultaneously making it easier for manufactured goods to be delivered to the interior.

In 1862, Finland's first railway line, connecting Helsinki with Hämeenlinna, also greatly improved transportation between Helsinki and the interior of the country. Eight years later, the St. Petersburg–Helsinki line would link the Finnish and Russian capitals. Soon, industrial goods produced in such fledgling industrial centers as Tampere, Forssa and Karkkila could find their way by rail to the Russian capital or to Helsinki's harbor and from there to markets as far away as England. Industrial production became much more profitable, and the output of Finnish textile mills, for example, increased more than 10-fold between 1840 and 1870.

During the second half of the nineteenth century, Germany, France and England became interested in Finland's vast forest resources and growing production of sawn goods. Finnish farmers had long used the cold and dark winters as a time to log their woodlands. Water-driven sawmills in Finland had been turning logs into lumber since the sixteenth century, but the founding of a steam-driven sawmill north of Oulu in 1860 opened a new chapter in the country's industrialization. Sawmill owners began buying more pine and spruce logs from farmers, knowing it would now be easier and cheaper to saw them and ship the resulting lumber to markets near and far. Between 1859 and 1873, paper mills opened beside rapids and waterfalls in eight different localities, and the first pulp mill started production in 1880. Most of the technological innovations that fed this growth were developed elsewhere, but by the late nineteenth century they had made the forest industry (lumber, pulp and paper) Finland's leading source of export revenue, creating knock-on demand for transportation, banking, industrial equipment and other goods and services.

The Birth of Finnish Separatism

All these advances were speeding proto-industrial Finland's transition towards a mature industrial economy, but that is not why Jussila calls 1861 an *annus mirabilis*. He claims that in 1861 "was born as if in a single breath" the unanimous opinion among Finns that Finland was a separate nation and not just a Russian province. He attributes this awakening to the publication of a polemic by Johan Philip Palmén in which the author claimed that Swedish laws of 1772 and 1789 establishing the form of government for Sweden's eastern provinces were, in effect, a Finnish constitution. Following Palmén's line of argumentation, Jussila argues, the country's elite began to think of Finland not as a province with privileges but as a nation with constitutional rights.

By this time, cracks were already beginning to appear in Finland's relationship with Russia. The widespread 1848 revolts against European monarchies sparked a conflagration of nationalism in many parts of the continent. Italy would be unified in 1861 and Germany a decade later. Poland tried unsuccessfully to break free from Russia in 1863, as it had once before in 1830, but Finland remained unfailingly loyal during the reigns of both Alexander I and Nicholas I. Nicholas had, at one point, admonished his civil servants: "Leave the Finns alone! That's the only province in my entire realm that hasn't given me one minute of trouble or dissatisfaction during my reign." But as Finland began to think of itself after 1861 as an increasingly separate and legitimate nation, mutual trust began to erode. Nicholas' son and successor, Czar Alexander II, who was crowned in 1855, had enough trouble with Finland that he was heard to grumble: "Finland is just like a little Poland."

Already in the 1850s, school and university reform laid the groundwork for nationalist consciousness and separatist thinking. The first public lower schools (folk schools) were opened, the first Finnish-language upper or secondary school (1858) was established, and a four-year Teachers' Seminary was opened. University reform in 1852 led to increased specialization and research into Finnish culture, language, history and natural science. A decree published in 1863 accorded Finnish, the language of "the common people," equal status with Swedish. Although their implementation would be contested and hampered by those who wanted to maintain the exclusive status of Swedish, these reforms opened the way for greater participation by the Finnish-speaking majority in public affairs.

In 1861, Finland's first modern newspaper, the Swedish-language *Helsingfors Dagblad*, made its appearance. A few Finnish-language broadsheets, such as *Maamiehen ystävä*, *Saima* and *Suometar*, all published by J. V. Snellman, and a Swedish-language paper, Zachris Topelius' *Helsingfors Tidningar*, had been circulated earlier. In addition to being sources of information, newspapers in both Finnish and Swedish would play an important role in shaping public opinion. Finns would go on to become enthusiastic readers of newspapers, third in the world in 2015 behind only the Japanese and Norwegians.

Finland's Diet had not convened once during the half century following 1809, but from 1863 to 1906, when the Diet was replaced by a single-chamber Parliament, it met 14 times. The result was a significant increase in political activity and public debate.

Another important stimulus to national development was the cultural awakening taking place at the same time. The song "*Maamme*" ("Our Land"), which would later become independent Finland's national anthem, was composed in 1848. The expanded version of the *Kalevala* was published in 1849 and the second part of *The Tales of Ensign Stål* in 1860. The first Finnish-language novel, Aleksis Kivi's *Seitsemän veljestä* (*Seven Brothers*), appeared in 1870. The first Finnish-language play to be performed, *Lea*, opened in 1869. A Finnish opera company performed regularly from 1873 through 1879 before succumbing to financial difficulties. Finnish artists studied in Germany, France and Italy, absorbing the influences of the Romantic Nationalist period that was already drawing to a close in those countries but would live on in Finland in the last years of the century.

All of this diverse activity can be understood as a collective response to the command, "Let us therefore be Finns!" If little Finland were to take its place in the rank of nations, as Alexander I had ordained, it would need every fiber of historic, cultural, economic, political, industrial and intellectual muscle it could muster.

Obstacles to Integration
(of Jews into Finnish Society)

Just as Finns were finally figuring out what it meant to be Finns, Peisach and his handful of co-religionists appeared in their midst. If the typical Finn was Lutheran, Finnish-speaking and lived off the land, these Jewish Cantonists tended to be shorter and darker than the local population, Yiddish-speaking, and many of them couldn't tell a heifer from a horseradish. It is hard to imagine a more complete contrast.

Unlikely as it would have seemed at the time, these Jews were in Finland to stay. Cantonists in Helsinki had used a prayer room in the Viapori Fortress during their military service, but once permitted to remain as civilians, they began to take the first tentative steps toward forming a proper congregation. In 1864 they established a *Chevra Kadisha* (Burial Aid Society). Three years later Naftali Zwi Amsterdam arrived from Lithuania to become their first rabbi. From 1870, the congregation rented a building in the working-class Siltasaari district near the first *narinkka* to serve as a synagogue.

In Turku, at first, Jewish soldiers used a prayer room in the Turku Castle. It wasn't until the late 1870s that there were as many as 70 permitted Jews living in the city, and they apparently held their prayer services in the homes of observant Jews. From 1880 to 1889, the congregants rented an apartment (two rooms and a kitchen) to serve as their first synagogue. They would not get their first rabbi until 1895.

Viipuri's congregation was only "officially" organized in 1872, when there were 120 Jews living in the city. Its first rabbi, however, may have been Berka Baranoff, who signed a birth certificate for a member of the congregation six years earlier. He was followed by Nochem Liebkind, who served as *shochet*[1] and rabbi until he resurfaced in 1895 as the first rabbi of the Turku congregation.

The *annus mirabilis* for Finland's Jews would have been 1856, when Alexander II decreed an end to the Cantonist system, not 1861. Although a law was passed in Russia in 1861 allowing Jews possessing university degrees to settle outside the Pale in order to serve in government or pursue jobs in commerce and industry, it had no standing in Finnish law, where the restrictions carried over from the time of Swedish rule still applied. Jews could still only live in cities and towns that had Russian garrisons and could only trade in goods of little value, such as used clothing, rags and trinkets. If a permitted Cantonist traveled to a market town in the countryside to peddle his wares, he could be summarily deported along with his family.

Jews in Finland could not hold public office, could not enter the civil service, could not have representation in the Diet, and could not testify in court. Finnish law reserved such rights for Lutherans and, begrudgingly, the Russian Orthodox co-religionists of the czars. There would be a law passed in 1889 granting other Protestant groups the same rights as Lutherans, but it did not apply to Jews, Muslims, or even Roman Catholics. Only after Finland became independent in 1917 and Jews were granted the right to apply for citizenship was the restriction against Jews publicly practicing their religion officially lifted. But as noted above, congregations in the three permitted cities were active long before then. In 1900, in fact, the City of Helsinki donated land on which its Jewish community could build a synagogue, stipulating that construction had to be completed within five years.

How could the city give free land for a house of worship to a community that was not even allowed to practice its religion openly? As evidence of how contradictory the thinking was at the time, when the congregation applied for loans and financial assistance from the state to build the synagogue, they were informed by the Treasury that no assistance could be provided because Jews could not, according to the law, settle in the country or form a religious community under the law of 1723. Yet the money was privately raised, the synagogue built and its doors ceremoniously opened in 1906 with Finland's Head of Church Affairs as well as governors and other high officials in attendance. The smaller congregations of Viipuri and Turku built their own synagogues in 1910 and 1912, respectively. By early 1919, all three congregations would finally have been officially registered and accorded legal status by the state.

For all the legal and administrative obstacles these Jews had to face, the greatest impediments to integration into the larger community were cultural. Traditional customs, religious practices and language created barriers that were hard to penetrate. A different question altogether was whether these Orthodox Jews cared to penetrate them or were happier to stay within their own tiny, inward-focused community. The Cantonist generation's primary interaction with the non-Jewish world was through their business activities and encounters with officials over the renewal of residence permits or efforts to ease the restrictive conditions under which they lived. Their homes were near the synagogue and the homes of other Jews, and socially they tended to mix with other members of the Jewish community.

From the tipping point in mid-century, Cantonist Jews found themselves trying to determine what their place might be in a society where Finns were trying to carve out a national identity for themselves within an empire that increasingly suppressed efforts at separation. Ahead were hard years that would be characterized by pogroms in Russia and political oppression in Finland, but in 1861, Finland's year of miracles, the outlook for the country and its Jews was, if not rosy, at least tinged with imagined opportunity.

Note

1. Kosher slaughterer (Yiddish).

Figure 8.1. Most of Finland's first Jewish settlers arrived as members of the Russian Imperial Army (Finland's Jewish Archives)

Born in Viipuri around 1857, at the age of 15, Rebecka married a significantly older retired soldier, a divorcé from Vilnius. The couple had seven children, two of whom died in infancy. They made their meager living at *Narinkka*. In 1891, at the age of 33, Rebecka was widowed and left alone with five young children. She continued at *Narinkka* but now developed the business into ready-made suits, which she imported from St. Petersburg.

Laura Ekholm*

---

*Boundaries of an Urban Minority, unpublished academic dissertation, University of Helsinki, 2013, p. 89.

~

CHAPTER EIGHT

Peisach Gets a Life

Viipuri, 1859—So Peisach, after five years in a Cantonist school and twelve years in the Imperial Army, is set free to look for work. He is not afraid of hard work or putting in long hours, nor is he a stupid man. But where to start?

Arbitrary and somewhat unclear restrictions on earning a livelihood apply to all but the "respectable" inhabitants (i.e., those belonging to one of the Four Estates) of Finland's class-based society although these rules will not be formally codified with respect to former Russian soldiers until 1869. Jews, of course, are not permitted to own land and, in any case, are required to live in cities, where their options for earning a living are restricted by law.

Economic historian Laura Ekholm, in her 2013 dissertation, *Boundaries of an Urban Minority*, writes:

> The Finnish Senate prepared an edict in 1869 on the means of livelihood permitted to Russian soldiers—whatever religion they adhered to—and their families throughout Finland. It stated that these people could pursue tax-free trade with baked goods, other self-made products and berries. Within the town, they could trade on these tax-free products, whereas second-hand clothes and used shoes, along with other used goods and cheaper linen, scarves and hats, string, filament, needles, and other tawdry items would receive the same taxation rate as that of Finnish citizens.[1]

The option of tax-free income appeals to Peisach, of course, but what does he know from berries? He has never baked a loaf of bread in his life, and his skill in handicrafts? *Bupkes!*[2]

With no marketable skills to rely on, the only natural occupation left for Peisach to pursue is that of the peddler: in other words, to begin selling second-hand clothing. At first he will have to work from home—once he finds a home—selling from house to house, but, as soon as he can, he will want to set up a stand in the *Punaisenlähteentori* market square or the *narinkka*, a labyrinth of stalls rented by Jewish merchants opposite one flank of the market. (There is still a large public space in Helsinki today known as *Narinkkatori* in honor of that city's parade ground that was turned into a large, flourishing *narinkka* by Jewish merchants.)

Viipuri, with fewer than 100 Jews, has only a modest *narinkka*. One former resident will remember Viipuri's *narinkka* of the early twentieth century when writing about the city of his youth:

> Life on the market was given its own special flavor by a fairly long, low, wooden building on the eastern edge along Vaasankatu next to Moskvin's stone building with its cone-shaped tower. There could be found the so-called *narinkka*. An open hallway along the walls of which merchants had their own tiny shops, side by side like in an indoor market, ran the entire length of the building..
> . . . A brisk trade in clothing was carried on in the *narinkka*, especially with people from the countryside, but city-dwellers also considered it a suitable place to look for appropriate apparel. Customers browsed the merchandise unrestrainedly and tried on suits, trousers and overcoats, each to his own taste.[3]

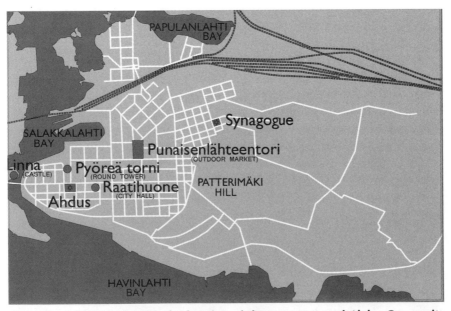

Figure 8.2. Viipuri, showing the location of the synagogue and Ahdus Community Center (Marja Leskelä)

Peisach teams up with two other Jewish veterans to pool their meager severance pay and rent a single room near the square in which to live. Hirsch, whose father was a tailor, knows how to handle a needle and thread. Moses is a born salesman. That leaves Peisach with the buyer's role, knocking on doors to ask if anyone has old clothes to sell for a few kopeks. In the evening in their ill-lit and poorly heated room, Hirsch teaches the others how to clean and repair the old garments and make them fit for resale.

At first they ply the streets and alleys of Viipuri, selling their wares, but before long the three neophyte businessmen have saved enough to rent a booth in the *narinkka*. The market brings them into contact with the segment of Viipuri's population that is too poor to buy tailored clothing. As farmworkers and laborers do not patronize their shops anyway, the members of the city's tailors' guild at first pay these Jewish peddlers little heed.

Spiritual and Personal Needs

Peisach and his roommates have no trouble figuring out what to do in their spare time. From Sunday morning to Friday afternoon they can be found washing, sewing, selling and buying. As *shabbos* approaches, however, they lay down their needles and primitive ledgers, wash, and prepare for lighting the candles, bless the bread, and enjoy their best meal of the week. Saturday morning these permitted Cantonists make their way to a shed in the yard of a tinsmith named Veikkanen, the son of Jacob Weikaim. Veikkanen is listed in official documents as having converted to Christianity, but one suspects that if Jews are holding prayer services on his property, the conversion and name change may have been a subterfuge designed to protect Veikkanen's business and family. By 1872, there are already too many Jews in Viipuri to fit into Veikkanen's shed when the High Holy Days come around. As former soldiers, they request and are granted permission to use a room in the Imperial Army Garrison for their services.

The curious contradiction of having their religion outlawed by Finnish statute but implicitly supported by Russian authorities will reappear time and again in the history of Finland's Jews. The reactions of the two sides indicate neither a deep antisemitism on the part of the Finns nor a fondness for Jews and Judaism on the part of the Russians. Rather they represent, on the one hand, the bureaucratic, do-it-by-the-book approach that Finnish civil servants took to applying the strictures of the old Swedish legal system and, on the other, the willingness of their Russian counterparts to overrule them at every possible juncture to show the Finns who was boss. It does not take long, of course, for Finland's Jews to learn how to manipulate this absurd game of one-upmanship to their advantage.

By saving every penny they make,[4] the three roommates manage, little by little, to assemble enough money to purchase a treadle sewing machine, a much-used but still serviceable Singer. The pace of work picks up, and after a few years the three men are able to rent rooms of their own.

Moses makes a trip to St. Petersburg and comes back with a wagonload of used garments, many of a better quality than Peisach has been able to buy in Viipuri. The men are tempted to expand their business, but they are already working to the point of exhaustion. The three ponder their collective financial situation while cutting and sewing in the evening and conclude that the next time Moses goes to St. Petersburg, he should look for more than clothing.

And so it is that on a bright and cold morning in March, 1870, Moses arrives at *Punaisenlähteentori* with a sleigh piled high with old clothes, and perched precariously on top are three very nervous young women. Moses has already chosen the one he will take for a wife. Peisach opts for her younger sister, leaving the third girl, who seems painfully shy, to the taciturn Hirsch. Moses explains that a *shadchen*,[5] a matchmaker, arranged for him to meet a number of eligible women of marrying age. The three he chose were from pious families and able to keep a proper Jewish home. Equally important, all three had been willing to travel with him to Viipuri in search of a new life.

Peisach is delighted with Feige. She has large dark eyes that pool beneath heavy brows. With her ample hips and plump arms, she seems somehow softer than the girls of Viipuri. Feige also turns out to be an excellent cook, a diligent housekeeper, and skilled with a needle and thread. As soon as arrangements can be made, they are married by Nochem Itzka Mowschew Aranow Liebkind, a *shochet* from Vitebsk who has moved to Viipuri earlier the same year. In addition to seeing to the provision of kosher meat for the growing Jewish population, Liebkind serves as rabbi and *mohel*[6] for the congregation.

Life is hard for Peisach and Feige. Although Peisach has a residence permit, he must renew it every three months at considerable cost. He knows that it can be revoked at any time and for almost any reason so he learns to keep his head down and stay out of trouble. If someone calls him a name, he pretends not to hear it. If one of the Finnish vendors in the market throws slops on his feet as he walks by, he doesn't react. He is not afraid of them, but he knows better than to draw attention to himself.

Peisach is not a tall man—his bowed legs see to that—but his years in the army have made him strong. He chooses not to regrow his *peyes*, but his beard is dark and full. He learns enough Finnish to conduct the business of buying and selling used clothes but beyond that has little contact with the good people of Viipuri.

Feige does her best to make a comfortable home within the limits of Peisach's modest income. She insists on keeping kosher and brought her own sets of dishes from St. Petersburg for that purpose. While Peisach was in the army, he had eaten what was given him. Although he tried his best to avoid pork, when a piece of meat was put in the pea soup and there was nothing else to eat, he ate the soup. Now he and his wife eat mostly black bread and soup made from beets, cabbage or potatoes, and for the *shabbos* meal, when they can afford it, they treat themselves to fish or chicken. They have only gruel in the morning, and, when they find time for lunch, it usually consists of bread and onions.

Feige helps Peisach with the cleaning and sewing of previously-owned clothes, but she constantly complains about the paucity of meat in their diet. Fourteen months after their marriage, Feige gives birth to a daughter, Chana. Far from her own mother, she obsesses over the baby's health. Chana's frequent bouts of diarrhea invoke fear of cholera, which had killed thousands in Finland 13 years earlier and would almost certainly be fatal to an infant. Sanitary conditions in the area surrounding the *Punaisenlähteentori* are poor. Feige must draw the family's drinking, cooking and washing water from the communal well, and the outhouse that they share with several neighboring families is impossible to keep clean and emits a foul odor that permeates the entire neighborhood. Despite Feige's fears, however, Chana thrives. She gets fat on her mother's milk and takes her first steps six weeks before her first birthday.

Now that they have families of their own, the three friends go their separate ways. Peisach and Hirsch open stalls of their own in the *narinkka*, and Moses becomes a full-time importer of used clothing from St. Petersburg. With Feige's help, Peisach begins to make enough money to feed his growing family (a second daughter, Mirjam, is born four years after Chana) and even save a little bit for a larger place to live.

Viipuri Grows and So Does Peisach's Business

Peisach's Viipuri in 1865 was a bustling multicultural commercial center, albeit a small one. Because of its natural harbor, Viipuri was already an important market town in the tenth century. Vikings, Vandals and Crusaders passing along the coast on their way to Novgorod or the Holy Land would have visited it. German merchants opened shops in Viipuri and stocked their shelves with provisions off-loaded from Hanseatic League ships plying the Baltic Sea. In the mid-sixteenth century, according to J.W. Ruuth's *History of Viipuri*, 61 percent of the city's inhabitants were of German stock, 19 percent were Swedish-speaking, and only 20 percent had Finnish as their native language.

Viipuri's population, excluding those living in the garrison, is only about 10,000 when Feige arrives there, but twenty years later it will have doubled. Unlike Helsinki, whose Swedish-speaking population is twice as large as its Finnish-speaking population in 1880, nearly 70 percent of Viipuri's population by then speak Finnish as their native language, only 20 percent speak Swedish, and the rest speak German or Russian. That is, except for most of the 100 or so former Cantonists and their wives and children, who would list their mother tongue, if anyone bothered to ask, as Yiddish.

Why is Viipuri growing so fast? Life in the countryside is hard at the best of times and almost intolerable during years when crops are poor. The famine of 1866–68 and the accompanying spread of disease result in the death of an appalling eight percent of Finland's population and drive people from the countryside to the cities in search of work. The government, still unwilling to grant residence permits to Jews other than former soldiers, is forced to turn for help to the Rothschild Bank of Frankfurt for a loan to buy grain and stave off an even worse catastrophe.

Viipuri's growth goes hand-in-hand with economic development. For Peisach the *narinkka* merchant, this means that more people are entering the wage economy. The new arrivals may be poor, but they no longer build their own homes, make all their own clothes or grow all their own food. Working class families, both agricultural and industrial, visit the *Punaisenlähteentori* market in search of serviceable second-hand items that fit their meager budgets. As they become a little more prosperous, they begin to want something better than other people's cast-off clothing but still cannot afford tailored garments. Unmet demand of this kind is known to stimulate innovation, and it isn't long before cheap but serviceable ready-to-wear clothing begins to appear in the market stalls.

Previously, the ready-to-wear clothing business in the Autonomous Grand Duchy had focused on the production of uniforms for soldiers of the Imperial Army. In the eighteenth century, each soldier had his own uniform made by a tailor, but by the time Peisach was serving in the military, needle shops and factories were turning out everything from undergarments to uniforms in standard sizes.

Military business is good business. The army buys in bulk and is always able to pay. When Russia's military investment was scaled back at the end of the Crimean War, many suppliers began using the resulting excess capacity to create ready-to-wear garments for the public. For some of Finland's Jews, the transition from second-hand clothing to ready-to-wear enabled them to escape poverty and take the first tentative steps on the arduous climb into the middle class.

By the time Feige *finally* [the emphasis is Peisach's] gives birth to a healthy son in 1888, the couple have three daughters: Chana (17), Mirjam (13), and Ida (2) and have lost three other children in childbirth. Mendel, the boy, is born as a birthday gift to his father, on the first night of Passover. He has a surprising head of dark hair, and from his first piercing cry is more demanding than any of the girls.

Peisach now employs a young woman, a daughter of the widow of another Cantonist, to help with the mending and washing of the secondhand clothing he sells, but his family is growing faster than his income. Moses is importing ready-to-wear garments from St. Petersburg instead of used clothing, doubling his income almost overnight. Feige has a cousin in St. Petersburg who has married into a family that makes hats and whose husband is willing to send shipments to Peisach at a price that will allow for a good mark-up. Peisach starts importing hats, and they sell so well that soon he opens a second stall that sells nothing else.

Now there is herring or chicken on the table several times a week and a rich *cholent* of beef, beans, potatoes and barley on the Sabbath. Peisach still has to renew his residency permit every third month, knowing that approval can be denied at the whim of the governor. Having outgrown the tiny apartment on the corner of Punaisenlähteenkatu and Pohjolankatu, the family has moved into larger two-room lodgings in Lallukankatu, three blocks away from the market. The girls all sleep in one room while Feige, Peisach and baby Mendel sleep in the other, which also serves as kitchen, living- and dining-room. Its only window looks out over a fetid courtyard where the outhouse is located. The building is not much nicer than the one they have left behind, but they are happy to have the extra room.

Viipuri's Jewish congregation keeps growing as additional Jewish soldiers and their families choose to remain in Finland after the completion of military service, which as of 1876 lasts only six years. More Jewish civilians are finding their way into the employ of the Imperial Army, too. There are complications, of course. The sons of Jews, even the sons of former soldiers, are not allowed to return to Finland after serving elsewhere in the Russian army. In another measure designed to keep the Jewish population from increasing, the sons and daughters of Jews, even the children of permitted Cantonists, are banished from Finland as soon as they marry. Despite these pernicious restrictions, as the pogroms of 1881–1884 spread fear and uncertainty among the Jewish communities of Russia, Peisach and his coreligionists have good reason to be thankful that they are living in the Grand Duchy and not in the Pale.

Opposition to Jewish settlement, however, is growing within Finnish society in the 1880s. Spearheaded by merchants fearing competition from Jews who have been granted the right to open shops, a movement arises to enforce strictly the 1782 regulation banning Jews from Finland unless they convert to Christianity. In 1886, the right of former soldiers to settle in Finland is revoked by the Senate. After more than a year, during which the status of Jews who have been living in the country up to that point under the protection of Czar Alexander II's 1858 decree remains unclear, the Senate votes to begin deporting them. Of the fifty-two Jewish families living in Viipuri, thirty-four are forced to leave the country within the first year. The only place they can go is across the border into Russia, where pogroms and repressive measures characterize the reign of the current czar, Alexander III. Among the first of those who pack their belongings and head eastward with heavy hearts are Peisach, Feige, and their four children.

The deportations are widely criticized in foreign newspapers, and, within a year, pressure from liberal politicians abroad and at home force the Senate to reconsider. Jews who are granted conditional residency permits by the Governor are once again allowed to remain. Their wives and children are included in the new regulations, but so are all the old restrictions.

Despite these setbacks, Viipuri's tiny Jewish community will somehow continue to grow and prosper. Half a century later, in 1939 to be exact, Viipuri's Jewish congregation, having more than doubled in size, will have built its own synagogue at Kalevankatu 31. Its *Ahdus* community center at Katariinankatu (later Linnankatu) 23 will be home to excellent concerts by Jewish musicians as well as plays and lectures in Yiddish. The Jewish community will have its own sports club, women's club, Zionist organization, and, of course, burial society and cemetery.

Unfortunately, the colorful narrative of Viipuri's Jewish community will reach its zenith and nadir at the same precise moment—the morning of 30 November, 1939—when three Soviet firebombs obliterate its synagogue on the first day of the Winter War.

Notes

1. Ekholm, Laura, Boundaries of an Urban Minority, unpublished dissertation, University of Helsinki, 2013, p. 51.

2. Nothing (Yiddish)

3. Tilli, Kalevi, *Viipuri: Muistoja kaipuuni kaupungista*, WSOY, Juva, 1985, pp. 23–24.

4. From 1860, when the Grand Duchy obtains the right to issue its own currency, the pennies are Finnish *penniä*, not Russian *kopeks*.

5. Matchmaker (Yiddish)

6. A person authorized to perform ritual circumcision (Hebrew).

Figure 9.1. Viipuri Youth Theater production at Ahdus, 1927 (Finland's Jewish Archives)

"Just so, Ruuben, that's what I want, too! To get away from here, far, far away!"

"I'm going to go when I get a little older. My uncle in Leipzig—the one who sent me this gold watch—has written about it to my mother. He is powerful and famous, a really accomplished lawyer. I'm going to become someone like that. I want to show what I can do, that I can rise to their level and even above. If you only understood how it feels to be pushed down all the time when your aspirations are upward and forward!"

"Yes, I understand!" shouted Haijele. Then she added thoughtfully, "I have an uncle in Leipzig, but he has never invited me to visit."

"That's a shame because one can't go far in this country although it isn't so important for you because you're a girl. It's different for me. I'm going to become a German. Jews have it good there, my father says. And then I'll come get you and take you there."

*Hilja Haahti**

---

*Haahti, Hilja, *Israelin tyttäret*, Otava, Helsinki, 1912, pp. 16–17.

CHAPTER NINE

~

Correspondence after Camp

Finland, 1936—Benjamin's prospects in the autumn of 1936 are much better than his paternal grandfather's were 75 years earlier. He has a home and family, enjoys full Finnish citizenship, and has a job which, while it may not excite him, is at least interesting most of the time. What he only vaguely realizes, however, is that political developments in an increasingly turbulent Europe could put all that at risk.

David has returned to his studies at the Polytechnic, working towards a civil engineering degree. He enjoys mathematics and physics and manages to pass his courses without too much difficulty, which is a good thing because he frequently devotes as much time and energy to Helsinki's night life as he does to attending classes and completing assignments. Although student life at the Poly includes plenty of social activity, David prefers the sophisticated atmosphere and excitement of Helsinki's dance halls and night clubs. Six foot (183 cm) tall and strong, he also meets other young men once a week at the Svenska Lyceum to play basketball, an increasingly popular sport that arrived in Finland only a few years earlier.

Rachel still has two years of high school left before she can take her matriculation exams. She would normally have been in her final year, but a bout of rheumatic fever when she was nine caused her to miss a year of school. Sometimes she dreams of becoming a doctor like Rosina Heikel, Finland's and the Nordic Countries' first woman doctor, but a nursing career seems more realistic. In her spare time, she devotes herself to WIZO's Turku branch, helping to organize meetings and fundraising activities.

Their triangular relationship from camp has remained decidedly asymmetric: Benjamin moons over Rachel, Rachel can't get David off her mind, and

David doesn't think much about either of them. Because they live in three different cities, there is no opportunity for the kind of casual interaction that could lead to deeper relationships. Instead, they have to rely on letter-writing. This creates particular problems for both Benjamin and Rachel, who must struggle with the gap between what they feel and what they dare to put down on paper.

As promised, Rachel is the first one to write.

Åbo, September 15, 1936

Dear Benjamin,

I must begin by apologizing for not having written sooner. I have been so busy with my new classes that I haven't had time to write to anyone from camp. I miss all our friends and hope we can meet again at camp next year. Do you know where it will be held?

I have decided to become a nurse so I am taking biology this year. There are only six of us in biology class. The teacher is really demanding. If it turns out to be too hard and I can't become a nurse, I think I might try teaching instead.

How is your work? I checked my father's Civil Guard hat, and, sure enough, the label says Eastern Finland Hat Factory! You must feel proud doing such important work. I hope you are enjoying it.

My father says that war is coming. He believes that since the Germans invaded the Rhineland and nobody stopped them, Hitler will think he can get away with whatever he wants.

Did you see that an American Negro won the 100 meter dash at the Olympics? Right in front of Hitler! I wish it had been a Jew! Some people here say that a few Jews were kept off our Olympic team even though they were good enough to have made it. I don't know if it is true, but some of my friends say so.

Have you heard from David? He promised to write me, but I guess he is too busy.

Well, I have to get back to my studies and then help my mother prepare for the holidays. Rosh Hashanah is just two days away. L'shanah tovah!

Your friend,
Rachel

Viipuri, October 9, 1936

Dear Rachel,

Thank you for your letter. I was beginning to think you wouldn't write. I have thought a lot about some of the things you said at camp. I guess I have a lot to learn. I still don't think David is right that Jews will never be fully accepted in Finland. At least here in Viipuri, I think we already are.

Last week I got to play my first game with *Kadur's* men's team, and I almost scored a goal. We beat a team from Käkisalmi 3–1. The coach said I played well. He is going to let me train regularly with the men from now on and says I have a chance to make the traveling squad next season. Most of the players are like ten years older, and sometimes they treat me like a kid, but I don't mind so long as I get to play.

The High Holy Days felt different this year. People here are really worried about what is happening in Germany and Palestine. One family we know is moving to America. They say things are going to get worse for Jews here, and they are getting out while they can. Are people in Turku thinking about leaving?

I guess that's all for now. Please write again. I haven't heard anything from David. I'll try to write him when I get a chance.

Yours truly,
Benjamin

Åbo, 17 December, 1936

Dear David,

Thank you for remembering my name day. I have to say, I was very surprised to receive your card. Although our family doesn't celebrate name days, I know when mine would be because there is a Finnish girl in my class named Raakel.

After the way camp ended, I didn't really expect to hear from you again. I probably shouldn't care, but I'm afraid I do. I'm still confused about the way you acted, like you cared about me sometimes and ignored me at others. I guess you do not really owe me an explanation, but you hurt my feelings, and I don't understand why. If you had just been friendly from the beginning without flirting with me, I wouldn't have felt that way, but you made me think you liked me, and then you embarrassed me in front of the whole camp by the way you chased after Naomi. I have to admit that I haven't had much experience with boys, but I think any kind of relationship should be based on respect. I don't know if you really don't respect me or just think it is okay to play with another person's feelings. I know that sounds terrible, but that's how it seems to me.

If I have misunderstood the situation, I'm sorry. I still have feelings for you, but I am trying to get over them. I would still like us to be friends, though, if that is possible. Please let me know what you think.

Yours,
Rachel

Viipuri, undated

Hi David,
How are things? I hope you are well. The picture on the other side is of the Viipuri Castle. It only takes about fifteen minutes to walk there from my house. Maybe you can visit sometime. Are you still in the Civil Guard? I'm thinking of signing up for the Youth Corps next summer. If you see any of the other campers, say hello from me.
    Your friend,
    Benjamin

Viipuri, undated

Dear Rachel,
I hope you are well. I thought you might like this picture of the Viipuri Castle. It is only about a fifteen minute walk there from my house. You said you visited it once, but I'm sure you haven't seen everything here. Viipuri is really a beautiful city. There are lots of interesting old buildings, but there are also some fine modern ones. We have a wonderful new library designed by Alvar Aalto. It just opened last year. There are museums and theaters, too. I would love to show them to you.
    Yours truly,
    Benjamin

HELSINGFORS, JANUARY 5, 1937

HEY BENI,
THANKS FOR THE POSTCARD. I'VE BEEN MEANING TO DROP YOU A LINE, BUT I'VE BEEN REALLY BUSY. I SHOULD PROBABLY SAY THAT I'VE BEEN STUDYING TOO HARD, BUT I REALLY HAVEN'T BEEN. THERE IS JUST SO MUCH TO DO HERE. I GO TO CLUBS A COUPLE OF TIMES A WEEK. LAST NIGHT I WENT WITH SOME FRIENDS TO A RESTAURANT CALLED HEIMOLA HALL WHERE THE DALLAPÉ ORCHESTRA WAS PLAYING. I MET A CHICK THERE WHO CAN REALLY DANCE. JUST MIGHT HAVE TO GO AND SEE IF SHE'S THERE AGAIN TONIGHT!

SPEAKING OF GIRLS, HOW ARE YOU DOING? ANY ACTION IN THAT SLEEPY LITTLE BURG OF YOURS? REMEMBER WHAT I TOLD YOU. YOU'VE GOT TO BE THE ONE TO MAKE THE FIRST MOVE. YOU WON'T GET ANYWHERE WAITING AROUND FOR A CHICK TO LET YOU KNOW SHE'S INTERESTED.

ARE YOU PLAYING ANY FOOTBALL? I GET MOST OF MY EXERCISE ON THE DANCE FLOOR, BUT I'VE STARTED TO PLAY BASKETBALL, TOO. I'M NOT VERY

GOOD YET, BUT I LIKE THE EXERCISE. THE OTHER GUYS ON OUR TEAM ARE ALL STUDENTS, AND WE HAVE A GOOD TIME TOGETHER. WE'RE JUST PRACTICING NOW, BUT NEXT SEASON WE PLAN TO JOIN A LEAGUE.

HJK WON THE FOOTBALL CHAMPIONSHIP THIS YEAR, BUT I GUESS YOU KNOW THAT. MY DAD AND I USUALLY GO TO THEIR GAMES. IF YOU BECOME GOOD ENOUGH TO PLAY FOR THE VIIPURI WOLVES, I CAN SEE YOU PLAY WHEN YOU COME TO HELSINKI. THEN YOU COULD STAY FOR A COUPLE OF DAYS, AND I COULD INTRODUCE YOU TO THE LITTLE SISTERS OF SOME OF MY GIRLFRIENDS. WHADDYA SAY?

I DON'T SEE MUCH OF THE GANG FROM CAMP. I DON'T REALLY HANG AROUND WITH THE JEWISH CROWD THAT MUCH. MOST OF MY FRIENDS ARE FROM THE UNI. BUT YOU'RE STILL MY BUDDY, OF COURSE, AND I'LL ALWAYS BE GLAD TO SEE YOU IF YOU MAKE IT TO THE BIG CITY.

DON'T DO ANYTHING I WOULDN'T DO!

DAVID

Viipuri, January 11, 1937

Dear Rachel,

I have been thinking a lot about you lately, maybe too much. Sometimes at work I realize I am daydreaming when I should be paying attention to what I'm doing. Fortunately I haven't messed up any of the good stock in the shop yet, but I'm going to have to be more careful.

Mother says I used to be like that when I was younger, too, but I know I wasn't thinking about girls then. This probably sounds stupid, but I can't help it. I had a dream about you, too. We were walking down the allée at Vidablick, only this time we were holding hands. David came walking up the allée from the other direction, and you dropped my hand as soon as you saw him. I guess you can tell how I felt when I woke up.

Now there is a real war going on in Spain, and the only question seems to be where the next one will break out. What is the world coming to? Mameh says that there is a Jew from Helsinki who is in Palestine fighting with the *Haganah*. Some of my friends talk about going, but I don't think any of them will really do it. How can we hope to defeat the British and the Arabs at the same time with just a few volunteers?

I probably won't be able to go to camp next summer because of work. I guess that means I won't be seeing you for a long time. I wish you could come here, but I guess you are too busy with school. I miss you and hope you are well.

Yours,

Benjamin

Viipuri, February 3, 1937

Dear Rachel,

It has been almost three weeks since I wrote, and you haven't answered. I hope I my stupid letter didn't make you mad. I probably shouldn't have told you how I feel. I don't want to do anything to hurt our friendship. Now I'm afraid you don't even want to be friends any more. Please write and tell me that isn't so.

I am putting in really long hours at work. Business is booming, and we all have to work extra hours in order to complete all the deliveries on time. I am pretty tired, but that's better than not having enough work.

I don't really have anything else to say except that your friendship is important to me, and I don't want to lose it. I'm feeling really sad that I might have messed it up by writing what I did. Please forgive me.

Yours,
Benjamin

Åbo, 14 February, 1937

Dear Benjamin,

I'm sorry I didn't answer your previous letter sooner. Please believe me that it was not because of anything you wrote. No girl can have her feelings hurt by being told that someone likes her. I have to admit that I already suspected you had some feelings like that at camp, but you never said anything. I do like you, of course, but as a friend. I wish I could say that I feel the same way about you as you say you feel about me, but no girl can control her feelings that way. At least, I can't.

I know what you mean, though, about how hard it is to care about someone who doesn't feel the same way about you. That's the way it has been with David and me. He has only written me once the whole time since camp. He probably has lots of girls in Helsinki and hasn't thought about me at all. I feel so stupid not being able to get him out of my mind, but what can I do? If you have any good ideas, please tell me.

I am convinced now that studying to be a nurse is the right choice for me, even though it will be hard. I think helping others is the most important thing anyone can do. Sophie Mannerheim visited our school in January. I really admire her. When I am a nurse, if there is a war in Palestine, I will definitely go. I could never bring myself to shoot anyone, but I could care for the sick and wounded.

I don't want to think such gloomy thoughts. The days are getting brighter, and it won't be long before the ice and snow begin to melt. For now, it is wonderful to be able to ski in the sunshine. Do you like to ski?

Don't feel bad. Let's keep writing. Maybe it will make both of us feel better.
Yours truly,
Rachel

HELSINGFORS, FEBRUARY 16, 1937

HI RACHEL,

SORRY I HAVEN'T WRITTEN YOU. I'VE BEEN REALLY BUSY WITH MY STUDIES. ENGINEERING IS HARD, AND THE TEACHERS REALLY PILE ON THE ASSIGNMENTS.

I'M SORRY IF I HURT YOUR FEELINGS AT CAMP. I GUESS I'M NOT THE MOST SENSITIVE GUY IN THE WORLD. I JUST DON'T TAKE THINGS AS SERIOUSLY AS YOU DO. I THINK YOU ARE REALLY SWELL, AND ANY GUY WOULD BE GLAD TO HAVE YOU FOR A GIRLFRIEND. I'M JUST NOT READY FOR THAT KIND OF THING. NAOMI DIDN'T MEAN ANYTHING SPECIAL TO ME, BUT SHE WAS FUN TO BE WITH. I THINK THAT CAMP IS A PLACE TO MEET A LOT OF NEW PEOPLE AND HAVE A GOOD TIME.

ANYWAY, OF COURSE WE ARE FRIENDS, AND I'LL BE SURE TO LOOK YOU UP IF I COME TO TURKU. ARE THERE ANY GOOD DANCE HALLS THERE? MAYBE I CAN GET YOU AWAY FROM YOUR BOOKS FOR A NIGHT OUT ON THE TOWN. I HAVE BEEN LEARNING THE JITTERBUG AND SOME JIVE STEPS. I SAW A MOVIE CALLED *THE SINGING KID* WITH AL JOLSON AND CAB CALLOWAY. MAN, THAT CALLOWAY CAN REALLY SWING! THE DALLAPÉ ORCHESTRA HAS A NEW SONG CALLED "BUGLE CALL RAG" THAT IS REALLY HOT. HAVE YOU HEARD IT?

I'D BETTER GET BACK TO MY STUDIES NOW. TAKE CARE, AND REMEMBER TO HAVE SOME FUN.

DAVID

Åbo, March 5, 1937

Dear David,
Thank you for answering my letter. You seem to be really busy. My life is pretty boring in comparison. I guess I am just old-fashioned. Mostly I study and help my mother, but sometimes I have to work at my father's store if one of the salesgirls is sick. I have also started singing in Turku's Jewish Choir. We practice twice a week and are not allowed to miss rehearsals unless we are sick. We will have our spring concert in April. There is even some talk about holding a joint concert with the Helsinki Jewish Choir next fall. Then maybe you could hear us.
I have decided to apply to the Lotta Svärd. Medical Lottas are already getting training for what to do in case of war. I think it is important to be as prepared as possible. Father says we are headed for war and is glad he doesn't have any sons

who would have to fight. He says the next war will be fought with airplanes and bombs. I can't imagine how horrible that would be.

I have to get back to my studies. It sounds like you are very busy, between studying and dancing.

Anyway, I'm glad we can still be friends. Don't be a stranger.
Rachel

Viipuri, March 22, 1938

Dear Rachel,

How have you been? I know you must be busy. I don't have much to write about. Things are a little hard at home. We have a couple from Germany living with us, the Scheins. They are about *Mameh*'s age or maybe a little older. They said they had to leave Berlin because life is getting too difficult for Jews in Germany. I don't know how long they are supposed to stay with us. Herr Schein says they are going to America the first chance they get. The good part is that my German is really improving. They don't speak Yiddish so we have to speak German together. Herr Schein was a lawyer in Berlin, but he doesn't know what he will do in America. He can't speak any English. I think they used to be pretty rich, but they don't have any money now. They had to leave everything behind when they left Germany. *Mameh* has even given Frau Schein some of her old clothes. *Mameh* didn't know them before they came to Finland, but the congregation asked if they could stay with us until they leave for America. They are staying in Jakob's and my room, and we are sleeping in the kitchen.

I haven't heard anything from David. If I get a chance, I would like to go to Helsinki. I still haven't ever been there except for a few hours in the train station on the way to and from camp. It would be great to have a few days to visit the city. *Tate* told me the synagogue is beautiful and I should see it if I ever get to Helsinki. I can't believe it has already been four years since he passed away. It has been hard for *Mameh*, trying to look after all of us without him. My older sister, Mirele, and I try to help by giving her the money we earn from our work, but it is barely enough to put food for everyone on the table. If the congregation didn't help out, we would never be able to feed the Scheins.

Football season is going pretty well. I finally scored a goal for the men's team. I was really proud because it turned out to be the winning goal of the match. I'm starting to get more confidence. I've grown quite a bit since last year, and that helps, too. We are only in the 2nd division, but some of the players are really good. I don't know if I'll ever be good enough to play in the 1st division, but I'm going to try as hard as I can.

I shouldn't be writing about football. I know you think it's boring so I'll close now. I hope your studies are going well. Please write if you have the time.

Yours,

Benjamin

* * *

The arrival of refugees from Germany, Austria and Czechoslovakia, a trickle at first but increasing rapidly as the situation in Central Europe deteriorates, makes it impossible for even the most optimistic of Finland's Jews to ignore the clouds on the horizon. Jews have enjoyed the rights of citizenship in Finland for less than twenty years, and the treatment of their co-religionists in countries where they have lived for generations, prospered and assimilated into society sends a cold shiver through the Jewish communities of Viipuri, Helsinki and Turku.

The Jews are not the only Finns to feel unsure of the future. Only recently has communist agitation, orchestrated from Moscow, been brought under control in Finland, and it seems like yesterday that an armed uprising by the right-wing Lapua Movement was quashed. Finland has been independent for less than a generation, and the cement holding society together after the horrific Civil War has not set completely.

Although the persecution of Central European Jews has unsettled Finland's Jewish community, Benjamin, Rachel and David, like most teenagers, are focused more on their own lives than on the future of their country. Yet when the storm comes, they will set aside their personal priorities and devote themselves to the defense of their nation even though it had denied their grandparents and parents basic civil rights because of their religion.

Figure 10.1.   Helsinki's Jewish Choir, 1933 (Finland's Jewish Archives)

Master tailor Leo Jakobson's family came within a hair's breadth of ending up on the list of those to be deported. The family had lived peacefully for several years in a tiny wooden house on the fringe of Viipuri in an area known as Kolikkoinmäki. One morning, a sheriff showed up unannounced. He said he had received harsh criticism from Governor Gripenberg because a Jewish family had been allowed to live outside the city limits. . . . The governor ordered them to move into the city within 24 hours. Fortunately, they found a vacant rental apartment. Then they waited anxiously for the decision on the renewal of their residence permit. Living in a forbidden area would have been reason enough for deportation. Many Jews had been denied permits simply because of a single illegal sales trip outside the city. For some reason, however, the governor was merciful in this case.

Max Jakobson*

**Väkivallan vuodet*, Otava, Keuruu, 1999, p. 156.

CHAPTER TEN

~

Benjamin Recalls His Family's Return to Viipuri

I think the year my grandparents lived in St. Petersburg was terrible for Bubbe Feige even though she originally was from there. She took their banishment from Viipuri as a personal insult. Zayde Peisach was different; he sort of lived inside his own head. I don't know if it really mattered to him where he was living. At least that is how my grandmother always described him, kind of fartrogn, absent-minded. Anyway, Zayde apparently never thought much about getting back to Finland. He just resigned himself to whatever fate God had planned for him. It was Bubbe Feige who got them back.

She loved to tell the story in later years, but Mameh told me everyone kept it a secret from Zayde Peisach while he was alive. Bubbe was furious that they had been deported. She hated living with all her children in her sister's tiny apartment and not having a home of her own. The first few months, she said, she couldn't believe what had happened. During the day, she was busy with housekeeping and looking after the children, but at night, she would lie awake, searching for some way to reverse this terrible injustice. She knew she couldn't rely on Zayde Peisach to do anything about it, but she was determined not to give up until they were allowed to return to Viipuri.

The Finnish government wouldn't listen to protests from Jewish families that had been denied residence permits, but Bubbe thought the Russian authorities might. She was afraid local officials wouldn't pay any attention to her, either, so she went right over the heads of all of them to Governor General von Heiden. The first time she went to his office, his secretary said he was too busy to see her. Instead of giving up, she returned the next day and the next. She just waited in the anteroom, knitting socks, until on the third day von Heiden came walking out while she was sitting there. Bubbe stood up and, without waiting for an introduction, announced that she was the wife of a loyal Russian soldier who had been treated unfairly by the Finnish government. Right there in the waiting room, waving her knitting in the air the way she used to do when she was excited, she began to tell her story. Her husband had served the czar faithfully and been banished on a technicality. He was charged with doing business in Lappeenranta but had only gone there looking for herbs in the marketplace so he could make medicine for his sickly daughter's allergies.

Count von Heiden actually listened to her, who knows why? He certainly couldn't have cared much about the fate of my grandfather and probably didn't believe the story Bubbe Feige had just made up. When I told this story once to a history teacher from the Jewish school, he said that von Heiden didn't like Viipuri's Governor Gripenberg. Maybe he wanted to show him that Russia had the power to overrule Finnish decisions and protect its former soldiers. Anyway, von Heiden asked his secretary to write down Bubbe Feige's story and promised to look into the matter.

Bubbe made up stories to tell Zayde Peisach about where she had been all the time she was waiting for von Heiden. St. Petersburg had changed so much since she had moved to Finland . . . she had trouble finding the right shops for everything she needed . . . and so on. Most likely Zayde Peisach hadn't even noticed. Anyway, about two months after Bubbe Feige spoke to the Governor General, a soldier showed up with a letter for Zayde Peisach. He was terrified at first, but when he read the letter he started to cry. The banishment decree had been lifted, and he was free to return to Viipuri with his family. They moved back in 1889 in time for Chanukah, and the Viipuri officials never bothered them again. In fact, Zayde was given a special residence permit that only had to be renewed once a year instead of every three months!

Bubbe Feige certainly had a lot of chutzpah.[1] In Russia, they don't respect you if you don't fight for what you want. That's like Finland in the Winter War. Stalin thought his troops would just waltz into Helsinki in a week. He was surprised when we fought back and gave the Russkies all they could handle. Finns call that kind of toughness sisu,[2] but I say when you are fighting one against ten, it's chutzpah!

Zayde Peisach lost everything when he was deported. His friend Moses left for America not long after Zayde had asked him to look after his belongings, and no one ever heard from him again. Was this Moses deported, or did he just get fed up and decide to leave? Who knows? Anyway, Zayde never found out what happened to his belongings. He had no money to start his own business again. He was 60 years old, and his health was failing. He had rheumatism, which made it almost impossible for him to thread a needle, and bad knees, probably from walking all the way to Finland as a young man and then standing all those years in the market. He finally found work as a sales clerk in Isak Kuschakoff's general store, and that's where he worked until his heart stopped in 1901. He was 71. Bubbe Feige was much stronger. She was almost 90 when she died.

Kuschakoff's store was quite successful, everyone in Viipuri knew it. Not just the Jews, the Finns used to shop there, too. Kuschakoff's son, Doni, was my father's age. They played together and became good friends. Years later, Doni got their maid, who wasn't Jewish, pregnant. In those days, that kind of thing happened in families that could afford servants. Usually, the maid went away after the family made some kind of financial settlement. To everyone's astonishment, including my father's, Doni insisted on marrying the girl, Olga, her name was. They were young at the time, maybe not even twenty. Anyway, the whole congregation turned its back on them. Doni's family read the kaddish[3] and sat shiva for him, and his name was removed from the congregation's membership rolls. That was the way it was in those days. His crime wasn't getting the maid pregnant, it was marrying a shiksa. Today, almost every Jewish family in this country has a son or daughter who has married outside the faith.

Tate was probably the only Jew who stayed friends with Doni. It helped that by that time Zayde Peisach was no longer around to make a fuss about it. Doni later changed his name from Kuschakoff to Kuusakoski and started his own business, buying scrap metal and melting it down for resale. Today that company is huge, maybe the biggest recycling company in Northern Europe, and still owned by Doni's descendants.

That's the funny thing. It seems that the more rules the Finns made to keep Jews down, the harder we worked and the more successful we became. How many times did the sons of Cantonists who came here with nothing become successful businessmen? All in just two or three generations! People say that Jews are successful because they have a lot of money, but none of those Cantonists had not even one penny to start with. All they had was ambitsye un bashtimung,[4] *ambition and determination! The people with money in Viipuri were the ones who owned sawmills, exported lumber, and owned the ships that delivered wood to customers as far away as England, and Jews weren't allowed in those businesses. Doni Kuschakoff was able to get rich because he chose a business nobody else wanted to be in, buying and selling junk that other people threw away.*

Most Jews never got rich, though. They worked like my father and grandfather and me, cutting and sewing and selling. My father used to complain about how hard life was, but I see it different. Maybe we didn't get rich, but we were much better off than the Jews from Germany and Austria and other countries who did get rich at first and then had everything stolen from them by the Nazis. We got to keep what we earned, even if we had to pay a lot of taxes, and if we saved something, we could pass it on to our children. All my grandchildren today live in nice homes and drive nice cars, not fancy, maybe, but nice. Not one day goes by that I don't feel thankful for having been born in Finland. It wasn't Paradise for us Jews, but it wasn't that other place, either.

Notes

1. Audacity, nerve (Yiddish)
2. Perseverance, grit, tenacity (Finnish)
3. Mourner's prayer (Hebrew)
4. Ambition and determination (Yiddish)

Figure 11.1.   The so-called Cossack Riots of 1902 in Helsinki (Finland's National Bureau of Antiquities: Einar W. Juva)

One of the Bolshevik's most important newspapers, *Proletaaria*, was printed recklessly . . . by the *Työ* newspaper's presses in Viipuri, some twenty editions. Lenin, himself, was in Viipuri supervising the work and editing the paper. Finnish railway workers then smuggled the papers into Petrograd [St. Petersburg]. Afterwards, Lenin shifted his activities to western countries. In Berlin, he registered at a hotel as a Finnish cook.

Veijo Meri*

---

*Ei tule vaivatta vapaus, Otava, Helsinki, 1995, pp. 201–202.

CHAPTER ELEVEN

~

Mendel's Childhood

Viipuri, 1888—Thirty-two years after the first Cantonist Jews are permitted to settle in Finland, Peisach and his family are forcibly evicted from it. Their crime? Being Jewish (or more accurately, not being Finnish, a status which is denied them precisely because they are Jewish).

1888   Baby Mendel is just two months old when Feige wraps him in swaddling clothes and takes him, along with Peisach and their three daughters, to live in her sister, Golde's, apartment in the Kolomna district of St. Petersburg.

1889   Mendel is little more than a year old and just taking his first steps when he and his family are surprisingly allowed to return to Viipuri.

1893   At five years of age, Mendel is neither old enough nor in the right city to be admitted to Finland's first Jewish school when it opens in Helsinki.

1894   Dr. Axel Johan Lille appeals to the Burgher Estate to support the granting of citizenship to Finland's Jews. Elsewhere in Europe, France's Dreyfus Affair is dominating the headlines.

1895   Seven-year-old Mendel starts school in Viipuri.

1896   Theodor Herzl publishes *Der Judenstaat*, which will spark the birth of the Zionist movement.

1899   Eleven-year-old Mendel overhears his father talking angrily with two other men about Czar Nicholas II's "February Manifesto," which strips away much of Finland's autonomy and the decision-making power of its Diet, ushering in the first oppressive period of Russification.

1901   Mendel, nearing his thirteenth birthday and long-awaited *bar mitz-vah*, is sleeping soundly when Peisach suddenly sits bolt upright in bed, blurts out "*Sh'ma Yisrael . . .*" and keels over dead from a massive heart attack.

1902   At 14, and a man according to Jewish tradition, Mendel leaves school to work at Steinbock's hat factory and help support his family. Although he now thinks of himself as a worker, he will not be attending the founding meeting that year of Viipuri's Workers' Party.

Return to Viipuri

In 1889, Peisach is almost 60 when he and his family return from their year-long exile in St. Petersburg. Penniless, bitter and disappointed, the former Cantonist and neophyte clothier goes to work at Kuschakoff's store, shorn of his dream of having a successful business of his own. As Kuschakoff pays him by the hour and Peisach needs the money, he spends six long days a week at the store, leaving only *shabbos,* which he nevertheless spends in *shul,*[1] for his family. Feige is only 44, but miscarriages and stillbirths have aged her beyond her years. She has grown heavy and suffers from bouts of depression although she has no name for the debilitating sadness that descends on her like a thick fog and lasts for days. Regardless, she soldiers on, holding the family together as best she can.

Mendel is a difficult child. Before he learns to crawl, he howls in frustration at being stuck in one place. Later, he pads across the floor on his hands and knees until he sees something he wants on a shelf or table, then he screams because he can't reach it. The worst comes once he learns to pull himself up and stand by holding on to furniture but has not yet figured out how to walk. He takes a tentative step, tumbles over, bangs his knee or scrapes his elbow, yells, pulls himself up, screaming all the while, and repeats the whole scenario until he is bright red in the face and his little limbs are purpling with bruises.

Feige can't stand it when Mendel screams. Nor can Peisach. The only one who can deal with him is the middle daughter, Mirjam, and when she is not around, all the others can do is turn away and clap their hands over their ears until Mendel grows tired of protesting.

Mirjam is patient, but there is more to it than that. She seems to be able to anticipate Mendel's frustration before it gets a firm grip on him, allowing her to create a speedy diversion. Perhaps for this reason, Mendel is calmest when Mirjam is within reach. Mirjam enjoys watching over her little brother, and Feige gladly relinquishes some of the responsibility for Mendel's care to her daughter.

Even as he approaches school age, Mendel rarely plays like other children. His idea of playing is to take things apart. If he sits quietly for more than a few minutes, Feige checks to see what he is dismantling. And invariably, once he has taken something apart, he has a screaming fit if he is not able to put it back together again.

By the time he turns seven and starts school, Mendel resembles a little old man more than a child. His default mood is seriousness. His mouth is never completely closed, although that may be because of a persistent sinus condition, and he walks slightly stooped over, his dark eyes peering out from under bushy eyebrows. Except when they are bullying him, the other children in his class mostly ignore him.

After school, Mendel spends hours on his own, scouring the neighborhood for things he can sell. Finland is becoming more prosperous at the end of the nineteenth century, and people who have a little money to spend on consumer goods have also begun to throw things away that can potentially be reused: empty bottles, a length of wire, broken tools with a salvageable wheel or handle. Mendel convinces his mother's friend Ester Mitnik to let him display a little basket of these found objects, carefully cleaned and polished, at her market stall, and occasionally one of Ester's customers buys something from it for a penny or two. Mendel squirrels the proceeds of these sales away in a folded piece of cloth that he keeps in a chink between rough boards in the wall. By pulling out and replacing a bit of the dried moss insulation, he is able to keep his hiding place secret at first, but he checks on it so often that before long his sisters all know where it is.

Another of Mendel's peculiarities: unlike other children, he does not spend the pennies he earns on sweets or toys. He earns money not to spend it but to possess it, a passion that will not release him from its grasp for as long as he lives.

At school, Mendel distinguishes himself as one of the best in his class at mathematics but, despite an excellent memory, he is a desultory student in his other subjects. He also gains a perverse reputation as a fighter, or rather as someone with whom others enjoy picking fights and who, despite his diminutive size and lack of skill, never backs off. The provocations are always the same: some slur related to his Jewishness, his nose (which is, of course, the same thing) or his family's Russianness. And because he is so easily goaded, beating him up becomes a favorite sport of certain older schoolmates.

There is one other Jewish boy in his school, Schmuel Rubenstein, but nobody bothers Schmuel. He goes quietly about his business, rarely attracting attention to himself, and the others leave him alone. And then there is Liba Leventhal, one of the prettiest and most popular girls in the school.

Two years older than Mendel, she is vivacious and the very opposite of self-effacing Schmuel Rubenstein. Later in life, Liba and Schmuel will claim that there wasn't much antisemitism at all in Viipuri; Mendel will say there wasn't much else.

Why is Mendel a magnet for bullies? Perhaps because he is aggressive when he should compromise, noisy when he should be silent, and questioning when he should let well enough alone. He is so antagonistic that a black eye and split lip seem to be part of his personality. Peisach tries to reason with his son, explaining how he survived the harsh years in the Cantonist school and the army by making himself as invisible as possible, but the root of the boy's problems is not to be found in reason. Feige recognizes in Mendel some of her own obduracy, but when she tries to talk him out of one of his moods, they invariably end up at loggerheads. By the time he is ready to begin studying for his *bar mitzvah*, his father is growing weak and absent-minded, and his mother is at her wits' end.

Hard Times

Peisach's salary from Kuschakoff's general store is barely enough to feed his family, keep them in second-hand clothing, and pay his dues to the congregation and its burial society. After he dies, the family is deprived of even that meager source of regular income. Feige, who previously earned a bit of extra money from sewing work she occasionally did at home, now offers to do piecework on a regular basis for several tailoring shops.

Chana, the oldest and prettiest of the sisters, has married Simon Harkavy, a brother of the famous writer A.A. Harkavy. They have settled in St Petersburg, where Harkavy works as a history teacher. Feige misses her eldest daughter terribly but is happy to see her well married and looks forward to the arrival of grandchildren.

Mirjam, the middle sister, is cheerful and industrious. After leaving school, she worked as a seamstress for a dressmaker and helped around the house when she wasn't working. Two years before her father's death, she married Faivel Fridman and moved with him to New York. Peisach's death leaves only Ida and Mendel at home with Feige. Sickly Ida gamely tries to help her mother but is allergic to so many things that her efforts often end up with Ida lying in bed, a wet cloth over her mouth and nose, coughing and sniveling until exhaustion brings merciful sleep.

Feige worries about Ida. Specifically, she worries that she will never marry. Ida is frail, but there is a sweetness about her and a tendency for people who meet her for the first time to want to protect her. One of those is Hanoch Zinik, a young doctor who is working in the Vyborg garrison. When he starts to court Ida, Feige cannot believe her good luck. A doctor! He will be able to look after her daughter in every way, providing a good home and helping her grow stronger. No one suspects that in 1918 Hanoch will be the one to bring home the influenza virus that will strike Ida down in a matter of days.

Chana tries to help her mother by sending a few rubles from St. Petersburg from time to time. Mirjam wants to help, too, but for the time being it just isn't possible. Years later, Faivel's clothing business will become successful enough for Mirjam to be able to send a little money to her mother, but during their first years on Orchard Street, his pushcart barely produces enough to cover the rent on their tiny tenement flat and put some cabbage soup on the table. They survive thanks to the sewing skills Mirjam learned from her mother and the dressmaker, which enable her to find work in a sweatshop called the Triangle Shirtwaist Factory.

Mendel at 13 becomes the man of the family. Peisach's death has more practical than emotional significance for his son. Mendel had never been close to his father, an introverted man who hardly seemed to be present, even at the dinner table. Only when they walked together to *shul* had Mendel occasionally felt that his father might be proud to have a son to walk by his side. They rarely talked. What would they have talked about?

Mendel's *bar mitzvah* is modest even by the standards of the poorest segment of Viipuri's tiny Jewish community. The reception is held in their cramped home, where only a few months earlier the family was sitting *shiva*[2] for Peisach. Besides the family, only Rabbi Segall and Ester and Chaim Mitnik are invited. Feige makes *gefilte fisch, kugel,* and a blueberry *babka* that is her specialty. Rabbi Segall gives Mendel a *Siddur*[3] on behalf of the congregation, and Feige has sewn him a handsome linen shirt. His sisters have pooled their resources to purchase a fine leather purse, which immediately becomes his most cherished possession.

And then Mendel leaves school. Feige has spoken to the wife of Meyer Steinbock, whose family has just returned to Viipuri and opened a hat factory and shop on Pohjolankatu. The Steinbocks were deported at the beginning of 1889, several months after Mendel's family. Despite having been relatively successful in business in St. Petersburg, Steinbock chooses to return to Viipuri as soon as the opportunity arises. He is looking for an errand boy: someone to do packing, make deliveries and clean the premises. At the urging of his wife, he gives Mendel the job. The work is not very exciting, but Mendel makes sure to keep his employer happy so he can collect his tiny salary each week. He turns it all over to his mother, who gives a few pennies back to him whenever she can afford to do so. In this way, his tiny leather purse slowly fills with coins.

Young Mendel's hyperactivity is well-suited to his job as delivery boy and packer. The work keeps him in nearly perpetual motion. At the same time, it leaves his mind free to absorb everything that goes on in Steinbock's workshop. He watches closely the cutters in the back room and peppers them with questions so frequently that Jakubovitch and Löfberg threaten to use their shears to circumcise him a second time if he doesn't shut up and leave them alone. Only old Berko, an ancient former Cantonist from Bialystok with a gray beard reaching almost to his belt, takes a liking to Mendel and patiently answers his questions in a mumbling monotone that keeps time with the deliberate pace of his cutting and sewing. Although Mendel is not allowed to handle the tools or fabric, he slowly but surely begins to absorb the basics of the trade.

Russification

Mendel was born during the reign of Czar Alexander III, who ascended the throne in 1881 after the assassination of Alexander II. Unlike his father, who freed Russia's serfs and was considered a benevolent and progressive ruler by the Finns, Alexander III was a conservative nationalist. The wave of pogroms in the Pale of Settlement following the assassination of Alexander II may have received at least tacit support from Alexander III's imperial palace. One of the czar's advisors supposedly suggested that the way to deal with the empire's Jewish problem was to baptize a third of them, starve a third of them to death, and deport the rest.

Finland's history under the czars can be characterized in an oversimplified way as a roller coaster ride: up with the liberal Alexander I, down with the conservative Nicholas I, then up again with Alexander II, and down again with Alexander III. Under the last czar, Nicholas II, instead of heading up once again, the roller coaster continued hurtling downward, taking consensus on how to react to Russian oppression with it. Finland's nationalist movement split between those preferring gradual development of Finnish society *within* the Russian Empire and those who advocated for outright independence. Rising pressure for separation on the Finnish side was met by reactionary measures and increased pressure for integration under both Alexander III and Nicholas II. The two periods of greatest oppression and revocation of previously granted rights were 1899–1905 and 1908–1917. In English they are known as the periods of Russification.

What was there about Finland that so irritated the czars and Russia's law-makers? By the last quarter of the nineteenth century, Finland had its own parliament, its own money, its own railway system, its own customs duties, its own postal system, and its own school system and university. It also boasted a strong civil service and an expanding industrial economy. In cultural achievement, as well, Finland was entering a golden age. The Finland Pavilion at the 1900 Paris World Fair, designed by Lindgren, Gesellius and Saarinen, attracted international attention to Finnish crafts, art and architecture. Akseli Gallèn-Kallela received a gold medal for his paintings of scenes from the *Kalevala*, and works by Albert Edelfelt and Pekka Halonen were also exhibited. That such a pavilion existed in the first place was remarkable: Finland, after all, was just a glorified Russian province, not a country.

The Uppity Postal Worker

Author Veijo Meri recounts a story that gained widespread credence at the end of the 1880s. Most likely apocryphal, it nevertheless helps explain what the Russian leadership found so provocative about Finnish behavior. In the story, Czar Alexander III's yacht is anchored in Virolahti Bay, some 50 kilometers west of Viipuri. One of the czar's guests, having written a letter to someone back in St. Petersburg, has himself rowed ashore so he can mail it. To his chagrin, the young woman in the local post office refuses to accept the letter because the envelope has a Russian stamp on it, not a Finnish one. The visitor pulls out his purse and offers to pay for Finnish stamps, but he has only rubles and kopeks with which to pay. Once again, the young woman shakes her head. She will only accept Finnish currency. As a consequence, the letter cannot be mailed.

All this conversation, of course, takes place through an interpreter because the visitor speaks no Finnish and the postal worker no Russian. According to Meri, when the frustrated customer returns to the ship and tells his story, the other passengers have no trouble sympathizing with him. This kind of supercilious behavior is all too familiar.

Within the empire of the omnipotent czar was an area where Russian stamps and money were not accepted. It was confirmed, when they consulted their memories, that the same thing had happened to many other Russians in Finland. Just thirty kilometers from Russia's capital city, Russian passengers heading to Finland and the West by train had to clear customs at what was, for all intents and purposes, an international border. That was why even public officials in Finland could not understand or speak Russian. They had different laws, different customs, their own border and their own postage stamps. Finns related to Russians indifferently or even standoffishly. Did Finland not belong to the Russian Empire? Had it not been conquered in 1808–1809? It seemed not. A Russian felt as if he were entering an unfamiliar land, a foreign country.[4]

Meri concludes: "Radical nationalist politicians and newspapers began demanding that Finland be conquered all over again."

Although there are no indications that preparations were actually made to invade the nominally Autonomous Grand Duchy, a movement to pull the upstart Finns back into the fold certainly got underway. The so-called Postal Manifesto of 1890, coupled with efforts to create a uniform currency and customs duties for Russia and Finland, presaged tougher measures to come under Czar Nicholas II. In 1899, he promulgated the so-called February Manifesto, in which he decreed that, with regard to laws applicable to the Russian Empire, Finland's Diet had only consultative rights and not the rights of refusal or noncompliance. The February Manifesto was a top-down "declaration of non-independence," Finns felt that practices and privileges long recognized as rightfully theirs were being withdrawn arbitrarily.

University students mobilized across Finland in 1899, collecting 523,000 signatures or signatory marks on a petition expressing concern about the effects of the February Manifesto, quite a remarkable accomplishment in a country with a total population of fewer than three million. Two years later, a group opposed to the Russification efforts focused on passive resistance to what they saw as the illegal conscription of Finnish men into the czar's army. They became known as *Kagaali*, a name that Antti Blåfield in *Loistavat Erkot* claims was originally a Russian slur derived from *kahal*, the name for the council of ruling Jewish elders in *shtetls* of the Pale such as the one that gave Peisach up to the *chappers*.

Both sides were caught in a spiral of resentment and hardening positions. Complicating this increasingly confrontational situation was the emergence of socialist ideology on both sides of the border. Revolutionary socialism was brought to Finland at the end of the nineteenth century by workers in the printing trade who had been exposed to it while working in Germany. Finland's Workers' Party, founded in Turku in 1899, changed its name to Finland's Social Democratic Party and adopted an overtly socialist program in 1903.

Whereas Finland's bourgeois political movements aimed to unite all Finns under a patriotic banner, socialism promoted internationalism and class consciousness in place of national unity. Members of the nationalist parties— Old Finns, New Finns and Constitutionalists—were predominantly middle or upper class, Swedish-speaking and well educated. They were certainly not interested in a class-based revolution or the downfall of capitalism. The country's factory workers and landless farm workers, on the other hand, were mainly poor, Finnish-speaking and poorly educated, and their priorities were better living and working conditions and, in the case of the farm workers, the redistribution of land.

Now Finland's political landscape featured three tendencies: a reformist movement that was trying to achieve change within the existing political framework, a growing and increasingly radical nationalist movement struggling to achieve independence for Finland but within the existing class structure, and a small underground internationalist movement plotting the overthrow of the capitalist system. All these efforts ran counter to the determined efforts being made by St. Petersburg to bind Finland ever tighter to the increasingly inward-looking Russian Empire and its autocratic monarchy.

The Jewish Question

Finland's Jews, meanwhile, were looking to improve their own insecure position. They still had to renew their residence permits every third month, paying 15 times more for it than Christian applicants. A motion to improve their status had been brought before the Burgher Estate of the Finnish Diet for the first time in 1872 by liberal reformer Leo Mechelin. He recommended the repeal of the statutes that placed Jews outside the scope of laws governing other residents of the country but did not specify what rights he felt they should enjoy. Other liberal-minded Swedish-speakers also spoke up on behalf of the Jews. By the turn of the century, when Swedish speakers accounted for less than 13 percent of Finland's population, they had begun to realize that discrimination against the Jews could lead to discrimination against other minorities . . . such as themselves.

Even the whole of Finland's population could be seen as a minority when viewed in the context of its powerful neighbors. Dr. Axel Johan Lille, editor-in-chief of the liberal Swedish-language newspaper *Nya Pressen*, made this clear in his address to the Burger Estate in 1894:

> I don't appeal to the Burgher Estate solely on behalf of the Jews living here but on behalf of our entire country as well. We are, ourselves, a people small in number, living surrounded by difficulties and threats from all sides. Danger threatens us specifically from the most powerful direction. That is all the more reason for us to avoid oppressing others when we find ourselves in a more powerful position.[5]

Other segments of the population, however, were not so well disposed toward the tiny Jewish population in their midst. When news of the persecution of Jews and the spread of pogroms began to arrive in Finland, the May 28, 1881 edition of Uusi Suometar, proclaimed that "Russia knows what it is doing," The following year, influential Finnish politician Agathon Meurman delivered a venomous diatribe to the Peasant Estate:

> Only a blind man could deny that the Jewish question is a question of world domination. With ironclad determination, Jews advance toward this goal. Everywhere . . . they suck in the material forces from around them . . . [I ask you to join in moving] that the prohibition on Jewish settlement in our country be rigorously upheld, and that the law that permits soldiers who served here to live in our country be repealed, and that those Jews, who live here without any legal right, be ordered to leave.[6]

There were those in the business community, as well, who felt that even a few Jews were too many for Finland to tolerate. Botanist and Member of Parliament Oswald Kihlman (later Kairamo) proposed that Jews be paid to emigrate. In August 1883, the Tampere Businessmen's Association held a meeting in Viipuri. The prepared introduction to the meeting included the following invidious comparison:

> It is said that our humanity requires us to accept, even grant citizenship rights to, Jews. There is no basis for such talk. No humanity requires a people to take in that which produces its ruination nor that which makes it susceptible to the danger of ruination. People on board ship who fall ill with the black plague are held in quarantine, nor has anyone ever argued that humanity requires those suffering from the mortal plague to be allowed to enter cities or permit infected goods to be sold. The Jewish question is, therefore, not at all to be seen from the point of view of humanity but directly in answer to the question: Is there anything to be feared from allowing Jews to enter our country?[7]

The debate continued, with heated contributions by both defenders and detractors of the Jews. Professor J.R. Danielson-Kalmari, a member of the Clerical Estate, worried in 1894 that rising antisemitism would have a deleterious effect on Finland's image at a time when Russian oppression was increasing.

> And should this Finnish Jewish question be judged by the civilized world, assuredly then would the sympathy that our people enjoy at present disappear. And furthermore, with what force can we promote our own people's efforts against oppression and violence if our own conscience is troubled by the feel-

ing that there are citizens in our midst, be they merely the children of a foreign people, whom we have placed outside the law?[8]

Finland's Jews were in the peculiar position of being discussed on all sides but having no part in the discussion. Perhaps this was a good thing, for it seems unlikely that any arguments they might have made would have proven persuasive. In any case, the net result of all these proposals and counter-proposals was that while everything else in Finland seemed to be in flux, nothing changed for the Jews. The highly restrictive 1782 directive left over from the days of Swedish rule—already rescinded by this time in Sweden—remained in force.

Notes

1. Synagogue (Yiddish)
2. Seven-day mourning period observed in Jewish homes (Hebrew)
3. Prayer book (Hebrew)
4. Meri, Veijo, *Ei tule vaivatta vapaus*, Otava, Helsinki, 1995, p. 86.
5. Jacobsson, *op. cit.*, p. 299 (translated by the author)
6. *Ibid.*, pp. 163–64.
7. *Ibid*, p. 197.
8. Torvinen, Taimi, *Kadimah*, Otava, Keuru, 1989, p. 70,

Figure 12.1. Helsinki's synagogue in 1908 (The Finnish Museum of Photography: I.K. Inha)

Opposition to Judaism was "normal" in Finland both, for example, in the contemptuous way of speaking about Jews in everyday language and popular culture as well as in the opinion that it was self-evident to consider Jews inferior to Christians and to refuse to take in Jewish refugees.

*Teuvo Laitila**

---

*Uskonto, isänmaa ja antisemitismi, Arator, Tampere, 2014, p. 11.

CHAPTER TWELVE

~

A Little Bird

Viipuri, 1902—When we left Mendel, he had just turned 14 and was working for Steinbock as an errand boy. Soon the leather purse his sisters have given him for his *bar mitzvah* begins to swell with the few coins he keeps after turning over most of his earnings to his mother, but the more he earns, the more he wants. When Feige hears from her friend Rosa Klimscheffskij that young Juda Eckert is looking for an apprentice cutter for his hat factory, Mendel, who had watched Steinbock's cutters with fascination, jumps at the chance to learn the trade.

You may wonder how Mendel, who spent so much of his time at school nursing knuckles swollen from frequent blows of the teacher's ruler, manages to earn a sufficiently positive recommendation from Steinbock (of course, all the Jewish merchants in Viipuri know each other and compare notes on customers, suppliers and employees) for the job. The answer is simple. As much as he hated school, he loves "the real world" of business. This is a passion that is somehow hard-wired into the soul of this serious— one might almost say joyless—young man. Unlike most teenagers, who live largely in the present, Mendel lives almost exclusively in the future, using the present only as a stepping-stone towards the next in a succession of goals he sets for himself. His overall objective is clear. He will not only be successful, he will become rich!

Once ensconced at Eckert's, Mendel quickly masters the skills required of a cutter's apprentice. He is careful and precise, able to follow instructions, and he has calmed down enough to be tolerated by the older cutters in the shop. Eckert makes men's hats in the style of the day: Ascot caps, fedoras, bowlers and homburgs. But the company's best customer is the

Russian Imperial Army, which regularly orders military headgear in large lots for new recruits. Russia is building up its army in anticipation of the war that everyone senses is coming, and that means more business for Viipuri's ready-to-wear clothing suppliers.

Mendel figures out a better way to block some of the hats and thinks too much of the felt is being wasted in the way the brims are cut. Unsurprisingly, no one in the workshop pays any attention to his suggestions. The cutters and blockers have no interest in changing the way they work, and they let Mendel know in no uncertain terms that he should mind his own business. Deeply offended, Mendel nevertheless continues to explore ways to make hats more efficiently and economically.

Mendel, it seems, has become as curious a teenager as he was an indifferent schoolboy. And although his main interests are in making hats and money, other questions increasingly bother him. One is: Why are Jews treated so badly? At first he thinks the problem is only a personal one, then a local one, and eventually a Finnish one. Gradually, however, he learns about the pogroms in Lithuania, Byelorussia, Poland and the Ukraine. He even hears in letters from Mirjam to their mother about discrimination suffered by Jews in the United States. Why? What have the Jews done to make the rest of the world hate them so? Most of the Jews he knows lead quiet lives. They don't drink, curse, fight, steal or otherwise disturb the peace—at least not nearly to the extent that Viipuri's other inhabitants seem to—yet they get no respect. He knows how much this bothered his father, and it begins to bother him in much the same way.

Curiosity

The other big question that elbows its way into Mendel's consciousness is sex. What to do, where and when, but above all, how? He knows what girls look like—after all, he has three older sisters, and they all lived in just two rooms—but since his voice changed, he has never been alone with a girl. As soon as he turns 17, he begins looking for the right girl to introduce him to the mysterious pleasures of male-female relationship.

The girl Mendel eventually finds is not a girl at all but a young woman and, although he doesn't know it at the time, the mother of two small children. In exchange for some of his hard-earned and carefully hoarded savings, she takes him up to a small room on *Ristikiventie* in the *Kolikkoinmäki* district. It is a warm Saturday night in early June, and Mendel has told Feige that he wants to watch the sunset from the top of *Patterinmäki* (Battery Hill). Entering the woman's home, Mendel is horrified to find the two infants sleeping on a straw mattress on the floor, but the woman says not to worry, they won't wake up. She strips off her clothes and lies down on the low and narrow bed. The room smells rank, the sheet is filthy, but the woman is young, perhaps barely twenty, and not at all unattractive.

Self-consciously, Mendel begins to disrobe. The evening sun is high enough in the summer sky to illuminate the room through the small four-pane window facing the hill. He has never felt particularly at ease with his own body, and the presence of the sleeping children doesn't help. Gathering his courage, he disrobes, approaches the bed, and lies down next to the naked woman. She seems to expect him to know what to do, and for what seems to Mendel like the longest time, they both just lie there, saying nothing and keeping still. Finally, she reaches across his body and begins arousing him with her hand. Her touch is abrasive and makes him contract reflexively at first, but before long he is erect and breathing heavily. She places his hand on her breast and then drops her own between her legs. Mendel feels her large nipple growing firm between his fingers. Silently, she rolls on top of him and slowly lowers herself onto him. He isn't inside her more than a minute or two, her hips moving forward and back insistently, before he explodes. And then it is over. She gives him a rag to wipe himself with, and without another word passing between them, he is dressed and out the door.

As he wanders slowly back across the hill to the sports field, he feels both elated and ashamed. The experience was degrading, no doubt about it. The woman was only doing what she had to do to feed her children. He doesn't know her name, and she probably wouldn't even remember him if they happened to run across each other in the street in a week or two. But he has made it through the ordeal without completely humiliating himself, and he thinks he might have some idea what to do should the occasion arise in the future. But one thing for sure, he will never pay for sex again. Maybe if he had an older brother to advise him . . ., but he doesn't so it is useless to think about it. As in everything else in life, Mendel has to make his way alone.

In addition to having shed his virginity, Mendel has finally made two real friends: Doni Kuschakoff and Viktor Jakobsson. Doni has six sisters and three brothers, all older than he. His father has turned a small tannery and a candy factory into a large wholesale and retail dry goods business in Viipuri. When Peisach was still alive and working for Doni's father, the two boys often played together. As the youngest child in his family, Doni usually got his own way, and as a teenager still gets to do more or less what he wants. He has his own small sailboat, and on summer evenings after work, the two young friends sometimes sail out to Viipuri's commercial harbor on the island of Uuras in Viipuri Bay with some bread and cheese and a bottle or two of beer from the local *Yhdysolut* brewery. Mendel, who had never been in a boat of any kind, learns from Doni how to maneuver the small craft in open water and before long can pilot it through narrow straits and dock it as well. Doni has no trouble getting girls to go sailing with him, but for some reason he doesn't invite Mendel to join him when girls are coming along. Mendel's only romantic outings on the bay take place in his fevered imagination.

Viktor Jakobsson is the youngest of four brothers: Moses Jakobson, Santeri (who, like Viktor, spells his name Jakobsson) and Jonas Jakobson. Their family can trace its lineage back to the first Jews to settle in Finland, the Weikaims, and Santeri and Jonas will make a mark for themselves as pioneers in the struggle for Jewish emancipation. Moses and Viktor, on the other hand, go into business. Viktor, in fact, will later become managing director of a large hat factory in Viipuri. He is serious, like Mendel, and shares Mendel's dream of growing rich. The two of them often take long walks together, dreaming of how to build successful businesses in the increasingly competitive Viipuri environment.

Mendel is ambitious. He sees other merchants doing well and wants a piece of the action. Almost from the moment he leaves Steinbock's to begin working at Eckert's, he dreams of having his own hat store and factory. Now his savings habit is put to good use as he begins the Sisyphean task of assembling enough capital to make his dream come true.

Visit to Helsinki

Young Mendel still attends *shul* every week and keeps kosher, but he is clean-shaven and only wears a *yarmulke* when in *shul* or at Jewish community events. While he doesn't look much like a typical Finn, he doesn't look much like the bearded Cantonists of his father's generation, either. Unlike Peisach, he speaks fluent Finnish in the Viipuri style, with colloquial traces of the Savonian and Karelian dialects in the way he talks.

A major event in young Mendel's life is his first trip to Helsinki at 18. He and his friend Viktor are selected by the congregation to accompany Viktor's older brothers to the Third Russian Zionist Congress, where Santeri Jacobsson will make contacts that will serve him well in his struggle to obtain civil rights for Finland's Jews. In addition to carrying the older men's bags and running errands for them during the meetings, Viktor and Mendel are to attend the general sessions as youth representatives.

Mendel, who has never been on a train before, brings Karelian rice pies, hard-boiled eggs and two bottles of water for the long ride. At first, he stares in fascination as the view from the window changes from Viipuri's seascape to the woodlands of Finland's interior. As it grows darker, he turns his attention to the conversation of the two older passengers. Jonas Jakobson, a lawyer, wants to talk about art, music and literature, but his brother Santeri redirects the conversation at every turn to matters of economic and political injustice.

Mendel doesn't know much about politics. During the previous summer, he had met an ardent socialist named Vladimir, who was producing a Russian-language newspaper called *Proletaaria*. It was printed by the same people who produced Viipuri's own workers' paper, *Työ*, and then apparently smuggled into Petrograd. Mendel attended a couple of discussion groups led by Vladimir but lost interest when he realized that Vladimir was only interested in one point of view: his own. Viktor's older brother Santeri, on the other hand, answers every question patiently and encourages Mendel to express his own opinions.

The Zionist Congress overwhelms Mendel. Everyone is dressed in fine clothes, and the meeting hall is decorated with colorful banners. Viktor points out Gruenbaum, Motzkin and Jabotinsky to Mendel. Some of the speeches are interesting, some incredibly boring, and Mendel struggles to understand the much-debated difference between Diplomatic Zionism and Synthetic Zionism.

The best part of the trip, by far, is visiting Helsinki. The Helsinki congregation's beautiful new synagogue on the ridge behind the *narinkka* has been opened for almost four months, and Mendel is amazed by its splendor. How can it be possible? Jews aren't even citizens and yet here is a magnificent building, owned by the descendants of Moses and housing beautiful Torah scrolls actually produced in Finland. Mendel struggles a bit to communicate with members of the Helsinki and Turku congregations, who speak Swedish instead of Finnish. Some of them have relatives in Viipuri and ask after them in Yiddish.

Mendel and Viktor spend part of each day wandering the streets and the *narinkka*, visiting the harbor, the Senate Square, and the Esplanade. They marvel at the electric-powered trams and even see an automobile, which they later identify as a Mercedes Simplex. They visit the Senate Building where Bobrikov was shot two years before and the cavernous Lutheran cathedral, which, despite its impressive exterior, seems an antiseptic, Spartan place to them in comparison with the magnificent synagogue with its delicate balconies, imposing chandelier, and ark flanked by the two snarling, crowned lions of Judah.

Feygele

When he turns 19, Mendel is finally promoted to hatmaker and given a proper salary by Juda Eckert. He gives Feige three-quarters of it each month, which not only covers the family's basic living expenses but allows Feige to visit her sister in St. Petersburg (she refuses to call it Petrograd) for the first time since Peisach passed away. Mendel saves almost all the rest, but he is already beginning to realize that it will take an eternity to earn enough for him to start a proper business. Not one to give up easily, he decides to work harder and spend even less.

And then everything changes, slowly at first but nevertheless with a certainty that surprises him. Walking home from work one evening, with his back sore from bending over the cutting table all day, he notices three girls walking towards him. Two of them he has never seen before, but one is vaguely familiar. She is slim, dark and quite animated until she notices him. Then she stops talking and looks down until he has passed the girls by. He thinks he hears her voice pick up again further down the street, but he cannot be sure. Who is she? And why were the girls carrying large sheaves of paper under their arms?

Later that night, it comes to him. She must be Zipora, the younger sister of Jankel from his *bar mitzvah* class. How old is she? 14? 15? Something about her intrigues Mendel, and he decides to walk home again the same way at the same time in the hope of crossing her path again. When he finally does see her again, though, it is not in the street but at the *Mon Repos* Park. It is a beautiful September Sunday, and Mendel is walking by himself as he often does on a Sunday afternoon when Doni is sailing with some girl and Viktor is otherwise engaged. As he approaches the statue of Väinämöinen playing the *kantele*,[1] he notices a young girl sitting on the grass with a sketch pad in her hand. Over her shoulder he can see that with only a few strokes of her pencil, she has already brought the old man to life.

As he walks closer to get a better look, he is astonished to realize that the artist is little Zipora. When she sees him, she quickly closes her portfolio and busies herself with her pencil case.

"Don't stop," says Mendel. "It's really good. You're Zipora, aren't you? I know your brother, Jankel."

"Yes, I know."

"Where did you learn to draw like that? It's like you made the statue breathe. I couldn't do that in a million years."

"I take art classes. Thank you for the compliment, that's very kind of you, but I know it really isn't any good."

"But it is!" blurts out Mendel. "I wish I had some talent like that."

"I'm sure you do. You are just being modest."

Only when Zipora says the last words does she look up. For a moment, all Mendel can see are her eyes. They catch the sunlight like amber, hold it for an instant, then darken as she looks away again.

"I was just getting ready to leave," says Zipora.

"Can I w-walk with you?" Mendel manages to stammer.

"I don't know. I guess so." She begins to gather her things.

Zipora reminds Mendel of a *feygele*, a little bird. Everything about her is delicate. She has a tiny waist, slim ankles and a pianist's fingers. Rising from the ground, she seems almost weightless.

They walk through the park, past the fortress, across the bridge, then along the shore past Salakkalahti up Pohjolankatu to Kalevankatu and the two-story stone house where Zipora's family lives. And neither one says a word, not a single word, until Zipora thanks Mendel for walking her home.

Turning toward his own home, Mendel is really angry with himself. What made him so shy with this young girl? There is nothing intimidating about her at all, not like some of the girls he knows. Yet the longer he tried to think of something to say, the harder it became to start a conversation. Had she felt the same way, too? Or was she just waiting for him to begin, wondering if he even had anything to say?

The next week, walking home, he sees Zipora and the same two girls coming his way again. This time she looks at him, smiles, and he thinks she may even be blushing a little. He greets them all in what he hopes is an appropriately jaunty manner and continues down the street. But as soon as the girls are out of sight, he does a little pirouette right there in the street and whistles the rest of the way home.

Their courtship proceeds slowly. Mendel is like a lovesick puppy, wanting to spend all his spare time with Zipora. She, however, is much more cautious and unwilling to commit herself. And, of course, she is young. Mendel is impatient but realizes that moving too quickly will only make things more difficult. His only consolation is that she obviously likes being with him. Their friends grow accustomed to seeing them together and begin to speak of them as a couple.

Zipora's father is a successful doctor who moved to Viipuri from Vilnius, Lithuania with his family when Jankel was an infant and before Zipora was born. Mendel worries that he would never approve of a poor hatmaker as a suitor for his daughter. Yet when Mendel calls at their home to take Zipora walking in the park or to a museum or concert, her father always seems polite and friendly. Her mother, too, is welcoming. Mendel makes it a point to get to know her brother better and is greatly relieved when Jankel says his parents are more interested in knowing that the man who marries Zipora is a good person and a good Jew than whether he is rich.

And so it is that when Mendel finally asks to speak to Zipora's father in 1912, he finds that the good doctor not only approves of him as a future son-in-law but is prepared to set Mendel up in business with a small hat factory and shop of his own. The wedding is a more lavish affair than anything Feige or Mendel have ever seen. Chana arrives from St. Petersburg with her husband and two sons, and Ida attends with her husband, but, sadly for Mendel, Mirjam is in New York, too far away to make the journey. A letter from her arrives in time for the wedding, however, wishing the couple well. She includes a prayer that the Lord will watch over Mendel and his Zipora as He has watched over her. She recounts how only weeks after she left her job the previous year to help Faivel in his clothing business, the factory where she had been working burned down, killing nearly 150 employees, including all those in her department who were at work that day.

Mendel and Zipora are married in the fine wooden synagogue on Kalevankatu that was built two years earlier. Gathered around the *chuppah*,[2] the guests watch as the ambitious hatmaker breaks the glass to commemorate the destruction of the Holy Temple in Jerusalem. And once this solemn moment has been properly observed, the dancing begins. Viktor is there, of course, dancing at Mendel's side, but Doni is absent. He has been banished from the congregation and the ranks of the faithful for having married his six-month pregnant Olga.

The late-afternoon sun shines approvingly on the revelers and Viipuri, but ferocious storm clouds are already forming to the east and south. Political oppression, world war, class struggle, civil war and violent revolution . . . all will rain down on the political landscape in the tumultuous years to come.

Notes

1. A Finnish zither
2. Canopy under which bridal couple stand during traditional wedding ceremony

Figure 13.1. Some second generation Finnish Jews began to prosper and enter the middle class (Finland's Jewish Archives)

In 1921 Moscow's Chief Rabbi, Jacob Maze, met with Trotsky, Leon Davidovitsch Bronstein. The rabbi spoke on behalf of Russia's Jews. Trotsky answered him, as he had previously done, that he was a revolutionary Bolshevik and didn't consider himself a Jew.

Rabbi Maze had his own view of the matter: "The Trotskys make revolutions, and the Bronsteins pay the piper."

*Dan Steinbock**

**Yö*, Werner Söderström, Porvoo, 1985, pp. 38–39.

CHAPTER THIRTEEN

~

Upheaval

Helsinki & St. Petersburg, 1898—Russia and Germany enjoyed friendly relations so long as Czar Alexander II's uncle, Kaiser Wilhelm I was alive. After he dies in 1888, however, the situation deteriorates to the point where both sides began arming in preparation for war. Russia's mounting fear of German aggression has serious consequences for Finland. Can the czar depend on Finnish loyalty in a situation where the empire feels itself threatened? Why, the Russians wonder, do the Finns keep protesting over such trivial issues as postal services, customs borders and the Finnish *markka*?

In 1898, Czar Nicholas II appoints Major General Nikolai Ivanovich Bobrikov Governor General of Finland with a mandate to quash the Autonomous Grand Duchy's separatist tendencies and speed up its reintegration into the empire. After his first visit to acquaint himself with the Autonomous Grand Duchy, Bobrikov reports: "Everything indicates that Finland has nothing in common with the empire, and it seems to me as if I were traveling somewhere abroad. And yet, this territory forms the closest and most strategically important borderland to the empire's capital city." The next year, the czar promulgates his infamous February Manifesto, and the Russification of Finland begins in earnest.

The Finnish writer and architect who designed the Helsinki synagogue, Jac Ahrenberg, claimed that Finland owed its unification to the railway system and Bobrikov: the railway united Finland geographically and commercially, and the harsh actions of the Governor General between 1898 and 1904 united it politically as Finns came together in opposition to Russian oppression. Russia insisted that the interests of the empire took precedence over any privileges previously accorded to its Finnish province; the Finns held fast to the position that they had constitutional rights stemming from eighteenth century Swedish legislation as well as from promises made by previous czars. It did not take long for this conflict to turn ugly.

Finland's separate postal system had been reabsorbed into the Russian Imperial Post in 1890. Now the Finns would lose their currency and their customs barrier with Russia, too. Another major step backward, in the eyes of the Finns, was taken when the neophyte Finnish military, created by the Military Service Law of 1878, was absorbed into the Russian Imperial Army and Navy. The Finnish Diet had specified from the outset that Finnish soldiers were not to be deployed outside Finland without its consent, but after 1899 it became clear that the czar would send them wherever he pleased. Bobrikov wanted to quintuple the number of Finnish soldiers and created a draft lottery, which was introduced in 1902.

The draft was met by widespread passive resistance. In Helsinki, for example, only 57 out of 870 draftees reported for service. April 18, 1902, a small crowd assembled in Helsinki's Senate Square in front of the police station to protest the conscription of Finnish men into the Russian army. Mounted Cossacks, swinging knotted ropes and sabers, were sent to disperse the gathering. Numerous bystanders were injured as the horses drove pedestrians into narrow side streets in what became known as the Cossack Riots. The Cossacks only withdrew when angry workers from nearby factories rushed to the aid of the victims.

Popular resistance eventually succeeded in having the draft rescinded, but in lieu of providing recruits, the Finns were required to make a large financial contribution to the Russian military. Meanwhile, Bobrikov was elevating Russian to the status of an official language in Finland and asserting the right of Russians to fill Finnish government positions. Freedoms of speech, assembly and association were suppressed. Bobrikov became the face of heavy-handed Russification in Finland, for which he paid the ultimate price. June 16, 1904 he was assassinated in the stairway of the Senate Building by a young Finnish patriot named Eugen Schauman.

Bobrikov's political assassination did not change the course of Russification, but the abortive Russian Revolution of 1905, the Russo-Japanese War and the General Strike of 1905 did. The assassination of Russian Secretary of State Vjacheslav Konstantinovich von Plehve by a bomb thrown by a Russian socialist, massive strikes at the end of 1904, and widespread discontent in almost all sectors of Russian society led to a chaotic situation in St. Petersburg. January 22, 1905, soldiers in front of the Winter Palace opened fire on a huge demonstration of workers petitioning for a minimum wage and an 8-hour workday, killing hundreds and provoking a general strike that spread from Russia to Poland and Finland.

Later the same year, Russia foolishly sent its Baltic Fleet halfway around the world to do battle with the Japanese. The subsequent destruction of the Russian navy in the Russo-Japanese War left St. Petersburg without adequate naval protection. Russia began to shore up fortifications along Finland's Baltic coast and added new defensive positions further inland to protect against possible German attack and invasion. Under these circumstances, political unrest in Finland posed a significant threat to Russian security. In an attempt to restore calm and appeal to Finnish loyalty, Czar Nicholas II did an about-turn. The conscription of Finnish men was halted, freedom of speech and the rights of assembly and association were restored, and Russification was put on the back burner for a while.

Security Vacuum

When Finland's own military units were disbanded during the first five years of the twentieth century, the responsibility for maintaining law and order fell entirely to Russia's civil and military police. By 1905, however, even these units were on strike, creating a security vacuum into which stepped citizen groups calling themselves National Guard units, or in the case of university students, the Civil Guard. The National Guard was made up at first of both workers and representatives of the middle class, but it wasn't long before these ad-hoc militias reorganized along class lines as the Red Guard and Civil (White) Guard.

Finnish workers had already begun organizing at the national level at the end of the nineteenth century. When Finland's Diet of Four Estates was abolished in 1906 and replaced with a single-chamber parliament as part of the relaxation of Russification, the socialists were the only ones with a national organization ready and able to wage an effective electoral campaign. The Social Democratic Party won 80 of 200 seats in the 1907 parliamentary election, with the Old Finns winning 59, the Young Finns 26, the Swedish Party 24, the Agrarian Union 9, and Christian Labor 2. The Social Democrats' victory indicated widespread discontent among the poorer segments of Finland's population, but constitutionalist parties still held an overall majority.

A second period of Russification began in 1908 with changes in the way issues concerning Finland were handled in St. Petersburg. Instead of the governor general taking matters directly to the czar, all initiatives were channeled through the Russian Council of Ministers. Two years later, when the Russian

Duma reaffirmed by a vote of 164–23 that Russian legislation had the power of law with respect to Finland, conservative Russian delegate Vladimir Purishkevich shouted out, "*Finis Finlandiae!*" ("That's the end of Finland!").

By 1914, when a comprehensive program of Russification was announced in the Finnish Press, World War I was the center of both Finland's and Russia's attention. Approximately 600 Finns enlisted in the Russian army, either hoping for a career in the military or some bread to put on the table. Some may also have thought that a thankful czar would restore Finnish autonomy. Most Finns, however, realized by this time that their only hope for an end to oppression was for Russia to lose the war.

Some were ready to take up arms and fight for Finland's liberation from Russian rule. With tens of thousands of Russian troops on Finnish soil, though, there was no way to organize armed resistance within the country. Sweden's neutrality ruled that country out as a training ground as well so in February 1915 the first Finnish volunteers made their way to Germany for training. As their numbers swelled to nearly 1,900, they were formed into the 27th Imperial Prussian Jaeger Battalion and sent to the Eastern Front. More than 1,200 of them would later fight in Finland's Civil War on the side of the White Army.

Although Finland was not directly involved in World War I, the presence of as many as 100,000 Russian troops on Finnish soil and the intensive efforts to build fortifications along the coast were constant reminders that the outcome of the struggle would strongly influence Finland's future. The proportion of Finns still believing that the best way forward was to demonstrate unquestionable loyalty to the czar was shrinking as political movements on both the internationalist left and the nationalist right began to display increasing opposition to the Russian monarchy. The presence of so many well-armed Russian troops, however, kept this opposition from morphing into insurrection.

Bread and Politics

The onset of war interrupted merchant shipping on the Baltic Sea. Finland's export traffic to Russia, which accounted for 39 percent of its export business, was largely by rail and therefore unaffected, and the delivery of an additional 8 percent to Sweden was still possible. Exports to the U.K. (22 percent), Germany (11 percent) and the rest of Europe (28 percent), however, were reduced to a fraction of their 1913 level.

Finnish suppliers of arms, machinery and clothing for the Russian war effort were able to maintain and even increase production at first. So were

Finnish paper mills, which had long been the principal suppliers of Russia's paper. On the other hand, lumber producers were unable to make deliveries to their largest markets, Great Britain and Germany, or find replacement customers in Russia or Sweden as those countries had ample forests of their own. The sharp drop in the demand for their lumber caused hardship for Finnish farmers, who depended upon logging for their livelihood.

Finland, which produced only 40 percent of its own food, needed export income to purchase grain and other essential foodstuffs. Supply channels from the West and South were cut off, and war-torn Russia was unable to meet Finland's needs. By 1917, grain and flour imports had been reduced from a prewar high of 363,000 tons to just 22,000 tons, and annual grain consumption per person plummeted from 220 kilograms to just 70. Factories that had been supplying the Russian Army saw their orders dry up, and work on the construction of fortifications, which had provided employment for 100,000 Finns, was halted.

The revolutionary uprising that began March 7, 1917 in the Russian capital changed the political calculus. World War I had already weakened Russia to the point of collapse, and, with the exception of a few units in Petrograd loyal to the czar, the army was no longer willing to support an ineffectual monarchy. Within a week, Nicholas II abdicated and Russia descended into chaos. A provisional Russian government was formed under Prince Georgy Lvov, who was soon replaced by Menshevik leader Alexander Kerensky. The provisional government restored Finland's rights and granted it increased autonomy, but these concessions satisfied neither independence-minded Finnish conservatives nor the socialists, who were themselves split between reformists and revolutionaries.

Finland's socialist movement had won a majority of 103 seats out of 200 in the 1916 parliamentary elections but refused to form a government. A coalition government finally emerged with Social Democrat Oskari Tokoi at its head in March 1917. Economic instability and social unrest, however, led to Parliament being dissolved in August. In the ensuing elections, the Social Democrats lost their majority. Angered by being maneuvered out of power, they were now ready to collaborate with the Bolshevik government that came to power in Russia following the November Revolution. Finland's Constitutionalist parties, on the other hand, which had been prepared to cooperate with the provisional government, refused to work with the Bolsheviks at all. The scene was set for a rupture in Finland's civil society.

Russia's inability in the midst of civil war to exercise control over its provinces presented Finland's Parliament with the opportunity to seize control. A government headed by strict constitutionalist P.E. Svinhufvud voted unanimously for the immediate establishment of the Republic of Finland. On December 6, 1917 Finland declared independence without having to fire a shot.

Russia's Bolshevik People's Commissariat recognized Finland's independence the last day of 1917, after which Sweden and Germany rapidly followed suit. Finland was now independent, but was it governable? Russia's Bolsheviks expected the Finns to join a Socialist Union under Soviet leadership; the West hoped Finland would become a capitalist buffer against the spread of communist ideology.

In Finland, the two sides begin to draw apart and prepare for armed conflict. On the revolutionary side were the landless 40 percent of the rural population and the growing number of industrial workers. On the opposing side were the 40 percent of the rural population who owned their own land as well as students, civil servants, white collar workers and business owners. The remaining 20 percent of the rural population, the tenant farmers, were evenly divided between the two sides. The newborn country appeared to be split right down the middle.

Independence

Finland had gained its independence, but what about its Jews? While the rest of the population in December 1917 is celebrating the country's emancipation from Russia, its 1,600 Jews are still in limbo, resident aliens even though most of them were born in Finland and have never lived anywhere else.

Events in 1908–1909 illustrate the absurd situation in which Finland's Jews found themselves. At the end of 1908, Finland's Senate could not find the time to process applications for residence permit extensions for 40 Jewish families before hurriedly adjourning for Christmas break. As a consequence, all 40 families—120 persons in all—were deported in early 1909. News of their banishment spread quickly around Europe, drawing attention to the fact that Finland's Jews still did not enjoy the protection of civil rights. The issue was raised in an embarrassing context when the Finnish government, desperate to gain access to European financial markets, tried to borrow money from England's J.C. Hambro and Son (later Hambros Bank), which was owned by a Jewish family.

When the Danish Jew, scholar and ladies' man Georg Morris Cohen Brandes finished a brief lecture series at Helsinki University in 1908, he remarked in his concluding address: "I have stayed here four days although I should have stayed no more than three. I have delivered lectures here although by law I am only allowed to sell used clothes. I may not get married here, but the authorities can hardly prevent me from falling in love."[1] On a subsequent tour of the United States, Brandes spoke disparagingly about the Finns' "medieval treatment" of their Jewish minority.

In an attempt to counteract all this negative publicity, Finland's Constitutional Committee proposed the elimination of all restrictions imposed on Jewish residents. Parliament approved the motion in November 1909 by a vote of 112–43, but Parliament still had no authority to implement changes of this kind without the approval of the czar. The matter was never brought before Czar Nicholas II, and so Finland's Jews remained without civil rights for nearly a decade until Finland could extract itself from the Russian Empire.

In many ways, however, the lives of Finland's Jews had improved dramatically in the early years of the twentieth century. It has already been mentioned that by 1912 the Helsinki, Turku and Viipuri congregations had all built new synagogues and were practicing their religion openly. The construction of impressive places of worship is just one indication that the children of the Cantonists were prospering in ways their fathers' generation could not have imagined.

Finnish society at the time of independence has progressed from being one of Europe's poorest in 1861 to one with average European living standards. From 1880 to 1900, the number of Finns working in industry more than doubled, from 134,875 to 288,343, and continued to grow rapidly in the early part of the twentieth century, reaching 459,751 in 1920. The passage in 1879 of a law rescinding restrictions on how a citizen could earn a living made it possible for increasing numbers of enterprising young Finns—excluding, of course, Jews and others without civil rights—to gain access to civil service jobs and professions on the one hand and opportunities for entrepreneurship on the other. With better employment often came such benefits of modern living as internal plumbing and electricity. While the increasingly conservative ownership class struggled to protect its vested interests, and the working class became increasingly radical in its demands for a more egalitarian social order, the middle class put its faith in progress, modernity and the promise of social mobility.

A More Prosperous Generation

Within the Jewish community in the early years of the twentieth century, some families caught the rising tide and made their way out of poverty. Only one generation removed from their Cantonist origins, Finland's Jews count no sawmill owners or shipping barons among their number, but they can point to the remarkable success of one of their own in the brave new world of securities trading. Four years after the modern Helsinki Stock Exchange is established in 1912, Moses Skurnik founds a stock trading company called Ab Börsförmedling. Skurnik, the uncle of future Medical Major and Iron Cross nominee Leo Skurnik, makes more than 22,000 share purchases in the next two years alone and becomes the leading trader on the rapidly growing exchange. In addition, he succeeds, along with Erik von Frenckell, a member of the aristocracy who would later become a member of the International Olympic Committee, in acquiring the Helsingin Osakepankki [Helsinki Joint-Stock Bank] in a hostile takeover. Without Frenckell serving as front man for the acquisition, Skurnik, as a Jew, would have been prevented by law from carrying out the operation.

Skurnik's meteoric rise will prove the exception within the Jewish community. The path to prosperity for most of its members will lie through more traditional forms of commerce. Having started out in the rag trade, they will stitch their way forward with needle and thread. Nevertheless, as schooling becomes available, others will find their way to university and into professions that were off-limits to Finnish Jews in the nineteenth century. In 1915, Viipuri's Isak Pergament and Jonas Jakobson are among the first Finnish Jews to obtain academic degrees: Pergament becomes a doctor and Jakobson a lawyer.

In Helsinki in 1915, there are more Jews who list their profession as musician than there are Jewish doctors, dentists and engineers combined, but the total number of professionals pales beside the number working in commerce. Many entrepreneurs have already left their market stalls behind and are either setting up clothing or textile shops in the center of town or working in those owned by their co-religionists as salesmen, tailors or office workers. Whereas before independence many of Finland's Jewish rag-trade entrepreneurs relied largely on orders from the Russian Imperial Army, the appetite of the rising middle class for consumption has created a lively market economy that continues to grow after 1917.

A survey of Viipuri's Jews in 1915 reveals that there are 270 of them living in 102 households of which 56 consist of families and 46 of single individuals. Occupations are listed as follows: 33 merchants, 14 shop assistants, 11 hatmakers, two peddlers, two seamstresses and two tailors. In addition there are two engineers, two sugar agents, two photographers, two manufacturers and 13 others with single listings ranging from tanner to rabbi. One of the hatmakers is Mendel.

What Goes Up . . .

In 1913, with the money provided by Zipora's father, Mendel rents a workshop at Pellervonkatu 5, three doors down from *Punaisenlähteentori*.

It comes with a tiny two-room flat on the second floor with a bathtub in the kitchen and electric lights. By the first time Feige visits, Mendel has procured a bed, table and four chairs, and Zipora has managed to furnish their little apartment with curtains, linen and cookware from her parents' home. Mendel swells with pride as his mother praises the housekeeping skills of his young bride.

Business is booming. Viipuri has become not just Finland's but all of Europe's leading port for the export of lumber. People have money to spend. So does the Imperial Army, which is gearing up for war. There are some 10,000 Russian soldiers in Viipuri, and a couple of thousand pioneers are working on fortifications, and all of them need hats!

Mendel still lacks the special machines required for his factory. As he tries to figure out where and how to acquire them, Judah Eckert is caught selling hats with counterfeit labels, falsely claiming that they were made in England. The English have their own Consular Section in Viipuri, and a Deputy Consul, amazed at such labels as "English style London" and "The Melrose, made from pure Scotch wool and knitted in a Scotch faktory," has asked the police to investigate. When their search turns up stacks of such labels in Eckert's office, the matter is referred to court. Eckert is forced to close while the case is being adjudicated, and to pay his bills, he needs to sell off some of his equipment and stock. Mendel seizes the opportunity. The price is right, and one of Eckert's young cutters even agrees to work for Mendel, at least until the case is settled.

Now Mendel can try out all the ideas he has dreamed up while working for Steinbock and Eckert. To his delight, he finds that he really can make quality hats cheaper than his competitors, but because demand is growing and Eckert is temporarily out of the picture, he can sell everything he makes without discounting the price. In the first year, he makes enough to pay for the equipment and supplies he bought from Eckert as well as hire a skilled blocker. Mendel, himself, now spends much of his time in the shop or negotiating with his main customer, the Imperial Army.

Ten months after their wedding, Zipora prepares a dinner of Mendel's favorite meal, *tefteli* with *kasha kugel*. It isn't *shabbos*, and Mendel was only expecting some broth with a dumpling or two in it. Zipora tries to protest that it is nothing special, but her subterfuge collapses almost as soon as they sit down. Mendel is going to be a father!

At first Mendel is struck dumb with wonder by the news. A father! In the same way a dying man's whole life is said to flash before his eyes in a few seconds, Mendel sees in fast-forward all the things he will do with his child, their child, all the things his father never had the time or inclination to do with him. He picks Zipora up from her chair and dances around the room with her, ignoring her protests as he whirls her around. Suddenly he stops, embarrassed, realizing that his little wife is actually pregnant, fearful that spinning around like that may not be the best thing for her or the baby.

For the next six months, Mendel won't let Zipora do anything. He gets a young girl to clean and cook three days a week and do the shopping. Zipora is not strong, and Mendel worries about her health. Nevertheless, the pregnancy progresses normally, and Zipora complains of nothing more serious than morning sickness. Feige comes to help out several times a week. She has five grandchildren by now, but all of them are far away in Petrograd or New York. She has never even seen the American ones except in a photograph Mirjam sent in a small Chanukah parcel the previous year. Now she will have a grandchild right here in Viipuri, one she can care for, one who will bring joy to her declining years.

. . . Must Come Down

It was not to be. The baby, a girl, is stillborn at the end of the seventh month. Zipora's father reassures her that she will yet have healthy babies and this kind of thing happens all the time. Nevertheless, Zipora collapses into depression. She stays in bed for nearly two weeks, and even after she finally gets up, she is listless and refuses to go out. She wears the same drab *shmata*[2] day after day and pays little attention to her hair. Sometimes, she spends hours staring out the tiny back window onto the barren yard or the larger front window facing the street, watching people hurrying foolishly back and forth as if time and place still mattered. The young servant girl is now coming six days a week as Zipora shows no more interest in housework than in her appearance.

Mendel has no idea what to do and moves quietly around their home like a tenant who is afraid of disturbing his landlady. He puts in long days in the shop and factory, seeking refuge from his own sorrow in hard work. Nothing in his life has prepared him for the profound melancholy that engulfs him. Zipora would have known how to comfort him under other circumstances, but he cannot expect any help from her now. He has to be the strong one, and the effort it takes is almost more than he can muster.

And then one day, returning upstairs in the early afternoon to retrieve one of the ledgers with orders from the previous year, he finds Zipora sitting by the window with her drawing pad on her lap and a pencil in her hand. The giant hand squeezing his heart relaxes its grasp just a bit as he realizes that his wife is beginning to heal. He puts his own hand gently on her shoulder and watches in silence as she sketches the clouds silently grazing the rooftops across the street. Then remembering why he returned to the apartment in the first place, he picks up the ledger, turns and hurriedly descends the steps to the shop where his impatient customer is waiting.

Business during the war years is better than ever. Mendel's hat factory is now well-known, and customers looking for the best quality seek out his store. One of his hats earns a bronze medal at the 1914 Baltic Exhibition in Malmö, and he thinks about entering one of his fedoras in the competition at the San Francisco World's Fair in 1915 but is so busy that he never gets around to it. Encouraged by his success and by demand that is outgrowing his limited production capacity, Mendel borrows money to expand his business. He rents a floor in the neighboring building for a proper factory and turns the former workshop into a hat store. He also hires a second blocker, a second cutter and a salesgirl. His expenses are much higher now, but he calculates that he will be able to turn a profit again within a year.

At the end of 1916, Zipora has another miscarriage. This time it comes much earlier in her pregnancy, and both she and Mendel are better prepared. Nevertheless, the loss is a heavy one. Mendel asks himself why God would take the life of an unborn child. What use is it to attend *shul* regularly and observe all the commandments? Mendel is no Job. If he is keeping his part of the bargain with God, he and his Zipora should not be denied the family they so desperately want.

And then comes 1917 and the Russian Revolutions. First, Czar Nicholas II abdicates in February, then the Provisional Government that replaces him falls to the Bolsheviks. Professor Markku Kuisma, in *Venäjä ja Suomen talous 1700–2015 (Russia and Finland's Economy 1700–2015)*, emphasizes the enormous economic impact the fall of the Imperial order has on Finland:

> The February Revolution in Russia didn't put an end to war, mayhem or hunger. Nor did it stop the Russian Empire's disintegration process and ever-deepening chaos. What it did put an end to was the income-producing military fortification work in Finland and so made tens of thousands of workers unemployed.[3]

Taking advantage of the chaos in Russia, Finland declares independence. Bloody civil wars erupt in both Finland and Russia, the border between the two countries is sealed, and Finland's trade with Russia plunges like a train hurtling off a trestle bridge into a chasm. Trade with the West is also next to impossible because of continuing WWI hostilities on the Baltic Sea. As a consequence, Finland is no longer able to import the food it needs to meet the requirements of its population.

Most significantly for Mendel, the Imperial Army stops paying its bills. Mendel has meticulous records of what he is owed but absolutely no way to enforce collection. Mendel's father-in-law, who has invested heavily in business ventures of his wife's Russian relatives, loses everything. So does Mendel, who cannot meet his monthly payments to the bank. On the brink of financial success, Mendel suddenly finds himself staring into a financial abyss.

Notes

1. Jacobsson, *op. cit.*, p. 342
2. Rag, old garment (Yiddish)
3. Kuisma, Markku, *Venäjä ja Suomen talous*, Siltala, Helsinki, 2013, p. 170.

Figure 14.1. Red terror in Viipuri struck at the provincial prison on February 27, 1918, just before the Whites took over the city and fighting ended (Finland's Military Museum)

Civil wars are more brutal than wars between states because it is possible to respect the soldiers of enemy nations—they are only doing their duty—but the enemy in a civil war is either a revolutionary and a traitor or an exploiter and an oppressor. They are shown no mercy.

Max Jakobson*

*Väkivallan vuodet, Otava, Helsinki, 2003, pp. 51–52.

CHAPTER FOURTEEN

~

Civil War

Viipuri, 1917—Mendel has been too busy grieving over the loss of his business to pay much attention to politics. Tuesday, September 11, 1917, as he heads toward the main market, however, Viipuri's social fabric is unraveling in a way he cannot ignore. A crowd has gathered along the shore road near the bridge leading to the old fortress. Curious to know what is causing the commotion, he pushes his way through the throng until he reaches a vantage point from which he can see the bridge clearly. Some twenty or so older Russian soldiers, officers apparently, are being herded onto the bridge at gunpoint by younger men. Then, to Mendel's amazement, the young soldiers begin pushing and kicking the older ones off the bridge and into the water, finishing off their grisly business by shooting those who manage to stay afloat. The executioners will later explain that they were giving the officers, who were known for their sadistic treatment of enlisted men, swimming lessons!

It takes a long time for the city to settle down after this mutinous act. For a while, no one seems to be in charge of the 12,000-man Viipuri garrison. Groups of idle Russian soldiers congregate in the streets and cafes, and it is impossible not to notice that some of them have been drinking. The good citizens of Viipuri keep their wives and daughters at home until order is restored in the garrison and city life more or less resumes its everyday rhythms.

Russian newspapers, which arrive by train each morning from Petrograd, are eagerly scanned throughout the autumn for the latest political developments. The paper of November 8th brings shocking news: the previous day, Bolshevik forces succeeded in overthrowing Kerensky's provisional government. According to the report, the revolutionaries were led by a certain Vladimir Ilyich Ulyanov, who goes by the *nom de guerre* Lenin. There is a picture of this Lenin addressing a crowd of workers in the Russian capital, and Mendel is astonished to recognize him as the same Vladimir who led the discussion group he attended two years earlier. How strange to think that the high-strung propagandist writing his underground paper in Mendel's city is now the head of the government of almighty Russia!

It does not take long for Lenin's revolution to spin off both opportunity and threat for Finland. Less than 30 days after the Bolsheviks seize power in Russia, Finland takes the opportunity to declare independence. With no army of its own and tens of thousands of well-armed Russian troops garrisoned on Finnish soil, Finland cannot extract itself from the Russian Empire militarily. Russia, however, has been fighting World War One since 1914 and its own civil war since March. Its soldiers and sailors in Finland are tired, dispirited and worried about what is happening at home and show little desire to intervene in Finland's affairs.

Joseph Stalin, in his capacity as People's Commissar for Nationalities, officially recognizes the right of the Finns, like other national minorities in the former Russian Empire, to self-determination. He adds that Finland should, of course, agree to a voluntary union with Bolshevik Russia. When that does not happen, he will complain in January 1918 that the Council of People's Commissars had only been forced to grant Finland independence because the Autonomous Grand Duchy's proletariat "had failed to take power due to vacillation and inexplicable timidity,"

Finland Takes Up Arms

German control of the Baltic Sea continues to block Finnish trade with the West, and Russia's civil war closes the eastern border to trade with the East. The collapse of the Russian monarchy puts an end to fortification construction in Finland and employment for those working for or supplying the Imperial Army, throwing more than 70,000 Finns out of work. The combination of hunger, inflation, and large numbers of unemployed young men creates a highly inflammatory situation. Red and White militias, now called the Red Guard and Civil Guard, respectively, mobilize once again. By January 1918 both sides boast forces of some 35–40,000 men.

January 25, 1918, the seven-week-old Finnish government officially transforms the Civil Guard into the nation's army. The following day Lieutenant General C.G.E. Mannerheim is named its Commander in Chief. Born into Finland's Swedish-speaking nobility, he had entered the Nicholas Cavalry School in St. Petersburg at the age of 20 and served the ensuing 30 years in the Russian Imperial Army, rising to the rank of Lieutenant General and Commander of the Sixth Cavalry Corps during World War I.

In his first move as Commander in Chief of Finland's army, Mannerheim orders the 40,000 or so Russian soldiers still in Finland to lay down their arms and return to Russia. Most of them eventually do so, but 7–10,000 Russian soldiers, some of whom are still garrisoned in Finland and others who cross into the country from Petrograd, end up fighting on the side of the Red Guard. January 27, Finland's left issues orders for the imprisonment of the Senate, thereby demonstrating that its indecisiveness in December owed more to lack of preparation and the speed with which events overtook them than to "vacillation and inexplicable timidity," A revolutionary government is formed, and the first military operations of what will become a full-fledged civil war begin.

Finnish society, united for years in opposition to czarist repression, now splits along class lines. On the Red side, unresolved grievances and shortages of food and work propel the radicalization of industrial workers and landless peasants. The Whites—primarily independent farmers, students, and members of the middle class who have seen their prospects diminished by the economic downturn—fear that Bolshevik agitation and radicalization of the poor will threaten not only their economic interests but Finland's recently proclaimed independence.

Figure 14.2.   Red and White Finland, January 1918 (Marja Leskelä)

Geographically, although there are pockets of opposition in each territory, the country is roughly divided between White Finland in the largely agricultural North and Center and Red Finland in the more industrialized South. The Reds hold Tampere and Viipuri at the outset of hostilities and take control of Helsinki on January 27, causing the government to evacuate hastily to Vaasa in the White stronghold of Ostrobothnia. At the same time, a Finnish People's Delegation emerges in Helsinki to lead the revolution. From the outset, the Reds face serious military challenges as their ragtag volunteer force has very few trained officers, and too many of the Russian officers who join them can only communicate in a language that most of the Finnish troops they command cannot understand.

Fighting is concentrated in and around the three Red urban strongholds: Tampere, Helsinki and Viipuri. Because the Petrograd-to-Viipuri railway functions as the Red Guard's lifeline for weapons and other supplies, the area east of Viipuri becomes an important battleground. The first firefight takes place there on January 27 when White forces ambush a Red Guard ammunition train arriving from Russia.

The ensuing war will last three and a half months and leave approximately 37,000 dead. Healing the rifts in civil society caused by this conflict will take decades, herculean efforts on the part of courageous leaders, and three more costly wars.

Whites Take the Initiative

The Whites concentrate at first on training their own recruits and disarming Russian Army units in the territory they control. February 11, 403 Finnish commissioned and 727 non-commissioned officers who have been serving in Germany's 27th Imperial Prussian Jaeger Battalion return to Finland, providing the White Army with some badly needed leadership.

Mannerheim was horrified by the Bolshevik revolution and feels that Russia can only be returned to stability through the re-imposition of its monarchy. As a patriotic Finn, he also believes that Finland might be able to win the gratitude of Russia, including permanent recognition for its independence and a secure eastern border, by taking the former St. Petersburg militarily and restoring it to legitimate imperial rule. Mannerheim personally experienced the post-revolutionary chaos in Russia and believes such a plan is realistic even though the Finnish army, consisting of the Jaegers and poorly armed volunteers with only minimal training, is not even in control of its own country at that point.

February 1918, Commander-in-Chief Mannerheim proclaims an oath that will haunt his country long after the Civil War ends. "I will not sheathe my sword until all fortifications are in our hands, law and order prevails in the country, and the last of Lenin's fighters and hooligans are driven out not only of Finland *but from Ladoga and White Karelia as well*" [italics added]. The last part of this boast creates expectations in the Jaegers and other Finnish ultranationalists that Mannerheim will lead them in a campaign to create a Greater Finland that will include territory which, while home to people who may be culturally and linguistically related to the Finns, has never been part of Finland. Writer Veijo Meri has noted that in one respect the vision of Greater Finland's advocates was the same as that of the Bolsheviks: both desired the unification of Finland and Karelia. Where they differed was that the former envisioned Greater Finland as a free and independent republic while the latter expected it to be a subservient part of what would become the Soviet Union.

Before Mannerheim can cleanse Petrograd of its Bolshevik "fighters and hooligans," he first has to deal with the revolutionary forces at home. He had previously considered the Finnish Jaegers to be traitors—they left the Autonomous Grand Duchy of Finland illegally to train in Germany and fight against the Russian Army in WWI while Finland was still part of Russia—but, with the exception of a handful of fellow Finnish officers from the Russian Army and a few volunteers from Sweden, they are the only trained and battle-hardened officers he has. With Jaeger officers leading the way, the Whites move south from Vaasa at the end of February until they reach Tampere in mid-March. There begin three weeks of the most intense fighting of the war, culminating in a rout of the Reds in which 1,800 are killed and 10–12,000 captured. The defeat starts a retreat eastward by the Reds and their supporters that will end in tens of thousands being captured and thousands more fleeing across the Russian border.

In the meantime, the German and Bolshevik Russian governments sign the Treaty of Brest-Litovsk, ending WWI hostilities between them. Russia cedes control of what are today the Baltic States, Belarus and Ukraine to Germany. In an attempt to weaken its traditional enemy and stop the spread of communism, Germany steps up its support for Finland and Poland, both of which are in the process of breaking away from Russian control. Berlin lets the Finnish government know that a formal request for assistance will result in German troops being sent to help put down the Red insurrection. Mannerheim distrusts the Germans and wants to do the job without foreign help. Without his knowledge, however, a letter from the Senate asking for Germany's assistance has already been delivered to the German High Command.

A German expeditionary force of 9,500 men under General Rüdiger von der Goltz lands April 3, 1918 at Hanko on Finland's southern coast and begins marching towards Helsinki. Fifty German warships and transport vessels wait outside the Hanko harbor. The Finnish People's Delegation decamps from Helsinki to Viipuri as soon as the Germans set foot on Finnish soil. One week later, German troops arrive at Helsinki's outer line of defense. After three days of fighting, the Germans parade through the capital. Now all attention is focused on Mendel's city as Mannerheim's White Army rushes eastward to liberate the last Finnish territory controlled by the Reds before the Germans can get there.

Viipuri under Siege

Even before war breaks out, Mendel notices the growing number of armed men in Viipuri's streets with red cockades pinned to their hats. They gather daily in front of the workers' hall on Punaisenlähteenkatu near the *narinkka* and can be seen entering and leaving the railway station at all hours of the day and night. January 19, 1918, Mendel and Zipora are awakened by gunshots several blocks away from their home. The next morning, Mendel learns that a firefight had broken out when members of the Red Guard raided Pietinen's Carpentry Shop on Karjalankatu. Viipuri's Civil Guard had been using Pietinen's as an ammunition factory and weapons depot. Two men from each side are killed in the shootout.

Mendel, already despondent over his own personal problems, becomes increasingly pessimistic about Finland's situation and the fate of its Jews. Whenever there is unrest, the Jews somehow get blamed. He reverts to his father's old defensive tactics, walking in the shadows with his head down, looking no one in the eye. Throughout February he waits for something terrible to happen. Unable to find work after the loss of his business, he is reduced to accepting charitable assistance from the Jewish congregation to feed his family, which once again appears to be growing. At the worst possible time, Zipora is again with child. The specter of another miscarriage hangs over the destitute hatmaker, who finds it impossible to have any confidence at all in the future.

Mendel hears reports of heavy fighting to the east of the city in the Karelian Isthmus. He keeps the news from Zipora, but she hears it anyway. Surprisingly, she seems to bear up under it better than her husband does. The suffering she endured has made the sheltered little bird a stronger woman. Her depression is only a memory now, and she tries to reassure herself and her husband that this time she will bring a healthy baby into the world.

Fighting is soon reported along battle lines from Ahvola to the north of the city as far as Valkjärvi in the southeast, but the only fighting in Viipuri itself is among drunken Red Guard soldiers outside the Arista Restaurant. Some of the city's prominent industrialists and members of the Civil Guard have gone underground, but otherwise life goes on more or less as before. As time passes, however, banks close one after another, business activity grinds to a halt, and food becomes increasingly scarce. Rumors circulate about White victories in the West, but no one knows whether such reports are reliable or just wishful thinking on the part of those who are spreading them.

Something else Mendel and Zipora do not know is that her father has secretly been visiting the battlefields near Ahvola to treat White soldiers in need of medical attention. To do so, he has had to cross the battle lines repeatedly. One night in late February, on his way back to Viipuri with two young members of the Civil Guard, they are surprised by a Red patrol and executed on the spot. Zipora's mother learns of her husband's death when an officer of the Civil Guard calls at the house to inform her that the body has been recovered for burial. Although the family knows that terrible things have been happening all around them, the unexpected news is a shock to them all. Once again, Mendel worries about his wife's reaction, and once again she surprises him. Zipora feels the loss deeply, but she channels her grief into caring for her distraught mother, who takes sick soon after hearing the news.

The doctor's death increases the pressure on Mendel to find a job. Zipora has always managed somehow to put food on the table. Without telling Mendel, she has pawned her jewelry with a Russian pawnbroker. Now she has nothing left that anyone would want to buy.

The flight eastward of Red Guard troops and their families intensifies in mid-April after the fall of Helsinki. Viipuri remains under Red control, but the White army is rapidly approaching. April 24, Viipuri's Civil Guard members receive the command to come out of hiding. They free prisoners held in the Swedish School and take the *Patterinmäki* stronghold by surprise. There are too few of them to hold it, however, and before long they are surrounded and forced to surrender.

Mendel and Zipora, like everyone else, hear the sounds of gunfire as the Reds retake *Patterinmäki* Hill, but the sound of White artillery fire can also be heard in the distance. That same evening, the first White forces make their way into the city, and the following day the members of the Finnish People's Delegation, their tails tucked cravenly between their legs, debark for Petrograd on the last ships to make it out of the harbor, leaving behind those they have led into defeat.

Revenge

War is never pretty, especially when the fires of conflict are stoked by deep-seated class resentment and, in Finland's case, the long-smoldering ethnic animosity between Swedish and Finnish speakers. According to historian Markku Kuisma:

The most brutal acts [on the White side] were probably committed by the upper-class Swedish-speaking Whites, who hated and disparaged the Finnish-speaking populace as an inferior race. The same spirit permeated the Jaegers, who committed atrocities in Viipuri, where ethno-racist hatred was aimed primarily at Russians (and Jews or anyone who didn't represent pure 'White' Finnish ethnicity) and by extension at 'impure' Finnish Reds. The latter were no longer humans but belonged to the same category as Russians and Jews, filthy and bestial beings and therefore to be purged.

Red terror clearly included, in addition to what inevitably happens in warfare, outbursts of class hatred, long pent-up bitterness and revenge. And when guns were put in the hands of young men, giving them unthinkable power for once to show the upper class who was who, and strong drink, lack of discipline and breakdowns in communication were added to the picture, we see that fighting each other for the most part were civilians, not professional armies—as is always the case in civil war.[1]

On April 28, 1918, inebriated Reds, sensing that the end is near, attack the provincial jail. Singling out 30 people—guards and any of the prisoners they take to be on the side of the Whites—they execute them in cold blood. The next day the White army takes control of the city. White soldiers, most of whom are from far away in the North or West of Finland, begin "cleansing" the city of Russian soldiers and anyone with connections to the Red Guard. In addition, they round up numerous Russians and men of Russian extraction, some 5,000 of whom live in Viipuri. Most are Finnish citizens, but some—including, of course, the city's Jews—are not. The White soldiers scour the city for "suspects," picking them up from the street, rousting them out of hiding places, and pulling them unceremoniously out of workshops and homes. One of those seized in this fashion is Mendel, who is returning from a meeting with the congregation's representative responsible for assistance to indigent members of the Jewish community.

These "Russkies" are herded onto the Parade Ground, where they are made to line up. Sobbing women and children who have followed the men are soon forced by the soldiers to leave the area. Fortunately, Zipora doesn't seem to be in the crowd. Mendel is terrified but tries not to show it. He reasons that he has done nothing that could be held against him, having stayed as far from the conflict as possible. Now his survival will depend on how suspicious he looks to the White soldiers scanning the ranks of "suspects,"

Soldiers are walking along the rows, picking out individuals they decide might be Red Guard, Russian soldiers in civilian clothing, or otherwise sympathetic to the Red cause. One of the Finnish soldiers, a tall man with bad skin and an ugly scar running from under his right eye to his jaw, stops in front of Mendel and stares hard at him from an arm's length away, obviously considering what to do. It takes a nearly superhuman effort for Mendel to maintain his composure. Showing either too much fear or too little could convince the soldier that he has something to hide. The man stands there for an unbearably long time, his scarred cheek twitching while he tries to make up his mind. For whatever reason, he eventually turns his gaze away and moves on down the row. After he leaves, Mendel is seized by uncontrollable trembling and a shortage of breath, realizing that for the moment at least, the Angel of Death has passed him by.

More than 200 men, some of whom should more accurately be described as boys, are pulled roughly out of the ranks and marched off to the Hamina Road. A few hundred meters beyond the Fortress Bridge, they are led to the left over a steep embankment. With no further ado, they are lined up and gunned down, each and every one of them. Then their bodies are stripped of anything of value. Among the victims are several people Mendel knows. Two of them are Jews, Mooses Reiman and Markus Wainer. They had nothing to do with the Red Guard or leftist politics. They were ordinary shopkeepers, heads of families. Killed for what?

Mendel walks home in shock, still shaken by the knowledge that he has come within a hair's breadth of execution. What kind of a place is this for his child to be born into? That night he tells Zipora about what happened, but he tells it as if he were only a spectator. He knows that even this edited version will be upsetting enough for his pregnant wife.

The next afternoon, word quickly circulates throughout the Jewish community. "Tonight they are coming for us!" A Lutheran minister, at the risk of his own life, has informed the head of the congregation that some of the Jaeger officers are planning to rid Viipuri of its Jews. Mendel hurries to the office of one of his former customers, Mikael Sjögren, who has a large property with a barn and a root cellar big enough to hide several people. Sjögren agrees to lock Zipora, Feige and Mendel in the cellar for the night. It is damp and cold in there, but Mendel brings blankets. Well before dark, Sjögren turns the key in the large padlock outside the door, promising to let them out once the coast is clear.

The Steering Committee of the Jewish congregation appeals for help to Kaarle Nestori Rantakari, Viipuri's Acting Police Commissioner. As a younger man, Rantakari had encouraged students to throw eggs at a Jewish professor and demanded the deportation of all Jews from Finland. That was in Helsinki, however, and Viipuri's Jewish delegation doesn't know about it. In any case, Rantakari has apparently outgrown his youthful antisemitic prejudice. He listens patiently to their entreaty. Although as police commissioner he has no authority over army matters, Rantakari decides to intervene in the name of maintaining civic order.

That evening, in a surprise move, the police lock down the entire Viipuri garrison. The furious Jaegers find themselves unable to leave their garrison while fearful Mendel, Zipora and Feige crouch in Sjögren's root cellar. The next morning, Sjögren brings them some bread and cheese and ensures them it is safe to return home. Although Viipuri's Jewish community is nervously on guard for several more nights, nothing happens. Finland's only pogrom has been prevented by the prompt intervention of a reformed antisemite.

Ugly Aftermath

Throughout Finland, many who fought in the Red Army or supported those who did are not so lucky. Those suspected of having been in leadership positions are summarily executed as soon as they are caught or try to surrender. Nearly 80,000 ordinary Red Guard soldiers, family members and supporters avoid execution but end up in fetid prison camps. Finland is still suffering from a shortage of food, and 16 percent of the prisoners will die of hunger or disease. In certain notorious camps, the mortality rate will be much higher.

Trials of dubious impartiality are arranged, resulting in the conviction of 70,000 of those being held. Of those convicted, 555 are sentenced to death, but as time passes and emotions begin to cool down, only 113 are actually executed. A few prisoners are condemned to long periods of incarceration, but most are given conditional sentences or eventually granted clemency and released.

Those who flee to Russia seem to fare better, but Professor Kimmo Rentola estimates that 20,000 of them eventually fall victim to Stalin's terror. In other words, almost four times as many Finnish Reds will be killed by Soviet authorities as died in battle during the Civil War.

The war and the treatment of prisoners, which ranges from inadequate to intentionally cruel and retributive, will spread a dark stain across Finnish society in the decades following 1918. And as if fratricidal warfare, hunger and economic collapse were not enough, the Spanish Flu sweeps over the country in waves in 1918, 1919 and 1920, inflicting widespread devastation on the Finnish population. Approximately 210,000 people (8 percent of the population) contract the disease, and 20,000 perish. One of those who succumbs is Mendel's sister, Ida.

When all these catastrophes and their psychological after-effects are added together, it can truly be said that 1918 deserves to be called an *annus horribilis*.

Emancipation

And yet, in another of those curious twists of fate that seem to bind Finland and its Jewish population together in paradoxical ways, 1918 is the year in which Finland finally grants its Jews full civil rights. Technically, the law allowing Jews to apply for citizenship is passed by a Parliamentary vote of 163–6 in early December 1917, but the outbreak of civil war prevents it from being implemented. It will not be until September 10, 1918 that 38-year-old Moses Kotschack, founder of Suomen Sotilaspukimo Oy (Finnish Military Clothiers, Ltd), becomes the first Jew to be granted Finnish citizenship with all the rights and responsibilities that go with it.

Those who see the glass as half empty complain that Finland is the last European country to grant citizenship to its Jews. Those who see it as half full say that the emancipation of the Jews is among the very first initiatives to attain the force of law once Finland declares independence and can enact its own legislation.

Mendel hears from his friend Viktor Jakobsson about the law even before it is ratified. Viktor explains that it does not automatically grant Finnish citizenship to Jews, only gives them the right to apply for it like any other foreigners. But Mendel is not a foreigner. He was born in Finland and has never lived anywhere else. Why can't they do the right thing and make all of those who were born here citizens right away? What if he applies and is turned down? He knows he should be happy, but he can't help worrying that it may all end in disappointment once again.

In any case, no one has a chance to apply for citizenship before war breaks out and Finland's *annus horribilis* lurches from one disaster to another. Nevertheless, Mendel will always remember 1918 as one of the most wonderful years of his life. Not because of Jewish emancipation; nor because he, Zipora and Feige survive the war; but because in the early hours of the morning of June 29, Zipora gives birth to a healthy baby girl. The war is over, citizenship is a possibility, and the cloud of childlessness hanging over Zipora and Mendel has lifted.

Zipora is not sure what name to give her baby, but Mendel has already decided. They will call her Mirjam.

Note

1. Kuisma, Markku, *email correspondence with the author, April 28, 2016.*

Figure 15.1. German Baltic Sea Division troops during the Battle of Helsinki (Public domain)

. . . a strong state would spare the country a recurrence of the disaster that had recently befallen it. A hereditary monarchy free of the crises that so often plague a republic would provide the necessary stability. Those that took part in the rebellion had to be denied access to power. The necessity of maintaining a consistent foreign policy also recommended a monarchy; the monarch would assure continuity despite a shifting balance of power in Parliament. Germany offered the only hope of withstanding a strong Russia. Since Finland was in an exposed position on Russia's doorstep, German support was essential. The selection of a German prince as Finland's monarch was the solution.

*L. A. Puntila**

---

*The Political History of Finland 1809–1966, Otava, Keuruu, 1975, p. 112.

142

~

CHAPTER FIFTEEN

Finland Lurches Right

1918—Although Finland's Civil War ended in May 1918, when fighting stopped and the last Russian soldiers left the country, the nation's future was still anything but secure. Researcher Arto Jokinen has written that Finland began preparing for war with the Soviet Union in 1918: in other words, as soon as the Civil War ended. The notion that the two wars were causally connected would be given its clearest formulation by Marshal Mannerheim in his first official Order of the Day on November 30, 1939 at the start of the Winter War. "This war is nothing other than the continuation and epilogue of our War for Independence."

Finland's Radical right (and some on the not-so-radical right as well) felt that the victory of the White Army was undermined by the policies of the post-war government. Ultranationalists demanded a complete purge of leftist elements from Finnish political life. They also still expected General Mannerheim to lead them in the liberation of Eastern Karelia from Bolshevism as he had sworn in his *February 23, 1918 Order of the Day*. When those expectations were disappointed, many of them turned to extra-parliamentary attempts to "finish the job,"

The nationalists' argument was that the historic, cultural and linguistic affinity of Finns with the peoples of Karelia and Ingria—they were of the same "tribe"—justified the annexation of the Karelia and Ingria provinces. This would be the position taken by the Academic Karelia Society (AKS), founded in 1922, which became a potent force in Finnish politics. The vast majority of Finnish-speaking university students enrolled as members, taking the following pledge: "I devote myself to the fatherland on behalf of Finland's national awakening, Karelia and Ingria, and the ideal of a Greater

Finland. As I believe in the greatness of God, I believe in our great father-land and its future."

War and terrorist rampages on both sides of the political divide had seri-ously frayed the country's social fabric. In the late spring of 1918, prison camps held 80,000 dispirited industrial and farm workers, former convicts, unemployed youth, and others who had fought in or supported the Red upris-ing. Across the border, thousands of Red refugees, backed by the Soviet gov-ernment, were plotting ways to foment revolution in their former homeland.

Bolshevik Russia had only recognized Finland's independence because its leaders assumed that a proletarian-led revolution in the country would lead to the creation of a socialist state and voluntary union with socialist Russia. Early in 1918, Russian soldiers had been dispatched from Petrograd to sup-port Finland's Red forces. How would Finland's powerful neighbor react now to the young nation's insistence on independence?

As it turned out, the greatest immediate threat to Finland's post-war inde-pendence came not from its recent enemy, Russia, but from its ally, Germany. Kaiser Wilhelm II had supported Lenin's Bolsheviks in order to undermine the stability of Russia under Kerensky's Provisional Government and because his enemies were supporting Russia's Whites. He was not, however, eager to have a strong communist state in Germany's backyard. The German military also feared that the English, who landed at Murmansk on the Barents Sea in March 1918, would use the Murmansk-Petrograd Railway to mount an at-tack on German forces in the Baltic countries, a precursor of fears that would shape German strategy in World War II. German troops still in Finland at the end of the Civil War quickly moved to establish strongholds in Viipuri, Kouvola, Kemijärvi, Helsinki and Rovaniemi, all important rail hubs or ter-minals, and nearly 100 German officers were named to important positions in the newly formed Finnish Armed Forces.

Many Finns felt this German presence was necessary. Even after the last Russian soldiers left Finnish soil, Finland's victorious Whites remained focused on the potential threat from the East. Future President Juho Kusti Paasikivi wrote presciently at the time: "Finland's independence depends on Germany's support. . . . When the time comes, an attack will come from the Russian side just as surely as summer is followed by autumn and winter." German troops were welcomed as guarantors of Finland's independence, but skeptics noted that should the relationship sour, they could quickly turn into a formidable occupying force.

Germany was admired by educated Finns as the center of European cul-ture. German had long been the first language (after Swedish and Finnish) taught in Finnish schools. German universities educated Finnish engineers, civil servants and doctors, and the German military trained Finnish officers. Finnish schools and universities were modeled after their German counterparts, and Finland maintained strong industrial and commercial ties with Germany. Finland's established Evangelical Lutheran Church, which counted 98 percent of the population as members, had its roots in German Reformation theology. The father of modern Finnish Lutheranism, Mikael Agricola, had studied under Martin Luther at the University of Wittenberg.

During the immediate post-war period, Germany also exerted a disproportionate influence on Finland's economy and external relations. In 1918, Germany accounted for 43 percent of Finland's exports, a huge percentage. An agreement signed March 7, 1918 astonishingly prohibited Finland from entering into relations with any third country without Germany's prior approval. Altogether, civil war, the presence of strategically placed German troops, the pressure of disadvantageous trade agreements, and Germany's interference in Finland's foreign affairs had transformed Finland in less than half a year from an Autonomous Grand Duchy of Russia into what was effectively a fledgling protectorate of Germany.

Hard Shift to the Right

Not surprisingly, Finland lurched to the right after the defeat of the Red forces. When Parliament met for the first time after the end of the Civil War in May 1918, 40 of its elected Social Democrats had fled to Russia and an additional 50 were in prison camps. Only one was allowed to take his seat. The political right and the government were now one and the same, free of even token opposition from the left. Although the conservatives were able to pass their legislative agenda unopposed, they realized that they had to do so in a hurry because at the next elections, scheduled for March 1919, the Social Democrats were sure to return in force.

Unhappy that the country had not opted for an even more authoritarian response to what he saw as continuing threats to civil society, General Mannerheim resigned from his post as Commander in Chief of the army after the war and moved to Sweden. In the autumn of 1918 he visited France and Great Britain in an attempt to win recognition for Finland's independence. Meanwhile, many Finns who had supported the creation of a democratic republic only a year earlier now questioned whether a republican government could be relied on to eliminate revolutionary tendencies and preserve order. Pehr Evind Svinhufvud, acting as Regent until presidential elections could be held, led the faction arguing that Finland would be best served by becoming a monarchy. Parliament voted October 9, 1918, before the Social

Democrats could return, to make Finland a kingdom, but where would they find a suitable king?

The crown was offered to Prince Friedrich Karl of Hesse, a brother-in-law of Kaiser Wilhelm II, in October 1918. He was not Finland's first choice, but when all the other candidates declined or were ruled out for one reason or another, he was the last one left standing. Friedrich Karl, who would have become King Fredrik Kaarle, asked for time to consider the offer.

One month after Friedrich Karl began mulling over the invitation, Germany's republicans toppled Kaiser Wilhelm II. The fall of the German monarchy and its replacement by a republic dampened Finland's enthusiasm for taking on a German as its king, but the offer could not be unilaterally withdrawn. Finland's Prime Minister, Lauri Johannes Ingman, wrote the prince a personal letter in which he hoped Finland's offer would be rejected. When Friedrich Karl officially declined to accept the crown in December 1918, the wind was taken out of the monarchists' sails. By that time, Mannerheim had replaced Svinhufvud as Regent, the last German troops had withdrawn from Finland, the German officers in the Finnish army had returned home, and the restrictive trade and political treaties between the two countries were rescinded. Finland had been saved by geopolitical circumstances beyond its control from becoming a satellite of Germany.

Much was riding on independent Finland's first elections, held in the spring of 1919. Could the pieces of Humpty Dumpty be put together again after a bitter internecine struggle? Would a stable democratic republic emerge after the monarchist fiasco? The answers to these questions would depend largely on the behavior of Social Democrats, who once again won the largest number of seats (80/200) of any party. Mannerheim lost the country's initial presidential election, in part because Social Democrats were unwilling to give their support to the former head of the White Army. He was beaten by law professor Kaarlo Juho Ståhlberg, a staunch democrat, who championed the country's respect for the rule of law. Stung by the electorate's rejection and resentful of Ståhlberg's refusal to support a military campaign to liberate Petrograd and Karelia, Mannerheim withdrew, albeit temporarily, from public life.

Obstacles to Reunification

For reconciliation to occur, the rural and industrial workers who had risen up in revolt would have to feel that progress could be achieved by parliamentary means. A law establishing an eight-hour workday had been passed a week before Finland's independence. Now it would have to be enforced. Finland's economy was in terrible shape. The border with Russia was closed, and trade agreements with Germany were no longer valid. The painful process of rebuilding would have to be carried out within the new legal limitations on how much labor employers could demand from their workers.

Another issue requiring urgent attention was the redistribution of land. A law passed in July 1918 gave tenant farmers the right to redeem some of the land they were cultivating. Four years later, new legislation known as *Lex Kallio* would enable landless peasants to acquire property at reasonable prices. These measures would help correct longstanding abuses and ease rural unemployment by creating 126,000 new farms and smallholdings.

A third long-smoldering issue was the comparative status of the Swedish and Finnish languages. Finnish had only been accorded official language status in 1902. Following independence, Finnish nationalists sought to bypass Swedish altogether and make Finnish the only official language. Opponents of such a move included the 11 percent of the population whose native language was Swedish and those Finnish speakers who feared that such a decision would isolate Finland politically, commercially and culturally from Scandinavia. The Social Democrats and Swedish People's Party successfully lobbied for Finland's 1919 constitution to designate both Finnish and Swedish as official languages and ensure that public services would be provided in both languages. This farsighted decision, while mandating expensive and labor-intensive investments in bilingualism, effectively defused one of the country's most divisive and long-standing conflicts.

Also requiring urgent attention was the need for a formal peace treaty with Russia. To be resolved were Finnish claims to Petsamo on the Barents Sea and conflicting demands for territory in Eastern Karelia. Compromises were written into the Treaty of Tartu, which formalized relations between Finland and Soviet Russia in October 1920. Finland received Petsamo but had to relinquish Repola and Porajärvi, Finnish-speaking municipalities on the Karelian border. The latter concession stoked paramilitary efforts by Finnish ultranationalists to create an uprising in Karelia and attach it to Greater Finland.

Most pressing of all unresolved issues was the need for reconciliation between Finland's Reds and Whites. Although most of Finland had not been touched by actual warfare, which was limited to a fairly narrow swath of the country, it had been almost impossible for anyone to remain neutral in a class-based conflict that inflamed emotions on both sides. Ten to twelve thousand Red prisoners were either executed or died of hunger or disease in prison camps. Of the 68–70,000 survivors, a few remained imprisoned into the 1930s while almost all the rest were either pardoned or given conditional sentences and released by 1921. Civil rights were restored to 40,000 former Red prisoners the same year. Although these actions were necessary to start the healing process, they were not sufficient to complete it. For many, the animosity proved to be difficult or impossible to overcome. In 1919, when a law making military service mandatory for all young men took effect, the sons and younger brothers of former Red Guard soldiers were excluded as unreliable. Most would have felt, in any case, that they were being forced to serve in what was, for them, an enemy army.

Figure 16.1.   Cooking class at the Ahdus Jewish Community Center in Viipuri (Finland's Jewish Archives)

It was *Yom Kippur*, I had my *tallit* and *siddur* with me at the front, and I told my commanding officer that I wanted the day off and nobody should bother me. I found a place and began to pray, but I was not completely alone. There was a Russian prisoner with me, one of those who was sent each morning to help repair the road. I always had one of them help me sort the company's laundry.

I closed the door, but suddenly it opened and the prisoner came in. I gestured for him to leave, but he kept returning. Finally, he asked me what I was doing. I answered, "I'm a Jew, I'm praying."

With that, he began to cry. He said, "I'm also a Jew, but I don't know anything about my religion. All I know is that my grandfather used to say something like *'Sh'ma Yisrael.'"*

The whole time I was praying, he just stood there, this Jewish prisoner, listening.

*Salomon Altschuler**

---

*Interviewed by the author, Helsinki, 9 July, 2014.

~

CHAPTER SIXTEEN

Benjamin Thinks
Back on Hard Times

It seems like every generation in our family had to start over again at some point. Zayde Peisach was deported and lost everything. Tate, after WWI and the Independence War, he lost everything, too. It must have been hard for him. He was ambitious, impatient and unconditional. Absolutely unconditional! There was only one way for everything: his way. It wasn't easy being his child, I can tell you.

Maybe he was that way because of how it was when he was growing up. Bubbe Feige used to tell me how hard life was for them when she got married. Life was hard for everyone back then, but antisemitism made it worse for the Jews. Things got so bad that during the Civil War we almost had a pogrom in Viipuri. That was two years before I was born. If they had succeeded, I wouldn't be here today. Fortunately, the chief of police, a decent man, Baruch hashem, heard about it and told the Jews to hide.

Right after Old Man Lifson moved his factory from Sortavala to Viipuri, Tate began working there. He needed a job badly, not just for the money but so we could become citizens. Our family had lived in Viipuri for over 60 years, but Jews had only just become eligible to apply for citizenship, and it mattered a lot if you had a job when you applied. We got our papers in 1923, but some of our friends didn't get theirs until much later. Even knowing someone who was a socialist was reason enough for the police to label Jews "suspicious or undesirable elements," and everyone knew Santeri Jacobsson.

Somehow, our papers were finally approved, and I officially became a Finn when I was three years old. I think it helped that Tate was in the Civil Guard. On the other hand, he was a Zionist, which probably explains why it took so long, more than five years. Some people had to wait even longer. Eventually, though, except for the ones who moved away, all of us became citizens.

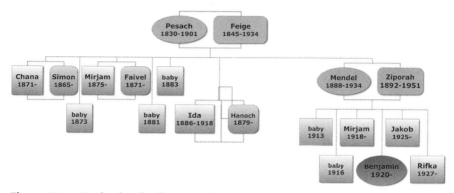

As a boy, I was Bubbe Feige's favorite, the oldest son of her only son. Once all her children were married, she went back to the market on Punaisenlähteentori, helping her friend Ester Mitnik sell clothes and remnants. After school, I would rush to their stall and "help," too. Bubbe always had some kind of treat for me in her bag, but I had to promise that I wouldn't tell Mameh about it.

I started working as an apprentice at Lifson's, that was in 1934. I was really lucky to get the job even though the pay was almost nothing. It was during the Depression, and finding any work at all was difficult. Old Man Lifson had liked Tate, and maybe he just took me as a favor to Mameh. Lifson's son, Aron, was a few years older than me. He was studying already, but we played football together. He was a good athlete and much more popular than I was. I was shy.

I was happy working at Lifson's, but Zayde's generation had no choice. They made money the only way they could, selling second-hand clothing. But already their children had more opportunity, and some of them became lawyers, doctors, and musicians. By the time I was growing up, we had doctors like Apter, Seligson, Pergament, Steinbock, two Skurniks and Zewi; lawyers like Jakobson and Maslovat; the composer Pergament-Parmet; wonderful singers like Sissi Seleste and Nina Ronni, whose real names were Seligson and Rubanowitsch; and the ballerina Sari Jankeloff. So many I can't remember them all. There were musicians like Naum Levin, Henach Kjisik, the brothers Sal, Pej and Jack Manuel and their sister, Rosie Andrew, and film stars like Hanna Taini, whose real name was Schlimowitsch, and Jacob Furman, who was younger, and later there were writers like Mindele London, Daniel Katz and Dan Steinbock. We had our own Jewish orchestras, choruses and dance bands. Just think! How many Jews were there in Finland? Maybe 2,000 is the most of us there ever were at one time in the whole country. I say it's amazing how much we have done.

I liked to sing and play the piano, and I liked to act, too, but I had no talent, not anyway the kind you need to make a career out of it. And there was no way to *earn a living playing football, even if I had been good enough, which I wasn't. Not like today. Oy vey, the money those professional athletes make today! I did pretty well in school as far as I went. I wanted to continue, but what could I do? After Tate died, I had to get a job to help Mameh so after she talked to Lifson, I became a hatmaker like my father.*

Even though we had to work sometimes from eight in the morning to six or seven in the evening, I liked it. I enjoyed working with my hands, and my mind was free to think about whatever I wanted. Sometimes I would go over the lines for a play I was going to act in, but mostly I thought about Rachel or what I would do on my days off. There were a couple of Finns working for Lifson, and they really liked working for a Jew because they got two whole days off every weekend. We were closed on shabbos and on Sundays. Workers in shops owned by Finns had to work on Saturdays.

Antisemitism didn't play much of a role in my life. I worked for a Jewish hatmaker, played football in a Jewish sports club, and acted and sang at Ahdus. Where would I experience antisemitism? Maybe in the Civil Guard I heard a few comments, but there had always been some who talked like that in the Guard. To me, it wasn't personal, and I didn't pay much attention.

Some of my friends, though, felt the situation kept getting worse. There was a lot of talk about leaving, going to America or Palestine. The Zionists wanted to go to Palestine and fight, or at least they said they did. Tate's sister, Tante Mirjam, went to America, but that was before I was born. I never met her. I probably have lots of relatives over there, but I don't know any of them. That's what happened, families split up. My own daughter, Ruut, moved to Israel after the Yom Kippur War, and two of my grandchildren still live there. I used to see them once in a while but not so often after Ruut's funeral. She died fourteen years ago. I remember because it was right after those meshugenah[1] *Arabs flew their planes into those towers in New York. I wish I had never seen such a thing!*

So much hatred in the world! Who can ever explain a Hitler or a Stalin, all the people they killed? And they had the chutzpah to make a treaty not to fight each other until after they had divided up all the land lying between their countries. And what was that land? Mostly it was the Pale of Settlement, home to millions of Jews. They wanted the land but without the Jews. That's where all the trouble started. Maybe that's the reason Stalin and Hitler were both so interested in Finland. There was a lot of land here, too, but only 2,000 Jews. It wouldn't be so hard for them to kill all of us.

Note

1. Crazy (Yiddish)

Figure 17.1.   S. Dubkoff's tailoring workshop in Viipuri (Finland's Jewish Archives)

Schmuel ran into significant speed bumps in developing his business operations as the general rules concerning the freedom to establish an enterprise and earn a living did not extend to Jews. Until 1918 they were listed as Russian citizens temporarily residing in our country. According to the laws and regulations in force at the time, their business opportunities were limited on the basis of their nationality, ethnic background and Jewishness.

In reality, the first and second generation of Skurnik entrepreneurs faced double, or actually triple, challenges at the end of the 19th and beginning of the twentieth centuries as they tried to adjust to Finnish society. First of the all, the times were generally challenging. Second, the societal environment was hostile, and third, Finnish society placed tight restrictions on their lives and business activities.

Samuli Skurnik*

---

*Narinkkatorilta Kiestingin mottiin, Paasilinna, Juva, 2013, p. 75.

CHAPTER SEVENTEEN

~

Mendel Becomes a Citizen

Viipuri, 1918—Mendel emerges from Sjögren's root cellar more determined than ever to succeed in business and provide a good home for his growing family. The problem is where to start? He has no job, and it isn't the best market for hatmakers. For the rest of 1918, he scours Viipuri for steady work, but no one is hiring. To keep some bread and the occasional sardine on the table, he helps repair the storefronts of those Jewish merchants who have been able to keep their businesses going. On several occasions, in return for a small commission, he travels to Latvia to pick up textiles and clothing ordered by Viipuri's shop owners. Prohibition is about to be imposed, and a local restaurant owner offers Mendel a considerable sum to smuggle spirits into the country with the textile deliveries. Mendel does not even consider it. The way things are, he already worries each time he goes abroad that he might not be allowed back in the country. Then what would become of Zipora and little Mirjam?

Mendel would like to apply for Finnish citizenship, but he knows it is futile to do so until he can find a steady job. A few members of the Jewish community register dummy corporations as a way to prove that they are employed. Once they get their papers, they dissolve the companies. Even this simple subterfuge is beyond Mendel's reach as he has no money to pay the lawyers, notaries and corporate registration fee.

Financial distress and the death of two cherished family members cast a pall over Mendel's family. Feige has a hard time dealing with the loss of Ida, whom she had patiently nursed through a sickly childhood. Her fervent hope was that having a doctor for a husband would shield Ida from further health problems, but it turns out that no one is safe from the ravages of this epidemic. The Spanish Flu spreads rapidly throughout the country, sending more than 20,000 Finns to an early grave.

In Sortavala, at the northern tip of Lake Ladoga, a hatmaker named Lifson is sitting *shiva* for his wife Hane, one of those struck down by the disease. He is left with two boys to look after, Mikael 8 and Aron 2, and now that the border with Russia is closed, his East Karelia Hat Factory is in the wrong place. It should be closer to its remaining customers, who are all in Finland. At the end of the prescribed grieving period, Lifson packs up his business and family's possessions and moves with his two sons to Viipuri. Before long he is joined there by Hane's younger sister, Paula, who becomes his wife, as is the custom.

Lifson, who will later call himself Simon Livson, must find skilled workers quickly. He has large orders to fill for the newly formed Finnish army. Mendel meets Lifson at an event to raise funds for the purchase of a building to serve as a community center for the Jews of Viipuri. Mendel, who has no money to contribute, is doing his part by serving as a greeter and usher at the fund-raiser. Towards the end of the evening, Congregation President Isak Pergament introduces the two hatmakers to each other, and the following Monday morning Mendel is already helping his new employer set up shop at Karjalankatu 23. Lifson's business will now be known as the Eastern Finland Hat Factory, and Mendel begins work as a senior cutter.

Promise Renewed

Mendel has a job, the Jews have civil rights, and both Finland's Civil War and World War I are over. Now is the time for Finland, its Jewish community, and Mendel to focus on establishing themselves, creating wealth, and putting history's troubles behind them.

In 1918, Finland's Jews acquire a collective voice, a newspaper called *Judisk Krönika*, founded by Israel-Jakob Schur. In its inaugural issue, dated November 15, Schur writes on behalf of his co-religionists:

> We undertake to fulfill all the duties that befall us as they do the rest of the country's population; although we are prepared whenever our country calls to sacrifice everything we possess for the happiness and success of our fatherland and as loyal citizens not only to live but to die for the general good . . ., we are [also] committed along with our brothers elsewhere in the world, we have our own culture . . . but all this does not prevent us from being at the same time loyal citizens on whom the country can calmly rely.[1]

This declaration of dual loyalty—to Finland, on the one hand, and to the concept of a Jewish people, on the other—appears almost exactly a year after the publication of Great Britain's Balfour Declaration, which, for the first time in history, commits a great power to supporting the Zionist cause. "His Majesty's government view with favour the establishment in Palestine of a national home for the Jewish people, and will use their best endeavours to facilitate the achievement of this object." The *Judisk Krönik's* editorial, in keeping with the times, renews the strong pledge made on behalf of Finland's Jews by Dr. Axel Johan Lille to the Burgher Estate in 1894 but balances it with the Jewish community's commitment to Zionism.

Not all Finns are happy about the new legal status that has been accorded to the country's Jews. In 1921, a Finnish translation of *The Protocols of the Elders of Zion* is published. Originally issued in Russia in 1903 and purporting to be a Jewish blueprint for world domination, the fraudulent and largely plagiarized *Protocols* are intended to fan the flames of anti-semitism. Their appearance in a Finnish-language edition does not bode well for Finland's Jews or the welcome they will receive now that they are finally allowed to move freely around the country. Fortunately, it will not be widely distributed or read.

Because at this point they have still never seen or talked to a Jew, most Finns are susceptible to misconceptions spread through antisemitic propaganda. According to numerous accounts from the period, those who actually have dealings with Jews are more likely to appreciate them as businessmen providing a valuable service than to view them as pariahs. Jewish shops are known for offering suitable quality merchandise and service at a reasonable price. The claims in antisemitic literature that Jews manipulate financial markets, dominate the press, and are responsible for the excesses of both capitalism and socialism make no sense in the Finnish context, where even the most successful Jews are likely to be small businessmen or professionals focused on pursuing stability and security for themselves and their families.

Starting Anew

By the end of 1919, Mendel has left behind the chaos of Civil War, the collapse of his business, and the deaths of his sister and father-in-law. He is a free man (though not yet a citizen) in a free country and has a good job and a healthy family. He would like to have a hat factory of his own, though, and a bigger family. If the former seems beyond his reach for now, the latter does not. Zipora is once again pregnant. January 30, 1920, between 3:00 and 4:00 in the morning, she gives birth to a fine baby boy at home with the help of a woman from the congregation who serves as midwife. Eight days later, Rabbi Nahum Maslovat performs the *bris*,[2] and the child is given the names Benjamin Eliezer.

Mendel applies for citizenship for his family and himself in 1921. For some reason, it takes two more years for the application to be approved, but at last he, Zipora, Mirjam and Benjamin have a homeland. What, Mendel wonders, would his father have made of all this? Jews being granted Finnish citizenship? Jews openly celebrating religious festivals, publishing their own newspaper, and enjoying Viipuri's lively *Ahdus* community center? How strange it would have seemed to the bitter Cantonist for whom life had been something akin to the Finnish practice of treating various ills by sitting naked on a nest of stinging ants. Peisach has survived, but he never loses the feeling of being beset by painful attacks from all sides.

Foreign trade picks up quickly after the war as soon as it becomes safe to ply the Baltic Sea again. By 1923, the value of Finland's total annual export trade is almost nine times greater than for all of 1917, 1918 and 1919 combined. Viipuri, always at the center of the commercial action, has once again become Europe's number one port for exporting wood.

Now that Finland's Jews are free from all restrictions on how they may earn a livelihood, the rising economic tide lifts their boats the same way as it does the boats of other Finns. In Helsinki by 1930, according to economic historian Laura Ekholm, 48 percent of the Jewish community will consist of entrepreneurs or self-employed individuals and their families while the remaining 52 percent will mostly be wage earners working for the first 48 percent. That some of the entrepreneurs turn out to be quite successful is clear from records showing that the top ten taxpayers in the Helsinki congregation (owner/managers of textile wholesale companies, a textile factory and a garment retail business) will account for 45 percent of the congregation's tax revenues.

Stone houses are replacing wooden homes and offices in the better neighborhoods of Finland's cities, and a number of Jews can be found living at some of the most desirable addresses. The growing middle class attends concerts and theater performances. In Viipuri, a young man with spare change in his pocket might take a girl for a romantic ride around the city in a horse-drawn cab or treat her to a silent movie such as *Kihlaus (Engagement)* or *Koskenlaskijan morsian (The Rapid-shooter's Bride)* at the *Salama* or *Scala* cinemas. Radio broadcasts begin in 1926, bringing news and music right into the home.

Mendel now sees life not in terms of restrictions but of limitless possibilities. His sister Mirjam writes from New York that Faivel has made enough money to sell his peddler's cart and open a women's apparel store called *Lovely Lady*. The letter contains a sepia picture of the shop with its proud owner and his wife standing by the shop's display window. Mirjam writes that having left her sewing job, she now helps her husband with the bookkeeping and inventory. Mendel is happy for his sister and brother-in-law, but he cannot help feeling a little jealous. When will his turn come?

Zipora has her hands full with Mirele, as little Mirjam is called. Apparently Mirele does not like the idea of competing with a baby brother for Zipora's attention, and she makes her displeasure known by screaming, biting, kicking and generally making life miserable for both Benjamin and their mother. Mendel often comes home in the evening to find Zipora exhausted and at her wits' end. On *shabbos*, after he returns from *shul*, Mendel takes Mirele for long walks in her stroller in the hopes of allowing Zipora some peace and quiet while Benjamin naps. Little Mirele seems to enjoy spending time with her father. She babbles cheerfully as he pushes her along the path in *Mon Repos Park*, where he first saw Zipora making sketches of the statues.

Mendel's love for Zipora is now augmented by waves of gratitude that wash over him from time to time. She has given him a wonderful family, and he knows it has been anything but easy for her. She has had to adapt to circumstances far more difficult than those to which she had been accustomed before marrying him, but she never complains. He feels there is so much he owes her. He will start, he decides, by finding the family a new apartment, one with running water, an indoor toilet and electricity.

Tough Love

Benjamin is a sweet child. Even as a baby, he causes his parents much less trouble than Mirele. And when a younger brother arrives before Benjamin's sixth birthday, Benjamin exhibits neither Mirele's aggression nor the impatience that had characterized Mendel as a child.

Mendel is mystified by Mirele and Benjamin, who are as different from one another as Cain and Abel. He notes with concern that Benjamin readily gives in to Mirele when she bullies him for something. When he searches his own childhood for clues to how a father should react to such behavior, he comes up empty-handed, realizing that Peisach had never really paid much attention to him or his sisters. Mendel does not want to be that kind of father, but good intentions cannot replace the lack of a role model. When he tries to discipline the children, he has no confidence that he is doing the right thing. Somehow, Mirele seems to sense his uncertainty and finds ways to exploit it. Zipora tells Mendel not to worry, that he will become surer of himself with experience, but he doubts it and dreads the day when his teen-age children will have an even greater need for a father's steadying hand.

Zipora worries about how Benjamin will adjust to school, but when the time comes, he trots off happily alongside his older sister to Repolan kan-sakoulu,[3] the local primary school. His teachers send home good reports and give him top grades in comportment. The only critical comment is that he sometimes daydreams when he should be concentrating on his lessons.

Benjamin is not, strictly speaking, daydreaming. He is composing sto-ries. Sometimes they are about kings and ships and armies, sometimes about animals and trolls and fairies. When he tries to draw pictures of what he is imagining, though, his hand won't follow his mind's instructions. When he is in second grade, two army airplanes collide over Viipuri. The pilot of one of them is thrown from his aircraft and falls through the roof of Benjamin's school. The pilotless plane crashes and explodes in the middle of Torkkelinkatu, narrowly missing Pursiainen's crowded cafe. For the next year Benjamin draws nothing else but colliding and burning airplanes and falling pilots. Years later, as he scans the sky for enemy aircraft from Pat-terinmäki Hill as a plane-spotter for Viipuri's anti-aircraft gunners, he will remember the shock of the explosion and the thump of the pilot's body smashing through the roof.

One day in the spring of 1930, Benjamin, who is ten and in fourth grade, is accosted by four older boys while walking home from school. One of them, a tough kid named Saarvala, knocks him down and pushes his face in the mud, saying, "Dirty Jew, that's what you get!" Benjamin tries to clean himself up before going home, but he can tell by the horrified look on his mother's face that he hasn't succeeded very well. As soon as she washes him off and makes him change his shirt, she hurries down to the shop to get her husband.

Mendel's first reaction is to grab Benjamin roughly by the arm and set out to find his assailants. Why didn't his son try to fight back? It is no excuse that there were four of them and he was alone. If he lets them take advantage of him without defending himself, he will soon find himself being beaten up by half the neighborhood.

Luckily for Benjamin, they do not find the boys who bullied him, but Mendel is not satisfied. Instead of returning home, he takes his son to the Viipurin Nyrkkeilijät (Viipuri's Pugilists) gym and signs him up for boxing les-sons. Benjamin tries to tell his father that he doesn't want to learn to box and that it will only make things worse, but Mendel is determined. No son of his is going to let other boys push him around!

Benjamin hates the boxing lessons, and, predictably, he isn't very good at it at first. He doesn't want to hit anyone, and he certainly doesn't want any of the other boys hitting him, either. But to his own surprise and that of everyone else, after a few months of trying to avoid beatings by the other boys in the group, he begins to be able to hold his own in the ring. It turns out that what he lacks in punching power and killer instinct, he more than makes up for in agility and balance. He learns to slip punches, leaving his opponents clumsily off balance. Sometimes he gets through an entire round of sparring without getting hit even once. The coach, who despaired at first of having another boy in the group who is only there because his father forces him to attend, begins to see some potential in Benjamin.

Once Benjamin realizes he doesn't have to hurt opponents to win, he begins to enjoy boxing. The first time *Viipurin Nyrkkeilijät* arranges a tournament against *Viipurin Voimailijat (Viipuri's Gymnasts)*, Benjamin surprises everyone by easily beating a boy who is a year older and a head taller. Benjamin doesn't hit the other boy very often during the three rounds, but his opponent hardly hits him at all. That evening, when he shows his father the tiny medal he earned, one would have thought it was a Finnish Championship trophy the way Mendel beams and praises him. Zipora, who never made a secret of being unhappy about the boxing, is nevertheless delighted by the sign of a bond beginning to grow between father and son.

Plans and Disappointments

The Eastern Finland Hat Factory prospers during the 1920s, and Mendel gets a small raise in salary every second year, allowing him in the autumn of 1928 to move his family into a flat in a three-story stone building with modern conveniences at Sammonkatu 37. It is big enough for him to bring Feige to live with them as he has wanted to do since his father died. She still goes to the *Punaisenlähteentorin narinkka* to help Ester Mitnik, but she is not one to enjoy living alone, and he thinks having the children around will cheer her up.

He tries to save enough money to start his own business again, but his income can barely keep up with the growth of his family, which now includes four children: Mirjam, Benjamin, Jakob and six-month-old Rifka. His one hope is that his brother-in-law Faivel will become rich enough in New York to be able to lend him the money he needs to start his own workshop and salesroom. Mendel decides that on his next birthday he will ask Faivel for the loan.

Six months before Mendel, whose hair prematurely shows a few streaks of gray, turns 42, the bottom falls out of his plan. On October 29, 1929, shares on the New York Stock Market lose 12 percent of their value in record heavy trading. Faivel, who got carried away by the early success of *Lovely Lady* and the prospect of fortunes to be made in the bull market of the 1920s, has compiled a modest stock portfolio on margin. When the market crashes, he loses everything. In order to repay even part of his debt, Faivel has to sell his store and all his inventory. He will spend the rest of his life as a representative of Schenley Industries, traipsing from bar to bar in Jersey City and Hackensack with a bag of samples on his back, taking orders for whiskey, bourbon and rye. When he dies 16 years later, he will leave his Mirjam just $700 and his grandfather's gold pocket watch and fob.

For once, Finland's remoteness works to its advantage. The Great Depression is slower arriving in Viipuri than in the great capitals of America and Europe, but arrive it eventually does, bringing with it social unrest and strikes. The number of unemployed grows, and those lucky enough to have work often find their hours shortened and their paycheck reduced.

By the time of Benjamin's *bar mitzvah*, however, which takes place on his thirteenth birthday, January 30, 1933, Finland is already beginning to recover. Benjamin has developed a love for football, where his ability to anticipate the moves of opponents and his skill at dodging and feinting make him difficult to defend. He has left boxing behind, but the experience has accomplished what Mendel had hoped for.

Benjamin knows now that he can overcome fear and find ways to survive in a threatening world. As fate will have it, he will need all the defensive skill and confidence he can muster in the years to come. At the very moment when Benjamin is reading his *bar mitzvah* portion from the Torah scroll to the assembled congregation in the Viipuri synagogue, an Austrian World War I veteran with a squeaky voice and a truncated moustache, the previously jailed leader of the failed Beer Hall Putsch and author of *Mein Kampf*, is being sworn in by President Paul von Hindenburg as Chancellor of Germany.

Notes

1. Schur, Israel-Jakob, editorial in *Judisk Krönika*, November 15, 1918.
2. Ritual circumcision
3. Folk or primary school (Finnish)

Figure 18.1.   July 7, 1930, supporters of the Lapua Movement descended on Helsinki in a show of force that became known as the Farmers' March (Tampere City Museum archives)

If we in Finland have made out all right and sometimes been seen to be clever, I think it has a lot to do with the fact that we have a big neighbor who has forced us to think a little and reach at least a minimal consensus within our own society. Finns aren't any better than Norwegians or the Dutch or anyone else, but because of our geopolitical position, we've had to stay on our toes. This joint border has created opportunities that we would never have had without it.

*Matti Klinge**

*Interviewed by the author, Helsinki, 22 October, 2012.

CHAPTER EIGHTEEN

~

Finland Recovers

1920—A major step in securing recognition for Finland's sovereignty is taken when the country gains admission to the League of Nations in 1920. Is Finland finally ready, then, to take its place in the rank of nations as Czar Alexander I had ordained more than a century earlier? It has been joined by other newly created independent states from the Baltics to the Balkans as old empires collapse and borders are redrawn in the name of national self-determination, but many observers feel that the odds are stacked against the survival of these fledgling countries. E.H. Carr in Britain and Walter Lippmann in the United States, for example, will warn that these new states are too small and weak to defend themselves against the strategic interests of the major powers.

A 1915 editorial in Sweden's *Afton-Tidningen* had insisted:

Should Russia, under pressure of exceptional circumstances, temporarily give up Finland, its first task after that will be to win it back. The blood which Finland would shed to free itself from Russia will be shed in vain. In the course of time, Finland can never defend itself as a free country.[1]

In 1922, *The Economist* will publish a map showing Finland as part of Russia. When Finland's Ambassador to the U.K. protests, he is told by the magazine's editor, "We don't change our maps in response to every passing phenomenon!"[2]

Newly independent Finland sets out to prove *Afton-Tidningen* and *The Economist* wrong. Although most Finns have no illusions about the external threats they face and the internal divisions they need to overcome, all but those diehard communists still harboring hopes of creating a Soviet Socialist Republic of Finland rally around the task of nation-building. Nationalist fervor is directed towards improving the quality of education, strengthening trade and industry, achieving international success in sports and culture, and building a military capable of deterring external aggression.

Radicalism vs. the Rule of Law

During the 1920s, the Social Democratic Party, shorn of its most radical elements, gradually returns to its role as the acknowledged standard-bearer of the working class. The parliamentary right is led by a coalition consisting of the Agrarian League, the republican National Progressive Party and the monarchist National Coalition Party. Working together and governing in various combinations, these parties find ways to fend off the challenges from the radical extremes at both ends of the political spectrum during the turbulent 1920s and 1930s and lead the country back to stability and the rule of law.

The evolving maturity of the country's democratic commitment can be seen in the actions of two of its storied leaders, each of whom risks the scorn of his own party to keep the ship of state on course. Väinö Tanner, a pioneer of the Cooperative Movement and long-time chairman of the Social Democratic Party, opposed the armed uprising that led to the Civil War, earning him condemnation from the radical left and the Soviet Union. In 1927, while serving as Prime Minister, he is called on to substitute for ailing President Lauri Kristian Relander at a Civil War anniversary parade. For reviewing the Finnish Army and Civil Guard, which are still anathema to the left, with honor, Tanner is branded a traitor to the working class by those with the bitterest memories. He is excluded from the leadership of his own party for four years following the parade, but his unequivocal action sends a clear message that it is time to put the grudges of the Civil War to rest and get on with building a unified country.

Five years later, President Pehr Evind Svinhufvud faces an even more difficult situation when the Young Communists begin organizing provocative meetings and demonstrations in the province of Ostrobothnia, a bastion of White Finland. Leftist activity has been increasing as the effects of the Great Depression are felt by members of the agricultural and industrial working class, provoking a counter-reaction in which angry mobs forcibly strip off the red shirts of communist demonstrators. This right-wing activism coalesces into the Lapua Movement, a radical nationalist groundswell that is primarily anti-communist and anti-socialist but also, inevitably, unfriendly to Jews.

Unhappy with the reunification politics practiced by centrist parliamentary parties, the Lapua Movement resorts to vigilante actions such as kidnapping opponents and spiriting them across the Soviet border before releasing them. In July 1930, the Lapua Movement organizes a "farmers' march" in Helsinki that draws 12,000 participants from the countryside. Three months later, Lapua activists kidnap former President Ståhlberg and his wife with the intention of "deporting" them, an act that is broadly condemned by the Finnish public.

In 1932, a group of armed men summoned by the Lapua Movement—some accounts say there are hundreds, others report more than a thousand—descend on the village of Mäntsälä 60 kilometers north of Helsinki, intent on disrupting a meeting of the local Social Democratic Labor Association. When the meeting begins despite their protest, shots are fired at the Workers' Hall where the meeting's participants are assembled. The protesters refuse a police order to disperse, prompting the Lapua Movement's leadership gathered in nearby Hämeenlinna to send a telegram to President Svinhufvud announcing that they will be unable to maintain order among their followers unless the government resigns and the political orientation of the country changes. Additional men, including members of the Civil Guard, hurry to Mäntsälä to join what is rapidly turning into an armed rebellion.

President Svinhufvud, an archconservative who served as head of the elected (White) government during the Civil War and marched with the Civil Guard for many years, issues an order for the rebels to "obey the law and your oath" and commands the head of the Civil Guard to read it over the radio. When the latter refuses to do so, Svinhufvud goes on the airwaves himself. He orders the protesters to return home and dispatches Civil Guard member Martti Pihkala to make sure the order is carried out. The rebellion fizzles, and Pihkala later sends an invoice to the Finnish Parliament that reads: "For putting down one rebellion: 5,000 markkas."

By their courageous stands, Tanner and Svinhufvud, two politicians on opposing sides of the political divide, play important roles in preventing the kind of radicalization that is growing stronger elsewhere in Europe from taking hold in Finland. The Lapua Movement is banned in 1932 and replaced by the Patriotic People's Movement (IKL), a minor political party with Nazi tendencies that never gains significant popular support. With the Finnish Communist Party banned as well, communists try to infiltrate the Social Democratic Party but are prevented from exerting much influence by Tanner's firm control of that organization. Extremism has been blunted at both ends of the political spectrum, causing the nexus of political power to gravitate naturally toward the center.

Recovery

As Europe emerges from the Great Depression in the mid-1930s, trade increases, and Finland, still needing to export forest industry products in order to buy food, fuel and manufactured goods, prospers. Finland's gross national product per capita had already doubled between the end of the Civil War and 1929. Wages had risen, too, but not as fast. As a result, protracted and often violent strikes are organized, culminating in the stevedores' and dockworkers' strike of 1928 that lasts almost a year.

Under the able stewardship of Bank of Finland president Risto Ryti, who serves from 1923 through 1939, Finland's economy begins to revive as early as 1933. In 1934, Finland starts paying back the eight million dollars it borrowed from the United States between 1918 and 1920 to ease post-war food shortages. It will later be widely praised as the only country to repay in full its reconstruction loan debt with interest. Aided by the 1935 creation of a timber-exporting cartel, the European Timber Exporters Convention (ETEC), Finnish sawn goods again find their way to western markets. All these signs of recovery help convince Finnish consumers to look ahead instead of backward.

Although the country's social fabric is still fragile during the early 1930s, important steps have already been taken to increase fairness and redress serious grievances stemming from social inequality. In 1906, Finland became the first European country to extend the franchise to women. Shortly after the nation gained independence, it passed an eight-hour workday law. The cooperative movement accounts for one third of total retail trade by the 1930s, making it possible for the families of industrial and agricultural workers to increase their participation in the country's economy through membership (ownership) in everything from local shops and restaurants to cooperative banks and credit unions. By the end of 1935, unemployment has declined from 82,626 in 1932 to only 17,718.

Every municipality has been compelled from 1921 to provide free primary schooling, and all children are required to attend through grade six. The Religious Liberty Act is passed in 1922 and the land reforms embodied in Lex Kallio begin to be implemented. In the 1930s, universal military service brings young men of varying backgrounds together in a way that will hasten the demise of the rigid, centuries-old class society. Social and economic progress even begins convincing many of those whose fathers fought on the losing side of the Civil War that their young nation is worth defending. No less an icon of the right than Marshal Mannerheim eventually delivers a speech arguing that it is time for people to stop asking on which side everyone fought in 1918.

But if Finnish society is showing signs of settling down in 1933, the Soviet Union and Germany are both in turmoil. As many as 5.5 million Soviet citizens die from hunger during the 1932–33 famine caused by the U.S.S.R.'s forced collectivization of agriculture. Another 247,157 are executed by the end of 1938 in Stalin's Great Terror and 386,798 killed in operations to repress former Kulaks.

Meanwhile, Germany is suffering from catastrophic levels of inflation and unemployment. There are 5.4 million unemployed in Germany in 1933. By borrowing heavily and confiscating wealth from German Jews and other "enemies" of the Third Reich, then pouring money into public works and rebuilding the military, the national socialists are able to achieve full employment by 1938. An early part of the Third Reich's public works program, implemented soon after Hitler becomes Chancellor in 1933, consists of building concentration camps at Dachau, Oranienburg, Sachsenhausen and Ravensbrück. Originally intended to hold left-wing and union activists, they will be ready when train-loads of Jews, Roma, homosexuals and other "undesirables" begin to arrive.

Germany's rapidly increasing military strength reawakens Soviet anxiety over the vulnerability of Leningrad (as the former St. Petersburg and Petrograd is now called) to attacks from the South via the Baltic States, from the West via the Baltic Sea, and from the North via Finland. In 1932, Finland and the Soviet Union sign a mutual non-aggression pact, which is extended in 1934 to last through the end of 1945. As the decade progresses, though. the Soviets begin pressuring the Finns to make territorial concessions in order to create a deeper buffer zone against possible attack from the West and North.

Finland begins strengthening its military capability in order to be able to mount a credible defense of its borders. The Finns (3.7 million in 1939) never expect to be able to beat the Russians (170 million) in head-to-head combat, but they hope to be able to hold off attacking forces long enough for help from friendly nations to arrive. To this end, able-bodied males are required to undergo one year of military service, followed by reserve obligations lasting until the year in which they reach the age of 60. Between 1918 and the start of the Winter War in 1939, more than half a million Finns (13.5 percent of the total population) undergo basic military training.

For many in this lightly populated northeast corner of Europe, the last years of the 1930s are a period of hope. Finally, there is light at the end of the tunnel for a continent that has suffered through a bloody conflict followed by a crushing economic collapse. Few are farsighted enough, however, to recognize that the light is an onrushing train called World War II, picking up speed as radical ideologies in Berlin, Rome, Tokyo and Moscow stoke its boilers.

Notes

1. Quoted in Jakobson, Max, *Väkivallan vuodet*, Otava, Helsinki, 1999, p. 56.
2. *Ibid.*, p. 60.

Figure 19.1. In 1906, the Third Russian Zionist Convention was held in Helsinki (Finland's Jewish Archives)

The worst antisemites in Viipuri were the Swedish-speakers. The Jewish boys who went to the Swedish school had a hard time. There was one teacher there who was very antisemitic. Our rabbi's son sat in the front row, right in front of him. One day the teacher asked him, "Maslovat, do you know what separates Jews from asses?"

Maslovat looked straight at him and answered, "Yes, I do. It's the teacher's desk!"

The teacher became furious and shouted, "Out!"

Maslovat answered back, "Yes, I'm leaving and going straight to the Principal's Office."

After that, the teacher never mentioned donkeys again.

Salomon Altschuler*

**Interviewed by the author, Helsinki, 9 July, 2014

CHAPTER NINETEEN

~

Benjamin Reflects
on the Rise of Zionism

I never managed to Visit either Turku or Helsinki before the war. I wanted to, but there was no way. I didn't have the money or the time.

I couldn't stop thinking about Rachel. Was I in love with her? I thought I was, but what did that mean? I never saw her, had never kissed her, and the only communication we had was by letters that we exchanged less frequently as time went by. She was studying to become a nurse, and I. . . . I was just a cutter in a hat factory. For sure, she would marry someone like David, someone with an education and a profession and what our mothers called "prospects," all qualifications I didn't have.

Luckily, there were other things in my life like football, theater, and keeping food on the family table. Jakob and Rifka were too young to work so it was up to Mirele and me to do what we could. Our salaries were small, but luckily so were our family's needs.

I was growing taller and stronger and playing regularly on Kadur's men's team. We practiced three times a week from April to October. During the 1938 season, I began to be able to beat even some of the better players to the ball, especially in the air, and my teammates began passing to me more often. I wasn't the best player on the team, but I wasn't the worst, either.

In the winter I usually had a part in a play at Ahdus. We were very serious about our acting, or maybe that's not the right way to say it. We had fun, but we also tried to perform as well as we could. Sometimes we had directors from the National Theater, and we wanted to show them how good we were. It was a matter of pride for the whole Jewish community.

I had friends, of course, but with work, football, acting and my responsibilities at home, I didn't have much time for socializing. And then there was the problem of money. There was no way I could go with the others for summer weekends to the beach at Terijoki or justify spending my hard-earned salary in Viipuri's restaurants. Mameh always told me to go and have a good time, but I knew how hard it was for her to get by with the money we gave her. It might have been different if Rachel had wanted me to visit Turku, but that wasn't going to happen.

Mameh tried to get me to spend more time with Jewish girls from our own congregation. Some of them were nice enough, but I couldn't get interested in them in the way she wanted. What saved me was that Mameh worried much more about finding a husband for Mirele. It didn't matter so much if a boy took a long time to find a wife, but for a girl it was different. Mameh felt she needed to find a good Jewish husband for Mirele and quickly. My sister was really headstrong, and Mameh was right to worry.

Before 1938, we were too worried about what was going on in Palestine and just across the border in the Soviet Union to pay much attention to what was happening in Germany. But after the Anschluss, all of a sudden refugees started arriving from Austria. Finland allowed them into the country without visas at the time, but that changed when the Nazis refused to let Jews return once they left. Most Finns didn't want them staying here, anyway.

At first, we only knew what was in the papers. We didn't know anything about the concentration camps. What was happening in Germany and Austria seemed far away. After the Scheins moved in with us, though, it was suddenly right there in my home!

The Jewish communities of Helsinki, Turku and Viipuri offered to look after refugees until other countries could take them. I think we got some financial help from Jews in America, too. Mameh was one of the first in Viipuri to take in a family, but by the spring of 1939, practically every Jewish family in Viipuri had someone living with them. After the Scheins, we had others, too: the Hirschfelds, the Beerwalds, I can't remember all the names. Jewish businessmen gave them work, too, whenever they could. Everyone was helping as much as possible.

We thought things couldn't get worse, but, Riboyne shel oylem,[1] were we wrong! First the police turned away the Jews on that ship, sent them back to Germany. Kekkonen was Interior Minister then, and he didn't want to take any more Jews. He said Finland had enough Karelian and Ingrian refugees already and didn't need to take in Europe's Jews as well.

Some Finns claimed that Jews were communists, and that's why they shouldn't be let into the country. Schmegege![2] Almost all the Jewish families I knew either owned or hoped to own their own businesses. They wanted to be part of the capitalist economy, not overthrow it.

Anyway, only three months after Finland closed the door to Jewish refugees came Kristallnacht. Even some of Finland's newspapers that usually had only

good things to say about Hitler wrote about how synagogues were burned and de-
fenseless Jews were beaten by mobs and killed. Thousands were sent to concentra-
tion camps, too, and there was nothing we could do to help. No one could believe
that the Germans, with their great culture, could turn into such monsters, but we
know now that was just the beginning.

We Jews saw Germany as a problem, but most Finns were looking to it for a
solution. All of us were worried about the Russkies, and many people hoped the
Germans would take our side like they did in 1918. Back then, Mannerheim might
have beaten Finland's disorganized Reds without the Germans' help, but as we soon
found out, fighting Stalin's powerful and disciplined Red Army more than thirty
years later would be different.

I was just 18 at the time. My friends and I weren't much interested in politics.
We thought that even if Russia and Germany went to war, Finland could stay out
of it. That was what a lot of the politicians were saying, but it was just alevay-
gedanken, wishful thinking.

One person who wasn't fooled by any of it was Jabotinsky. When he came to
Finland in the spring of 1939, he said that it didn't matter what would happen
in a war, the Jews would be the big losers. The way the Nazis were persecuting
Austrian and German Jews showed that assimilation didn't work. Our only hope,
he said, was to force open the gates to Palestine. Only in a Jewish homeland could
we be safe.

Tate agreed with Jabotinsky. From very young, he was a committed Zionist. He
was very bitter about what had happened to Zayde Peisach, how he was deported
and lost all his money. He felt that Jews would never get a fair chance in Finnish
society. A lot of Viipuri's other Jews were Zionists, too. Some of them thought a
Jewish homeland would be a good thing but weren't ready to move there. Others
were ready to go as soon as they got the chance.

You see, there were different kinds of Zionists when I was growing up. There
were the Labor Zionists, who thought if we Jews could send enough people to farm
the land in Palestine, we would eventually make it our own country. A second
kind, the Revisionists, argued that no one would give Jews anything. They felt we
had the right to set up a Jewish state on the Biblical lands of Judea and Samaria
and were ready to fight to take back what rightfully belonged to us. And then there
were those who took everything in the Bible literally and believed it was wrong to
try and do anything because the return to Jerusalem could only take place when the
Messiah arrived. We had all kinds in Viipuri.

Jonas Jakobson was chairman of our congregation and participated in the Third
Russian Zionist Conference. It was held in Helsinki in 1905 or 1906, I don't
remember exactly. All the big names were there, from Jabotinsky to Shimshon
Rosenbaum. Tate went with Jakobson and Hillel Zall to Helsinki, and he told me

that it changed his life. He was just a young man at the time. Like Zayde Peisach, he felt uncomfortable being a Jew in a society that didn't want us, but instead of making him depressed like his father, it made him angry. He resented everyone who had oppressed his people: Russians, Finns, even the Jews who were afraid to stand up for their own rights. From the moment he heard Jabotinsky speak, he became a follower. That's the way Tate was: all or nothing. Of course, there really was only one Zionist movement until Jabotinsky founded the Revisionist Movement years later, but the two trends were there from the beginning—compromise or fight—and Tate was a fighter.

I don't think Tate really respected his father. Bubbe Feige said she always felt that Tate needed to be disciplined, but Zayde Peisach wasn't that kind of father. If his son didn't do what he was told, Zayde just shrugged his shoulders and muttered something to himself, she said. Tate took advantage and became very independent. He joined the Civil Guard, and later I joined it, too. He couldn't understand how his father could have been a soldier and not be prepared to fight for his rights.

The Labor Zionists in Viipuri organized agricultural camps so young Jews could learn to be farmers. Of course, there were no Jewish farmers in Viipuri so they had to find Finns from the countryside to be teachers. The idea was that some of us would make Aliyah, go to Palestine to build a society where Jews could be free.

The Revisionists came later. In Viipuri, they founded a branch of their youth organization, Betar, and conducted military training. This was in the 1930s. They had to be careful because the police were always watching them. Jonas Jakobson's son Leo was a Betar group leader and a member of the Civil Guard, but that was after their family moved to Helsinki. He was a little older than me. He left after the war and became a university professor in the United States.

The Betarists were too serious for me. They lived in Viipuri but acted like they were already fighting in Palestine. I hated the military training and wouldn't join even though Tate was furious with me. Instead I joined the Civil Guard, but for me that was more like being in the scouts. It was one of the things lots of boys did, join the Civil Guard youth program. Still, I didn't like the military part of it, the marching and saluting, even if it was not as serious as Betar. I would rather read or play sports. Sometimes Tate had to make me go. He said every generation had its own war to fight, and I needed to be ready for ours. I thought he was a little crazy at the time, but it turned out he was right.

Notes

1. Master of the world, often used like "Oh my God" in English (Yiddish)
2. Nonsense, simpleton (Yiddish)

Figure 20.1. Civil Guard practicing maneuvers in the late 1930s (Mäntyharju Museum)

We Finnish Jews are and remain a loyal part of Finnish culture, the Finnish fatherland, and the people of Finland. We are ready . . . to fight faithfully side by side with our Finnish brethren, to shed our blood and die on behalf of that country we have learned to love and its people, whom we call our own.*

---

*From *Hatikwah*, a Helsinki Jewish Congregation paper from 1935, quoted by Torvinen, Taimi, in *Kadimah*, Otava, Helsinki, 1989, p. 128.

CHAPTER TWENTY

~

Loyalty Parallax

Maksima Island, February, 1940—Salomon Klass was both a Finnish patriot and an ardent Zionist. He served in the Civil Guard in his Helsinki neighborhood as a young man and was promoted to company commander before being forced out in 1933 by rising antisemitism in the ranks. After transferring to a more tolerant unit, where he served until 1935, he left for Palestine to join the Jewish underground resistance to British occupation. He stayed there for four years but when called up to serve in the Finnish Army two months before the start of the Winter War (1939–1940), he returned home immediately to fulfill his military obligation.

Klass eventually rose to the rank of captain. According to one of his older brothers, Henrik: "[Salomon] was truly a legendary soldier. The others called him a fanatic warrior. He wasn't afraid of anything! He always had to be out in front and the rest of the troops behind him."[1]

As company commander in charge of the defense of Maksima Island in Lake Ladoga, the largest lake in Europe, Salomon Klass nearly lost his life. His company, greatly outnumbered by repeated waves of Soviet attackers, had few weapons and limited supplies with which to defend themselves. Writing later about one attack on the island, he recalled:

> . . . the Russians approached the island using tanks as snow plows. They advanced by zigzagging, leaving high snow banks to protect the infantrymen who were following behind. Our artillery had saved a few shells for such an occasion and opened fire when the tanks were halfway to the island. Some of the tanks fell through the shattered ice while others suffered direct hits. That was enough for the rest of them, who turned tail. 'You can relax, we'll help when

you need it,' said the fire direction officer. [Klass then added,] That was the first and last time those boys had ammunition for us.[2]

By the last week of February 1940, the Finnish troops were exhausted and rapidly thinning out. Casualties in some units were running as high as 50 percent. The Soviets continued to put pressure on Maksima Island.

On the 23rd the Russians charged, and now on the 24th I got a much-needed respite. All afternoon I reorganized our defenses. Fallen Russkies were piled up in heaps behind the new line. They looked like snow-covered boulders. I shuttled back and forth between the hill and the command bunker. At one point, one of the boulders suddenly got up, its rifle flew forward, and then the boulder fell once more. How patient those Russkies were, lying there like dead men for the longest time, waiting for the right moment to rejoin their comrades! Perhaps there were many other 'boulders' just waiting to be saved.

[Lieutenant] Salmi was fit for combat again on the 24th and able to resume command. He waited for me at the base of the hill, surrounded by his command group. I crawled down the hill to explain the situation to him and where the lines of defense had been set up. I warned him and the other men about staying out of the enemy's line of fire as they made their way up and over the little ridge ahead of us. Then I crawled back up, assuming that he would follow, but looking backward I saw that Salmi had remained at the base of the hill. Ignoring my own warning, I got up on my knees and waved for him to follow. A Russky, alert to the situation from behind his machine gun, scored a direct hit. A bullet to the head sent me reeling ass over tea kettle so that my feet were in the air and my head in a snow bank.[3]

The bullet entered Klass' skull and exited through his eye, taking his eyeball with it. When the truce ending the Winter War was agreed to on March 13, 1940, Salomon Klass was recuperating in a military hospital. Of the 60 men who had made up Klass' company at the start of the war, only 15 were still alive.

A Differed Kind of Risk

Although Klass was entitled to invalid status and retirement, he chose to return to the military in the autumn of 1940. His duties at first were limited to training recruits and planning defensive positions along the eastern front. When the Continuation War broke out at the end of June 1941, however, Lieutenant Klass took charge of Infantry Regiment 11's First Company which, like Leo Skurnik's unit, was subordinated to Germany's Army Norway. Their job was to push eastward across the border from the village of Suomussalmi into Eastern Karelia.

The Soviets had dug themselves in at the base of a hill along the road leading north from Kiestinki. Klass and his battalion were to prepare the way for a German assault on the hill. Finnish artillery began with coordinated fire lasting about one minute. When the firing stopped, the Soviets, thinking that the German attack was beginning, crawled out and started to advance. Klass and his men sent them scurrying back into their foxholes. This scenario was repeated seven times until the Soviets no longer knew whether to advance or retreat. Then the Germans attacked. Klass writes that by that time the outcome was no longer in doubt.

> After the fighting comes the time for burying the dead and handing out medals. Second Class Iron Crosses were pinned on many lapels. A list of names was sent at the request of the Germans. . . . When I met Colonel Valden,[4] I asked if it was necessary to accept that medal, and he said 'No' right away and promised to try to have my name removed from the list. [Instead] I was awarded a [Finnish] 3rd Class Freedom Cross, of which I already had two.[5]

Later, Klass received a visit to his bunker from the German commanding officer:

> Our share of the fighting was over when Colonel Pilgrim and his staff came to our tent. The colonel was the head of the German division. Lieutenants Oesch and Timonen pretended to be 'sawing wood' in the corner of our tent. Now they jumped up and tried to get the buttons on their jackets straightened out. As for me, there was nothing I could do to cover my threadbare trouser knees. Why Pilgrim came to my tent can probably be explained by the fact that our battalion was generally spoken of as Klass' battalion rather than Paavola's. [Major Paavola] was never seen in the briefings and always sent me instead.
>
> Colonel Pilgrim thanked us for the work we'd done. I asked him to take a seat and offered him coffee and 'plywood.'[6] We talked about this and that until he suddenly asked if I came from one of the Baltic Countries. My way of pronouncing German resembled the German spoken there. I answered that I was born in Finland, learned German in school, and that my parents had, indeed, immigrated from Latgale in Latvia. Picking up steam, I couldn't resist adding that I am Jewish and my mother tongue is actually Yiddish, a language resembling German. Perhaps that is why my German is a little different from normal German. Everyone stared at me. The colonel rose, took my hand, and said: 'Ich . . . I have nothing against you personally although you are a Jew.' At the same time, he straightened his arm in a Nazi salute, said, 'Heil Hitler!,' and walked out of the tent.[7]

In his account of the incident, Klass added drily that Oesch and Timonen suggested that he had taken an unnecessary risk by speaking out in this way.

Zionist Stirrings

Salomon (Shalum) Klass (1907–1985) was the sixth of eight children born to Jerechmiel Klass, a furrier, and Bassja Braine Klass, who appears to have tended the family's store. They moved from Latvia to Helsinki between the arrival of Moses, their first-born, in 1899 and Henrik (Henach), their second, in 1901, and lived there until their deaths in 1964 and 1955 respectively.

Salomon Klass attended school in Helsinki. Like many of the young Jews who would later serve in the Continuation War, Klass got his first military training in the Civil Guard. How was it that he and so many other Jewish schoolboys ended up joining what was essentially a paramilitary organization? The narrator of the television documentary *"David: Stories of Honor and Shame"* asked Samuel Hirschovits, a Jewish veteran of the Continuation War, that question.

> *Narrator:* "Was there a contradiction between the values of Judaism and those of the Civil Guard?"
>
> *Hirschovits:* "Not at all. It never occurred to us. It was more a question of patriotism. That is why we all joined and were even given a certain amount of training. We never thought about war. It was more like a hobby for us."[8]

But another veteran interviewed in the same documentary, John Anker, suggests that not everyone viewed the Civil Guard training as a hobby.

> *Anker:* "Before we entered the Winter War, I had been in the Civil Guard. There was a former teacher named Bolotowsky, the grandfather of the present chairman of the congregation. He invited some of us Jewish boys who had been called up for military service over for a cup of coffee. He also gave us a short speech. 'Boys, now that you are going to war, remember this: Try to learn all you can about warfare. You never know, Palestine might need you one day.'"[9]

Vladimir (Ze'ev) Jabotinsky, the firebrand Revisionist Zionist leader, traveled to Helsinki in May 1939 to speak at the invitation of his old friend, Jonas Jakobson. Jakobson's eldest son, Leo, a group leader in the Revisionist Zionist's *Betar* youth organization, was almost certainly in the audience. Apparently Leo's younger brother, Max, was there, too, because he later recalled the speaker's words and the audience's reaction in his history of the period, *Väkivallan vuodet [Years of Violence]*:

> Jabotinsky began with a merciless analysis of the international situation. "Unavoidably ahead of us is a great-power war," he said. "If it doesn't break out dur-

ing the current year, it will certainly begin in 1940. It will be the most horrible war in the history of the world, spreading from Europe to the other continents."

After this, Jabotinsky transitioned to a consideration of the fate of the Jews. "We don't know," he said, "whether Germany will win this war or not, but even if Germany loses in the end, it will do everything in its power to destroy Europe's Jews. We must prepare for this," he proclaimed. "Palestine's gates must be opened to immigrants, by violent means if necessary. Everywhere our young men must organize militarily and learn to handle weapons in order to defend themselves. There is no time to lose. Act now!"

The speech shocked the listeners. Most of them said, "He's exaggerating, he's crazy, nothing like that can happen."[10]

Max Jakobson would serve Finland as a distinguished diplomat and become a strong candidate to replace U Thant as Secretary General of the United Nations in 1971. Ironically, Finland's highest-ranking Jewish diplomat of all time lost the nomination to Austria's Kurt Waldheim, who was later revealed to have been less than candid about his membership in the paramilitary *Sturmabteilung* (Brown Shirts) and complicity in Nazi atrocities during his service as a wartime officer in the *Wehrmacht* in Greece and the Balkans.

Dual Identity

Salomon Klass had already spent the four years prior to Jabotinsky's speech as a volunteer in Palestine, where he participated in underground operations against the British. That Klass was willing to risk his life for the creation of the State of Israel and then again for the defense of Finland reflects the double loyalty felt by Finland's Jews. They were at one and the same time Finnish Jews and Jewish Finns: Finns when it came to nationality but Jews when it came to their global, historical identity. This dual patriotism defined Klass and many of his contemporaries in much the same way as outsider status had defined the Cantonists who had arrived a century earlier. It also made some Finns—especially those in the State Police hierarchy—suspicious of the loyalty of Jews to the Finnish state.

Theodor Herzl's publication of *Der Judenstaat* in 1896 is generally credited with giving birth to the Zionist movement. The first World Zionist Congress was held in Basel the next year. Russian Zionists began holding their own congresses soon after, at a time when the persecution of Jews in their country was becoming uglier and more violent. In 1903, the viciously antisemitic and totally spurious *Protocols of the Elders of Zion* was published, and the first bloody Kishinev pogrom took place. By the time the Third Russian Zionist Conference was supposed to be held in St. Petersburg in 1906, the 1905 Revolution had made it impossible to get permission for such a gathering in the Russian capital so it was moved to the more provincial setting of Helsinki.

Attending the conference were future Zionist leaders such as Jabotinsky and Yitzhak Gruenbaum. Jews had already achieved citizenship status in most European countries. The Jews of Sweden, Norway and Denmark, for example, had enjoyed citizenship for more than half a century, during which time many of them had focused on assimilating into the surrounding society. Cynics said at the time that a Scandinavian Zionist was someone who was prepared to pay for another Jew's boat ticket to Palestine.

Finnish Jews' Dilemma

The typical experience of Finnish Jews was very different from those of their Scandinavian coreligionists. To begin with, Finnish Jews still lacked basic civil rights in 1906. Whereas the Jews of Copenhagen or Oslo at the start of the twentieth century could confidently (if short-sightedly) plan for the future of their families, their counterparts in Helsinki, Turku and Viipuri knew that they could still be deported at the whim of local officials. Finland's Jews longed for a safe, permanent place they could call home. While they had not given up hope that Finland could become such a place one day, they had to deal with the reality that the government under which they lived was not even prepared to offer them permanent resident status.

In *Taistelu ihmisoikeuksista* [*The Struggle for Human Rights*], Santeri Jacobsson argues that 1905–1906 was a watershed period in the effort to achieve Jewish emancipation in Finland:

> [Before 1905, the priority] was rather a fight for residency rights. Jews were not demanding full citizenship from the authorities. They were initially content to hope anxiously that [Peasant Estate representative Agathon] Meurman's proposal for the mass deportation of Jews would not be implemented in one form or another.
>
> 1905 provided the Jewish question with different content. Finland was in the thrall of the Russian Revolution, which shook up the ostensibly calm society. The [Finnish] people . . . rose up against Russian oppression and their own reactionaries. Attempts were made to reorganize internal conditions so that the common people would be able to participate in governing. Large groups demanded similar voting rights for men and women in local and national elections, a single-body parliament in place of the four-estate Diet, an eight-hour work day, and sovereign power for the parliament . . .
>
> The general excitement also had an emboldening effect on the Jews. . . . They decided to organize open public meetings around the country to explain

their unjust plight. . . . The goal was to demand complete citizenship rights for those Jews who were born in [Finland] or had lived there for a long time. In this way, the Jewish question entered a new phase, the road to emancipation, in the public arena.[11]

Not all Jews shared Jacobsson's enthusiasm for the struggle for citizenship. Some feared the reaction of both the Finnish public and the Russian state. Jews were a tiny minority, and gradualists worried that activism would lead not to emancipation but to renewed oppression.

Jacobsson's campaign was launched at the same time as Zionism was coming to the attention of the authorities in Finland. Although Zionism was not focused on changing local conditions, the authorities nevertheless saw it as a potential threat. According to Jewish Studies scholar Simo Muir:

[Russian Zionism at the time of the 1906 congress was] a kind of moderate, centrist Zionism, later mocked by revisionists as 'drawing-room Zionism.' Let's live comfortably and provide some financial support and send a few youngsters [to Palestine], so that someone does something there. Contributions were made. Scholem Bolotowsky said that most [Finnish Jews] were in this 'general Zionism' stream, moderate and traditional.

The '06 Helsinki program was about 'Gegenwartsarbeit,' what is to be done here and now, both in Palestine and in the Diaspora. In Russia, of course, Zionism was driven completely underground after the revolution, but in many of the Baltic countries, Poland and others, there were lots of organizations, lots was done. Hebrew was studied, literary societies were formed, and international Zionist informational activities were launched. In Helsinki, of course, the Jewish scouts [Riddargossarna, later Kefir] and sports club Stjärna [later Makkabi] were largely Zionist organizations.

Both the Viipuri and Turku congregations founded leftist Zeire Zion organizations. Though the Helsinki Zionist organization, Agudas Zion, chose to follow centrist General Zionism, in the 1920s all three joined together to form a Central Organization of Jewish Zionists, which published a monthly bulletin called Zionistiska Månadsbulletin.[12]

Despite the leftist Zionism of the Viipuri and Turku congregations, those communities included many upward-striving families and small business owners who tended to espouse conservative social and political values. This conservatism was reinforced by the strongly Orthodox nature of religious practice in the country's synagogues.

Funds were collected in Finland for Zionist causes from at least 1906. Zionist youth organizations such as Turku's Zeire Zion and Kadima, Helsinki's Hatchijo, Kadima and Keren Kajemet le'Israel, and Viipuri's Agudas Zion, Zeire

Zion and Ha-zair Ha-zioni were founded in the decades following the 1906 conference, accompanied by WIZO (Women's International Zionist Organization) branches in all three congregations. The staunchly Revisionist federation *Hazohar* took root in Helsinki (1934) and Viipuri (1937).

Special attention was paid to the indoctrination of Jewish youth. Agricultural training was organized to prepare young people for work on *kibbutzim* in Palestine. Young Jews were also encouraged to attend summer camps run by the *Skandinaviska Judiska Ungdomsförening* (Scandinavian Jewish Youth Association), where they could learn more about Zionism and perhaps also find suitable mates.

The Promise

During the same time as antisemitic literature, imported from both East and West, was portraying the typical Jew as effete, unwilling to dirty his hands, interested only in money and yet, contradictorily, an agent of international socialism, young Finnish Jews were training in the Civil Guard, winning medals in weightlifting and boxing competitions, and even, as in the case of Salomon Klass, joining the underground resistance movement in Palestine. Some of these young men undoubtedly drew inspiration from their grandfathers, who, despite having been conscripted as children against their will, were still proud of having served in the czar's army. Others likely saw themselves as young pioneers in a Zionist movement that could establish a safe haven for their families and future generations.

Revisionist Zionism found itself aligned against international socialist tendencies in the Jewish diaspora at the same time as Finland was facing a growing threat from its communist neighbor, the U.S.S.R. The following comment appeared in the 1934 Helsinki Revisionist Zionist publication *Hazohar*:

> . . . we know that every healthy nation strives to rely on its own powers, we know that love for the fatherland and a sense of mutual belonging are the most important components of a people's iron will, and this knowledge makes us powerful in our belief in the future. We Revisionists attempt to awaken patriotism because it is the only thing that brings our work to life. We do not accept internationalist movements; rather, we believe blindly in our people's mission . . .[13]

The fatherland they were writing about was Israel, but it could just as well have referred to Finland. In preparing for the struggle to liberate Palestine, these young Finnish revisionists were also preparing to defend Finland. Just as their dedication to the armed struggle to drive the British out of Palestine was understood to be their duty as Jews, taking up arms in defense of the fatherland played an unquestioned role in their responsibility as Finns.

Finnish Labor Zionists believed in the importance of moving to Palestine but not primarily to engage in armed resistance. They focused on working the land, founding settlements, and resuscitating Hebrew as the spoken language of the Jewish people. They were more willing than the Revisionists to negotiate their way into statehood. Consequently, the young men in this movement were less likely to belong to the Civil Guard or focus on their potential readiness for combat. Their obligation to defend their country, however, was the same as that of any other Finnish citizen, and they performed their military service in the same way as other young men their age.

When military training turned into actual warfare in 1939, these young Jews—whether Revisionist, Labor Zionist or assimilationist—had the additional burden, laid heavily upon them by previous generations, of proving to the rest of the population that they were just as patriotic and worthy of citizenship status as other Finns. Having campaigned for citizenship for so long, Jews wanted to show that the country's trust in them had been well-placed. According to historian Hannu Rautkallio:

> The Winter War was the Finnish Jews' 'war of independence,' in which they finally redeemed their Finnishness. The Winter War was the culmination of their assimilation, and it carried a high price when calculated by the number of Jewish men who fell in the war.[14]

According to *Suomen juutalaiset sotilaat ja lotat Suomen sodissa 1939–1945* [Finnish Jewish Soldiers and Lottas in the 1939–1945 Wars], a total of 327 Jewish men (242 soldiers, 52 non-commissioned officers, 18 commissioned officers, 15 medical officers) and 21 members of the Women's Auxiliary served in the Winter, Continuation and Lapland Wars. Twenty-three of them fell in the line of duty, fifteen in the Winter War and eight in the Continuation War. The casualties suffered by the Jewish population represented the highest *per capita* loss of all religious denominations and minorities in Finnish society.

These deaths, depriving a tiny community of many of its most vigorous young people, constituted a high price for Finland's Jews to pay. It was a price already foreseen in an 1885 appeal read to the Clerical Estate on the Jews' behalf by Dr. William Gabriel Lagus, a lawyer and historian. In their letter to the lawmakers, the Jews claimed that their descendants, if granted the right to remain in Finland, would become staunch defenders of their country.

For us, the fathers of families who arrived here from the Empire about 30 years ago, it no longer matters how you decide our fate as most of us have arrived at the edge of our graves, and the end of our days is approaching. But consider, Noble Gentlemen, that we also have children, and parental hearts beat warmly in our chests. And how painful will the knowledge be—when the moment comes to bid farewell to our loved ones—that the same fate, the same scorn that we have had to endure, will also be our children's share. . . . our children were born and raised here and have thus adopted this country's ways and customs and learned to love it even to the extent that they have almost completely forgotten the ways and customs of their own faith. We are fully convinced that if our appeal is listened to, our children and descendants, having realized that Finland has been zealous in pursuit of their best interests and motivated by no more than this realization, will fulfill their duty as diligent and faithful citizens.[15]

When the war finally came, the grandchildren of those who made this appeal remembered and stood firmly behind the commitment their forefathers had made on their behalf. There was another explanation, too, for the readiness of Finland's Jews to take up arms in defense of their country. With German troops moving through the cities where Finland's Jews were living, the protection provided by the Finnish government for all its citizens, regardless of religion or ethnic background, was the Jewish community's only guarantor of survival. Flight or refusal to serve by individual Jews would have cast a shameful reflection on the honor and loyalty of the entire Jewish community and potentially put the life of every Jew in Finland in danger.

Mahal

After the three wars, Finland's Jews were rightfully proud of their contribution and their country. Not one of Finland's Jewish citizens ended up in Nazi concentration or death camps. Of all continental Europe's combatant countries, no other could make a similar claim. But for many of Finland's Jews, the struggle had not ended with the end of World War Two. Now it was Palestine, not Finland, which needed their help.

Many volunteers who participated in the post-WWII struggle for the liberation of Palestine were *mahal*, members of the diaspora who came from abroad to join the fight. Twenty-eight *mahal* were Finnish Jews, many of whom had fought in the Winter and Continuation Wars. They departed Finland together in 1947 under the pretext of attending an agricultural camp in Sweden. Instead, they would undergo training under the guidance of two seasoned *Haganah* instructors before traveling via Italy and then slipping surreptitiously into Haifa's harbor on the SS *Argentina*. They were later joined by six more Finnish Jews, who arrived via other routes. Of the 34 volunteers, five were women. By percentage of their country's Jewish population, there were more Finns in the struggle to create a Jewish state than volunteers from any other nation.

One soldier who might have been expected to be among them was missing: Salomon Klass. He had more than fulfilled his responsibility as a Zionist as well as redeemed his share of the promise to defend Finland made by the men of the Jewish community in 1885 on behalf of their sons and grandsons. He had fought bravely, won numerous honors, been seriously wounded, and returned to fight again. But after years in the Civil Guard, a four-year stint in Palestine prior to WWII, and service in all three of Finland's wars between 1939 and 1945, he had had his fill of the military and enough of Finland, too.

Klass emigrated to Sweden, where he worked in the fur trade. Having spent most of his adult life at war or preparing for it, Klass finally walked away. Idealism and eagerness to sacrifice, after all, are traits more likely to be found in young men than in those in their forties who have been severely wounded and seen their comrades killed in battle. He had been a true war hero and a source of pride to the Jewish community. Now it was time to get on with his life.

Notes

1. Recorded interview of Henrik Klass by Hannu Rautkallio, January 2, 1989.

2. Quoted by Lokki, Jouni from the war diary of Salomon Klass in *Synopsis: Sotasankari Salomon Klass*, p. 9 (translated from the Finnish by the author).

3. *Ibid.*, p.10

4. Should be "Walden,"

5. *Ibid.*, p. 14.

6. Dry crisp bread

7. Klass, Salomon,*Minnen från Vinterkriget och Fortsättningskriget 1939–1945*, unpublished memoir, p. 14–15.

8. *Daavid: Stories of Honor and Shame*, documentary film by Taru Mäkelä, ForRealProductions in cooperation with the Finnish Broadcasting Company's Channel 2, 1997.

9. *Ibid.*

10. Jakobson, Max, *op. cit.*, p. 188.

11. Jacobsson, Santeri, *op. cit.*, p. 333.

12. Muir, Simo, interviewed by the author, March 14, 2012.

13. *Hazohar*, 1934.

14. Rautkallio, Hannu, *Suomen juutalaisten aseveljeys*, Tammi, Helsinki, 1989, p. 53.

15. Jacobsson, Santeri, *op. cit.*, p. 226.

Figure 21.1. **Nursing students in Viipuri before the Winter War (Maria Juntura's collection)**

My sister said that once when she was at Aulanko, a German soldier came up to her with tears in his eyes and said that he was opposed to all the horrible things that the Nazis were doing to the Jews. He could see that my sister was a Jew. That all German weren't Nazis, and that they, too, were unable to do anything about the situation.

In general, we weren't afraid of them. I remember walking one time with my father down the Esplanade, and Germans came walking up the other way, and we sang: *"Es geht alles vorüber, es geht alles vorbei, erst geht der Führer und dann die Partei"* [Everything is transient, everything comes to an end, first will go the Führer and then the Party]. They looked at us in amazement but didn't say anything.

Hanna Eckert*

*From an interview (German corrected) in Paju, Imbi, *Suomenlahden sisaret*, Like, Helsinki, 2011, p. 205 and Muir, Simo, *Ei enää kirjeitä Puolasta*, Tammi, 2016, p. 162.

CHAPTER TWENTY-ONE

~

Rachel Makes a Decision

Turku, 1937—"Are you certain you want to be a nurse? You know nurses aren't allowed to marry. What sense does it make to spend years studying so hard and then give it all up as soon as you find a husband?"

"I know, Mother, I know," says Rachel, "but I want to do something important."

"Don't you think what your father does is important? People need good clothes, you know. And what about me? Isn't it important to raise a family?"

"Please, Mother, that's not what I meant. I do think what you and Father do is important, but the way the world is right now, I don't know whether I would even want to raise a family. What kind of a future is there for a Jewish child if a Hitler or a Stalin takes over Finland? Then our only hope will be Palestine. I can help if I'm a nurse. Even if there is no fighting, there will be plenty of work, building a new and better society. And there won't be any stupid rules like the one about nurses not being able to marry. You know as well as I do that the only reason they don't want nurses to get married is so they can be made to work long hours for low wages and won't take time off to have babies."

"Oh! How you talk sometimes! This isn't Germany or Russia. As far as I know, Hitler and Stalin have no interest in Turku. There are lots of things you can do here besides being a nurse. You know how hard your father has worked so that you and your sister can have a business to take over when you are ready. You've been helping in the shop since you were little, and you know how things are done. It would please him so much to know that you wanted to carry on the business."

Rachel has had this conversation with her mother, in one form or another, many times, and she knows where it is heading.

"And stop that nonsense about not wanting a family. Of course you do. You are beautiful and smart, and you know there are several handsome young men in the congregation who are interested in you, but you won't even give them a chance. I don't know why you are so stubborn."

"I'm not being stubborn. I just don't want to marry someone I don't love."

Rachel's mother looks lovingly at her daughter. They are folding sheets that have just come out of the mangle and smell as fresh and soft as a summer meadow. "You know, you can learn to love someone, Rachele. Your Grandmother Zivia had never even seen your grandfather before they married, and they lived happily together for more than 40 years. I knew your father before we married, of course, but I don't think I really understood what it was to be in love with him until you were born. You young people have such romantic notions. Marriage is about so much more than love. It's about security, family and preserving tradition. Love is just part of it."

"Maybe so," Rachel admits, "but it's the most important part to me. I don't want to find myself in bed with someone I find repulsive."

"Don't talk like that! You make it sound so vulgar. I'm not trying to force you to do something against your will, but you have to be realistic if you want to have any kind of life at all. Look at Tante[1] Bluma, you don't want to end up like her, living alone your whole life."

Rachel rolls her eyes. "Tante Bluma, always Tante Bluma. You make it sound like the only alternatives are marrying someone you don't love or never marrying at all. No thank you! I'm going to find someone I can love and who loves me, too. If that can't happen here, I'll go to Palestine or the ends of the Earth to find him."

For all her apparent self-assurance, Rachel is worried. Try as she might, she has not been able to get over her infatuation with David. He hasn't written more than a couple of times. What if she never finds someone to take his place in her heart? That no longer seems like such an unlikely possibility. Then being a nurse, even if it means never marrying, would be better than marrying just to please her parents and the congregation.

Chava

Rachel and Chava are sitting in the Café Hansa, drinking strong coffee with lots of sugar and pouring out their hearts to each other as they regularly do on Thursdays after school. Chava lights up a Twenty Gold, glancing all the time around the room to make sure no acquaintances of her parents are

among the cafe's patrons. The subterranean meeting place for Turku's artists and bohemians rarely attracts any of their families' bourgeois friends or
acquaintances, making it easier for Rachel and Chava to indulge themselves
and share secrets.

They have been best friends for as long as either can remember. As their
final year of school ticks toward matriculation exams and decisions that
will impact on the rest of their lives, they have drawn even closer together.
Rachel mentions her recent discussion with her mother and her frustration
with the expectations her parents have for her. She knows, however, that
her problems pale in comparison with Chava's. Her friend is deeply in love
with a businessman from Tampere who is a dozen years older. Not only that,
he is a divorcé. And not only that, he is a goy.[2] Her parents know nothing of
the relationship and will surely never approve. Chava is not as close to her
parents as Rachel is to hers, but she dreads the scandal and certain break with
her family that will follow. She has two younger sisters and suspects they will
also turn their backs on her as soon as her parents do. Her plan is to finish
school before announcing that she is leaving for Tampere.

Rachel tries to be supportive, but she is deeply suspicious of Chava's
lover. She has only met him once. He is certainly handsome and seems
nice enough, but she senses something unsettled about him, something
not entirely trustworthy. She doesn't doubt that Chava loves him, but her
friend is impetuous and doesn't always think things through before acting.
"If I said something like that to Chava," she thinks, "I would sound exactly
like her mother," and so she keeps her reservations to herself. Anyway, she
knows that Chava has made her decision, and nothing Rachel says is likely
to change her mind.

Rachel, on the other hand, is far from sure about her own future. She has
been thinking about nursing school and has come up with a plan she now
haltingly reveals to her friend. She will apply to the Surgical Hospital Nursing School in Helsinki. Rachel's idea is to explain to her parents that they
have a program for Swedish-speaking students and offer the opportunity to
specialize in surgery, which interests her. When not required to sleep in the
school's dormitory, she could stay with her Tante Bluma, who lives alone in
a large apartment in the center of town.

Chava learns back in her chair, puffs theatrically on her cigarette, sweeps
her long auburn hair over her left shoulder with her free hand, and whispers
conspiratorially across the table, "This wouldn't have anything to do with
the possibility of seeing David more often, would it?"

"Oh, how could you think that?" Rachel sputters, but she realizes that her
reaction has only confirmed Chava's suspicion. "Well, maybe a little," she

shyly admits. She takes a sip of cold coffee. "But I'm not naive. I know I don't mean anything to him, and he probably has lots of other girlfriends. At least I will be able to find out for certain that there is no hope, and maybe then I can get over him once and for all. I just hate going on like this, thinking I'm in love with someone I hardly know and never see. It's almost as bad . . ."

". . . as bad as being in love with a divorced *goy?*" finishes Chava with a chuckle. "Not on your life!"

Rachel can't help laughing. She has to admit that her friend's situation is much worse than hers, but that isn't much help. She feels the way she feels, and she can no more put herself in Chava's shoes than she can feel the hunger of the starving Armenians when her parents insist she finish everything on her plate and be thankful she isn't one of them.

Chava has always been popular with the boys, and that has given her a boldness and self-assurance Rachel lacks. Rachel is popular, too, in a quiet and unobtrusive way, but she has always measured herself against the most popular and self-confident girls in school and found herself lacking. At the same time, she has always been very demanding—"picky," her mother calls it—about boys, and since meeting David she has turned away even the most innocent overtures from schoolmates or young men in the congregation. During the past year, Benjamin's letters have become increasingly open about his feelings for Rachel. If only David felt for her the way Benjamin says he does! But he doesn't, and although Benjamin's letters are in some way reassuring to Rachel, she has no romantic feelings for him.

Rachel has to admit that she can't even be sure that moving to Helsinki will mean that she will see David more often. He did come to that choir concert in Helsinki the previous winter and stayed to talk with her at the reception afterwards. He was chatty and friendly, but he never came to see her in Turku after that. In the year since camp, that was the only time they met. What makes her think living in the same city will make a difference? She isn't the kind of girl to go chasing after a boy. She will probably be even more miserable in Helsinki than she has been in Turku, but she feels she has to find out. Anyway, the nursing school in Helsinki is the best in the country. What does she have to lose?

Looming Threat

Between the end of the 1936 SJUF camp at Vidablick and Rachel's graduation from Åbo *Svenska Flicklyceum*, Turku's only Swedish-speaking high school for girls, the world had become a darker place. Stalin had launched what would come to be known as the Great Terror in August 1936 by putting numerous generals and secret police officers on trial. Among the first to be condemned and executed were former members of the first Soviet Politburo Lev Kamenev (born Rozenfeld) and Grigory Zinoviev (born Hirsch Apfelbaum), both Jews. Leon Trotsky (born Lev Davidovitsch Bronstein), also a Jew, avoided the show trials (but not assassination) because he was abroad in exile.

While Stalin's purge of Soviet leadership and the army high command eliminated (among others) many Jews in prominent positions, Hitler was claiming that Bolshevism's goal was "to replace mankind's leadership strata with Jews," Jews found themselves targeted on both sides of the dictatorial divide with no one to take their side. Four months after the March 1938 Anschluss created a flood of desperate Jewish refugees from Austria, President Roosevelt convened an international conference in Évian-les-Bains, France to discuss the situation. Of the 32 nations in attendance, only the Dominican Republic proved willing to increase substantially the number of Jewish refugees it would accept,[3] thus condemning many of those attempting to flee Nazi terror to eventual extermination.

Finland, paradoxically, was emerging at the same time from one of the most threatening and chaotic periods in its history into a considerably more stable one. While Stalin and Hitler were solidifying brutal one-party rule in the territories they controlled, Finland was forcefully rejecting dangerous radicalization and reconfirming its commitment to democracy and the rule of law. If either the Communist Party or Lapua Movement had been allowed to gain a firm foothold in Finland, Rachel would have had much more pressing matters to worry about than her studies and her love life (or lack thereof). It will not be long, to cite just one terrible example, before the entire Jewish community of neighboring Estonia will be completely wiped out. First some 10 percent of its members are deported to Siberia after the Russians take over, then all those who are unable to flee before the Germans arrive are murdered by Nazi killing squads and their Estonian collaborators. If Rachel had been born just 175 kilometers to the Southeast, in Tallinn instead of Turku, her fate would be the same.

Notes

1. Aunt (Yiddish)
2. Gentile
3. President Rafael Trujillo saw the move as a way to increase the immigration of white people to his country.

Figure 22.1. August 19, 1938, the *SS Ariadne* is turned away from Helsinki Harbor with 56 Austrian Jewish refugees aboard (Lehtikuva Photo Service)

One time *Hauptsturmführer* Eggers asked me how many Jews are there in Finland.

I said there were close to 2,000.

Eggers responded: "So few! Are they still living?"

An *Obersturmführer* who was present chimed in: "Not, in any case, for much longer!"

*Olavi Viherluoto**

*Finnish State Police Passport Inspector Olavi Viherluoto in his report on his official December 1–12, 1941 visit to Estonia as reported in Silvennoinen, Oula, *Salaiset aseveljet*, Otava, 2008, pp. 237–238.

CHAPTER TWENTY-TWO

~

David and the Refugee Situation

Helsinki, August 12, 1938—"Dudel, Dudel, get up!"

Something's the matter. Has her boyfriend suddenly shown up? David tries to remember what happened the night before. He was at the Rio, dancing and having a good time. Did a young woman he met there take him back to her place? Which one was she? And why is she calling him by his family nickname? She is shaking him now, and her pleading becomes more urgent.

"Wake up! Fabu[1] Stiller called. They need you at the harbor."

David rolls over, forces himself to open his eyes, and realizes he is in his own bed. He has been dreaming, and it is his mother who is shaking him.

"A boat is coming with Jews from Austria. He needs boys from *Kefir*[2] to help with the baggage."

Mumbling reflexively, "Mama, let me sleep a little more," David pushes aside the covers and begins to get up. His head aches and his mouth is dry, but he knows that if Farbror[3] Stiller has said "Come!" he has to get going.

Abraham Stiller's authority comes not from money (although he is a wealthy man), nor from temporal power, but from the respect accorded a man of principle. He does not cut an imposing figure. In fact, he is known for his careless way of dressing in rumpled suits, quite the opposite of his dandyish younger brother Moses, who is, by this time, deceased. The brothers differed in many ways. Moses moved to Stockholm, changed his name to Mauritz, distanced himself from his Jewish roots, became a film director, discovered a 17-year-old drama school student named Greta Gustafsson (known later by her stage name: Garbo), apparently lived with her for a while, moved to Los Angeles for three years, made three unsuccessful films, and returned to Stockholm, where he died in 1928. Abraham, on the other hand, is a successful businessman—although it is his wife, Vera, who is mostly responsible for the success of their clothing business—and Orthodox Jew who has dedicated his life to Zionism and helping others. In addition to serving as liaison between the Finnish authorities and the country's Jews, he helps the Jewish community establish useful contacts abroad.

By the summer of 1938, Stiller has already been active for some time in marshalling support for the growing number of Jewish refugees arriving from Central Europe, but the eight days beginning August 12th will severely test the limits of his ability to provide protection for Jews seeking temporary asylum in Finland.

David arrives, a little the worse for wear, at the Helsinki Harbor shortly after 10 a.m. If everything had gone according to plan, the young men from Kefir would already have begun loading the refugees' baggage onto trucks for delivery, first to the Jewish School, and then on to the homes of the families with whom they would be staying. Louis Levinsky, Jussi Kersch and Harry Matsoff are already standing near the ship, ready to help, and travelers are descending the gangway to the dock, but there seems to be a problem with respect to the Jewish passengers.

"It's unbelievable," Jussi tells David. "All the Jews have been sent back onto the ship by passport control. Nobody seems to know what is happening. We've been here for an hour, and none of the Jews have been allowed off the ship."

The scene is chaotic. On the deck of the SS *Ariadne*, men and women cry out for help to the crowd below. Abraham Stiller sends an urgent message to Sylvi-Kyllikki Kilpi, an influential Social Democrat and Member of Parliament, who hurries to the harbor and boards the ship. In the previous year's election, the Social Democrats won enough seats to be included in a governing coalition for the first time in a decade. Kilpi argues forcefully with the police for the refugees to be allowed to disembark but to no avail.

Nothing more happens that day, and the frustrated young men return home in the afternoon, leaving the negotiations to Stiller and Kilpi. In David's home that evening, the mood at the *shabbos* dinner table is somber. The prayers remind the family that God looks after His people, creating for them the fruit of the vine and bringing forth bread from the earth, but this evening in the forefront of everyone's mind is fear that the refugees on the *Ariadne* will be forced to return to Stettin to face persecution or worse.

Once the main course has been consumed and David's mother has gone to the kitchen to fetch the cake, David addresses his father. "I have been thinking about making *Aliyah*," he says, "and joining the *Haganah*. It's criminal what is happening to our people, and no one will stop it. The only answer is for us to have a homeland of our own. It is my duty to go."

His father replies calmly, "I don't disagree with you, Son, but you are still young, and you have your studies to complete. You will be able to do much more for our people as an engineer than as a farmer or fighter in the underground. There are plenty of others who will be ready to fight when the time comes. I am proud that you feel this way, but you need to be rational, not emotional. For now, the best thing is to concentrate on your studies."

"But Father, what if it were us on that boat? What if Zayde had ended up in Vienna instead of Helsinki? Would there be anyone to stand up for us?"

"Let Fabu Stiller take care of this for now," his father insists, glancing toward the kitchen. "There will be plenty of time for making *Aliyah* later in your life. Let that be the end of it. I don't want you upsetting your mother."

Two days later, the young men have been called back to the harbor early in the morning. "Look!" shouts Dado Wardi, "they're coming!" This time, to everyone's relief, the refugees are allowed on shore. David notices that they are well-dressed and well-mannered although emotionally drained by their recent experience. The worst is over, they have been granted temporary refugee status, contingent upon the Jewish community taking responsibility for their upkeep. Seven of them are sent to Turku, nine to Viipuri, and almost 50 are lodged in Helsinki.

David had originally been annoyed at being dragged out of bed on a Sunday morning, but he realizes how desperate these people are and has been touched by their plight. They have left their homes, their businesses and the world they know in order to escape Nazi persecution. If only Palestine could be turned into a Jewish homeland, he thinks, people like this wouldn't have to beg for entry into a country that doesn't really want them.

Boys Will Be Boys

The next Wednesday, about an hour after the evening meal, David's 13-year-old brother Rafael, whom everyone calls Rafu, cautiously pushes open the door to David's room. David can tell that Rafu has something on his mind, but he waits patiently until the younger boy is ready to begin. After the *Ariadne* incident, Rafu had asked David and their father why the Jewish passengers had not been allowed to disembark. David could tell that the younger boy was not satisfied with their explanation. As an older brother, he had not done a very good job of putting Rafu's mind at ease.

Now Rafu has a confession to make. "Promise you won't tell anyone?" David nods. "Last night, two of my friends and I took an air rifle and shot out some windows in the German School. No one knows who was responsible, but I guess the first ones they suspect will be us boys from the Jewish

School. I'm pretty sure I'm going to get called into Schlüter's office tomorrow, and I'll get at least a month's detention if he finds out I was one of the ones who did it."

The Jewish School is only a couple of blocks away from the German School, and there have been occasional dust-ups between boys from the two schools. Rafu is certainly right that the older Jewish boys will be the first ones suspected of committing the vandalism.

David wants to smile, but he knows the situation calls for him to remain serious. This is exactly the kind of thing he would have wanted to do at that age but never dared because he was so careful about maintaining his reputation.

"You know that something like that can't be kept a secret for long," David says. "One of your friends will brag about it, and the word will get around in no time at all. I'm glad you told me and not someone else."

David can see that the younger boy is having a hard time maintaining his composure. Rafu is impulsive, prone to acting first and worrying about the consequences later. Now the realization that he will have to answer for his actions is setting in. David can imagine that his greatest fear is what will happen when their father finds out.

"Look, Rafu, when you do something like that, you have to be prepared to take your medicine. If you know that you are going to be found out anyway, the best thing to do is make the first move. Tell Faija⁴ yourself before he hears it from someone else. He'll be mad, of course, but he'll respect you for telling him. He understands that feelings are running pretty high right now. You can expect to be punished, but it will be worse if he finds out from the school.

"As for the Principal," he continues, "wait until he calls you in. Tell him you know it's about the windows in the German School and that you were one of the ones who did it. You don't have to tell him who the others were, even if he says you do. Just say that you did it and are willing to accept your punishment. I know that sounds harsh, but if you think about it, that's your best choice."

"That's pretty much what I thought you'd say," says Rafu. Although he hangs his head dejectedly, he seems relieved to hear it. "I really understand why you want to go to Palestine, though. It is terrible to see everything that is happening and not be able to do anything about it."

"Yeah," responds David, "but breaking windows in the German School is only going to convince people that Jewish boys are troublemakers. The IKL will use it as another argument to show that Jews can't be trusted. Sometimes actions can end up having consequences that are the opposite of what you are trying to accomplish."

They talk for a while longer, then David hugs his younger brother, and Rafu returns to his own room. If Rafu feels better after talking with his brother, the conversation has the opposite effect on David. His world is becoming more complicated and uncomfortable all the time. He had wanted to concentrate on his studies and social life, but the political situation, both domestic and global, keeps intruding in ways that are difficult to ignore.

Ariadne Redux

One week after David was first called to the harbor, the SS *Ariadne* returns. This time David has been warned in advance and goes to bed early the night before. He need not have bothered. Interior Minister (later President) Urho Kekkonen has issued orders not to let any of the 56 Jewish passengers off the ship. Rony Smolar, in his biography of Abraham Stiller, describes the scene David witnessed that morning:

> Among the refugees were those who had obtained transit permits and tickets for passage from Sweden to the United States. They only wanted to travel via Finland because of shipping line connections. Nevertheless, they were not allowed to disembark. Official Finland was not in the least interested in where the Jewish travelers would end up.
>
> The turning away of families with children, the elderly, and the sick created dramatic incidents as several passengers threw themselves overboard in a hopeless attempt to avoid deportation, and one slashed his wrists. With great expectations, refugees who had arrived earlier came to the harbor to greet relatives and acquaintances. Many became hysterical at dockside. Numerous passersby stopped and criticized the harbor officials for their heartlessness.[5]

This time attempts to reverse the officials' decision fall on deaf ears. Smolar writes that Kekkonen had not wanted to create "a Jewish Question" for his country. The government had decided a few days earlier that Austrian travelers could no longer enter Finland without a visa, and none of the Jews on board had one. As the S/S *Ariadne* turns away from Helsinki's harbor and sails past the Porkkala Peninsula, three of its 56 Jewish passengers hurl themselves into the sea and drown rather than return to Stettin.

David is deeply shaken by the *Ariadne* affair. He sees it as further evidence that the Jews in Finland, even those like him who have been born and raised in the country and enjoyed citizenship almost their entire lives, cannot be sure that the country will provide them with the same protection it gives its other citizens. Although all the government explanations are about official processes, he suspects that antisemitism is at the root of it all.

Another Voyage of the Damned

The *Ariadne* incident is followed nine months later by the better-known case of the MS *St Louis*, a German ocean liner that sets sail for Cuba May 13, 1939 from Hamburg with 937 Jewish refugees on board. It reaches Havana on May 27 but is denied access to the docking area. Only the 22 passengers who have valid Cuban visas are allowed to disembark. The ship then leaves Havana, traveling slowly up the U.S. coast from Florida with the remaining 915 Jews on board while Jewish advocates plead first with President Roosevelt to allow the passengers to enter the United States and then with Canada's Prime Minister Mackenzie to provide asylum in that country. Both refuse, and the *St. Louis* returns to Europe, where it docks in Antwerp, Belgium. Three hundred of the Jewish passengers are granted entry into the U.K., but the remaining 619 end up in Belgium, France and the Netherlands, all countries that are invaded and occupied by the Nazis the following year.

The voyage of the St. Louis is covered widely in the world's press. Whether President Roosevelt does not want to antagonize anti-immigration voters as the election for his third term approaches, or whether he is afraid that the struggle against fascism will be harder to sell to the American people if it is seen as primarily about the fate of Europe's Jews, he and his government turn their backs on the refugees. The justification given by the Finnish officials who reject the Ariadne's passengers is different. The country had taken in as many as 30,000 refugees from the Karelian and Ingrian regions of the Soviet Union after the anti-Bolshevik uprisings of the early 1920s. It is argued that those cultural and linguistic kin of the Finns have a greater call on the country's generosity than the coming flood of Jewish refugees from Central Europe. The extent to which this is just a rationalization and antisemitism is the real reason for both the MS St. Louis and the SS Ariadne being turned away is as difficult to prove as it is to refute.

Notes

1. Uncle (term of respect and endearment, truncated form of Farbror or Father's brother)
2. The Helsinki Jewish Boy Scout Troop
3. Uncle (Swedish)
4. "Dad" (slang, Swedish)
5. Smolar, Rony, *Setä Stiller*, Tammi, Helsinki, 2003, pp. 101–2.

Figure 23.1. Abraham Tokazier (nearest the camera) finishes "fourth" in the Helsinki Olympic Stadium's inaugural track meet (Finland's Jewish Archives)

"Listen Thune," Jary asked in a disbelieving voice, "what did that announcement say? I must have heard wrong."

Thune and Lindemark exchanged glances again. Both remained silent, the speechless moment would not end, the situation was vexing in the extreme.

The silence pained Thune.

"No Jogi," he said softly. "You heard right. They put Salomon in fourth place."

"They can't do that," said Jogi in a weak voice. "Shlomo won. Everyone saw it. It was announced when they crossed the finish line. The others aren't placed right, either. Ruikka crossed the line ahead of Marttinen. Everyone saw that, too."

"I'm terribly sorry," Thune said.

He had the unpleasant feeling that he had experienced all this before and that the whole conversation, too, was already familiar. He shrugged the unpleasantness from his shoulders and added optimistically, "It will certainly be corrected."

*Kjell Westö**

Kangastus 38, Otava, Helsinki, 2013, p. 113.

~

CHAPTER TWENTY-THREE

Benjamin Becomes
the Man of the House

Viipuri, 1934—It has been raining off and on for three days, and a North wind chills the small, dark cluster of mourners slowly wending their way back from the cemetery in Ristimäki toward Sammonkatu. Although it is August, the powerful gusts that propel the horizontal rain can make it seem like November. A carriage has been hired for Zipora, Feige and the two little ones, but Mirele and Benjamin walk with the handful of descendants of Cantonists and other immigrants from the Pale who have accompanied Mendel on his final journey.

Although Mendel is only 46 when he suffers his fatal aneurysm, his life is barely eight years shorter than that of the average Finnish male of his day. This is little consolation to Zipora, who still has two small children to care for and no income of her own. Mendel's burial insurance covers the cost of a modest funeral, but where will she find the money for all the rest? Mendel always handled the family's finances. Zipora has no idea whether her husband had either savings or debts. She fears she will never be capable of managing the family's finances by herself, but she knows there is no choice. She must find a way.

The clatter of the horse's hooves and the jolting of the carriage make it hard for her to focus her thoughts, but the feeling of insecurity persists. Zipora's relationship with her husband had occasionally been difficult. Her own parents had never seemed to argue or hardly even disagree about anything, leaving her ill-equipped to deal with the normal misunderstandings and conflicts that occasionally arose over matters large or small. She eventually learned to live with a temperamental husband, she realizes, but nothing has prepared her for living without him.

At the apartment, she makes sure everything is in place before the members of the *Chevra Kadisha* (burial society) arrive, bearing hard-boiled eggs, pots of lentil stew and platters of sweets and fruit. Mendel did not have many friends, but there will be one or two of his colleagues from the hat factory, and the Lifsons will almost certainly make a courtesy call at some point. Several of the neighbors can be expected to stop by and perhaps also one or two of the men with whom Mendel played chess at *Ahdus* on Sunday afternoons.

By the time the required seven days of mourning have passed, Zipora cannot wait to get out of the oppressive apartment. The familiar bustle of the *Punaisenlähteentori* market reassures her that life goes on. Helping the children cope with their father's death also distracts her somewhat from her own grief, but once the younger ones are back in school and the older two are at work, she realizes that the ache of loneliness stalks her every idle moment.

Little Rifka has been waking up in the middle of the night, trembling from bad dreams. Mirele and Benjamin are on their best behavior, helping whenever there is something for them to do. Nine-year-old Jakob is the one Zipora is most concerned about. Whatever he is feeling, he keeps it inside. His mother tries to talk to him, but Jakob, who never mentions his father, stays locked in a sullen and uncooperative mood.

When Zipora's father was murdered, when she lost the first young lives she had nurtured in her womb, Mendel was always there to provide her with a space in which to grieve and recover in her own way and time. Now that he is gone, she suddenly has to be the one to keep the tent standing in the strong wind. As if looking after the needs of her children under such circumstances is not enough, Zipora also has Feige to worry about. Her mother-in-law has not been well since the death of her son. She takes to her bed, but instead of gradually regaining her strength, she slowly allows life to slip away. One afternoon in the early days of the new year, when Zipora takes some tea to her mother-in-law's room, she finds Feige slumped over in bed, a book face-down on the floor. She must have died earlier in the day because her body is already cold.

Turning to God

At 44, Zipora is still a good-looking woman. She hardly weighs any more than she did before her first pregnancy, and her hair is still dark and thick. Although she has never worked for pay a day in her life, she has often thought that she could do many of the jobs she has seen other women doing. She is not prepared to find out if this is true just yet, though. First she needs to make sure that the children are settled.

Benjamin, at age 14, has begun an apprenticeship at the Eastern Finland Hat Factory. In keeping with his new role in the family, he takes it upon himself to help his mother with the family finances. He knows where his father kept the ledger and bills. Evenings, he sharpens a pencil and sits with his mother at the kitchen table, adding up the expenses and explaining to Zipora what the numbers mean. Where has this serious young man learned bookkeeping skills? Although he never dreamed of owning his own hat factory, he sees that more than the ability to make hats is needed to be successful in business. With the help of Lifson's accommodating young assistant office manager, Benjamin has started schooling himself in the basics of double-entry bookkeeping during the lunch break. He and Mirele have agreed to turn over most of their meager incomes to their mother for as long as necessary, and Benjamin figures that they should be able to manage for a while by keeping expenditures to a minimum.

Although Zipora is grateful to her older children for their support, she worries about her ability to be both mother and father to all four of them. In the spring of 1935, she hears from Eva Abramovitsch that Mirele has been seen more than once with a young man who is not from the congregation. When her mother confronts her, Mirele is indignant. Does her mother think that the only boys in the world worth talking to are Jews? There are hardly any Jewish boys her age in Viipuri, and the ones there are couldn't be less interesting. Zipora orders her to stop seeing the boy, and Mirele, of course, cries that she will see who she wants and her mother can't do anything about it. She is almost 18 (in fact, she has yet to turn 17), and her mother should stop treating her like a baby!

Zipora realizes that Mirele senses her mother's uncertainty and is taking advantage of it to challenge her authority. Now, more than ever, Zipora misses Mendel. At a loss for answers, she turns to the congregation's beloved rabbi, Hirsch Nahum Maslovat. Rabbi Maslovat is a warm and expert counselor. In addition to offering guidance to the bereaved widow, he asks his wife, Bassia, to speak with her. The Maslovats also have four children, all fully grown, so the two women have plenty to talk about. Zipora begins visiting the rabbi and rebbetzin[1] regularly, the former for spiritual and the latter for both practical and emotional guidance.

Zipora's parents were culturally Jewish but not very observant. Her rationalist doctor of a father had attended services twice a year, on *Rosh Hashanah* and *Yom Kippur*. She had never known her mother to set foot inside the synagogue. They kept kosher at home, but prayer was not really a part of their lives. Under Rabbi Maslovat's tutelage, Zipora begins to draw nearer to the source of communal wisdom and strength that has sustained the Jewish people through centuries of trials and tribulation.

Benjamin is confused by his mother's newly found religiosity. In fact, he is confused by a lot of things. He feels deeply obligated by the vows he took a year earlier at his *bar mitzvah*, but he cannot help noticing the many contradictions between the commandments of the faith and the behavior of the congregants. He notices small things—the way some Jews talk about others, for example—and finds it increasingly difficult to devote himself to prayer. The situation comes to a head with the unexpected death of Rabbi Maslovat in October 1935. He had served the Viipuri community as rabbi, cantor, *shochet* and *mohel* for 33 years. Searching for a new rabbi was never going to be easy, but Benjamin, who is entitled to participate in meetings as an adult member of the congregation, is shocked and repulsed by the politicking and intrigue that surface as various factions vie for control of the selection process. Eventually, a Latvian rabbi, Haschea Scher, is chosen. Benjamin misses Rabbi Maslovat and finds his replacement to be pedantic and distant. When the Winter War breaks out three years later, Rabbi Scher will disappear without notice. Once hostilities have ended, he will send a pathetic letter from Riga, pleading with the congregation to be reinstated to his post.

Assimilation

During the 1930s, Finland's Jewish community is being pulled from within in many different directions at once. While Zionists are campaigning for the return of Jews to Palestine, others feel that the whole Zionist movement is utopian nonsense and all efforts should be focused on integration into the surrounding society.

One sign of assimilationist momentum in Finland during the 1930s is the prevalence of name-changing. Antisemitism is on the rise, and it is probable that some Jews change their names in order to hide their Jewishness. Many families have already stopped giving their children traditional first names such as Mordechai, Schmuel, Ljuba and Schenja and are naming them Daniel, Leo, Hanna or Rosa instead. Now a significant number begin adopting Finnish-sounding surnames as well. Researchers Simo Muir and Laura Ekholm suggest several reasons for the change. Many Jews are involved in business, where it is desirable to have a name that customers can pronounce and remember. The most common reason, though, may be related to the association of many Jewish surnames with their owners' Russian ancestry. The outsiders most subjected to negative stereotyping in Finland, after all, are not Jews but Russians. Many Jews are apparently eager to distance themselves from their Russian past and the widely held perception that Russian Jews play a central role in communist leadership. Thus, for example, Schlimowitsch becomes Kamras, Abramovitsch is transformed into Raamo, Besprosvanni (which, in Russian, means "person with no name" and was apparently bestowed upon a Cantonist child by the army) is shortened to Vanni, and Klimscheffskij is changed to Katro.

For poor people, upward economic mobility can be assumed to play a role in enabling assimilation. The number of Jews in Finland grows by nearly 20 percent between 1920 and the beginning of WWII, from 1468 to approximately 1800. Over the same period, the number of Jewish-owned businesses in Helsinki doubles from approximately 60 to about 120. This steady growth in entrepreneurship, which actually starts just after the turn of the century and lasts with only a few brief interruptions until 1950, corresponds to an increase in wealth. Jews move out of poverty and into the middle class or from the lower to the upper middle class. As wealth makes Jews more socially acceptable to the urban Finnish middle class, intergroup dating and intermarriage become more common. While a sign that Jews are becoming more acceptable in some Finnish circles, this trend raises serious concerns within the Jewish congregations. The Jewish population is already so small that intermarriage, given the strict rules of Orthodox Judaism, risks undermining the community's already fragile basis for survival.

Antisemitism

While economics is fueling assimilation, there are entrenched institutional forces militating against it. Certain institutions—the universities, the army and, to some extent, the established church—are less tolerant of Jewish "otherness" than the society at large. All of them have deep historical ties with Germany, and all of them are slow to condemn the excesses of Nazi ideology and practice. Leo Skurnik, who would later be one of the Jewish soldiers to turn down an Iron Cross, studies pharmacochemistry at Helsinki University. When the time comes for him to choose a doctoral dissertation topic, Professor Paavo Simola, a Nazi sympathizer who knows Skurnik is a Jew, offers him only craniometry, a subject totally unrelated to medical chemistry and the very pseudoscience Nazi propagandists are using to "prove" the inferiority of Jews and other non-Aryans. Blocked from pursuing his dream of becoming a research scientist, he leaves the faculty and becomes a doctor.

A few years later, Israel-Jakob Schur clears the doctoral pre-examination process at Helsinki University and defends his thesis on the Jewish practice of circumcision in the light of Old Testament and rabbinic literature.

Although dissertations that pass the pre-examination are almost never rejected, Schur, who will lose his only son, Boris, in the Continuation War, is turned down not only in Helsinki but again at Åbo Akademi. Some of the professors who reject Schur's scholarly work openly sympathize with national socialism and maintain contacts with German antisemitic ideologues.

The officer corps in Finland's army in the 1930s includes many of the Jaegers who fought for Germany in WWI and returned to fight in the White Army in 1918. Naturally enough, some of them retain a strong attachment to Germany and sympathy for the militarism and anti-communist politics of its Fascist government. A number of Jews gain admission to Finland's Reserve Officer School (RUK) in the years leading up to 1933 and again at the end of the decade, but during the intervening years no Jew is able to earn an officer's commission. Historian Hannu Rautkallio recounts how Rafael Steinbock and Natan Maislisch, for example, are accepted into RUK in 1934. Having successfully completed the training course, however, they are informed on the eve of the promotion ceremony that they will not be among the graduates and have instead been issued tickets for that night's "milk train" back to Helsinki. They return to their units with no explanation as to why they have been denied their commissions.

In sports, as well, Jewish athletes are increasingly subject to discrimination in the late 1930s. At the inaugural track meet held in Helsinki's new Olympic Stadium in June, 1938, Abraham Tokazier crosses the finish line in the 100-meter race ahead of the other competitors, but when the winner is announced, he is judged to have finished fourth. Although daily papers publish pictures with such captions as "Photo that testifies to the mistake" and "Winner placed fourth!," the faulty result is never corrected, and it will take 75 years for the appropriate Finnish sports authorities to issue an apology to the Jewish community.

In 1939, Salomon "Jack" Kotschack, a champion tennis player, and five other Jews are dismissed from the exclusive *Westend Tennis Stadion Klubb* on the grounds that they have not paid their fees. The club's records indicate that 122 out of the 200 or so club members had not paid their fees at that point, but only the six Jews are expelled. Like the Tokazier affair, the expulsion of the Jewish members from the Westend club draws considerable attention from the press. The club's founder, Arne Grahn, claims in a letter to *Helsingin Sanomat* that Kotschak has been dismissed for bad behavior. He makes no mention, however, of the other five Jews, causing *Tennis* magazine to respond:

> If one member of the Jewish race has conducted himself in an inappropriate manner, it does not mean that all the Jewish members should suffer for it. Until

a plausible explanation for this has seen the light of day, one, though uniniti-ated, has to continue to believe that the Westend TSK, a member of the FLTF [Finnish Lawn Tennis Federation], can pursue racial policies with impunity.[2]

The treatment of Skurnik and Schur, Steinbock and Maislisch, and Kotschack and Tokazier shows that there are clearly pockets of active an-tisemitism in Finland during the 1930s. What is perhaps more indicative of the degree of acceptance that the country's Jews have achieved in just twenty years of citizenship, however, is that there are so few such incidents that come to the attention of the public at a time of increasing antisemi-tism throughout Europe, and in the cases where they do, there is often a swift reply from someone outside the Jewish community in defense of the injured party. And if the institutions that should object to antisemitic be-havior often remain silent, it is also true that independent Finland never enacts openly discriminatory legislation of any kind. Finland will soon wel-come German troops onto its soil as co-belligerents in the fight against the Soviet Union. This lack of legalized antisemitism and insistence on fidelity to the rule of law make it possible for Finland to maintain some degree of moral separation from Germany's Nazi policies while soldiers from the two countries are fighting side by side.

Clash of the Titans

The same year Hitler becomes *Reichskanzler*, 1933, Franklin D. Roosevelt is sworn in for the first of his four terms as President of the United States. By this time, Joseph Stalin has been the head of the Soviet Union for nearly a decade, Benito Mussolini has wielded dictatorial power in Italy for almost as long, and Hirohito has been emperor of Japan for seven years. Of the strongmen who dominate the political scene during WWII, only Winston Churchill, who had been Chancellor of the Exchequer from 1924 through 1929, will have to wait until 1940 before becoming Prime Minister of Great Britain.

Although Finland is smaller than all those great nations, it produces not one but three men who rise above the others to form an unlikely triumvirate of wartime leadership. There are others, of course, who make important con-tributions, but the fate of the country can be said to rest largely in the hands of these very different individuals who play crucial roles in the country's un-steady development during the 1930s. One is a military officer, one a banker, and one a politician and leader of the cooperative movement.

Gustaf Mannerheim was already 50 years old when he took command of the White Army in 1918 and will be 72 when the Winter War breaks out.

He is an aristocrat, explorer and career soldier who speaks Swedish, Russian, German and French as well as some English but speaks Finnish only halt-ingly. He had served 30 years in the Russian Imperial Army and is deeply antipathetic toward communism. As a younger man, he did not think much of democracy, either, and would gladly have seen Finland adopt a more au-thoritarian form of government. He is cautious, however, and though offered the opportunity, was not prepared to take control of the country by extra-legal means. Instead, as the revered leader of the victorious White Army in the Independence War of 1918, he used his authority to rein in radical ten-dencies on the right as he moved towards a more centrist position in Finnish politics. Mannerheim, who works behind the scenes as chairman of Finland's Defense Council throughout most of the 1930s at the request of Presidents Svinhufvud and Kallio, preparing Finland to defend itself against external aggression, will serve as Commander in Chief of the Armed Forces from 1939 through 1944 and President of the country from 1944 to 1946.

Väinö Tanner is fourteen years younger than Mannerheim and from a very different background. The son of a railway brakeman and a tenant farmer's daughter, he managed to graduate high school and study business and law at university. He joined Finland's 15-year-old Social Democratic Party in 1904, just after it changed its name from the Finnish Labor Party and adopted a socialist program. He serves as a Member of Parliament (1907–10, 1914–17, 1919–27, 1930–45, 1951–54 and 1958–62) and managing director of the Helsinki Cooperative Society Elanto (1915–1946). He also holds the posts of Prime Minister (1926–27), Finance Minister (1937–39 and 1942–44), Foreign Minister (1939–40), Supply Minister (1940) and Minister of Trade and Industry (1942–43). Tanner, who had refused to take part in the 1918 Civil War, fights throughout the 1920s and 1930s for better living and work-ing conditions for Finland's industrial and agricultural workers, champion-ing by parliamentary means many of the reforms that those on the radical left argued could only be achieved through armed revolution. His greatest contribution, however, is in leading Finland's working class back into the political mainstream. In 1937, the Social Democratic Party is welcomed into a governing coalition with the Agrarian Party with Tanner serving as Finance Minister.

Risto Ryti, eight years younger than Tanner and twenty-two years younger than Mannerheim, is one of ten children of a well-to-do farm owner from southwestern Finland. He studied law and holds the following political of-fices: Member of Parliament (1919–24, 1927–29), Finance Minister (1921–24), Prime Minister (1939–40) and President of Finland (1940–44) during the decisive years of the Continuation War. He also serves with distinction as head of the Bank of Finland (1924–39 and 1944–45). During the war years, he will skillfully guide Finland on a pragmatic course that makes possible the speedy resumption of relations with the democracies of the West after the hostilities end.

Strength in Unity

Mannerheim is staunchly conservative, Tanner a committed socialist, and Ryti a center-right liberal. What they share, however, is more important than their differences. They all distrust both Stalin and Hitler as well as the radical political ideologies they espouse. All three are essentially pragmatic men but also men of principle. What they all understand is that a divided Finland has no chance whatsoever of defending itself. Only if everyone pulls together can Finland hope to hold its own. To that end, it becomes a national priority to put an end to the Civil War's divisions and create a strong sense of national unity.

The romantic nationalism that ripened under the Fennoman statesmen, writers, artists and composers of the nineteenth century will now be harvested to nourish a growing sense of shared national history in the first generation coming of age after independence. National pride, although necessary, is not sufficient to prepare Finland for its coming trials. As the likelihood of war increases, Finland will need a clear strategy to avoid being sucked into the conflict. First of all, the country's defensive capabilities will have to be improved. Mannerheim emphasizes this necessity at every turn, and Bank of Finland head Ryti locks horns with the Commander in Chief over the latter's insistence that Finland should borrow money to upgrade its badly outdated military equipment. Mannerheim also feels that a close relationship with Sweden is vital because 1) it is the only country capable of providing aid in a hurry, and 2) it is clearly in the Swedes' self-interest to prevent Finland from becoming a battleground with the Soviet Union.

Despite their disagreements over defense spending, the triumvirate of Mannerheim, Tanner and Ryti understand that Finland must do whatever is necessary to maintain its territorial integrity. Finland's long border with the Soviet Union and Baltic shoreline leading almost to Leningrad as well as its year-round port on the Barents Sea and its rich nickel mines in the Kola Peninsula will make it strategically important to both the Soviet Union and Germany in case of conflict between them. Should Finland be invaded and occupied, there is a strong likelihood that it will permanently lose its sovereignty.

Many Finns think that a strengthened Germany will be able to keep the Soviets in check and, even were Germany to attack the Soviet Union, enable Finland somehow to stay above the fray as it had in World War I. Hitler has made it clear as early as *Mein Kampf* that his primary interest is in expanding to the east, but he first needs to solidify his control of Western Europe to ensure that he will not have to wage war simultaneously on eastern and western fronts. Stalin, for his part, is aware of Hitler's intentions and needs time to build up the Soviet military before the Germans attack.

In August 1939, Finland's optimism about being able to maintain neutrality while everyone else takes sides is shattered when Germany's Foreign Minister, Joachim von Ribbentrop, and Russia's Foreign Minister, Vyacheslav Molotov, announce the signing of a non-aggression treaty between their countries. The Molotov-Ribbentrop Pact states that Germany and Russia will neither attack the other nor aid any country doing so. In reality, it is a cynical and thinly disguised ploy by both countries to carve out the time they need to prepare to battle one another.

Particularly disastrous for Finland is a secret protocol in the pact which divvies up the territories of Poland, Romania, Latvia, Lithuania, Estonia, and Finland into German and Soviet spheres of influence. The secret protocol does not remain secret for long. On the first day of September 1939, Germany invades Poland. When Russia doesn't retaliate, the other buffer states between the two military behemoths understand that their existence is also threatened. Under duress and in quick succession, Estonia, Latvia and Lithuania sign mutual assistance agreements with Moscow, allowing the Soviets to station 75,000 troops in those countries. Pressure is already mounting on Finland to agree to similar terms.

Notes

1. Rabbi's wife
2. Gashe, Malte and Muir, Simo, "Discrimination against Jewish Athletes in Finland," in Muir, Simo & Worthen, Hana (ed.), *Finland's Holocaust: Silences of History*, Palgrave MacMillan, Basingstoke, 2013, p. 140.

Figure 24.1. The Viipuri Jewish Sports Club Kadur's football team before its October 11, 1931 game with VVY. Back row, left to right: Samuel "Sava" Gurovitsch, Dadu Rosenberg, Salomon "Pepe" Katz, Wolf Karni (Koseloff), Jonas Jonka Maslovat and Salomon Altschuler. Middle row, from the left: Oskar Wainer and Leo Kaplun. Bottom row, from left: Mooni Salomon Gurovitsch, Mikko Gurovitsch and Hesekiel "Heku" Katz. Kadur lost the game 1–5 (Finnish Jewish Archives, National Archives of Finland)

Previous scars had healed in the moment of danger. Finland's prickly and freedom-loving people rose up now, united and single-minded, to save its beloved fatherland. During its first two decades of independence, a strong basis for the continuous positive development of Finnish society and the well-being of its citizens had been established.

Kalevi Tilli*

*Viipuri: Muistoja kaipuuni kaupungista, WSOY, Porvoo-Helsinki-Juva, 1985, pp. 152–3.

CHAPTER TWENTY-FOUR

~

Benjamin Recalls
His Adolescent Years

I was never close to Tate. Mostly, I guess, it was because we just weren't interested in the same things. I liked sports and music, and he didn't. What he liked, I never knew. He just worked and went to shul. If he did anything else, I never knew about it, except, of course, play chess at Ahdus and read books and newspapers. When he was home, if he wasn't eating or sleeping, he was reading. The best times were when he would tell us about what he had read. That was what I liked most, to hear him talk at the dinner table about history or politics or religion. He could get really excited about ideas. I learned more from him than I did from school, but we never did things together like other boys did with their fathers. We never went fishing or to football games, but I learned early not to expect anything like that.

It was Mameh I was close to, Mameh and Bubbe Feige. Bubbe Feige used to read to me when I was little and tell stories like "The Fisherman's Wife" and "The Rabbi and the Poor Cobbler," Those were my favorites. She had lots of stories. She said she heard them from her own grandfather when she was a child. He came from Pinsk and had been a tanner. His hands were like shoe leather, she said, and his beard came all the way down to his waist. By the time she was growing up, he couldn't see any more, she said, but he could tell a different story every day. She tried to remember them all, but it was too long ago. I didn't mind. I loved hearing her tell the same ones, over and over.

Maybe the reason why I was so close to Bubbe Feige was that she made me feel special, like I was her favorite. She always wanted to know what I was doing and what I wanted to be when I grew up. Mameh would ask, too, but sometimes it seemed like she didn't even listen to my answers. She was always so busy. She had to look after Jakob and Rifka, of course, and then there was Mirele. Mirele was what you would call a handful. She was always doing something she wasn't sup-

posed to. I think too much energy was what she had. We were told to come straight home after school, but Mirele almost never did. She always had some explanation.

After Tate died, olev hashalom,[1] Mameh couldn't control Mirele at all. She just did whatever she wanted. Mameh called what she was doing "running around," A few times she would come home and Mameh could tell she had been drinking. Oy, gevalt![2] Mameh would cry and scream, but it did no good. Mirele was working as a seamstress at Pukimoliike (Clothing Store) Rosa on Torkkelinkatu, and she thought she was grown-up enough to do what she wanted. Bubbe Feige prayed for her, but that didn't seem to do much good, either. Mirele was going to do things her own way. She was never a bad person, just a little wild. I was never like that.

In some ways, I was jealous of my sister. She had lots of friends and somehow seemed to be more free. I was always going to football practice or rehearsals. I had a few friends there, but there was never time to do anything else with them. Most of the football players were older than me, anyway. When the football season was over, I didn't see them anymore. It was the same with the actors, who were even older, except for Salomon Eckert, who lived in my building. He was a real friend even though he was older, too, but he fell in the Winter War.

You could say that I was a mama's boy, but I felt like I had responsibilities. After Tate died, I was the man of the house. It wasn't like I could start telling Mirele what to do or anything like that, but I didn't want Mameh to have any more problems so I tried my best to do what Mameh wanted. For me, it was easy. I really didn't want to do any of the things Mirele was doing, anyway.

But that didn't mean that I didn't have problems. There was Rachel, of course, but that situation seemed farfaln, you know, hopeless. What could I do about the way she felt? Maybe there could have been something, but if there was, I never figured it out. Instead, I just tried to keep from thinking about her all the time and feeling bad.

There was one girl at Lifson's, a shop girl named Tamara. She had dark eyes and long, black curly hair. Everyone thought she was really pretty. I guess I thought so, too, but somehow that wasn't enough. Bella from the office told me that Tamara liked me and wanted me to take her out, but I just couldn't bring myself to ask her. I was too stuck on Rachel.

Another problem that really bothered me was religion. I was Jewish, for sure. I kept kosher, I went to shul, I did all the things Jewish boys my age did. But when I tried to pray—not just repeat the prayers we had all memorized but really talk to God—I couldn't find the words. When I was younger, I thought praying meant asking God for things, like, "Please make me a better football player." Then it became more like negotiating a deal. "If You make Rachel love me, I promise to spend more time in shul and follow all Your commandments." Then came all the meshugas in Germany and Spain and Russia. I thought, how could an all-powerful God who saw and knew everything allow such things to happen? I knew I was supposed to be thankful in my prayers, but that became harder to do as the news got worse.

At the same time, Mameh was becoming much more religious. Tate had always been the one to go to shul, but after he died Mameh was going not just on shabbos but during the week a few times, too. I went with her sometimes on shabbos, but it was just for her sake. When I sat in shul and tried to pray, the sounds came out all right, but the words had no meaning. I had lots of questions, but instead of answers, all I got was more questions.

I never thought God didn't exist. I don't know how people can think such a thing. But I couldn't reach Him. I knew the problem had to be with me, not with God, but what help was that? I could have used someone to talk to, but there was no one. I told Mameh, and she wanted me to talk to the rabbi. If Rabbi Maslovat had still been alive, I probably would have gone, but I didn't like Rabbi Scher. There was something about him I didn't trust. Anyway, I thought I already knew what he would say, and it wouldn't help. I never told Mameh I wouldn't go talk to him, but I never went.

It wasn't a good time to be questioning my faith. People started saying there would be a war, and I knew that if they were right, I would have to fight. It was like when Saarvala's gang was bullying me. I didn't want to fight, I just wanted them to leave me alone, but no matter what I did, Tate said, the only way to make them stop was to fight back. And, as usual, he was right. That's the way it seemed with Finland and Russia. They were going to bully us, and sooner or later we would have to fight to make them stop.

And then there were the Jews and Germany. I could see how some Jews could escape from the Nazis, but all of them? Germany was going to make life miserable for every last Jew it could get its hands on. Wouldn't they have to stand and fight sometime, too?

Anyway, Finland couldn't run away from Russia, that was for sure, and the Russkies were acting like they were sure we wouldn't defend ourselves, we would just give them whatever they wanted. I had learned at the boxing club that you can beat someone bigger than you if you are quicker and smarter. You can jab and duck before he hits you. But how do you jab and duck and hit back when it's bombs and tanks that are coming at you?

I know people who say that the best time of their life was when they were 17 or 18 or 19 years old. For me, those years were in some ways the worst, even worse than the war. When the war came, we had no choice. No matter what we thought, we all had to fight. But during the years before the war, it didn't seem like there was anything we could do. We just had to wait for things to get worse. And they did.

I had joined the Civil Guard Youth Corps, but I didn't really like most of it. Everyone said the Guard would get us ready for the army, but the marching seemed stupid, and the sports were like child's play compared to the training we did at Ka-dur. I could see that the men in the Guard were learning to shoot and practice skills they could use in a real battle, but we weren't allowed to do any of that. Maybe we would have been more enthusiastic if our instructor hadn't been such a putz.[3] Everyone hated him. He would make us run in place, dive on our stomachs, jump back up and keep running every time someone did something he didn't like. It didn't matter what we were doing or where we were, he would all of a sudden yell "Hit the ground!," and we all had to do it that very second. I can still see his face turning bright red as he yelled at us. Diktonius was his name. We called him Dickhead but not, of course, when he could hear.

One thing I learned from Dickhead, though, came in useful in the army: don't stand out from the crowd. If you were better than the rest, he would give you extra duties, but if you couldn't do what everyone was supposed to do, you would get punishment. Better to be just average. I felt sorry for the ones who were in terrible shape. Dickhead really gave them a hard time. But the Youth Guard was still only like a club, two times a week, not like in the real army. If you couldn't take it, you could quit, and some did. But the word got around pretty quick in Viipuri, and nobody wanted to be known as too soft for the Youth Guard.

Looking back at it now, all the signs were there in 1938. First, there was the Anschluss and then Czechoslovakia. There were wars in China and Spain. Italy deported all the Jews who weren't already citizens before WWI. And then came Kristallnacht. Some people said these things had nothing to do with Finland, but Marski[4] knew better. He ordered mobilization and extra reservist training. You don't do that unless you think there is a real chance something is going to happen.

The only good things that happened that year were in sports. Helsinki got the 1940 Olympics, and Joe Louis knocked out Max Schmeling, in the first round it was. We all thought Schmeling was a Nazi. Now I know he refused to join the party and even helped to hide some Jewish children during the war, but at the time we were all happy to see him lose. Hitler was always bragging about how Germans were a super race. Hah! Their champion got knocked out by a shvartze![5]

My grandchildren tell me I shouldn't use that word any more. They think I mean something bad when I use it, but I don't have anything against them. I don't have anything against Germans or Russkies, either. The war ended 70 years ago. You can't blame people who weren't even alive for the terrible things that happened then. Maybe their grandfathers killed some of my friends and relatives, but maybe I killed some of their grandfathers. We were just doing what we were ordered to do and so were they.

In some ways, we were lucky. When I think about the poor Estonians, I can't imagine what it was like for them. First the Russkies occupied their country and took their young men into the Russian army. Then the Nazis invaded, pushed the

Russkies out, and took all the young Estonians who were left into their own army. All the Estonians wanted was for their country to be free. But when the Russians pushed their way back into Estonia on their way to Berlin, those Estonian boys in German and Russian uniforms were sent to kill each other. That must have been really terrible, zeyer shreklekh. At least when the time came for us to fight, we Finns didn't have to fight each other. We were all on the same side, and we knew what we were fighting for, and that was to defend our own country.

Notes

1. May he rest in peace (Hebrew)
2. Help! (Yiddish)
3. Good-for-nothing person, slang for "penis" (vulgar, Yiddish)
4. The country's affectionate name for Field Marshal Mannerheim
5. A black person (vulgar, Yiddish)

Figure 25.1. Members of the Helsinki Jewish Congregation's Youth Group on an excursion to Tallinn in 1930 (Finland's Jewish Archives)

It is important to point out that Finland was first of the Central and Eastern European countries to extract itself from the war; the only one that was never occupied; the only one that maintained its independence and democratic system; the first to carry out parliamentary elections even before Germany surrendered; the only one where, after the armistice was signed, no one was executed . . .

Max Jakobson*

---

*"Toukokuun 9. päivä," *Helsingin Sanomat,* 7 May, 2005, p. 2.

CHAPTER TWENTY-FIVE

~

Europe in Turmoil

Viipuri, 1937—Because in 1937 Benjamin is still an apprentice, he remains bound to the Eastern Finland Hat Factory. Only in 1939, if he successfully completes his apprenticeship, will he be free to seek work as a salaried cutter and blocker. No matter, he really has no place to go and no intention of leaving home or Lifson's at this point anyway.

Benjamin now does much of the same work as the master cutters and blockers and enjoys their grudging approval of his skills. He has mastered the various tricks of the blocker's trade by watching the older craftsmen carefully and diligently copying the way they work. He gives almost all the money he earns to his mother to help with the upkeep of the family. Some young men might have resented the need to do so, but Benjamin has gladly shouldered his role as man of the house. Anyway, his hobbies do not require him to spend much on himself although he has recently used most of his meager savings to buy a fine new pair of football boots which he polishes nightly with a homemade mixture of soot and tallow.

Benjamin is not the only apprentice working at the hat factory. Novitsky—he must have a first name, but everyone calls him Novitsky so Benjamin never learns it—is two or maybe three years older than Benjamin. He lives on the far side of Kolikkoinmäki in one of Viipuri's poorest neighborhoods. He gets little respect from the other workers at Lifson's, in part because he shows up for work in the same dirty clothes day after day and because his attitude towards the hatmaker's craft is decidedly less reverential than Benjamin's. He does what he is told, but he shows little enthusiasm for the work.

One Tuesday evening in May, Benjamin and Novitsky find themselves alone in the Karjalankatu workshop, finishing up some hats to be delivered the next day. The two have rarely talked much before, but Novitsky seems particularly eager to tell Benjamin about his visit to the port city of Kotka the previous weekend.

"My uncle took me there to see an exhibition about the Spanish Civil War. It's unbelievable! They are dropping bombs on villages and cities, killing innocent women and children. The pilots don't even see who they are killing. They just drop bombs from the air and then fly away. It's not like fighting at all, just slaughter."

Benjamin has heard about the war but hasn't thought much about it. They are attaching brims to fedoras, and Benjamin listens to Novitsky without looking up from his work.

"Somebody has to stop them," Novitsky continues. "I'm thinking of going there to join the Republican army, but don't tell Old Man Lifson. He'd probably fire me on the spot."

"You can't do that," Benjamin blurts out. "It's illegal to fight in another country's war. If the State Police find out, you probably won't ever be able to get back into the country."

"I don't know if I want to come back," says Novitsky, absent-mindedly placing back on the table the brim he should be attaching to the hat in front of him. "There are volunteers coming from all over the world. It's not like I'm doing something so important here. I've thought for a long time about going to Russia, but Spain is where the action is now."

"But you have a good job here," says Benjamin. "You'll lose that, too."

"Good job? What do I have to show for my work? Not even enough to rent a place for myself. I still have to sleep in a shitty room with my three brothers. You think I like wearing the same clothes every day? Since my father lost his hand in an accident at the mill, all my money has gone to pay for food for the family."

Benjamin doesn't know what to say. He is as surprised by Novitsky's willingness to confide in him as he is by the older boy's rhetoric. Novitsky has never indicated any interest in politics before although, now that Benjamin thinks about it, this particular workplace would not be the first place anyone would choose to express the kinds of views Novitsky is voicing.

"How could you think about going to Russia?" Benjamin asks. "Haven't you heard about what's been happening in Karelia? They say that anyone with any connection to Finland is being executed or sent to Siberia."

"You don't really believe that, do you?" sneers Novitsky. "They are living a better life than you or I ever will if we stay here, that's for sure."

"I don't know," answers Benjamin. "It seems to me things are getting better here. Jews are citizens like everyone else with the same rights. Business is picking up, and people have more money to spend."

"Some people do, but I certainly don't. You can sit here, if you want to, and make hats until the brown shirts take over Viipuri, but I don't intend to. The first chance I get, I'm going to Spain."

"But how will you get there?"

"I'll find a way. You'll see!"

With that, Novitsky apparently feels he has finished the work he stayed to do. Benjamin notices that some of the brims haven't been attached yet and points this out as Novitsky prepares to leave. "You can finish them if you want to," he says. "I've had enough." Benjamin hurries to finish his own work, but Novitsky's lies unfinished on the table.

Unsettling Times

The next morning, Benjamin is surprised to find Novitsky in his usual place and the previous night's unfinished hats now fully sewn and neatly packed. Novitsky looks questioningly at Benjamin to see whether the younger boy will say anything about the previous evening, but Benjamin acts as if nothing has happened. And in some sense their conversation might as well not have taken place because Novitsky doesn't leave the hat factory, and not a word about it is ever spoken again.

It would be wrong to think that nothing changes, however. Benjamin, who has scarcely paid any attention to the radio or the newspaper, finds himself increasingly curious about the news not only from Spain but from Germany and Russia as well. He remembers Rachel's rebuke: "If you don't think about things, someone else will do the thinking for you." In his own way, Novitsky was saying the same thing.

Benjamin doesn't think he agrees with Novitsky, but he realizes that he doesn't know enough to be able to argue effectively with him. Pictures in the newspaper from the siege of Madrid and the bombing of Guernica certainly seem to support Novitsky's claim that the Nationalists are willing to slaughter civilians in order to gain the upper hand. On the other side, there are disturbing reports about churches being destroyed, priests murdered and nuns raped by Republican soldiers. How is it possible to know who is right when such horrible things are being done by both sides? If he gets the opportunity, he will definitely try to learn more.

For some time now, Benjamin has been troubled by the thought that right or wrong don't seem to have much to do with how disputes are resolved. At the individual level, maybe, but when he looks at countries, he sees only the powerful doing whatever they can get away with. He could never be a communist, but there certainly doesn't seem to be much reason to trust any of the other parties, either.

And where is God in all this? How can He allow innocent people to be bombed and raped? Benjamin has heard how terrible the Great War was, but at least most of the killing was done by soldiers shooting other soldiers. Now it seems bombs are being dropped from airplanes on women, children and old people who are going peacefully about their own business. In Germany, Jews are being driven out of universities and civil service jobs just for being Jews, and synagogues are being destroyed while the police stand by and let it happen. Why?

Silver Lining

Closer to home, Benjamin recognizes that his family's financial situation is growing worse. Mendel's meager savings have been exhausted. Benjamin's position does not pay enough to support the family, and Mirele cannot be relied on for her contribution. Zipora begins contemplating a move from their comfortable apartment on Sammonkatu to a sublet in a multifamily building on the outskirts of Viipuri. The younger children will have to change schools, and the living conditions will be considerably more primitive, but there is no alternative. Or so she thinks until she receives an urgent message one day requesting her presence at *Ahdus*.

Worried that one of her children is in some kind of trouble, she wraps a shawl around her shoulders and hurries along Linnankatu to the community center. When she arrives there, she finds Rabbi Scher, Jonas Jakobson and two strangers, a slim and elegantly dressed man who looks to be in his fifties and a plump, pleasant-looking woman of indeterminate age. Next to the man are two bulging suitcases wrapped with baling wire.

Jonas Jakobson introduces Zipora to Chaim and Beila Schein, who have just arrived from Berlin. He explains that they have had to leave Germany because of rising antisemitism and are hoping to get visas to travel to America. In the meantime, they have asked the Viipuri congregation for help. Jakobson knows that Zipora needs financial assistance, and the congregation has agreed to pay a reasonable sum for room and board for the duration of the Scheins' stay. Chaim Schein explains in High German that he is a lawyer who got into trouble with the German authorities for protesting the illegal seizure of one of his Jewish client's property. He assures Zipora that he and his wife will be no problem and won't be staying long.

Zipora requires no time to consider the offer. The Scheins' arrival means that she and the children won't have to move, at least for now. Before the evening meal, the new members of Zipora's household have been installed in Benjamin and Jakob's room and the boys' possessions stored in boxes in the hallway until a better place can be found. Jonas Jakobson has given Zipora a first installment on the rent, enabling her to send Jakob to buy a chicken for a proper welcoming dinner. At the table, she beams proudly as her tenants praise the meal and Benjamin shows off the German he learned in school.

Making Ends Meet

The childless Scheins grow close to Zipora's family, but after a couple of months their U.S. visas arrive. Their departure is a tearful one: They promise to write when they get settled and tell what life in America is like. Zipora has lost touch with Mendel's sister, Mirjam, but she gives Beila Schein the last address she had for her in case they might be able to find some news about her.

By the time the Scheins leave, the flow of refugees has quickened. Soon Austria is swallowed by Germany, and not long afterward, *Kristallnacht* leaves hundreds of German Jews dead and more than 30,000 detained in concentration camps. The exodus becomes a stampede as even thoroughly assimilated Jews flee Nazi persecution.

Some of those displaced Jews seek refuge in Finland, and the urgency of their plight makes it hard at first for the government to turn them away. The new arrivals are typically penniless, having fled with little more than the clothes on their backs. The Helsinki, Turku and Viipuri congregations, with financial assistance from the American Jewish Joint Distribution Committee, agree to take responsibility for the upkeep of Jewish refugees allowed into the country. Although some of her Central European boarders only stay a few weeks before moving on, Zipora has no trouble replacing them, and her economic situation stabilizes.

Another source of potential financial stability briefly materializes when a widower from the congregation begins to show some interest in Zipora, but the prospect of providing upkeep for her large family eventually puts an end to his advances. Zipora decides this is just as well. She is nearing fifty and is growing resigned to her lot.

Benjamin is still pining for Rachel two years after camp, still blocking hats for Lifson, still helping his mother as much as he can. His football career suffers a serious setback when a late tackle by a burly opponent fractures his ankle. While recuperating, he decides to spend the time that would have been devoted to football practice in learning to sing and play the piano. Benjamin has a pleasant tenor voice that is slowly but surely descending into baritone range. He joins the *Ahdus* Choir and convinces the director to give him piano lessons in exchange for helping with set-up and clean-up at choir practice and concerts.

Benjamin graduates from the youth corps to full membership in the Civil Guard after turning 18 in 1938. He still finds the drill and military discipline juvenile, but the European political situation is growing increasingly unstable, and young men need to be ready to serve their country. In the spring of 1938, Germany annexes Austria and Italy invades Albania. Less than half a year later, Britain and France acquiesce in Germany's annexation of Czechoslovakia's Sudetenland with Britain's Prime Minister Neville Chamberlain reassuring the world that "peace for our time" has been secured. Despite Chamberlain's claim, the situation for smaller European nations looks increasingly precarious.

Finland, while doing its best to stay out of any war, fears the worst. The immediate threat is from the East, where its 1,300-kilometer-long border with the Soviet Union must somehow be defended in case the Soviets should decide to attack. Fortification of the Eskellinen Line (later called the Mannerheim Line) across the Karelian Isthmus had begun years earlier, but the work was never finished. Now, the Academic Karelia Society mounts a fundraising drive to support the voluntary resumption of the work, which will get underway in earnest during the summer of 1939. Nearly 70,000 men and more than 2,500 women will take part. The project will be largely financed by people all over the country contributing their salary for one day—May 16, 1939—to the cause. Although some politicians feel the effort is unnecessary, Field Marshal Mannerheim considers it essential: militarily to the defense of the country and politically to the strengthening of Finland's hand in its negotiations with Moscow.

One of those who will spend two weeks digging trenches in the narrow isthmus between Lake Ladoga and the Baltic Sea during the summer of 1939 will be Benjamin, but that is still more than a year away as he "graduates" from the Youth Corps to the adult Civil Guard and prepares to spend his two-week summer vacation in 1938 as a counselor at Youth Corps camp.

Figure 26.1. Syväranta on the shore of Tuusula Lake (Courtesy of the Syväranta Lotta Museum)

I never went to the Jewish School because it was Swedish-speaking, and my mother's relatives convinced her that Finnish was the language of our country's future. They sent me to a Finnish-speaking school, *Helsingin yhteiskoulu ja reaalilukio*. Once, at a class reunion, my classmates asked me if I had ever been teased about being Jewish. Not once! No one ever said anything bad to me about it. I always felt welcome in that school.

We spoke Swedish at home, and attending school in Finnish wasn't exactly easy for me at first, but I managed somehow. I eventually came to speak Swedish, Finnish, English and German, and I studied French, too, but I never really learned to speak it. Oh, and I learned how to buy potatoes in Russian.

At that time, there were horrible rows between Swedish-speaking and Finnish-speaking Finns. We used to walk down the Esplanade, the Swedish speakers on one side and the Finnish speakers on the other. But the language problem was already dying down by the time I was in high school.

At the same time, we had groups like the Academic Karelian Society and the Patriotic People's Movement. I'll never forget one of my classmates had invited me over one Saturday evening, and when I got there her parents were going to an IKL meeting, and they had their black uniforms on. There were these two creatures standing there, and none of us said a word.

Hodie Figur*

---

*Interviewed by the author, Helsinki, 30 May, 2013.

CHAPTER TWENTY-SIX

~

Lotta Training and
Civil Guard Youth Camp

Helsinki, Summer 1938—While David is waiting on the dock for Austrian refugees to debark from the SS *Ariadne*, Benjamin is camping in the woods southeast of Viipuri with the Civil Guard Youth Corps, and First Lieutenant Adolf Eichman is taking charge of the newly created Central Agency for Jewish Emigration in Vienna. Rachel, for her part, is attending a six-month nursing course for members of the Lotta Svärd[1] organization at Syväranta College in Tuusula some 25 kilometers north of Helsinki, where future "Medical Lottas" are receiving leadership training as well as advanced instruction in bandaging, patient care, and the treatment of wounds. They also attend lectures about medication and nutrition. Their teachers are doctors and nurses, and the course is quite demanding.

Rachel is excited to be taking the first concrete steps towards a nursing career. There are twenty-three young women in Rachel's class, most of whom are from Helsinki or the surrounding area. They will be housed for the first three weeks of the course in the elegant two-story wooden villa where their classes will also be taught. In signing up for the program, all have vowed to report for assignment without delay should their country find itself at war.

Gaining admission to the Women's Auxiliary of the Civil Guard had not been easy for Rachel. In principle, the Lotta Svärd organization still accepts only Christian applicants, but the organization's leadership has begun to exhibit some flexibility with respect to highly qualified candidates. Rachel's high school diploma puts her in the top echelon of applicants, and her father's long-time membership in the Guard tips the scales in her favor. She knows she will have to attend Christian prayer sessions as part of her daily routine but reasons that no matter what words she is required to mouth, God will know what is in her heart.

Rachel has multiple reasons for enrolling in the six-month course to become a Medical Lotta. Almost immediately after it ends, she will begin a three-year program at the Helsinki Surgical Hospital Nursing School. The summer course will help her prepare for the rigorous demands of nursing college. And should war break out before she finishes her studies, she will have a place waiting for her in the national defense network as a Medical Lotta. She also recognizes—although she doesn't mention it to anyone—that the practical experience she gains in the training course would prove useful should she end up some day in Palestine, taking part in the struggle to create a Jewish homeland.

Even after graduating second in her class at the Åbo *Svenska Flicklyceum*,[2] Rachel had not been certain of a place in the nursing school of her choice. She had her mind set on the Helsinki Surgical Hospital program, though, and refused to entertain the possibility that she would not get in. Even before the official notification of admission to the course beginning in January 1939 arrived, Rachel had asked to stay with her Tante Bluma during those times when she was not required to be in the nurses' residence, and the older woman had replied that she would be delighted to have her niece as a companion. On the way to Syväranta, with her acceptance letter in hand, Rachel had left clothes and books she would need at nursing school in her aunt's spacious apartment on Helsinki's busy Bulevardi.

Gaining her parents' blessing to leave for Helsinki was almost harder than gaining admission to the school. Her mother was dead set against it. Why should Rachel leave home when there was an excellent nursing school in Turku where she could study in Swedish? It wasn't proper for a young single woman to live alone in a big city like Helsinki. Rachel reminded her mother that she would be living in the hospital's nursing residence, where there was strict supervision, and with Tante Bluma, never alone, and there would be no time for anything but studying anyway. Doesn't her mother trust her? In the end it was her father, realizing that Rachel wanted to test her wings a bit and had found a relatively safe way to do so, who prevailed.

Rachel was not the only one to set off on adventure as soon as school ended. Her friend Chava left Turku for Tampere before the ink on her diploma was dry. Rachel hasn't heard a word from her and worries that all might not be well. Chava clearly expects her lover to marry her, but Rachel has her doubts. She could never imagine doing what Chava has done, but Rachel is not about to judge her. She just hopes her friend won't end up being hurt too badly. One thing is certain, Chava's reputation has been ruined. If it turns out that her impulsive friend has made a mistake, it will be one from which she will never fully recover.

Syväranta

A late spring snow has lightly dusted the first pale, unscrolling leaves of Syväranta's aspens and birches. Lake Tuusula is still covered with ice, but even the hardiest ice fisherman no longer dares venture out on its fragile surface. Despite the unseasonably cool temperature, the lengthening days and welcome return of nourishing sunlight remind the young women that summer is on its way.

The future Lottas sleep in bunk beds in two large dormitory rooms on the second floor. Rachel is surprised to find that few of her fellow students have gotten beyond sixth grade. Most will become practical nurses after completing the course and can expect to spend their time feeding patients, making beds and emptying bedpans. Rachel realizes she must be careful not to create the impression that she thinks her education makes her better than the others, but she has already told some of them she will begin studying to become a registered nurse as soon as her Medical Lotta training has been completed.

Rachel finds the first three weeks at Syväranta frustrating. After the classical education she received at the *Lyceum*, she has been looking forward to hands-on practice in first aid and patient care. Instead, she finds herself sitting once again in a stuffy classroom each morning, listening to lectures on anatomy, hygiene and the standard of comportment required of all Lottas. The doctors and nurses teaching the courses are certainly well qualified and enthusiastic, but there is little information to add to what she already learned in her high school biology classes. Several of her course-mates, however, find it hard to follow the lectures, and Rachel gladly helps them with their assignments.

In the afternoons, the program finally turns to practical instruction. The young women learn to disinfect wounds and staunch bleeding; apply bandages, tourniquets and splints; and treat patients for shock. The afternoon hours fly by as the future Medical Lottas in their grey uniforms and spotless white aprons practice bandaging one another, trying to imitate with recalcitrant gauze strips the wrinkle-free wraps that their experienced instructors have produced.

In the evening, when not engaged in tutoring others or completing her own assignments, Rachel sometimes takes long walks along the tranquil shore of Lake Tuusula, listening to birds that have recently returned from their winter homes in the South and are beginning to build nests and trill for mates. At these times, her thoughts inevitably turn to David. She is conscious of being closer to him now although she hasn't written to tell him about her move to Tuusula or acceptance at nursing school in Helsinki. He hasn't contacted her in almost a year, and she is determined not to be the one to make the first move.

Rachel's feelings for David are the source of immense frustration. He has many of the characteristics she looks for in a man. He is handsome, smart, sophisticated and resembles her father more than any young man she has ever met. Has he not taken a romantic interest in her because she is not his type or simply because he doesn't know her well enough? Wouldn't he look at her differently if he got to know her better? Her experience at camp makes her think he does not find her entirely unattractive, but what to do? That was already two long years ago, and nothing has happened in between. Adding to her confusion is the knowledge that, as a nurse, she will not be allowed to marry. Of course, should she decide to marry anyway, she can always abandon her career and stay at home to raise the children.

Fortunately, the rigorous training program leaves little time to worry about such things. Students have to wash, dress, and clean their rooms before assembling at 7:45 a.m. for the flag-raising ceremony, morning prayers, and breakfast. The day then proceeds with lectures, followed by lunch and an afternoon of making and remaking hospital beds, splinting each other's limbs, disinfecting imaginary wounds, and giving injections to a mannequin they call, for some reason, Lauri.

At the conclusion of the three-week-long introductory phase of the program, Rachel and her coursemates are transferred from Syväranta to the nearby Hyrylä Garrison Military Hospital to gain practical experience. At first, they merely follow nurses on their rounds, running errands and performing the simplest tasks, but they all feel the thrill of carrying out their first official duties, however menial. Before long, they actually become involved in basic patient care although their tasks are still limited to washing and feeding those who cannot help themselves in addition to the less glamorous changing of sheets and bedpans. Nevertheless, the future Medical Lottas are helping real patients, and this first personal contact feels at the same time both professional and tantalizingly intimate.

The Role of Sports

David is an enthusiastic sports fan, the kind who routinely opens the morning's *Uusi Suomi* to the sports page before turning to the national and international news. His interest in sports comes from his father, who began taking him to Helsinki Jalkapalloklubi football matches as soon as David started school. Since then, the two of them have rarely missed a match when HJK plays at home.

David, himself, is a pretty good athlete. He represented Helsinki's *Judiska idrottsförening Stjärnan* (renamed *Makkabi* in 1934)[3] in both soccer and track and field as a teenager but has not participated in sports competition since he entered university. He keeps in shape, though, by playing basketball with friends during the school year and performing chores such as chopping wood at the family's lakeside cottage during the summer.

Finland began making an international name for itself in sports even before it became independent. In track and field, Hannes Kolehmainen won the 5,000 and 10,000 meters and cross-country competitions in the 1912 Olympic Games in Stockholm. Paavo Nurmi, the Flying Finn, set 22 world records between 1920 and 1932, won nine gold and three silver Olympic medals, and at one point was undefeated in 121 straight races at distances of 800 meters and above. At the 1924 Olympics in Paris, *Stjärnan's* Elias Katz teamed with Nurmi and Ville Ritola to win the 3,000 meters team race and finished second to Ritola in the 3,000 meters individual steeplechase. Another stellar Jewish athlete, Viipuri's Wulf "Wuli" Gurevitsch, won the Finnish Heavyweight Boxing title in 1930 and finished fourth in the European Championships the same year. In the 1920s and '30s. there were many outstanding Jewish competitors in table tennis, wrestling, weightlifting, bandy and team handball. In 1930, the *Stjärnan* football team earned promotion to Finland's Championship League but was relegated to a lower league after a single season.

Why is success in sports so important? For Finland, it has proven to be the surest way to gain international recognition in spite of the isolating effect of the country's location and language. It has always been a matter of great pride to Finns when one of their athletes or teams proves to be among the best in the world. The country was virtually unknown in 1920, when it competed in its first Olympics as an independent nation. Finland was surprisingly successful in those games, winning 34 medals (15 gold) and ranking fourth in the world behind the U.S., Sweden and Great Britain. Four years later, Finland placed second in the first Winter Olympic Games and second again in the Summer Olympics with a medals total of 37 (14 gold), behind only the United States. In 1936, Finland still finished fourth and fifth on the medals board of the Winter and Summer Olympics, respectively.

For Finland's Jews, success in sports has an added dimension. The Cantonist generation was plucked from an inward-looking *shtetl* environment in which Talmudic scholarship, not physical prowess, was the measure of a man.

Then came the bloody nineteenth century pogroms and the rise of Zionism. Many of the Cantonists' grandchildren have grown up with the understanding that they will need strength and endurance to build and defend a Jewish homeland. It is no accident that weightlifting, wrestling and boxing are among the sports in which Finland's "Muscle Jews" excel in the 1920s and 1930s as they prepare for the serious challenges to come.

Olympic Fever

Finland had only been independent for 15 years when Helsinki applied along with Rome, Barcelona and Tokyo to host the 1940 Summer Olympic Games. A dark-horse candidate, Finland counted on its unprecedented success in international competition to compensate for its obvious drawbacks as a small, relatively poor and out-of-the-way nation. Two years later, to support its bid, the city began building an Olympic Stadium large enough to house the opening and closing ceremonies and the all-important track and field events. Although Tokyo, and not Helsinki, was selected to host the 1940 Olympics, the stadium is completed on schedule and opens to much fanfare in June 1938, two months before the SS *Ariadne* is turned away from Helsinki's harbor.

It is at the Olympic Stadium's inaugural track meet that *Makkabi's* Abraham Tokazier is cheated of victory and placed fourth behind three runners he has clearly beaten. The unresolved incident quickly fades from public view, but it continues to fester painfully in the collective consciousness of Finland's tiny Jewish community. Rumors circulate that a high-level Nazi delegation, guests of Finland's Athletics Federation, was in the stands that day. Could the "mistake" have been planned in order to avoid sending "the wrong kind of message" to Hitler's Germany?

Less than a month after that race, Japan, in the midst of the intensifying Sino-Japanese War, relinquishes its right to host the 1940 Olympics. In extraordinary session, the International Olympic Committee awards the games to Helsinki. The sports-crazy Finns will be given a chance after all to show not only what they can do in competition on their home turf but how well they can organize such a huge international event. Helsinki and all of Finland are immediately swept up in Olympic fever!

Meanwhile, as war rages in East Asia, Germany annexes the Sudetenland. The Third Reich has now extended its power over all of Austria and part of Czechoslovakia without a shot being fired or any of the western democracies making a move to intervene. And then in November 1938, just one month before Finland celebrates the 20th anniversary of its independence, German mobs, instigated and led by Nazi paramilitary forces, burn over

1,000 synagogues and destroy nearly 8,000 Jewish-owned shops in a massive orchestrated orgy of violence that becomes known as *Kristallnacht*. When the broken glass is cleared away, news that more than 90 Jews have been murdered and tens of thousands detained in camps finds its way into western newspapers. Finland's *Helsingin Sanomat* reports that "the Third Reich wants to deprive its Jewish populace of the possibility of living," and *Uusi Suomi* writes, "Everything points to the total destruction of Germany's Jews in a single generation if they aren't given the opportunity in one way or another to leave the country."

Despite the best efforts of the country´s Jewish congregations and Social Democratic Party, Finland will not play a major role in providing safe passage for Central Europe's Jews. By the end of 1938, Finland has granted asylum to a paltry 183 Jewish refugees. The number of asylum seekers grows slightly, eventually reaching a total of about 370. All but 17 of those arrive before mid-1941, when Finland's status as a cobelligerent of Germany removes it from the list of acceptable destinations for those fleeing Nazi terror.

David is at first shocked and then enraged by *Kristallnacht*. Although he is about as thoroughly assimilated into Finnish society as any practicing Jew can be, he now has to admit that assimilation provides no protection when rabid antisemitism becomes state-sponsored policy, nor is a civilized populous necessarily immune to the contagion of hateful incitement.

For David, at least, the events of the summer have extinguished his enthusiasm for Finland's Olympic preparation. He cannot avoid drawing not-so-subtle connections from the cold-hearted refusal to let the Ariadne's passengers disembark and the blatant erasure of Tokazier's victory to the events of *Kristallnacht*. Finland has a long history of military, cultural and commercial cooperation with Germany. If the growing instability leads to war in Europe, which way will his country turn? And if it turns toward Germany, what will that mean for Finland's Jews?

Civil Guard Youth Camp

Benjamin, who has turned 18, now stands 188 cm (6'2") tall and weighs 90 kilos (nearly 200 pounds). His dark hair curls at the ends when it grows too long, but his mother keeps it neatly trimmed and straight for him. He walks with the loose-limbed gait of an athlete, but when sitting or standing he displays the erect posture of someone who has also had some military training.

As he boards the train for Perkjärvi on the Karelian Isthmus, he has no way of knowing that almost exactly three years later he will find himself marching as a Finnish soldier through the same countryside. For now, he is merely a volunteer in the Civil Guard, assigned to assist with running a two-week encampment for the Youth Guard of Viipuri. He graduated from the youth organization to the adult Guard more than a year ago, but now he will spend his summer holiday helping to run the camp and looking after the 15- and 16-year-olds who are jostling each other on the Viipuri Station platform and jabbering excitedly to one another.

Benjamin has mixed feelings about his role as a camp officer. He has not enjoyed being ordered around by the officers in the Civil Guard. He is prepared to do his duty, but he doesn't want to be put in a position to command others. He could not refuse this assignment, though, and since the boys are so much younger, his consolation is that he is really more of a camp counselor than an officer. Marttinen, who is the officer in charge of the group, and Hölttä, who is also Benjamin's superior, can dispense the orders. Benjamin will focus on trying to keep the smaller boys from being bullied by the bigger ones and the bigger ones from getting into trouble.

Fitting Civil Guard training into his crowded schedule of activities—football, theater and work—has been challenging from the start, but Benjamin accepts it as one of his responsibilities as a Finn and as a Jew. It was what his father had wanted. Since independence, every Finnish male has had to serve in the military, and training in the Guard is a good way to prepare for the experience, Mendel said. Now maybe that preparation will turn out to be useful. Finland has proclaimed its neutrality, but should there be a war, there is no guarantee that the Finns will be able to avoid being drawn into the conflict.

While David is worrying primarily about Germany, Benjamin is much more aware of the threat posed by the Soviet Union. At Perkjärvi, he and the boys will be about halfway between Viipuri and the Russian border. He has heard that the Red Army's long-range cannons could conceivably shell Perkjärvi from emplacements at the border, which is less than 40 kilometers away. While there was no reason to think Stalin is planning anything like that, the very idea makes Benjamin nervous.

Benjamin and the boys are setting up tents on the shore of Perkjärvi Lake when Olympic Stadium officials steal victory from Abraham Tokazier in the 100-meter dash. There are no newspapers or radios in the forest to convey the news so Benjamin will not hear about it until he returns home after the encampment. For two weeks the only world that exists for the boys and their leaders is their campsite and the surrounding fields and woodlands where they play their war games. They cook their own food, go on long marches, practice digging foxholes and crawling under barbed wire. They use compasses and crude maps to locate "targets" in the woods and learn to make their way through the forest at night.

For Finnish youngsters who grew up on farms in the country's heartland, most of these assignments would be child's play, but these are city boys from Viipuri. A few of them may have learned how to start a fire in order to heat the saunas at their families' summer cottages, but survival in the forest is a new experience for all of them. The unit's first aid kit gets plenty of use as blisters swell and cuts get infected, but fortunately no one gets seriously hurt.

Benjamin notices the first day that one of the boys, a chubby 15-year-old, consistently lags behind the others. Benjamin begins to join him at the rear during maneuvers, encouraging him to keep up as best he can. Hölttä tends to yell at the boy, whose name is Kaskinen, and Benjamin can see that yelling doesn't help at all. It turns out that Kaskinen is asthmatic and prone to attacks from overexertion. Trying harder only makes matters worse.

By the campfire later in the week, Kaskinen confides to Benjamin that he hates the Guard, but his father won't let him quit. He says what he really likes is drawing, but his father says you can't make a living drawing pictures, and there is a job waiting for him in the bank where his father is a manager. Kaskinen says he hates his father and thinks about running away, but he knows it would hurt his mother. Benjamin doesn't know what to say but tries to reassure the younger boy that things have a way of working themselves out over time.

Kaskinen's story makes Benjamin realize that his own life has been pretty easy by comparison. His own father was assuredly a difficult man, and Mendel's early death forced Benjamin to leave school and go to work, but Benjamin enjoys his job, and family life has never had the kind of drama for him that Kaskinen's story suggests.

Benjamin's biggest problem continues to be his unrequited love for Rachel. He continues to write her, and while she doesn't always reply promptly, she never leaves a letter unanswered. Now she has moved to Helsinki or somewhere nearby to study nursing. She still writes about David occasionally, but she doesn't seem to have heard from him, and there is no mention of anyone else who might be considered a romantic interest. The absurdity of his infatuation is not lost on him. He hasn't seen her in two years. Just as he has changed in the past two years, the girl he is in love with must no longer exist. He tries to imagine what she looks like now, how she dresses, how she talks, but it is hopeless. All he can see is the 17-year-old girl she was at Vidablick, not the 19-year-old woman she must have become.

Mirele keeps trying to get Benjamin to pay attention to some of her friends or their younger sisters, but he isn't interested in any of them. The cute ones are silly, and the serious ones aren't very attractive. Anyway, he isn't looking for a girlfriend.

Notes

1. Finland's Women's Auxiliary Corps 1920–1944
2. Swedish Girls' Upper Secondary School of Turku
3. Today Finland's Makkabi is arguably the oldest continuously functioning Jewish sports organization in the world, which would certainly not have been the case had Finland been occupied by either the Soviets or the Germans during the war.

Figure 27.1. From left: Pej Manuel (Isak Manulkin) and Rosie Andrew (Rosa Manulkin) with one of Finland's most popular vocalists of all time, Olavi Virta. (Finland's Jewish Archives)

During the 1920s and 1930s, [President Kyösti] Kallio, [Minister Väinö] Tanner and [Marshal G.C.E.] Mannerheim were very influential in ensuring that Finnish society developed into a democracy. It began with Lex Kallio, the law that enabled the peasants to become independent farmers. And Tanner understood what was at stake. When he was prime minister, he reviewed the military parade. And then there was Mannerheim, who was instrumental in seeing that the fate of the Red prisoners was resolved in a reasonable way.

The 1930s saw the reunification of Finnish society, or should I say its "democratization," Then came the Soviet attack, which was felt to be unjust. But it wasn't just the Soviet attack that reunited the people, it was the whole societal development that preceded it.

Finland's former Chief of Defense General Jaakko Valtanen*

---

*Interviewed by the author, Helsinki, 3 September, 2013.

~

CHAPTER TWENTY-SEVEN

A Night on the Town

Helsinki, April 1939—She is on a tram, returning from the hospital to the student dormitory on Mikonkatu in the center of Helsinki, when she sees him. She has been gazing out the window at the buildings and people without really paying any attention to them, her mind still on the nutrition lecture she has just attended, thinking about how much there is to learn about ordinary things one never thinks about such as whether or not the food you have been accustomed to eating since you were a child really provides you with a balanced diet. And then there he is, walking in the same direction as the tram along Turuntie towards the magnificent new Parliament Building.

As the tram slows to a stop at the National Museum, Rachel impulsively stumbles to the pavement and crosses quickly to the sidewalk, half walking and half running in his direction. It is only then that she realizes he is not alone. There is a woman on his arm, and they are chatting as they stroll leisurely along. At that very moment David looks up, and there is nothing Rachel can do but continue walking in their direction, trying her best to hide her confusion.

"Rachel? Is that you? What a surprise! What are you doing here?" David seems pleased to see her.

Rachel struggles to find the right posture, the right tone of voice. "Hi David," then, somewhat awkwardly, "I'm studying nursing at the Helsinki Surgical Hospital."

"Sorry, this is Heli. Heli, let me introduce you to Rachel. Rachel and I were at camp together almost three years ago. We have only seen each other once since then, at a choir concert early last year."

The two young women exchange greetings, eyeing each other as carefully as good manners allow. Heli is obviously not thrilled by the chance encounter.

"Why haven't you gotten in touch?" David asks. A small frown appears on Heli's almost perfectly round face, which is framed by cascading platinum curls. She is wearing a tightly belted gray jacket that flares over her hips and, jauntily tilted to one side, a bright red beret that matches the color of her shoes.

"I've been ever so busy and imagine you have, too," Rachel replies. She realizes that color must be rising in her cheeks. She has never been very good at controlling the way emotions show in her face.

"We have to get together sometime. How can I reach you?" David enquires.

Rachel gives him the address of the nurses' residence and makes up an excuse about being late for a meeting with her aunt (who lives, of course, in the opposite direction from the one in which she is walking). They say goodbye, and Rachel cannot help noting that Heli has stopped trying to restrain her show of displeasure. Although Rachel thinks that Heli's reaction is a bit childish, she would have to admit, if she examined her feelings more closely, that she is not entirely displeased to have produced it.

More importantly, David seemed happy to see her. He had asked for her address. After waiting impatiently for so long, refusing to make the first move in his direction, Rachel may just have accomplished what she secretly longs for by her impetuous descent from the tram.

As she loops around behind the museum and the Parliament Building so as not to bump into them once again, she begins to imagine a future meeting. The lid on the Pandora's box of hopes and anxieties she has struggled to keep fastened since camp now springs wide open. Rachel realizes that the more she expects, the worse will be her disappointment if things don't work out. She is young, though, and David is still her first and only love. He is handsomer than ever, and seeing him in his own environment, the big city in which Rachel still feels so like a visitor, makes him seem more mature and worldlier than ever. Of course he has other girlfriends, Rachel expected as much. But there is undeniably a little more spring in Rachel's step as she passes the Old Church on Lönnrotinkatu and heads back to her dormitory.

Anticipation

For the first time since her training program began, Rachel has a hard time paying attention in class. The combination of the first warm days of spring and the possibility that there will be a note from David when she returns to Mikonkatu make it hard for her to concentrate. Perhaps he will ask her to join him for the annual *Vappu* (May Day) celebration. She has heard about how exciting *Vappu* is in Helsinki, and the thought of experiencing it with David produces a little shiver of anticipation.

He doesn't contact her before May Day, however, and Rachel joylessly watches the crowd streaming down the Esplanade as the warm holiday evening brings out the revelers. Prohibition is now a dim memory. Hip flasks and bottles peer out of pockets and bags when they are not being passed from hand to hand. Before long, Rachel realizes that the streets this evening are not the place for an unaccompanied young woman and returns dejectedly to her room and books. She does not enjoy alcohol and doesn't understand why so many of her countrymen need to drink to excess in order to have a good time. As much as she finds the behavior of the drunken men distressing, it is the women who drink too much for whom she reserves her harshest judgment. She could never act like that nor respect anyone who does.

Thursday, May 3. A note from David is waiting for her at the dormitory when she returns from class. She doesn't want to open it in her room, where her roommates will be able to see her reaction, so she takes it with her to the street and walks to Kaisaniemi Park, where she can find a bench and some privacy.

The note is short but does not disappoint. David will be at Kappeli, a cafe on the Esplanade, at 3:00 p.m. on Saturday. If Rachel is free, would she please join him? If she is busy, there is no need to reply. He will simply take his coffee alone and move on to take care of other business.

Rachel goes to the public sauna at the Yrjönkatu swimming pool on Friday evening. It makes her feel clean and fresh and helps her relax, but it also forces her to struggle mightily the next day to make her hair behave. As she walks slowly along Mikonkatu Saturday afternoon so as not to arrive too early at one of Helsinki's finest cafes, she tries to dampen her expectations by reminding herself that if she hadn't happened to notice David on the street that day, he probably never would have made the effort to contact her.

Entering Kappeli, she finds David waiting for her at a window table. He has on a crisp white shirt, striped blue and red tie, and a dark blazer with some kind of crest on the pocket. The practiced gentleman, he stands immediately, holds her chair for her, and calls the waitress over to take her order. Rachel, who is not used to such treatment, orders a hot chocolate and a cinnamon bun. David orders coffee and a Karelian rice pie with egg butter.

Rachel has been worried about holding up her end of the conversation, but she needn't have been concerned. David is a skillful conversationalist. Rachel remembers their discussions about Zionism and assimilation at Vidablick, but David leads the talk in a different direction.

"What have you seen and done since you've been here?" he asks.

"Actually," Rachel replies, "I don't have much spare time. I've walked around the center of town a little, but I haven't done much else."

"Do you like art? You should go see my cousin's paintings. He's just returned from Paris, and some of his latest work is hanging in the Artek Store on Fabianinkatu. It's really amazing!"

"Your cousin? How wonderful! Who is he?"

"His name is Sam Vanni. He's older than we are, and he's from Viipuri. He's actually a distant cousin on my mother's side, and I have only met him once. His paintings are really modern, full of color and strong shapes. They're not like anything I've ever seen. I don't understand what they mean, but I feel like I can look at them for hours. You really should go. And while you're there, be sure to look at Aalto's furniture, too. Some of it is really keen."

Rachel can't help feeling how unsophisticated she is in comparison to David. She doesn't know anything about art. There was only one painting in her parents' home, and that was a landscape her parents had purchased from a Russian artist who was selling his work from door to door. She didn't like it very much, but over the years she had gotten used to it hanging in the parlor.

"Can you get out of that dormitory of yours for an evening on the town? I'd love to take you dancing," David asks.

"Oh, I'm not a very good dancer. I don't think you would have a very good time," says Rachel.

"Nonsense! I'm sure we'll both have a great time. Let's make it next Friday, shall we?"

Excited, and at the same time terrified, Rachel lets David talk her into accepting, and so it is that the following Friday, she hurries home from classes to prepare for her night out. All week she has been buffeted by alternating gusts of apprehension and elation. She knows she should be happy. An evening with David! How many times has she dreamed of just such a possibility? And yet she can't free herself from the nagging fear that it will somehow end in disappointment.

Rachel's First Taste of Night Life

Rachel decided what to wear as soon as David invited her. Actually, she doesn't have much choice: a white blouse with a lace collar, a black pleated skirt suitable for dancing, and her best black pumps. Oh, yes, and a navy blue and gold scarf with a classic equestrian design for a touch of color. Because she would have to be back in the dormitory by 10:00 p.m., she asks for and receives permission to spend the weekend at Tante Bluma's.

She isn't quite sure what to tell her aunt but finally settles on saying she is going to hear some music with a friend. She has her own key and tells her aunt not to wait up for her.

David is already waiting for Rachel at the bottom of the steps leading up to the *Mikado* when Rachel arrives. He has a special surprise for her. Jack Manuel's Swing Masters will be playing tonight with Rosie Andrews as the soloist. Jack Manuel's real name is Jacob Manulkin, and Rosie Andrews is the stage name of his sister, Rosa. The band's saxophonist, Pej Manuel, is their brother, Isak. The Manulkins are members of the congregation, and David has known the whole family for as long as he can remember.

David has reserved a table in advance, asking to be seated near the dance floor. Rachel orders salmon while David chooses the pepper steak and then selects red wine for himself and white for Rachel, over her protestation. Rachel is overwhelmed by the surroundings, the couples speaking loud enough to be heard over the music, the women showing off their stylish outfits, and David, paying attention to no one but her.

David reveals that he will be reporting for military service in the autumn. In the meantime, he intends to enjoy himself. Earlier today he attended his last lecture, and now it will be more than a year before he returns to the classroom. He will need two more years to complete all his course work before he can sit his exams, and he insists the year away from the books will do him good. He hopes to be selected for Officers Training School, he says. Until recently, it has been almost impossible for Jews to be admitted, but now it seems that the doors are open once again. He wants to join the artillery so he can put his math and physics skills to good use. First, though, he has to make it through basic training. He has heard that one out of every four recruits is rejected ahead of time or else fails to make it through the first two months, but he is confident he will succeed.

"Aren't you afraid?" Rachel asks. "What if there is a war?"

"That's exactly the point," he replies. "If I'm an officer in the Artillery Corps, I can do something important. If I ask for a deferment now and then get drafted when the fighting begins, I'll just be canon-fodder like all the rest of them. That's not for me. There are enough farm boys to carry rifles and dig trenches."

"You sound like you think it is some kind of adventure. To me, the whole idea is horrible."

"Of course I don't think it will be fun, but there is a big difference between crouching in a foxhole at the front line with thousands of Russkies coming at you and being in charge of a battery of artillery on a hill overlooking the battle scene. If I have to go, I want to be in a position where

I have some control over what is happening. But let's not talk about such things. It's time to dance. May I?"

"Remember what I told you," Rachel says as David offers his hand to help her up. "I'm really not a very good dancer."

"I'm sure you're just being modest. This is a slow fox trot so it won't even test your skill."

He is right. David is a good dancer, and Rachel is relieved to find that she has little trouble following his lead. She is nervous at first but gradually begins to relax and enjoy the music. Can she really be dancing with David, her dream come true? She enjoys the dancing and the music, but something is missing. Rachel can't put her finger on what it is. She is having a good time, but maybe it's that she expects to be swept off her feet, and that doesn't seem to be happening . . . at least not yet.

When the music ends, Jacob Manulkin announces that the band will be taking a break. Instead of leading her back to the table, David takes Rachel to meet the musicians. The Manulkins are a handsome family, especially Pej. Rosa seems sweet, not stuck up at all despite being a famous singer. David invites her back to their table to sit with Rachel while the young men go out back for a smoke. Rosa asks Rachel what she does and says how much she admires nurses and the important work they do. Rachel asks what it is like being a singer in a dance band, and Rosa says that she has been singing with her brothers since she was little so it seems natural. At first she liked the attention, but her life is consumed by the practice and the gigs in clubs and restaurants. Sometimes she wishes she could lead a "normal" life. The admirers who try to see her after the show can be a problem, too. Fortunately her brothers are there to help out whenever someone gets a little too enthusiastic.

When David returns, he asks the women if they would like a drink. Rachel still hasn't touched her wine, and Rosa says she doesn't drink while performing. David orders two Metropol cognacs, which surprises Rachel since he is the only one drinking. When the cognacs arrive, he downs the first with surprising speed but leaves the second untouched for the time being.

When the Swing Masters begin the second set with a lindy hop, David once again leads Rachel onto the floor. Rachel is musical, but unlike most city girls her age, she hasn't spent hours practicing the latest dance steps. She tries to follow David's lead but has trouble figuring out what she is expected to do. Embarrassed, she asks David halfway through if they can sit down. He is obviously disappointed but returns to the table, where the second cognac is waiting for him. "We'll just have to stick to the slow dances," he says graciously.

When the next slow dance comes, Rachel notices that David is now pressing her closer to him than he did the last time. Once again, she feels that should make her happy, but for some reason, it doesn't. Perhaps it is the strong smell of cognac on his breath, which she finds unpleasant.

What started as a dream come true gradually degenerates into something very different. David wants to show off on the dance floor, and when Rachel doesn't cooperate, he begins paying more attention to the cognacs that continue to arrive at their table than to her. At first she blames herself, but as he becomes increasingly tipsy, her annoyance is redirected at David. They still dance the slow dances, but when David's hand on her back begins wandering lower than etiquette would deem appropriate, Rachel has had enough.

"David, don't!"

"What?"

"Your hand, it doesn't belong there."

"Why don't you relax? We're su-supposed to be having fun."

"Well, this isn't my idea of fun. You're drunk, and I don't like it. If you don't mind, I'm going to leave. Anyway, I told my aunt I'd be in early."

"Don't go. The night is still young."

"I'm sure you'll find someone more suitable than me to enjoy the rest of it with."

David pulls himself together enough to offer to take her home, but Rachel wants to be free of that horrible cognac smell and insists that she can walk the three or four blocks to her aunt's apartment by herself.

She is already in tears by the time she exits the restaurant. She has failed completely. It was a mistake to think she could satisfy someone like David. His interest in Naomi should have warned her. While they perhaps think alike about Palestine and their responsibilities as Jews, they obviously have very different ideas about other things. What kind of woman is he looking for anyway? And then she is struck by the sobering thought that he isn't looking for anyone. The whole idea of a romantic relationship has existed only in her imagination. How could she be so naïve?

By the time she reaches her aunt's apartment, she has stopped crying. Fortunately, she doesn't use much makeup so her face is relatively easy to wipe clean. Putting her feelings back in order, however, will be much harder.

The Soviets Ratchet Up the Pressure

One week before Rachel flees the *Mikado* and her disastrous evening with David, Jabotinsky told Helsinki's Jews that a great war was inevitable, Jews would be the losers no matter what happened to Germany, and young Jewish men should learn how to use firearms and prepare to take Palestine, by force if necessary. The very same day, the ill-fated Jews on the S.S. *St. Louis* departed from Hamburg for Havana.

Jabotinsky wasn't the only one convinced that war is likely. A year earlier, a junior official in the Soviet Embassy in Helsinki named Boris Yartsev (real name: Boris Rybkin), had informed Finland's Prime Minister A. K. Cajander that the Soviets, who have assumed since 1935 that Finland would join the Germans if the latter were to attack Russia, were now absolutely certain that Germany was planning to attack the Soviet Union. It would invade Finland on its way to attack Leningrad, and the U.S.S.R. would not wait at the border for them to arrive. At the first sign of potential German aggression, the Soviets would send troops into Finland to prevent the Germans from landing.

National Defense Council chairman Mannerheim demands that Finland borrow three million dollars from the United States to upgrade the country's defenses. The request is turned down. Finland needs to focus all its financing efforts on preparations for the 1940 Olympics, he is told. Mannerheim submits his resignation but, having made clear that he cannot be held responsible for the outcome should his poorly equipped forces be routed, allows himself to be talked into retracting it by President Kallio. Without money for rearmament, Finland has only manpower with which to prepare its defense. A law is passed making all residents 16–60 years old subject to compulsory service in the national interest.

All the while, Soviet behind-the-scenes pressure on Finland and the Baltic countries to make territorial concessions or allow Soviet military units to be stationed on their soil is mounting. Chief negotiator J.K. Paasikivi and Field Marshal Mannerheim both recognize that the Soviets have legitimate historical and geopolitical reasons to be concerned about the proximity of Finland's border to their second-largest city, but Foreign Minister Eljas Erkko insists that Finland's promise not to allow any nation to use its territory to attack the Soviet Union should suffice and rejects any attempts at compromise that include territorial concessions. Referring to the decision by Estonia, Latvia and Lithuania to allow the Soviets to station troops on their soil, Erkko tells Soviet Ambassador Derevjanski: "Finland will not accept agreements such as those to which the Baltic States have submitted." Paasikivi will later call the Winter War "Erkko's war,"

Finland continues to hope for a diplomatic solution or, if a war should break out between Germany and the U.S.S.R., to stay out of it. A major effort is made to get Sweden to agree to a mutual-defense pact. While expressing sympathy for Finland's dilemma, Sweden is not prepared to make any commitments that might draw it into a war on Finland's behalf. France and England are engaged in discussions with the Soviet Union about creating an alliance to oppose German expansion. Should the alliance become a reality and the Soviets launch an attack, Germany will be left as the only potential guarantor of Finland's sovereignty.

Given the Soviets' assumptions, Helsinki's attempts to reason with Moscow probably have no chance of succeeding. Stalin and Hitler share the Manichean view that countries are either allies or enemies, politics is a zero-sum game, and neutrality does not exist. The Soviets make increasingly pressing territorial demands, starting with access to a few fairly insignificant islands and a readjustment of the border near Leningrad and ending with the demand to garrison troops on the Hanko Peninsula in Southwest Finland. Even Mannerheim, the same general who once promised to drive the Bolsheviks out of Petrograd, suggests ceding a few indefensible islands to placate the Soviets, but no one is prepared to accept the possibility of Soviet troops stationed on the mainland to the west of Helsinki. J.K. Paasikivi works tirelessly to find compromises that will satisfy both the Soviet leadership and Finnish government but to no avail. No country has ever agreed to cede any of its own territory just because its neighbor feels it needs to strengthen its own borders, and the Finnish people, encouraged by Foreign Minister Erkko and already fed up with Soviet interference in Finland's internal affairs, are hardly amenable to satisfying what they see as unreasonable Russian demands. As Parliamentary elections to be held in July approach, no politician wants to be seen as bending to Soviet pressure.

June, however, is a difficult time to be pessimistic in Finland. The sun rises before 4:00 a.m. and sets around 11.00 p.m. in the South of the country and doesn't set at all in the North. After a long winter, the sunlight acts as a powerful anti-depressant. In 1939, it might be said that the powerful rays also blind the population to certain unpleasant realities that will be made all too obvious in the dark days of the coming winter.

Figure 28.1. Terijoki Beach between Viipuri and St. Petersburg during the beautiful summer of 1939 (National Board of Antiquities)

The Finnish people, who had until now intentionally isolated themselves in their own surroundings, didn't believe there would be a war. Most Finns didn't follow world politics. A large majority couldn't afford to subscribe to newspapers, or if they did subscribe to a paper, it was only the local news that interested them.

Young families' time and effort were devoted to earning a living. Family life was closed. There was something dirty about politics, which made women exclaim, "Oh! How dreadful!" These kinds of attitudes had, of course, protected us from radical movements, but they were also responsible for the war coming as an incomprehensible surprise. Even after Germany attacked Poland, we spoke of the 1940 Olympic Games, which were supposed to take place here.

*Eila Pennanen**

---

*Wagner, Hans and Pennanen, Eila, *Kesä 1939*, Gummerus, 1999, p. 17.

~

CHAPTER TWENTY-EIGHT

The Magical Summer of '39

June 1939—The summer of 1939 in Finland is a time of hope and aspiration set against a backdrop of fear and anxiety. National per capita income has doubled since the fratricidal 1918 War, rising for the first time above the European average. Finland still has a way to go to catch up to living standards in neighboring Sweden and the rest of Scandinavia, but it has left behind the poorer countries of Eastern and Southern Europe.

The unification politics practiced by the coalition government installed early in 1937 has succeeded in further marginalizing the radical movements on the left and right. Neither communism nor fascism has been able to inspire a significant popular following. An indication of how far the politics of the left has moved towards the center is the reversal of the Social Democrats' position calling for the dissolution of the despised Civil Guard. The Guard is now recognized as playing an important role in Finland's national defense. At the opposite end of the political spectrum, the 1939 Parliamentary elections will see the fascist-sympathizing IKL party, which wins just eight seats out of two hundred, continue its decline towards total irrelevancy.

The 1930s has witnessed the transformation of Helsinki through the construction of solid monumental buildings that embody the country's new-found confidence in its place "among the rank of nations," Earlier visitors to the capital would have noted the neoclassical beauty of the Senate Square with its towering cathedral, but that style harked back to an earlier time and place. The buildings of the 1930s, even those with classical elements in their design, are forward-looking. J.S. Siren's Parliament Building combines neoclassical elements with local materials, creating a massive national symbol of stability and strength. Borg, Järvi and Lindroos' Central Post Office and Sigurd Frosterus' Stockmann's Department Store also combine solid formalism with modern functionality. Lindegren and Jäntti's marvelous Olympic Stadium with its elegant outline and distinctive white tower, although still awaiting finishing touches in 1939, has already been hailed as the most beautiful stadium in the world. The Malmi Airport is ready to receive the expected flood of participants and visitors for the 1940 Olympics. Meanwhile, in Viipuri, Alvar Aalto's newly opened City Library has been globally acclaimed for its modern functionalist design.

Finland continues to attract attention through its success in diverse international competitions. Ester Toivonen, the first in a long list of international beauty contest winners from Finland, is crowned Miss Europe 1934. Five years later, Taisto Mäki sets world records in the 5,000 and 10,000 meter races, and F. E. (Frans Eemil) Sillanpää is awarded the Nobel Prize in literature. Finns take great pride in these accomplishments, but rising above all else is the euphoria that has gripped the country in anticipation of the 1940 Olympic Games. All eyes will be on Finland as the world's best athletes descend on the capital for the world's premier sporting event.

Finland has not one but two national athletic governing bodies, the Finnish Workers' Sports Federation (TUL) and Finland's Gymnastics and Sports Federation (SVUL), representing the political left and right, respectively. After 1931, cooperation between the two broke off, making it impossible to assemble all the country's best athletes on national teams for international competition. As a result, the biannual Sweden-Finland Track-and Field Championships were not held as planned in 1935 and 1937. This contest, which allow the Finns an opportunity to outshine their big brothers to the west, are of great patriotic significance. The Finns won the first (1925) and fourth (1931) encounters but narrowly lost the two intervening contests (1927, 1929). In anticipation of the coming Olympics, the two Finnish federations finally agree to field a combined team for a reprise of the event to be held in Stockholm. The symbolic reunification of the country athletically has repercussions on the playing field. With its best athletes on board, Finland beats Sweden by ten points, bolstering optimism about the host country's chances in the coming Olympics.

The finishing touch to the 1939 summer idyll is added by the weather. The days are warm, the sun shines almost every day, and when it rains, it seems to rain only at night. Wheat and rye ripen in the fields, hay is harvested and stacked, and farmers who have been able to acquire land as a result of the previous decade's land reforms can look forward to a bumper harvest.

David Gets Ready for Military Service

In July, David receives his orders to report Tuesday, September 5th for his 350 days of compulsory military service. As a student in good standing at the Polytechnic, he could ask for a deferment, but waiting until he graduates would make him considerably older than the other conscripts. Over his father's objections, he decides to face the grind of basic training before he gets any older. He might also gain some additional motivation to finish his studies after a year away from the classroom. Finally, if a war is coming, and it increasingly looks as if it might, he would rather be properly trained than drafted to fight at the last minute.

David is initially assigned to an infantry regiment with the other young men who live in the same conscription district, but he petitions to be assigned to a field artillery unit instead. When several young men who have been provisionally assigned to artillery units fail the physical exam, he gets his wish and is ordered to report to Riihimäki, 70 kilometers north of Helsinki, for artillery training.

Basic training involves marching, running, close-order drill, breaking down and reassembling rifles, calisthenics and, of course, hazing. In the artillery corps, though, the focus shifts relatively quickly to the specific tasks required of artillerymen in the field. The recruits are split into three groups: Communication, Fire Direction, and Gun Line. Those assigned to Communication are then divided into telephone and radio teams: the former learn to string and maintain telephone lines between the forward observers and the battery while the latter learn how to transmit and receive Morse Code. The Gun Line members operate the artillery, learning to load, aim and fire the big guns quickly and efficiently.

David chooses to serve as a forward observer in the Fire Direction unit. He will be located where he can see the battlefront and communicate precise coordinates for the location of the enemy to the battery's operational team, which hardly ever has a line of sight to its target. Since the first volley rarely hits its target exactly, he will then calculate and communicate how the trajectory needs to be corrected so that the Gun Line is able to strike its mark.

David has no trouble with military discipline, the physical demands of training, or learning the skills required of a forward observer. He chafes at the hazing but eventually decides that it is probably justified as a way to weed out those who are not physically or psychologically tough enough to withstand the rigors of combat. He has his sights set on Officers' Training School and knows he cannot afford any disciplinary entries in his record. With single-minded resolve, he manages to control his temper even when frequently forced to do extra calisthenics by an antisemitic junior officer named Peltonen who clearly feels that Jews don't belong in the army.

After attending Helsinki's Jewish School and the Polytechnic, the army experience is a mind-opener for David. He bunks with young conscripts, many of whom have had only a few years of elementary schooling and have been working on farms, in factories or on the docks since they were teenagers. David has never lived away from home or mixed with such a diverse group. To his surprise, he enjoys getting to know some of these young men even though they seem to have little in common with him. Among the recruits he encounters no antisemitism beyond the usual misconceptions and curiosity. It is only some of the officers who give him a hard time. Even the latter leave him alone once he shows that he can perform as well as the others and doesn't complain.

David's bunkmate and best friend is the son of a farmer from the tiny village of Naappila in South Central Finland. Heikki has never met a Jew before, and some of his questions are naïve or awkward, but it is obvious that they are caused by ignorance, not malice. He listens to David's explanations with evident interest, and before long, the two young men are planning to visit one another's homes after they finish their service.

Rachel Spends Her Summer Teaching First Aid

Rachel finishes her first semester at the Helsinki Surgical Hospital Nursing School in the middle of May. She has passed all her courses with good grades and is more confident than ever that she has made the right career choice. After three days with Tante Bluma, during which she shops for summer clothes, she boards the train for Turku and three weeks with her parents. She is delighted to be able to wear something other than her nursing uniform for a change, and she feels quite pleased with herself as she takes her seat in the second class carriage in her new skirt and blouse and opens the latest copy of *Kotiliesi* magazine, which she purchased from the kiosk at the Helsinki Station.

The third week of June, she will report for her summer job, traveling to various Swedish-speaking communities in the South to train beginner Lottas and younger Little Lottas in basic first aid skills. The way the courses are organized, she will spend two weeks in one location before moving on to the next. By the middle of August, she will return to Helsinki for the start of the fall semester at the nursing school.

Looking back over her first half year, Rachel has reason to be satisfied. The course work has been demanding, but she has clearly been one of the better students and received more than her fair share of the praise handed out by the teachers. From the first day, she has been impressed by the professionalism of the staff and will be pleased to report to her parents on her progress. Her relationship with Tante Bluma has also been a source of pleasure. Her aunt has a surprising sense of humor and a progressive outlook that Rachel did not expect to find in the older woman.

The weeks at home pass quickly. Rachel tries to visit with old friends but finds that many of them have left Turku. She asks discretely about Chava but no one else seems to know what has become of her. Rachel doesn't want to call on her friend's parents. She always got along well with them, but the way Chava left home, she is sure they would not be especially happy to see her. She decides that if she gets near Tampere, she will do a little detective work. All Rachel has to go on is Chava's lover's first name, but she suspects that it might not be too hard to find someone in Tampere who knows where her beautiful friend can be found.

Rachel's teaching program involves the basics of hygiene, disinfecting and bandaging wounds, splinting broken bones, and what to do if a patient is suffering from shock. She has always liked teaching and enjoys using her newly acquired nursing experience to help others. Some of the older volunteers seem disappointed at first to find such a young teacher, but by the end of the week she has usually won them over by her businesslike approach and pleasant demeanor. She likes working with the school-age Little Lottas best of all. Their enthusiasm and eagerness to please make the hours fly by quickly.

In order to keep expenses at a minimum, the Lotta Svärd organization arranges for its instructors to be housed with local members. In this way, Rachel makes many new acquaintances. Her hostesses are always gracious, but problems arise when pork is brought to the dinner table or meat and milk or cheese are served together. Because Rachel is one of the first Jewish Lottas in the entire organization, no one has thought about how to deal with the discrepancies between the typical Finnish diet and what she can eat. At the nursing school dormitory, she can merely avoid anything that isn't kosher, but as a guest in someone's home, her refusal to eat the main course is a cause of embarrassment for all concerned. Some of her hostesses quickly adapt, with fish or chicken replacing meat for the rest of the week. In most instances, however, the meat remains, and Rachel makes do with potatoes and vegetables.

Her busy schedule makes it easier for Rachel to put that horrid evening with David out of her mind. She is more ashamed than angry. What did she expect? She doesn't really know David very well and had created an idealized version of him that was a product of wishful thinking. He hadn't done anything different from what most young men would probably have done. All that is behind her now, and she finally feels free from the infatuation that had held her in thrall for almost three years.

Enthusiasm for nursing and teaching fill the void where her longing for David had resided. She will become a surgical nurse, maybe even end up teaching some day at the Surgical Hospital Nursing School. And if she never marries? Now that she has gotten to know her Tante Bluma better, the prospect doesn't seem so frightening after all.

Benjamin Spends Midsummer Digging Trenches

Benjamin continues to grow, filling out to 191 cm (6'3") and 93 kilos (205 lbs). He has recovered fully from his broken ankle and become one of the best players on Kadur's men's football team, which is challenging for the leadership of the second division with a chance for promotion to the first. Old Man Lifson has praised his work at the hat factory and said that if all goes well, he will offer Benjamin a regular salaried position at the end of the year.

There is a break in Kadur's schedule around Midsummer, and Benjamin has decided to join the volunteers who are building fortifications along Finland's eastern border. He has heard from others in the Guard that it should be like a vacation with free transportation, room and board in return for two weeks' worth of healthy exercise. Thousands of young men and women are signing up, the men to do the digging and heavy lifting and the women to cook and serve the meals. Benjamin had enjoyed the Youth Guard encampment the previous summer at Perkjärvi and looks forward to seeing more of the beautiful Karelian Isthmus.

Mirele still lives at home, but she and her mother barely speak. Sometimes Mirele goes out and doesn't return until the the early morning hours. Zipora threatens to throw her out of the house as she knows her husband would have done, but when Benjamin begs her not to, Zipora relents. As angry as she is with her daughter, she does not want do anything to make the situation worse. She worries, though, that Mirele's behavior is having an adverse effect on Rifka, who is now 12 and is already on her way to becoming a young woman.

Benjamin is assigned to fortification work near Kiviniemi, due east of Viipuri and only about 20 kilometers from Lake Ladoga as the crow flies. To get there, he has to take the train all the way north to Elisenvaara and then change trains to come back down to Kiviniemi at the narrow point where the Vuoksi empties into Suvanto Lake on its way to Lake Ladoga. The Mannerheim Line runs on both sides of Kiviniemi along the northern shore with the

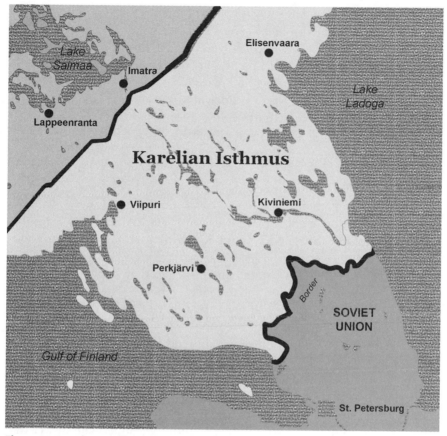

Figure 28.2. The Karelian Isthmus (Marja Leskelä)

waterway serving as an additional obstacle should the enemy attack from the south. Kiviniemi was a narrow isthmus separating the Vuoksi and Suvanto Lakes until 1857, when it was cut through to allow the water to run down to the east and empty into Lake Ladoga. The narrow strip of land on either side of the rapids would form a tempting target for troops trying to break through the Finnish defenses.

During the train ride, Benjamin gets to know some of the others from Viipuri who are on their way to Kiviniemi. At Elisenvaara, they are joined by more volunteers from Imatra and Lappeenranta. Their spirits are high as they descend the train at Kiviniemi Station, where they are greeted by Civil Guard officers who march them towards the camp by the shore of the Vuoksi, west of the rapids. On the way, they pass army troops already at work constructing concrete bunkers and artillery emplacements along the Mannerheim Line.

After arriving at the tent site, dropping off their bags and downing a quick meal of pea soup and crisp bread served by Lotta volunteers, Benjamin and the other young men are handed shovels and set to work digging. Half of them dig trenches and the other half begin creating deep anti-tank embankments near the shore. Stout logs and massive boulders embedded in and in front of the ditches will at least slow down tank and troop advances, allowing the soldiers in the trenches to hurl explosives at the tanks and direct machine gun fire at the advancing foot soldiers.

The men strip off their shirts, and soon the dirt is flying. There isn't a cloud in the sky, and the volunteers have to be reminded to take water breaks so they don't get dehydrated. The work is hard and would certainly advance quicker if there were heavy earth-moving machinery available, but the combination of good weather, camaraderie, and the knowledge that they are performing an important service to their country keep the men from complaining.

The two weeks pass quickly, and almost before they know it, the volunteers are boarding trains again for the journey home. They not only hope but believe the fortifications will never be needed though they realize that preparedness is the best form of prevention.

The first week of August, the army will hold extensive military exercises in the Karelian Isthmus. Addressing the troops at their conclusion, Field Marshal Mannerheim will say that "those who have dreamed of lasting peace are beginning to wake up and understand the harsh reality of the twentieth century." The next day, addressing the troops as they assemble in Viipuri for the return to their garrisons, Prime Minister Cajander will answer that fortunately Finland has used its scarce resources to increase the wealth of the country and its citizens instead of "wasting it on rearmament," As a result, he argues, "We are more or less a unified people . . ."

Although the general and the politician seem to be insisting on diametrically opposed priorities, it will turn out in the end that both of them are right.

End of Innocence

The idyllic summer of 1939 ends abruptly on August 23rd with the signing of the Molotov-Ribbentrop Pact. Suddenly help from Germany in forestalling an attack by the Soviets is no longer an option. Russia has been pressuring Finland for territorial concessions since the early spring, and Germany urges Finland to comply, but hard-liners headed by Finland's Foreign Minister Eljas Erkko and Defense Minister Juho Niukkanen insist that the Soviets will not attack neutral Finland to gain a few islands or extend its border a few kilometers to the west. Everyone agrees that allowing the Soviets to take control of the Hanko Peninsula is unacceptable. Marshal Mannerheim, justifiably concerned about the state of Finland's military readiness, recommends a more flexible approach to the negotiations but to no avail.

World War II begins the first day of September with Germany's invasion of Poland. Seventeen days later, Russia attacks Poland from the east. Recognizing that their defenses are totally inadequate to resist Soviet pressure, Estonia (September 28), Latvia (October 5) and Lithuania (October 10) buckle under to Soviet pressure and sign military aid agreements. Soviet troops are hastily dispatched to all three countries, and Soviet ships and aircraft arrive at Baltic harbors and airfields. At this point, even the most optimistic Finns begin to understand the seriousness of the situation, but President Kallio, Foreign Minister Erkko and others reiterate that Finland won't agree to the kinds of arrangements being implemented in the Baltic States.

October 5, 1939, Finland receives a "request" from Molotov to send a negotiator to Moscow to discuss "concrete political issues," Four days later, a tiny delegation consisting of Finland's envoy to Sweden, J.K. Paasikivi, Foreign Ministry Department Head Johan Nykopp and Colonel Aladár Paasonen depart for the Soviet capital, where they will be joined by envoy Aarno Yrjö-Koskinen. By now the whole nation recognizes that the future of the country is at stake. Paasikivi will make two more trips to Moscow, accompanied each time by Finance Minister Väinö Tanner, to try and convince the Soviets that Finland can guarantee the integrity of its borders without Soviet "assistance," Leaving for the final negotiations to be held November 9 in the Kremlin, Paasikivi, Tanner and Rafael Hakkarainen are accompanied at the Helsinki Railway Station by more than a thousand well-wishers, who send them off with a heartfelt rendition of "A Mighty Fortress is Our God,"

Tension increases with each failed effort to stave off war. The Soviets hold fast to their demands while Finland's parliamentary majority clings stubbornly to the belief that there will not be a war, "at least not in winter!" When conservative politician and future Prime Minister Edwin Linkomies visits Mannerheim's home in early November, however, he notices that all the picture frames on the walls are empty. The realist Mannerheim has removed his valuable paintings and stored them in a bomb shelter for safe keeping.

Figure 29.1. Finnish anti-aircraft emplacement in the Winter War (Finland's Military Museum)

Viipuri was a great place for children. I had lots of friends. We lived on the *Punaisenlähteentori* Square, right in the center of the city, and my father owned a hat store on the corner of Karjalankatu and Torkkelinkatu. Sometime in the 1950s, I went back to visit my father's grave. The Jewish graveyard had a stone wall around it, and I easily found my father's grave there, but later, sometime in the '60s or '70s, the Soviets destroyed it. They turned the graveyard into a parking lot.

Ruth Hasan*

---

*Interviewed by the author, Turku, 31 August, 2012.

~

CHAPTER TWENTY-NINE

Benjamin Recalls the Start
of the Winter War

I had spent the night before on Patterinmäki (Battery Hill), watching for planes. It was bitter cold, ayz-kalt. We couldn't light a fire to keep warm because the Russkies would see it from the sky. Otherwise, nothing much happened that night. The sky was clear most of the time, but we didn't see even one plane. Then it started to get too cloudy to see just before the day shift took over. That was about six in the morning. I got home a little before seven, and I was so cold and tired that I fell asleep without taking off my clothes or eating. I was sleeping when the sirens went off just before nine o'clock. Funny how I can remember details like that more than 75 years later but not where I put my glasses half an hour ago . . .

Before I could put on my coat and boots, explosions shook the house. Boom! Boom! S'iz geven a balagan![1] Windows shattered, glass was flying everywhere, and the air was filled with smoke and dust. The sound of the bombs going off, it was terrible. Mameh and Rifka and Jakob had left weeks before, but Mirele was still in Viipuri and—unusually for her—at home. I told her to get into the cellar and stay there until she heard the all-clear. I could see she was afraid, but she wouldn't go. Stubborn she was, my sister. I couldn't make her do what she didn't want so we headed together to Civil Guard Headquarters.

The streets were a mess. I could see buildings on fire but not one firefighter. Police were trying to get people off the streets, but they kept coming outside. Most of them looked like they were lost. Suddenly came a loud noise from the sky. I looked up and saw planes. I knew them all, the Russky planes, and these were Tupolev SB's. They seemed to be moving in slow motion, like in the movies. I remember I could see the red stars on the bottom of the wings and then the bomb hatches opening.

We dove for cover, Mirele and me, and we ended up in a coal chute. There was a loud clap like thunder, and mud and brick and glass were flying everywhere. We could hear more explosions, too, going further and then further away. Then they stopped, and we knew they had dropped all their bombs.

We must have looked like a couple of shvartzes, Mirele and me, when we climbed out of the chute, covered in dirt and coal dust. We saw a few people who had been cut by flying glass but nobody who was badly hurt. We weren't hurt at all so we wiped ourselves off as well as we could and hurried to headquarters.

Russky planes had been flying over Viipuri for weeks already. Everyone saw them. We thought it was to scare us and the government. Probably they were checking their maps and looking to see how we would react. No one believed the Russkies would really attack us. We were a peaceful country. Everyone could see that there would be war in Europe, but most people still thought Finland could stay out of it. Just to be sure, though, almost all of Viipuri's women and children had already moved to the countryside. Except for the Jews, that is. They mostly went to stay with relatives in Helsinki or Turku.

I was only 19 when the war started. Since the summer, I had been a plane spotter in the Civil Guard, counting how many Russky planes flew over, what kind they were, that sort of thing. Because I had a regular day job at Lifson's, I was usually on night shifts. That meant I might have to go sometimes 36 hours straight without sleep if Old Man Lifson needed me the next day, but I was young and didn't mind because I felt I was serving my country. Lifson was very patriotic and usually let me come in a little late after a night on watch anyway. That all changed when the fighting began.

We knew we would have problems if they attacked us. Even if we knew they were coming to bomb us, we wouldn't have been able to do much about it. Machine guns and rifles, that's mostly what we had, and they weren't much use against the big Soviet bombers. We had five batteries of heavy anti-aircraft artillery for the whole city, and sometimes some of the guns didn't work or there wasn't enough ammunition for them.

When we were practicing what to do, the gunners would send me to get ammunition from the storage cellar, but that was the closest I got to shooting. Mostly I was on blackout patrol, making sure that people covered their windows or put out their lights, things like that. It was hard to get some people to understand how serious these rules were. Of course, when the bombing started, then they understood.

Mameh, Jakob and Rifka had left for Helsinki on a train six weeks before the bombing began. They only had a few hours to pack what they could carry with them. Mameh wanted to take so many things. Mirele really had a hard time convincing her to take only what she would need until they could return. It was winter and really cold so they needed to take warm clothes. Mirele stayed behind with me to cook for the Civil Guard. We promised Mameh we would take care of the apartment. Before Mirele and I also had to leave, we were able to send a few more of Mameh's things to Helsinki, but it really didn't matter so much by then. We understood that we would all have to start our lives over.

When I reported to my Civil Guard unit the day the war began, I was assigned to the Ristimäki District to keep the refugees moving along the St. Petersburg Road into the city. On the way there the whole sky was glowing bright red from fires burning in different parts of the city. Faster than people were leaving Viipuri, more were coming in. They came on foot or by bicycle, some on kicksleds, some pulling carts or leading cows. Most of them had no idea where they were going or where they would get their next meal. Our job was to move them along toward the City Center. Those who couldn't fit into the railway cars and were strong enough to walk would be sent over the Castle Bridge and onto the Siikaniemi Road heading to the west. Such a sad sight, nishto gedacht, those Karelian peasants trudging along with the few miserable belongings they could carry.

After the war started, I hardly ever went back to our apartment. I slept most nights in the Civil Guard Headquarters and ate in the canteen where Mirele was cooking. She never showed much interest in cooking at home, but I guess she learned enough from Mameh to be able to help. Merele almost never stayed at the apartment, but I didn't ask where she was staying, and she never told me.

After two days in Ristimäki, my unit was sent back to the main railway station. Trains filled with soldiers came all the time from the west, and refugees and wounded soldiers kept coming from the east. The Russkies kept trying to bomb the railway station, but most of the time their aim wasn't so good. They hit it a few times, but luckily most of the bombs fell into the harbor or the fields on the other side. Sometimes trains full of refugees had to wait in the yard for days because of traffic or the track had been blown up. If a bomb had hit the train yard then, hundreds, maybe more, would have been killed.

It was bitter cold, and the wind blew through the sides of the railroad cars. They were cars for cattle or freight, not people. Although there was a small stove in most of them, they didn't give much heat. We had to bring wood for the stoves and food for the people in the cars, and we could see they were nearly freezing.

After a while, everything calmed down. Most of the women and children had already left the city. The railway station, hospital and cemetery were the busiest places. Fighting was going on not far away, and most of the bombing was where the fighting was. Still, they say almost 5,000 bombs fell on Viipuri during the Winter War, and that doesn't include the shelling from the "phantom guns,"

Along with the bombs the Russkies dropped meshugenah leaflets. They said things like: "Comrades! Put down your guns and return home to your wives and girlfriends!," "Save yourselves from starvation! We have bread for you." and "Long live the friendship of the Soviet and Finnish peoples!" Friendship, hah!

A good thing it was that the bombing began on a Thursday! If it had been a Saturday when everyone was in shul, the bombs that hit the synagogue would have wiped out the entire congregation. Although we didn't realize it at the time, the war would bring an end to Judaism in Viipuri anyway. The congregation scattered when we lost the city the first time. Some went to Turku, some to Tampere, and some to Helsinki. Some tried to come back in 1942, but after Viipuri fell again in 1944, it was all over.

Isak tells me that there's a tiny new Jewish congregation in Viipuri now. I'm glad, but it doesn't have anything to do with me. They must all be Russian Jews who moved there long after we left. All the old families are gone.

What's left isn't Viipuri at all. A ruin it is, just a name from history with a few people scrabbling in the remains of what was once a marvelous city like cockroaches in a pantry that was abandoned long ago. It's sad how a place can grow for years and years, it can prosper and have a wonderful life of its own, and airplanes can come along one day and bomb it off the face of the Earth. Hiroshima, Dresden, Viipuri, you can find them all on the map today. You can even buy a ticket, book a hotel room, and pay a visit. But you won't find the real place anymore. Only shadows you'll find. It's a shande un a charpe, *a shame and a disgrace.*

Note

1. It was a chaotic situation (Yiddish)

Figure 30.1.   Karelian evacuees on the road to Viipuri (Finland's Military Museum)

Peace was a harder blow than war. Nobody cried about the war, but the peace. . . . That blow felt at the start too hard to take until we began to learn to understand that our sacrifice had not been in vain.

Marja Mosander*

---

*Kun onni muuttaa suuntaa, Like, Helsinki, 2010, p. 198.

CHAPTER THIRTY

~

The Winter War Begins

November, 1939—Special Envoy J.K. Paasikivi's third and final effort to negotiate some way out of Finland's impasse with the Soviet Union takes place November 9, 1939. With him in Moscow are Finance Minister Väinö Tanner and diplomat Rafael Hakkarainen while across the table sit Soviet Foreign Minister Vyacheslav Molotov and Josef Stalin. The Finnish delegation's room to maneuver is severely limited by the knowledge that their country's parliament and President as well as popular sentiment are all dead set against territorial concessions. The Soviets, for their part, cannot understand what popular sentiment has to do with the matter or why Finland's leaders need to seek parliamentary approval before making commitments that, Molotov argues, are clearly in their country's best interests. To the Soviets' way of thinking, Finnish reservations are simply excuses for refusing to recognize the Soviet Union's legitimate right to ensure the integrity of its borders.

Paasikivi understands the seriousness of the situation. He wrote years later:

> I believed [at the time] that Stalin would have preferred to reach an agreement without military confrontation. It was possible, however, for matters to take such a turn that the Russians could create additional difficulties. Also, Molotov's having revealed the Soviet Union's demands in his October 31 speech was apt to complicate matters because now a reduction in Russian demands would be seen as their backing down from Finland in view of the entire world.[1]

The mutual non-aggression pact signed by Finland and the Soviet Union in 1932 and extended two years later is still in force as Paasikivi heads home empty-handed on November 13th. In principle, at least, the agreement prevents the Soviet Union from resorting to military intervention to get what it cannot squeeze out of Finland through negotiations. In practice, it merely causes the USSR to resort to subterfuge: in this case, shelling one of its own border outposts in order to create the impression that it has been attacked by the Finns.

One week after Paasikivi returns home, the Finnish government authorizes the demobilization of a large number of those serving in the field army (which, fortunately, is not implemented before the Soviets attack) as a cost-saving measure. The people of Viipuri who previously left the city are so confident that there will be no war that by mid-November many are returning to their homes, and schools are reopening. On the Soviet side of the border, however, actions are being taken that show such optimism to be misguided. November 26 at 3:00 p.m., a Soviet commando team headed by Major Pavel Okunev of the People's Commissariat for Internal Affairs fires five mortar shells at Mainila, a village on its own side of the border. At the time, there are no Finnish artillery units anywhere within range of Mainila, but the Soviets claim that the attack, resulting in the death of four Soviet border guards and the wounding of nine more, has been carried out by the Finnish army. Two days later, a note is delivered to Finland's envoy in Moscow, Yrjö-Koskinen, informing him that as a result of the alleged Finnish attack, the non-aggression pact is no longer in force.

Surprise Attack

At 6:50 in the morning of November 30, massive artillery shelling awakens Finnish soldiers in their defensive positions on the narrow Karelian Isthmus. The Soviet 7th and 13th Army Corps charge across the border northwest of Leningrad. Before the morning is over, Soviet planes have carried out bombing raids on 16 civilian centers in Finland, killing 110 people and wounding hundreds more. At a total of nine points from the Baltic to the Barents Sea along the 1,300 kilometer-long border between Finland and the Soviet Union, coordinated Soviet ground attacks begin pushing westward into Finland.

The Soviet military has prepared for this conflict by massing 400,000 men along the border. Many times that number can be called upon should reserves be needed. Finland, for its part, has only 265,000 men in total available for field duty and only enough rifles for 250,000 of them. Soviet superiority in heavy armor and aircraft is even greater with Finland outnumbered at least 40:1 in tanks and 20:1 in planes. The Finns have only some 270,000 artillery shells available at the start of the war, roughly the same amount as the Soviets will fire at them during a single day of the heaviest fighting of the war.

Despite the overwhelming odds in the Soviets' favor, the Finnish lines hold surprisingly well at first. The defenders are either able to repel the attackers or mount counter-attacks in instances where they suffer initial setbacks. In order to break through the resistance of their tiny adversary, the Soviets will find that 400,000 soldiers will not suffice. They will eventually have to deploy one third of their total overwhelming military might.

Finland desperately needs help. As weeks pass, supplies dwindle and its soldiers battle exhaustion. The besieged country's defensive strategy is designed not to defeat its outsized adversary but to hold it off long enough for help to arrive, but where will help come from?

In the mazurka of international politics, it seems that everyone has a dancing partner but the Finns. Finland had proposed a coalition based on the concept of Nordic neutrality, but Denmark and Norway felt that it was unnecessary. Sweden, which is Finland's natural ally in this situation, clearly wants to prevent its neighbor from becoming a battlefield, but when the Soviet Union strongly objects to the coalition and Germany threatens military intervention, the Swedes back off as well. Germany, which supported Finland in 1918, is (temporarily and hypocritically) a Soviet ally in 1939 and prevented from helping in any overt way by the conditions set down in the Molotov-Ribbentrop Pact. Allied Powers France and Britain are mired down in a trench war with Germany in the West. Although they consider coming to Finland's aid in a thinly disguised effort to interrupt the crucial supply of Swedish iron ore to the Nazi war machine, they know such a move would antagonize the Soviets, whom they hope to recruit to their own side in the fight against the Axis Powers. When Britain and France finally offer to send expeditionary forces to Finland despite these concerns, the Norwegian and Swedish governments refuse to grant them safe passage across their territory so the promised help never arrives. For its part, the United States, intent on avoiding entanglements that would drag it into the European war, stays officially on the sidelines but provides crucial military aid . . . to the Soviets.

Nearly 9,000 fully equipped volunteers eventually arrive from Sweden as do food and arms for the beleaguered Finns. Another 3,000 volunteers—most of them from Denmark (1,000), Norway (700), the U.S.A. (375 Finnish-Americans), Hungary (350), Soviet Karelia and Ingria (350) and Estonia (100)—also show up to fight on the Finnish side. The British finally agree to sell the Finns 32 fighter planes, 24 Bristol Blenheim light bombers, 17 Westland Lysander reconnaissance planes, and 25 howitzers as well as 50,000 hand grenades and 10,000 anti-tank mines and give them 10 outdated Gloster Gladiator bi-planes. The French agree to supply 145 planes, 496 artillery pieces, 5,000 machine guns, 400,000 hand grenades and

200,000 rifles. Because the British and French arms are promised so late and have to be shipped across reluctant Norway and Sweden, however, much of it never arrives before the end of the war. The U.S. approves a $10 million loan package for Finland but specifies that it can only be used for agricultural and civilian supplies when what the Finns need most are weapons and ammunition. All in all, the assistance from the international community—most of which must be purchased—is both too little and too late.

Finland's most reliable ally in the Winter War turns out to be the weather. The winter of 1939–40 is one of the coldest on record, descending more than once to –40° C (also –40° F) and rising above the freezing point only a few times during the entire war. It is equally cold for both sides, of course, but the Finns are both more used to the conditions and better equipped to withstand them than the Soviet troops, who are insufficiently prepared for protracted winter combat. The Finns in their defensive positions sleep in tents or bunkers heated by wood stoves while the Russians sleep, for the most part, in unheated foxholes. Many of the Soviet prisoners taken by the Finns are found to be suffering from frostbite and pneumonia. Gordon Sander recounts the following extreme—and undoubtedly apocryphal—example in *The Hundred Day Winter War*:

> The next day [January 5] there was the grotesque report via Stockholm of a Finnish patrol on the Salla front in eastern Lapland, which had suddenly come across a detachment of 150 Russian troops. The Finns made ready to engage the soldiers—until they realized that they were all frozen.[2]

Even with winter on their side, the Finnish troops cannot hope to hold out indefinitely against overwhelming odds. In a courageous effort no one thought possible, they maintain their defensive positions for three and a half months. In the end, though, they will be forced by overwhelming numbers, vastly superior firepower, and the limits of human physical endurance to sue for peace.

Civil Defense

Benjamin's family had already split up in mid-October, when all those not working in essential industries or defense were encouraged to leave the city. Early snow covered the ground even though there were still leaves on the trees. This was a sign, said some of Viipuri's older residents, that many young people were going to die before long.

Zipora, Jakob and Rifka depart for Helsinki, where they are housed by the Jewish Congregation with an elderly couple. The space in the couple's tiny home on Lapinrinne becomes available for the evacuees from Viipuri when

Austrian refugees who had been staying there receive visas for entry into the United States. Zipora has to share with Rifka so Jakob, now 14, can have his own room, but she is thankful to have found a place in a Jewish home near both the synagogue and the Jewish School.

Zipora had wanted Benjamin to leave with them, but he is needed in Viipuri, working at Lifson's Eastern Finland Hat Factory by day and alternating between plane spotting and street patrol for the Civil Guard most nights. The Civil Guard has been transformed into the Civil Defense Corps, which reports to the army, and his unit is charged with helping civil authorities maintain order in the city. Mirele, who has signed up to help with cooking and cleaning at a Civil Defense Corps canteen near the railway station, also decides to remain in Viipuri. To Benjamin's surprise, his headstrong sister seems to settle down in the chaotic environment leading up to the war. Later, she will deliver food to the trainloads of injured soldiers who pass through Viipuri on their way to military hospitals far from the front. From what Benjamin can tell, she shows up on time and does her work without complaining, pretty much the opposite of the way she behaved before the crisis.

Once the fighting starts, Benjamin no longer has time for making hats. During the first week of the war, Viipuri sucks in a pulsing flow of wounded soldiers and ragged homeless Karelians from the east, then pumps them westward by rail, truck or on foot. The procession advances solemnly under a sky that glows red from the buildings set afire by incendiary bombs that rain down at frequent intervals on the city and harbor. The bombing of cities is a new kind of warfare, unfamiliar to the people of Finland except through radio and newspaper reports of the bombing of civilians in the Spanish Civil War. Most of Viipuri's women and children have left for safer destinations, and many of the men are at the front, leaving a shell of a city inhabited primarily by those who are maintaining important functions such as the rail connection between Karelia and the rest of Finland. Most of the rest are men who are too old, too young or simply unfit for one reason or another for military duty.

Benjamin has been trained in the Guard as a plane spotter, but as soon as the fighting begins, he is replaced on Patterinmäki by a young Lotta and assigned to new tasks. The first is easy enough: keeping the refugees moving steadily along the road into the city. He finds it incredibly sad, the old people carrying bundles hastily tied together and often leading a single cow, the bereft mothers with young children in tow. The columns proceed in eerie silence, the only sounds being the occasional sobbing of a small child or a few words of urging for a cow that has stopped by the roadside to eat some grass.

One man, who asks for help in locating the rest of his family, says he sent them on ahead because he could not leave before doing something he didn't want them to see. "I spent the most o' me life clearing and tilling them fields and building a house and barn with me bare hands. *Perkele*,[3] if we have to leave our home, I ain't going to let them Russkies have it!" he says. Having doused the buildings with kerosene, he freed the animals and then set fire to the whole place. Benjamin later learns that the man's desperate gesture wasn't necessary. Finnish soldiers retreating towards the Mannerheim Line have been systematically burning the farms and villages in their path in order to slow the enemy's progress and deny him shelter.

During the worst of the bombing that first day, the flour mill in Ristimäki is hit by an incendiary bomb that explodes less than 200 meters from where Benjamin is stationed. He and the other Guard members in the area are immediately ordered into the burning mill to salvage as much of the valuable flour as possible. A light rain begins to fall, and the flour dust covering the young men who are carrying the sacks to the nearby train yard turns into a gooey paste. American troops were given the nickname "doughboys" in 1846, but it applies literally to Benjamin and his Civil Defense Corps unit as they shuttle stickily between the mill and the train yard 93 years later.

At the end of the first week of war, a strange convergence in the Jewish and Gregorian calendars provides a poignant reminder to Finland's Jews that fighting against overwhelming odds has always been their lot. In 1939, it happens that the first day of Chanukah falls on December 6, Finland's Independence Day. Benjamin has hardly been to *shul* the past two years except on the High Holy Days and to recite the *kaddish* for Mendel and Bubbe Feige on their respective *yahrzeits*.[4] Now the anniversary of the liberation of the Second Temple of Jerusalem from Syrian oppression in 165 B.C., coinciding with the anniversary of the liberation of the Finnish people more than 2,000 years later from centuries of Swedish and Russian domination, makes him wish he could share the day with his family and co-religionists. The synagogue, however, has been destroyed on the first day of bombing, the rabbi has fled the country, and Zipora and the younger children are far away in Helsinki. He suspects there will be some kind of gathering of the few Jews remaining in Viipuri at *Ahdus*, which is still standing, but he knows Mirele won't want to attend, and he finally decides that fulfilling his duty in the Civil Defense Corps is more important than any obligation to light Chanukah candles. He is surprised to realize that this decision makes him feel a little guilty, but he reckons that Judah Maccabee and his brothers, who were warriors after all, would probably have done the same thing.

Trains, Fires, and Politics

Benjamin's next assignment is to help the officials who are doing their best to make sure that trains moving through Viipuri don't bunch up in the train yard. Stationary trains are sitting ducks for the Soviet bombers and fighter planes that swoop down out of the clouds, machine guns rattling, whenever they can penetrate Viipuri's anti-aircraft defenses. Soviet bombers have been blowing up railway track and bridges throughout the Karelian Isthmus and beyond, causing dangerous traffic back-ups while repairs are made. The work is slow and difficult in the freezing cold, and some of it can only be carried out when cloud cover keeps enemy planes from attacking the repair crews, but there is an urgency to the reconstruction because supplies and reinforcements need to reach the front, and delays in transporting the sick and injured result in a steep increase in the number of deaths.

When there is no traffic in the train yard, Benjamin joins some of the Guard Boys from the I/SK Battalion in a warehouse several blocks away on Vesikaivonkatu, where they are filling bottles with a mixture of alcohol, gasoline and tar and stuffing cloth wicks in the necks. The bottles will be sent to the front, where they will be used to knock out tanks and other armored vehicles. Some of the boys have started calling them "Molotov cocktails," just as they call the bombs that rain down on the city "Molotov's breadbaskets,"

Sometimes Benjamin is called on to help put out fires, too. The city's fire brigades are not prepared to fight so many conflagrations at once. In addition, Soviet fighter squadrons occasionally follow up the bombing with strafing runs to hamper efforts at containing the damage, leaving firefighters dead or wounded and forcing the city to turn to volunteers and the Civil Defense Corps for help. As winter progresses and the city's water pressure drops, water freezes in the fire hoses, and fires frequently burn out of control. The work is hard and dangerous, but the worst part is finding charred bodies in the burned-out buildings. The lingering smell of death, which never completely leaves his clothing, gives Benjamin recurring nightmares in which he finds Rachel's disfigured corpse among those of the unfamiliar victims.

Benjamin manages to stop by Lifson's, where the hats, tools and supplies are being packed up in preparation for a move to Kuopio in North Savonia. Aron Lifson and his older brother, Mikael, have both been called to the army. The few remaining workers are nailing boards over mattresses that have been placed against the two shop windows on the Pohjolankatu side of the building, the only ones that haven't been shattered. Novitsky is gone, no one knows where. By mid-December, Lifson and his hat factory will be gone, too.

Viipuri's Civil Defense Corps has become increasingly skilled at alerting the population in advance to enemy bombing raids. Shrill sirens send those people left in the city scuttling for air raid shelters. But two days before Christmas, mysterious explosions, always in clusters of six, begin to rock the city with no warning at all. The inhabitants learn that the silent assassins are shells from Soviet 155 mm "phantom cannons" at Perkjärvi, 40 kilometers away. These attacks usually come at night and, although not particularly accurate, sow a new kind of fear in the hearts of the residents because they arrive unannounced.

One evening at the Civil Defense Corps canteen where he is eating after a particularly strenuous day in the train yard, Benjamin finds himself sitting across from a former primary school classmate he hasn't seen in years. Veikko spent two years writing for the *Karjala* newspaper after finishing his studies but now serves as an assistant to Viipuri's mayor, who is doggedly trying to keep city services functioning. Their conversation inevitably turns to the suffering caused by the bombing of the city.

"Why," Benjamin asks Veikko, "do they keep bombing this place anyway? They must know that almost all the women and children have left and the men are at the front."

"My guess is that Otto Wille Kuusinen has convinced Stalin that all of us are just waiting for the chance to rise up and throw off our chains. The bombing is probably meant to scare everybody and destabilize the government so the revolution can begin."

Benjamin takes another forkful of potato and gravy, then shakes his head in disbelief. "That's crazy. I can see that most people are really scared, but I think the bombing has just made everyone *more* determined to chase the Russkies back home and force them to leave us alone."

Both young men toy with their food for a while before Veikko continues, "My guess is that Molotov is just using Kuusinen and his puppet regime as an excuse to avoid negotiating with our government by saying that only the so-called Finnish Democratic Republic is legitimate."

"But no one even knows about this Finnish Democratic Republic. Can they just make up crap like that and expect people to believe it?"

"Yeah, I guess they can," Veikko concludes, sounding a bit tired. "Between Hitler and Stalin, I don't think either of them gives a damn about the truth. Hey, I've got to get back to my office. It was nice to see you. Maybe I'll run into you here again sometime. Stay safe! Adios!"

Before the war began, Benjamin thought the Soviets were just trying to force the Finns to hand over some territory that would strengthen their own borders. After all, that was what the negotiations had supposedly been about. After they attacked not only in Karelia but in several places along the border much further north, though, he began to wonder what they hope to accomplish. If they have already set up a puppet communist government for Finland, it can only mean that they intend to take over the whole country. People who have been saying that from the beginning must be right after all!

Once again, Benjamin wonders why he needs someone else to open his eyes to what seems obvious to others. And that makes him think of Rachel. Where is she? What is she doing? Is she all right?

Bombs over Helsinki

Rachel arrives at the Helsinki Surgical Hospital Nursing School on Paci-uksenkatu a little after 7:00 a.m. the morning of November 30, 1939. She has an anatomy exam at 10:00 o'clock and wants to go over her notes one more time before the test begins. Rachel is particularly proud of her grades in anatomy and wants to do well in order to improve her chances of being selected for training as a surgical nurse.

By 9:00 o'clock she has reviewed the most difficult material and decides to step outside for a little fresh air. She bundles up once again and emerges into the cold morning's sunrise. She hasn't walked even half a block when a loud roar surprises her. Looking up, she sees three huge planes flying from right to left and so low she thinks they might actually hit some of the trees at the top of the hill.

Even before the fierce detonation of the first bombs, she hears machine-gun fire and then the sharp clack of anti-aircraft shells exploding in the sky. She knows she should run back inside and into the hospital's bomb shelter, but for a long moment she remains frozen in place, mesmerized. It is really happening! The war that everyone said wouldn't take place has begun!

When she finally comes to her senses and rushes into the hospital, the place looks like an anthill that has been kicked open. Hospital staff and students scurry between the wards and the bomb shelter, shepherding patients to safety. Rachel rushes to the post-op recovery room, where the patients are bed-ridden and unable to get to the bomb shelter. She pushes the beds closer to the back wall, away from the windows, then arranges pillows and blankets as protection against flying glass or other debris should a bomb explode nearby.

Instead of going to the bomb shelter, herself, she elects to stay with the frightened patients. One elderly woman in particular can't seem to stop crying. Rachel sits on the side of the woman's bed, holds her hand, and tries to calm her. The woman keeps moaning, "We are all going to die! Why has

God forsaken us?" But the hospital is far enough from the center of the city that its buildings, staff and patients will survive these first bombing runs of the war.[5] Whether or not God has forsaken them, however, won't be decided for another 104 days.

Surprising Success

Soviet military strategy consists of four overall objectives, all of which Stalin expects to accomplish in a matter of days: 1) push Finnish forces away from Leningrad in a drive across the Karelian Isthmus and capture Viipuri, Helsinki and other population centers in southern Finland; 2) cut Finland in half at the middle, preventing aid from arriving overland from the North or West; 3) secure the Liinahamari port and the mineral resources in the North, and 4) gain control of the eastern Baltic Sea. Finland's defensive priorities are to bottle up the Soviet offensive in the South until help can arrive while preventing the enemy from splitting the country in two.

The Soviets attack in multiple westward probes. The Red Seventh Army Corps thrusts up the Karelian Isthmus in the South while the Eighth Army tries to sweep over the top of Lake Ladoga and attack the Finnish defensive positions from the rear. In the center of the country, the Ninth Army attacks in a pincer movement, its southern forces driving from Joensuu and Tohmajärvi towards Oulu on the West Coast and its northern units descending from Salla towards Tornio at the top of the Gulf of Bothnia. In the far North, the Fourteenth Army quickly takes the port city of Petsamo and sweeps down towards Nautsi on the Norwegian border.

Finland's defensive stronghold in the South is the Mannerheim Line, the string of fortifications looping in a northeasterly arc across the Karelian Isthmus from the shore just east of the mouth of Viipuri Bay to Taipale on the shore of Lake Ladoga. The Soviet forces outnumber their Finnish adversaries on the isthmus by more than 2:1 (250,000:120,000) and bring 2,000 pieces of artillery (the Finns have 250), 1,500 tanks and more than 1,000 airplanes to the battle. This huge imbalance in manpower and firepower forces the Finns to fall back to the Mannerheim Line from their positions near the border. Once they do, however, they manage to repel the Soviet attacks on the Karelian Isthmus during the first two months of fighting.

The Soviet Eighth Army throws seven divisions and a tank brigade against a Finnish defensive force the size of three divisions at the top of Lake Ladoga in an attempt to circle behind the Finnish forces. It achieves some early success but is stopped at Kitilä and the Kollaa River, far short of its objective of outflanking the Finnish defenses.

Under the leadership of General Paavo Talvela, Finnish forces score their first major victory at Tolvajärvi the second week of December. By destroying the Soviets' 139th Infantry Division (more than 4,800 dead, 1,500 seriously wounded, 2,300 missing), Talvela's troops demonstrate that the Soviets are not unstoppable and the Finns can hold their own.

Further north still, the Soviet Ninth Army at first forces the heavily out-numbered Finnish troops to retreat on all fronts. Arriving at Suomussalmi and Kuhmo, the attackers find them burned to the ground. In a parallel thrust, the Soviet 122nd Division pushes from Salla to Kemijärvi but is brought to a halt by outnumbered Finnish defenders. Then it sends the 372nd Mountain Infantry Regiment hooking north and west to Pelkosenniemi. To everyone's surprise, the Finns succeed in pushing the 372nd back to Märkäjärvi, where it remains bogged down until the end of the war. Next, in a series of daring moves in the Suomussalmi region, an undermanned Finnish reserve division cuts off the attackers' supply and communication lines. Soviet troops, unable to communicate with one another, are trapped in disadvantageous positions without food or shelter in bone-chilling weather.

H. M. Tillotson describes the tactical approach employed by Finland's 9th Division's commander, Colonel Hjalmar Siilasvuo:

> Siilasvuo made a flanking move to cut the road running westwards from Raate towards Suomussalmi. He thus separated the still advancing 44th Division from the 163rd, which was sheltering from the weather in the ruins of the vil-lage. The point where Siilasvuo cut the road combined the features of a road block and ambush. It was a mile-wide isthmus between Lakes Kuivasjärvi and Kuomasjärvi. The only route around the road block accessible to the Russians would be over the ice of the frozen lakes. Once on the ice, the enemy would be at the mercy of the Finns' carefully sited machine-guns.[6]

The 44th Division gets piled up along the Raate Road. Resolved not to waste scarce men and equipment, Siilasvuo sends small groups of attackers through the woods instead of confronting the column head-on. Gordon Sander breathlessly describes the Finnish attack:

> *Suomis* (submachine guns) blazing, *puukkos* (hunting knives) unsheathed, Siilasvuo's soldiers [cut down] several dozen men along with several hundred wailing, mortally wounded horses. Rearing and panicking, the surviving ani-mals threw the rest of the Russian column into confusion. . . . Russian troops sleeping by the road were suddenly enfiladed from fifty points. . . . The pan-icked, disoriented Russian troops fired into the woods, but there were no Finns there. Like phantoms, they were here, there, everywhere.[7]

Meanwhile, the Soviet 163rd is holed up in the remnants of Suomussalmi, its lines of communication and logistics severed and its supplies almost exhausted. Having unsuccessfully tried to break through the Finnish lines to the north, the 163rd hunkers down in Suomussalmi, waiting for help from the 44th that never arrives. Tillotson recounts the outcome:

> Soviet soldiers of 163rd Division, many having thrown away their weapons, formed long columns and began to shamble away to the northeast across the ice of Lake Kiantajärvi. The Finns showed no mercy to the would-be invaders. In an operation of almost surgical precision, Siilasvuo's men reduced the 163rd Division to a rabble of dazed individuals with thoughts only for survival. While around 9,000 reached the safety of the frontier, another 5,000 Russian dead were counted in and around Suomussalmi at the end of December.[8]

Some estimates put casualties from the combined Suomussalmi-Raate Road battles as high as 30,000 killed or wounded though the actual number may be closer to half that, while the corresponding Finnish casualty figure is only around 2,000. A huge amount of military equipment is abandoned in the retreat. Along the Raate Road alone, the Soviets leave behind 53 tanks and armored carriers, 71 artillery pieces, 16 anti-aircraft machine guns, 260 trucks, 20 tractors, two cars, 15 motorcycles, 47 field kitchens, 106 machine guns, 190 submachine guns and thousands of small arms. A bemused Sander recounts how Moscow Radio announced that if the Finns didn't return the Soviet equipment they had recovered at Suomussalmi and Raate, the Kremlin would declare war on Finland!

These victories provide an adrenaline boost that enables an entire nation on the brink of exhaustion to maintain its fighting spirit for another two and a half months. The scope of the debacle gives birth in Finland to the popular notion that "ten Russkies are no match for a single Finnish soldier,"

At the tactical level, the Finns clearly get the best of the aggressors in the first month of the war. Hordes of inappropriately dressed Soviet soldiers, easily detected against the snow in their dark overcoats, are mowed down in appalling numbers by Finnish rifle and machine-gun fire while Finnish ski troops, clad in warm, all-white camouflage, seem to appear out of nowhere. Expecting a quick victory, the Soviet high command has neglected to provide proper winter gear for its troops.

While most Finnish troops are led by battle-hardened former Jaegers who fought in WWI, the brutal Stalinist purges of the 1930s have depleted the ranks of Soviet officers with operational experience by as much as 80–90 percent, all the way down to the level of regimental commander. In numerous battles, Finnish officers outmaneuver their Soviet counterparts, trapping them in *mottis*. Meanwhile, Stalin has forbidden his troops to retreat for any reason, even when faced with entrapment. This inflexible approach leads to huge numbers of Soviet soldiers being killed or captured. Moreover, the Soviet troops, many of whom are from Byelorussia and Ukraine, have no real idea why they are fighting. They have been told that Finland started the war, but no one has come up with a satisfactory explanation for why a country of 3.7 million would attack a neighbor of more than 160 million. While some of these conscripts are undoubtedly patriotic and loyal to Soviet leadership, what motivates others to keep moving forward in suicidal waves are the guns aimed at their backs by the ruthless political commissars assigned to every unit.

As 1939 draws to a close, and Europe's Western Front is quiet, the whole world seems to focus its attention on Finland. In this David v. Goliath struggle, tiny Finland continues to defy all expectations. The Finns are clearly the sentimental favorites among spectator nations, but heartfelt admiration is not translating itself into military support. They have forced the Soviets to hunker down in defensive positions, but 72-year old Finnish Commander-in-Chief Mannerheim knows that his men and supplies cannot last much longer. The Soviets have suffered many times greater casualties than the Finns, but they have a seemingly limitless supply of men to send against Mannerheim's troops, whose resources are already stretched to the limit. The mighty Soviet Union is surely not going to allow itself to be humiliated for long by its tiny neighbor, and, in any case, it will just be a matter of time before the last Finnish bullet will be spent.

Reassessing the Situation

As Finland sinks deeper into the war, the locus of decision-making power that would normally belong to Parliament is held ever more firmly in the hands of a tiny coterie of leaders. Parliament has been evacuated to Kauhajoki in the Northwest on the first day of bombing, leaving the President, Prime Minister and war cabinet in the capital. No important decisions can be made without the approval of Commander-in-Chief Mannerheim, who is several hours away in Mikkeli, because the army's performance is crucial to bringing the Soviets to the negotiating table. Parliament is informed about decisions that have been prepared and presented by a tiny inner circle of decision-makers. Parliament's greatest contribution during the Continuation War may reside in providing negotiators with an excuse for delaying certain key decisions "until they can be approved by Parliament as required by Finnish law."

President Kallio accepts the resignation of Prime Minister Cajander as soon as the war begins and persuades Bank of Finland President Risto Ryti to form a government. Ryti chooses Väinö Tanner to be his Foreign Minister and gives J. K. Paasikivi a post as minister without portfolio. While radical ideologues in Berlin, Rome, Moscow and Tokyo have the world plunging deep into a previously unthinkable Second World War, tiny Finland's key decision-makers—Ryti, Tanner, and Field Marshal Mannerheim—recognize that their job will be to determine the best time and way to sue for peace. The dilemma they face is that, on the one hand, neither the Finnish people nor their troops will accept anything that looks like capitulation so long as Finland seems to be holding its own. On the other, the Soviets are unlikely to agree to back off once they have broken through Finland's defenses. Survival depends on a delicate balance of military success and outside help. In early January, neither seems likely to materialize although both are just plausible enough to make decision-making at the highest levels excruciatingly difficult.

Notes

1. Paasikivi, J.K., *Toimintani Moskovassa ja Suomessa 1939–1941*, Werner Söderström, Porvoo / Helsinki / Juva, 1979, p. 92.

2. Sander, Gordon, *The Hundred Day Winter War*, University Press of Kansas, Lawrence, 2013, p. 200.

3. The name of the devil, a powerful curse word in Finnish

4. The anniversary of the death of a relative (Yiddish)

5. Of the three Soviet bombing raids on Helsinki that day, only the third succeeds in causing significant damage. It results in the death of 91 civilians and the destruction of several buildings, among them the Soviet Embassy.

6. Tillotson, H.M., *Finland at Peace & War 1918–1993*, Michael Russell (Publishing) Ltd., Norwich, 1993, p. 140.

7. Sander, Gordon, *op. cit.*, p. 191.

8. Tillotson, *op cit.*, p. 141

Figure 31.1. Finnish ski troops in their white camouflage outfits (Finland's Military Museum)

What do I remember most from the war? It was the incompetence of our army, as it could not deal with a handful of Finns in a proper manner and in good time. They [the Finns] showed us how to fight a war.

George A. Prusakov, Soviet medic*

What needs to be told, in my opinion, is just this: the Finns put a beating on the Russkies twice and the Germans once, and that's how it was! Seen from a larger perspective, that's the truth. No matter what amazing things happened during the Winter and Continuation Wars, that was the outcome. And there are a million different stories connected to it.

Lieutenant Colonel (ret.) Leo Skogström**

---

*Quoted by Sander, Gordon A., in *The Hundred Day Winter War*, University Press of Kansas, p. 31.

**Interviewed by the author, Lotinapelto, 15 August, 2013.

CHAPTER THIRTY-ONE

~

Finland's Survival at Risk

January, 1940—As the Winter War enters its second month, David is on a train to Vaasa on Finland's West Coast. Having completed basic training with Field Artillery Regiment 3's (KTR 3) reinforcement division and survived numerous bombing raids on Riihimäki's railway hub and army garrison, he is headed for Non-commissioned Officers Training School (NCOTS) at the Vaasa Army Reserve Training Center. Although Finland's army is already stretched to the limit by the manpower demands of the war, no effort is being made to rush into battle those young recruits who have not completed their training.

David has never been so far north before. January, though, isn't the best time of year to be introduced to this charming coastal city. The wind blowing off the frozen Gulf of Bothnia seems to slice right through the warmest clothing. One thing in Vaasa's favor, regardless of the weather, at least from David's point of view, is that a majority of the city's inhabitants are Swedish-speaking and so is its garrison.

Non-commissioned officers' training consists of a four-month course designed to prepare participants to lead small fighting units into battle. Because men who were previously rejected for service for minor reasons have now been called up, he finds that his course includes some men as old as 40. The core of the training program consists of four segments: 1) general leadership training, 2) tactical combat training, 3) physical training, and 4) specialty training in the use of weapons.

David is encouraged by his countrymen's early success in pushing back against the Soviet onslaught. Unbeknownst to him, however, the Soviet military has decided to treble the size of its force on the Karelian Isthmus. If Stalin and Molotov were annoyed by the Finns' refusal to accept their "reasonable" demands in October and November, they are furious now at the damage to the glorious Red Army's prestige inflicted by tiny Finland's successful resistance. Nothing less than crushing the Finnish defenses will erase that humiliation.

To be selected for Reserve Officers School (ROS), David knows that he will need to be twice as good as the other applicants. He is surprised to find that hazing at NCOTS is actually more intense than it was in basic training, and he chafes at the evident sadism of a couple of the officers. Already in Riihimäki, he noticed how members of minorities seem to elicit special attention from drill sergeants. Growing up as a member of a double minority— a Swedish-speaker and a Jew—he became accustomed to dealing with this kind of prejudice. It made him tougher, and he is confident that will be able to deal with it in the military, too. Like all his coreligionists, he is constantly being judged not just as an individual but as a representative of the entire Jewish people. If he wants to get into ROS, he will have to prove himself worthy of being selected despite the long-standing prejudice against the idea of a Jew becoming an officer.

The course work dealing with leadership, David feels, consists mostly of boring and self-evident platitudes, but the operational training for those in the Artillery Corps he finds fascinating. There are segments on field artillery tactics, map reading, reconnaissance, fire direction and measurement, equipment transport, battery operation, and munitions handling. The part he most enjoys is the intensive training in fire direction theory and practice. The mathematical skills required ensure that only those with a mastery of algebra, geometry and trigonometry can accurately and quickly determine the fire direction coordinates for indirect fire, which have to be calculated in angular mils (1/6283 of a circle).

Most of the officer candidates with the requisite mathematical skills seem to lack natural leadership ability, and those with leadership skills are rarely very good at the math. Despite the preconceptions of several of his instructors, David rises quickly to the top of his class. He is frequently called upon to demonstrate solutions to difficult problems and is also chosen by his classmates to captain teams in intra-squad games and lead platoons in orienteering competitions. He enjoys the leadership role and observes his best teachers closely in order to determine what makes a good officer.

Although Finland has surprised the world by holding off repeated Soviet attacks, rumors abound of a massive build-up of troops behind the border. David wonders whether there will still be a war left for him to fight when he finishes his training. Perhaps the question he should be asking, though, is whether there will still be a Finland to defend by that time.

David assumes, in any case, that no matter how and when the Winter War ends, he will sooner or later be called on to fight in Palestine. For the past three years, Palestine's Arab population has been engaged in a violent struggle against the British Mandate in an attempt to staunch the influx of Jewish immigrants into the territory. In 1937, Britain's Peel Commission recommended the partitioning of Palestine into Arab and Jewish states, a solution that the Arabs rejected because it allocated large stretches of Arab land to the projected Jewish state and folded the remainder into the Hashemite Kingdom of Jordan. In the Arab uprising, terrorists began targeting Jewish settlements along with infrastructure such as oil pipelines and railways.

Between 1919 and 1939, the Jewish population in Palestine has grown from only 75,000 to nearly half a million out of a total population of some 1.6 million. Palestine's Jews have their own paramilitary organization, the *Haganah*, which works alongside the British troops to quell the Arab uprising. A splinter group from the *Haganah*, called *Irgun*, has begun carrying out terrorist attacks not only against Arab settlements in retaliation for attacks against Jews but also against the British. As the situation spirals out of control in 1939, and the Arab-Zionist London Conference ends in failure, the British renounce their previous intention of partitioning Palestine. At the very time when Jews in Europe are facing escalating Nazi terror, Jewish immigration to Palestine is sharply curtailed.

David follows these developments on Swedish radio and the BBC. He feels that the British are reneging on the promise of the Balfour Declaration and that the creation of a Jewish state will now require a protracted armed struggle against multiple enemies: the British, the Palestinian Arabs and the Arab states of the Middle East. Whatever happens to Finland, the end of the Winter War is unlikely to mean a return to the classroom for David any time soon.

Tender Care

December is the darkest month, with the sun rising in southern Finland only around 9:30 in the morning and setting already by 3:30 in the afternoon. Farther north, it doesn't rise or set at all for almost two months. During the war, black-out restrictions make some of the simplest tasks, such as driving, extremely challenging. The cold and dark severely complicate many of the tasks that need to be carried out quickly in response to enemy attacks.

It is under just such conditions that Rachel begins work December 3 at the Kiljava Sanatorium on the shore of Lake Sääksi a little more than 50 kilometers north of Helsinki. The facility, which only opened a year earlier, has been converted into a military hospital, and Rachel has been assigned by the Lotta Svärd to assist the nurses on Kiljava's Orthopedic Ward. Simple bone-setting and splinting are done at field hospitals near the front, but the seriously wounded and cases requiring specialist attention are evacuated by train to army hospitals in the interior such as Kiljava.

By the middle of December, Kiljava's wards have begun to fill up. Many of Rachel's patients are in traction or otherwise bed-ridden with serious injuries. A big part of her job is feeding, bathing and adjusting the position of patients in bed so as to minimize the risk of bed sores and infection. Rachel isn't a big woman, and the physical demands of the job leave her exhausted at the end of each long shift. Worse than the physical strain, though, is the emotional toll that the work takes on the nurses.

Rachel is deeply moved by the plight of the young men on her ward. Several have had one or both legs amputated; others still have both legs but will never be able to walk again without the use of crutches. The worst cases are those with spinal cord injuries that have left them paralyzed. One, a handsome young lieutenant named Jukka, is paralyzed from the neck down. Nurses and Lottas have to administer his medicine, turn him over several times a day, change his diaper, wash and feed him, and see that he drinks enough. He is not in physical pain, but he has just begun to realize how serious the prospect of life as a quadriplegic is.

Whenever she has a spare minute on the ward, Rachel checks on Jukka and sometimes sits by his bed for a minute to talk with him. He has already told her that he is engaged to a girl from his home town, which is less than an hour away, but after visiting him once the week he arrived at Kiljava, she has not been back to see him. Rachel wonders what kind of girl would abandon her fiancé at a time like this and tries to comfort Jukka as best she can.

One day, the head nurse, whom everyone calls Sister Helmi, summons Rachel into her office. She is a gruff woman in her fifties, with a wrinkled face and raspy voice.

"Sit down, Rachel. We need to talk."

"Yes?"

"I have been watching you on the ward since you got here. You are skillful and diligent, but you need to change your bedside manner."

"I try to be as pleasant as possible, Sister."

"That's just the problem," continues Sister Helmi. "You can't be 'pleasant' with these boys. They don't understand. 'Businesslike' is the right way to treat them."

"Why is that?" asks Rachel. "We were taught always to be pleasant and respectful. Our patients have suffered so much. The least we can do is treat them in a friendly and pleasant way." She has always thought that the "businesslike" manner of Sister Helmi and some of the older nurses was a sign that they had been doing hospital work for too long and were no longer able to empathize with their patients. Sister Helmi reminds her of a prune. She is determined never to become like that herself.

"That's fine for dealing with the grannies in the Helsinki Surgical Hospital," Sister Helmi continues, "but with these boys it's different. Many of them will never have a normal life, and the sooner they come to terms with that, the better off they will be." She drops her voice ever so slightly. "Washing and feeding them bring you into intimate contact that can easily be misunderstood. I've seen it too many times. It just raises unreasonable hopes in their minds, and when they finally realize the way things really are, they come crashing down even lower than they were before. It's not fair to them."

Rachel is dumbfounded. Not fair to them? The whole idea seems ridiculous. Should she try to act mean and disinterested to all her patients because one of them might misinterpret her kindliness as an inappropriate sign of affection?

"I'm just trying to be nice. I'm sure I never do anything to give any of them the wrong impression."

"You may think that," Sister Helmi replies, "but these boys are hurting and lonely. The worse their injuries are, the more they need to feel that they are still men and attractive to women. I understand that you don't mean to do it, but you'll only hurt them more. Unless you are prepared to look after one of them for the rest of his life, you'd better back off and do as I say. Believe me, a purely professional manner is best for everyone in the long run."

The hardest hours in Rachel's young nursing career begin when she returns to her rounds after this rather one-sided discussion with Sister Helmi. On the one hand, everything the head nurse said makes sense; on the other, the cold-hearted approach she recommends—no, orders—Rachel to take goes against everything that attracted her to nursing in the first place. If she has to place herself above her patients, she isn't sure she wants to be a nurse at all. How can she take responsibility for her patients' feelings in that way? And yet, just like legs and arms, a soldier's heart can surely be wounded, and she certainly doesn't want to be responsible for anything like that, either.

It is time to give Jukka his evening meal, and Rachel nearly stumbles with the tray on her way to his bedside, so distracted is she by the dressing down Sister Helmi gave her. Jukka, too, can sense that something is wrong.

"What did that old Harpy say to you?" he asks. "I saw her call you into her room."

"It was nothing," Rachel replies. "We were just talking about some scheduling matters."

Jukka tries to engage her in conversation between bites of his liver casserole, but Rachel feels herself pulling away. She is unsure how to react, and that in itself is enough to erect a barrier between her and the young soldier that had not been there before.

"Hey, don't feel bad," Jukka says. "She gets on everyone. Maybe you don't see it, but I do. She never misses an opportunity to show somebody up, especially the young nurses. I think she was born crabby!"

Rachel cannot help laughing at the idea of a tiny, wrinkled, serious baby Helmi, and the laugh causes her hand to shake as she tries to spoon some liver casserole and lingonberry into Jukka's waiting mouth. Some of the bright red berry juice drips onto his nightshirt, and a stain spreads across his chest. The stain will never come out, Rachel knows, no matter how many times the shirt is scrubbed.

Uncertainty

Benjamin doesn't hear from his mother for almost three weeks after she leaves for Helsinki with Jakob and Rifka. The war has already begun by the time he sits down to read the reassurances in her long-delayed second letter that negotiations will certainly prevent the outbreak of hostilities. How much the world has changed in such a short time!

Zipora writes that she and the children slept for the first four nights in the Helsinki Jewish School on Ruoholahdenkatu, waiting for the congregation to find a place for them to stay. Then they moved into an apartment on Lapinrinne owned by an elderly couple. From there it is an easy walk for the children down the hill to the Jewish School. Classes will be more of a challenge for Jakob, who is in ninth grade, than for Rifka, who is still in seventh. Although the school has been changing the language of instruction year-by-year and grade-by-grade from Swedish to Finnish for seven years, the eighth and ninth grades are still being taught in Swedish, a language Jakob speaks only haltingly. Still, they all agree that in such uncertain times, it is better for both children to be in the Jewish School than to be among total strangers. There are a few familiar faces at the school, some of whom are also recent evacuees and others who left Viipuri earlier for the capital.

Some of Viipuri's Jews have moved in with relatives in Helsinki or Turku or been able to rent places of their own while others have been resettled by the government in Tampere. Those like Zipora and her children, who have neither family nor money, are dependent on the congregation for support. The Jewish community, having taken extraordinary measures to help hundreds of Middle European refugees fleeing Nazi persecution in the months and years leading up to the war, now digs even deeper to help Finnish Jews being driven from their homes in Eastern Finland by the advancing Soviet army.

Once Benjamin has an address for his family, he begins to write at least a few lines every day and sends off the resulting compilation every Monday. Zipora wants him to send clothes, bedding, and numerous other items from their home, but the post office won't accept packages weighing more than five kilograms, and each package costs twenty *markkas*. It will be cheaper and easier to send everything by train when he can get around to it.

Benjamin writes about how empty the city seems and how the bombs are not such a big problem because the air raid sirens usually give everyone plenty of warning. So as not to worry his mother, he doesn't bother to mention the shelling from the phantom canon. He writes that it is probably more dangerous to be in Helsinki than in Viipuri, at least for the time being. He had been really worried after he heard how many people in the capital had died in the first day's bombing and is greatly relieved to know that his family is okay.

The apartment has not been damaged, Benjamin writes, and he and Mirele are doing fine. He neglects to tell his mother how much time they are both spending in and around the train yard, certainly the most dangerous place in Viipuri. He mentions that there are problems with electricity, heat and water. Temperature in the apartment only reaches about 15 degrees (60° F) during the day, but it doesn't really matter because he and his sister are rarely there excerpt to sleep. The lack of hot water makes it tough to wash, but he and Mirele are both getting hot meals at the Civil Defense Corps canteen. Coffee and sugar are hard to come by, but otherwise there is enough food. Finally, he reassures her that they are keeping the apartment clean so it will be ready for them when everyone returns home.

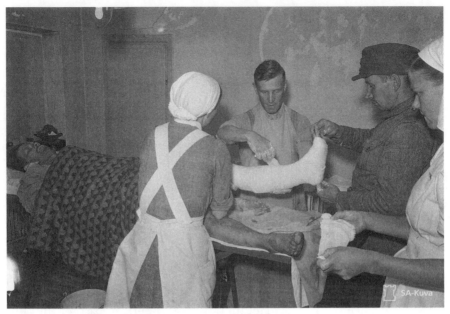

Figure 32.1. Medical Lottas helped with everything from applying plaster casts to emptying bedpans and bathing patients. (Finland's Military Museum)

In this field hospital, we saw the worst injured soldiers of the war. They were missing their hands, and we had to feed them, they were missing both legs and covered in blood and blood-soaked bandages. We stayed awake around the clock before we were able to sort out the chaos and provide each patient with some kind of care. One soldier had both arms and legs broken, and his tongue was lolling in some kind of frame, and the boy was crying in misery. It was up to the Lottas to provide basic care, and I saw how tenderly the young Lottas tried to feed this boy and spoke to him in a calming manner.

*Maire, a 25-year-old Lotta**

---

*Lehväslaiho, Reino, *Lottien Sota,* Werner Söderström Osakeyhtiö, Porvoo–Helsinki–Juva, 1988, p. 11.

~

CHAPTER THIRTY-TWO

Benjamin Remembers the Winter War

If you really want to know what people think, Mameh always used to say, you should look at what they do, not what they say. The same is true, even more true, maybe, for countries. Look what happened to Estonia. Before the Russkies attacked us, they sent soldiers, planes and ships to Estonia. It was supposed to be some kind of agreement, they said. To me it's not an agreement when someone is pointing a gun at your head and says, "Do you agree?" The Estonians said, "We agree," and look what happened to them: they lost their freedom. And the Jews of Estonia, the ones who didn't escape, they were sent to Siberia by the Russians or murdered by the Nazis.

The Russkies pointed guns at our heads, too, but we wouldn't agree to what they wanted so we had to fight. People thought we were brave to fight them, but what choice did we have? We knew what they were like, and we knew what would happen if we let them into our country.

Some people said it wasn't fair, but who ever said life would be fair? We Jews know about fair. Was it fair, what the Egyptians did to us? The Babylonians? This was the same thing, only the Russkies had bombs and tanks instead of spears and chariots.

Because I wasn't at the front in the Winter War, I never saw the tanks, but the bombs, they were terrible. And there were so many of them! Sometimes you could hardly see or breathe after an attack because there was so much smoke and dust in the air. After a while, there was shattered glass and brick everywhere on the streets and sidewalks so people just got used to walking through it. I ruined two good pairs of shoes that way with big holes in the bottom.

But even when there were no bombs, life was really tough. Nothing worked right. There was only electricity some of the time. The same for water. We tried to fix everything, but the more we fixed, the more they destroyed with their bombs. And it was cold, ayz kalt, that winter! Many times I had to sleep with my clothes on and even my overcoat to keep warm.

But the amazing thing was the people, they didn't complain. Everyone just did what they had to do. Some stores and restaurants stayed open almost to the very end and even a couple of banks. One restaurant I remember, Karjaportti, was hit by a fire bomb, and the whole upper floor burned, but they saved the ground floor, and three days later they were serving customers again. That was the Viipuri spirit!

One of my big problems was staying in touch with Mameh. It might take one or two weeks for a letter to get from Viipuri to Helsinki, and then another two weeks for the answer to get back to me! Sometimes she would complain that I hadn't written to her, but I had, every week. It was just that the mail was so slow in getting there. I knew someone who worked in the post office. He said they spent so much time sitting in bomb shelters they could never catch up on their work. There were always huge piles of mail, some waiting to go out and some to be sorted and delivered. Already they didn't have enough people to do the work because so many were in the army, and then a few got killed when a bomb hit the telegraph room in the Main Post Office Building.

Mameh worried too much about Mirele and me. I always told her to take care of Jakob and Rifka. We could take care of ourselves. When I had children of my own, I understood better. It doesn't matter how old they are, you still worry about your children.

For a long time, there were many people, maybe most people, who thought we would beat the Russkies. They said we would do to their whole army what Siilasvuo did to them at Suomussalmi and on the Raate Road. I always knew that was crazy. There were too many of them. I saw our dead and wounded soldiers coming through the train yard so I knew how bad the situation was. I have to admit, though, that sometimes I was fooled by the news, too. I thought maybe we could hold them off longer than we did, and maybe the Swedes or the Brits or somebody would come to help us in time. The radio said that the League of Nations had thrown the Russkies out in December. Everyone could see what they were doing. We knew the Germans were not going to help because of their meshugenah treaty, but we thought the Allies would. They let us down.

All through January we waited. It was pretty quiet in Viipuri. Every once in a while there were bombs or attacks from the phantom guns, but we got sort of used to it. And our defense at the front stayed strong. Then came February and the attack we were afraid of. The Russkies had brought more men and tanks, lots more, to smash through the Mannerheim Line. It took them two weeks of bombing and charges with thousands and thousands of men and tanks. When they finally broke *through at Summa our troops had no choice, they had to pull back. Before long we could hear the fighting as it came closer and closer to Viipuri.*

By then, we were all living like rats, spending most of our time in cellars. The bombing was terrible. The Russkies brought their big guns up close. I was sick most of the time, but I couldn't stop working. My throat hurt, my nose was running, and I had a cough that wouldn't go away. I should have gotten some rest, but we had to put out the fires and keep the trains running. Otherwise, it would be all over. Maybe I would sleep three or four hours, sometimes at night, sometimes during the day. That's how I caught the pneumonia. Now the shops were closed, and there wasn't much to eat. We heard that the Allies had promised to send troops, but we no longer believed that they would get here in time to save Viipuri, and we were right.

Mirele finally left for Helsinki. She had lost a lot of weight and looked terrible. I was really proud of her, how hard she worked. I could see she had changed a lot. I guess we all did. The war made you grow up in a hurry.

I stayed in Viipuri until the very end. I was supposed to go to Summa with the Guard Boys, but I was in the hospital by that time with the pneumonia. I only got out when we all had to leave Viipuri. If I hadn't been so sick, I probably wouldn't be here today. A lot of those boys, the ones who went to Summa, never came back. They had never been in a war and they were thrown into the worst battle of all. They were mostly just sixteen and seventeen, some even fifteen. It must have been awful. The Russkies broke through and just kept coming. They say the shelling never stopped the whole time. When we went back in '41, Summa looked like the moon, trees cut in half or blown out of the ground, big holes where the bombs fell. Shreklekh![1]

It was amazing that our men were able to stop the Russkies at all once they made it across Viipuri Bay, but, Got tsu danken, somehow they did. We were worried then that Viipuri wouldn't be able to hold out, but when the war ended, our flag was still flying on top of the castle tower.

That was the hardest thing for us. We never lost Viipuri in the war, we lost it in the peace. I still can't understand that. We kept the Russkies out, and they got it anyway. It was shameful! The best city in Finland, maybe one of the best in the world. It was never a Russian city. And now what have they done with it? They haven't even tried to rebuild. I think maybe they are still punishing Viipuri for standing up to them. That's the way they are.

I never shot at anyone in the Winter War, never even held a gun, but we all helped to fight the enemy in our own way. My job was to help keep the trains running, fight fires, and keep order in the streets. There were railway workers, police- and firemen, but without our help, they would never have been able to keep the city going. It's not a normal place, a city that is being bombed. But we never gave up. We did the best we could. In the end, we had to leave, but I remember looking back and seeing the flag, still there on the castle tower. I wish it was still there now, but what can you do? Life goes on.

Note

1. Terrible (Yiddish)

Figure 33.1. Viipuri during the final stages of the Winter War, March 1940 (Finland's Military Museum)

After Viipuri surrendered, our unit had a lot of interaction with German troops. My job included relaying weather reports to them, and I became buddies with one of the non-commissioned officers. We talked and went swimming together, and one time when we were sitting on the shore, we started arguing about National Socialism and Communism. I said that they were exactly the same, dictatorships. A little later, he asked me why I wasn't an officer, and I answered, "My hair is too dark,"

He asked, "What do you mean?," and I said, "*Ich bin Jude.*"

He turned bright red and didn't utter a sound for over a minute. Then I said to him, "I have one request. When I come to your tent or your area, don't tell your comrades that I'm Jewish. I'd really be in a difficult spot."

He put his arm around my shoulders and said, "If I told them you are Jewish, nothing would happen to you. You are a Finnish citizen. I'm the one they would shoot for fraternizing with a Jew!"

*Chaim (Harri) Mattsoff**

---

*Interviewed by Hannu Rautkallio, 10 January, 1989.

289

CHAPTER THIRTY-THREE

~

Finland Is Forced to
Accept a Bitter Peace

February, 1940—Stalin, who had insisted at the start of the Winter War that Kuusinen's People's Democratic Republic of Finland was the only legitimate government of the country, suddenly and unceremoniously abandoned the puppet regime on Monday, January 29. Responding to an appeal from Finland, delivered via Russia's Ambassador to Sweden, Alexandra Kollontai, the Soviet leader indicated that he was no longer opposed to entering into peace negotiations with Prime Minister Ryti and his government. Many of the world's newspapers that day featured stories of widespread German bombing raids on shipping along the British coast. Only one—the *Rochester* (New York) *Democrat and Chronicle*—led off with a banner headline reading "Finns Rout Air Attack on Viipuri," After a lull in the fighting, bombing runs over Karelia had begun again. If Stalin was truly interested in negotiating, he apparently intended to encourage the Finns to participate in the process by first hammering them into submission.

Three days later, the Soviets launched a massive assault on the Mannerheim Line. It began with saturation bombing in which some 300,000 shells fell on Summa, a key defensive position in the line, during one twenty-four hour period.

> "There had been nothing to compare with this since the German shelling of Verdun in 1915," writes H. M. Tillotson. "In the face of such fire the Finns' only tactical resort was to withdraw from their positions by day and reoccupy what remained of them at night. This at least reduced their scale of casualties and surprised the enemy when he tried to push forward with tanks and infantry at daylight."[1]

The Soviet Seventh Army had been reinforced to a strength of fifteen divisions, including five tank brigades and ten field artillery regiments. Some 2,000 bombers and fighter planes were thrown into the battle. The Finns had sixteen artillery batteries and only 12 anti-tank guns with which to hold off the main assault in the Summa sector. It still took until February 12th for the Soviets to break through the exhausted Finnish defense. Two days later Commander-in-Chief Mannerheim reluctantly authorized the withdrawal of troops to the next line of defense, ten kilometers to the rear. By the end of the month, a wedge had been driven into that defensive position as well, and a retreat to the so-called Rear Line, which ran through Viipuri Bay and the southern outskirts of the city, got underway.

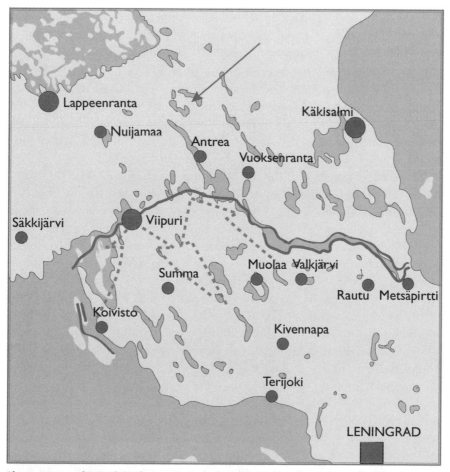

Figure 33.2. The Soviet 7th Army's push through the Karelian Isthmus in February 1940 (Finland's Military Museum)

The defense of the Karelian Isthmus was costly, but it convinced the Allies that the Finns were prepared to carry on fighting. March 1, 1940 the Allies finally promised to send 50,000 men if Finland would officially ask for them. Sweden and Norway immediately reacted by repeating that they would not allow safe passage for troops or equipment across their territory, and the Germans, who urged the Finns to sue for peace, controlled the sea routes.

Convinced that even under optimal circumstances the promised reinforcements wouldn't arrive in time, the Finns never sent the request for Allied intervention. Mannerheim had already decided instead to ask Ryti to open truce negotiations. He could see all-out war between the Axis and Allied powers approaching, and he didn't want Finland's valiant army to be completely wiped out. March 13, 1940, the Winter War came to an end.

Harsh Terms

Why did Stalin agree to a truce at a time when his men had finally broken through the Finnish lines and Finnish troops were obviously exhausted? Although the Finns had regrouped and would have continued to fight, the Soviets were now positioned to push across more favorable terrain towards Helsinki. The tactics at the start of the war clearly indicated that Stalin's objective was to occupy all of Finland. What had changed?

One theory suggests that the risk of having to fight the Allies if they came to the defense of Finland—he already knew war with expansionist Germany was inevitable at some point—was greater than any territorial advantage to be gained. Furthermore, were Finland to be conquered and occupied, a huge occupying force would have been needed to maintain control of its hostile population. It may also be that he feared that a negative reaction to his bullying tactics would turn away potential allies in the U.S., Britain and France. He would need them in the crucial fight to the finish with Germany. Comments he would later make also suggest the tiny opponent that fought back stubbornly against overwhelming odds had earned Stalin's grudging respect.

In any case, the Russian juggernaut stopped before reaching the pre-1809 border. Relieved at first to have the fighting come to an end, the Finns were shocked and dismayed by the punitive conditions demanded by the Russians in the peace negotiations. Finland was to cede eleven percent of its land, not all of which had been lost in the fighting. Included in the territory to be handed over were some of the nation's most productive farmland, factories and power plants as well as the country's second-largest city, Viipuri. Twelve percent of the population would have to be permanently resettled in what remained of the country. The Hanko Peninsula, 120 kilometers west of Helsinki, was to be leased to the Soviets for 30 years. And to add insult to injury, Finland was made to pay for damage that resulted from fighting on Finnish territory subsequently annexed by the Soviet Union.

So long as fighting continued, Finnish censorship (including strict control of the content of all correspondence between soldiers and their families) had continually emphasized the army's success in repelling enemy attacks and frequently reported foreign expressions of solidarity in order to maintain morale in the field and on the home front. When the war suddenly ended, and the unfavorable terms were announced, the public felt betrayed. Flags were lowered to half-mast throughout the country, and people cried openly in the streets.

President Kallio went on the air to explain the decision:

> Our people can rest assured that the government's intention throughout the peace process has been to prevent the continuous destruction of the Finnish people's vitality in this uneven struggle we have had to wage against a great power. In the light of our people's heroic defense and the conditions for peace imposed on us, we are overcome by deep sorrow at the dismemberment of our country, but our mind exhorts us to marshal all our forces for the single-minded reconstruction that will carry us forward toward the future.[2]

Adding to the Finns' distress was the growing scarcity of food. How would Finland feed 430,000 homeless refugees when the rest of the population was already scraping by with inadequate portions? Now there would be even less farmland for summer crops and fewer healthy men to do the planting. Coffee and sugar, which had already been rationed during the war, were joined on the list of regulated items by bread in May and butter, milk and meat by the end of the year.

The shock created by the harsh peace was felt most deeply by those who had sacrificed the most. Rachel was bombarded with questions she couldn't answer by patients on her ward. Would Soviet demands stop now, or were there more to come? Why had Finland agreed to such a truce when it hadn't been defeated? Many wondered aloud whether they had sacrificed their limbs, their youth and, in many cases, their future, in vain.

She tried her best to reassure them that Finland had retained its sovereignty in the face of overwhelming odds. Although Finnish Karelia had been lost, the costly struggle had ensured that the next generation of Finns would grow up as free citizens in their own democratic nation. No, she reassured them over and over again, their sacrifice had not been in vain.

David and his classmates at Non-Commissioned Officers Training School suffered a different kind of trauma. Many of them, like David, had chosen training over assignment to the front. When the war ended abruptly, they could not help feeling guilty about having spent the entire war in relative safety while so many others of their age were losing their lives in battle.

For David, the guilt was compounded by the heavy losses suffered by the Jewish community. Fifteen Jewish soldiers fell in the Winter War, many of them during the final seven days. Two of those were his good friends, Meier Kafka and Moses "Mosa" Smulovitz. All three were the same age, had played together as children and studied for their bar mitzvahs at the same time. David and Mosa had corresponded until the Soviet assault in February disrupted the delivery of mail. Mosa had been confident that Finland would win the war or at least force the Soviets to accept an honorable peace.

Benjamin had lost a good friend as well. Salomon Eckert, with whom he had acted in several plays at *Ahdus*, fell in February at Oinaala, a village just a few kilometers north of Perkjärvi. Benjamin's father had worked as a hat-maker for Eckert's uncle, and Salomon had been something of a big brother to Benjamin. Benjamin also had a namesake, a handsome second lieutenant from Viipuri named Benjamin Bassin, who was killed on the very last day of fighting. His body was never recovered for burial and still lies somewhere near Säkkijärvi (Kondratjevo), where he fell.

Benjamin grieved over the loss of his friends and his city, but he didn't suffer from the guilt feelings that beset David. Although he hadn't actually fought, he had survived his share of dangerous situations, including a potentially deadly bout of pneumonia, and contributed to the war effort through his work in the Civil Defense Corps. He had done the right thing.

Although he was exhausted, Benjamin knew he would be called to the army before long. In the meantime, he would go to Helsinki and rejoin his family. David, meanwhile, still had to finish NCOTS and see if he would be accepted at Reserve Officer School. Rachel would remain at Kiljava through midsummer, by which time most of the patients would have returned home or been transferred to other hospitals or rehabilitation centers. Then she would begin preparing for the fall semester at the Helsinki Surgical Hospital Nursing School.

Notes

1. Tillotson, H.M., *op. cit.*, p. 169,
2. President Kyösti Kallio's March 14, 1940 speech: https://histdoc.net/historia/kallio1940-03-14.html

Figure 34.1. The 1940 Independence Day commemoration ceremony at the Helsinki Jewish Cemetery and the graves of Jewish soldiers who fell in the Winter War (Finland's Jewish Archives)

There were about ten of us students [at Reserve Officer School] assigned as "head-waiters" to a restaurant in Niinisalo. It had been turned into a German officers' club because about a hundred low-ranking German officers had been brought from the Leningrad front to Niinisalo to learn about forest and winter warfare.

Among them were about twenty S.S. officers in black uniforms; the rest wore grey. Normally there were more men from the *Wehrmacht* than the S.S. I was in charge of the Germans' wine stock and making *Glühwein* [mulled wine]. One evening, two young German officers in grey uniforms came to give me instructions on how to make *Glühwein*. My *Glühwein* apparently didn't have enough of this or too much of that.

Just then, the "greys" and "blacks" started another fight. One of the young officers introduced himself to me. His name was von Moltke. He asked if I was familiar with the family. I said I'd heard of it. It was the name of a well-known family of German officers. He said, "I'm one of the descendants of that family, and I'll probably be one of the last officers bearing the name because I shall not live to see the end of this war." Then he added, "Those men in black uniforms, they are not officers, they are murderers. They're a disgrace to the military reputation of Germany, but they will probably be our future leaders."

Leo Jakobson*

**Daavid: Stories of Honor and Shame*, documentary film by Taru Mäkelä, ForRealProductions in cooperation with the Finnish Broadcasting Company's Channel 2, 1997.

CHAPTER THIRTY-FOUR

~

Finland's Fragile Truce

Spring, 1940—The day after the Winter War ends, *Pravda* and *TASS* both publish diatribes against the idea of a Nordic defense federation based on the principle of neutrality, undermining Finland's best hope of staying out of rapidly expanding World War II. But does Finland really want to stay out of the war? Had there been no Winter War, the answer would certainly be affirmative, but that costly conflict has made the question considerably more complicated.

In February 1940, Reichstag president Hermann Göring, in urging Finland to agree to end the Winter War, assured former Prime Minister T. M. Kivimäki that when Germany wins World War II, Finland will get back "with interest" whatever it has lost to the Soviet Union. It is probably safe to say that every Finn wants to regain the land that has been unfairly taken, but not all of them are prepared to go to war again to get it back. Heading the list of those for whom recovery of the lost territory is a priority, of course, are the Karelian and Hanko evacuees, who want to return home, even if many of their homes have been destroyed. Also eager to restore prewar boundaries are many of those Finns who are forced to open their homes to recently arrived Karelian refugees or give up land so they can be resettled. As one resident of a village where both Jewish refugees from Austria and Karelian evacuees were housed remembers today: "We saw the Jews as guests who were just passing through. Resettling the Karelians was a bigger problem because they were here to stay and would need land and houses of their own."[1]

Those who are eager to redress the wrongs of the Winter War and its truce agreement also include members of the Academic Karelia Society (AKS) and others with an ultranationalist agenda and a fierce attachment to Karelia, which they revere as the cradle of Finnish culture and identity. Industry and commerce want to reacquire Viipuri, Karelia's rich agricultural resources and factories, and the lost territory's hydropower potential. For its part, the military recognizes how much easier it would be to defend against attacks from the east if the eastern border could be redrawn to link Lake Ladoga, Lake Onega and the White Sea, leaving three relatively narrow isthmuses to defend instead of a long undifferentiated border.

In the spring of 1940, however, most Finns are focused not on regaining Karelia but on putting food on the table and returning to something close to prewar normality. While the Finnish Army has not been defeated, its soldiers and Lottas are exhausted and its supplies depleted. Access to Finland's export markets in the West are cut off by the war between the Axis and Allied Powers. Ryti, Mannerheim and Tanner would like to draw closer to the Allied Powers, but Germany and its ally, the Soviet Union, stand in the way.

Hurtling Forward

The Winter War's guns have not been silent for even a month when Germany invades Denmark by land, sea and air on its way to attacking Norway. After just six hours of sporadic fighting in which 16 Danish soldiers are killed, Denmark capitulates. The invasion of Norway takes longer, but the results are similar. Two months after the invasion begins, Norway is firmly in German hands. According to *Yad Vashem*, the World Holocaust Remembrance Center, most of Denmark's 7,800 Jews and Jewish refugees will escape to Sweden as the Germans pretend not to notice their departure, but 477 will be deported to German concentration camps, where 60 will die. Norway's 1,700 Jews are not so fortunate: 762 will be killed.

While still mopping up in Norway in mid-May, Germany attacks the Low Countries. Luxemburg is conquered in a day, and 1,950 of its 3,500 Jews are exterminated. The Netherlands resists for a week, after which more than 100,000 of its 140,000 Jews, an incredible 71 percent, will eventually be put to death. Belgium lasts ten days longer but the result is the same: the country is occupied, and 28,900 of its 65,700 Jews are murdered. France initially sends troops into the Netherlands and Belgium to stop the onslaught but gets beaten back. Pushing down through the Ardennes Forest, German troops subsequently make deep inroads into France.

By the end of May, all of continental Northwest Europe is in German hands. Sixteen days later, France's Prime Minister Reynaud resigns and is replaced by Maréchal Pétain. By midsummer, the Maginot Line has fallen, France has agreed to an armistice, and the country is divided into an occupied

zone and a "free" zone. Of the country's 350,000 Jews, 77,320 will be liquidated before the end of the war.

Only two and a half months after German soldiers first crossed into
Denmark, Nazi control of the Atlantic Coast extends from Nordkapp at
the northernmost tip of Europe to France's border with Fascist Spain in the
south. The western half of the Baltic Sea and access to the North Sea is controlled by the German navy. Finland's only theoretical opening to its crucial
export markets is the port of Liinahamari on the Barents Sea, almost 1,500
kilometers north of Helsinki over roads unfit for heavy traffic.

The Soviet Union, exercising territorial ambitions of its own, forces the
Baltic States to accept Red Army troops on their soil in early June 1940. Two
months later, popular front governments in Estonia, Latvia and Lithuania,
supposedly elected by overwhelming majorities, request membership in the
Soviet Union, effectively forfeiting their independence. Further south, the
U.S.S.R. demands that Romania hand over its Bessarabian oil fields.

Finland and Sweden find themselves completely surrounded by countries
at war (see map on p.19). Stalin continues to increase pressure on Finland,
reducing promised deliveries of grain to a trickle in order to force Finland to
grant the concession for nickel production from the Petsamo mines in the
Kola Peninsula to the U.S.S.R. Prime Minister Ryti recognizes that Germany
is the only potential remaining source of the grain his country needs to stave
off hunger. Mannerheim badly wants to keep Finland out of the conflict
among the great powers, but he knows his country needs to rearm in case
war comes to it anyway.

Although Ryti, Tanner and Mannerheim all distrust Hitler and find Nazi
politics abhorrent, they cannot avoid drawing three conclusions: 1) the current peace will not last long, 2) the abiding threat to their country's sovereignty comes from the Soviet Union, and 3) Germany is the only potential
source of protection should the Soviets move to seize control of Finland as
they recently did in the Baltic States.

Starting Over

Benjamin lacks a home of his own and employment. By the time he arrives
in Helsinki, he has already begun to wonder what he should do with the
rest of his life. He will not have to decide right away, however, as a notice
ordering him to report for military service in September is waiting for him
on his mother's dresser. Zipora is relieved to see her son but wonders why
he is so thin. He has neglected to write her about the pneumonia and says

only that the work was arduous and nourishing food hard to find during Viipuri's last days.

How she does it, he doesn't know, but Zipora somehow finds a chicken with which to make soup to welcome him home and fatten him up. In the absence of *matzo* meal, she makes some dumplings from millet flour. To Benjamin, the taste of her cooking is the best present she could give him, and he eats heartily. Jakob and Rifka tell him about school and pester him with questions about Viipuri and what he did during the war. When he asks about Mirele, though, he is met with silence. She is not staying at home, and Zipora doesn't know where she is. For the first few days after she came home, everything went well, but before long Mirele and her mother were at loggerheads again. After one particularly heated argument, Mirele packed her things and left. That was just days before the war ended, and no one has heard from her since.

Jakob insists on sleeping on the floor and giving his bed to his big brother. "It's only for a few days," Jakob says, "and I really don't mind." Benjamin had thought about going to the Civil Defense Corps headquarters and asking for help in finding a place to stay. He would rather be with his family, though, and allows himself to be talked into accepting his brother's offer. Being back with them all reminds him of how much he missed them after they left Viipuri even though he was too busy to realize it at the time. He will look for a room in a few days, but first he must find work for the summer.

On his fourth day home, Benjamin decides to redeem his promise to look David up if he ever got to Helsinki. He remembers the address from their correspondence and finds the house on Juhani Ahon tie in the Eira district but not without having to ask several people along the way for directions. David's mother is home and explains that her son is in Vaasa until the first week in June at NCOTS. After that, they don't know where he will be assigned. Benjamin thanks her and, after protesting at first, accepts her offer of a cup of real coffee, which her husband has obtained from a colleague in Stockholm.

Benjamin has never seen such a magnificent Jewish home and is more than a little intimidated by it. The Jews he knew in Viipuri lived in much more modest dwellings. There are carpets on all the floors, paintings on the high walls, and drapes framing the large windows. When David's mother asks what Benjamin plans to do, he explains that he needs to find work as soon as possible. It turns out that David's mother's second cousin is a furrier who makes coats and hats. He lost two of his best workers in the war and recently complained to her that he cannot find competent replacements. She gives

Benjamin his address and a note explaining that he is a friend of David's. Two days later Benjamin has a job as a cutter and blocker at Turkisliike [Fur Shop] Grünstein and has found a small room to rent on a weekly basis until September only a block away from where his family is living. Life is looking a little brighter.

The last time he was in Helsinki was the summer of 1936, and he was on his way to camp. That, of course, makes him think of Rachel. He hasn't heard from her since the war began, but he decides he will write her the first chance he gets. After all this time, what can he lose?

Winding Down

Rachel spends April helping patients prepare to leave Kiljava. By May, all the mobile patients have left, and she turns to the more difficult cases. One by one they are picked up by their families until only those unable to be cared for at home or who have lost contact with their families are left. Lilli, one of the remaining Lottas, spends all of her time trying to track down Karelian families that are scattered around the country so their sons can be reunited with them. Rachel stays on the ward, and her heart goes out to the few remaining soldiers who have such severe injuries that home care is out of the question for them. One of them is Jukka.

Rachel has tried to maintain the professional distance mandated by Sister Helmi, but watching Jukka slip deeper and deeper into depression is almost more than she can bear. His fiancée has never returned. Rachel also learns that Jukka's mother died giving birth to him. Then his father was killed in a logging accident when Jukka was only five, leaving him to be raised by an older sister. She, apparently, moved to Sweden with her children when the war began. Jukka dictates a letter for Rachel to send to the sister, but no answer ever arrives. Rachel realizes now and so, apparently, does Jukka, that he is, and will probably remain, alone for the rest of his life.

The Disabled War Veterans' Association has recently been created to take responsibility for the rehabilitation of veterans and provide long-term care for those who will never be able to look after themselves. The Association offers Jukka a place at Kyyhkylä Manor in Mikkeli, where veterans of the 1918 War have been housed since 1920. He is one of the very last to leave Kiljava, which is returning to its pre-war function as a sanatorium. Rachel accompanies Jukka to the ambulance that will take him to Mikkeli, and it requires all her self-control to keep from taking his hand as the gurney is wheeled out of the hospital. She does wave somewhat awkwardly and wish him well as he is lifted into the ambulance, but the gesture feels wholly inadequate, and

Rachel cries herself to sleep that night. She could never look after Jukka by herself, as Sister Helmi had warned, but denying him what little warmth and friendship she could have provided seems like a cruel and beggarly response to his loneliness, and it rends her heart.

One week after Jukka's departure, Rachel packs her bags, and prepares to bid farewell to the nurses and Lilli. The Lotta Svärd organization, however, has other plans for her. She is needed to assist in taking inventory at Kiljava, packing all the military property and preparing the hospital for reconversion. It isn't until the third week of June that she is finally driven to Hyvinkää to catch a train for Helsinki, where she will change for Turku. The summer of 1940 is neither exceptionally warm, like the previous summer, nor particularly cool. The mean temperature will hover around 15 degrees (almost 60° F) through the end of August, creating a sense of normalcy in stark contrast to all the incomprehensible things that have taken place since the magical summer a year before. Instead of the eagerly awaited Olympics there has been a horrible war. Could so much have changed in just twelve months?

The last time Rachel visited her parents' home, she was struggling to cope with the hurt and disappointment caused by David's behavior at the Mikado. How trivial all that seems now! She promises herself, as the train slices through the fields and forests of southern Finland, never to feel sorry for herself like that again.

Moving On

David waits for the longest time before checking the list on the bulletin board. He is pretty sure he knows what it will say, but he still doesn't dare read it right away. He missed the graduation ceremony with, of all things, the mumps, and was quarantined for fear of contagion. Although he finished the non-commissioned officer training course at the top of his class, and by all rights the list should confirm his assignment to Reserve Officer School, he remembers everything he has been told about Jews being rejected without cause. Now he is healthy again, but he still hesitates before consulting the list.

And there it is! He is to report in five days to the Forty-Seventh Class at Reserve Officer School in Niinisalo. That gives him just enough time for three days in Helsinki with his family. He hasn't been home since November, before the first day's bombing raids that changed everything. He recalls that he spent too much of that furlough partying with friends and acquaintances. Only when he left again for Riihimäki did he realize how disappointed his parents and Rafu were that he had not spent more time with them. This time, he decides, he will stay at home and rest up for the trials ahead at Niinisalo.

By the third day he is home, however, David needs to get out of the house and so sets out to visit the Jewish cemetery in Helsinki's Hietaniemi district. The afternoon is unseasonably cool, and sharp gusts of wind whip up tiny cones of leaves and dirt as he wanders among the graves of Cantonists and other ancestors. Those members of the congregation who fell in the recent war have been assigned a special place of honor just a few dozen paces down-hill from the gate and to the right. Their permanent headstones have yet to be installed, and the graves are high mounds of earth that have yet to settle. At the head of each one, a simple wooden marker in the shape of the tablets of the Ten Commandments allows David to identify those, including Mosa and Meier, whose remains have been returned home to their final resting place. He recognizes every name. Later, on the spot where he is standing, a slab of black granite, designed by his cousin Sam Vanni and Leo Engel, will memorialize their sacrifice.

Finland makes an enormous effort to recover the bodies of its soldiers, wash and dress them, and ship them home for burial. Graveyards are meticu-lously tended, and survivors make sure to adorn the graves with flowers and candles on appropriate occasions. Memorial Day falls two weeks after David leaves for Niinisalo. Surviving Jewish veterans and numerous other members of the congregation will gather at the site to honor their fallen comrades. As David walks pensively among the graves, however, he is the only one in the cemetery. A late sprinkling of spring snow imparts to the scene a solemn, ghostly aspect, and the whispers of the departed are muffled by the wind.

Note

1. Riihilahti, Pauli, in a presentation to the Vantaa branch of the Suomi-Israel yhdistysten liitto, March 17, 2016.

Figure 35.1. The Helsinki Jewish School in 1894 (Finland's Jewish Archives)

During the Continuation War, when the Germans were in Finland, we fled the city and were living in the North in places like Kemi, Tornio and Pietarsaari. I had an uncle who lived in Pietarsaari. He said he had a boat ready to take us across the Gulf of Bothnia to Sweden. There were Jews in the army, and the criterion was that Mannerheim had to give the order for all Jews to leave Finland, then we would go, but the order never came.

Jewish soldiers had their own synagogue at the front, and they were open about their Jewishness. My husband served in the army as a translator between the German and the Finnish armies. He spoke both German and Yiddish and said that he was Jewish. One officer told him that he was Austrian. Then he offered my husband a cigar and said, "This cigar is from before the Anschluss so it is OK."

*Ruth Hasan**

---

*Interviewed by the author, Turku, 31 August, 2012.

CHAPTER THIRTY-FIVE

~

Benjamin Reflects
on His Altered Status

I was a refugee but a refugee in my own country. I had to leave my wonderful city, the only home I'd ever known. I rejoined my family, but they were living in someone else's home, in someone else's city. It was a strange feeling, a modne gefil, like being lost and alone in a crowded place. Even the way people spoke here was different. But what could I do?

I think this was when I began to understand Zayde Peisach. I had always known the story of his exile in St. Petersburg, but to me it was just that, a story. I mean, I didn't know how it felt. Now I did. To be driven out of your home, not because of what you did but because of what others did to you, that's terrible.

At first you can't even imagine starting a new life. I was lucky. I was young, and I got a job in Helsinki almost right away. For the older people it was much harder. Some of them didn't find work for a long time, and that meant they couldn't get a home of their own, either. They had a good life in Viipuri, and then suddenly they didn't any more. Of course, the congregation helped, but no one who is used to working and being independent wants to live on charity. And then came war again. Oy gevalt!

My family, they were lucky. Most of the people we knew from Viipuri were sent to Tampere. Mameh, she wanted to go to Helsinki. She didn't think Tampere would be such a good place for a Jewish family. She got in touch with Counselor Jakobson. He had been the head of our congregation in Viipuri and would lead the Helsinki congregation during the next war. He agreed to help her find a place in Helsinki so my brother and sister could attend the Jewish School. Mameh had become more religious after Tate died, and she wanted the young ones to have a Jewish education. For Mirele and me, she knew, it was too late.

I had lost interest in the Viipuri congregation and in religion because of everything that happened in the years leading up to the war. I couldn't stand the way some people fought over power in the congregation. Power? Hah! Like crows fighting over crumbs spilled under a garden table, that's what they were. Who would have the best seats in shul on the High Holy Days, who would be chairman of what committee, gants kindish[1] is what it was!

But then came the war, and now I could see how everyone pulled together and helped each other. First they took responsibility for those fleeing the Nazis, then Jews who were evacuated from Viipuri and Sortavala, and finally the Russian Jewish prisoners during the Continuation War. Fabu Stiller and Bernhard Blaugrund were the ones they talked about, but I could see that everyone contributed what little they could. I don't say all the selfishness disappeared, but the generosity of even poor people was amazing. Mameh would never have made it without the help of the congregation. Even the old grandmothers who could hardly see any more would sit all day and knit socks and mittens for those who needed them. Women who used to show off their expensive jewelry were selling it so they could contribute to the welfare fund, and men were contributing money, can you believe, without talking about it!

That was when I began to find my Jewishness again. Not in shul, at first. I still had no interest in going there except on the High Holy Days. It was more like a sense of community, of knowing where I belonged. It was the food, the Yiddish, the music, even the jokes. Especially during the first year after losing our home, I somehow stopped being so critical. It wasn't easy. The Helsinki Jews spoke Swedish. Okay, most of them knew how to speak some Yiddish and Finnish, too, especially the younger ones, but they preferred Swedish. Until my Swedish got better, I often spoke Yiddish with the older ones.

I don't really know how to explain it. It wasn't like feeling we were better than the other Finns. I never felt that way. It was more like I began to feel that we Jews were a big family, the way everyone was helping take care of everyone else. We were doing our part to help Finland, every one of us, but then we were doing extra to help our own people, too. Losing our home and having to depend on others for help showed me how important that was. I kept thinking of the Karelians coming on foot into Viipuri with their few possessions. I could see in their faces how it must have felt to have lost everything, to be alone and helpless, leaving their entire life behind and not knowing what was in the future. And then it happened to me. I had to leave, and at first it felt like I had no place to go, either.

When I arrived in Helsinki, though, I realized I wasn't really alone. It wasn't like being in Viipuri, but there were some people we knew already there, and the congregation was very welcoming. Even if it was much bigger than ours had been, *it wasn't so different. I think the culture brought us all together. Jews had suffered much worse in other places and other times and still survived, and that gave us courage and hope. We would survive, too.*

Note

1. Quite childish (Yiddish)

Figure 36.1.   Left to right: Finland's Director of Sports Urho Kekkonen, Field Marshal Gustaf Mannerheim, Sweden's Prince Gustaf Adolf, Finland's Prime Minister Risto Ryti and Germany's Sports Director Hans von Tschammer und Osten, at the opening of a track meet in Helsinki, September 7, 1940 (Lehtikuva Photo Service)

A kind of enthrallment with Germany had taken over Finland in May [1941]. It didn't touch only the cultural and sports circles and the military leadership. . . . A majority of the population was leaning towards Germany.

General (retired) Pentti Airio*

**Aseveljeys: Saksalaiset ja suomalaiset Itä-Lapissa 1941–44*, Docendo, Jyväskylä, 2014, p. 92.

CHAPTER THIRTY-SIX

~

Hitler Changes His Mind

Summer, 1940—Commander-in-Chief Mannerheim wrote to his sister, Eva Sparre, at the end of the summer of 1940:

> We have experienced a summer full of threats and unrest. In order to avoid a new war, we have given in to demands that are not based in the peace agreement. Their purpose can only have been to destroy our country and create the same kind of farce that, skillfully directed, turned the residents of the Baltic States into slaves in a few hours. We live from day to day.[1]

In addition to the collapse of the free Baltic States, the summer sees the capitulation of France, Germany's continued unwillingness to provide aid, and a message from Sweden saying it will not grant Finland direct military assistance. On the domestic front, mounting provocation by the Finland-Soviet Union Peace and Friendship Society (a communist front organization supported by the U.S.S.R.) takes the form of huge and sometimes violent demonstrations during which participants shout "Long live Soviet Finland!" The ever-present Soviet threat is underscored on June 2 when two Soviet DB-3 bombers shoot down an unarmed Finnish commercial passenger plane, the *Kaleva*, en route from Tallinn to Helsinki. All passengers and crew members perish. The attack, which is witnessed by Estonian fishermen, is not acknowledged by Moscow.

What Mannerheim cannot know at the time, however, is that Germany's attitude towards Finland is about to change. In the early summer of 1940, once the Atlantic Coast has been secured by German forces, *Reichsminister* Göring assures Hitler that the *Luftwaffe* will be able to control the air space over the English Channel, clearing the way for the invasion of England. July 10, Germany launches the assault, code-named Operation Sea Lion. By August 20, however, the struggle for aerial supremacy commonly known as the Battle of Britain is going badly for the Third Reich.

A disappointed Hitler postpones the planned invasion of England indefinitely and pivots back to his temporarily neglected focus on wiping the Soviet Union off the map. Having told the *Reichstag* in July that Germany has no interest in Finland, he now reverses his position. Finland's recent agreement to sell 60 percent of its nickel production to Germany may have something to do with the change as does the Finnish army's potential importance in securing the *Wehrmacht's* northern flank during the reimagined invasion of the U.S.S.R.

Were Germany to have carried out its plan to invade Britain, Allied troops would have been tied down for months on Europe's western fringe, leaving the Soviet Union a free hand to take care of unfinished business in Finland. With the German invasion of Great Britain off the drawing board, however, another unprovoked Soviet attack on its tiny neighbor risks triggering Allied or even German military intervention on Finland's behalf. In saving Britain from the Nazis, the Royal Air Force has also saved Finland, at least for the time being, from renewed Soviet aggression.

Germany, which refused to come to Finland's aid during the Winter War, now begins providing assistance through a bilateral commercial agreement. No arms are included in the arrangement, but crucial grain supplies are secured. And then, August 17, 1940, a German lieutenant colonel named Josef Veltjens arrives in Finland with an astonishing offer from Göring for Marshal Mannerheim. Germany is prepared to sell arms to Finland in return for the right of passage across Finland for German soldiers moving between Germany and northern Norway. Germany, he points out, already has a similar agreement with Sweden. Because the part of the deal involving the sale of weapons is in violation of Germany's pact with the Soviet Union, deliveries will have to be made clandestinely via Swedish companies. Veltjens insists that no change has taken place in Germany's relationship with the Soviet Union, but as the latter is threatening Finland, Germany needs to act to secure its access to Finland's nickel reserves.

The Soviet Union has been pressuring Finland to allow its troops to travel by train between Leningrad and Hanko, where it has established the garrison and naval station it insisted upon in the Moscow Peace Treaty. Having secretly agreed to grant similar rights to German troops, Finland meekly acquiesces to the Soviets' demand.

Reserve Officer School (ROS)

When the Winter War ended, Finland was in desperate need of rebuilding its economy. It had a total of 365,500 men in uniform, and they were needed to plow the fields and man the production lines that would help the country get back on its feet. They would also be needed to build housing for the Karelian evacuees. Nine months later, the standing army has been reduced to 110,000 men with most of the rest put on active reserve. It is clear to all, though, that Finland will have to be able to mobilize its military reserves quickly if the Soviet Union threatens Finland's independence once again. Men who served with honor in the Winter War are expected be ready at any time for immediate redeployment, and many of those who were considered unfit for duty in 1939 are called back for new physical examinations. Should they be needed, these reserves amount to an additional 376,000 men, bringing the total number available for service to almost half a million.

With so much of its potential military manpower tied down in civilian activity, the high command recognizes what a tremendous challenge it will be to mold them quickly into efficient fighting units. A top priority, therefore, becomes training enough competent officers to lead the troops. Because many officers fell in the war, and the number of divisions is being increased from twelve to sixteen, thousands of new officers will have to be trained quickly to meet the army's growing need.

The first post-war Reserve Officer School class, ROS 47, begins training May 6, 1940 at Niinisalo, a garrison that sits north of a point midway between Pori on the West Coast and Tampere in the center of the country. David reports May 5 for the four-month-long course along with 1,103 other candidates, 98 of whom have been chosen for artillery training. If he successfully completes the course, he will receive his provisional second lieutenant's commission the first week of September.

In 1940, Finland's artillery operations have not yet developed to the point where, admired for their accuracy and tactical flexibility, they will be adopted by armies around the world. It will be three years before General Vilho Nenonen and Lieutenant Colonel Unto Petäjä revolutionize artillery science with improved fire direction cards and the trajectory corrections converter, tools that greatly simplify the task of fire direction officers while simultaneously improving the accuracy of the vectors they relay to the fire command. Without the benefit of these innovations to come, the candidates in ROS 47 still have to perform rapid calculations in their heads. David is especially quick and accurate in mental computation and quickly distinguishes himself in the classroom. He also performs well in physical training, finishing seventh out of the entire class in the traditional "Callus Marathon" from Niinisalo to Kankaanpää and back.

By coincidence, his bunkmate Johan is also an outstanding candidate, both in the classroom and the field. Johan's great-grandfather was an officer in the Czar's Guard, and the family's manor is among the finest in southwest Finland. He and David converse in Swedish, which creates a bit of tension between them and others in the barracks. Johan is one of the tallest officer candidates in the class at 196 cm (6'5"), and his generally stern demeanor keeps most of his classmates at arm's length.

Gradually, David and Johan are drawn to one another by mutual respect earned in the classroom and by their outsider status among the candidates, conferred on them by their mother tongue and additionally on one by his religion and the other by his social class. They begin spending time together, discussing the same things young men of all backgrounds do at a certain age when relaxing together. One day, though, their discussion turns away from women and sports to a much more serious topic. They have just finished their evening meal and have an hour of free time before they have to be in their bunks. Without either of them suggesting it, they find themselves walking along the shore of Lake Valkjärvi. It is the week after midsummer, and the sun is still well above the horizon, sending orange-tinted rays skittering across the rippled surface of the lake.

"Did you hear that Hitler has taken Paris?" David asks. "It doesn't look like anyone can stop him. Soon he will have his foot on the neck of all of Europe."

"And a good thing, too," replies Johan. "The sooner, the better. Then he can turn his attention to Russia."

"How can you say that? Look what he's done to the Poles and Jews."

"Yes, I know," says Johan. "He can be ruthless, and he certainly has some strange ideas. But he is the world's only hope to stop the rampant spread of communism. Stalin wants to take over the world, too, and I'd certainly rather have the Germans as my masters than the Russkies."

"But why do we need masters at all," asks David. "To me, they are both murderers."

"Maybe so," Johan continues, "but let's be realistic. Hitler is all about order and discipline. The other one sows confusion and chaos wherever he goes. Half of Germany was unemployed when Hitler came to power, and look at it now. Stalin took over a country where there were problems, for sure, but people had enough to eat. From what I hear, millions have died of starvation because of his absurd collective farming system. Anyway, I don't care so much about starving Russkies or Ukrainians, but I do care about what will happen to us. The Germans aren't a threat to us at all. The Russkies, on the other hand, have already attacked us once, and they didn't get everything that they wanted. If they attack us again, I'd rather have Hitler on my side than to have to fight them alone like we did before."

"Maybe Sweden, Britain or America will fight on our side. Germany isn't the only country with a strong military."

"Where were they when we needed them the last time? Now the Brits are holed up on their island, the Yanks are halfway around the world and thinking of no one but themselves, and the Swedes don't have the balls to stand up to Russia. That's how it is, and wishing won't change it," says Johan.

"Well, if the Germans do come here, it will mean the end for me and my people. Wherever the Nazis go, they round up all the Jews and send them to concentration camps. What they will do with us after that, no one knows, but it certainly won't be good. I have no love for communists," David insists, "but at least they haven't made the persecution of Jews a central part of their program."

"That's because so many of the communist leaders are Jews, themselves. Marx, Engels and Trotsky? All Jews! Hitler hates communists more than he hates Jews. He just recognizes that communism has a strong Jewish component. To wipe out communism, he has to get rid of some Jews."

Up to this point in this conversation, neither David nor Johan has raised his voice. Johan's last comment, though, crosses a line that risks turning the conversation from theoretical to personal. There is no way for them to continue without causing irreparable damage to their otherwise friendly relationship so they stop talking and walk back in awkward silence to their bunkhouse.

Anticipation

Benjamin doesn't know where to send his letter to Rachel so he sends it to her home in Turku. From there it makes its way to Kiljava but arrives just after she has left. By the time the letter is returned to Turku and she receives it, Benjamin has already become convinced she is never going to answer.

When Rachel does finally reply, she explains that she is spending the summer in Turku, helping her parents. She will return to Helsinki in the autumn to take up her studies again at the Helsinki Surgical Hospital Nursing School. Her tone is friendly but somehow distant, as if she is writing carefully, not with feeling. Nevertheless, Benjamin responds that he might be able to visit Turku at the end of the summer as one of his former *Kadur* teammates is now living there and has said Benjamin can sleep on his couch if he ever comes that way. Rachel's reply, which arrives without delay, is that it would be nice to see him, but she is moving back to Helsinki after the summer anyway, and maybe they should wait until then as she hardly has any free time in Turku, what with working in her father's store and helping her mother at home.

Rachel's letter drops like a wet blanket on Benjamin's enthusiasm. He would have been ready to leave immediately if she had said, "Come!" Instead, he writes that he hopes she has a nice summer and looks forward to seeing her in Helsinki, perhaps at the end of August. He adds that he has received his notice to report for military service and will be leaving the first week of September.

Rachel's next letter arrives August 17, explaining that she will be staying with her Tante Bluma on Bulevardi the weekend of the 24th and 25th before checking into the nursing students' hostel. They could meet at the lovely Café Ekberg at 9 Bulevardi. Would 2:00 p.m. on the 24th be okay? As soon as he reads it, Benjamin forgets his disappointment and dashes off a note to say that he will be there.

When the big day arrives, Benjamin puts on his best white shirt with a high collar, massages a dab of Brylcreem into his recently trimmed hair, and arrives at the cafe at quarter past one. By the time two o'clock arrives, he has already finished two cups of tea, and his neck is getting sore from corkscrewing around to look at the clock on the wall behind him. Rachel hasn't shown up.

At ten past two, he finally sees her walking towards the cafe. She is wearing a dark blue fitted skirt and white blouse with a light blue paisley scarf around her neck. Her dark hair falls in thick curls to her shoulders. She walks hurriedly to the door, opens it, and scans the room. Then she walks right past Benjamin without looking down. When she reaches the back of the room, she turns and walks past him again. Benjamin stands, awkwardly. "Rachel?"

She turns and looks up at him. "Benjamin?" A perplexed look comes over her face. "Benjamin, is that you? Gosh, you've changed!"

Remembering his manners, Benjamin pulls out a chair. "Please, sit down. You look wonderful!"

"I'm sorry I'm late. You know how it is. The one who lives the closest is always the last to arrive. I hope I haven't kept you waiting."

"Not at all. What would you like?"

While waiting for her Ravitol, a hot chocolate substitute made from roasted soy beans and sugar-beet molasses, Rachel continues to express her amazement.

"You've gotten so tall. When we were at camp, you were hardly any bigger than I was. I didn't recognize you."

"That was four years ago," Benjamin reminds her. "You've changed, too, but I would still have recognized you anywhere."

Rachel blushes slightly. She realizes that she was expecting to meet a boy, a slightly modified version of the Benjamin she knew at camp. Instead she finds herself sitting opposite a handsome young man who bears only a vague resemblance to that spindly camper she remembers. She regains her composure, however, and begins asking Benjamin about life in Viipuri during the war.

Benjamin tells her about the bombings and the shelling by the phantom gun, the fires and the suffering of the injured soldiers and evacuees as they came through the train yard, but he doesn't dwell on his own involvement. When she asks, he just says he did whatever he was ordered to do. The worst thing, he says, was having to leave the city without knowing whether he would ever be able to return.

Rachel then tells him about Kiljava. Mostly she talks about how skillful the surgeons were and how brave the soldiers. They rarely complained, and most of them accepted that their sacrifice was part of the price paid for keeping the country free and independent. She is looking forward to returning to class now that she has some practical experience under her belt.

"I am more certain than ever that I want to be a nurse. Being able to help people in need, it's a . . . a blessing. Maybe that isn't the right word, but I can't think of a better one. There really isn't any way to describe what it's like. I watched the nurses in the operating room when I was allowed to help. One time, a patient who stepped on a land mine was brought in with his leg blown off at the knee and his body filled with pieces of shrapnel. It was just awful. But somehow the nurses put aside their feelings and concentrated on what they were supposed to do. And some of the surgeons were just amazing! Then a couple of weeks later, I'd be helping that same patient get out of bed and learn to use crutches, and you wouldn't believe how he would be smiling and talking about all the things he was going to do after he got home."

"You must be really proud," Benjamin says. "I don't think I could do that. I felt really sorry for the wounded soldiers on the trains, but I mostly tried to think about other things. Otherwise, it just made me angry. I know we had no choice, and those who fought have every reason to feel that they accomplished something important, but I just think the whole business was . . . I don't know, senseless. In Viipuri, we weren't trying to hurt anyone. Those bombs weren't dropped on an army, they were dropped on a city that was just trying to survive. The people who were killed or hurt were mostly old men and young boys. I might feel differently if I had been at the front, but to me the situation in Viipuri wasn't war, it was more like the Russkies were shooting fish in a barrel."

"Let's not talk about the war. Tell me what you are doing now," Rachel insists.

"I've been working for a furrier, making hats. But in ten days I'll be in the army. From what I can tell, we'll probably be at war again soon. That's what I mean. It doesn't even do any good. People die, and cities are destroyed, and before long it's happening all over again. Nothing changes."

"Don't talk that way! If we hadn't fought, we would be just like the Estonians. From what I hear, anyone who doesn't agree with the government there gets shot or sent to Siberia. Here we can still say what we like and not worry that anything will happen to us."

Benjamin has the same kind of sinking feeling he had at camp when politics was being discussed. He can never find the right arguments. But when he looks in Rachel's eyes, he forgets about everything else. He is still hopelessly in love with her. If he thought that after four years his feelings might have changed, he was wrong. If anything, he is even more infatuated with her. And here he is, sitting across from her in a fancy cafe in Helsinki as if it is the most natural thing in the world.

"Don't you agree?" she asks.

"Sorry, agree about what? I guess I wasn't paying attention."

"What's the matter?"

"It's just that I'm so happy to see you," he confesses. "I guess I still have those same feelings I wrote about. I don't want to make things difficult, but I really would like to see you again when I come home on leave. I know you wrote that you have to be somewhere soon, but maybe next time we can go out for dinner or go to the cinema."

"That would be nice," Rachel admits, "but I don't want to lead you on. I'm not looking for the kind of relationship you mean, but I'm still happy to be your friend. I don't go out at all, really, so a film or a dinner would be a change. Let me know when you will be in town. Now I do have to go. It was lovely seeing you. Take care of yourself. Let's hope you are wrong about there being another war."

As he watches her walk briskly toward the center of town, Benjamin can't tell whether he is happy or sad. Rachel is even more beautiful, more charming . . . more everything than he remembered. Can it be that the first girl he ever liked will be the only one for him? And if she never comes around to feeling the same way about him, what then? He isn't even thinking about her career choice and the implication that she will never marry. Before it can even get to that point, she has to become interested in him, and Benjamin doesn't have a clue how to make that happen.

Nightmare

Benjamin leaves for Tammisaari and basic training at the Dragsvik garrison the first of September. At the end of the same week, Rachel receives a shock she will never forget. While riding the tram to school, she is astonished to see that all the main streets of Helsinki have been decorated with huge red flags bearing black swastikas on a white circle! What on earth can this mean?

Having seen its dream of hosting the 1940 Olympics destroyed by war, Finland has decided to revive the spirit of its people by hosting an international track and field meet in the new Olympic Stadium. Of course, Finnish Athletics Federation director Urho Kekkonen invites Sweden to participate, but to everyone's surprise an invitation is also extended to Nazi Germany. The choice is so unusual at the time that Lauri "Tahko" Pihkala, who sends the invitation on Kekkonen's behalf to Sweden's federation, feels obliged to write that everything has been assured "except the reaction of the Finnish public to the event," by which he certainly means to Germany's participation.

The event, dubbed Helsinki's mini-Olympics by the press, takes place the weekend of September 7–8. A press photo from the opening ceremony shows Kekkonen, Marshal Mannerheim, Sweden's Crown Prince Gustaf Adolf, President Ryti and Germany's *Reichskommissar für Turnen und Sport,* Hans von Tschammer und Osten, standing side by side as the German national anthem is played. Von Tschammer und Osten's right arm is extended forward and up in a Nazi salute while Mannerheim, in uniform, has his hand raised crisply to his cap. Behind them, at least three other Nazi salutes can be seen, presumably from other German officials in the VIP gallery.

The final tally of the two-day competition has Sweden victorious with 147 points, followed by Germany with 141 and Finland with 134. Despite the loss, Finland is left with a feeling of pride at having organized a successful event. Its Jews are left with the shocking realization that Nazi Germany is now being courted by the government as a potential partner. Finland is entering a period that Minister Paavo Rantanen calls "a seesaw of hope and fear" in his book, *Suomi kaltevalla pinnalla (Finland on a Slippery Slope).* President Ryti and his inner circle must try to balance asymmetrical relationships with superpowers that are already, or soon to be, at war with one another. To keep from falling off the seesaw, they will have to weigh all Finland's options carefully. In such circumstances, the interests of the country's tiny Jewish minority can hardly be expected to tip the balance one way or the other.

See-Saw

According to contemporary reports, the sudden arrival in Vaasa September 21 of German troops creates even more consternation than the mini-Olympics in Helsinki. Less than a year earlier, Germany had stood coolly by and let Russia pound Finland into submission. Now, uniformed German soldiers can be seen in the streets and cafes of Vaasa, waiting to board trains and trucks for Lapland and Norway. For many Finns, the news of their presence, reminiscent of the German expeditionary force that helped the White Army drive the Reds out of Helsinki in 1918, is more than welcome. "Just let the Russkies try to attack us again. This time, we won't be alone!"

Not all Finns feel reassured by the presence of the German troops, however. After the invasions of Denmark and Norway, knowledge that German troops have landed raises the specter of a potential Fascist putsch. Pro-German enthusiasm in military, university, church and cultural circles has occasionally spilled over into expressions of sympathy for racial policies and political methods at odds with Finland's democratic values. Will the power of the far right, which withered in the lead-up to the Winter War, be resuscitated in the nourishing embrace of the German military?

Word of the German soldiers' arrival hits the Jewish community especially hard. Although the soldiers are far away in the North and West, what is to guarantee that tomorrow they won't be in Turku and Helsinki? And if the news sends tremors through Finland's Jewish community, the shock is felt with greatest force by the Central European refugees still in the country. They came to Finland to seek a safe haven from Nazi terror, and now it seems as if it has followed them here.

The Soviet Union, as expected, reacts immediately to the news. Paavo Rantanen reports the following conversation between Foreign Minister Molotov and Ambassador Paasikivi:

Molotov: "Can I know how many German troops are being transported and to what region of Norway?"

Paasikivi: "All I know about it is what has been said in the official statement. We have also made an agreement with the Soviet Union concerning the transport of troops and military material to Hanko."

Molotov: "That is based on the peace agreement."

Paasikivi: "Nothing is said about that in the peace accord as has been stated several times. We required that the Soviet Union use sea routes to Hanko."

Molotov: "But the peace treaty doesn't forbid such an arrangement."

Paasikivi: "That means nothing in this case. We made the arrangement even though the treaty does not require us to do so."[2]

Everything seems to be in flux. Five days after German troops land at Vaasa, the first German arms shipments leave for Finland via Sweden, and Russian troops begin shuttling back and forth by rail across Southern Finland. Now there are both German and Russian soldiers on Finnish soil, and Finland is starting to rearm.

Notes

1. Rantanen, Paavo, *Suomi kaltevalla pinnalla*, Atena, Porvoo, 2012, p. 86.
2. *Ibid.*, p. 118

Figure 37.1. Helsinki's Isidor and Rafael Hirschovits on the Hanko Front as the Continuation War approached (Adiel Hirshovits' private collection)

Hitler is not the first Haman in Jewish history, nor is Berlin the first Susa. Until the present day the Jews have always had one response for such phenomena, and giving this response has always helped Jews to outlive their enemies. That response is unity.*

---

*From an editorial in *Ahdus*, the Viipuri Congregation's newspaper, No. 0, 1933, cited by Jukka Hartikainen in *"Viipurin juutalaisen yhteisön vaiheita,"* *Viipurin suomalaisen kirjallisuusseuran toimitteita*, Helsinki, 1998, p. 106.

CHAPTER THIRTY-SEVEN

~

Pressure Mounts

Autumn, 1940—Tammisaari lies on the Baltic Coast 35 kilometers from the municipality of Hanko. The border between the territory rented to the Soviets for thirty years in 1940 and the rest of Finland runs across the Hanko Peninsula halfway between Hanko at its tip and Tammisaari on the eastern shore, then fans out to the east and west through the archipelago. The peninsula is a sandy spit of land that looks a little bit like a mini-Italy without Sicily. Tammisaari, with its well-protected harbor and beautiful beaches, lies one third of the way to the tip on its eastern shore.

The Soviet Union's primary motive in demanding the Hanko Naval Base even before the start of the Winter War was to be able to seal off the mouth of the Bay of Finland. Hanko's harbor is open year-round, enabling ships to respond quickly to threats from the west, and coordinated crossfire from Hanko's coastal batteries and those of Estonia's Paldiski Naval Base just 81 kilometers to the south can effectively prevent enemy warships from entering the eastern end of the Baltic. Marshal Mannerheim recognizes Moscow's interest in protecting the approach to Leningrad and had earlier recommended offering Moscow the use of islands off the Hanko coast instead of the peninsula itself. His fear is that with Soviet troops stationed on the Finnish mainland, Finland's capital could find itself caught in a giant *motti* created by troops advancing quickly overland from both east and west.

Just days after the Winter War ends in an uncomfortable peace, Mannerheim and his staff meet to discuss next steps. The new border with the Soviet Union is going to be much harder to defend than the previous one, and the country's meager arms supplies have been badly depleted by the fierce fighting at the end of the war. Finland's only reliable military resource at this point is the continued willingness of its people to fight to defend their country.

A plan is drawn up to create a fortified line of defense that will run parallel to the redrawn border. The three most vulnerable stretches are the border on the Hanko Peninsula, the coastal sector west of Viipuri, and the waistline of Finland across which the Finns have been forced by the Soviets to build a rail line from Salla to Kemijärvi. Planning takes place in the late spring of 1940, and by mid-July there are already 10,000 men hard at work on the fortifications. The Salpa Line, as it will later be called, will become one of the largest construction projects ever carried out in Northern Europe. By November, there will be 35,000 men, mostly soldiers, providing the manual labor and 2,000 Lottas seeing that they are properly fed.

No Time to Waste

Benjamin's unit, part of the newly formed 13th Brigade, assembles in September at Tammisaari's Dragsvik garrison on the coast near Hanko. After all that he endured in Viipuri during the Winter War, basic training doesn't present much of a problem for him. His years in the Guard have prepared him for the discipline and the marching although he still doesn't enjoy either very much. The physical training is no more difficult than what he experienced with *Kadur's* football team, but he is surprised at how tired he feels after each calisthenics session or 5 km run.

An even bigger surprise for Benjamin is that he has been placed in a Swedish-speaking brigade. His Swedish is not very good, and at first he thinks about requesting a transfer, but on further reflection, he decides that the effort it will take to become fluent in Swedish will be worth it in many ways. Not only is it an important cultural language, it is the language of commerce in Helsinki. Furthermore, Helsinki's and Turku's Jews are almost all Swedish-speaking, and, last but certainly not least, so is Rachel.

After only three weeks in Tammisaari, Benjamin's unit moves to a camp just above the peninsula's ankle at Skogby, where they pitch tents that will house them throughout the winter. Their assignment is to construct a line of fortifications capable of preventing the Soviets from breaking out of their 115 km² enclave to attack targets on the rest of the mainland. Two days each week are spent in training, during which Benjamin learns how to take apart a bolt-action Mosin-Nagant M1891 and put it back together again. He practices cleaning and firing a Suomi submachine gun and learns how to fire an L-39 anti-tank rifle. He and the other recruits also learn how to communicate with one another and their officers on the battlefield and maneuver as a unit at night. The rest of the time the men are engaged in the same kind of work Benjamin performed a year earlier near Kiviniemi. They dig trenches, construct bunkers, build machine-gun nests, create tank obstacles composed of huge boulders in gap-toothed rows, string barbed wire, and generally try to turn the flat, sandy landscape frosted with coastal pines into as inhospitable terrain as possible for advancing enemy troops.

In much the same way he did both at school and in the hat factory, Benjamin parks his fears and aspirations in a separate, dreamlike space while his body goes about its army business. Hovering menacingly over the camp like a lazily circling kettle of vultures is the near certainty that Finland is headed once again into war. The older men in Benjamin's unit grumble about being taken away from their farms and families, but the young ones express an eagerness for battle that Benjamin finds troubling. Some of them seem to resent having missed out on the Winter War. Can they have already forgotten that so many who left for that war with the same enthusiasm they are showing now never returned or came home maimed or crippled?

Another thing Benjamin has a hard time understanding is the affection some of the men seem to feel for their weapons. They spend their precious spare time polishing and oiling their rifles and sharpening their knives as if they were gems. These men tend to be the quiet ones, older men with hard gazes and little time for the foolish chatter of the younger recruits.

Decisions

Unlike David, Benjamin has no desire to distinguish himself. On the contrary, he tries to sink as much as possible into anonymity, neither one of the best in his unit nor one of the worst. Nevertheless, one day well into basic training his platoon leader, Lieutenant Löfland, who fought with distinction in the Winter War, takes him aside during lunch break.

"I've been watching you, Son, and I think you would make a good officer. You have a good attitude, the men respect you, and you learn quick. I'm thinking of recommending you for non-com officer training. What do you say?"

"I'm flattered," Benjamin replies, "but I don't think I'm officer material. I'm quite satisfied where I am."

"But the army needs good leaders," insists Löfland. "I think you have what it takes, and I've been around long enough to know."

Benjamin doesn't know what to say and finds himself in an uncomfortable position. "I'm not a leader," he protests. "I've never wanted to tell other people what to do, and I certainly don't want to take responsibility for the lives of other men. I'm worried enough about myself, I mean, how I'll do if I find myself in combat. There are people who feel comfortable with that kind of responsibility. I guess I'm just not one of them."

"Everyone has doubts about how they will perform under fire before they experience it," concludes Löfland. "If I was you, I'd be proud to accept the challenge. And I can tell you this, Son, if you do find yourself in combat, you won't be happy being led by someone who can't do as good a job as you. Think it over before you decide."

Benjamin does think it over, but he doesn't change his mind. He will be as good a soldier as the situation requires, but he doesn't want life-and-death responsibility over others. His father, he knows, would have jumped at the chance and would be furious at him for refusing it. His father, however, is no longer around to be disappointed in him, and it is time for him to make his own decisions.

At about the same time as he turns down Löfland's offer, Benjamin begins formulating a plan for winning Rachel's affection. Their meeting at the cafe taught him that they need to do something together that will not only be enjoyable but provide subject matter for an evening's conversation. When he was working at Grünstein's, he had wanted to go to the theater but couldn't generate much enthusiasm for attending plays by himself.

Now he scans the Helsinki newspapers and sees that the National Theater is showing *Niskavuoren nuori emäntä* (*The Young Mistress of Niskavuori*), starring Kaisu Leppänen. He doesn't know the play, which is being performed for the first time, but he has heard that Hella Wuolijoki's previous Niskavuori plays were very popular with women. If he and Rachel see a play together, they will have something to talk about besides the threat of war or Benjamin's unrequited feelings. He will invite her to see the play and then to a restaurant for dinner afterwards. It will take most of his tiny savings, but what more important use for it can there be? He has already given most of the money he earned during the summer to his mother, and she and the children seem to be doing all right on the subsidies they receive. He certainly doesn't need any money in the army. He doesn't smoke, doesn't drink, doesn't play cards, and the only girl he cares about is the one he will be spending the money on.

Benjamin is scheduled to get a weekend pass the last week in November. He writes Rachel, inviting her to the theater, and to his delight, she accepts. As he counts down the days until his leave, he can hardly think of anything else.

Diligence

Rachel, on the other hand, marks the date in her almanac but hardly thinks about it until the end of November. She is too busy trying to stay on top of the considerable amount of work assigned for her courses. She is determined to maintain her standing near the head of her class so she will be selected for surgical nursing at the end of the basic nursing program.

Rachel notices that those students who served as Medical Lottas are easily distinguishable from those who didn't. They are more serious, more focused in their approach and more critical of any instructors whose teaching seems "too academic," Most of them are aware that they may be called on again before long to perform in field or military hospitals and realize from experience that precious lives will depend on their performance. Intent on being ready if needed, they tackle their assignments with an intensity that separates them from those who may still be wondering whether or not they have made the right career choice.

If another war breaks out, Rachel wants to be sufficiently qualified to be able to assist surgeons in operating theaters, not just wash and feed recovering patients. That means she will have to have completed most of the required course work, which would normally take two more years. To speed up the process, she takes additional courses on top of her normal work load, a practice only made possible by the sense of urgency communicated to the nursing school by the National Defense Council.

The only extracurricular activity Rachel permits herself is membership in the 100-strong Helsinki Jewish Choir led by Samuel Rubinstein and Isaac Skurnik. Although the Turku Choir was good, this one is larger and more professional. The three-hour practices transport her far from the demanding world of nursing and harsh memories of war to a virtual refuge of replenishing harmony. Rachel marvels at how many excellent Jewish musicians there are in Helsinki, especially now that talent from Viipuri has been added to the mix. Some of the other young women in the choir try to convince her to join in other activities such as WIZO meetings, but she declines. She knows from her involvement with the organization in Turku how much time that would take and is determined not to let anything interfere with her studies.

Although she accepted Benjamin's theater invitation, it was not without some reservation that she did so. She knows that he is not going to be satisfied with their "just friends" status, no matter what he says, which is sure to make the evening difficult at some point. Still in all, she likes him well enough and doesn't want to cut herself off from all social activity. Although she objects strongly to her mother's attitude about her becoming like Tante Bluma, she recognizes the risk of becoming a lonely old woman like her aunt or a prune like Sister Helmi. But what can she do? Apparently she was meant to be a nurse, not a wife.

Commission

David refuses to believe it until the cadet lieutenant's epaulette's are pinned on his uniform at the promotion ceremony. A Jewish officer in Finland's army! His grandfather had served in the Russian Imperial Army but as a recruit, not an officer. How many of his friends had told him that antisemitism in the military would make it impossible to get a commission? But here he is, ready to become a second lieutenant as soon as he completes the probationary period in his unit.

The second week of September 1940, he is assigned to the Third Army Corps' 4th Fortification Artillery Battery stationed southeast of Savonlinna in the lovely eastern Lake District. Camped on the shore of Uitonsalmi, his unit begins construction of two heavy artillery emplacements. David's background in civil engineering helps him win the respect of his men, even though he is younger than many of them and has never actually built anything more complicated than a few tiny bridge models out of sticks for a class at the Poly. Fortunately one of the men in the unit he commands is a mason, and several others are farmers who have built sheds, barns and even houses. David is only too happy to turn over the practical aspects of the construction to them and concentrate on the logistics, scheduling and ensuring that the structures conform to the drawings.

While David's team is building the battery emplacements, others are excavating sites for concrete bunkers, battle trenches and tank defenses. The days are cool, and when the sun shines, the work hums along. There is only one real complainer in David's platoon, a fisherman from Inkoo who insists that the whole effort is a waste of time and the Russkies will overrun the Salpa Line the same way they did the Mannerheim Line. Since he can't find anyone else to join in the bellyaching, the fisherman puts on a stoic face and grudgingly does his share of the work while grumbling under his breath. The men quickly develop a sense of camaraderie and mutual accomplishment, helped along by David, who frequently grabs a shovel or axe and participates in the strenuous work. He has an easy way of urging the men on and remembers to praise them when they make good progress.

David was initially worried about whether his men would object to having a Jew as their commanding officer, but no one seems to mind. It is likely, in fact, that some of them don't even realize that he is Jewish. Even the grumbling fisherman reserves his negative comments for the army, not for his platoon leader. For as long as he can remember—in scouts, sports, school and at university—David has either assumed or been selected for leadership positions and carries the responsibility lightly. He knows, of course, that the situation will be different should they find themselves at war, but in this work camp environment on the shore of Uitonsalmi, he feels comfortable in the role he has been assigned.

At night, in his tent, he tries to imagine the future. Will there be war with Russia again? Will he be needed in the fight for the creation of a Jewish homeland in Palestine? And what about when the fighting is over? If he survives, will he go to work in his father's import-export business, or will he try to find work as an engineer? First he would have to finish his degree, of course, but then he would also have to struggle to gain a foothold in a part of the Finnish economy where few Jews have gone before him. And what about a family? He has had more than his share of romances, to be sure, but has to admit that he has never been in anything like a long-term relationship. He has met several nice, attractive Jewish girls, and some of them would no doubt have considered David a good catch, but somehow nothing serious ever developed. Well, he is still young and will worry about that when the time comes.

Pressure Mounts

Concessions granted to the Soviets toward the end of 1940 only lead to additional ratcheting up of pressure on the Finnish government by Moscow. Petsamon Nikkeli Oy, the Finnish company operating the nickel mines in the Kola Peninsula, is owned almost entirely by Mond Nickel, the British subsidiary of International Nickel, the world's largest producer of the valuable metal. Germany previously got its nickel from Canada, but as hostilities increasingly interrupt shipping on the Atlantic, Hitler needs a more reliable source. In the spring of 1940, I.G. Farbenindustrie begins negotiating to receive 60 percent of Petsamon Nikkeli's production from Mond Nickel, at which point the Soviet Union starts demanding the entire concession, and Britain threatens to blockade the Liinahamari port, the only available harbor from which the nickel can be exported.

To avoid too great a dependency on Germany, which is now supplying Finland with both food and arms, Finland seeks a mutual defense alliance with Sweden based on both countries' commitment to political neutrality. Both Germany and the Soviet Union react immediately, the Soviets insisting that such an alliance would invalidate the Moscow Peace Treaty and the Germans opposing the idea because they fear loss of access to Sweden's iron and Finland's nickel and copper. As a consequence, the idea of the alliance is dropped like a hot potato.

The second week in November, Foreign Minister Molotov visits Berlin. During a meeting with Hitler, he insists that the Soviet Union, as agreed in the Molotov-Ribbentrop pact, has the right to deal with Finland as it wishes.

There can be no misunderstanding the Soviet Union's intention: it will deal with Finland as it has with the Baltic States. Hitler replies that further conflict in the Baltic region is not in Germany's interest, and another war between Finland and the U.S.S.R. would create a strain on relations between the Soviet Union and Germany. In other words, keep your hands off! It does not take long for this interchange, which infuriates Molotov, to be leaked to Finnish authorities.

In November, President Kallio, who is in such poor health that he is occasionally unable to fulfill his official duties, submits his resignation. Molotov keeps up pressure on Ambassador Paasikivi over Petsamo. In early December, he goes even farther, interfering directly in Finland's internal politics. Because of the prevailing political instability, the Finnish Parliament decides to have the electors from the previous presidential election choose Kallio's successor rather than for new electors to be chosen by popular ballot. December 6, Finland's Independence Day, Molotov wakes Paasikivi at his residence in Moscow shortly before midnight and summons him peremptorily to the Kremlin. In addition to inveighing against the proposed Finland-Sweden alliance and Germany's continued access to Petsamo's nickel reserves, Molotov issues the following thinly veiled threat: "We will decide, by who is chosen president, whether Finland wants peace with the Soviet Union." In case the message isn't sufficiently clear, he adds that Mannerheim, Svinhufvud, Kivimäki and Tanner are all unacceptable to Moscow.[1]

December 18, 1940, Hitler confirms plans with his general staff for Operation Barbarossa, Germany's massive assault on the Soviet Union. The following day, Prime Minister Risto Ryti is elected to replace Kallio, who collapses and dies while being escorted by a large crowd of well-wishers to the train that would have taken the exhausted President from Helsinki to his home in Northern Ostrobothnia.

Weeks earlier, Hungary, Rumania and Slovakia had formally aligned themselves with the Axis Powers, creating an unbroken boundary between the Baltic and Black Sea with Germany and its allies on the one side and the Soviet Union on the other and no neutral nations in between. For the time being, the Soviet Union's only European neighbors not committed to the Axis camp are Bulgaria and Finland. Bulgaria will sign the Tripartite Agreement with Germany, Italy and Japan on March 1, 1941. Finland, though invited, will refuse.

Note

1. Paasikivi, *op.cit.*, p. 127.

Figure 38.1. Finland's National Theater, designed by Onni Törnqvist-Tarjanteen (Matias Multamaa)

Niskavuoren nuori emäntä was well suited to the spirit of the interwar period. Its young principal characters represented the time of national awakening, and even the difficult love triangle ended in their marriage being restored and a future vision of it as a builder of Finnish society.

*Pirkko Koski**

---

*"Hella Wuolijoki kirjailijana ja kulttuurivaikuttajana," in *Niskavuoren nuori emäntä*, Suomen Näytelmäkirjailijaliitto, Helsinki, 2001, p. 10.

CHAPTER THIRTY-EIGHT

~

A Night at the Theater

Christmas / Chanukah 1940—Once autumn begins turning to winter, Benjamin starts coughing again. Although there is a small camp stove in the tent he shares with five other soldiers, the nights are cold and damp. Unwilling to complain about feeling weak and unwell, he continues to shoulder his full share of the heavy workload as if his cough and aching body were minor annoyances. When a fever sets in during the second week of November, though, he asks to see the camp doctor. Recognizing a relapse of the pneumonia Benjamin suffered earlier, the doctor orders him sent straight to hospital.

There are rumors about a marvelous new drug called penicillin, but it is not yet available in Finland. The only treatment is for individual symptoms of the dreaded disease: aspirin and poultices to reduce the fever, tea with honey to ease the cough, and enforced bed rest to help the body fight off the tendency of the lungs to fill up with fluid. About 30 percent of those who contract pneumonia die from it.

Benjamin had hoped to be sent to a hospital in Helsinki, where he could possibly see Rachel, but he is admitted to an army hospital in Salo instead. The building there is clean and bright, and the nurses are efficient and cheerful. Some of them had spent the war in hastily established field hospitals and are pleased to be working once again in a more structured and orderly environment. The doctors, too, are happy to return to peacetime routines without the constant demands of treating bodies riddled with bullets and shrapnel. Benjamin hardly notices these things, though, as the fever and his own antibodies battle to determine his fate. He longs for his mother's chicken soup but doesn't want her to know about the pneumonia. When the hospital asks whom it should notify about his illness, he says there is no one.

329

Benjamin is young and strong, though, and after only a few weeks of hospital rest is well on his way to recovery. The nature of the relapse, however, suggests that he has a persistent strain of the disease. After the fever subsides, the doctors keep him under observation in the hospital until they feel he is well enough to return to his unit, and he still hasn't been released by the time his scheduled weekend leave in Helsinki rolls around. He writes Rachel to tell her that his leave has been canceled and asks if their theater date can be rescheduled for the week between Christmas and New Year. He fears she may be going home then, but she writes back that she has two exams in January and will be staying in Helsinki to study. An evening of theater will provide a welcome break. She hopes he is feeling better and wishes him a speedy recovery.

When the time comes for Benjamin to return to Skogby, Lieutenant Löfland has arranged instead for him to be assigned temporarily to office work in Brigade Headquarters back in Tammisaari, where he can sleep in barracks instead of a tent and avoid physical exertion for a while. He gradually regains his strength and finally confesses to Zipora in a letter that he has been sick although he downplays the seriousness of his illness. He writes that he will be coming home on the 24th of December for six days.

The first day of Chanukah falls on Christmas Eve in 1940. Benjamin knows how happy his mother will be to have him home for a family holiday. He would love to have everyone there but doesn't dare ask about Mirele. He decides, though, that he will look for her when he gets to Helsinki, but how?

Knowing that many families will be celebrating during the week between Christmas and New Year, driving up demand for theater tickets, he asks a Lotta named Sirpa from the Communications Office who is going to Helsinki the second weekend in December if she would buy him two tickets in advance for a performance of *Niskavuoren nuori emäntä* on the 27th or 28th. The National Theater is right next to the Central Station so she won't have to go out of her way. She happily agrees, and he gives her the money for the tickets in a small brown envelope.

He also has to make reservations for dinner. He doesn't know anything about Helsinki's restaurants, but a young corporal from the city named Blomqvist is only too happy to provide some advice. When he hears that Benjamin and Rachel will be attending a performance at the National Theater and that Benjamin wants to make an impression with the choice of restaurant, he recommends either the Fennia or Seurahuone. Blomqvist warns that both are expensive, but Benjamin is determined for once not to let money stand in the way. As soon as Sirpa returns from Helsinki with the tickets, he writes to the Seurahuone requesting a table for two after the theater on the evening of the 27th.

Holidays

Zipora, Jakob and Rifka are waiting on the platform when Benjamin's train arrives at the Helsinki station. Rifka, especially, has grown and looks more like a handsome young woman than the girl who left Viipuri little over a year ago. Jakob insists on carrying Benjamin's bag, while Zipora interrogates her firstborn about his illness.

When they arrive at the home on Lapinrinne, Zipora has already laid out the menorah and the first two candles. Food is still scarce and kosher beef especially so, but Zipora has somehow found enough to make a *cholent*.

Benjamin hasn't had any contact with Jews or Judaism since he entered the army. As they light the first Chanukah candle and say the familiar prayers while the smell of the *cholent* being reheated in the oven fills the air, he is overtaken with emotion. Closing his eyes for just a moment, he is transported to the Viipuri of his childhood, his whole family is gathered around the menorah in their own home, and he still believes. How much simpler life was in those days!

The next morning, Benjamin wakes up early. He is surprised to find that Rifka is already preparing breakfast for the rest of the family. They talk quietly so as not to wake Zipora or Jakob, both of whom like to sleep late when they have a chance. Rifka tells her brother about the Jewish School. "It's really different from the schools in Viipuri," she says. "I didn't realize it last year because the schools were closed so much of the time. At home I knew everyone in my class, of course, but here I already know everyone in the whole school. It's like one big family, even the teachers. I really like it, and so does Jakob."

The mention of family reminds Benjamin of something. Lowering his voice even further to a whisper, he asks Rifka if anyone knows where Mirele is.

"I do," says Rifka. "I meet her every Tuesday after school at the restaurant where she works, but don't tell Mameh. She doesn't like us to talk about Mirele. She thinks she is bringing shame on the family. I think that's old-fashioned. Mirele just wants to be treated like an adult. She's already twenty-two, but Mameh treats her like she's still a child. Mameh thinks I stay after school for help with math, but I don't need help. I got a nine this term all by myself."

Benjamin tries to digest this all at once. The main surprise is how grown up Rifka is, maneuvering around her mother's restrictions in order to maintain contact with her sister. The other is that he won't have to do any detective work to find Mirele. Rifka can lead him right to her.

The restaurant where Mirele works is closed on Christmas, of course, but it will be open on Boxing Day. Shortly after lunch on the 26th, saying they are going to look at the window displays in the shops in the center of town, Rifka and Benjamin slip out of the apartment and head for the *Lasipalatsi* (Glass Palace) on Läntinen Heikinkatu. The HOK restaurant in the modern functionalist building on the far side of the parade ground where the *narinkka* used to be turns out to be huge, seating over 1,000 people.

By the time they arrive, lunch is no longer being served, and the tables are being set for dinner. Benjamin doesn't see his older sister at first—all the waitress are wearing identical uniforms—but Rifka spots her right away. Mirele's dark, shoulder-length hair is parted in the middle with tight curls at the temple like Garbo's in *Ninotchka*. She has changed, thinks Benjamin, as much as Rifka. No longer an angry teenager or self-effacing canteen worker, he recognizes that she has become a self-possessed beauty. She is obviously as delighted to see him as he is to find her, but she cannot get away until her break at 3:00 p.m. They agree to meet downstairs in front of the Bio Rex cinema as soon as she is finished.

Benjamin and Rifka use the intervening time to look at some store windows so they won't have to lie to their mother.

"Helsinki is impressive," says Benjamin, "but it isn't Viipuri. Somehow it seems, I don't know, colder."

"I know what you mean," adds Rifka. "Especially at this time of year. I think I miss the hyacinths in the windows most of all. They always made Viipuri look so festive at holiday time."

After they reach Kalevankatu, Rifka heads for home, leaving Benjamin to return to the Bio Rex to wait for Mirele. She appears at quarter after three, saying that some of the waitresses haven't shown up because of the holidays so the rest needed more time to set up for dinner. She takes Benjamin's arm and steers him to the railway station, where they find a booth in the Eliel Restaurant and began catching up on the events of the past nine months over ersatz coffee and a bun. Mirele admits that after she argued with their mother and left the apartment, she had a hard time getting on her feet. She has decided that she wants to study to become a secretary, but she needed a place to stay right away and some kind of a job to support herself in the interim. She walked from one restaurant and cafe to another until she found one that would give her work washing dishes. It wasn't until weeks later that she saw a notice that the HOK Lasipalatsi was looking for waitresses. After a two-week trial period, she was given the job. Now she is trying to save enough money for secretarial school. The dilemma is that she can't work and study at the same time because the restaurant requires her to wait both lunch and dinner, six days a week.

When she begins talking about her social life, her eyes narrow ever so slightly and her mouth grows tense. She has met several men, but they all seem to want just one thing. Why don't they understand that if a girl looks nice and acts friendly, it doesn't mean she is easy? She notices, however, that many of the waitresses seem happy enough to have men spend money on them. What they offer in return is anyone's guess.

Mirele adds that she has made friends with another waitress, a middle-aged woman from Käkisalmi, and they are planning to move in together in order to save on rent. When Benjamin asks whether she couldn't return home, she answers softly, "I've tried, Benjamin. Really, I have. Mameh and I are just like a match and gunpowder. I don't think she tries to make me upset, but she can't help it. I wish it weren't like that, but we just set each other off. I've made my decision, and I'll live with the consequences, but I wonder what will happen when Rifka gets a little older. She is such a good girl, but at some point she will want some breathing room, too."

"I think part of the problem is that Mameh has to deal with everything by herself," says Benjamin. "She used to rely so much on Tate. After he passed away, she was left alone with the responsibility for all of us. I know how hard it is for you, but try to understand how she feels. Life is hard for all of us now, but I think it is worst for her."

Mirele understands Benjamin's argument but for now sees nothing she can do to solve the problem. She is a modern woman, and her mother is old-fashioned. She is no more prepared to submit to her mother's restrictions than Benjamin is to start growing *peyes* and wearing a long black coat and wide-brimmed hat. Does Benjamin know that Zipora actually wanted to marry her off to the son of some woman she just met from the Helsinki congregation? No thank you!

Benjamin recognizes the old, rebellious Mirele taking over from the sophisticated Helsinki version and decides to abandon his efforts at reconciliation for now. He is confident that she will come around at some point, but it will take time. To change the subject, he does something he has done with no one else: he tells her about Rachel. Mirele immediately brightens up, asking all kinds of questions about how they met, what she looks like, what she does, and where she is from. For the first time, he realizes that he can't answer all the questions. He doesn't know all that much about Rachel and her family. Blushing with a combination of pride and embarrassment, he struggles to find words that tell enough about her without revealing more about his feelings than he is willing to admit even to his beloved sister.

Before Mirele returns to work the evening shift, Benjamin finds out where she is living and makes her promise to stay in touch. A dimension of admiration, based on her determination to make a life for herself on her own terms, has been added to the closeness he and Mirele developed during the war. He will probably have to make decisions like that someday, but for the time being he is in the army. In January, the period of military service will be extended to two years. For the next twenty months, the army will be making most of the decisions for him.

Theater

The following evening, Zipora and the children are amazed to see Benjamin dressed in a clean uniform, his hair neatly combed in place, and his shoes polished to a mirror shine. He tells them he is going to the theater but discloses nothing else. His history of theater participation at Ahdus provides enough cover for this rare excursion. Zipora insists that he eat something before leaving, but he says he isn't hungry and can always get something after the performance.

The nursing students' residence on Mikonkatu is so near the theater that he has agreed to pick Rachel up only twenty minutes before the opening curtain. He arrives, nevertheless, an extra ten minutes early and has to wait in the foyer for her to come downstairs. When she does descend the staircase, he is momentarily dumbstruck. She has curled her hair so that it falls in soft coils to her shoulders. The beige blouse and amber necklace she is wearing set off her dark eyes, and she looks, in a word, radiant. He helps her into her wrap, holds the door open for her, and offers his arm as they hit the sidewalk.

Rachel immediately asks about his stay in the hospital and whether he thinks he is fully recovered. He explains that he received excellent care and has been on temporary reassignment to an administrative unit, enabling him to avoid both the cold weather and unnecessary exertion. Now he is feeling strong again and ready to return to his original post when ordered to do so.

He has hardly had time to ask Rachel about her studies when they find themselves at the cloakroom, leave their coats and begin climbing to the upper balcony. They actually have quite good seats in the third row just left of center. Rachel, who has never been to a professional theater performance, is astonished by the elegance of the National Theater: the mural on the cupola, the gilt trim, the bright lights and plush red seats. Her excitement thrills Benjamin though he wishes it had more to do with him and less with the glamor of the surroundings.

The performance is the best Benjamin has ever seen. Eino Kalima's direction maintains the drama's tension between the needs of the individual characters and the larger themes of the preservation of the Niskavuori patrimony and the nationalist awakening. He is especially impressed by how Kaisu Leppänen transforms the shy and retiring Loviisa into a strong-willed and almost regal figure in the short time span covered by the plot. He is pleased to note that Rachel seems transfixed by the spectacle. She is obviously enjoying herself, and he can't wait to hear what she has to say over dinner.

The headwaiter shows them to a table in the Seurahuone's main hall. The *Mikado* is the only restaurant in Helsinki where Rachel has eaten although she has visited Turku's best restaurants with her family. Benjamin tries to act as if this isn't the first time he has ever been in a fancy restaurant, but he can't help feeling overwhelmed by his surroundings. He is smart enough not to pretend to be more experienced than he is and pays close attention to the waiter's recommendations. To his relief, Rachel asks for mineral water instead of wine, and he takes the same. They both order mushroom soup as a first course. Rachel then chooses pikeperch with mashed potatoes, and Benjamin orders the same.

Once the waiter has taken their order, Rachel exclaims, "This is terribly expensive, Benjamin. You really shouldn't have. Just the theater would have been enough. What a wonderful experience!"

"I'm glad you liked it. Don't worry about the cost. After four months in the army, I really need something like this. It's a big treat for me, too, and especially to be able to share it with you. I'm so glad you agreed to come."

Rachel senses the conversation is heading into dangerous territory and swiftly changes the subject. "The actors were really fabulous, and I especially like the way the women were portrayed as real people, not just as, you know, 'wives' and 'daughters.' One thing really bothered me, though. Why are Finns always portrayed as such crude and backward people? We aren't all like that. At first, Loviisa is such a passive wife. Then she gets upset with her husband, takes her son, and runs away into the forest. Everyone fears she is going to kill herself and the baby like some totally uncivilized Amazon. Then she comes back, magically changed into a stronger, noble person. Next that horrible Juhani, her unfaithful husband, runs off into the forest and drinks himself almost to death. Then he returns and has somehow become an honest and caring husband. Who can believe such nonsense?"

"I don't think it was meant to be taken so literally," answers Benjamin, "although 60 or 70 years ago people in the countryside may have been more like that than we think. To me, the message is that the forest is a source of strength. Finns were just beginning to think of themselves as a nation at that time. Remember what we learned in school: 'Swedes we are not, Russians we don't want to be'? They didn't have hundreds or thousands of years of culture, they just had the forest, the land, the lakes, the sea, and the myths that went with them. I think the play is trying to show that by going back to the forest, Liisa and Juhani get in touch with the source of the strength and wisdom of their ancestors. Something like our own people fleeing into the desert and then getting the Ten Commandments, going back to the basic things we believed in. It seems that is how we've survived as Jews whenever we have been threatened, by recommitting ourselves to our fundamental beliefs. Maybe the play is saying something like that for Finns."

Both of them fall quiet. Benjamin can't believe what has just happened. Where did that all come from? And Rachel seems astonished, too. After a moment, she breaks the silence. "That really makes sense. I never would have understood it that way, but I can see that you're right. I guess that is why they made such a big fuss about the politicians coming to the house at the end."

Just then the soup arrives, and Benjamin begins asking about nursing school. The soup is tasty, the entrées excellent, and chocolate cake and real coffee top off the meal perfectly. It is almost 11:00 p.m. when Benjamin accompanies Rachel to the door of the hostel. The evening has more than lived up to his expectations. Rachel thanks him profusely, saying she hasn't enjoyed herself so much in a long time. And that is when he almost ruins everything by asking her for a picture.

"So you can take it back to the army and show everyone that you have a girlfriend? No, I don't think so. I told you, Benjamin, I am happy to be your friend, but that's as far as it goes. If you think theater tickets and a fancy meal will change that, I'm afraid you're mistaken!"

He starts to explain, that isn't it at all, but quickly realizes his explanation will only make things worse. Reluctantly, he wishes her good night and trudges forlornly back to Lapinrinne, his short-lived elation burst like a soap bubble grown too big for the surface tension to hold it together.

Figure 39.1. Finnish commanders of the Karelian forces at the start of the Continuation War (from left): Lieutenant General Erik Heinrichs, Colonel Ruben Lagus and Major General Paavo Talvela (Finland's Military Museum)

"I hauled all the Passover dishes and *shabbos* tableware and pots and kettles and other stuff. They had to be watched over and held and lifted and carried. But it wasn't easy. At the Vaasa Station. . . . Have I told already what happened at the Vaasa Station?"

"Yes, you've told," said Vera in her fed-up tone of voice.

"At the Vaasa Station," continued Benno, "the bottom fell out of one of the boxes, and pots and kettles fell onto the platform, making a terrible clatter and rolling in every direction. I began gathering them up. At a little distance away stood some Germans, laughing at me. German officers. They laughed good-naturedly, and one of them, he was a lieutenant with a narrow Christ-like face, helped me pick up your Jewish Passover kettles from the ground. Of course, he didn't know what they really were. He got soot all over his hand from one of the pots, but he only smiled and saluted me with his sooty hand. Can you guess what I did?"

"We already know what you did," replied Vera wearily.

"I thanked him between gritted teeth, in Yiddish. The Christ-lieutenant wiped his hand with his handkerchief, which was decorated with a tiny swastika, and smiled back. I thanked him in Yiddish. Then he asked me if I originally came from Bavaria or the Tyrol as I spoke such peculiar German but so fluently. Hah! Peculiar German!"

"I still don't understand how that lieutenant couldn't see from your face where you come from," said Meeri.

"Well, he just didn't see," said Benno. "He wasn't completely with the program yet, you see, still just a young fellow. But I told him the truth straight to his face, like I usually do. I grabbed my cane and thought that if he starts to get difficult, at least I have my silver-headed cane. I'm still strong enough. Then I stood up straight and said right to him, 'I'm a Jew, you see.' But at the same time as I said it, the locomotive whistle blew, and the German didn't hear what I said. So I said it again, louder (*DER JID BIN ICH!*), but the damn whistle blew again and the lieutenant couldn't make out what I was saying. He raised his hand to his cap once more and walked back to where the other Germans were standing."

*Daniel Katz**

Kun isoisä Suomeen hiihti, WSOY, Porvoo, 1969, pp. 108–109).

~

CHAPTER THIRTY-NINE

Afraid of Being Eaten by the Bear, the Lamb Lies Down with the Wolf

January–June 1941—The new year begins with Benjamin back in Skogby, Rachel preparing for exams in Helsinki, and David on the shore of Uitonsalmi.

By this time, Sweden, Switzerland and Finland are completely surrounded by countries at war or under occupation. Sweden and Switzerland will stay out of the conflict, but Finland will not have that option. After nearly 240 years of simultaneously benefitting and suffering from its proximity to St. Petersburg/Petrograd/Leningrad, Finland will once again be dragged reluctantly into war with a Russia afraid of being attacked from Finnish soil.

This time, however, Finland's leadership is determined to do everything in its power to avoid the naïve mistakes that resulted in its lack of preparedness when the Soviet Union launched its surprise attack in November 1939. Their strategy involves trying to keep all options open for as long as possible. Markku Jokisipilä and Janne Könönen, in *Kolmannen valtakunnan vieraat*, write:

> Mannerheim specifically advocated and endeavored in his own undertakings to promote simultaneously a Nordic orientation, a foreign policy leaning towards the Western Powers, securing support from Germany, and a compromise-seeking pragmatic relationship with the Soviet Union.[1]

Not even a juggler as skillful as he could keep all those balls in the air at the same time for long.

President Ryti, in his memoirs, recounts a conversation with former President Svinhufvud, in which he listed what he felt should be Finland's priorities:

1) trust ourselves and do everything possible to strengthen our defenses, 2) develop especially our relationship with Sweden, 3) maintain good relations with Germany, 4) avoid all conflict with the Soviet Union and attempt to develop our relationship with it in the best possible way, and 5) and try by all means to remain outside the Great Powers conflict and avoid having our territory become a battlefield between them as well as maintain complete authority and decision-making power over our own affairs.[2]

This summary provides the clearest and most concise description of Finland's unachievable strategy in the spring of 1941. In practical terms, the Nordic Orientation has already been vetoed by Germany and the Soviet Union. The Western Powers are both physically isolated by Germany's occupation of western Continental Europe and unwilling to risk opening a northern front against the Axis Powers, leaving the Soviet Union and Germany to resolve Finland's status between them. Both have troops on Finnish soil and armies just across the border, the Russians to the east and the Germans to the northwest. There is no question in the minds of Finland's leaders, however, that the imminent threat to their country is posed not by the Germans but by the Soviets.

Finland's relationship with the Soviet Union is in the hands of diplomats and elected leaders. There is little commercial activity and even less constructive interaction between the two countries' military commands. Finland and Germany, on the other hand, have established close commercial ties and begun to strengthen military cooperation but avoided any kind of overt political interaction. Nevertheless, Hitler already assumes that the Finns will join Germany in the Barbarossa offensive and so, no doubt, does Stalin.

Once the Germans begin secretly supplying Finland's military with arms, Finnish protestations of neutrality begin to lose their validity. Although Finland would still undoubtedly like to stay out of World War II, it has begun sliding down the slippery slope to military alliance with Nazi Germany. While Ambassador Paasikivi is engaged in a defensive struggle in Moscow to ward off escalating Soviet demands, high-ranking Finnish and German officers are meeting with increasing frequency to discuss matters of mutual interest. In January 1941, Marshal Mannerheim sends his Chief of Staff, Lieutenant General Erik Heinrichs, to Berlin. Although there are conflicting reports about how much he learns during the visit, there is little doubt that General Franz Halder, the *Wehrmacht's* Chief of Staff, at least alludes to Barbarossa during their discussions. By mid-February, Colonel Erich Buschenhagen, Chief of Staff to General Nikolaus von Falkenhorst, Commander of the German forces in Norway, is on a two-week reconnaissance tour of Northern

Finland, and Halder is writing in his diary that negotiations over joint preparations for war will take place in March.

Mannerheim and Ryti believe that the Soviet Union will not be able to stand up to Germany militarily. As Soviet demands on Finland continue to escalate, Germany dangles tempting rewards for cooperation before the eyes of Finland's military leaders: the recovery of the territory lost in the Winter War, the addition of Eastern Karelia, and even the rights to whatever is left of Leningrad after the Germans have destroyed it. At first, all they ask for in return is for the Finns to commit sufficient forces to tie down Soviet troops along their border. Eventually these demands will increase to include demands Finland is unwilling to meet, such as participating in the obliteration of Leningrad and the annihilation of its inhabitants.

The Germans go so far as to offer Mannerheim command of the combined Finnish and German forces on the Finnish front. He refuses, unwilling to put himself as Commander in Chief of Finland's independent military in a position where he would have to take orders from Germany's High Command. Instead, Mannerheim subordinates Finland's Major General Hjalmar Siilasvuo and his Third Army Corps to von Falkenhorst and relinquishes command responsibility for operations in Finland north of Oulu and Kajaani to the Germans.

While Germany prepares to invade the Soviet Union, Finland continues to proclaim its neutrality and dig in for a defensive war, insisting that it will only fight if attacked. Although still unfinished, the Salpa Line fortifications are largely in place. The Finns realize, of course, that if Germany launches an offensive from Finnish soil, the Soviets are certain to retaliate. The Finns assume, however, that their defenses will never be seriously tested, not because there will be no war, but because the German *blitzkrieg* will push far into Soviet territory and force the Soviets into submission before a counteroffensive can get underway.

Operation Barbarossa

German plans call for Operation Barbarossa to be launched May 15, but setbacks to Rommel's campaign in North Africa and the need for intervention in Greece to bail out the hapless Italians result in its postponement. May 20, Nazi diplomat Dr. Karl Schnurre calls on President Ryti with confirmation that both Germany and the Soviet Union are preparing for war. Five days later, at Schnurre's invitation, General Heinrichs and five other top Finnish officers arrive in Salzburg, where they are briefed by Germany's Supreme

Armed Forces Command's Chief of Operations, General Alfred Jodl, on the planned invasion. The second week of June, large numbers of German troops begin arriving in Northern Finland from Norway and Germany, and less than a week later the newly constituted German XXXVI Army Corps is marching from Rovaniemi in Finnish Lapland towards the Soviet border. Finland, having already carried out a limited mobilization June 9, now orders a full general mobilization on the 17th, bringing the country's total number of men on active duty to 475,000.

On June 21, the evacuation of 45,000 Finns living near the Soviet border begins. That night, Finnish and German naval vessels prepare the coordinated mining of Estonian harbors and the Gulf of Finland, and Soviet troop transport between Leningrad and Hanko is suspended. At 2:30 in the morning of June 22, the Germans occupy Petsamo. Forty-five minutes later, German troops launch a massive coordinated invasion of the Soviet Union, attacking from Northern Finland to Southern Poland with a force of more than three million men, 3,600 tanks, 7,000 artillery pieces and 2,500 aircraft. Luftwaffe planes use Finnish air bases at Luonetjärvi, Malmi and Utti to refuel after bombing runs.

In retaliation, the Soviets bomb Finnish ships and airports and shell military installations. The Finns refuse to respond militarily at first, clinging to their claim of neutrality, but when the Soviets bomb Helsinki, Turku and a dozen other places on June 25, Prime Minister Jukka Rangell goes on the radio to confirm that Finland and the Soviet Union are once again at war. The situation resembles the start of the Winter War in many respects, but in two ways it is strikingly different. One is that this time the Finns are much better prepared. The other is that fighting alongside them[3] is another country, and not just any country but mighty Germany with its supposedly invincible war machine.

The *blitzkrieg* will last four years, not the two months many predict, and end in ignominious defeat for Germany and its comrade-in-arms, Finland. Is it a mistake for Finland to accompany the Third Reich on its adventurist campaign to wipe "Jewish Bolshevism" off the map? When President Ryti addressed his Cabinet earlier in June on the possibility of war breaking out between the Soviet Union and Germany, he explained that it could happen by midsummer but foresaw the fighting taking place somewhere between the Baltic and Black Seas, perhaps only later spreading to the north. In his memoirs, he wrote:

> I then explained Russia's policies both in Finland, where it has step by step attempted to destroy us during the period following the Winter War . . . and

everywhere else, where it has done everything it can to give birth to another world war and expand it in order, while staying out of the war itself, to weaken everyone else, finally to create revolutions and chaos everywhere and then, when it is more powerful, the opportunity to achieve its push for Russia's and bolshevism's world domination.

This kind of war, should it occur, could be of benefit to the entire world. It appears that Germany is the only country capable of defeating the Soviet Union or at least significantly weakening it, nor, perhaps, would it be damaging to the world should Germany weaken itself in the effort . . .[4]

These are the words not of a warmongering demagogue but of a rationalist Anglophile banker, thrust into the leadership of his country against his will. He has endured the weight of guiding his country through one unjust war and is doing all he can to avoid another.

It is never possible for one generation to put itself wholly inside the mindset of an earlier one, which makes it difficult for us to understand why Finland's leadership made the decisions it did in the spring and summer of 1941. The facts on record cannot adequately convey the fears, pressures and desires that animate history. Emotions fade over time, leaving the facts behind like bleached bones in the desert. We can try to understand the *who* and the *what* of history, but unless we also pay careful attention to the emotional context in which decisions are made, we can never understand the *why*.

Notes

1. Jokisipilä, Markku and Könönen, Janne, *Kolmannen valtakunnan vieraat,* Otava, Helsinki, 2013, p. 151

2. Rautkallio, Hannu, *Risto Ryti: Sota-ajan muistelmat,* Paasilinna, Juva, 2012, p. 107.

3. Hitler claims in a June 22 radio speech that they are "allied" [*im Bunde*], an assertion that is quickly corrected and never used again in official German communiqués.

4. Rautkallio, Hannu, *ibid*, p. 127.

Figure 40.1. Ansa Ikonen (left) and Tauno Palo (right) starred in "The Vagabond's Waltz" in 1941 (Suomen Filmiteollisuus SF Oy: Toivo Särkkä)

It was only during war that I fully came to understand what boundless power there is in music and song. I'm not talking about propaganda songs, that's another story, but about songs that for a second are able to free our thoughts from bleak, cold reality.

*Georg Malmstén**

---

*Quoted by Maarit Niiniluoto in "Sotavuosien 1939–45 viihdytystoiminta loi uskoa valoisempaa huomiseen," http://pomus.net/kehityslinjat/1939-1945, 6 July, 2016.

CHAPTER FORTY

~

Miracles Sometimes Happen

Helsingfors, January 5, 1941

Dear Benjamin,

I am truly terribly sorry for what I said at the end of the evening we spent together. It was thoughtless and ungenerous of me. I had a wonderful time at the theater and restaurant and appreciate all the trouble you went to. I was just so surprised when you asked for the picture that I reacted impetuously. I wish I could take back my words, but it is too late for that. I hope you can forgive me.

Thank you again for a wonderful experience. I will always remember it fondly.
Yours truly,
Rachel

"Ungenerous?" Benjamin can't get the word out of his head. Is that what she really thinks, that she should have been more generous?

As he lies awake at night in the tent he shares with five others in Skogby, he recalls a much warmer night at Vidablick in the tent he shared with David, Max and that other boy whose name he no longer remembers. He has been infatuated with Rachel since he lay awake then, thinking about her while David recounted his exploits with Naomi. He still lies awake thinking about her four years later. He has never once doubted his affection for her, but what about Rachel? He obviously still doesn't matter to her any more than when she confessed to him her feelings for David. What a fool he's been!

The ground is frozen solid, making it impossible to dig trenches, but construction of bunkers, gun emplacements and tank barriers continues. Benjamin is again strong enough to leave his temporary desk job and put in a full day's work strengthening the defense positions along the Hanko front. The rough living conditions and hard labor create a strong sense of camaraderie among the men in his platoon despite the differences in their ages and backgrounds. The behavior that bothered him when they first met has been replaced by an appreciation of the many good qualities the men display, such as generosity to one another and helpfulness.

Ah, generosity! He is still in a quandary about what to do about his feelings for Rachel. He knows that he has to make up his mind. If he goes on like this, he will not only make a fool of himself but probably be unhappy for the rest of his life. The only thing to do is to put an end to this one-sided romance. If he can manage to do that, maybe he can find someone else. It is hard for him to imagine such a scenario, but what other realistic path forward is there?

By the time February rolls around, Benjamin has made up his mind. The next time he goes to Helsinki on leave, he will meet Rachel and tell her that he won't be bothering her any more. They can still be friends, of course, but he has put his romantic feelings behind him. He has some doubts about whether that is entirely honest, but he must make it so, one way or another.

Vagabond's Waltz

Saturday, March 15. Benjamin meets Rachel at Kappeli, the same place she had met David almost two years earlier. They take a seat in the back and order hot chocolates. More than a meter of snow has accumulated in Helsinki, making it difficult to walk more than a few blocks, even in the center of town. Rachel says the hospital is full of people who have fallen and broken bones or suffered heart attacks shoveling the snow. Benjamin asks how her studies are going, and she says she is still hoping to be chosen for advanced studies as a surgical nurse at the end of the semester. He tells her about the new law that has extended the length of military service to twenty-four months. With the reorganization of the army now underway, he can expect to be assigned to a new regiment in the coming weeks.

This exchange of news is followed by an awkward silence, after which Rachel is the first to speak.

"You never answered after I sent you my apology. I really felt bad about what I said. I know I hurt your feelings, but I didn't mean it, really I didn't."

"That's okay," replies Benjamin. "I was the one causing all the problems. I just couldn't help it. I know it sounds silly, but I have been crazy about you since camp. But now I guess think it's finally time for me to grow up. If you had given me your picture, it would just have made things worse. You were right to refuse. Like you wrote to me once, no one can make themselves feel differently from the way they do. I finally understand that."

Having said what he came to say, Benjamin felt not relieved but depressed. Rachel didn't look so happy, either. Their meeting would end in absolute disaster if he didn't think of something.

"Look, all this serious talk isn't going to make for a very pleasant evening. What do you say we go to a movie? Everyone is talking about *Kulkurin Valssi* (*The Vagabond's Waltz*) with Ansa Ikonen and Tauno Palo. On my way here, I saw that it is playing at the Rex. Even in all this snow, that's not too far to walk."

"I'd love to!" responds Rachel. "I haven't been to the cinema in ages."

As they leave the cafe, Rachel takes Benjamin's arm. It gives him a start, but he realizes the sidewalk is slippery, and there are segments that haven't been cleared very well. Rachel is wearing boots, but they only cover her ankle. He tries to steer her along so she doesn't walk through any deep snow. The going is difficult, but there is no denying that Helsinki looks beautiful dressed in white.

They buy their tickets and ascend to the mezzanine. Aware that the balcony is the preferred location for lovers, Benjamin had hoped for seats on the ground floor, but the show is so popular with people of all ages that balcony seats are the only ones left.

The film is just what they need to pick up their spirits. *Kulkurin Valssi* is a fast-paced romantic musical adventure. Palo plays a Finnish baron in nineteenth century St. Petersburg who shoots a Russian prince in a duel after taking all his money in a card game. Afraid for his life, he flees to Finland, where he adopts a false identity as a vagabond. There follow escapades in the circus, a gypsy camp and a country manor. In each setting, the handsome vagabond wins the heart of a lovely lady but is forced by angry rivals to slip surreptitiously away. In the end he steals a bride—the daughter of the lord of the manor—literally waltzing her away from her wedding ceremony with the help of a band of gypsies. They flee to the baron's ancestral property, where the heroine realizes that her lover isn't a vagabond after all. Feeling betrayed, she threatens to leave him but is conquered by a kiss as the film ends.

This film is just silly enough to take Benjamin's mind off his misery. The action, singing and romantic nonsense distract him in much the same way his daydreams did at school. Then, about halfway through the film, a strange thing happens. A very strange thing. Benjamin suddenly feels Rachel's head resting on his shoulder. At first he doesn't even dare to turn and look. When he eventually does, though, he finds her smiling softly up at him. A few minutes later, she reaches over and puts her hand in his. By this time, Benjamin's heart is pounding so hard he can no longer hear the music.

What is going on? He knows it is a corny reaction, but could he possibly be dreaming? He tries to relax, but his confusion is too great. When the film ends and the lights come up, he is sure Rachel will drop his hand, but she holds it until they reach the door and has to put on her coat. She doesn't say anything, but that soft smile is still there, and her eyes twinkle in a way he has never seen.

When they've walked a little way, and the crowd has thinned, Benjamin guides Rachel under a portico and turns to look at her. "What's going on?" he asks.

"I don't know," says Rachel. "Something has changed, that's all. I guess I began to feel this way after the last time we were together."

"Is this because of what you said?"

"Don't be silly! It isn't *because* of anything. I just started feeling differently, that's all. I can't explain it. What you said in the cafe a little while ago, about having grown up, I think that's true but not the way you meant it. I had to stop thinking about you as the Benjamin from camp before I could see you the way you are now."

Benjamin is absolutely dumbstruck. He had asked to meet Rachel so he could tell her that he wouldn't be bothering her any more with his childish infatuation, and here she is saying what? That she actually has romantic feelings for him?

While he stands there, unable to put his amazement into words, she reaches up, standing on her tiptoes, and kisses him. He holds her to keep her from falling, or is it to keep himself from falling? And in that moment, his world changes forever.

Figure 41.1. Finnish Jewish War Veterans meeting in Helsinki in May, 2012. Back row, from left: Salomon Furman, Tevje Kagan, Abi Kagan, Boris Rubanowitsch and Hodie Figur (née Gottlieb). Bottom row, from left: Salomon Altschuler, Aron Livson and Harry Matso (Rony Smolar's private collection)

Fehlbaum and Zanco smiled, eyebrows raised in astonishment. "I don't remember the exact details," Fehlbaum said eventually. "The funny thing with memory is you don't remember the event, you remember the story again and again, and it then becomes fact."*

---

*Gregory, Alice, *Body of Work*, New Yorker, 1 August, 2016, p. 32.

CHAPTER FORTY-ONE

~

Benjamin on Heroism and Fear

I don't like it when they call us "heroes," Survivors, yes, but not heroes. Most of us, we were just doing what we were ordered to do. Some tried to do it well, and some tried to do as little as possible. I guess I was somewhere in between, sometimes doing things one way, sometimes the other. Most of the men I knew, in any case, were more interested in staying alive than in earning medals.

The war ended more than seventy years ago. How many people today were even alive then? Most Finns now have never seen a war, much less fought in one, so how would they know? You don't have to be a hero to follow orders. What choice do you have anyway? In a war, instead of ending up in the brig for disobeying, you might get shot.

I know what a hero is, though. There was this fellow in our company named Kajander, a cabinet maker. He didn't have much of a sense of humor, but he never bothered anybody, just kept pretty much to himself. At Kuuttilahti one day during the trench war, a live hand grenade landed in the bunker where some of us were resting. Nobody saw where it came from. Probably a scout from a Russky patrol got close enough to throw it in. Anyway, there was no place to run. Everyone just sat there, staring at it; everyone, that is, except Kajander. He grabbed his helmet and threw himself down on top of the grenade, put his helmet over it and then covered the helmet with his body. If it had exploded, there would have been nothing left of him to send home to his family except maybe his boots. Some of us would have been hurt, for sure, but he would have saved our lives. Luckily for all of us, the grenade was a dud. Even after we realized it was not going to explode, we couldn't move. We still sat there, shaking. All of us, that is, except for Kajander. He got up without saying a word, brushed himself off, put on his helmet, walked outside with the grenade, and threw it into the swamp.

If the grenade had exploded, Kajander's widow would have been given a Cross of Mourning and a widow's pension. Because it didn't explode, he only got the same Second Class Freedom Medal all the rest of us got for being at the front.

Then there was Forss, who took out a machine gun nest by pulling himself up a long, rocky hill near Karhumäki with almost no cover after taking two bullets in the leg. Our company had been ordered to take the hill. Who knows how many of us would have been killed if Forss hadn't knocked out that chatterbox. He lost so much blood he almost didn't make it, but he just kept going until he got close enough to blow up the gun and gunners. He could have been killed at any time. That's what I call heroism, not just living so long that people imagine you are a hero simply because you were in a war.

It's been a long time since all that happened, and so many things have changed. I guess it isn't surprising that no one understands. The young ones today play video games where they kill people and blow things up, but if they get killed, themselves, they just start over again or turn off the computer and put a slice of pizza in the microwave oven. How can they know what it is like being in a battle, having to keep going when you haven't slept or had a warm meal for days and artillery shells are ripping up the trees all around and the air is filled with smoke and blood and flying dirt and tanks are coming at you and you are almost out of ammunition? If it weren't for those little white pills they gave us, I can tell you, there were times when we would never have been able to keep going.

At the start of a war, you go off to fight for your country and freedom, but it doesn't take long for big ideas like that lose their meaning and you are fighting to stay alive and for the other men in your unit. Even the ones you don't like very much, you are ready to kill or be killed so that they can live. Maybe you don't realize it at the time, but looking back you see it. This little group of men. You eat, sleep, march and go to sauna together, week after week and month after month. They become your country and your family. Together you fight to survive.

Of course, I didn't understand any of this the first time I marched off to battle. We had been taught how to fire our guns and how to take cover. We had practiced what to do to protect ourselves from incoming mortar fire and how to blow up a tank. But no one taught us how to deal with the sight of the man next to you who has just had half his head blown off or his guts are hanging out. Or what to do when someone you've grown close to begs you to put him out of his misery with a bullet to the brain because his legs have been shredded, you are pinned down in what is sure to be a long fire fight, the medics can't get to you, and he can't stand the pain.

To tell the truth, before the fighting started I was scared. Scared of being killed, scared even more of being crippled, but also scared of killing someone else. I really didn't know if I would be able to shoot another person. Some of the other guys would talk about all the brave things they were going to do but not me. They acted *like the Russkies were less than human and so killing them would be easy, but I knew it wasn't like that. Anyway, I had relatives living in Russia. Some of the Russkies they were talking about might have been my cousins.*

What I learned later was that when you are actually fighting, you don't have much time to think. You just follow orders and react to what is happening around you. Most of the time you aren't fighting, though, and when you are waiting, that is when you imagine all the horrible things that can happen.

When the war first started, it was just the Germans and Russkies who were fighting. We stayed in our camp in Miehikkälä and waited for Marski to give us the order to move out. Even after the Russkies bombed our cities, we sat and waited. Maybe "sat" is the wrong word. We trained and built fortifications, but we weren't fighting. Two months we waited. And when we finally got the order to advance, we had to march almost to Viipuri before we met the enemy. There were some small Russky units trying to slow us down, but they never attacked where my company was. Still, we could hear the fighting, and every once in a while we would pass a dead Russky by the side of the road, so we knew we had to be careful.

Most of the men in my regiment were older and had already fought in the Winter War. They were happy to be getting revenge for what had happened. I kept thinking about Viipuri. We were going to take it back! My family and I would be able to go home, our wonderful city would be part of Finland again, and we would rebuild it so that it would be even bigger and better than it had been before the Russkies stole it from us.

Everyone said this would be the Summer War, over in two or three months at most. The Wehrmacht was the greatest fighting machine in the world, and we had given the Russkies a hard time all by ourselves only a year earlier. No one believed it would be much of a fight, but we were wrong. Got tsu danken,[1] we were wrong! If the Nazis had won the war, who knows what would have happened to Finland? What would have happened to us Jews, though, is certain. All of us would have been murdered.

Note

1. Thank God (Yiddish)

Figure 42.1. Some of the Soviet equipment captured in the "Billion-Markka Motti" (Finland's Military Museum)

I was the first Lotta to cross over into Russian territory. I was with a regiment. We were in Tenhola [near Tammisaari], and from there we walked all the way across Finland. We came to a place called Suistamo. I stayed there one night, and then we moved on.

At the time, we thought it would be a brief war, but it didn't turn out that way. We thought it would be over as quickly as the Winter War, but no! I was there for four years and four months!

Marta Holmberg*

---

*Interviewed by the author at her home in Helsinki, 21 November, 2013.

CHAPTER FORTY-TWO

~

Benjamin Goes to War

August 1941—Benjamin's war begins in earnest August 22 when JR 24 (24th Infantry Regiment) under Colonel Bertil Heinrichs heads out in pursuit of the Soviet 245th, which has begun to withdraw from the post-Winter War border between Finland and the Soviet Union towards Viipuri.

He has been part of JR 24 since the 13th Brigade was reorganized in preparation for war, and some of the men were assigned to other units. Like his former unit, the newly formed IV Army Corps' JR 24 consists largely of older Swedish-speaking veterans of the Winter War. It will later be called "the Jewish regiment" by some because it has more of them in its ranks than any other regiment. This is hardly surprising since it has been formed from residents of the province of Nyland, including Helsinki, where most of Finland's Jews live. For nearly two months, JR 24 has been manning defensive positions at Miehikkälä, about 50 kilometers west of Viipuri. Since the Continuation War broke out, the only action its men have seen has consisted of simulated skirmishes in training, but now they are headed towards confrontation with battle-ready Soviet troops.

As he marches towards Säkkijärvi (Kondratyevo) near the mouth of Viipuri Bay, Benjamin nervously scans the countryside on either side of the road for signs of enemy activity. Occasionally the Finns are forced to take cover as Soviet patrols harass them in delaying action designed to allow their comrades in the 245th to complete their rearward redeployment. There are a few casualties in other units, but Benjamin's platoon proceeds without any losses, arriving intact at Tervajoki (Bolshoye Pole) southwest of Viipuri on the evening of August 23.

By the time JR 24 reaches the shore of Viipuri Bay the next morning, Finnish troops to the north and east have secured positions in a wide arc around Viipuri about 15 kilometers from the center of the city. The three Soviet divisions stationed there initially plan to mount a stout defense of the city, but when the Finns break through their defenses from the northeast, the Soviets realize they are trapped and begin to look for a way out. Several times they attempt to push eastward along the St. Petersburg Road, but Finnish forces block their way. As Soviet defenses north of Viipuri begin to buckle, the only potential escape route left is along the railway and road to the port city of Koivisto (Primorsk) some 45 kilometers to the south.

The Soviet 43rd, 115th and 123rd Divisions holding Viipuri are all trapped in an increasingly vice-like grip that is rapidly tightening around them. As the Soviet troops prepare to break out toward the Koivisto Road, JR 24 receives the order to cross to the island of Uuras and team up with JR 45, which has already established a beachhead on the other side. Their mission is to complete the *motti* by sealing off the escape route.

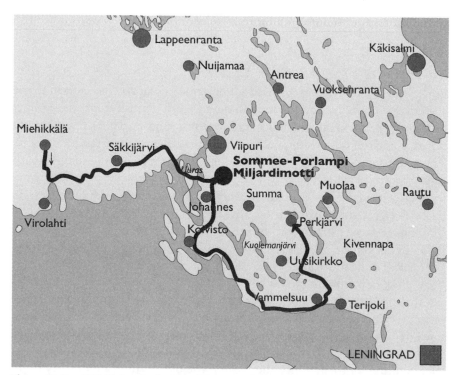

Figure 42.2.   JR 24 joins the battle of Sommee-Porlampi as Viipuri is recaptured (Marja Leskelä)

The first assault boats carrying JR 24 fighters toward Uuras are met with heavy machine gun and direct artillery fire from Soviet troops on the island, causing them to turn back. Soviet fighter planes flying overhead are driven off by Finnish anti-aircraft fire. Most of the Finnish troops will cross in assault boats, but pontoon barges consisting of two flat-bottomed boats supporting a platform lashed between them are needed to transport their equipment. Two of the barges are hit by artillery fire during the first crossing attempt, one sinks, and the men on board are lost.

To minimize further losses, the main crossing is delayed. On the 27th, JR 24 sets out from Keihäsniemi and Piispansaari at 23:00 hours in light rain, heading this time toward Lihaniemi on the eastern shore. From where he is crouching in the bottom of an assault boat, Benjamin can just barely make out the distant outline of the tower of Viipuri Castle over the water. His excitement at being so near home is dampened, however, by the sound of bullets skipping over the waves as the enemy fires blindly from Uuras in the direction of the narrow strait his boat is trying to cross. Although this is technically Benjamin's combat baptism; he isn't shooting at all, and the fire coming at him is random and, fortunately, inaccurate.

Closing the Gap

By 3:00 in the morning of August 28, Benjamin's company has crossed to the eastern side of the bay, but there is no time to rest. Finnish troops are rushing to take up positions in the fields and forest around Porlampi (Sveklovich-noye), some ten kilometers southeast of where Benjamin scrambles ashore. They must simultaneously prevent the flight of Soviet troops retreating south from Viipuri, block attempts by troops marching northwest from Leningrad to open an escape route for those trapped in the *motti*, and avoid getting themselves caught between them. JR 24 is assigned a sector that includes Ylä-Sommee (Sverdlovo) and the main inland road leading south, enabling JR 45 to cut off the rail link and shore road from Viipuri to Kovisto by taking control of nearby Kaislahti (Popovo) and Sommee Station (Matrosovo).

At first, Benjamin is glad to be away from the exposed shore and marching through the woods, but the situation turns chaotic as his company approaches Ylä-Sommee. The woods are already full of Soviet soldiers rushing towards Koivisto. They apparently are unaware that Finnish troops have already crossed the bay and are surprised to find Benjamin and his compatriots waiting for them. Once they realize the danger they are in, they begin shouting "Uraa" and attacking in several directions at once. Machine-gun bullets rattle through the trees, and mortar fire rains down incoherently, killing friend and foe alike. Benjamin is not prepared for the deafening noise or the dust, smoke and dirt that fill the air, making it difficult to breathe.

By August 29 the Finns have begun to stabilize positions that block the main roads leading south. Soviet troops attempting to use the roads are trapped or picked off, forcing those who can to regroup and attack through the woods. Word comes that JR 45 is holding firm along the coast road and JR 3 and JR 5 of the 12th Division are pushing in from the East. As the *motti* draws tighter, the Soviets are increasingly being funneled onto the battlefield where Benjamin and his regiment have taken up their positions.

During the first brief lull in the fighting, Benjamin's platoon is ordered to dig foxholes behind a low ridge. Rain has been falling off-and-on for two days, and the ground is soft, so it doesn't take long for the work to be finished. The men have their first meal of the day, even though it is nearly six in the evening. The field kitchens are still making their way across the bay so dry rations are the only food available. The rain is falling steadily now, and the temperature has fallen to 8° C (46° F).

Before long, the Soviets renew their attempt to push through the Finnish lines. Fighting continues with little interruption through the night. Not having slept in two days, the Finns are kept awake by little white pills provided by their German comrades-in-arms. Bottled under the name "Pervitin," the tablets contain a wonder drug with a peculiar name, *metamfetamiini*, which helps the troops fight off exhaustion.

Benjamin fires his rifle in the general direction of the attacking Soviets, but he is pretty sure he hasn't hit anyone yet. Some of the Winter War veterans patiently wait until an enemy gets within range, but Benjamin doesn't aim at individuals, only at noise or motion in the woods. During one particularly massive attack, the Finns are forced to pull back and call for help from the 45th, but a determined counterattack enables them to regain their original position.

August 29, sometime around what would be sunrise were it not so overcast, the Soviet pressure relents, and Benjamin looks for a place where he can nap for fifteen or twenty minutes. Seeking cover from stray bullets and shrapnel as well as shelter from the rain, he notices a large outcropping of rock and clump of alders in a small clearing nearby. Before lying down, he decides to walk once around the largest boulder, just to make sure he is alone. Holding his rifle at the ready, he creeps counterclockwise around it but doesn't get even halfway before he comes face to face with a Russian soldier. The Russian is even younger than Benjamin, perhaps 16 or 17. He is also holding a rifle, which is pointed straight at Benjamin. The boy has apparently been resting behind the rock, just as Benjamin intends to do. His red hair is cropped short, his uniform filthy, and his green eyes are fixed on Benjamin's trigger finger.

Time freezes, all noise ceases, and the two young men stare at each other as rain runs down their faces, each wondering what the other will do, knowing that the slightest misjudgment could prove fatal.

Benjamin will remember later that foremost in his own mind is that he will not be able to shoot first, even though he understands that shooting second is not an option. Apparently the young man facing him feels something similar because—after what seems like a very long time—he slowly and tentatively begins stepping backward across the clearing and into the woods. He never lowers his rifle or takes his eyes off Benjamin, but it is clear to Benjamin that his intention is to escape, not to shoot. Benjamin keeps his own rifle pointed at his young adversary until he is out of sight.

Then Benjamin sits down and leans back against the rock, his breath coming in rapid gasps as if he has just emerged from too long under water. Was he wrong to let the Russian go? He knows that he could have killed him if he had acted decisively. Why didn't he? Had he been afraid to pull the trigger? And why does he feel relieved that he didn't shoot him? That boy may live to kill who-knows-how-many Finnish soldiers or innocent civilians.

Billion-Markkaa Motti

August 29–30, the Finns fight to hold their positions as the Soviets mount attempt after attempt to break out of the woods where they are trapped. Pressure on all sides forces the Soviet troops into an ever more compact motti seven kilometers long and three kilometers wide along the road from Sainio to Sommee. Finnish heavy artillery arrives August 30 and begins pounding the road, causing the Soviet column to come to a halt and inflicting heavy damage on the besieged troops. A force of nearly 2,000 men brought from Leningrad tries to free the entrapped men by attacking from the south along the coast road but is intercepted and pushed back by JR 45.

By the afternoon of August 31, the Soviets have given up hope of salvaging their equipment and supplies and are concentrating on saving their lives by fleeing through the woods. Captured enemy soldiers confirm what the Finns have begun to suspect: the morale of the Soviet troops in the motti is collapsing.

Back in Viipuri, one year and 161 days after the last Finn left the city at the end of the Winter War, a victory parade is taking place. News that the country's second city is once again in Finnish hands circulates quickly among the soldiers in JR 24. Benjamin reacts to the recapture of his home town as if he has ingested several Pervitin pills at once. Although he hasn't had a night's sleep or a decent meal in four days, he is fully energized and ready for anything the Russkies might throw at him. Viipuri is ours again, he thinks, and we will be able to go home! Up to now, he has not shared his comrades' feeling that this war will end differently from the last one, but the liberation of Viipuri makes him consider for the first time that he might have been wrong. When JR 24 launches a multipronged attack on the Porlampi-Sommee *motti* that same afternoon, Benjamin joins in the attack with a new kind of enthusiasm. Finnish artillery pounds the Soviet regiments, and by the next day, Soviet soldiers are surrendering in droves.

The results of the Soviets' failed week-long struggle to retain Viipuri or escape to Leningrad are mind-boggling. Of the approximately 35,000 Soviet soldiers involved, some 7,000 have been killed in battle and 9,000 taken prisoner. On the Finnish side, by comparison, casualties total just 700 killed or missing and 2,700 wounded. The Soviets abandon a huge arsenal that includes 306 different pieces of artillery and 19,000 artillery shells; 246 mortars and 46,000 mortar shells; 272 machine guns, 55 tanks, 10,000 rifles and 3.4 million bullets; as well as 673 cars, 300 tractors and 4,500 horses.

After four days of nearly non-stop fighting, the Finnish troops are finally able to get some rest. Soviet prisoners are put to work burying the dead, clearing the roads and compiling an inventory of captured weapons and vehicles. September 1, the sun reappears, and little by little the terrain finally begins to dry out. Benjamin marvels that he has survived the cold and damp, the prolonged battle and sleepless days and nights, without falling sick again, but there is no sign of the cough that has twice laid him low. And despite his confusing confrontation with the young Soviet soldier and the probability that he still hasn't shot anyone, he feels proud that he has held his ground in the face of some pretty fierce attacks. Maybe, he thinks, being surrounded by experienced older soldiers helps. All he has to do is watch them and do as they do. So far, it has worked.

Sometime around 11:00 in the morning of September 1, as the fighting winds down, Benjamin is sent to the medical tent to ask for some gauze and disinfectant for his unit so old wounds can be cleansed and dressings replaced. On the way, he bumps into a medic named Gunnar Bergström, who had been with him in Tammisaari. While Benjamin is talking to Bergström, Lieutenants Krogerus and Wallenius rush up to them to report that there are Russkies in the woods just around the bend in the road. The four of them hurry off together and a few minutes later come across two men who are apparently sleeping soundly, covered from head to toe by their raincoats.

Bergström snatches off one of the raincoats while the others point their guns at the men on the ground. To everyone's astonishment, the uniform that has been uncovered reveals the soldier to be some kind of high-ranking Soviet officer. Bergström, who is an excellent wrestler, hoists the man to his feet like a scarecrow that has fallen from its perch and rapidly strips him of his 9mm Mauser, map case and canteen, the last of which is subsequently revealed to contain half a liter of vodka. The officer makes no attempt to resist and, although a bit startled to be awakened in this manner, seems remarkably calm and good-natured about the whole incident.

It turns out that the congenial officer is Major General Vladimir Kirpitsnikov, commander of the Soviet 43rd Division. The other man, considerably less even-tempered, is a political commissar named Terichov. The prisoners and maps are taken to 8th Division headquarters; their vodka rations, however, remain with Krogerus and Wallenius.

As it turns out, Kirpitsnikov will be the highest-ranking prisoner captured by the Finns during the entire Continuation War. After four years as a prisoner of war, he will be returned to the Soviet Union, where he will be immediately interned again. In 1950, almost nine years to the day after he is captured, Stalin will have him executed as a traitor to the Soviet cause.

A Step Too Far

While Benjamin was waiting to cross Viipuri Bay on August 23, Commander-in-Chief Mannerheim was reading a letter from Field Marshal Wilhelm Keitel, chief of the Supreme Command of the German Armed Forces. The letter expressed Germany's wishes that the Finnish army would join in the siege of Leningrad by pushing Soviet forces down the Ladoga Isthmus (between Lakes Ladoga and Onega) to the far side of the Svir River, eventually joining up with Germany's Army Group North arriving from the southwest. The next day, on a visit to Finnish Army Headquarters in Mikkeli, President Ryti will hear Mannerheim say that his troops on the Karelian Isthmus are prepared to cross the pre-Winter War frontier to establish a more defensible border, but they will stop short of Leningrad's outer line of defense. Meeting Keitel's request on the Ladoga Isthmus, on the other hand, would require a deep incursion into territory that has never been part of Finland.

Despite concerns some Finns have about joining forces with Nazi Germany in the struggle against the Soviet Union, there is still a broad consensus among its citizens that Finland is justified in retaking the land that was wrested away by force during the Winter War and subsequent one-sided peace negotiations. As soon as Finnish troops begin crossing "the old border" into territory that has never been part of their country during the first week of September, however, many in Finland and abroad begin to see participation in the war as an unjustified adventure with territorial expansion as its objective. In addition, most Finns had expected the war to be swift and the men to return home in time to harvest the crops. As summer turns to autumn, however, and no end to the fighting is in sight, many soldiers feel that they have been deceived. There are numerous cases of near-mutiny and desertion, hastily covered up by the country's censors, as some soldiers refuse at first to cross the old border and have to be threatened or bribed to continue advancing.

JR 24 spends three weeks after the Sommee-Porlammi battle in mop-up operations, making certain the Karelian Isthmus is clear of all Soviet troops. They march through Summa, where some of the men had fought during the brutal closing days of the Winter War, and Perkjärvi, where Benjamin served as camp counselor. The landscape presents a bleak reminder of the devastation of the Winter War. Trees are broken off a few feet above the ground, charred buildings lie in ruin, and the bones of men and horses left unburied by the Soviets litter the ground where they fell. Numerous villages and hectares of land have been levelled by fire. JR 24 makes its way through this desolate scenery to Syväjärvi on the coast by the last day of September, then turns around and marches back to Perkjärvi, where it has been ordered to board the train for Jessoila.

"*Perkele!*" curses Palmqvist when he hears that they are being sent to Jessoila. "That's almost in Petroskoi. We got no business there." He fought at Kitilä in the Winter War and knows the Ladoga Isthmus geography. Some of the other older soldiers begin to complain as well.

"We've already got what we came for," says Vikholm, a metalworker in a crane factory. "They should let us go home. She doesn't say so, but I can tell from my daughter's letters that they barely have enough to eat at home, and going to Jessoila won't put food on their table."

Benjamin hears rumbling like this all around but doesn't say anything. He doesn't like the idea of crossing the border, either, and he is certainly ready to go home, but he will obey orders. If his unit had been asked to march across the pre-war boundary, some of the men might well have refused. What would have happened then? He has heard that men have been arrested for refusing to cross the border, and rumor has it that some may have even been shot as traitors. JR 24 is spared the drama, however, because the men board the train at Perkjärvi, and the train only crosses the border the next night, by which time the men are asleep and, for the time being at least, the grumbling has given way to snoring.

Eastern Karelia

Having crossed into unfamiliar territory, Finnish troops set out to secure defendable positions across three isthmuses: the Karelian Isthmus between Leningrad and Viipuri, the Ladoga Isthmus between Lakes Ladoga and Onega, and the Maaselkä Isthmus between Lake Onega and the White Sea. Commander-in-Chief Mannerheim and his staff believe these moves, however politically questionable, are essential to protect Finland from incursion by its eastern neighbor.

Finland has already retaken all the territory on the Karelia and Ladoga Isthmuses lost during the Winter War. The troops holding the Karelian Isthmus have taken up defensive positions on the Rajajoki-Valkeasaari-Lempaala-Tappari line just outside Leningrad. By the middle of September, Finnish troops hold the entire north bank of the Svir River at the southern end of the Ladoga Isthmus as well, and an attack is being mounted on the city of Petroskoi (Petrozavodsk) on the shore of Lake Onega. By October 21, when JR 24 arrives at Selki southwest of Lake Seesjärvi after a twelve-day march through slush and mud, Petroskoi has been occupied and renamed Äänislinna, and only the Maaselkä Isthmus from Paatene (Pogosta) to Poventsa remains to be secured.

Benjamin's unit spends the next month in heavy combat along the southern edge of Seesjärvi in places called Jouhivaara, Karjalan Maaselkä, Liistepohja, Suurlahti and Maaselkä Station. Closing off this northernmost isthmus to protect Petroskoi from incursion from the north proves to be difficult and costly in terms of lives lost. Cold weather and stiff resistance by Soviet troops slow the Finnish advance, and it is December before Karhumäki (Medvezhyegorsk) and Poventsa are taken and defensive positions can be established.

By November 26, Benjamin's regiment has been depleted by death, injury, illness and desertion. His company has been on the front line at Suurlahti without interruption for ten days of heavy fighting. Unable to wash properly, the men are infested with lice. It is so cold in early December that guard-duty shifts are reduced to one hour at a time, forcing each man to stand watch at least twice a night and limiting sleep to two or at most three hours at a stretch.

It is during the battle for Liistepohja that Benjamin finally knows for certain that he has shot and killed a man. A Soviet company attempting to break out of the Liistepohja *motti* early one morning charges straight at the position defended by Benjamin's platoon. Having dozed off, Benjamin is rudely awakened by shooting and the dreaded "Uraa!" of the charging Soviet soldiers. Still only half awake, he grabs his rifle and rushes to his station. Before he reaches it, he sees an enemy soldier taking aim at the radio operator, Åkerman, who is crouched down by a tree, trying to establish contact with headquarters. In a reflex reaction, Benjamin raises his rifle and fires. The Russian throws his hands up, and his gun drops to the ground. He takes a step, falls to his knees, then crumples over on his face.

In the confusion, which lasts about twenty minutes before the Finns beat off the enemy assault, Benjamin returns to his habit of shooting blindly in the direction of noise and motion. After the fighting ends, though, he finds himself reliving in his mind what happened earlier. There can be no question about it, he has broken the most sacred of the Lord's commandments, and he has done it intentionally. He has gone over all the rationalizations many times but to no avail. The reality is that he has aimed his weapon, pulled the trigger, and killed another human being.

Now, more than any time since the war began, he wishes he could be with Rachel, to be held and consoled by her. But she is far away, and he is tired, cold and alone.

Figure 43.1. Among the Soviet prisoners of war taken by the Finns in the Continuation War and later handed over to the Germans were at least 74 Jewish soldiers (Finland's Military Museum)

They were all from the province of Pskov in White Russia, near the Latvian border. My grandfather came as a Hebrew teacher to Finland in 1915, as a private tutor for children of some wealthy families. When Helsinki's Jewish school was started up again in 1918, he became the school's first Hebrew teacher, married a local redheaded daughter of a Cantonist and had two sons. My uncle was born in 1920, my father in 1922. They were both in the Continuation War. On the other side, the Russian side, were at least one or two of their uncles about whom they didn't know anything, of course, because the Soviet Union was a closed society. They knew they had relatives, but they knew nothing about them. There were at least five brothers still in Russia. My understanding is that one of the uncles fell here in Finland, another fell on the German front, and the rest reached Berlin. Most of the Jewish soldiers in the Finnish army had relatives on the Russian side because the bulk of Finnish Jewry had come from Russia only one or two generations earlier.

Gideon Bolotowsky*

---

*Interviewed by the author, 27 March, 2012.

~

CHAPTER FORTY-THREE

Rachel Crosses the Border

Helsinki, June 1941—June 25, just before two in the morning, the shrill wail of the siren startles Rachel awake after only three hours of fitful sleep. She hastily throws her overcoat over her nightgown, fastening the belt and pushing her dark unruly hair under her cap as she rushes to the Helsinki Surgery Hospital's Recovery Ward. Three nurses join her and begin assisting the patients who can walk, hurrying them towards the air raid shelter. Fortunately, most of the inpatients have already been evacuated to other hospitals far from the capital, creating bed space for those who will be injured in the bombings to come.

The Soviets' main target in this first raid is Malmi Airport, just outside the city, but most of the bombs miss their target, falling on nearby fields or farm houses. Before a second assault can be mounted, anti-aircraft batteries and a squadron of Brewster Buffalo fighter planes drive off the attackers. Cocooned by this time in their underground shelter, the patients and staff can barely hear most of the explosions. Other cities don't fare so well. Rachel's home in Turku is spared, but her city suffers heavy damage as do Heinola, Kotka and Kouvola.

Rachel has had her bags packed for three weeks. Unlike her roommates at the nursing school, who argue that Finland will be able to remain neutral in the widening conflict between the Allied and Axis powers, Rachel has felt certain that Finland will be dragged into the war. Her name is still on the list of Lottas ready and willing to serve at the front in case of conflict. She could receive her new assignment at any time.

The next day, Finland's President Risto Ryti addresses the nation by radio. "Beginning yesterday, the Soviet Union, without provocation from us, has carried out systematic, widespread acts of warfare in all parts of our country and, as is their wont, targeted the civilian population. Thus has begun our second defensive struggle."[1]

Rachel wonders whether it is entirely accurate to say that there has been no provocation by Finland. Wasn't welcoming tens of thousands of German soldiers onto Finnish soil a provocation? She thought so even before they launched their attack on Soviet territory, but whether their presence was justified or not is a matter for history to judge. The war is a reality now, and she is ready to do her part.

First Assignment

The letter with her assignment to Field Hospital 28 doesn't arrive until June 29. It orders her to report to the main railway station July 1st to take the overnight train to Joensuu, 440 kilometers to the northeast. From there, she will be transported the final 70 kilometers by bus or truck to Tohmajärvi near the border. The hospital there, set up in a school, will serve Finland's 6th Army Corps under Major General Paavo Talvela and the German 163rd Division, known as the Engelbrecht Division, as they head east in the direction of Sortavala at the top of Lake Ladoga.

Rachel is startled to learn that she is assigned to a unit that includes German soldiers. It has never occurred to her that she may have to treat German soldiers or take orders from German doctors, but those are now very real possibilities. Her first reaction is that she should ask for reassignment. On second thought, she realizes that she has been given the perfect opportunity to prove how loyal a Jewish Lotta can be. Refusing the assignment would only convince those who never wanted to let Jews into the organization in the first place that they were right.

By the time Rachel arrives at Tohmajärvi and makes her way to the field hospital, groggy from lack of sleep and aching from rides in crowded railway carriages and the back of an army truck, two entire days have passed. The hospital is located in the Kaurila Primary School, which consists of a large building on a hilltop, an annex, a barn, a drying shed, and the home of the local druggist, where the nurses and Lottas sleep. Rachel will share a bedroom with two other medical Lottas. It is a clear, sunny day, and despite the unusual amount of activity taking place, the scene conveys an impression of rural calm and harmony to the arriving staff.

By noon the next day, beds in the main building are already beginning to fill up with wounded soldiers, and calm has given way to urgency. The most recent arrivals, awaiting treatment, are lying on pallets in the annex. The floor of the drying shed has been set aside for wounded Russian prisoners.

Because of her training at the Helsinki Surgical Hospital and experience in the Winter War, Rachel is assigned to the field hospital's Surgical Unit, where she helps the nurses administer ether and morphine, apply bandages and splints, and generally assists in efforts to limit the damage done to limbs and organs. With increasing frequency, she will be allowed to help in the operating rooms as well. There are nine doctors at the hospital (including two who are German), 14 nurses, and five Lottas. As German and Finnish troops push further into the area annexed by Russia after the Winter War, the number of wounded rapidly mounts, forcing the operating teams to work around the clock in 12-hour shifts. Because the hospital is still understaffed, doctors and nurses often find themselves working consecutive shifts without rest.

As a fresh arrival, Rachel is assigned a double shift the day after she arrives. Excitement carries her through the first twelve hours, but as the night shift progresses, she begins to realize that her reactions are slowing. A soldier who looks no more than a boy is brought in to have his left leg amputated. It has been shredded by shrapnel and shards of rock from a howitzer shell that exploded only a few meters away from him. Reacting instinctively, he had thrown himself behind a boulder when he heard the whistle of the incoming missile. The rock has saved his life, but his leg remained exposed and shattered in so many places that there is no hope of saving it. He is heavily sedated but moans from time to time in delirium as the doctor cuts through the tissue below the hip.

Rachel fears that in her exhausted condition, she could make a mistake that could be anything from embarrassing to fatal. The nurse in the preparation room at the time, a serious-looking wiry woman who is ten or maybe fifteen years older than Rachel, notices her yawning and hands her a small metal tube.

"Here, take this," the older woman says.

"What is it?"

"It's something the Germans use, it will help"

Rachel opens the tube and takes out a small white pill.

"Crush it and dissolve it in a glass of water. It works faster that way. I'll cover for you for a few minutes."

The Pervitin works quickly, and in no time at all Rachel feels wide awake and ready to continue. She helps bandage the young amputee and carry him into the recovery room. By the time she finally gets to eat and sleep, many hours later, she will have assisted in caring for four more soldiers who have had difficult operations. One of the men dies soon after being transferred from the operating table to the makeshift recovery ward. Two have wounds that are not life-threatening, but the fourth patient, a Russian soldier, has a head wound and fractured skull. His chances of recovery are slim.

Once again, as she had during the Winter War, Rachel wonders at the logic of trying to kill someone and then—if you only manage to wound him—attempting to heal him. As a nurse, she never questions her moral obligation to provide medical attention to anyone in need, but the absurdity of war is never more apparent than when she is tending to a wounded Russian soldier.

The pace of work at the hospital is punishing. The fighting up ahead is heavy, and the sound of artillery provides a harrowing accompaniment to the work. Not until the fourth day does she get a chance to go to sauna and wash her hair, followed by a full uninterrupted night's sleep.

Wake-Up Call

The corridors and wards are filled with a cacophony of cries in Finnish, Swedish, German and Russian. Finnish and German soldiers are treated and then sent away from the combat zone to military hospitals for further care or recuperation. Occasionally someone is sent back to his unit, but most of those with minor injuries have already been screened out at the first aid stations and never reach the field hospital. Russian soldiers who survive their wounds are sent directly from the hospital to P.O.W. camps.

During her second week at Tohmajärvi, Rachel has an experience that will haunt her for the rest of her life. She is on night duty in the Operating Room and has just finished putting the finishing touches on a Finnish soldier's full-arm plaster cast when a Russian soldier is brought in. He has a stomach wound, and those often require the trickiest interventions. As she turns and bends over the Russian to hold the mask while the nurse administers the ether, she recognizes something familiar about the face. There can be no mistake about it, the man is a Jew! His hair, his complexion, all his features proclaim his Jewishness. Startled, she quickly looks to see which doctor will be performing the operation. To her relief, Captain Järvinen is going to operate. What if it had been one of the Germans, Dr. Hoche or Dr. Bouhler? Would they have seen a patient on the table . . . or a Jew? Rachel has had no trouble with either of the German doctors, but she remains uneasy in their presence and has avoided contact with them outside the O.R.

So far no one has asked about her religion, but she suspects that some of the Finns are aware that she is Jewish. She has decided not to say anything, but if someone asks, she will answer truthfully. She has been taught never to deny her people or her heritage, and the events of the past few years have strengthened her conviction that she must speak out when the situation calls for it.

The operation is a difficult one, but somehow the Jewish soldier survives and begins to heal. A week later he is able to sit up and swallow some watery gruel. On her way back to her quarters at daybreak one morning after a relatively uneventful night shift, Rachel passes by the shed where the Russian prisoners are housed. On impulse, she steps inside and is taken aback by the smell. There are too many men in the small room, and there is only one tiny window for ventilation. Although there is little light in the room, she has no trouble finding the Jewish soldier. He is lying on his back with his head turned to the side, cushioned by his rolled-up jacket. "How strange," she thinks, staring at the face of the sleeping prisoner. "I have treated hundreds of soldiers, most of whom are my compatriots, yet this poor Russian is the only one who could be my relative. He is my enemy and yet my brother." She stands there, looking down at the convalescent soldier for several long minutes, then turns away with a heavy heart, closing the door quietly behind her.

Moving On

By the first week of September, the combined Finnish and German assault has reached the pre-Winter War border and is poised to advance across into unknown territory. Rachel and a team of doctors, nurses and Lottas have moved forward to set up a field hospital in Värtsilä on the banks of the Jänis River. To their surprise, when they reach the village, they discover that another field hospital team has preceded them and is already struggling to cope with the influx of patients. Rachel is among those assigned to help ease the workload at the hospital until their own unit can be set up and begin accepting patients.

Work shifts regularly stretch to 18 hours with little time for eating. It increasingly seems that just when the last head has been bandaged and the last broken bone set, a fresh truckload of wounded in need of immediate attention arrives from the front. Pervitin has become a supplement to everyone's diet. No one questions the wisdom of taking the pills or doing anything else that helps them cope with the exhausting routine. Anyway, the war will surely last only a few weeks more. Finnish troops have been advancing rapidly towards Leningrad from the west and north, and the Germans have already taken Smolensk and are heading towards Moscow.

The morale of the field hospital staff is strong. Although the work is exhausting, and the mosquitoes make sleeping problematic even when the schedule permits it, no one complains. All the usual hospital intrigues have been left behind, and the hierarchy that usually separates doctors, nurses and Lottas has been flattened considerably by shared hardships and challenges.

And then suddenly the flow of sick and wounded abates, perhaps because the fighting has moved further afield or because the rugged terrain and terrible roads have made advancing slow and difficult. In any case, on her first "free" day in Värtsilä, Rachel and some of her colleagues are sent into the nearby fields to cut, rake and stack the ripened hay. With all the men at war and food shortages looming as fields lie untended, Finland is forced to mobilize every possible able-bodied person to harvest crops. Rachel has never worked on a farm before, and the hay rake chafes and blisters her hands, but the summer day in the fields is among the happiest she has spent since leaving Helsinki. In the evening, she and two other Lottas pick blueberries in the woods in back of the hospital and swim in the peaceful Juvanjoki River before retiring for the night. As dawn is breaking the next morning, enemy planes drop bombs that obliterate the blueberry patch where only hours before she had been laughing and gathering the finger-staining fruit, but they miss the hospital. Huge red crosses on white backgrounds have been painted on the roofs of all the hospital buildings, but apparently the Soviet pilots don't consider these signs a reason to spare the occupants.

Instead of setting up their own field hospital in Värtsilä, Rachel and the team from Tohmajärvi now leapfrog ahead to Suistamo. The hospital is located on the shore of Lake Ladoga, and the nearly constant shelling of Sortavala at the northern tip of the lake booms in the distance. Before the first patients arrive, Rachel has time to swim in the lake and wash her hair again. Her skin is covered with bedbug bites, making it look as if she has a blotchy rash. She washes her clothes and hangs them up to dry in the sun, but she knows that the battle against this persistent enemy won't be won by a single washing.

When the first patients arrive the next afternoon, they are mostly men who have contracted a particularly virulent form of dysentery. This is a debilitating condition but not life-threatening in most cases. There is no effective medicine for the condition available in the field hospitals. Also, the staple army meal of dry crisp bread and pea soup is not the easiest on the digestive system. Recuperation is slow, and return to the front line can take anywhere from a few days to two weeks.

After ten consecutive days of long hours on the wards, Rachel gets another "day off" to go scavenging for food with two of the ambulance truck drivers. One of them has spotted what appears to be a deserted kolhoz[2] a few kilometers away. They arrive to find potato and cabbage fields that clearly have not been tended for a while. Apparently the inhabitants abandoned the farm ahead of the advancing Finnish and German troops. Rachel and the men easily fill the baskets they have brought and several more they find in one of the outbuildings. In the root cellar they also discover baskets of apples, which they add to their booty.

Into Eastern Karelia

The drivers will return to those fields many times, but Rachel has already been informed that her unit is once again moving forward. It is the beginning of September, and the troops to which her field hospital is attached are on the march towards the Svir River. Another team arrives in Suistamo to take their place.

Rachel has not had much time for reflection, and the hectic days and nights have kept her focused on the demands of the operating theater. But now she hears from a Lotta with the replacement unit that Finnish troops have retaken Viipuri, and she suspects that Benjamin's regiment has taken part in the battle. Her unit has moved so fast that mail has reached them only once since the end of July, and the one letter she received then was from her parents. Of course, Benjamin has been too busy to write, or maybe his letters just haven't reached her yet. Then she realizes that she has only written him two letters since Tohmajärvi. That evening she sits down with her suitcase on her knee and composes a letter into which she tries to cram all the experiences and feelings of the past several days. For the first time, she feels afraid for her life, not that she will be killed by a bomb or a sniper but that Benjamin might be taken from her and her life be destroyed in that way. She realizes now how deeply she loves Benjamin and prays that the Lord will watch over him.

The next destination for Rachel and Field Hospital 28 is Aunus (Olonets). On the trip from Suistamo, over roads that only barely deserve the name, she sees for the first time the full extent of the devastation this war is exacting. They pass forests and villages burned to the ground, bombed-out bunkers and trenches by the road, littered with the rotting bodies of Russian soldiers and horses, lying as they fell. The rancid smell of decaying flesh is overpowering.

This depressing environment does nothing to allay her fears for Benjamin's safety. She doesn't want to imagine him as one of the severely wounded she has treated, but in her dreams that night and many times afterwards she imagines tending to him, nursing him back to health, and sending him off to the safety of a military hospital near the Swedish border. When she wakes up and realizes it was just a dream, she doesn't know whether to feel relieved or afraid.

The only remedy for what ails Rachel is work, and once she arrives in Aunus, the hectic pace of work takes her mind off morbid thoughts. She decides, though, to be sure to write more often to Benjamin and hopes to hear from him the next time mail is delivered. The war was supposed to be over by the fall, but here it is September, and the wounded keep arriving by the truckload. Surely, they will all be home by the end of the year?

Notes

1. Virkkunen, Sakari, *Ryti: Suomen tasavallan presidentti*, Otava, Helsinki, 1985, pp. 104–5.
2. Collective farm (Russian)

Figure 44.1. Fire direction station high up between two trees on the Eastern Front (Finland's Military Museum)

Father [Jussi Nemes, formerly Nemeschansky] was traveling with one of his friends, an officer named Topi Korpivaara. They were on their way back from leave in Helsinki to the Svir River sector by train, a trip which probably took over 20 hours. They were sitting in a car reserved for officers and were joined at some point by a group of German officers. They began talking with one another, and the same old question was brought up once again by one of the German officers: *"Wo haben Sie so gut Deutsch gelernt?"* (*Where did you learn such good German?*)

Jussi, of course, since he was cheeky and wanted to needle them a bit, replied: *"Ich habe in der jüdischen Schule gelernt"* (*I studied it in the Jewish School*).

A deathly silence followed. The silence was broken by a click, the unmistakable sound of a pistol's safety being released. Then Topi, who was sitting next to Father, turned to the German officer and asked, *"Haben Sie etwas dagegen?"* (*Do you have something against that?*) to which the German quickly replied that in no way did he have anything against it. Topi's act of courage and friendship touched my father deeply, and he never forgot it.

Joel Nemes*

---

*Interviewed by the author, Helsinki, 29 June, 2012.

CHAPTER FORTY-FOUR

~

David's Battlefront Diary

19 June, 1941 Juurikorpi—We received our marching orders at 19:00 hours. Departure at 21:00 in light rain. Boys in high spirits despite cold weather, glad to be on the move. We proceeded via Hamina to Rakila Manor. Fire direction at the head on bicycles, followed by our guns, then fire team on bicycles, and ammunition trucks bringing up the rear. Lottas waiting for us at Rakila with hot pea soup and "plywood,"

Midsummer, Virolahti. Used the days here for much-needed training and practice. Focused on calculation speed and fire direction accuracy. Finally able to familiarize ourselves with the new howitzers, too. Captain Sirola personally led exercises twice to make sure everyone is working well together.

29 June, Virolahti. 07:40 enemy shelled several targets in our sector. We answered their fire with a few rounds, then moved our battery back about 1.5 kilometers to await further orders near an old observation tower. First live fire experienced by those of us not in the last war! Received the order to shell Laitsalmi Island dock and the torpedo and artillery boats tied up there. I had a direct line of sight from the tower, and we hit a torpedo boat with our first volley! It didn't sink but listed badly to starboard. That boat won't be going after our ships any time soon! The others shoved off before we could recalculate and reload. Have to make the whole fire chain much faster.

8 July, Tuherrusjärvi. Sent a scout patrol behind enemy lines to look for potential battery placements. Those boys never engaged the enemy but brought a 40-kilo wild boar that they shot on their way back to camp. Not kosher, I guess, but still delicious! Vanya[1] sent greetings to us last night in the form of mortar fire. No damage to fire direction or gun line, but one of the soup kitchens took a direct hit and Cook Pitkäranta was hit in the leg (only a "sick-leave" wound).

15 July, Valkjärvi. Ordered to begin daily shelling of enemy troops and batteries. Vanya launched several attacks against us, but we sent him packing. Accurate incoming mortar fire forced our battery to move a few hundred meters to a more sheltered position behind the hill to our left. After that, we continued to harass the enemy without worrying about getting hit. We are now able to change fire direction in under 30 seconds and accurately fire off five rounds in twelve seconds!

24 July, Valkjärvi. After a 30-hour firefight, everything is calm. Vanya is apparently pulling back further. Most of us took a swim in the lake today, then lay in the sun on the shore to dry off. Koskivirta caught three pike, the biggest almost 3 kilos.

2 August, Hyttilä. Spent four days building bunkers. Last night, division staff rewarded us with a show. Entertainment provided by JR 45's brass band and singing by Sgt. Reine Hallaperä. Enjoyable evening.

21 August, Kolmekantajärvi. From my fire direction lookout, I heard loud explosions on the other side. Vanya must be blowing up his own bunkers and retreating back across the border.

24 August, Kehäsniemi. Took up position near the shore and began shelling Ykspää and Tienhaara. Neighboring battery shelling Viipuri's South Harbor. JR 45 preparing to cross Viipuri Bay. We will probably follow.

26 August, Porkansaari. Advanced to loading dock early in the morning, but squadron of 15 enemy planes prevented embarkation. Finally got first guns loaded onto a pontoon barge at 21:00 hours. Fire direction went ahead in assault boats. By midnight first guns had been moved off the beachhead to Rauhala. Our boys headed towards Kaislahti and Ylä-Sommee but Uuras is still in enemy hands. Heavy fighting in direction of Kaislahti.

29 August, Ylä-Sommee. 04:30 hours on 28 August, Nyström saw a Russky column advancing from Ala-Säiniö. 8th battery scored a direct hit on vehicles at the head of the column. Two hours of heavy fighting followed. Vanya threw mortar, direct fire and tanks at us, but our batteries continued to hammer them until he gave up and retreated, leaving some pretty big guns behind as well as a lot of dead bodies. Meanwhile Russkies also attacked Koivisto-Viipuri Road in Kaislahti sector. Fierce battle in heavy rain all day long from Ylä-Sommee to Sommee Station. Nyström and his men were caught in a *motti* for over 30 hours until Hollström's platoon was able to free them. Fighting never stopped so our guns never got the chance to cool down. Finally brought in antitank guns and mortars to join the fight around noon today. Before evening, we got the news that our flag is flying over Viipuri Castle again!

1 September, Ylä-Sommee. It's over. Some of the enemy have managed to slip through our lines, but thousands have surrendered. The amount of equipment they left behind is staggering, from tanks to big guns to rifles. Our unit has suffered only seven wounded, none seriously. Six of our own guns are out of commission, rifling destroyed when they overheated from constant firing. Replaced them with best captured pieces we could find.

3 September, Rautanen. Chasing Vanya to Koivisto. Finally got a replacement for the injured runner we lost, a small, dark man named Salonen. Says he spent last two years in jail but wouldn't say for what. Wasn't on the job for three days before he brought two big sacks full of carrots and cabbage he "found" someplace. Then I heard he was selling honey to the men. Have to keep an eye on him. In the afternoon, a recon patrol returned to the command post with seven prisoners while I was there. One spoke pretty good Finnish and explained that they had gotten separated from their company, spent two days without food, and had been trying to get to Koivisto. The captain ordered the patrol to take them to the sand pit behind the tents. When they left, he told me he wanted to use the one who spoke Finnish as a translator so he could help with interrogating other prisoners. A few minutes later, we heard a submachine gun barking in back of the tents. Lieutenant M. had interpreted the captain's order as "take them to the sand pit and finish them off," I was shocked but didn't have much time to think about it before we were on the move again.

3 October, Viipuri. We all thought that after cleaning out the last pockets of resistance on the Karelian Isthmus, we would be going home. Instead, we were put on a train, destination unknown. First Kouvola-Mikkeli-Pieksämäki and then headed east to Joensuu-Maaselkä-Veskelys, where we arrived the evening of the 4th under bright moonlight.

9 October, Veskelys. Set off marching toward Tsalkki in year's first snowfall. Constant artillery fire somewhere to the east. Ground still not frozen yet so very slippery. Made only slow progress with guns getting stuck in deep ruts or sliding off the road and having to be pushed back out of the ditch. Don't have nearly enough ice calks for all the horses. What will we do if we come to steep hills?

23 October, Selki. Reached Seesjärvi Lake yesterday. Assignment: support JR 45 as it tries to take Karjalan Maaselkä. Today fought off surprise attack by Russky infantry. At first we thought it was just a patrol but then saw about 200 men advancing towards us and realized it was a planned attack. Luckily

Lt. Mattila brought us 30 Jaegers from JR 4 for support. It was already getting dark, and we couldn't really tell what the enemy was doing. We held on until 21:30, when Lt. Alfthan arrived with some more men. He asked, "Are there Vanyas here?" We said there were, and he answered, "Then I guess we should drive them off!" Throughout the night additional reinforcements arrived, and the next morning Alfthan kept his promise. The Russkies took off through the swamp, leaving almost 350 dead. We lost 15 men.

26 October, Karjalan Maaselkä. Finally able to position our batteries and begin firing. Incoming mortar fire is fierce. We have lost some good men. I set up a good fire direction station, but the Russkies keep cutting the telephone wire to the gun line as fast as it can be mended by our communications guys, and I keep losing contact. Hope to get a radio set up so we won't have to rely on the telephone lines.

11 November, Tsalkinselkä Field Hospital. I'm strong enough to write again. My shoulder wound seems to be healing, and I don't have a temperature any more. Captain Degerth came by to see me this morning. He told me that we took Karjalan Maaselkä but at a heavy cost. We lost 369 men, most of them from JR 24. I hope not anyone I know. The Russkies lost more than a thousand. He said I was lucky. A little bit lower and the bullet would have pierced my heart or lungs. As it was, it entered above my collarbone in front and exited through my back. Didn't hit any bone or vital organs, and I never lost consciousness, but the doctor says I lost a lot of blood. The real danger was from the fever, but now that's gone. Funny, I never was seriously sick in my life or had to be operated on. Well, now I have, but I should be able to rejoin my unit in a couple of weeks. It's not so bad here in the field hospital, and some of the nurses are really nice, but I want to get back. I hear the men are already on their way to Suurlahti.

16 November, Paatene (Pogosta). Moved yesterday from Tsalkinselkä Field Hospital 23 to the rest house in the Paatene Folk School. Most of the others here are on three-day leave, but there are four of us recuperating from wounds. There are only straw pallets instead of real beds, but everything is clean and well maintained and the food in the canteen is pretty good. There is an old piano in the canteen, and last night a sergeant named Pohjola played for almost two hours, everything from Chopin to Gershwin. Hope he is here again tonight. Tomorrow there is going to be a film shown during the afternoon and a dance performance by a local Karelian folk dance group in the evening.

6 December, Karhumäki (Medvezhyegorsk). We made it here for Independence Day! Vanya put up a stiff defense, but here we are. I only got to

join the action when it was almost over. Marski wanted us to take all three isthmuses, and it's taken less than half a year! Our neighbor to the east will never be able to surprise us again the way he did in '39. Now it's just a matter of waiting for Leningrad and Moscow to fall. What will happen after that, nobody knows.

Note

1. A common derogatory term used by some Finnish soldiers to speak of Russians in general.

Figure 45.1. The execution of Ukranian Jews at Babi Yar near Kiev in September 1941 (dpa picture alliance)

During the Independence War in 1918 I assured Finnish and Eastern Karelians that I would not sheathe my sword until Finnish and Eastern Karelia were free. I swore this in the name of Finland's yeoman army, trusting in its brave men and Finland's self-sacrificing women.

Independence War Fighters, Illustrious Winter War Veterans, My Courageous Soldiers! A new day has dawned. Karelia is rising. Among your ranks march its own battalions. Free Karelia and Greater Finland gleam before us in the enormous maelstrom of world historical events. Let Providence that directs the fate of nations allow Finland's army to fulfill the promise I made to the clans of Karelia.

Soldiers! The soil onto which you are stepping is drenched in the blood and suffering of our people. It is holy land. Your victories will free Karelia, and your deeds will create for Finland a great and prosperous future.

*"Mannerheim"**

Commander in Chief's Order of the Day No. 3, Mikkeli, 11 July, 1941.

CHAPTER FORTY-FIVE

~

Finland Walks a Tightrope

Karelia, Autumn 1941—By the time David's unit closes in on Karhumkäki, Finland has accomplished almost all its military objectives on the Karelia and Ladoga Isthmuses. Even the previously Soviet-occupied Hanko Peninsula is once again in Finnish hands.

Finnish troops already occupy the Karelian Isthmus right up to the outer defenses of Leningrad as well as a broad swath of territory around the top of Lake Ladoga and down to the Svir River on the Ladoga Isthmus. Responsibility for the sector of the Ladoga front where the Svir River empties into Lake Ladoga is assigned to Germany's 163rd Division, known as the Engelbrecht Division, which was held in reserve while the Finns battled from Sortavala to the Svir. South of Leningrad, Germany's Army Group North, under Field Marshal Wilhelm Ritter von Leeb, is now firmly entrenched between the Bay of Finland and Pähkinälinna (Schlüsselburg) along the outskirts of the city.

Hermann Göring has twice said that Finland will get all of Karelia once it has been taken/retaken from the Soviets and suggested the second time that the ruins of Leningrad will be included in the package. Field Marshal Mannerheim and President Ryti like the idea of occupying all of Karelia, but they are much less interested in Hitler's plans for Leningrad: *der Führer* intends to starve the inhabitants and raze the city to the ground. To complete the encirclement of Leningrad and prevent its defenders and inhabitants from being resupplied overland from the east, the Germans insist that Finnish troops push south from the Svir River to join up with Army Group North, which has advanced to Tikhvin, some 60 kilometers away. In response, Commander-in-Chief Mannerheim replies that Finland has already kept its promise: the Finnish Army has advanced to the Svir River as he said it

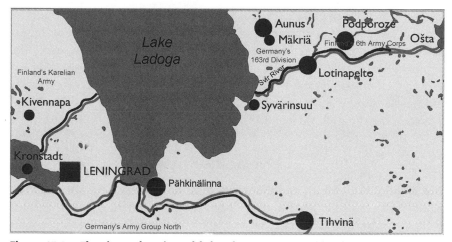

Figure 45.2. The siege of Leningrad left only a narrow corridor for supplies to reach the city from the east (Marja Leskelä)

would, and it is up to the Germans to keep their own commitment by joining them at Lotinapelto if they want to complete the encirclement.

Mannerheim then tells General Waldemar Erfurth, the German liaison officer at Finnish Military Headquarters, that he does not want to attack any more. When the Soviet High Command becomes aware of Mannerheim's position, it is able to redeploy troops from the Finnish border to contain Germany's Army Group North.

So near and yet so far. Because the siege ring is never fully closed, the Soviets can maintain a meager lifeline to Leningrad via Lake Ladoga and the narrow corridor left open between the Finnish and German lines. The Germans' siege of the city, which lasts until January 1944, is by design the most murderous in history. Of Leningrad's 3.3 million inhabitants at the start of the war, 1.4 million are evacuated during the first two years. At least that many civilians and soldiers perish, mostly by starvation.

When the Germans withdraw from Tikhvin in early December 1941, the Finns along the Svir River front are hunkered down in their defensive positions. Mannerheim diverts his attention to the North, mounting an offensive aimed at capturing Petroskoi, a city which is important to the Finns but figures nowhere in the German plans. By the spring of 1942, Mannerheim sends General Erwin Engelbrecht's 163rd Infantry Division back to the north, far from Leningrad. The Germans had promised a *Blitzkrieg*, but the fighting has already been going on for nine months with no end in sight. Nevertheless, procrastination and reluctance to meet Hitler's demands[1] have to be carried out with great tact as Finland is still heavily dependent upon German grain and military support.

Even with the crucial German aid, however, Finland's economy is on the verge of collapse. With 16 percent of able-bodied males in the army and trade interrupted by the war, neither agriculture nor industry is able to supply the country's basic needs. By the end of 1941, when the attacking phase of the war is over, the army begins releasing soldiers born before 1912 from service, slowly at first but with increasing speed in the spring of 1942. By the second week of March, more than 71,000 men will have been allowed to return home.

Tightening the Screws

Meanwhile, in Germany and the territories it has annexed, all Jews over the age of six have been forced from the beginning of September 1941 to attach yellow stars to their clothing. The same month, Russian and Polish prisoners are murdered in the first tests of the Auschwitz (Oświęcim) gas chambers. As the industrial method of exterminating humans is still in the developmental stage, however, the September 29 and 30 massacre of 33,771 Ukrainian Jews from Kiev has to be carried out the old-fashioned way. They are rounded up and told they are being resettled. Then they are taken to the Babi Yar ravine, where they are ordered to put down their luggage and strip naked. One of the truck drivers who take them there later describes what happened:

> Once undressed, they were led into the ravine which was about 150 meters long and 30 meters wide and a good 15 meters deep. . . . When they reached the bottom of the ravine, they were seized by members of the *Schutzpolizei* (Security Police) and made to lie down on top of Jews who had already been shot. . . . The corpses were literally in layers. A police marksman came along and shot each Jew in the neck with a submachine gun.[2]

With the bodies in the Babi Yar ravine still warm, Leningrad still under siege, and Smolensk and Kiev already in German hands, the *Wehrmacht* redirects its efforts toward Moscow. Two million German soldiers reach the gates of the Soviet capital by the beginning of November. There the attack stalls, first in the mud and then in temperatures that drop to –45 C°. The Germans, expecting their *Blitzkrieg* to accomplish its goals long before the onset of Russian winter, lack proper clothing, equipment and logistical support for snowbound warfare so far from home. The Soviet counter-offensive that begins in early December 1941 pushes the German troops 100 kilometers or more from the city by January 7. Compounding the problem for Germany, Japan's December 7 attack on Pearl Harbor has brought the United States into the war in an active combatant's role alongside the Soviet Union and its allies. Finland's leaders begin to doubt seriously whether Germany can win the war.

Finnish law requires all foreign citizens (potential spies and fifth column members) to be resettled during the war away from major cities, the Soviet border and the coastline. With German soldiers moving through Turku and Helsinki, Finland's Ministry of the Interior speeds up the relocation of Jewish refugees to the countryside. Representatives of Helsinki's Jewish Congregation meet with State Police Chief Arno Anthoni and agree to a plan to resettle many of the Jewish refugees in and around Hauho, Lammi, Tuulos and Luopioinen some 135 to 160 kilometers north of the capital. The area, where a number of Central European Jews are already lodged, has many large farmhouses that take in summer boarders and can accommodate new arrivals on short notice. The refugees, however, will have to find and pay for their own accommodations. Unfortunately, many of those with jobs in Helsinki or Turku will not be able to continue working. Compounding the problem, the American Jewish Joint Distribution Committee suspends its support for the refugees. Finland's tiny Jewish congregations will have to find ways to make up the deficit on their own.

Both the 350 or so Jewish refugees and Finland's own Jewish citizens are well aware that their co-religionists, packed into ghettoes in Polish cities, are dying of overwork, hunger and disease. Some have relatives with whom they are still able to correspond at this point although the letters (in both directions) are heavily censored and can only hint at what desperately needs to be told. Unbeknownst to most of the world, during the second week of December 1941 at Chelmno near Lodz, the first dedicated extermination camp begins its awful work, and six weeks later, at a conference in the Berlin suburb of Wannsee, senior Nazi officials from various ministries will hear Chief of the Reich's Main Security Office (RSHA) Reinhard Heydrich explain in detail the plans for implementing *Endlösung*, the wretched Final Solution to what Hitler has called The Jewish Question. No one will raise a voice in opposition.

And yet, strange as it may seem, the lives of Finland's Jewish citizens on the home front at this time differs little in most ways from the lives of their non-Jewish neighbors. Yes, they have to expend extra energy raising funds to support the Jewish refugees in the countryside. And, yes, they may by aware that some Jews in Lithuania, Latvia and Estonia have already been murdered by German *Einsatzgruppen* forces, sometimes aided by local Self-Defense Committees, although surely not that the number of victims already totals more than 185,000. But Finnish Jews are at the front, soldiers in Finland's army, and they and their relatives remain outwardly confident that their government will ensure that no Finnish citizens or refugees under the protection of the Finnish state will be subjected to racially motivated persecution or put to death.

Daniel Weintraub, who has studied the Helsinki Congregation's archives from the war years, says that the concerns recorded and preserved from that time are amazingly pedestrian. With so many young men at the front, asks a group of concerned mothers, could the congregation organize more social activities for its young people so young Jewish women would not be tempted to spend too much time with men from outside the Jewish community? Given the shortage of food on the home front, where can families get the matzo[3] meal they need for Passover?

Do the archives reflect the full range of fears, doubts, rumors and assumptions circulating through the Jewish communities of Helsinki, Turku and Tampere at the end of 1941? Undoubtedly not. Books such as Simo Muir's *Ei enää kirjeitä Puolasta* (*No More Letters from Poland*) and Rony Smolar's *Setä Stiller* (*Uncle Stiller*) as well as Taru Mäkelä's documentary film *Daavid* make that clear. There is, nevertheless, a concerted effort being made to focus on the positive: Finland's Jews are being allowed to defend their country and being treated like all other citizens. It is essential that nothing be done to jeopardize that status, a situation that requires a collective refusal to admit publicly to any anxiety about the future other than that shared by all Finns about the outcome of the war.

Jewish soldiers at the front, of course, are faced with radically different circumstances. Some of those who speak Yiddish or German are brought into close contact with German soldiers when they are assigned to serve as interpreters, and Jewish doctors treat sick and wounded German soldiers. Their experiences range from harrowing to comical, but there are no records of serious incidents or murderous consequences.

During the attacking phase of the war, three of Finland's Jewish soldiers—Harry Matsoff, Elis Nemeschansky and Rafael Sklarsky—do make the ultimate sacrifice for their country. They are felled, however, not by German assassins but by Soviet fire.

Notes

1. Had the farsighted Mannerheim accepted the proffered command of all German military operations in Finland, his refusal to advance from the Svir to Tihkvin would have been rank insubordination and potentially punishable as treason.

2. Berenbaum, Michael, *The World Must Know: The history of the Holocaust as told in the United States Holocaust Memorial Museum*, Johns Hopkins Press, 2006, pp. 97–98.

3. Unleavened bread (Hebrew)

Figure 46.1. Jewish soldiers gathered for shabbos services at the Kuuttilahti field synagogue on the Svir River front. Back row, left to right: Herman Berman, Leo Epstein, Daniel Wardi (Waprinsky), Bernhard Kapri, Abner Zewi, Jacob Manuel, Ruben Stiller, David Wardi (Waprinsky) and Samuel Chalupovitsch. Front row, left to right: Isak Smolar and Abraham Scheiman (Rony Smolar's personal collection)

One day I was summoned to our company's command bunker. I had grown a long dark beard, and I told my commanding officer that I couldn't meet a German officer looking like that. He replied, "Salomon Altschuler, I am giving you an order!" My gut was churning because the Germans kept looking at me closely. In the evening, the orderly returned and told me the German officer wanted to see me again, this time in private. I reported as ordered, and for a few minutes we exchanged pleasantries. Then the mood changed, and he said to me, *"Du bist kein Finne"* (You are no Finn).

I replied, *"Herr Oberkommandeur, ich bin ein Finnischer Soldat, aber ich bin Jüde"* (Lieutenant, Sir, I am a Finnish soldier, but I am a Jew).

How can a Jew be in the Finnish Army? he asked.

I answered that we were born in Finland, and it was our duty to serve in the army. Then he told me—I still remember it to this day—*"Ich bin kein SS, ich bin kein SA, ich bin Wehrmacht"* (I'm not SS or SA, I'm regular army). He said he had nothing personal against Jews. On the contrary, he found it hard to believe what was happening to them.

A couple of years later I was at a train station when an orderly ran up to me and said, "Salomon, there are some Germans leaving across the way, and one of them is shouting "Altschuler!" I went to see, and there was this same lieutenant. He gave me his business card and told me to come visit him after the war if I got to Germany. He was shipping out for home.

*Salomon Altschuler**

---

*Interviewed by the author, Helsinki, 15 May, 2012.

~

CHAPTER FORTY-SIX

Tent Synagogue
on the German Front

12 September, 1942—"*Mir haben sich do farsamelt zu faiern Rosch-Haschono,*"
intones Abner Zewi, a bespectacled math teacher and son of the Turku Congregation's rabbi, who holds the rank of corporal in Benjamin's regiment.
"We have gathered here to celebrate *Rosh Hashanah.*"

The year is 1942, the setting an army tent on the Svir River front that
serves as a field synagogue, and the circumstances unique in the annals of
World War Two. Zewi is addressing fifteen Finnish soldiers, fifteen Jews who
have come to spend this holy day in prayer.

He continues in Yiddish.

We are very grateful to our Finnish brothers-in-arms for enabling us to celebrate one of our holiest days. It is an interesting and unique case in these
days that our people and our religion are still respected in a small country on
this continent. We shall never forget the day we are celebrating here. This
teaches us two things. First, we learn that Jews always remain faithful to their
religion and their people, wherever they are and whatever the circumstances.
Second, this shows us that Judaism cannot be exterminated so long as a single
Jew still exists.

Another year of affliction and suffering for the entire world and especially
for our people has come to an end. We have experienced a year of persecution
and oppression. . . . Today, while celebrating *Rosh Hashanah* in a tent, far from
our homes, we hope for a new year of better times for our people and humanity
as a whole. . . . For two thousand years already we have wandered in the world
without a home and without a country. May it be God's will that the years of
our diaspora come to an end and our people be granted redemption.

. . . We wish and hope that the new year will be a year of life and peace for the people and country of Finland. We hope that the Finnish people will be set free from suffering, famine and poverty. We pray that our families will not suffer and will overcome all difficulties. We ask the Holy One to help all our Jewish brothers wherever they are. We also hope that, at long last, our dreams, cherished for generations, of being again like all nations and of a Jewish state flourishing in *Eretz Yisrael* will come true. . . .

In conclusion, I wish you all a year of life and success, a year of peace, bless-ing and livelihood. We express the same wish for our families and all Jews in Finland and all over the world. May the year 5703 be a year of peace, redemp-tion and consolation. Amen.[1]

The 15 celebrants, who have gathered from various units along the Svir Front, respond with heartfelt "Amens" of their own. Among them, two men are surprised to recognize each other. Six years after their shared camp expe-rience at Vidablick, Benjamin and David find themselves once again in the same tent. Neither has previously known that the other is nearby.

This time the talk is not of girls, sports and food but of redemption and survival. More than fourteen months into the German Army's lightning attack that was to wipe the Soviet Union off the map, Finnish soldiers are mired down in stultifying trench warfare that shows no signs of abating. Far to the southeast, the Germans are now three weeks into their ill-fated assault on Stalingrad, but along the Svir River, Finnish and Soviet troops are playing cat-and-mouse, each holding the other in place but neither making a serious move to advance.

In need of spiritual replenishment, David has come to the *Rosh Hashanah* service at a God-forsaken place called Kuuttilahti. His role as an officer is proving much more challenging than he expected. He can handle the physi-cal grind and the pressure under fire. What is taking its toll, though, is the emotional strain caused by the loss of men under his command. Even worse is the nagging suspicion that had he exercised his authority more effectively, he might have been able to prevent some of the deaths and injuries. This kind of uncertainty is new to him. Outwardly he still maintains the same air of self-assurance, but inwardly he is in turmoil.

Benjamin, on the other hand, has come to the prayer tent primarily for companionship. There is something comforting and reassuring in this time of uncertainty about being surrounded by *lantzmen*, fellow Finnish Jews who share the same traditions and concerns. For the first time in years, he even finds consolation in the prayers chanted in unison. Perhaps the location and *ad hoc* nature of this mini-congregation make the prayers seem more authentic than in the structured environments of the Viipuri and Helsinki synagogues with their petty squabbles and annoying hierarchies.

Unusual Neighbors

Kuuttilahti was once a branch of the Svir River that ran into Lake Ladoga. Blocked off eons ago by silt at its mouth, it is now a long and narrow inlet with Soviet troops camped along the southern shore and Finnish troops on the opposite bank. When the Soviets are pushed across the Svir in September 1941, responsibility for the sector between Kuuttilahti and Lake Ladoga is given to Germany's 163rd Division. In the spring of 1942, worried about German pressure to complete the stranglehold on Leningrad, Field Marshal Mannerheim sends the Germans back to Northern Finland, and the Ladoga end of the Svir front is assigned to Benjamin's JR 24.

The last members of General Erwin Engelbrecht's 163rd Division will depart Kuuttilahti by 7 June, but JR 24, with the largest number of Jewish soldiers of any Finnish regiment, has already arrived in mid-April and set up camp alongside the Germans. Only a month before, all JR 24's soldiers older than 40 were reassigned to a separate regiment, which was then disbanded and its members sent home as part of an effort to relieve the manpower shortage on the home front. There are still more than enough Jews left in the Eighth Division, though, to enable a *minyan* to be formed on any given Sabbath. The field synagogue has been erected by Corporal Isak "Sholka" Smolar, who petitioned his division's headquarters to allow Jewish soldiers to set up their own house of worship. When the request was granted and a tent provided for the purpose, Smolar brought a *Torah* from Helsinki to be read during services. "Sholka's Shul" was born.

The field synagogue is a unique phenomenon, a Jewish house of worship on the Third Reich's eastern front. In a 1988 interview with Historian Hannu Rautkallio, Isak Smolar explained:

> I got five or six men to help me pitch the tent. It was the kind that officers used, with windows and a wood-burning stove in the middle. That's where we met every Saturday, and an official order went out saying that all followers of the faith of Moses were free to assemble at the synagogue every week. Lots of guys showed up there who didn't attend *shul* at home very often. They came to the field synagogue enthusiastically because they knew they would meet their buddies. They sat around, read, attended proper services, and the next Saturday they met again. I'm sure those memories stayed with each one of them for as long as they lived. The *shul* was maybe a kilometer or a kilometer and a half

from the front line. . . . The Germans were a few hundred meters or at most a kilometer to our left, and the war was going on![2]

Sholka's son, Rony Smolar, adds that his father told him about curious German soldiers occasionally visiting the synagogue, always respectfully.

My father said he often talked with German soldiers about the significance of the synagogue, and the matter seemed to interest them greatly. The Germans at no time tried to desecrate the field synagogue, nor were there any incidents caused by it even though Jewish soldiers were in daily contact with their foreign brothers-in-arms.[3]

On 12 September, 1942 (the 1st of Tishrei 5703 in the Hebrew calendar), however, there are no Germans present. The prayer tent holds only 16 Jewish soldiers celebrating the arrival of the new year.

Role Reversal

After the morning service, Benjamin and David take advantage of the midday break to walk along the Kuuttilahti embankment and catch up on the years that have passed since they last saw one another.

"My mother says you came by our place two summers ago, looking for work," David begins.

I was looking for *you*," Benjamin replies, "but she helped me get a job with a cousin of yours. I spent the summer as a cutter at Grünsteins' until I had to report for service. They were really nice to me. I don't know what I would have done without that job. Mameh and my younger brother and sister were living on assistance from the congregation. After I got the job, I was able to help out. Your mother told me you were in Vaasa at Reserve Officer School."

"Actually, it was non-com training," corrects David. "I went from there to ROS at Niinisalo. Now I'm in charge of an artillery battery at Lake Sekeenjärvi. I was a fire direction officer at first, but we lost several officers in the fighting up north, and I got a field promotion. What about you?"

"Me? Just a foot soldier. I've been making hats since I left school. I guess you have finished university already."

David lets out a little self-deprecating laugh. "Not even close. I'm maybe halfway there. For me, the war came along at the right time. I wasn't really motivated to study. Now I realize you have to take advantage of every day because you never know what the next one will bring. How about your social life? You finally got a girlfriend?"

Now it's Benjamin's turn to search for the right tone of voice. "I'm sure you remember Rachel from camp. We've been together since last winter. Or maybe that's not the right way to put it since we haven't actually been together very much. I was on the Hanko front at first, and I've been doing the three-isthmus tour since then, but we write each other regularly. She's a Lotta somewhere north of here."

"Hey, that's swell!" replies David without missing a beat. "She's a great girl. We met once in Helsinki a couple of years ago, but I haven't seen her since."

That's funny, thinks Benjamin. She never mentioned it. "What about you? Are you married? I don't see a ring."

"Far from it," admits David. "I've had girlfriends, but I've never had what you could call a serious relationship. I wonder sometimes if there is something wrong with me. I'm worried that I may never find the right girl, I mean one who is willing to put up with me for longer than a few weeks."

"That's crazy," says Benjamin. "You're handsome, smart and come from a good home. I think any girl would be happy to have you for a husband."

"It's not that," concludes David. "There's something that always seems to happen after a couple of dates. Maybe I'm not cut out to be the marrying kind. I'm really envious of you. To have a girl like Rachel and be able to plan a future together, I don't know if I'll ever have that."

Benjamin is astonished. David envious of him? He remembers the way David put his arm around his shoulder at *Vidablick* and offered him brotherly advice. Now he is saying that shy and awkward Benjamin, who listened to David's advice but could never have imagined following it, is the successful one.

Just then there is a loud explosion nearby. David jumps, causing Benjamin to chuckle.

"It's just some of the boys fishing. They're not supposed to use hand grenades, but if the cook wants to make fish soup for dinner, the officers look the other way."

"Oh," acknowledges David. "I wondered why there was no sound of incoming ordnance before the explosion. I'm used to knowing what's on the way by the sound it makes as it approaches."

"Yeah, the Russkies fire all kinds of stuff at us here," Benjamin explains. "The biggest problems, though, are caused by the patrols they send out at night to snatch anyone who isn't careful. We lost someone one evening a couple of weeks ago when he went without his gun to get water. Of course, we do the same thing to them. You have to be really careful on guard duty. Vanya is just on the other side of Kuuttilahti, and on a rainy or foggy night, he can sneak across in about twenty minutes. If you doze off or lose your concentration, you can wake up dead or captured. Sometimes they attack our positions in the Glada Hörnan sector or back at the Brick Factory, but they haven't tried to cross here in force because most of the time we have a clear view of the other side and our machine-gunners would see them coming."

Uncertainty

Rosh Hashanah finds Rachel with five other Lottas, four nurses and seven doctors at a field hospital in Aunuksenlinna. She has been given the day off to observe the holiday in whatever quiet and personal way she can, but there has been heavy fighting near Lotinapelto the night before, and wounded soldiers are awaiting care not only outside the operating room but in the improvised emergency waiting room set up to handle the overflow. With a heavy heart, she recognizes that this new year will begin not in prayer and reflection but in determined attempts to limit the damage inflicted by one man on another. And it isn't just men. In one case, she was astonished to find, when stripping the clothes off an enemy soldier to treat his wounds, that the patient was, in fact, a woman. Female soldiers, their hair cropped and their breasts bound, fight alongside men in the Soviet Army.

Not all days are this hectic. Rachel occasionally finds time to practice with the Aunuksenlinna mixed choir or participate in women's gymnastics classes. She joins hospital staff members in mushroom-gathering trips and half-day visits to nearby villages such as Mäkriä and Tuulos whenever she can. But as the winter of 1942–43 approaches, she finds herself thinking gloomy thoughts. It has been more than a year since she followed the troops across the old border into Soviet territory and even longer since she has seen Benjamin. On Radio Aunus, Pekka Tiilikainen frequently reminds everyone how happy the people of Eastern Karelia are to have been liberated by their Finnish kin, but Rachel finds most of them to be suspicious and withdrawn. They are also obviously hungry. Even the field hospital's food supply is now inadequate. Rations for the prisoners have been reduced, and sometimes the potatoes and turnips delivered to the kitchen have spoiled before they arrive. No one—not even the doctors and nurses—gets enough vitamins to meet normal daily requirements.

The first snow of winter arrives on October 24. Although it makes the days lighter, it does little to brighten Rachel's mood. She worries about Benjamin. She knows he isn't far away, but they haven't been able to see each other. Every time a truckload of wounded soldiers arrives, she gets a sinking feeling in her stomach. Will he be among them? If he is hurt, how badly? Despite her fears, she continues to get letters each week telling her that he is fine and his sector is relatively calm. But as she writes to tell him how well she is doing and not to worry, she realizes that he must be doing the same thing. Each is determined to protect the other's feelings. War and the censors leave little room for the luxury of honest correspondence.

Turning Point

While the Finns and Soviets facing each other across the Svir River in Benjamin's sector are mostly content to lob a few mortars at each other and send exploratory patrols into each other's territory, 1,500 kilometers away German and Soviet troops are engaged in a battle that will have a decisive impact on the outcome of the war. German troops cross the River Don and reach the outskirts of the city of Stalingrad on the banks of the Volga River the last week of August 1942. For the next two and a half months, the attackers lay waste to the city, capturing some 90 percent of it. In the process, they leave themselves open to encirclement. During the ensuing two and a half months, Soviet defenders surround, hammer and starve the German forces, killing, wounding or imprisoning nearly a million of them. In addition to the heavy losses, the defeat punctures the myth of German invincibility. Finland's pragmatic leaders begin to foresee themselves caught on the horns of a future dilemma: how to extract their country from its alliance with, and dependency on, Nazi Germany without being overrun by the Soviet Army.

Unwelcome Visitor

For Finland's Jews, 1942 is full of frightening omens and events. SS *Reichsführer* Heinrich Himmler visits Finland twice during the first eight months of the year. In March, he spends six days touring the northern battlefronts at Kiestinki and Uhtua, where Leo Skurnik and Salomon Klass earned the Iron Crosses they refused to accept. He arrives directly from Poland, where his subordinates are already operating extermination camps at Belsen, Majdanek, Sobibor and Treblinka. Himmler's second visit lasts from July 29 to August 6. It is during this visit that Himmler reportedly asks Prime Minister Jukka Rangell what Finland intends to do about its Jewish problem. Rangell replies, according to his own postwar testimony, that Finland's 2,000 Jews are respectable people whose sons are serving in the army like any other Finns. Rangell claims to have concluded the conversation by insisting, "*Wir haben keine Judenfrage*" [We have no Jewish question], and that Himmler supposedly never brings up the subject again.

Rumors circulate throughout the Helsinki Jewish community that Himmler has demanded a list of Finland's Jews along with their addresses. Louis Levinsky, a member of the congregation who served in the war, says that Jac Weinstein took the Helsinki Congregation's membership records home with him and hid them every night to ensure that they didn't fall into the wrong hands, but Finland's State Police surely had lists of their own. In a 1954 article in *Uusi Kuvalehti*, the former head of Finland's Information and Censorship Bureau, Kustaa Vilkuna, writes that Himmler's hosts did their best to ensure that his visit would inflict as little collateral damage as possible on Finland's image as a civilized nation. Aware of Himmler's interest in archeology, they took their guest to various sites and museums to distract him from politically sensitive matters. Nevertheless, claims Vilkuna:

> The second objective of Himmler's visit was to get his hands on Finland's Jews. It was only later, on Thursday October 22, when I observed the normally good-natured and vigorous Prime Minister Rangell's atypical concerned expression, that I understood what pressure President Ryti, (Foreign) Minister (Rolf) Witting and he had been under in evading the proposal from Hitler that was communicated by Himmler: Finland's Jews were to be sent to Germany! Because of the difficult food situation and our otherwise sensitive position, it was not possible to bang fists on the table and shout "No!," The matter was skirted around, referred to Parliament, which would only meet in the autumn, etc.
>
> The autumn rolled around but the government did nothing. Now some neuropath in the Gestapo inner circle [apparently referring to State Police Chief Arno Anthoni] came up with the idea of "police action," which would require neither approval from, nor a stand by, the Parliament or the government as a whole. At a time when the war was demanding the daily sacrifice of our best men, the entire Jewish question seemed insignificant to most of the people of Finland, especially that kind of "police procedure," But what did a few of our leaders know about the seriousness of it? A lot!
>
> You see, some highly skilled men carried out an unbelievably daring and successful seizure during Himmler's visit. They simply photographed the contents of the world's most closely guarded secret police chief Himmler's briefcase, including all its most interesting papers. (But let it be said right away that I had nothing to do with this matter. It was carried out by soldiers . . .)
>
> In this black briefcase were, among other things, a list of Finland's Jews, nearly 2,000 names. In the autumn of 1942, it was clear that since mass deportation could not occur, that the Gestapo could demand that our Jews be handed over in small batches of various sizes on different kinds of charges to be prosecuted and convicted in Germany. This knowledge perhaps gave additional weight to the strong reaction that immediately arose in response to

police activity leading to the first deportations. It also supported our government's efforts. Hundreds of people subsequently avoided a terrible fate.[4]

Whether or not this espionage caper actually takes place and influences
Finnish policy as Vilkuna suggests is highly questionable. No paper trail from
the time exists, and the account was only published years later, when Finland
was trying to rebuild bridges with the international community. What is certain is that Himmler's presence in Finland in 1942 leaves the country's Jews
anxious and unsure of just how safe they can be in a society that receives the
chief architect of the Holocaust as a guest of honor.

Between Himmler's two tours of the North, just as the last members of
Germany's 163rd Division are packing their bags and heading from the Svir
River to Lapland, an even more dramatic visit takes place in Imatra some
60 kilometers north of Viipuri. On the fourth day of June, as Commander-
in-Chief Mannerheim is celebrating his 75th birthday, a surprise guest,
none other than *Reichsführer* Adolf Hitler, arrives in time for lunch. This
social call is intended as a sign of Hitler's respect for Mannerheim and
perhaps to tie him closer to the war effort at a time when the German
juggernaut has been ignominiously beaten back from the gates of Moscow.
It is no longer in Finland's interest nor Mannerheim's, however, to flaunt
close relations with the German leader, and the unannounced visit causes
Hitler's host considerable consternation.

Two months later, the secretary-general of the World Jewish Congress,
Gerhart Riegner, sends a telegram from Geneva to the organization's presi-
dent, Rabbi Stephen Wise, in New York City. The message, which is shared
with the U.S. State Department and British Foreign Office, confirms to
the West that Hitler is now determined not to resettle but to murder all of
Europe's Jews. Later in the year, information smuggled out of Poland by Jan
Karski will lead to the publication by the Polish government in exile of *The
Mass Extermination of Jews in German Occupied Poland*. It won't be until 17
December, however, a full 132 days after Riegner sends his telegram, that the
Allies belatedly issue a public condemnation of Germany's genocidal inten-
tions and threaten retribution against those involved.

In Finland, of course, these revelations are accorded no official recognition at all. How could they be? The country's soldiers—including its Jewish
soldiers—are still fighting side by side with German troops against their
common Soviet enemy.

Notes

1. English translation by Isak G. Zewi from the Yiddish original, copies of both provided by Simo Muir to the author.

2. Taped interview with Hannu Rautkallio, June 6, 1988

3. Interviewed by the author, May 24, 2012.

4. "Suomen juutalaiset ja Himmlerin salkku," *Uusi kuvalehti*, November 12, 1954, pp. 8–9 (translated by the author).

Figure 47.1. In 2000, at the dedication of this memorial, Prime Minister Paavo Lipponen apologized on behalf of the Finnish State and all Finns for the rendition of eight Jewish asylum seekers to the Gestapo in 1942 (Finland's Jewish Archives)

Troubled and clearly nervous, Julius Wilder sat in the deep armchair. Stiller urged him to unburden his heart, which seemed difficult at first.

Wilder said, "My permit to travel here to Helsinki expires this evening, and the bus back to Paippinen leaves soon. Mr. Stiller, I am afraid that all of us [Jewish refugees from Central Europe] will be arrested and sent to Germany. I heard a threat to this effect today from [State Police Chief Arno] Anthoni. I went to speak to him about getting a permit to move to Helsinki. He said that Helsinki is already full of dirty Jews and that I should get the hell back to the countryside and not bother him any more with requests. Then he threatened to arrest us all and send us to the death camp at Dachau in Germany. He added in German that we would find hot places for us there. That [Lieutenant Ari] Kauhanen was there, too. He said that soon there wouldn't be any more Jews in Finland because they all would be taken away."

*Rony Smolar**

---

*Setä Stiller, Kustannusosakeyhtiö Tammi, Helsinki, 2003, pp. 181–82.

CHAPTER FORTY-SEVEN

~

"Those Eight"

Monday, 6 November, 1942—By 6:30 a.m., several Finnish State Policeman have already boarded the SS *Hohenhörn*, a German cargo ship bound for Tallinn with 27 prisoners who are to be handed over to the Gestapo in the Estonian capital. The morning is extremely cold. In *Kuoleman Laiva S/S Hohenhörn* (*Death Ship SS Hohenhörn*), Elina Suominen (later Sana) quotes one of the policeman as saying: "When they had stood on the deck for almost an hour, I said to the Germans that they should be taken inside. Otherwise, they would freeze to death. But the Germans said. 'Let them stand there all the way to Tallinn. If they freeze, it will save gas!'"

Post-war accounts claim there were actually only 24 prisoners and that three family members—the wife and year-old son of Georg Kollmann and the 11-year-old son of Heinrich Huppert—are voluntarily accompanying men who are being deported. Suominen shows that, on the contrary, Kollmann and Huppert have been ordered to leave the country "with their families," The Kollmanns and Hupperts are Jews, as are three other deportees: Hans Korn, Elias Kopelowsky and Hans Szübilski. Two months after Riegner's telegram warned the world of the Nazi's "Final Solution," Finland is knowingly handing over eight Jewish refugees to that country's genocidal network of internment, labor and liquidation camps.

The shameful deportation of these eight Jewish refugees stains Finland's reputation. Fifty-eight years later, Finland's Prime Minister Paavo Lipponen will apologize on behalf of the government and all Finns for the act. But why was it allowed to happen in the first place?

Role of the State Police

Before 1938, citizens of Germany, Austria, Latvia, Czechoslovakia, Hungary, Estonia and Norway—those countries from which Jewish refugees came to Finland—could enter for short stays without visas. As Nazi persecution of Jews increased, and German occupation of Western Europe closed off land and sea routes to the west one after the other, the only point of departure from which it was possible for Central and Northern European Jews to sail to lands where they might be safe was the northern Finnish port of Liinahamari.

At that point, there were still more than 14,000 former refugees from the Russian Revolution, most of them from Karelia and Ingria, living in Finland. The Finnish government claimed that it had a greater responsibility for them than to the Jews fleeing Nazi oppression and took measures to discourage "Central Europe's flood of refugees" from heading to Finland. The hasty imposition of visa requirements was one of those measures, resulting in the 56 Jewish refugees on the SS *Ariadne* being turned away from Helsinki and returned to Stettin in August 1938.

Between the Winter and Continuation Wars, as Finland began to draw closer to Germany, President Ryti authorized the head of the State Police to handle "at his own discretion" such matters as the deportation, prohibition on leaving the country, and granting of residency and work permits for foreigners. The only official with higher authority in these matters was the conservative Interior Minister, Toivo Horelli. Only a few days before Ryti issued this instruction, an antisemite named Arno Anthoni was named head of the State Police. With Anthoni authorized to deal with the refugees as he saw fit and only the Nazi sympathizer Horelli in a position to countermand him, the stage was set for some ugly business.

Horelli was named Interior Minister in May 1941, six weeks before the Germans launched Operation Barbarossa. When hostilities broke out, he ordered all the Central European refugees, including political refugees as well as Jews, moved out of Helsinki to the countryside "to avoid contact and possible conflict with the Germans," At first, the refugees were primarily concerned in their new surroundings with making ends meet on the meager allowance provided, by the hard-pressed Helsinki congregation in the case of the Jews, or by the Social Democratic Party in the case of the political refugees.

Finland, however, with 16 percent of its population in the military, was suffering from a severe labor shortage. A law requiring able-bodied civilian men between the ages of 18 and 55 to work on the home front when called upon to do so was enacted in 1939 but not enforced until 1942, when the age range was expanded to include all males between 15 and 65. Approximately 40 of the 100 or so Jewish refugees living in the countryside fit into this category. In March 1942, they were ordered to report for work and sent to Kuusivaara and Alakurtti near Salla in the Northeast. Although the Jews had originally been moved to the countryside to keep them away from contact with Germans, these locations near the front were paradoxically in territory controlled by the German military.

Unaccustomed to hard physical labor and lacking adequate clothing for outdoor work in weather as cold as −25° C, the Jews found themselves working 10-hour days on road-building and tree-planting crews. After three months near the front, they were moved to Kemijärvi to work on building the Salla-Kemijärvi Railway. Here they stayed only a month. At the end of July, the State Police turned them over to the Domestic Armed Forces headquarters, which sent them to the island of Suursaari (Gogland), smack in the middle of the Baltic Sea. There, they were set to work making barbed wire frames with their bare hands.

Detestable and Unnecessary

Some of the refugees gain the ear of politicians and influential individuals, who try to intercede on their behalf. This activism enrages State Police Chief Anthoni, who initiates deportation procedures against some of those he finds most annoying. Although he will claim that the deportations have nothing to do with the deportees' religion and are strictly a police matter, many of the Jews he targets have no criminal record and are guilty, at most, of minor infractions such as failing to renew their residence permit on time.

October 27, 1942, nine Jewish refugees are bundled onto a truck on Suursaari at 6:30 p.m. with no information about where they are being sent. Escorting them are soldiers armed with automatic weapons. The truck delivers them to the dock, where they board a small ship. One of the crew members recognizes one of the prisoners, Dr. Walter Cohen. In exchange for a prescription, the crewman [who apparently has a venereal disease] tells Dr. Cohen that they are being taken to State Police headquarters on Ratakatu in Helsinki and agrees to mail a postcard for him. Cohen hastily scribbles, "Nine men today to Ratakatu, hopefully you can meet us" and addresses the card to Abraham Stiller in Helsinki.

The card arrives Friday, October 30 and propels Stiller into action. He hurries to Ratakatu and asks to meet with Anthoni or his deputy, Aarne Kauhanen, but is told neither is there. No one will even confirm whether the refugees are being held in the police headquarters. The congregation's

Samuel Maslovat approaches the Commander in Chief's adjutant, General Heikki Kekoni, to arrange an audience with Mannerheim. Kekoni conveys the appeal but returns to say that although Mannerheim calls the matter "detestable," he can do nothing about it because two high-ranking officials have told him that the refugees are spies and the government knows what it is doing. While it is not clear with whom the Commander in Chief has spoken, both Foreign Minister Witting and Interior Minister Horelli will later publicly justify the action as the expulsion of spies.

Stiller next seeks an audience with President Ryti, who sends a message that the matter is the province of the Interior Minister. At a seeming dead end, Stiller contacts Social Democratic Member of Parliament Sylvi-Kyllikki Kilpi. The next day, Social Democratic Party Secretary Aleksi Aaltonen asks Finance Minister Väinö Tanner to intervene to prevent the deportation. Tanner replies that it doesn't fall under his jurisdiction, but since both Prime Minister Rangell and Interior Minister Horelli (along with State Police Chief Anthoni) are in the countryside hunting elk, Tanner is the senior minister on duty. Anxious to prevent an action that has the potential to cause serious damage to Finland's reputation, Tanner orders the deportation delayed until Monday, by which time the others will have returned.

On Monday, the matter is discussed in chambers by the Council of State. Apparently Minister of Social Affairs Karl-August Fagerholm threatens to resign if the refugees are deported and Horelli to resign if they aren't. Finland, in the midst of war, cannot afford to have its fragile coalition government break up over the fate of a few Jewish refugees. Prime Minister Rangell promises to find a solution to the problem, and neither minister resigns.

Articles appear in the *Sosiaalidemokraatti* and *Helsingin Sanomat* newspapers extolling the importance of respecting the rights of asylum seekers and reminding readers that many Finns have themselves benefited from that protection in the past. The Jewish refugees cannot be returned to their own countries because the citizenship of all Jews has been revoked by the Nazis, and in any case the refugees have been forced on their departure to sign a pledge never to return. Under international law, deportees can only be forcibly returned to their country of origin. There is no way the planned deportations can be made legal.

The State Police, for their part, have already informed the Gestapo in Tallinn that the refugees are on their way. The political intervention on the refugees' behalf creates an embarrassing situation for Anthoni that needs to be resolved quickly. After each case is summarily reviewed, only Kollmann and Szübilski of the nine brought from Suursaari are finally "approved" for deportation. Huppert, Korn and Kopelowsky are brought later to Ratakatu and added to the list.

Ironically, Finland's respect for bureaucratic procedures and the rule of law actually work against the arguments for the refugees' release in this instance. Although many influential leaders—among them President Ryti, Field Marshal Mannerheim and Finance Minister Tanner—find the deportation order morally repugnant and contrary to the best interests of the republic, they are unwilling to overstep the authority of the officials whose responsibility it is to decide such matters.

The morning of 6 November, despite the unflagging efforts of Abraham Stiller and numerous others, the SS *Hohenhorn* departs from Helsinki harbor and heads to Tallinn with eight Jews (and 19 others, most of whom are Estonians) on board. The Jews will be sent from Tallinn via Berlin to Auschwitz. Only Georg Kollmann will survive.

Figure 48.1. Card game in a Finnish bunker, 1941 (Adiel Hirshovits' private collection)

When father [Salomon Steinbock] was at the front during the Continuation War, he was in a place where there were also German troops. He was an officer so he ate his meals in the officers' mess where the German officers ate as well. Father was dark and had a large nose, so there was no need to guess. Everyone could see that he was Jewish.

When the Germans came into the room and saw Salomon sitting there eating, they announced in loud voices that they would not eat in the same place as a Jew. Father's Finnish officer colleagues replied that as far as they were concerned, the Germans could eat outside if they wanted to. Father never forgot that!

Janiki Steinbock*

---

*Hartikainen, Jukka, "Ei unohtanut upseeritovereidensa tukea," in Lagerbohm, John (ed.), *Sata sotakohtaloa*, Otava, Helsinki, 2011, p. 97.

CHAPTER FORTY-EIGHT

~

Benjamin's Recollections of the Trench War

They never stopped harassing us, never got tired of attacking, especially at night. Oy yoy, the night was the worst. And they were everywhere, absolutely everywhere.

We would wake up in the morning covered with little red spots. The bedbugs, we never did figure out how to get rid of them for even a day. The lice, too, they would get in the seams of our clothing. The little ones you couldn't even see. The big ones you could crunch with your thumb and forefinger when you found them, but the little ones were too small. The only thing we could do was to sit in the sauna long enough to kill the ones in our hair and then leave our clothes there for four or five hours. Of course, even after we killed them all, others would take their place the next day, sucking our blood.

With the bedbugs, of course, you couldn't take your whole bed to the sauna. Some people said you could get rid of them by spraying vinegar on your bed, but we never had any vinegar. Others said alcohol would do it, but the men who had alcohol didn't want to waste it on bedbugs. All that was left was to get used to them, but no one I knew ever did.

And it wasn't just the bedbugs and lice, there were snakes and rats, too. Where we were in Kuuttilahti, there were lots of adders. You had to look before you stepped or sat, or you might get bitten. The rats were mostly after our food, but if you surprised one in a corner, it would give you a terrible bite. There were water snakes, too, sometimes really big ones, but they weren't dangerous. We kept our boots on most of the time because of the adders. After a while, we learned where they liked to make their nests and which rocks they liked to lie on when the sun was shining, but they could be anywhere, and they looked so much like the ground and the rocks that they were hard to see. If our camouflage had been as good as theirs, the Russky planes would never have spotted us.

There were bears, too. A few times one came into our camp, looking for food. When that happened, some of the men would try to track it down and shoot it. Twice they succeeded, and we had fresh meat for a while instead of our usual rations of pea soup and porridge. And sometimes we had fish and eels, too, from Kuuttilahti. When we were in heavy fighting, we sometimes had to go days without a proper meal, but during the trench war we usually ate pretty well.

What I remember most, though, after the lice and bed bugs, is the boredom. When we first got to Kuuttilahti and took over the sector from the Germans, they had already finished the dugouts and trenches. Some of the bunkers they left behind were really nice: strong and comfortable. And the Germans even built an outdoor cinema with a concrete projection room. They had their own graveyard, too. The graves were in absolutely straight lines, and every cross had a plaque with a name in neat letters. You could tell how that was important to them.

But because our sector was ready for us when we took over, there wasn't that much left for us to do. At first, the officers made us do all kinds of exercises like take our guns apart and put them back together over and over again, but after a while they got tired of it, just like us. We still had to stand guard and gather and chop wood to heat the dugouts and for cooking, and we had to collect water from the well twice a day, but after that we had plenty of free time.

We played sports, of course, to stay fit. We skied in winter and played football, volleyball or basketball when the field we built was clear and dry enough. David played on a basketball team called the Kolmen Kannaksen Koukkaajat (the 3-Isthmus Outflankers) made up of the best players from our Division, the 8th. They even competed for the National Outdoors Championship in 1942. They had Nils Fabritius and Max Jakobson on the team and made it to the finals, but many of them couldn't get leave when the finals were played so they had to forfeit. David said he didn't get to play that much because the shoulder that was shot hadn't completely healed, but he still got to go with the team so he could help out just in case too many players got in foul trouble or were injured.

Mostly, the men in my unit just played cards or whittled. They played games called Seiska (Sevens), Paskahousu (a Finnish version of Shithead or Shed) and Skruuvi (Vint or Russian Whist), using cigarettes for chips. We all got three cigarettes every day with our rations so even if you lost everything one day, you could get in a game the next day. They weren't real cigarettes with real tobacco, but they were the best you could get during the war. I didn't smoke or play cards so I sent mine home to Mameh. She said they were better than money. She could trade them for hard-to-get things she needed because cigarettes were so valuable.

Gambling was different at the front because it felt like you were always gambling with your life so losing a few cigarettes didn't matter. I remember one day, the Russkies were shelling us pretty hard. Everyone ran into the bunkers except

Sjöblom. His bunkmates kept yelling at him to get inside, but he just sat on a stump, smoking his pipe. Shells were exploding all around. One made a direct hit on Sjöblom's dugout, killing three men and wounding the rest. When the shelling finally stopped, Sjöblom was still sitting on that stump, smoking, dazed but unhurt. If he'd done what they said, he probably would have been a goner.

Most of the men seemed to believe that when your number came up, that was it. It didn't matter whether you were careful or not. Myself, I always thought it was stupid to take chances.

I liked to read, but after a while I had finished every book in camp. I didn't play cards so I decided to learn to whittle, just to pass the time. The first week, I almost cut off a finger on my left hand. It took a long time to heal properly so I had plenty of chance to watch how the other guys did it. Some of them were really good. They were making beautiful little things like bowls or boxes with delicate covers. They would carve designs into them, sometimes with animals or flowers. I knew I could never do anything like that, but I did make a few things good enough to give to Mameh and Rachel. The secret was to be patient and careful. Once I understood that, I was able to finish some projects without ruining them or hurting myself. I was pretty proud of one dish I made. I copied the idea from one I saw in a display at regiment headquarters. But even if I copied the design, I was still proud because I had made it with my own hands.

I wanted to give the dish to Rachel myself, but we were never able to meet. It was frustrating because for a few months she wasn't that far away. I couldn't get leave for the longest time because the older men all had more seniority and got to go ahead of me. And Rachel, she had so much to do at the field hospital that she couldn't get away. All we could do was write to each other. I think during that time, she had it much harder than I did. She tried not to show it in her letters, but I could tell that all the bloodshed and suffering was getting to her. And then, all of a sudden, she was transferred to a military hospital in Oulu. That's the way it was. One day you were stuck in a place for what seemed like forever, and then, without warning, you had to pack up and move. Although I really wanted to see her, I was happy for her when she was moved to Oulu. It was far away from the front and much safer than Aunuksenlinna. If the fighting ever got really bad, it would be easy for her to get from Oulu to Sweden.

Of course, as luck would have it, only a couple of weeks after she was transferred, I got my first leave. I wasn't able to go to Oulu so I went to Helsinki to see Mameh, Mirele, Rifka and Jakob. It seemed like it took forever to get there. First I had to walk to Pisi. Then I got a ride on an army truck to Mäkriä. From there, I took a bus to Sortavala, a Studebaker K 25 it was. There wasn't enough gasoline for civilian vehicles so the busses all ran on wood gasifiers. One of the passengers had to ride next to the gasifier and shovel wood chips into it the whole way to keep the fire going. The gasifiers were better than nothing, but they didn't give the bus much power. If it had to climb a big hill, we all had to get out and push. It took twice as long to get anywhere as it did before the war, but it was still better than walking!

Being in Helsinki was really strange. There were shortages of lots of things, and there weren't many men around, but otherwise you wouldn't know there was a war going on. People were walking in the streets and shopping and going to the cinema like everything was normal. Life was hard for Mameh, but it had been hard for her for a long time already. Rifka and Jakob were growing fast. They tried to help Mameh as much as they could. I felt bad for them when I thought about my wonderful childhood in Viipuri and compared it to what life was like for them in Helsinki during the war, but it didn't seem so bad to them. At least that's what they said.

Mameh and Mirele still weren't speaking so I had to go find Mirele again at the restaurant where she was working. She was worried that she would be laid off because with so many men away at war, business was really slow. She had started visiting wounded soldiers in the hospital on her days off. She said she had begun thinking about moving to Sweden or maybe even to the United States. She couldn't see any future for herself in Finland. I didn't know what to say to her. During the war, it wasn't that easy to leave the country, but in 1947, she moved to Trollhattan to work in the new Saab factory there, installing seat cushions. She married a foreman from the factory, had four children and died of cancer at the age of 63. Her husband, Stefan, told me the last months were awful. I went to see her a few times in Sweden, but she never came back to Finland, not even for Mameh's funeral.

Jakob kept talking about joining the army. He had just turned 17. I said he should finish school first, but I could see he wasn't going to listen to me. As for Rifka, she was becoming a young woman, and Mameh was worried about her, of course. She didn't want her running off the way Mirele did. I didn't think Rifka would do that, but I could see that the longer the war went on, the more likely it would be that she would start doing things Mameh wouldn't approve of. There just wasn't any kind of social life for a young Jewish girl in Helsinki at that time, and sooner or later she would want to get out of the house.

The biggest shock from being home was hearing news about what was happening in the rest of Europe. On the front line, the only news we got came from Aunus Radio, battlefront newspapers like Karjalan Viesti, or letters from our families, and we knew that everything was heavily censored. The Germans were our allies, and nothing could be published or even written in letters that was critical of them. Some people in the congregation had managed to maintain contact with relatives in the Polish ghettoes or correspond with those who had made it to America. No matter how hard the censors tried to remove everything they thought might be damaging to Finland's relationship with Germany, people managed to read between the lines. We still didn't know about the death camps, but the Jews in Helsinki were for sure worried about what would happen if the Germans won the war. Although no one was leaving yet, some were making plans to get away to Sweden if things took a turn for the worse.

After just a few days at home, then, it was the same long journey back to the front by train, wood-powered bus, army truck and the long walk from Pisi to Kuuttilahti. As much as I had looked forward to going on leave, it had been strange to be away and somehow felt good to be back in my unit. There is no way to explain it, but I just felt out of place in the city. Somehow I belonged at the front, even though I hated so many things about it. I wanted the war to be over, I wanted to be with Rachel, but since neither of those things was possible, the best place for me until something changed was Kuuttilahti.

Figure 49.1. [Left] Pages from Chaje Steinbock's patient book at the Oulu Military Hospital. (Aviva Nemes-Jalkanen's personal collection) [Right] Cousins Chaje Steinbock and Dina Poljakoff. (Margait Halutz's personal collection)

My Darling
Who you are to me,
I have told you.
What I am to you,
I have never asked.
I don't want to know it,
and don't want to hear it
because knowing too much
can destroy happiness.

I tell you only this,
and you should think about it,
I would give you all
your heart desires.
You are like the woman
I have loved above all others.
I never thought
such a thing could be.

I tell you only this,
and you will understand,
We will one day meet again.
Mark my words.
Don't forget them.
In wartime they are written,
written for you.

Your Rudi*

*Entry in Chaje Steinbock's patient notebook (Aviva Nemes-Jalkanen's personal collection)

CHAPTER FORTY-NINE

~

Rachel Meets the Steinbocks

Oulu, Spring 1943—In the August 28, 1940 issue of *Kansallinen Työ*, the news-paper of a short-lived National Socialist Party political party called the Finn-ish National Work Organization, a contributor hiding behind the pen name *Monttööiri-Matti* (Matti the Mechanic) issued a call for others to join him in forcibly evicting a Jewish doctor from the Oulu County Hospital. That doctor was Alexanteri "Sascha" Steinbock, born in St. Petersburg in 1894 and raised in Viipuri. After graduating from high school, Steinbock moved to Helsinki to study medicine. There he met Gulle Pergament, who was four years older. They married in December 1918, and their only child, a daughter born seven-teen months later, was given the name Chaje Meri Steinbock.

Alexanteri and Gulle Steinbock moved to Oulu on Finland's Northwest Coast in 1937 so Alexanteri could take up a position at the Oulu County Hospital. Chaje was about to begin medical school in Helsinki, where her cousin on her mother's side, Dina Poljakoff, was studying dentistry. Dina and Chaje were born only months apart and grew close as teenagers. Both would serve as Medical Lottas: Chaje joined her father in Oulu, where the County Hospital had been converted into Military Hospital 32; Dina served in Helsinki at the Central Military Hospital of the Finnish Armed Forces known as *Tilkka*.

At the start of the Continuation War, Chaje was dating Elis Nemeschan-sky and Dina was courted by Fred Stiller, who was the fourth of Abraham and Vera Nemeschansky Stiller's six children and Elis' first cousin. While serving on the Hanko front in 1941, Elis was felled by a sniper's bullet. He had asked his younger brother, Jussi, to take care of Chaje if anything were to happen to him. Chaje and Jussi were subsequently married as were Dina

Poljakoff and Fred Stiller: a pair of male cousins marrying a pair of female cousins. In the tiny and tight-knit Finnish Jewish community, such intertwining of families was not unusual.

Alexanteri Steinbock served as a doctor in both the Winter and Continuation Wars and rose to the rank of Medical Major. *Monttööri-Matti* never succeeded in driving him out of Oulu, but the Germans did.

Close Contact

During the conflict's trench warfare phase, pressure on the Aunuslinna Field Hospital subsides, and Rachel is transferred to Military Hospital 32, where her skills as a surgical assistant are badly needed. The hospital takes in seriously wounded Finnish and German soldiers, many of whom require long periods of convalescence. As a result, the nurses and Lottas in the hospital are often in close and extended contact with soldiers who have been without female companionship for months or even years.

Chaje and Rachel—the former grew up in Helsinki, Berlin and Viipuri, the latter in Turku—have never met. Both know that there are only a handful of Jewish women among the more than 90,000 Lottas serving in various assignments. Not surprisingly, it does not take long for them to find each other and become friends and confidantes.

Rachel, who is assigned to work directly under Chaje's father, quickly learns that Alexanteri Steinbock is a difficult man with a reputation among the hospital staff for tyrannical behavior. Unlike the doctors she has worked with in Aunuksenlinna, he is gruff and a demanding task master. Although they recognize that he is an excellent surgeon, the nurses under his command are so afraid of making mistakes and incurring his wrath that the atmosphere in the operating theater and on the recovery ward is frequently tense. After watching him berate a nurse for an infraction Rachel thinks is insignificant, she decides to be sure to show up early for work each day in a freshly washed and pressed uniform and check all the instruments and supplies to ensure that everything is in order before he arrives. By taking extra care to conform to his expectations, she manages to stay below the temperamental doctor's radar most of the time.

As Rachel and Chaje get to know one another, their talk migrates from work towards their personal lives. Before it does, however, Rachel asks about the relationship between patients and Lottas in the hospital. She tells Chaje about Sister Helmi and her own excruciating experience with Jukka. It looks, she says, as if the distance between caregivers and patients is not so strictly enforced in Oulu.

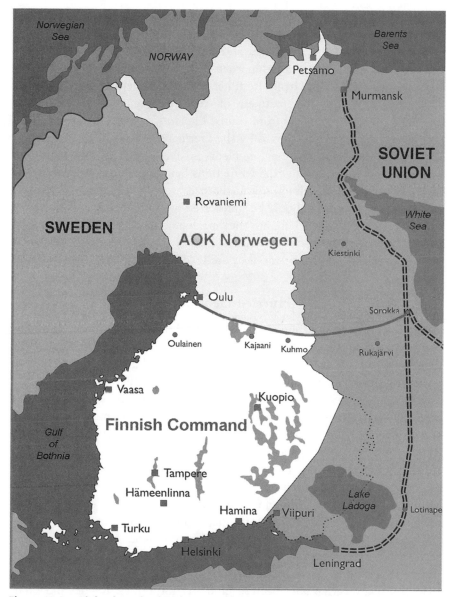

Figure 49.2. Finland north of Oulu was under German command (Marja Leskelä)

Chaje admits that some of the nurses have allowed themselves to become involved with patients, especially with some of the German officers. Because she expects to be married soon, she has found it easy to keep potential suitors at a distance, but some of her patients have made it clear that their feelings for her go beyond gratitude. This has caused her a few moments of discomfort, but by and large the soldiers in her care have behaved with consideration and dignity. She suggests that if Rachel is mindful of the risks and does nothing to encourage the men, she shouldn't have any problem.

However, a troubling situation that will affect them both has already begun to arise. Chaje has heard from her father that German authorities are demanding an end to the treatment of Aryan patients by non-Aryan doctors and nurses. Even nurses from nearby Lapland, many of whom are short and dark, are apparently viewed by the Germans as suspect in this regard. Although there have been no incidents so far, Dr. Steinbock fears that should some German soldier die while he is being operated on, there could be big trouble. Already the hospital administrators are reportedly discussing whether the Steinbocks should be transferred to another hospital.

Rachel is incensed. Where are they, in democratic Finland or Nazi Germany? Can German pressure result in Finnish staff being forced out of a Finnish hospital, simply because they are Jewish?

Hurried Departure

Before Rachel even has time to get accustomed to her new surroundings, she has to move. On the afternoon of March 21, a high-ranking German official tells Military Hospital 32's director, "If I were you, I'd have that Steinbock removed from here and preferably by tomorrow morning. Otherwise, I can't vouch for his safety." This was no *Monttööri-Matti* making vulgar threats he probably couldn't carry out but a military official in the powerful German army warning about a situation that would have international repercussions if it were allowed to take place.

At 6:50 a.m. the next day, Rachel and the three Steinbocks board the morning train with all their possessions. Their destination is Oulainen and Military Hospital 60. Oulainen is only 100 kilometers away, but it is a small town tucked quietly into the countryside, and its military hospital is safely to the south of the area under German military command.

An hour and a half later, hospital officials are waiting at the Oulainen station to welcome Dr. Steinbock. After they take the surgeon and his wife to look at quarters that have been secured on short notice, Rachel and Chaje are shown to a room they will share in the hospital's nursing quarters. Because they arrive as "extra" Lottas and have no immediate duties, they have some time to arrange their things and try to digest all that has happened in the past 24 hours.

Chaje, who is pretty and vivacious, is less inclined than Rachel to emotional outbursts, but the threat implied in the German officer's "warning" still has her beside herself with anger. "How dare they!" she sputters as she pulls the sheets tightly over the corners of her bed, knowing full well the answer to her rhetorical question. "My Jussi is somewhere in Eastern Karelia, fighting their stupid expansionist war, and they are saying that my father and I aren't good enough to treat their soldiers? Well, we have been treating them for almost two years, and not once has there been a complaint against either of us."

"You know as well as I do," says Rachel, "that none of this makes any sense. Finland is stuck with the Germans because no one else would help us. And there are plenty of cowards who will do whatever they ask. Sometimes I think only Marski dares to stand up to them. What scares me is that anyone who wants to curry favor with the Nazis can use us as scapegoats. Look at what happened with those refugees who were deported a few months ago. Whether it was the State Police or the Ministry of the Interior or both of them, they just did what they wanted even though it was against official policy. What did it matter what happened to a few Jews?"

"Did I tell you about my cousin, Dina?" asks Chaje. "She is a great person, funny and smart. You'd like her. She graduated from the *Svenska flicklyceet i Helsingfors* (Helsinki Swedish Secondary School for Girls) and won all kinds of medals for running and gymnastics, both at school and with Makkabi. Since the war started, she has been serving as a Medical Lotta at *Tilkka*. Several months ago, she told me the Germans wanted to give her the Iron Cross! Can you imagine? She said it had something to do with a German ship that hit a mine and blew up. Most of the crew members were shredded to bits by the blast. They brought the ones who survived to *Tilkka*, and Dina was one of those who worked night and day for days on end to save as many of them as they could."

"Did she accept the medal?" asks Rachel, clearly astonished.

"Of course not, but she didn't say anything about it at first. She wanted to see if they were really going to give it to her. She said she only believed it when she saw the medals being laid out along with the names of the recipients. Then she took off as fast as her legs would carry her. What sense does it make? First they want to give her a medal for treating their wounded, and then they won't even let us touch their precious Aryan soldiers."

"What bothers me the most," insists Rachel, "isn't the way the Germans act. We know what they are like. But how can our own army give in to their demands?"

"I think they are just scared," says Chaje.

"Well, I'm glad to be out of Oulu," concludes Rachel. "I've never treated German patients or even Russian prisoners any different from our own boys, but I'll be just as happy if I never see another German for the rest of my life!"

No More Trouble

Rachel and the Steinbocks are made to feel welcome in Oulainen. The hospital is delighted to have another skilled surgeon and two experienced Lottas with medical training and couldn't care less about their religious affiliation. All of them serve there with no more incidents of the kind that drove them from Oulu.

As the rail line passes right through Oulainen, Rachel is able to visit her parents several times during her stay there. She never does get together with Benjamin, though. They write frequently to one another, but as time goes on, each secretly begins to wonder what will happen if and when they are united again. It is said that absence makes the heart grow fonder, but will they have grown apart in ways neither can imagine?

Dr. Steinbock will return to the Oulu County Hospital after the war and participate in the planning for its conversion into the Oulu University Hospital, one of the finest in Northern Europe. Chaje and Jussi will settle in Helsinki and have three children, two daughters and a son. And Rachel? She dreams of getting married, having children, maybe studying medicine like Chaje, but everything will depend on the outcome of this seemingly endless war and Benjamin's fate.

Figure 50.1. Germany's Reichsführer Adolph Hitler, Finland's Commander in Chief Gustaf Mannerheim and Finland's President Risto Ryti on Mannerheim's 75th birthday in June 1942 (Finland's Military Museum)

Ryti's term of office ended on March 1, 1943. He had been branded a "war president" and his chances to lead the country to peace seemed scant. In addition to Ryti, Mannerheim alone enjoyed the prestige necessary to serve as head of state, and the latter's name was mentioned during preparations for the elections. In the end, it seemed probable that the war would continue for some time. Finnish plans to disengage began to drag on, and it seemed advisable to save Mannerheim until the likelihood of peace was greater.

L. A. Puntila*

First of all, there was no information at all about whether the Soviet Union was in the least prepared to make peace and if it was, were the conditions such that the Finnish population could be convinced to accept them. At the time, it wasn't possible in advance to know what Germany's reaction would be if Finland seriously tried to withdraw from the war. It was clear, however, that Germany's reaction would be strongly negative. But would Germany go so far as to use force against Finland and occupy the country? At that point, Germany still had sufficient resources to do so.

Edwin Linkomies**

---

*Puntila, L. A., *The Political History of Finland 1809–1966,* translated by David Miller, Otava, Helsinki, 1975, p. 178.

**Linkomies, Edwin, *Vaikea aika*, Otava, Helsinki, 1980, p. 219.

CHAPTER FIFTY

~

The Worm Turns

Behind the Scenes, 1943—In November 1942, not long after Rommel is defeated a second time at El Alamein and the German advance across North Africa halted for good, German forces besieging Stalingrad on the banks of the River Volga since August are surrounded by Soviet troops. Cut off from their supply lines, they run out of food and ammunition and by February 2, 1943 are forced to surrender. The battle costs the Axis Powers 850,000 men killed, wounded or captured and is generally considered to be the turning point in the war. As Churchill later commented about the significance of this period of the war, "Before Alamein we never had a victory. After Alamein, we never had a defeat."

In Leningrad, however, the situation remains critical for inhabitants trapped in the siege. While some supplies can be brought in and manage to keep the city from collapsing entirely, the provisioning is not enough to eliminate starvation or enable defenders to lift the siege, which will last another year. Finnish troops, meanwhile, remain in their defensive positions along the Svir River in Eastern Karelia and along the Rajajoki-Valkeasaari-Lempaala-Tappari line in the Karelian Isthmus, neither attacking nor withdrawing.

The German 6th Army's surrender at Stalingrad is followed the very next day by a meeting at Finnish Army Headquarters in which Finland's Chief of Intelligence, Colonel Aladar Paasonen, opens by saying Germany is going to lose the war and Finland must find a way out, even if it means accepting the harsh conditions of the 1940 peace as permanent. Three days later, a new Finnish government is sworn in with Henrik Ramsay replacing Foreign Minister Rolf Witting and Leo Ehrnrooth taking the place of Interior Minister Toivo Horelli. There can be little doubt that the changes are meant to send a message to the West and the Soviets that Finland's political ship is changing course. February 15, Risto Ryti is chosen by a vote of electors to an abbreviated second term as President. Having prosecuted the war, he will now have to find a way to withdraw from it with minimal damage to the independence of his country.

Speeding Up the Final Solution

Perhaps sensing that time is running out, Hitler and Himmler have accelerated their efforts to rid Europe of its Jews. New concentration camps have been opened by the summer of 1943: Bergen-Belsen and Kaufering in Germany, Vught in the Netherlands, Kauen in Lithuania and Klooga in Estonia, and a new crematorium has been added at Birkenau. May 19, Berlin is declared *Judenrein* (free of Jews). Jews are being transported from, among other places, France, the Netherlands and Greece to feed the ovens awaiting them in Poland.

Poland has become the focal point for Jewish suffering. In addition to being home to the most destructive internment and extermination camps, it has the largest concentration of Jews in cramped and fetid ghettoes. At first, there are as many as 400,000 inhabitants packed into a 3.3 km² compound in the center of Warsaw, the biggest of the Nazi-created ghettoes. In the summer of 1942, some 250,000 of its inhabitants are shipped to their death in Treblinka's gas chambers.

January 18, 1943 a massive uprising begins when the Germans try to carry out a second round of deportation from the Warsaw Ghetto. The occupants had voted not to resist the first round in 1942 after being told that the deportees would be resettled, but now they know they are being sent to death camps instead. Some of them manage to obtain weapons from Polish sympathizers and meet the German troops with armed resistance. Although hugely outnumbered, the Jews manage to continue fighting for four months, by which time most of the Ghetto has been burned to the ground by the Nazis. Some 13,000 Jews die in the uprising, and the survivors are sent to death or concentration camps. May 16, as a final gesture of contempt, the attackers blow up Warsaw's Great Synagogue.

Dr. Simo Muir, whose book *Ei enää kirjeitä Puolasta* details the attempts by Helsinki congregation activist Bernhard Blaugrund to assist his relatives in Poland and keep track of their whereabouts, writes under the chapter heading *Helsinki, 1943*. "The *subconscious* [emphasis added] concern for many years over their fate began to take its toll on Bernhard's health." Blaugrund is probably as familiar as anyone in the Jewish community with what is going on in Poland, but in 1943 there is no indication that he or anyone else (with the probable exception of those in military intelligence or the military High Command) knows about the Warsaw Ghetto uprising or the mass killings being carried out in the death camps.

What would Benjamin and David have thought, hunkered down in their positions to the northeast of Leningrad, if they had known about the Warsaw Ghetto uprising and demolition or the extermination camps of Auschwitz-Birkenau, Belzec, Chelmo, Majdanek, Sobibor and Treblinka? More to the point, what could they have done?

The question never arises because of the effectiveness of censorship in Finland, the decision by the Germans not to press for the deportation of the country's Jews or even its Jewish refugees,[1] at least for the time being, and the absence in Finland of any legislation or regulations singling out Jews or other minorities for special treatment. In fact, Finland takes the unusual step in the early spring of 1943 of granting citizenship to 110 of the 150 Jewish refugees still in the country at the time, a unique action among countries cooperating with the Third Reich.

The treatment of Jews in countries allied with Germany varies widely during the war years, ranging from the virulent antisemitism of Romania to the decision by Bulgaria to allow the deportation of more than 11,500 Jews in Bulgarian controlled parts of Greece and Macedonia but not of its own Jewish citizens. In independent Hungary, some 20,000 Jews without Hungarian citizenship are deported to Poland in 1941, but the mass deportation of hundreds of thousands of Hungarian Jews who are citizens won't get underway until after Hungary is occupied by Germany in 1944.

A communiqué from the German Ambassador to Finland, Wipert von Blücher, to the German Ministry of Foreign Affairs at the end of January 1943 shows that Finland's "Jewish question" is still being discussed in official German circles. The document sheds some light on this remarkable diplomat's contribution to Germany's reticence to demand that Jews in Finland, which is still an important ally, be handed over immediately for extradition.

> Although official circles are silent and the Finnish press doesn't write about the matter, either, still Germany's Jewish policies alienate the Finnish people from us. We saw last October how sensitive the Finns are in this area, when rumors of the deportation of some Jews produced such a strong reaction that Germanophile Interior Minister Horelli's position has hung in the balance since then. Relations between Germany and Finland are already under pressure, and adding an extra burden during such a difficult period might produce a dangerous effect.[2]

With so few Jews in question—barely 2,000—the risk apparently is seen as greater than the reward. Anyway, should the Nazis win the war, they can easily resolve Finland's tiny "Jewish problem" once the fighting is over.

First Peace Feelers

March 20, the U.S. Chargé d'Affaires in Finland, Robert Mills McClintock, offers American services to facilitate peace discussions between Finland and the Soviet Union. A few days later, Foreign Minister Ramsay delicately broaches the subject of a separate peace in Berlin and is sharply rebuffed by his German counterpart, Joachim von Ribbentrop, who reminds him that Hitler's objection was all that saved Finland from being completely overrun in 1940 and is all that stands between it and the same fate now. Sensing that the Finnish government's resolve to support the war is weakening, Ribbnentrop demands that Finland sign an agreement with Germany that commits both sides to fight to the end together.

Finland is now in a doubly dangerous position. Its future is tied to the fortunes of a cobelligerent the Finns no longer believe can win the war, but if they try to negotiate a way out of the conflict, they must take into account the huge number of well-equipped and battle-ready German units stationed in northern Finland. What will they do? Three times during the spring of 1944, the Germans demand that Finland sign Ribbentrop's agreement, and each time the Finns procrastinate. Meanwhile, pressure across party lines is growing for a peace initiative. In August, the so-called Peace Opposition sends President Ryti a demand to sue for peace without delay. The message is leaked to the Swedish press, causing an angry reaction in Berlin. Fortunately for Finland, Germany has more pressing worries as summer turns to autumn than Finland's uncertain stance. The Allies invade Italy, Mussolini is removed from power, the new Italian government declares war on Germany, and Hitler's overstretched army is forced to invade Italy to prevent the Allies from rolling up the country unopposed.

Germany is not the only country whose resources are overstretched. Even after sending the oldest servicemen home, Finland still has 450,000 men on active duty at the end of 1943, far more than the economy can tolerate. The coming of age for military duty of a new cohort in 1944 will do little to ease the pressure. Finland has already suffered more casualties than during the catastrophic Winter War, and there is still no end in sight.

The last weekend of November 1943, Stalin, Churchill and Roosevelt meet in Tehran, the first time that Stalin and Roosevelt meet face-to-face.

They agree on plans and dates for an Allied invasion of France and the establishment of a new Western Front in the spring. They also settle on the postwar division of spheres of influence, granting Stalin hegemony over Eastern Europe in return for his continued commitment to maintain pressure on the Eastern Front. The Declaration signed by the three leaders and published at the conclusion of the conference, expresses the commitment of the Soviet Union, Great Britain and the United States to work together to win the war and create an enduring peace. The document hints at the creation of a body like the United Nations to create "a world family of Democratic Nations,"

With all the main extermination camps operating at full capacity, more Jews than ever are being murdered at the end of 1943. Of the Jews, however, there is no mention at all in the Tehran Conference's Declaration.

Notes

1. The eight refugees handed over in 1942 were deported on the initiative of the Finnish State Police, apparently without any overt German request or pressure.

2. Jonas, Michael, *Kolmannen Valtakunnan lähetiläs: Wipert von Blücher ja Suomi*, Ajatus Kirjat, Juva, 2010, p. 269.

Figure 51.1. Without German deliveries of grain, the difficult food situation in Finland would have become catastrophic (Finland's Military Museum)

As an invalid, I wasn't in the army, but I kept pondering [the question of what would happen to us Jews] from many different angles.

"We are Finnish citizens, and we are treated, officially at least, as equals . . ."

My thinking went like this: "If Germany wins and we are destroyed, Germany would direct its hate only at Jews and Gypsies and the like. But should Russia win, it would be a disaster for the whole country. Then we would all be equal."

Samuel Maslovat*

*Daavid: Stories of Honor and Shame, documentary film by Taru Mäkelä, ForRealProductions in cooperation with the Finnish Broadcasting Company's Channel 2, 1997.

CHAPTER FIFTY-ONE

~

The Beginning of the End

Karelia, Spring, 1944—The new year begins with the order to begin fortifying the VKT (Viipuri-Kupparsaari-Taipele) Line, Finland's third and rear-most line of defense across the Karelian Isthmus. Marshal Mannerheim has begun to worry that the Finns will once again find themselves facing the Soviets alone and is beginning to prepare as best he can for the possibility. Two weeks later the siege of Leningrad collapses, and Germany's Army Group North begins withdrawing in a southwesterly direction to Estonia's Lake Peipus and Lake Narva, leaving the Finnish Army exposed from the South on both the Karelian and Ladoga Isthmuses.

Meanwhile, Finland's partnership with Germany unravels as mutual trust continues to evaporate. Germany and Finland still need each other, but by the spring of 1944 both realize that their shared interests, based at the start of the war on assumptions of a German victory, no longer exist. In the light of Finland's repeated refusal to rule out the possibility of seeking a separate peace, Germany unilaterally suspends the delivery of desperately needed supplies. With nowhere else to turn but Sweden, Finland finds its stores of grain, fuel and ammunition dwindling.

Soviet Ambassador to Sweden Alexandra Kollontai has been acting as a go-between in secret preliminary discussions concerning the possibility of a peace settlement between the Soviets and the Finns since early November 1943. Neither side, however, is willing to accept what the other considers a reasonable offer. In February, Stalin resorts to his favorite form of persuasion, brute force, to convince the Finns to lower their expectations. On three separate occasions—the nights of February 6, 16 and 26—the Soviets unleash massive bombing raids on the civilian population of Helsinki.

Waves of bombers (785, 406 and 929 of them on the first, second and third nights respectively) drop a total of 2,600 metric tons of explosives on the Finnish capital.

Benjamin and David's families experience their worst month of the war. They spend the nights when the bombings occur huddled in dank air raid shelters. Because of the sheer number of attackers, Finnish anti-aircraft defenses that proved so effective in the Winter War cannot prevent most of them from getting through. The first night proves the most destructive, after which defense tactics are revised. Instead of trying to shoot down all the attacking planes, anti-aircraft fire is skillfully used to divert the attacks from the most vulnerable parts of the city.

The raids are destructive, but the damage could have been much worse. Civilian casualties from the three attacks total 146 killed and 346 wounded. If Stalin assumes that bombing would break the will of the Finnish people, he is mistaken. If anything, it strengthens their determination to resist. Stalin would prefer to settle matters with the Finns as quickly as possible so he can focus on the Germans, but there are no signs that they are any more prepared in March to agree to the punitive terms of the Soviet peace offer than they were in January.

Between Scylla and Charybdis

Germany's ally Hungary, meanwhile, has also been secretly negotiating a peace agreement with the Soviets. In March, when Hitler finds out about those talks, he orders the invasion of "traitor Hungary," The country's bloodless occupation meets no resistance, but as a consequence, more than 437,000 Hungarian Jews will be sent to Nazi gas chambers. At the end of March, when Erfurth tells Mannerheim that Germany will intervene militarily should Finland reach a separate peace with the Soviet Union, the example of subjugated Hungary is staring Finland's decision-makers in the face.

Despite repeated requests, Germany refuses to provide Finland with any more arms, leaving Ryti, Mannerheim, Tanner and their colleagues squeezed between a rock and a hard place. The Russians are likely to attack if the Finns don't agree to harsh peace terms, and the Germans are likely to attack if they do. In both cases, the very existence of the country is threatened. The Finns, as they did in 1940–41, face a choice between unacceptable alternatives—"between cholera and the plague" is the metaphor that is commonly used—in a war in which they have no desire to participate. As Foreign Minister Ramsay puts it in a letter to Finland's Ambassador to Germany, T.M. Kivimäki, weighing the merits of accepting Russian conditions rather

424   ⌣   Chapter Fifty-One

than committing to a hopeless German cause: "It is being said here that the first alternative is the same as suicide and the second like being murdered."

June 6, 1944, everything changes once again. The Allies launch Operation Overlord, landing some 150,000 assault troops on the beaches of Normandy. With the enemy pressing in from the east, west and south, Germany desperately needs to maintain control of the Baltic Sea to the north and keep the Soviets tied down along the Finnish border. The only way to do that is to revive arms and grain shipments to Finland, but Hitler doesn't want to do so without a promise that the Finns won't pull out of the war.

Professor Kimmo Rentola has documented that Stalin was intent on destroying Finland as an independent state. Hitler, had the Germans defeated the Russians, might have done so as well. Great Britain and the United States, the only powers that could have been expected to speak up meaningfully on behalf of Finland's sovereignty, had their hands tied by the Tehran Conference agreement. Sweden remained sympathetic but unwilling to risk its own future by committing itself to the life-and-death struggle of its neighbor.

Such was the unenviable situation facing Finland's political and military leaders on June 4, 1944 when they gathered at Enso near Imatra to celebrate Marshal Mannerheim's 77th birthday. Five days before, Mannerheim had received a letter from Hitler, once again refusing to provide arms unless Germany could be sure Finland would use them exclusively and unstintingly against their mutual enemy. According to Professor Henrik Meinander in *Suomi 1944*, Mannerheim complained to German Liaison Officer Erfurth that unless Germany would provide Finland with more weapons, Finland would lose the war.[1] On the other hand, as Ramsay concluded in his letter to Kivimäki: "Is it any reason to commit suicide that one is afraid of being murdered?"

A decision had to be made, one way or the other, but who would make it, and what would the decision be? Would Finland prefer to be dashed against the rocks of Scylla or those of Charybdis? It may have seemed impossible for those sitting around the table at Finnish Military Headquarters in Mikkeli to decide, but they would not have long to wait before events beyond their control would force their collective hand. The end was drawing near more rapidly than any of them believed likely.

Note

1. Meinander, Henrik, *Suomi 1944: Sota, yhteiskunta, tunnemaisema*, Siltala, Helsinki, 2009, p. 175.

Figure 52.1. Sholem Bolotowsky standing watch on the Svir River front (Gideon Bolotowsky's private collection)

Although there had been advanced warnings, the Russian offensive took the Finnish High Command by surprise. During May there had been indications of an attack in the making, and on 1 June Finnish Army Intelligence warned that an offensive was to be expected within 10 days. Four or five days before the attack the Russians began radio silence—an almost infallible sign. But the Army operations chief was not convinced, and his judgment carried the greatest weight with Mannerheim.

Earl F. Ziemke*

**The German Theater of Operations 1940–1945*, Department of the Army, Washington, D.C., 1959, pp. 278–279.

CHAPTER FIFTY-TWO

~

Waiting

They say it was unexpected, but we knew, be'emes[1] we knew. Our men came back from patrol on the far side of the river, and they told us. Columns of men, whole battalions, on the move. Tanks, guns, some of them so big, they said, you could take a shower in the barrel! All heading towards the river.

Headquarters had sent the older men home and broke up our regiment three months before. They said younger men were needed on the front. You could see that some of the older guys were really mentally and physically farmatert,[2] but they were still tough, and they knew how to fight. I would rather have had them in the trenches with me any day, but of course, I had nothing to say about it. Some of the young guys they sent, you could see they were scared. Every time a grenade exploded somewhere, they would dive for cover. What would they do when the real fighting started? We would find out soon enough.

I was afraid they would send Jakob to the front, too. It turned out there was something wrong with his feet, the arches were too high so he couldn't march very far. It's called plantaari something, I can't remember. Anyway, he ended up in Lappeenranta, writing reports for the Propaganda Office until they had to withdraw. He was one of the lucky ones. They were always evacuated ahead of the fighting. I don't think Mameh could have taken it if anything had happened to him.

As everyone knows, the Russkies started their attack on the Karelian Isthmus. First they sent in the bombers, then the artillery shelling began, and after that came the tanks and infantry. The same thing happened to us on the Svir River, but for some reason it didn't start until almost two weeks later. But when they came, they came hard. We knew they would come, we just didn't know when.

My new unit was stationed in a town about halfway between the two big lakes, Ladoga and Onega. We had a bridgehead there on the far side of the Svir, and we figured it was one of the places they would try to cross. David's unit was somewhere in back of us, near Kuujärvi, ready to provide artillery support, but they didn't have much ammunition, and neither did we. There was nothing we could do but dig our emplacements a little deeper, stare at the water, and wait.

Notes

1. For sure (Yiddish)
2. Tired (Yiddish)

Figure 53.1. After the bombing of Helsinki in February 1944, many families sent their children to safety in Sweden (Pressens Bild /Scanpix / Lehtikuva)

As we were walking down *Aleksanterinkatu*, we saw some Germans marching in the middle of the street. There was a clattering noise, and *"Eins, Zwei, Eins, Zwei . . ."* I remember having my hand in my mother's hand and looking up at her. She looked ever so sad, holding my hand really tight. Then we turned into a narrow street, away from it all.

Mary Davidkin*

**Daavid: Stories of Honor and Shame*, documentary film by Taru Mäkelä, ForRealProductions in cooperation with the Finnish Broadcasting Company's Channel 2, 1997.

~

CHAPTER FIFTY-THREE

Against Overwhelming Odds

Karelia, June 9, 1944—The Allied Powers smell blood. With the Normandy invasion, the war that began nearly five years earlier when Germany invaded Poland enters a new and potentially final stage. Soon the Race to Berlin will begin, and Stalin wants to be sure to arrive before the British and Americans take full possession of the German capital. First, though, he needs to deal with stubborn, annoying Finland.

Having learned their lesson from the Winter War, the Soviets prepare carefully this time for their assault on the Finnish lines and throw over-whelming fire- and manpower into the fray. By the first week of June, 450,000 battle-ready Soviet soldiers are positioned along the front compared with only 235,000 men spread out along the Finnish side. The Red Army aims its first thrust at the Karelian Isthmus with the intention of destroy-ing the troops there and retaking Viipuri. To hold off an attacking force of 260,000 men on the narrow isthmus, the Finns at first have just 44,000 men on the front line and some 32,000 backing them up. The Soviets enjoy over-whelming superiority in airpower, too, and bring to the battle some twenty times more artillery than the defenders can muster. Furthermore, Soviet intelligence and the element of surprise enable the attackers to hit hardest at points where the Finnish defense is least prepared to withstand the shock.

Despite bombing raids on June 9 by more than 1,000 aircraft and intense artillery shelling, the Finnish defenses on the Karelian Isthmus hold at first. The next day, when the Soviet infantry assault begins, the main line is breached in the Valkeasaari sector. The Soviets fire 354,000 artillery shells at Finnish troops, who can only manage to return fire with 3,700 of their own. As Soviet soldiers pour through the gap, the Finnish forces begin to retreat to their second line of defense, the Vammelsuu-Taipale Line. By 15 June, that position has been lost as well, and the Finns are retreating towards the Viipuri-Kupparsaari-Taipale (VKT) line, the second-to-last string of fortified positions standing between the Karelian Isthmus and the plains leading to Helsinki.

The week of June 18–24, 1944 proves to be one of the most dramatic of the war and plays a decisive role in determining the fate of independent Finland. Saturday, June 16, Commander-in-Chief Mannerheim issues a troubling Order of the Day in which he tells his troops, "You know that the Fatherland's fate is in your hands. . . . You have—we all have—previously withstood tough blows together, and we will do so now, too." The next day, Wednesday, Viipuri falls like a toppled domino, after which the Finnish command orders its beleaguered troops to make a stand north of the city. Thursday, on the far side of Lake Ladoga, Finnish units begin withdrawing from positions south of the Svir River in anticipation of the long-awaited Soviet attack on the Ladoga Isthmus.

Fierce defensive battles in the days leading up to Midsummer (Saturday) buy time for the arrival of reserves from the Ladoga and Maaselkä Isthmuses as well as some who had been under the Commander-in-Chief's personal command. In *Finland at War*, authors Vesa Nenye, Peter Munter and Toni Wirtanen explain:

> The battle for the critical Tali and Ihantala sectors was to be the largest the North had ever seen. Soon 200,000 soldiers would be involved in the fighting, condensed into a battleground 12km wide and 15km deep. If the Red Army could get past these last choke points, and cross the old Moscow Treaty borders, both Stalin's political and military goals would soon be fulfilled. From there, the Soviets would be free to strike deep into the undefended Finnish heartland.[1]

Buoyed by reserves that arrive at the last minute and assisted by terrain that is more favorable to defenders, the exhausted Finns valiantly and unexpectedly hold their ground.

Behind the Scenes

Meanwhile, the government is frantically scrambling for a workable peace option. Gustaf Mannerheim, who has just turned 77, is considered the only figure with sufficient credibility both at home and abroad to lead Finland out of the war. He has concluded that his army is no longer capable of effective resistance to Soviet pressure and joins those pressing for a peace initiative. When queried about whether he would consider serving as President in place of President Ryti should the latter step down, he replies that he would not because he considers the situation hopeless. Defeat, he argues, is "not a matter of days but of hours,"

Although Stalin had given General Leonid Govorov overwhelming forces with which to crush Finland's Karelian Isthmus defenses, massive attacks on the Tali-Ihantala line on June 22 and 25 fail to break through the Finnish positions, and by the 29th Govorov is asking for additional troops. Stalin refuses. Some combination of the remarkable Finnish defense at Tali, successful counterattacks from Ihantala, and surgically accurate Finnish artillery shelling made possible by the recent adoption of the army's innovative fire direction corrections converter result in the assault on the Karelian Isthmus being gradually wound down to a standstill. Nevertheless, the Soviets have blunted one of the daggers pointing at Leningrad. The remaining dagger— the troops along the Svir River front—still needs to be neutralized for the Soviets to be able to concentrate fully on the coming battles further south. June 21, bombardment by 350 planes and a three-hour artillery and rocket barrage from some 1,800 big guns begin to soften up Finnish troops along the Svir River in anticipation of a Soviet crossing.

Efforts to sway Finland to accept or reject a separate peace with the Soviet Union reach a watershed June 23, Midsummer Eve, when a Soviet ultimatum arrives from Moscow via Stockholm at the same time as a competing German demand is delivered personally in Helsinki by German Foreign Minister Ribbentrop. The Russian message states that Moscow is prepared to consider a separate peace with Finland but only in conjunction with the latter's unconditional surrender. The German offer is to provide crucial military aid and grain but only upon publication of a promise by the Finnish government to stop negotiating with the Soviet Union and commit to fighting alongside Germany to the end.

Stalin apparently assumes that Finland no longer has the will to fight. Many Finnish politicians, reckoning that Germany will lose and Finland will be left to face the Soviet Union alone if it cannot reach a peace agreement, are leaning toward surrender. Marshal Mannerheim, however, encouraged by signs that the Tali-Ihantala defenses are holding and the possibility of acquiring additional arms from the Germans, now wants to prolong the resistance.

Necessity, the Mother of Invention

Unconditional surrender would require submission to harsh conditions dictated by the victors. Mannerheim now vehemently opposes such a course and presses the government to do whatever is necessary to obtain the required military aid in the shortest possible time. Committing to the doomed German cause, however, not only offers little hope of avoiding the same Soviet ultimatum, or worse, when German resistance finally collapses but will make it virtually impossible for Finland to continue claiming that it is waging a parallel war solely in its own interests, not Nazi Germany's. Given the growing sentiment for peace, it would be almost impossible to obtain Parliament's approval for such a commitment.

Under mounting pressure from both camps, President Ryti signs a pledge that as Finland's President he will not agree to a separate peace with the Soviet Union, nor will any individual or government named by him agree to a ceasefire or enter into peace discussions without the approval of the German government. The promise is conditional upon the provision of further German military and food aid. Late on the evening of June 26, three years to the day after he went on the radio to tell the Finnish people that the Soviets had attacked Finland once again, President Ryti hands the signed letter to Ribbentrop.

Although discussed behind closed doors in the Council of State,[2] the matter is never brought before Parliament. As such, the commitment intentionally binds only Ryti and officials named by him, leaving open a back door through which a later President can exit the alliance. Finland gets the arms and support it needs to continue fighting (although it is probable that the aid, which never reaches the levels promised by Ribbentrop, would have been provided anyway at some point, even without Ryti's letter). Of particular importance are new anti-tank weapons as well as other munitions which have been depleted to dangerously low levels. The *Luftwaffe's* Detachment Kuhlmey arrives June 17 and proves to be a huge help in countering the Soviets' dominance in the air, but the additional assault gun brigade and infantry division that arrive from Germany as a consequence of Finland's renewed commitment only engage the Soviets briefly before being recalled home a month later.

Germany is certainly acting primarily in its own self-interest and only circumstantially in Finland's by trying to prolong the fighting in the north. Nevertheless, Ryti's action defuses a situation that had seemed intractable. Significantly rearmed, Finland once again focuses its attention on holding off Soviet attacks and defending its 1940 border.

To Stay or Go?

Almost all of the fighting during the Continuation War has taken place on the Soviet side of the post-Winter War border and away from Finland's population centers. For the most part, Finland's civilians have only been in immediate danger from occasional attacks in border regions by Soviet partisan patrols and in urban areas during bombing raids, the worst of which so far were carried out over numerous cities at the outbreak of the war.

Even though most adults had no intention of fleeing the country during the war, many were concerned about their young children. Already in December 1939, the first so-called "War Children" were evacuated to safety in Sweden. During the ensuing war years, nearly 80,000 Finnish children under the age of 14 would be taken in by families in Nordic countries, the vast majority—72,000—in Sweden.

Finland's Jews steadfastly remained in Finland during the Continuation War despite the presence of German troops on Finnish soil. It was clearly understood that flight by any significant number of them would jeopardize the position of the rest, who would no longer be seen by the general population as sharing their plight or being committed to their society's values. Having finally achieved a previously unreachable degree of acceptance in Finnish society through their great sacrifice and unstinting participation in the Winter War, most Jews are not prepared to risk losing that status by putting personal interests above those of the larger polity (first the congregation, then the nation). Antisemitism has not found fertile ground in the country during the war despite Finland's relationship with Nazi Germany, and the Jews have no desire to do anything that might cause it to flare up again.

As Finland's predicament grows more threatening, however, the country's Jews begin to make contingency plans in case the country should be overrun or the threat of hostile German occupation should become a reality. In 1943, the Helsinki congregation's Jac Weinstein visits Stockholm to discuss whether Sweden's Jews would be willing to care for the Jewish congregations' young children and the Jewish refugees still in Finland should the need arise. It isn't until the intensive bombing of Helsinki begins in February 1944, however, that the Jewish community feels it can make a move without drawing undue attention to itself. The departure of thousands of other Finnish children ensures that no one will notice a few dozen Jewish children joining the exodus.

As throngs of children with name tags around their necks are put aboard trains bound from Helsinki for Tornio on the Finland-Sweden border, the Jewish community charters a plane and sends the first 30 or so of its children to Stockholm to be cared for by Swedish Jewish families. They travel by plane not because their parents are unwilling to send them with the other children but because Tornio is in the sector of Finland under the command of German troops. By 1944, the community knows enough about what has been going on in German-occupied territories to take whatever measures necessary to avoid any and all contact between their offspring and representatives of the Nazi regime.

When they send their children to Sweden in February, Finland's Jews are still confident that their own government won't hand them over to the Germans. Nevertheless, some Jews begin negotiating with fishermen who could take them to Sweden on short notice if they suddenly need to get out of the country. The country's young Jewish men are still at the front, however, and mass emigration would certainly leave them and any other Jews who stay behind in an exposed position. Would some members of the Jewish community now be willing to save themselves by throwing others overboard?

When publication of President Ryti's June 26 letter ties the country's fate to Germany's in what looks like an irreversible downward spiral, the dilemma in which Finland's Jews find themselves grows more pressing. Germany's fortunes continue to decline, and no one can be sure what Hitler will do if Finland, despite Ryti's promise, opens negotiations for a separate peace with Moscow. Will the Germans occupy Finland as they occupied Hungary only months before? And if they do, won't they send all the Finnish Jews to death camps as they did with hundreds of thousands of Hungarian Jews?

Notes

1. Nenye, Vesa, Munter, Peter and Wirtanen, Toni, *Finland at War: The Continuation and Lapland Wars 1941–45*, p. 223.

2. The equivalent of the U.S. or U.K. Cabinet.

Figure 54.1. When the Soviet attack finally began on the Karelian Isthmus and then the Ladoga Isthmus, it was massive and relentless (Finland's Military Museum)

When rumors started circulating during the Continuation War that Finland's Jews would all be sent to Germany, my father's commanding officer took him aside and told him that should such a situation arise, he would warn him a day ahead of time so he would have time to pack his bags and get away.

Adiel "Adi" Hirschovits*

One day I got a phone call from the managing director of a company called Maan Romu. My brother was in the headquarters of the antiaircraft regiment in Kotka. "Could you tell your brother that both of you need to be ready. If the order comes, a car will come to fetch you." I wondered what this was all about, and he said, "Don't worry, I'll get back to you later." That evening, at midnight, he called and said, "The danger's passed." He'd been informed of Himmler's plan. All the Jews, even the soldiers, would be rounded up. There were two ships waiting at Katajanokka [harbor in Helsinki] to take [us] away.

Aron Livson**

*Interviewed by the author, Helsinki, 20 June, 2013.

***Daavid: Stories of Honor and Shame,* documentary film by Taru Makela, ForRealProductions in cooperation with the Finnish Broadcasting Company's Channel 2, 1997.

CHAPTER FIFTY-FOUR

~

All Hell Breaks Loose

Svir River, June 21, 1944—Er.P 18[1] scout teams return from sorties across Soviet lines south of the Svir River with increasingly alarming reports. Not only are troops massing near the river with tanks and artillery but channels have been hacked through the reeds on the southern shore and assault boats and barges hidden in coves and inlets from which they can be quickly launched. Nevertheless, an eerie sense of calm prevails. There has been no increase in shelling, the days are warm and sunny, and the greatest source of provocation is Tiltu's[2] inane babbling, broadcast at maximum volume from behind Soviet lines.

The night between June 18 and 19, the Finns begin silently withdrawing from positions south of the river, leaving behind only skeleton troops to mask their retreat. As the last troops make their way to the northern shore, demolition teams blow up bridges spanning the Svir to deny their use to Soviet troops. Three munitions experts are killed when Soviet planes attack them as they are planting explosives on the Pidman Bridge, causing the charges to detonate prematurely; otherwise, the withdrawal proceeds without major incident. There is no longer any way to keep the Finns' departure secret nor any need to do so.

Benjamin is standing watch at Uslanka on the northern shore of the Svir in the early morning hours of June 21, looking forward to being relieved soon and getting some coffee substitute, crisp bread and sleep, when the sound first reaches him. Although it is obviously coming from far away, it is not like the usual sound of artillery fire along the river. For one thing, there are no gaps between volleys, just an uninterrupted pounding. For another, the volume keeps increasing. It seems to be coming from the direction of Lotinapelto, but that is some 25–30 kilometers away, too great a distance, he thinks, to be carrying this far upriver at such volume. Then enemy planes appear in the sky, and bombing begins somewhere nearby, probably the bridgehead at Vaasenijoki.

Are there any signs of enemy activity on his stretch of river? Not yet, anyway. He peers anxiously through his field glasses at the far shore, curtained in morning fog, trying to detect the slightest movement. While he is scanning the river, his relief arrives, a tall, stooped-shouldered soldier named Föhr.

"They're comin' across at Lotinapelto," he tells Benjamin. "Backström says we're all to pack and be ready to leave at a moment's notice."

So it's not just shelling! Russkies have crossed the river, and fighting has started on this side already. Sleep is out of the question, but there is still time to return to his dugout for something to drink.

"Does anybody know what's going on?" he asks his bunkmates as he gulps down his ersatz coffee.

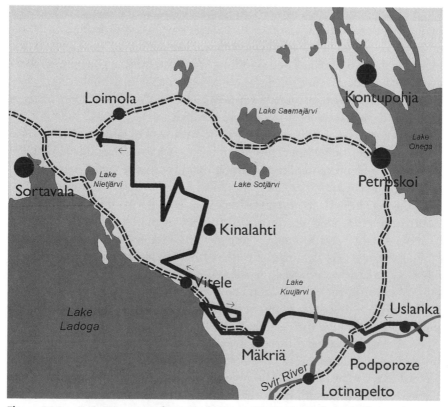

Figure 54.2.   Er.P 18's retreat from Uuslanka to Nietjärvi (Marja Leskelä)

No one answers. As often happens, the officers haven't yet explained to the men what is happening. The latter can only assume from the abandonment of their forward positions south of the river the past two days and the ominous booming of the big guns that the massive attack the scouts have been warning them to expect is finally underway.

Tactical Retreat

What they are not fully aware of is how serious the situation has become on the other side of Lake Ladoga (censorship has effectively prevented the spread of discouraging news). The Finnish High Command, though, knows that the future of the country depends first and foremost on the army's ability to bottle up the Soviet advance through the Karelian Isthmus toward the capital and heartland. At the risk of seriously weakening defenses on the Ladoga Isthmus, four of the eight divisions in Eastern Karelia have been reassigned to assist the embattled defenders desperately trying to hold their positions behind Viipuri Bay and along the Vuoksi. Instead of fighting to hold their own positions, the remaining units on the undermanned Ladoga and Maaselkä Isthmuses are ordered to conduct a staged withdrawal towards the prewar border. This delaying tactic requires a disciplined and coordinated retreat, inflicting maximum damage on the attackers while yielding ground as gradually as possible.

Like everyone else, Benjamin wants to go home. After nearly four years in the army, though, and the loss of more comrades than he cares to count, he doesn't want to be chased there like a dog with his tail between his legs. He hasn't heard yet that Viipuri has fallen again and is still confident that the Russkies can be prevented from pushing inland from the Svir.

In fact, by the time Benjamin shoulders his pack and rifle and heads toward the road from Podporozhye to Mäkriä, Soviet troops are already pushing Lotinapelto's defenders north of the city. Soviet marines have also crossed near Kuuttilahti, and Mikulski's 99th Army Corps is probing the outskirts of Podporozhye. As the main thrust of the Soviet attack at Lotinapelto advances rapidly towards Mäkriä, there is a serious risk that Benjamin's battalion and the entire 8th Division could be trapped in a *motti*.

By early evening, instead of engaging the enemy at Podporozhye, Benjamin is hurrying along the road to Mäkriä, looping well behind Lotinapelto. The last time he was on this road, it was the early spring of 1942, and he was on his way to Kuuttilahti as part of the sweep towards Leningrad and what seemed like certain victory. The objective is different now: to prevent the Soviets from breaking through the Finnish defenses, charging up the lake shore towards Pitkäranta and Sortavala, and delivering a fatal blow to the Vuoksi defenses from the rear.

During the first two days of fighting, the Finnish troops maintain contact with the enemy while retreating slowly towards the partially fortified but unfinished PSS (Pisi-Saarimäki-Sammatus) Line. Benjamin and Er.P 18 are positioned in reserve near Mäkriä, ready to support either the troops being pushed back from Lotinapelto or those trying to halt Soviet advances through the coastal sector from Kuuttilahti to Aunuksenlinna and the shore road. Should everything go as planned, they will gradually join the other withdrawing troops at the PSS Line and hold it for as long as possible.

Panic

Everything does not go as planned. The previous winter, war games had been organized to prepare for the eventual withdrawal from the Ladoga Isthmus. At the time, the risk of Soviet naval troops on Lake Ladoga landing behind the lines in the area around Vitele and Tuulos was recognized, but as a result of Finland's reallocation of troops and equipment away from Eastern Karelia and the subsequent reorganization of the remaining forces, the contingency measures for such a strike were never implemented.

June 22, at 8:40 p.m., Finnish lookouts at the Haapana Lighthouse notice a huge flotilla of more than 50 vessels of various kinds and sizes approaching from the south. The convoy spends the night off the coast of Alavoinen, out of the range of the Finnish light artillery in the area. Before morning, troops from the transport ships begin boarding landing craft. At 4:15 a.m., Soviet bombers launch an attack on the shore around Tuulos, supported by fire from the flotilla's five gunships. A little more than an hour later, the first Soviet marines land on the beach three kilometers north of the mouth of the Tuulos River. The shore road is less than a kilometer from the waterfront. If the 3,367 attackers can quickly establish a beachhead, push inland, and cut the shore road and rail line, they will be in position to trap the Finnish defenders retreating in their direction.

The sound of heavy fighting to the rear of their position is one of the scariest things any combatants, but especially those being pushed backward, can experience. Soldiers who less than a week before were hopefully discussing rumors of peace negotiations are now fighting for their lives under increasingly chaotic conditions. Unable to take their supplies with them, they are blowing up ammunition dumps and setting fire to warehouses. Three transport trains, trapped by the attackers near Tuulos, where the shore road and rail line are now controlled by the Soviets, are also blown up by the Finns to prevent them falling into enemy hands.

Near Pisi, the PSS Line begins to collapse. Disciplined withdrawal turns into panic, as one soldier later reported:

> Our chaotic escape from Pisi could have cost us the whole 3rd Battalion if the troops could not be brought under control. The road, which was in poor shape to begin with, was now packed with artillery pieces, cars, carriages and individual soldiers milling about. The only thought everyone had was: 'Those who can, save themselves!'[3]

Finnish troops mount two unsuccessful counterattacks on the Tuulos beachhead before the second wave of Soviet marines hits the shore at 2:25 p.m. Already, the bridgehead is so wide and deep that the landing craft are effectively out of range of Finnish machine-gun and direct artillery fire. Attempts to retake the beachhead fail, but the constant pressure exerted on the Soviet forces keeps them contained within an area some five kilometers wide and three kilometers deep.

Er.P 18 is ordered to head for Tuulos the morning of 23 June to help push the Soviet marines back into the sea. That evening, though, when they reach the outskirts of Alavoinen, the order is remanded, and they are turned back towards Pisi to staunch the flight of panicky Finnish troops. Coastal sector defenses have broken down completely, and soldiers are making their way however they can toward the distant Finnish border. June 23 is Midsummer Eve, the second-longest day of the year. Normally, it would be quite light, even at midnight, but the night is stormy. Chilling winds whip off the lake, driving rain horizontally into the faces of the tired Finnish soldiers. By now, they are running on Pervitin and adrenalin, and their only consolation is that the wretched weather keeps the dreaded Soviet ground attack planes from taking to the skies.

As Benjamin's column advances through the woods, he sees a figure darting from tree to tree about 50 meters away. Detaching himself from the formation, Benjamin runs ahead of the figure and points his rifle at him.

"*Ruki ver!*" he shouts. "Hands up! Stop where you are!"

"I'm one of ours," comes the reply in Finnish. The man stops, though, and reluctantly raises his hands. Benjamin approaches and sees that the man has on a filthy Finnish uniform and looks like a Finn, square-jawed and blond.

"Where is your unit?"

"*Perkele!* Don't know and don't care. Scattered from here to damnation, I guess, those that are still alive. Put down that gun, Boy!"

At the word "Boy," Benjamin notices that the man is probably twice his age. Must be one of the soldiers who was sent home and then recalled at the last minute.

"Not going to do that, not just yet. Where do you think you're going?"

"What does it matter? We're all going to be killed. The Russkies are right up our asses, and now there are Russkies in front of us, too. Shoot me, if you want. A Finnish bullet can do the job as well as a Russky one."

"You're coming with me to Division Headquarters. If you're willing to fight, I'm sure you'll get by with just a chewing out. Where's your gun?"

"Somewhere back there. Didn't have any more bullets anyway so I didn't see any reason to keep it. What's it to you what I do? You're not even an officer."

"I'm a Finn and a soldier. We need every last man we have. I don't think my life is worth any more than yours, but I've got family to think about, and you probably do, too. They're the ones we're fighting for. Come on, let's get going. This way, and don't try anything funny."

Search for a Defendable Position

The man is not the last Finnish soldier at whom Benjamin points his rifle during the following week. Some are nearly delirious with fear and lack of sleep. All are disoriented and unable to provide any rational explanation for their actions. Although Benjamin and his battalion are occasionally able to restore some kind of order to the sector, frightened men continue to burst onto the scene, lost, leaderless and confused. Because the ground is swampy, the Soviet pursuers cannot move with all their equipment as fast as the fleeing foot soldiers, but their pursuit is relentless. Their field guns constantly shell the retreating Finnish troops, who rarely have time to set up the few guns they have taken with them to provide answering fire. When they do, the hastily fired rockets sometimes fall on their own men instead of the enemy. There aren't enough first aid stations and soup wagons, and information about where they are supposed to be located is unreliable. Most soldiers haven't had a hot meal since the Soviet attack began, and only the seriously injured make it through the triage for medical attention.

The breakdown of the shore sector's defenses necessitates withdrawal from the entire PSS Line to avoid encirclement, but the shore road remains blocked. Fortunately, a temporary road the Soviets know nothing about was hastily hacked out of the forest during the winter as part of the defensive preparations, making it possible to bypass the beachhead and blocked road at Tuulos. The roadwork was never finished, however, and in the heavy rain, trucks, artillery, horses and men get bogged down in the mud. Nevertheless, the escape route cut from south of Tuulos to Suurmäki and on to Vitele provides a lifeline for the retreating troops. The sound of thousands of weapons—rifles, machine guns, mortars, howitzers and cannon from the gunboats—all firing at more or less the same time along the beachhead, drives the soldiers on as they slog through the muck.

The further north the battle spreads, the more confusing the situation becomes for the doggedly advancing Soviet pursuers and the exhausted and confused Finns. It is often impossible to know whether the men on the far side of a hill or stream are friend or foe without closing within firing range. The Finns tend to stay away from open spaces, preferring to move through the forest. The Soviets seem to stick to the roads. Nobody likes the bogs, but the Finns cross them when that is the quickest way to put distance between themselves and their pursuers.

While the Finnish 6th Army Group has been concentrating on slowing the Soviet push up the coast of Lake Ladoga, the 7th Division has been withdrawing from Äänislinna on the shore of Lake Onega. The two streams of retreating soldiers form a ragged defensive line stretching from Vitele on the Ladoga coast to Jessoila on the shore of a lake called Säämäjärvi. The evening of June 28, Benjamin and his unit take up a position at Kinalahti on a ridge above a lake called Sinemuksa, where, for one blessed night, there is no contact with the enemy.

Almost as soon as they arrive at Kinalahti, the rain stops, and the slowly setting sun bathes everything in gold. The surface of the lake is still and unblemished, the woods a dark green blanket over hills left behind by the glaciers. For just a moment, the war seems far away. Sitting on an outcropping of granite worn smooth by the elements and looking out over the Karelian countryside, Benjamin's thoughts turn to Rachel. Does she know where he is and what he is going through? He hopes not. How can she understand what this past week has been like for him?

Throughout the attacking phase of the war, as Benjamin marched through the three isthmuses, he was happy to drive the enemy ahead of him, shooting as little as possible and actually aiming at someone only when he felt it was necessary to save his or a comrade's life. Now he is shooting to kill and feeling an undeniable sense of satisfaction when he knows he has hit his mark. He has even turned his gun on Finnish soldiers, ready to shoot if they refuse to rejoin the ranks and do their duty. Luckily, he hasn't had to shoot any of them, but he has no doubt that he would do so if necessary. He never could have done that before. How much he has changed during these years! There is something hard in him now, something that Rachel will surely find strange and upsetting when they meet again. How can he explain to her what has happened? He hardly understands it himself.

And what about Rachel? Has she changed as well? It can't be easy, dealing with the wounded and dying, day after day after day. On the front, it is natural to become hardened to death. It is as much a part of life as eating and sleeping. When one of your buddies is killed, you react. Nothing like a violent burst of submachine gun fire to vent your anger. In a hospital, though, is there any way to purge such feelings? The bodies just keep arriving. Some can be sewed back together, but others can't. What does that do to a tender heart?

Final Stand

Benjamin and the remaining members of his unit arrive at the U Line the evening of July 10 after three weeks of confusion, danger, hunger and sleep deprivation. Stretching some 50 kilometers from Pitkäranta on the shore of Lake Ladoga to Loimola on the shore of a lake named Nietjärvi, the U Line has been built to serve as a fortified last line of defense for the retreating Finnish forces, struggling to prevent the advancing Soviet troops from breaking through where the isthmus widens out to expose the undefended interior of the country. The commanders of the 5th, 7th and 8th Divisions send word to their troops that there will be no withdrawing from these positions. They will either succeed in holding off the Soviet charge or fight to the last man in a final attempt to save their country from being overrun.

Although the U Line has never been completed, it does offer the protection of trenches, dragon's teeth fortifications in some places to hold off tanks, and barbed wire strung along its entire length. Located at the foot of high granite outcroppings in several sectors are thick-walled concrete bunkers and machine gun nests. Fifteen artillery batteries back up the line. Half of them are concentrated around Pitkäranta, though, and only one is in the sector near Loimola where Er.P 18 takes up its position.

Soviet troops regroup along the U Line and begin their attack July 10. The remains of four entire Soviet army corps line up opposite the remains of just three Finnish divisions. The defenders understand what is at stake. If they are unable to halt the Soviet advance, everything they have fought for will be lost. Five days of furious attack and counterattack cause heavy losses on both sides, but the Finnish defenses hold.

July 15, the Soviets initiate a renewed massive attack along the U Line with the dreaded song of the "organ gun," a mobile multiple rocket launcher whose firing sounds like weird organ music. One of the defenders later described the attack:

> After the overture, a wave of tanks rolled in against our bunkers, and behind them flooded a brown mass of infantry. Machine guns replied by spitting out one belt of bullets after another. Those attackers who survived by taking refuge between the National Firewood company's piles of stacked firewood found themselves in Hell on Earth. The piles caught fire and in an instant roared into 100-meter tall flames. I didn't see a single one escape the trap.[4]

An eight-inch railway gun knocks out several of the Soviet tanks, causing those not destroyed or knocked over by the explosions to turn tail and flee. During fighting on the 15th, the Finns fire more artillery volleys along the U Line than on any single day during the Tali-Ihantala defensive battle.

Fighting rages for a week from Pitkäranta to Loimola. At Nietjärvi, where Benjamin is positioned, the Soviets push through and secure some four hundred meters of that sector's poorly fortified defenses. The Finnish troops are exhausted, and the Soviets believe their adversaries have lost their ability to fight. Benjamin's unit is one of those called on to prove them wrong. Over the next two days, the Soviet troops that have broken through the Finnish lines are partially surrounded. Fighting through the corpse-littered trenches, brandishing Suomi submachine guns and flame-throwers, the Finns drive the attackers back meter by meter until they have retaken the portion of the line that had been lost, leaving nearly 2,000 Soviet casualties in their wake.

By July 18, the fighting along the U Line has quieted to a stand-off. Soviet attackers skirt around the northern end of the U Line and head for the final showdown of the Continuation War at Ilomantsi on the Finnish side of the pre-Winter War border. After pushing through Finnish defenses, two Soviet infantry divisions end up in a motti. Although they are eventually able to break out with the help of last-minute reinforcements, they suffer some 5,000 casualties.

Less than a month later, the depleted Finnish and Soviet troops on all fronts are settled into defensive positions, awaiting a political resolution to a struggle that seems so resistant to a military one. Benjamin is physically and mentally exhausted, drained by the battering he and his unit took in their withdrawal from the Svir River to the U Line. Miraculously, Benjamin has survived unscathed, save for two holes in his sleeve where pieces of shrapnel passed through without so much as scratching his skin. Not all have been so fortunate. With so many men separated from their units in the chaotic conditions, it is hard to get an accurate picture of the losses, but it looks as if about half the troops that left the Svir River are holding down the new defensive positions at the top of the isthmus. How many of the missing are dead, wounded or among those who chose to run rather than fight won't be determined until later.

Notes

1. When JR 24 was disbanded on 1 March, 1944 and its older members discharged, the remaining soldiers were reorganized into a separate battallion, the 18th or Er.P 18.

2. A female Soviet propagandist named Aino Kallio, born in Finland, who broadcast messages over Moscow radio urging Finnish soldiers to desert.

3. Nenye, Vesa, Munter, Peter and Wirtanen, Toni, *op cit.*, p. 257

4. Satamo, Seppo, *Leijonalipun komppania*, Edita, Helsinki, 2007, p 442.

Figure 55.1. Accurate artillery fire was one of the keys to Finland's success in holding off the final Soviet assault (Finland's Military Museum)

When the Continuation War ended, everybody was being discharged. We had withdrawn from Karelia and were near Hamina. I got a phone call through to my wife, and she asked me, "When are you coming home? All the others have come already." It was a Tuesday, and I told her, "We're coming Friday." "Fantastic!" she said. The company commander said to gather up all our gear, we were being sent home.

And the irony of it all was that that same evening came a phone call from headquarters with the notification that we had to leave for Lapland. The idea was that the young ones would go to Lapland and the older ones get to go home, and so we were sent to Lapland. I choked up then, but I thought that if God has helped me thus far, maybe He'll still be there for me if I have to go to Lapland. Otherwise, if I'm taken prisoner, and the Germans know I'm a Jew, they'll torture me to death. But thank God, I never came in contact with a single one after that!

Salomon Altschuler*

---

*Interviewed by the author, Helsinki, 9 July, 2014.

CHAPTER FIFTY-FIVE

~

What Price Peace?

Helsinki, August 1, 1944—While Soviet troops were mounting what would be their final unsuccessful assault on Finnish positions in Eastern Finland's Ilomantsi sector, Commander-in-Chief Mannerheim was concluding that German aid would be insufficient to sustain his army's defensive struggle much longer. He told President Ryti that it was time for the country to renounce its commitment to Germany and reach a separate peace agreement with the Soviet Union. July 27, Soviet Ambassador to Sweden Alexandra Kollontai informed Sweden's State Secretary for Foreign Affairs, Erik Boheman, that the Soviet Union was ready to negotiate with the Finns, including guarantees that Finland would remain independent and not be occupied. The only precondition was that the war-time Finnish government had to be replaced.

Finland had fought first and foremost to maintain its sovereignty. If the Soviets were ready to grant assurances of its survival as an independent nation, further loss of life made no sense. July 28, on a trip to Army Headquarters in Mikkeli, President Ryti and Finance Minister Väinö Tanner reached a gentlemen's agreement with the Commander-in-Chief: Ryti would resign, Mannerheim would agree to replace him, and Tanner would ensure that Parliament approved the deal.

The next day, President Ryti signed his letter of resignation, effective August 1. Prime Minister Linkomies would serve as Interim President until Mannerheim could be elected by Parliament. Four days later, a new government, headed by Antti Hackzell and shorn of anyone the Soviets considered objectionable, was sworn into office.

The new government walked a tightrope for three weeks. President Mannerheim told Germany's Field Marshal Wilhelm Keitel that he felt in no way constrained to abide by the commitment his predecessor had made. Nevertheless, although Bulgaria and Romania broke off relations with Germany, Finland made no public move to do so. Instead, the Finns continued using discrete Swedish channels to communicate with Moscow. August 30 the response to Finland's peace proposal arrived in the form of a list of Soviet demands, the main points of which were withdrawal of Finnish troops to the border dictated by the 1940 Moscow Peace Agreement, the ceding of Petsamo and its nickel mines to the Soviet Union, and the eviction of all German forces from Finland by September 15. Any German troops still in the country after the 15th were to be taken prisoner by the Finns and handed over to the Soviets.

Parliament was called into session September 2 to consider the demands. Although President Mannerheim felt certain the timetable for driving the Germans out of the country would be impossible to meet, Parliament approved the conditions in principle and authorized the beginning of detailed peace negotiations. Late that evening, Prime Minister Hackzell went on the radio to explain to the nation that Finland had no choice but to end its military cooperation with Germany and was prepared to agree to Soviet conditions for peace.

Unpleasant Surprises

The Soviets and Finns agreed immediately to a cease-fire that would begin the morning of September 4. The Finns strictly obeyed the agreement, but the Soviets continued firing up and down the various front lines until the following day. This widespread breach of the cease-fire before it had even been implemented sent a chill through the Finnish leadership. A greater surprise, however, awaited the Peace Delegation in Moscow. In addition to the conditions already conveyed at the end of August, Finland would now have to demobilize its army (reduce it from 531,000 men on active duty to 42,000) within two months, rent the Porkkala Peninsula just west of Helsinki to the Soviets for 50 years, ban organizations the Soviets considered "fascistic" (among them the Lotta Svärd and Civil Defense Corps), rehabilitate the Communist Party, and make U.S. $300 million in war reparations payments to the Soviet Union in addition to settling with the Soviets the remaining debt Finland owed Germany for food and military equipment it had been allowed to purchase on credit.

The full weight of the demands was crushing. There were still 214,000 German soldiers in Finland. There was no way they could be forced out of the country within the prescribed two-week time frame, and the country was in no mood to begin fighting a war against its former comrades in arms to speed up their departure. Soviet occupation of the Porkkala Peninsula, which was within artillery range of Helsinki, would pose a constant threat to the security of the country. And how could a war-torn country with its economy in tatters hope to come up with $300 million[1] within the required five year window?

Of equal concern, perhaps, was the high-handed way the Soviet Union was acting. It agreed to a cease-fire and then didn't respect it. It dictated peace conditions and then, after they were agreed to in principle, unilaterally added many more. With its back to the wall, Finland had no choice but to agree to whatever demands the Soviets made. What guarantee would they have, though, that these demands would be the last or respected over time?

Finland's immediate problem, however, was what to do about Germany, which still held over 700 kilometers of front line in the Northeast and controlled almost all of Northern Finland. September 2, Foreign Minister Enckell informed Germany's Ambassador Wipert von Blücher that Finland was breaking off diplomatic relations with Nazi Germany. He thanked Germany for its support during the war but indicated that Finland's survival was at stake. At the same time, he informed Blücher that it was no longer possible for Germany to have a military presence in Finland. Later the same day, a letter from President Mannerheim to Adolf Hitler, explaining that it was the former's responsibility to lead his country in the direction of peace, was handed to General Waldemar Erfurth.

The Germans had feared a separate Finnish-Soviet peace for some time, and a plan for withdrawal through Northern Lapland to Norway was already in existence. By the time the peace accord was signed, German troops had begun preparing for their departure. Continued control of Petsamo was one of their key objectives, but an autumn campaign by Soviet troops, driving through the Kola Peninsula, put an end to German hopes of retaining the region's crucial nickel reserves. Sweden was unwilling to allow German troops safe passage across its territory, leaving Norway's Finnmark along the coast of the Barents Sea as the only possible exit.

Evacuation would require marching through Lapland from Oulu and Hyrysalmi in the south via Rovaniemi and Kemijärvi to Enontekiö and Karigasniemi. Neither the Finns nor the Germans had any enthusiasm for fighting with their former allies so they secretly agreed to a scenario whereby the Germans would retreat, and the Finns would occupy the positions that had already been abandoned, giving the impression that they were in hot pursuit. This "pretend war" lasted only two weeks before the Russians threatened to cross the border and chase the Germans out themselves if the Finns weren't prepared to do the job in earnest.

The ensuing seven-month real war was characterized by broken promises on both sides, scorched earth tactics on the part of the Germans, and begrudging aggression from the increasingly angry Finns. By the time the last Germans crossed the Norwegian border during the final week of April 1945, the Finnish Army had suffered 774 killed and nearly 3,000 wounded. The Ger-

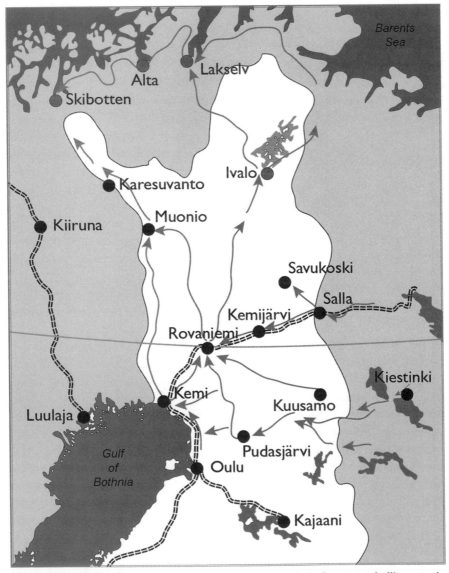

Figure 55.2. German troops headed for Norway with their former co-belligerents in pursuit (Marja Leskelä)

man casualty figures were similar but with the added loss of some 1,300 men taken prisoner during the fighting and eventually handed over to the Soviets.

The end of the Lapland War finally closed the third and final chapter of Finland's participation in WWII. The Winter, Continuation and Lapland Wars cost the country, directly and indirectly, the lives of some 94,000 citizens, more than 80,000 of whom died in battle or as a direct result of their wounds. Another 200,000 were wounded but survived. Taken together, the dead and wounded made up a whopping 7 percent of Finland's total population.

A final shameful chapter in the "cooperation" between the Finns and Soviets, dictated by Moscow, consisted of Finland handing over to Soviet authorities its German and Soviet prisoners as well as citizens of Soviet satellite countries who had fought on the Finnish side. The Soviet prisoners, having survived awful conditions in Finnish P.O.W. camps, would be imprisoned anew by Stalin for having been taken alive rather than fighting to the death. Volunteers from Soviet Karelia, Ingria and the Baltic Countries who fought valiantly alongside Finnish troops were detained and handed over to Soviet authorities. Engineers on Finnish trains transporting them across Finland to the border apparently slowed down on the way so that those who dared could jump off. Few of the deportees who stayed on board ever returned home.

On Pins and Needles

From the moment President Mannerheim informed the Germans that he did not feel bound by former President Ryti's commitment to carry on with the war, the entire population was on tenterhooks. What would the Germans do? Would they try to occupy Southern Finland in order to maintain control of the Baltic Sea and protect the withdrawal of their troops through Estonia, Latvia and Lithuania?

If most people were worried, the country's Jews were doubly concerned. Many had already made contingency plans to leave in case of emergency. Their young children, and in some cases their elderly parents, had been sent to Sweden. The liberation of the Majdanek death camp in July 1944 by the Soviets had given the world a first glimpse of the full horror of the Holocaust, but tight censorship kept the news from appearing in the Finnish media. Many of Finland's Jews and the 150 or so Jewish refugees still in the country nevertheless feared the worst.

Several Jewish soldiers, including Medical Captain Leo Skurnik, were among those whose service was extended in the effort to drive the German troops out of Lapland (Skurnik later told his son that the Lapland War was the only one of the three in which he participated wholeheartedly). The rest of the Jewish population, meanwhile, watched closely to see in which direction the fighting would move. To their relief, at least, there were no more German soldiers walking the streets of Helsinki or Turku.

With the arrival of the Allied Control Commission, headed by the feared Andrei Zhdanov, during the last week in September, the Jewish community was put in a delicate position. Simo Muir points out in *Ei enää kirjeitä Puolasta* that there was a fear the plight of the eight Jewish refugees turned over to the Gestapo in 1942 would be used by the War Crimes Tribunal to make it seem as if Jews had been systematically mistreated in Finland. Were that to happen, popular sentiment could easily turn against the Jews. In an effort to forestall such a possibility, the Helsinki congregation's Central Board published a memorandum describing the position of Jews in Finland during the war. Muir writes:

> According to the memorandum, the rights of Jews had in no way been violated, and [the Board] painted a very positive picture of Finland's actions without mentioning even a single word about the handing over of Jewish refugees to the Germans, let alone the plans to flee to Sweden.
>
> The memorandum was published in the Finnish press and sent to foreign papers and Jewish organizations such as the World Jewish Congress. Finland's officials were very grateful for the actions of the Central Board . . .[2]

It wasn't until December 6, 1944, however, the 37th anniversary of Finland's Independence, that the enduring tension in the Jewish community was finally broken in a dramatic way. A huge Independence Day celebration had been organized at the Helsinki Exhibition Hall, but President Mannerheim chose not to attend and sent Prime Minister J. K. Paasikivi[3] to deliver the principal address. Instead, the President attended a much more modest Independence Day memorial service being held at the Helsinki Synagogue.

Benjamin and Rachel are both in attendance. Benjamin is seated with the other veterans near the *bimah*,[4] and Rachel is upstairs, of course, in the balcony with the Lottas and other women. There is hardly a dry eye in the synagogue as Marshal Mannerheim, in full dress uniform, hands Congregation President Leo Wainstein a wreath in memory of the 23 Jewish soldiers who made the ultimate sacrifice for their fatherland in the Winter and Continuation Wars.

Hannu Rautkaillio, in *Suomen juutalaisten aseve*ljeys, writes:

> By his intervention, Mannerheim resolved the dilemma in which the Jewish community had been caught and out of which it felt powerless to extricate it-

self. Rabbi E. Berlingher, who had traveled from Sweden to attend the service, praised the marshal for his 'firm stand at the fateful hour of Finnish Jewry.'
. . .

The impression was gained by the Finnish Jews and the world at large that the 'rescue' of Finland's Jewry had been due to the marshal's active intervention. With his statesman's experience and vision, Mannerheim, for his part, understood how the victorious Western allies would condemn the Nazi crimes against the Jews. Finland had not shared in the guilt—and this truth had to be made plain to the whole world.[5]

Benjamin certainly feels this way and shares the unbridled admiration of his co-religionists for "Marski," as Marshal Mannerheim is affectionately known. He has no way of knowing that Mannerheim could have insisted that the deportation of eight refugees be stopped if he had been willing to take a "firm stand at the fateful hour" against the country's antisemitic Interior Minister and Head of the State Police but chose not to intervene.

In fact, Marshal Mannerheim gave no sign of being especially interested, one way or another, in "the Jewish question" until, as Rautkallio puts it, it became important to send a message to the West. He was focused, as were Ryti and Tanner, on the pragmatic challenges of preventing the occupation of Finland and preserving the sovereignty of the Finnish people. After all, that was his job and his mandate.

Like Abraham Lincoln—who is credited with freeing the slaves in the United States but admitted in a letter to New York Tribune editor Horace Greeley that his interest was in preserving the Union—Mannerheim would do what was necessary to save his country. Lincoln wrote:

My paramount object in this struggle *is* to save the Union, and is *not* either to save or to destroy slavery. If I could save the Union without freeing *any* slave I would do it, and if I could save it by freeing *all* the slaves I would do it; and if I could save it by freeing some and leaving others alone I would also do that. What I do about slavery, and the colored race, I do because I believe it helps to save the Union; and what I forbear, I forbear because I do *not* believe it would help to save the Union.[6]

Substitute into this text "Jews" (or Tatars or Roma) for "slaves" and "nation" for "Union," and the text reflects Mannerheim's as well as Ryti's and Tanner's single-minded focus. The Jews were undoubtedly no more important to them than any other Finns . . . but perhaps no less so, either.

Finland's leaders well understood that a tiny country that had been so recently and violently divided between Reds and Whites and between

Finnish- and Swedish-speakers would be unable to defend itself against outside aggression unless its people were united in the struggle. If even the tiniest minority of Finnish citizens were exposed as a group to official discrimination or outside threat, a chain reaction might occur in which other groups would wonder when their turn would come. Every individual, no matter what her or his background or beliefs, had to feel safe, respected and a part of the national project. The delicate fabric of national unity could be unraveled by pulling on a single thread.

As Commander in Chief, and later as President, Mannerheim emphasized this point at every opportunity. The example below happens to be from a certificate signed by him that accompanied a "Laatokan Karjala" medal awarded to Medical Captain Leo Skurnik in 1940 for his service in the Winter War.

Soldiers of Finland's Army. I have fought on many battlefields, but I have never seen soldiers the likes of you. I am as proud of you as I would be of my own children, as proud of the men of the fells in the North as I am of those from the expanses of Ostrobothnia, the forests of Karelia, the hills of Savonia, the fertile fields of Tavastia and Satakunta, and the young men of the grassy groves of Nyland and Southwest Finland. I am as proud of the sacrifice made by the factory worker and the youth from a poor cottage as of those made by the more affluent. . . . Our nation withstood its trial by dint of iron will. I thank the fathers and mothers of fallen heroes, I thank everyone who fought in the line of fire as well as those who served on the home front.[7]

As Benjamin and Rachel sit in the Helsinki *shul* and marvel at the appearance in their midst of the dapper 77-year-old hero and leader who personifies the determination of the Finnish people to remain free and independent, they can't help thinking what a strange and wonderful thing it is that Finland has survived . . . and stranger still, so has its tiny but resilient Jewish population.

Notes

1. The demand—to be met with goods, not cash—was calculated according to the prewar exchange rate, which essentially doubled the effective value of Finland's obligation. Struggling to meet the tight payment schedule, Finns were occasionally heard to remark: "The Russkies took our land, the Germans took our women, and the Swedes took our children. At least we still have our debt!,"

2. Muir, Simo, *Ei enää kirjeitä Puolasta*, Tammi, Helsinki, 2016, pp. 169–70.

3. Prime Minister Hackzell had suffered a debilitating stroke during the September peace negotiations in Moscow and was forced to step down immediately.

4. Raised platform in a synagogue from which the Torah is read during services

5. Rautkallio, Hannu, *Suomen juutalaisten aseveljeys*, Tammi, Helsinki, 1989, pp. 205–6.

6. Letter to Horace Greeley, http://www.abrahamlincolnonline.org/lincoln/speeches/greeley.htm

7. Mannerheim, C.E.G., excerpt from the certificate accompanying the Laatokan Karjalan medal awarded to Leo Skurnik and now in the possession of his son, Samuli Skurnik.

Figure 56.1. Independence Day, December 6, 1944. The Continuation War has ended, and President Mannerheim, accompanied here by Helsinki Jewish Congregation chairman Leo Wainstein, attends a memorial service in the Helsinki Synagogue (Finland's Jewish Archives)

The way I see it is this: it is the responsibility and requirement of every Jew to defend the country he has chosen to live in. We are Finns, we enjoy the rights and privileges of Finns, and we also fulfill our obligations. Take World War I for example. How many Jews fell on the French side, how many on the German side? No rumbling was heard then about Jews shooting at each other. And lots of them were lost on both sides. Complaints about Jews fighting against the Russians in Finland are completely childish to my way of thinking.

*Jacob Apter**

---

*Interviewed by Hannu Rautkallio, 18 December, 1988.

~

CHAPTER FIFTY-SIX

And Then?

It was finally over, at least for me. We had brought back as much of our gear and equipment as we could carry out or drag behind us. We tried really hard, too, not to leave any of our fallen comrades behind, but we couldn't get to all of them. There was nothing we could do when the Russkies were overrunning our positions. Aaach! Even now, I can't forget how that felt.

Anyway, I came home, or rather I went to Helsinki. Home for me would always be Viipuri, and there was no going back there anymore.

Some were not as lucky as me. They got sent to fight in that meshugenah war in Lapland. Even some Jews had to go. Salomon Altschuler, John Anker, Leo Kaplun, Leo Skurnik. It must have been horrible for them, but at least they all came back alive. Jews chasing Nazis through the countryside, like in some kind of bad joke…

Rachel was already in Helsinki when I got here. She had started school again. I was worried she would feel different about me, but I shouldn't have. She was the faithful kind. In all the years we were married, I never looked at another woman, and I don't believe she ever had thoughts about another man. That's how it was in those days. We had a wonderful life together. Today, young people change wives and husbands like it's nothing. Once Rachel and I got married, we both knew it would be forever.

That doesn't mean we had no problems. Sure we had. Rachel was the kind who always wanted to talk about feelings. For me, that was hard. Rachel always tried to get me to talk about the war. It will help, she said. But I couldn't do it. Even now I don't want to talk about it. Sometimes the children would ask me, too, but after a while they understood that I wouldn't have anything to say. Better to let those memories alone and not stir them up. No good can come of it.

David was wounded near Vieljärvi. Ground attack planes were shooting at them, and he was trying to get a horse and cannon off the road and under cover in the woods. The horse was hit, and when it fell, it pulled the cannon over on David's leg. Broke it in three places. He was lucky to get out alive, but he could never walk without a cane after that. He moved to Israel right after independence. Got married there, twice, and finally had a daughter with his second wife, Nataly. He eventually became quite rich, something to do with irrigation systems.

After our daughters—Ruut, Zivia and Sara—were all in school, Rachel went back to study again. She became a doctor, a children's doctor. Oh, how she loved that work! As for me, I made hats until I couldn't see to stitch and my hands were too swollen and stiff to hold a needle. It wasn't like being a doctor, but it was honest work. Making something, I always thought that was important. Nobody makes hats in Finland any more. Everything comes from China now.

I miss Rachel terribly. They say time heals all wounds, but that's shtus, nonsense. I think of her every day. When you do everything together for so long, you don't ever get used to being alone. At least I haven't.

Another thing that makes me sad is to see how the Jewish community here is struggling to survive. It's not antisemitism that is killing us now but the opposite. Too many young people are marrying outside the faith. Even my own daughter, the middle one, Zivia, married a goy, a good boy and a good husband, but still . . .

And then there are all the ones, like my Ruuti, who moved to Israel. They went to build a strong Jewish homeland, but by leaving they made the community here, where they were born and grew up, weaker. There are so few of us here, and everyone who moves away leaves a hole that we have no way to fill. Sara was the only one who stayed here and married within the faith, but then the cancer took her away, too.

We fought so this country would be safe for our children and grandchildren. Marski appreciated that. When he was asked by the Germans to turn us over to them, he told them, "Over my dead body!" He did, that's a fact! He saved us from the Nazis. But where is the Marski today who will save us from ourselves? For years the congregation has been shrinking. There are not even 90 children in the Jewish School. Even if they all stay in the congregation and don't intermarry or move away, that's not going to be enough to replace me and the other alter kockers.

What would our fathers and grandfathers say if they could see this? They worked so hard to make a place for themselves and us. They had to put up with antisemitic laws and institutions and antisemitic behavior from so many people. We have it so much better now. Our young people don't realize what is was like when Jews first came here or even before the wars. Maybe that is why some of them don't feel the same as we did. When the Germans asked us why we looked different from the other soldiers or spoke German with an accent, we told them to their face. We said, "We are Jews!" How many would do that today?

But we will survive. Somehow we always do. A few of the children of my friends, the sons and daughters of men who fought in the Continuation War, now spend some of their time in Germany. They bought apartments there. Who would have thought? So if there is a place for Jews in Germany, maybe there is a future for Judaism in Finland, too. I hope so. Our story is a wonderful story. It would be terribly sad for it to end.

Figure 57.1. From left to right: Harry Matso, Wolf Davidkin, Pej and Toja Manuel, Mary Davidkin, Pesach and Sara Blankett at the 5th World Assembly of Jewish War Veterans, 1988, in Jerusalem (Adiel Hirshovits' private collection)

It would be particularly anachronistic and unreasonable to blame Finland as a nation and a people for what Germany and its allies did to their Jewish populations. Although the Holocaust has become the most powerful and universal symbol of state cruelty and political violence, and recognition of it is a precondition to participation in current European historical discussion, Finland's position with regard to it is indeed exceptional. As far as Finland's historical conscience is concerned, hatred of Russians (*ryssäviha*), the concentration camps of Eastern Karelia, and the outrageously high death rates among Russian military prisoners taken by the Finns are more essential than antisemitism, Auschwitz and the destructive racial war on the Eastern Front.

Markku Jokisipilä and Janne Könönen*

---

*Jokisipilä, Markku and Könönen, Janne, *Kolmannen Valtakunnan vieraat*, Otava, Helsinki, 2013, pp. 496–497.

CHAPTER FIFTY-SEVEN

~

Aftermath

Jerusalem, March 1988—The notice promoting the opportunity to attend the Fifth World Assembly of Jewish War Veterans in Jerusalem, February 28–March 3, 1988 arrives in the mail at the end of the previous November. If members of Finland's Jewish War Veterans' Association sign up early enough for the trip, they can get a special discounted rate from El Al. Benjamin's first thought is that he and Rachel could combine attending the conference with a visit to Ruut, Avram and the grandchildren. "It has been six years since our last visit, much too long."

Secretary Harry "Haki" Matso is proposing a two-week trip, which would give Benjamin and Rachel time to see everyone except, of course, Tani. Tani has moved to San Francisco, but Ruut and Avram are still living in Gevim, and Avi and Dorit now live in Tel Aviv. The children wanted to leave the kibbutz as soon as they were old enough to attend university, and none of them apparently has any intention of moving back.

Benjamin loves visiting Gevim. The sunshine, food and atmosphere in the kibbutz, like in a huge extended family, make him feel relaxed and welcome. He doesn't particularly agree with some of the politics and philosophy of the place, though. How could Ruut and Avram give up their children to collective child-raising that way? They didn't even sleep in their parents' home! And the idea that everything has to be shared just seems to turn the simplest decisions into major debates involving the whole community. He doesn't think he could live like that, but for a vacation it is a *mechaje*.[1]

Benjamin and Rachel have visited Gevim twice since the Yom Kippur War. It will be strange to visit now, when the grandchildren aren't there, but they will be able to spend a few days with Avi and Dorit in Tel Aviv before driving down to the Negev. Then they will have time for a leisurely visit with their daughter and son-in-law before heading over to Be'er Sheva and then up to Jerusalem via Hebron. They might even detour via Masada and the Dead Sea on the way.

Rachel is thrilled at the prospect of the trip. The older she gets, the harder it is for her to be so far from her oldest daughter and the three grandchildren. But what can she do? You want your children to be independent, no? Anyway, the most important thing is that they are all healthy and getting on with their lives. As long as there isn't another war with the Arabs. Gevim is so close to Gaza . . .

* * *

Tel Aviv has grown a lot since their last visit, and so have the grandchildren. Gevim, on the other hand, is shrinking and aging. Some of the original kibbutzniks complain about the attitude of the young people, thinking only about themselves and their careers. The youth answer that their years in the military are enough of a sacrifice for the general good of the country, and they can do more for society by being successful and creating wealth for the nation than by being stuck on a kibbutz as cheap manual labor for the collective. The feeling of solidarity among those that stay on is still strong, however, and the kibbutz is more prosperous than ever. Ruut and Avram are both healthy, and the time seems to fly by for Benjamin and Rachel even though there is nothing for them to do but play cards, schmooze with some of the older kibbutzniks or relax by the pool.

By the time Benjamin and Rachel arrive in Jerusalem Sunday evening, they are well-fed and well-rested. They are looking forward to seeing former Finnish soldiers and Lottas who have moved to Israel. Surely some of them will be attending the conference, too.

Their room on the fourth floor of the Hotel Laromme on Ze'ev Jabotinsky Street has a spectacular view of Mount Zion. The Assembly, which opens Monday morning, is being held in the hotel, and Haki, Congregation President Wolf "Wova" Davidkin and his wife, Mary, have already settled into their own suite and spent a few days visiting the city. Mary Davidkin, née Grünstein, is a first cousin of Boris Grünstein, whose father, Jakob, employed Benjamin in his fur business between the wars, and the Davidkins have been good friends of Benjamin and Rachel for years. Both the Davidkins were *machal*, volunteers in Israel's War of Independence, so the visit has special meaning for them.

The Assembly has been organized as a celebration of Israel's 40th Anniversary. There are delegations attending from Australia, Belgium, Canada, Denmark, France, Great Britain, South Africa and the United States as well as Israel and Finland. The program includes sessions on such topics as "Israel's Accomplishments in Agriculture, Industry, Technology and Tourism," "International Terrorism," "The Meaning of Israel to World Jewry," "Israel's Defense," and "Towards Peace." Speakers include such familiar and distinguished names as Abba Eban, Shimon Peres, Yitzhak Rabin and Prime Minister Yitzhak Shamir.

Tuesday morning, the Finnish delegation, reinforced by Pesach Blankett, who lives in Israel, lays a wreath at the eternal flame in the World Holocaust Remembrance Center, *Yad Vashem*. Benjamin wonders why so few of the Finnish veterans living in Israel have shown up. When he asks Davidkin, he is surprised to hear that not a word has been heard from most of them, neither about the morning's solemn act of remembrance, nor about possible attendance at the Assembly. Strange that Jews have come all the way from Finland but so many of those living in Haifa or Tel Aviv wouldn't make the effort. Maybe, like some Finns, they just don't bother to write and will show up anyway.

* * *

More than 183,000 Russian Jews have immigrated to Israel since the war so it is no surprise that there is a large delegation of Soviet veterans at the Assembly. Another very visible group consists of dozens of Americans wearing garrison caps and jackets embroidered with their names and American Legion post number. Rachel, Benjamin, the Davidkins, Matso and Blankett are the only Finns in attendance. Benjamin discovers one possible reason the hard way when a small group of Russian veterans approaches him and Rachel after lunch on Wednesday, the third day of the Assembly. After inspecting Benjamin's participant badge, one of the Russians says, "So you are Finnish?"

"Yes," says Benjamin. "My name is Benjamin, and this is my wife, Rachel."

"I never understood why you attacked us," says his interlocutor, without introducing himself. "Such a little country, picking a fight with a big neighbor like us. What did you think you could gain?"

"Attack you? You can't be serious. Of course we didn't attack you. Stalin made up that whole thing about us firing on Mainila. Nobody would have been dumb enough to do something like that."

"But still you fought us twice," adds another of the Russians. "Why didn't you just agree to cooperate? So many of us died for nothing."

"Look," replies Benjamin. "I was only a foot soldier, but it was clear even to me that Stalin was not going to stop until Finland was wiped off the map. All we wanted was to be left alone. Anyway, I don't want to argue about what happened. I didn't come all the way here to fight the war all over again."

"Why *did* you come?" interjects the first Russian, "You were our enemy. In fact, you are the enemy of every single person here except those in your own delegation. You have some nerve. You should have all stayed home!"

And with that, the Russians turn on their heels and march off, leaving Rachel and Benjamin feeling as if they have just been caught in a freezing rain shower with no umbrella. When they rejoin Haki and the others, they hear that they, too, have had similar unpleasant discussions about their role in the war. Is that why they were invited? So they can be held up to ridicule by all the others?

*　　*　　*

That evening, Rachel and Benjamin skip the dinner at the Laromme. Benjamin had written to David as soon as he booked their flights. David's reply said he was too busy to attend the Assembly, but maybe they could meet for dinner. He subsequently booked a table at Fink, a tiny bar and restaurant on Ha'histadrut Street in the Downtown Triangle.

Although the reservation is for four, David shows up alone. His young wife, his second, has decided to stay at home with their daughter, who has a cold. David still has a visible limp and walks with the aid of a silver-headed cane, but he is vigorous and hasn't lost any of his thick, dark hair. His short-sleeved shirt, open at the collar, bears an embroidered monogram, and the Rolex on his wrist says all that needs to be said about his financial situation.

Most years, David has responded to Benjamin's New Year's card with a card of his own, but he has never been much of a correspondent. Benjamin got the impression that David's first marriage was difficult, but his second and the arrival of a child, his first, have given David a new lease on life. The friends haven't seen each other in over forty years. In fact, Rachel and David haven't met since that unfortunate evening at the *Mikado*.

They spend the first half hour over gin and tonics, catching up on the intervening years. Benjamin, however, can't get the unpleasant incident with the Russian veterans out of his mind. He tells David how shocked he was when the Russian said that the Finns were enemies of all the other attendees, as if they were still at war and on the wrong side. Doesn't anyone understand what kind of situation Finland was in at the start of the war?

"Actually, no," says David. "They can only see it from their own perspective. Looking at it that way, we were simply on the wrong side, allies of the epitome of evil."

"But we weren't allies! You know that. We were fighting our own, separate war."

"When Finns and Germans crossed the border together, no one but us saw it as separate armies fighting separate wars. How could they? In fact, if you ask me, that's a pretty weak justification, like saying we were a drifting log on the rapids of history. The truth is, we were fighting to acquire Greater Finland. That's what Marski and the AKS said, and that's what we would have gotten if we had won the war. If Germany had won the war, that is."

"Come on," interjected Rachel for the first time. "What choice did we have? We were being squeezed on all sides. It might have been different if Sweden would have agreed to a full military alliance, but by ourselves we couldn't stand up to either the Russkies or the Germans. The Russkies already had troops massing all along our border. We had to choose one side or the other, and we already knew what the Russkies wanted. Sometimes you have to choose between the lesser of two evils, and that's what Finland did. If we had sided with the Soviet Union, Stalin would simply have swallowed us. You know that."

"The problem," argues David, "is more complicated than that. The Soviet Union and Germany weren't just countries at war, they represented aggressive, radical ideologies. Of course, neither was acceptable to us, but by siding with Germany, Finland was saying to the world that we could live with Nazism but not with communism."

"No we weren't," fires back Rachel. "Finland never created an opening for Nazism. We needed help in pushing the Russkies back from the border, and that's what we got. That and food to keep us from starving. It had nothing to do with Nazism."

Benjamin has been effectively pushed out of the conversation, overwhelmed by a sense of *déja vu*. They are sitting once again around the dinner table at *Vidablick,* and Rachel and David are debating the responsibilities of young Zionists while Benjamin sits tongue-tied in admiration. He listens as his wife and friend ratchet up the debate. There are just six tables in the restaurant, and all are full. Although Rachel and David are speaking Swedish, which the other diners are unlikely to understand, the volume and tone of the conversation have drawn everyone's attention, making Benjamin feel self-conscious.

"Look," says David, "I know all those arguments. I'm not somehow on the other side. I just don't think sweeping uncomfortable truths under the carpet is going to help. Finland made a choice, and there is no way to separate out some parts and keep the rest, just like you can't marry someone and decide you're only married to her or his good qualities. You are stuck with the whole person, for better or for worse."

"That's a stupid argument," retorts Rachel. "Making a political alliance is not like getting married, and a country isn't like a person. We are stuck with this stupid 10-year Friendship, Cooperation, and Mutual Assistance Agreement with the Soviet Union, but that's because we have no choice. We aren't married to them. We just have guns pointed at our heads. It doesn't mean we like communism or support what goes on in the Soviet Union."

David doesn't bat an eye. "Call it a shotgun marriage, if you like, but your example actually proves my point. Finns may think they are completely independent from the Soviet Union and are making their own decisions, but the rest of the world doesn't see it that way. Although Finns aren't locked up behind the Iron Curtain in quite the same way as the Poles, Czechs, Hungarians and East Germans, they certainly aren't free to act any way they want when it comes to international politics."

Rachel's voice rises a bit higher, and the veins stand out in her neck as she replies. "We're talking about 1941. If we weren't free to make our own decision then, we would be part of the Soviet Union now. That's why we all fought, to keep our independence. Whether we ended up with Greater Finland or reduced borders, it was our independence that mattered. If we hadn't fought, we would have lost everything in the first days or weeks. To me, the shame of it all is not what we did but that the U.S. and U.K. fought alongside the Soviet Union. They only did that to have a better chance of winning. Their choice was completely different from ours. And the result is the horrible situation Eastern Europe finds itself in today!"

"O.K.," says David, lowering his voice as the food arrives at the table. "Of course, I understand all that. I am just trying to help you both understand where those veterans were coming from today. Every time they see an old picture of a Finnish warplane with a swastika on the side . . ."

"You know perfectly well," Rachel interrupts, "that the Finnish Air Force adopted the swastika many years before because it was on the plane given to us at the end of the Civil War by the Swedes. It had nothing to do with the Nazis. National socialism didn't even exist at the time."

"You're not listening to what I'm saying," David rejoins. "I know where the swastika came from, but none of these veterans from other countries does. The planes, the joint operations, the pictures of Finnish and German officers eating and drinking together . . . you name it, they all convey a sense that Finland had no problem with what the Nazis were doing. Maybe your arguments would be fine for convincing most people, but the Assembly you're attending is not made up of most people. These are Jewish veterans, men who, like us, lost comrades in the trenches. Some lost limbs in the war. More to the point, most of them lost relatives in the gas chambers. To them, they weren't just fighting any enemy, they were fighting a genocidal force that was trying to exterminate our people and came pretty close to succeeding."

"But we didn't know about that," says Benjamin, re-entering the conversation for the first time. "You didn't know about it, did you?"

"No, how could I? We were in the forest the whole time. But the press and radio in the rest of the world were operating under a completely different set of rules. They were using every atrocity to stoke the anger of their people against the Germans. Jewish soldiers in other armies knew far more than we did. Do you really want to know why most of the Finnish veterans living here are not at the Assembly?"

"We've been wondering about that."

"It isn't because we are afraid the other veterans will say we were the enemy. We've been through that many times. A fact is a fact: we were on the other side. The bigger reason is that we are blamed, especially here in Israel, for prolonging the Holocaust."

"What?" exclaim Benjamin and Rachel in unison, their faces contorted in grimaces of disbelief at what they just heard.

"Yes," continues David. "People say that by fighting on the German side, we made it possible for them to allocate fewer troops to the Northern Front and place more soldiers along the rest of the Eastern Front. While the Germans would have swept through the Pale anyway, we were fighting alongside them during the years when two thirds of those Jews were being shot or gassed or starved to death. Since thousands and sometimes tens of thousands were killed every week, if we helped perpetuate the war by even a week or two, that could be seen as costing many thousands of innocent Jewish lives. All of the Finns here in Israel have had to face that argument many times, and none of us wants to go through it again. Of course, it has nothing to do with 'why' we fought, but there is no way to argue against the conclusion that our participation may have had consequences none of us could ever have imagined. I'm sorry. I can see you are horrified, but that's what you can expect in the next couple of days. Better to hear it from me first."

* * *

That night, Rachel falls quickly asleep, exhausted by the debate with David and long-suppressed memories brought up by seeing him again. Benjamin, though, tosses and turns by her side, unable to relax. Despite his wife's spirited defense, David's argument won't let go of him. If his participation in the war allowed the Nazis to kill even one Jew, how could he live with that? Of course he wasn't trying to make it easier for the Nazis to murder Jews, but what if that really was one of the results, the unintended consequences, of his military service? What if the Russkies he was fighting could really have been liberating extermination camps instead of trying to retake the Ladoga Isthmus?

As a Finn, he knows he did the right thing. In fact, he did the only possible thing. But as a Jew? Everyone had said that Finland's Jews finally redeemed their citizenship through their participation in the war, yet the old question that bedeviled his father's and grandfathers' generations has not been fully answered. Is he a Jewish Finn or a Finnish Jew? When push comes to shove, is it possible to demonstrate absolute loyalty to both Finnishness and Jewishness? He loves his country and was willing to risk his life for it. He loves his people, too, and is horrified by the thought that someone could feel he has betrayed them.

Is this really what the whole Zionist struggle has been about, not just providing a safe haven for Jewish refugees but resolving the enduring conflict over loyalty for a people in perpetual diaspora?

*   *   *

The last day of the Fifth World Assembly of Jewish War Veterans is also the first day of Purim, the celebration of the Jewish people's miraculous escape from annihilation during the reign of King Ahasuerus of Persia. In the story of Purim, Haman, Viceroy of the Empire, is prevented by Ahasueras' queen, Esther, from carrying out a murderous plot to kill the kingdom's Jews. Unbeknownst to the king, who has selected her in a kind of beauty contest, his queen is a Jewess. The story is quite convoluted but ends with perfidious Haman hung from the gallows he had constructed for Esther's uncle, Mordechai, and the Jews killing their enemies instead of being massacred.

By staying faithful to both her king and her people, Esther keeps the former from making a terrible mistake and saves the latter from a fourth century BC version of the Holocaust. As he drinks his coffee and eats *hamentaschen*[2] with Rachel and the Davidkins in the Hotel Laromme coffee shop an hour before leaving for Ben Gurion International Airport and the flight home, Benjamin ponders the similarities between Esther's predicament and that of Finland's Jews. She had to keep her Jewishness a secret at first, but she emerged a heroine, honored throughout the ages for her transformation from a subservient wife into a decisive and forceful savior of her people. Acting within an alien culture and in opposition to the oppressive intentions of one of its most powerful leaders, she was able to protect the Jewish people and restore them to their position as a respected minority within the empire.

Hadn't it been somehow similar, what he, Rachel and the other Jewish soldiers who fought for Finland's sovereignty, had done? Hadn't they, too, shown by their actions that loyal Jews deserved to be respected, not just as citizens but as Jewish citizens? No one, he thinks, can be held responsible for collateral damage from his actions if they result from situations he couldn't possibly know about at the time. Otherwise, action would be impossible. And if there can be no responsibility, there can be no guilt.

He looks admiringly at Rachel, his queen. How little has changed, he thinks. After all these years, she can still hold her own in the toughest argument, and I, I still only figure out what to say long after the discussion is over, when it is too late. What would have changed if we Jews had refused to fight in the Continuation War? We certainly had no power to influence our country's decisions, nor would a couple of hundred Jews less at the front have freed up a single Allied soldier to fight elsewhere or liberate a single death camp prisoner.

If we had refused to fight, Marski would have had no reason to protect us. Those of us who didn't flee to Sweden would have been rounded up and handed over by Anthoni to the Gestapo. We would have saved the Nazis the trouble of putting an end to Judaism in Finland. We would have done the job for them.

Notes

1. A delight (Yiddish)
2. Traditional Purim pastry made with poppy seeds and honey

~

Acknowledgments

I could not have undertaken or successfully completed this six-year project without the generous financial support of the Kone Foundation and the provision of office space and facilities by KONE Corporation.

I would like to thank the Finnish Jewish WWII veterans (Salomon Altschuler, Hodie Figur, Abi Kagan, Tevje Kagan, Aron Livson, Louis Levinsky, Harry Matso and Boris Rubanowitsch) and family members of those no longer living (Gideon Bolotowsky, Leif Furman, Michel Grünstein, Margalit Halutz, Ami Hasan, Ruth Hasan, Adiel Hirschovits, Aviva Jalkanen, Dan Kantor, Daniel Katz, Laura Kaspi, Feige Kjisik, Joel Nemes, Jacob Seela and Laila Takolander) who graciously consented to be interviewed. Several veterans outside the Jewish community (Åke Gagneur, Marta Holmberg, Seppo S. Jokipii, Sven Wager and Göran Westerlund) also provided valuable insights.

I am indebted to numerous military experts (General [Ret.] Pentti Airio, Admiral [Ret.] Juhani Kaskeala, Colonel [Ret.] Ari Raunio, General [Ret.] Jaakko Valtanen, and Colonel [Ret.] Leo Skogström) and historians (Dr. Laura Ekholm, Prof. Matti Klinge, Prof. Markku Kuisma, Prof. Karl-Erik Michelsen, Prof. Eino Murtorinne, Dosent Simo Muir, Dr. Vesa-Matti Määttä, Dosent Hannu Rautkallio and Helsinki Jewish Coeducational School History Teacher Daniel Weintraub), who provided invaluable assistance and guidance as did other experts (Jukka Hartikainen, Ruth Messinger, Elina Sana, Samuli Skurnik, Rony Smolar) and friends (Charley Hart, Antti Herlin, Franco Oliva, Kyösti Tasa and Daniel Terris).

I would be remiss not to acknowledge the debt I owe to Taru Mäkelä for her magnificent 1997 documentary, *Daavid—tarinoita kunnista ja häpeästä*

(*David—Stories of honor and shame*), which preserved the voices and stories of many Jewish war veterans who were no longer alive when I started my research, and the late Väinö Linna, whose epic trilogy, *Täällä pohjantähden alla* (Under the North Star) first introduced me to the rich emotional undercurrents that nourished national development during the period when the country's Jews first made a place for themselves in Finnish society.

Most of all, I want to express my appreciation for the way the Helsinki Jewish Community embraced this project and contributed to it in more ways than I can mention.